Thomas Erskine

Speeches of Thomas Lord Erskine

Reprinted from the five volume octavo ed. of 1810. With a memoir of his life. Vol. 1

Thomas Erskine

Speeches of Thomas Lord Erskine
Reprinted from the five volume octavo ed. of 1810. With a memoir of his life. Vol. 1

ISBN/EAN: 9783337094898

Printed in Europe, USA, Canada, Australia, Japan

Cover: Foto ©Raphael Reischuk / pixelio.de

More available books at **www.hansebooks.com**

SPEECHES

OF

THOMAS LORD ERSKINE.

REPRINTED FROM THE FIVE VOLUME OCTAVO
EDITION OF 1810.

With Memoir of His Life

BY

EDWARD WALFORD, M.A.

IN TWO VOLUMES.

VOL. I.

LONDON:
REEVES & TURNER,
100 CHANCERY LANE,
AND
196 STRAND.
1870.

PREFACE.

THE Speeches of Lord Erskine being in constant demand, on account of their great value both to admirers of English oratory and also to students of the law, have of late years become extremely scarce, and the few copies which have been offered for sale have consequently increased to a price which has placed them beyond the reach of many who would otherwise have been glad to avail themselves of their contents.

The Publishers have, therefore, brought out a new edition of these Speeches, in a far cheaper and more compact form than that in which the work originally appeared. At the same time, they have endeavoured to avoid the objection to which the majority of modern reprints are liable, we mean that of overcrowded type.

This edition, it is hoped, will have also one additional merit, with regard to the accuracy with which it has been reprinted from the original edition, which has been followed *verbatim*, with the exception of a few typographical errors which had escaped the notice of the former Editor. On another ground this edition may claim superiority, as in the original the Speeches were printed without regard to the order in which they were delivered: the reader, however, will find them arranged here in strict chronological order.

Of Lord Erskine's Speeches, it may be said with truth that they are models of perspicuity and eloquence combined, and such as well become "the foremost of English advocates." They afford the best examples of sound legal and practical reasoning; and they derive additional value from the fact that most of them were delivered in connexion with the most important legal cases in which the real principles of our Constitution have been involved. It is almost superfluous to remind the legal reader what great services Lord Erskine has rendered to posterity by his advocacy and assertion of the "Liberty of the Press," and by his definition of the "Law of Libel," or that, in his day, he was the principal agent in the work of improving the state of the law on these all-important subjects.

A Memoir of Lord Erskine is, for the first time, prefixed to these Speeches. It will be found to contain many facts derived from authentic sources, which, so far as the Publishers are aware, have never yet appeared in print.

LONDON, *August* 1870.

CONTENTS OF VOL. I.

———◇———

LIFE OF LORD ERSKINE.

THOUGH the eminent lawyer, a selection of whose speeches is contained in these volumes, was one who never rose as a lawyer to the level of such men as Lord Mansfield, and was inferior to many men of his own age as a Parliamentary debater, yet there are few persons who will dispute the verdict of his fellow-countryman, and eventually his successor on the Woolsack, Lord Campbell, who pronounces him, in his " Lives of the Chancellors," " without an equal in ancient or modern times as an Advocate in the Forum."

A younger son of the noble house of Erskine, Earls * of Buchan, Thomas Erskine was born on the 10th of January 1750, in a " small and ill-furnished room," in an upper " flat " of a lofty house in the old town of Edinburgh. His family, who derived their name from, or possibly gave it to, the lands of Erskine on the banks of the Clyde, were connexions of the still older house of Mar,—of whom Lord Hailes says that their earldom dates from times anterior to history. But the Earls of Buchan, in the seventeenth and eighteenth centuries, had scattered to the winds a large portion of their hereditary wealth, so that, according to Lord Campbell, an income of £200 a year was all that was left to Henry David, the tenth Earl, on which to maintain and bring up his family. His Countess, however, Agnes, second daughter of Sir James Stewart of Goodtrees, in the county of Midlothian, was a woman of great energy, high character, and piety; and she struggled nobly with the disadvantages of her husband's narrow means. She brought her children up in a somewhat strict Presbyterian faith, as befitted the descendants of a religious house

---

* It is remarked by Sir N. W. Wraxwall, that if Lord Erskine had been the son of a Marquis instead of the son of an Earl, he never could have been called to the bar.—*Memoirs*, vol. i., p. 153.

which had suffered much in the Covenanting cause. Still the "flat" which she occupied with her husband and children was frequented not only by eloquent Presbyterian divines, but also by leaders of the "Parliament House," and by members of the best families who wintered in the Scottish metropolis.

A child of high spirit and very good abilities, young Tom Erskine was sent to the High School of his native city, where it is recorded that he rose to be "Dux," or, as we should say in England, "captain" or head-boy in his class. But unfortunately, in spite of its educational advantages, Lord Buchan found "Northern Athens" too expensive a place to live in, and accordingly, in 1762, removed with his children to St Andrews.   Here at the grammar-school, under a Mr Hacket, Tom Erskine maintained his early character for ability; but he does not appear to have been very industrious, since he picked up little Greek beyond the alphabet, and never attained to more than a very moderate stock of Latin. He was, however, fond of reading the English writers, both of prose and verse, and he devoured whole volumes of travels, voyages, and plays with avidity. After leaving school, he attended several courses of lectures in the classes of mathematics and natural philosophy at the University of St Andrews, but he never appears to have become a member of it by formal matriculation.

It was his early wish to have entered one of the learned professions; but the family purse was not well-lined enough to admit of this idea being realised ; so it was settled that he should be a midshipman. He vainly strove against this destination, and indeed went so far as to try, through his relatives, to obtain instead a commission in the army without purchase : but the fates were against him, and to sea he was forced to go. Accordingly, in the spring of 1765 he was put under the charge of Sir David Lindsay, then captain of H.M.S. *Tartar*, with whom some little interest had been made on his behalf through his uncle, the Earl of Mansfield. Having been duly fitted out with his blue jacket, cocked-hat, and sword, he joined his ship at Leith, and spent four years very pleasantly and happily, if we may judge from allusions in his letters, in cruising about the American station and in various parts of the West Indies. On returning home, however, at the age of nineteen, he found, on his ship being paid off, that he had no chance of going to sea again except as a "middy," and this did not suit his pride, as he had been employed by his captain as acting-lieutenant.

His father died in 1767, and he again thought of entering a learned profession: but the scantiness of his inheritance prevented him from entering either of the English Universities; so, through the interest of the Duke of Argyll, he was glad to obtain an ensign's commission in the "Royals," or "First Regiment of Foot." But the purchase-money absorbed all his means. The first two years of his military life were spent, not on foreign service, but in barracks at various towns in England and Ireland. He appears, however, to have made good use of his leisure in one respect; for on the 29th of April 1770, when only just twenty years of age, he married a young lady of good family and connexions, though not much more wealthy than himself, the daughter of Mr Daniel Moore, M.P. His wife accompanied him to Minorca, whither his regiment was ordered, and where he spent two years, busily employing himself in going through a course of English literature. Lord Campbell tells us that he also "showed the versatility of his powers by acting as chaplain to the regiment, the real chaplain being absent on furlough." No doubt the extemporary prayers to which he must have listened, and in which he probably joined, at his mother's house, here stood him in good stead.

Returning to England in 1772, we find him mixing in the society of London, in which he was well fitted to shine even at that time; and he was a constant frequenter of the *salon* of Mrs Montagu in Portman Square, where he used to meet most of the literary celebrities of the day, including Dr Johnson; and, if we may believe Boswell, he was bold enough on one occasion to maintain a contest of words against that Goliath of criticism on the subject of the slaughter of the Assyrian host under Sennacherib by the destroying angel.* Fired with literary ambition, or a zeal for the army, or both, he now became an author, though anonymously. The title of his work explains the author's purpose, and shows that from very early convictions he was a genuine Liberal and Reformer. It was entitled, "Observations on the Prevailing Abuses in the British Army arising from the Corruption of Civil Government; with a Proposal to the Officers towards obtaining an Addition to their Pay. By the Hon. —— ——, an Officer. 1773." The

* Boswell's Johnson, ii. 177.

pamphlet had a large circulation. "The name of its author (says Lord Campbell) was well known, though it did not appear on the title-page; and he acquired much celebrity by the boldness and eloquence with which he had pleaded for his profession."

In 1773 he was promoted to the rank of lieutenant; but there seemed to be little or no chance of a war; and in peace he knew that he could not afford to purchase his commission as captain. It so happened, one day in the following year, that his regiment was quartered in a town where his relative, Lord Mansfield, was Judge of Assize. He came into court, was invited to sit by the Judge's side on the bench, and afterwards to dine with his Lordship at the Judge's lodgings. He communicated to Lord Mansfield his early desire in the direction of the bar; and finding no discouragement in that quarter, and on the contrary great sympathy from his mother, he resolved to carry out his design. Accordingly, in April 1775, he was admitted as a student at Lincoln's Inn, and in the following January entered Trinity College, Cambridge, as a fellow-commoner. At Cambridge, however, he did not follow the studies of the place; but concentrated his attention upon English litera-ture, in which he proved his ability by carrying off the college prize for English declamation.

While still a student at Cambridge he contrived to keep his terms at Lincoln's Inn, and became a pupil, at first in the chambers of Mr Justice Buller, then a special pleader, and after his elevation to the bench, in those of Mr George Wood, afterwards a Baron of the Exchequer. At this time he lived in small lodgings in Kentish Town, at the foot of Hampstead and Highgate Hills, and he had the greatest difficulty in keeping the expenses of his young and increasing family within his slender means. In the evenings he used to take part in the debates of the Robin Hood, Coach-makers' Hall, and other "spouting shops," which, according to the custom of the time, were attended by shoemakers, weavers, Quakers, law-students, and members of Parliament, each person paying six-pence, and being entitled to a glass of porter or punch, and in which there is said to have been often a display of high oratorical powers.*

Though he never became a profound jurist, yet, with his lively imagination, he had a sound and logical understanding; and his

* Lord Campbell's Lives of the Chancellors, viii. 241.

legal commonplace books, which are still in existence, show that at this period his application to the studies of his newly-adopted profession was close and unremitting. Hence his progress was respectable, if not brilliant; and in a very short space of time he was able to collect and arrange the authorities upon most questions of law which he had to consider, and so to arrive at a thorough comprehension of the issue at stake.

He was called to the bar in Trinity Term 1778, but continued working in the chambers of Baron Wood until the following month of November, when, by one of those extraordinary chances which from time to time happen in some paths of life, he was suddenly called upon to defend Captain Baillie, the Lieutenant-Governor of Greenwich Hospital, against whom an action was brought for publishing statements relative to the abuses of that institution, and which were construed into a reflection on Lord Sandwich, then First Lord of the Admiralty. A fee of a guinea was dropped into his hand as a retainer, and the case came on before Lord Mansfield. The expectation was, that the Solicitor-General would have no difficulty in making the rule absolute, and that Captain Baillie would lose his cause. But the speech of young Erskine, contained in the first of these volumes, at once electrified the Court and the audience. The rule was discharged with costs; Erskine's fame as an advocate was established, and his fortune virtually made.

Briefs and fees now flowed in upon him in a golden stream; he practised in the King's Bench, and there were few more popular barristers in Westminster Hall than Thomas Erskine. In January 1779 he gained fresh credit as counsel for Lord Keppel, who was tried by a court-martial, and whose acquittal he secured, and from whom he received a present of £1000 as a mark of his gratitude. In the spring of this year he joined the Home Circuit, and soon found himself fully employed. In the same year he appeared at the bar of the House of Commons against a bill which very nearly touched the liberty of the press,—the bill introduced by Lord North, vesting the right of printing and issuing almanacs in the Stationers' Company and the two Universities of Oxford and Cambridge. The bill was rejected by a large majority, and mainly through his eloquence, which converted Lord North's brother-in-law from a supporter to an opponent.

We next find him, in 1780, engaged as counsel for Lieutenant Bourne, R.N., who was brought before the King's Bench for sending a challenge to his commanding officer, Admiral Wallace; and in the following year for Lord George Gordon, who was tried before Lord Mansfield for high treason on account of his share in the Protestant Riots of 1780. Here, too, in spite of the whole power of the Crown being put into force against the prisoner, and of a somewhat severe and unfavourable summing up from the Judge, he obtained for his client a verdict of " Not guilty." This acquittal, it need scarcely be added, gave a heavy blow to the law of constructive treason, as laid down by the Tory judges of the time.

In 1783, on the formation of the "Coalition" Ministry, he entered Parliament as M.P. for Portsmouth, his Whig friends being anxious for the assistance of his eloquent advocacy in the House of Commons; and it is not a little singular that both he and his rival and successor in the Chancellorship, John Scott, afterwards Lord Eldon, made their maiden speeches in the same debate,— that on Mr Fox's famous India Bill. But Erskine's speech was tame,[*] and fell somewhat flat upon the ears of his audience, who possibly expected that in St Stephen's he would equal the flights of his eloquence on the other side of Westminster Hall. He spoke, however, again, and with better effect, on the second reading of the bill, and ably contended for the right of Parliament to control the proceedings of the East India Company.

The bill was lost in the Lords, and the "Coalition" Ministry resigned. On the accession of Pitt to office, Erskine spoke in support of Fox's motion (January 1784) for going into a committee on the state of the nation. He again spoke against Pitt's India Bill, which he contrasted with that of Fox, and of which he prophesied that it would "prove the ruin of the East India Company, and lead to the oppression of the inhabitants of Hindostan, till they would rise and shake off our yoke." It need hardly be added, that subsequent events have proved that Erskine's words were all but realised in' fact a short time before the formal transfer of the provinces of India from the Company to the Crown, ten years ago. He again spoke on the motion for stopping the supplies in consequence of the King's refusal to dismiss his

* Sir N. W. Wraxall's Memoirs, ii. 436.

Ministers. The motion was carried, but Pitt resolved to appeal to the nation. Parliament was dissolved, and failing to secure his re-election at Portsmouth, Erskine remained for seven years out of Parliament.

Perhaps it was well for him that such was the case. He had not made any great success in St Stephen's; but though he had been only five years at the bar, he had already obtained a patent of precedence which entitled him to wear a silk gown, and to sit within the bar. He had already refused to hold junior briefs: and while he wore a stuff gown, a number of "juniors"—many years his seniors in point of age—were thrown out of business, as, consistently with professional etiquette, they could not be retained with him in any cause. Accordingly his silk gown was not merely a compliment and an honour, but of positive service to himself and to others.

He now began to be in most extensive request, not merely on his own circuit, but elsewhere; and accordingly he laid himself out for "special retainers," by which he was taken to the assizes in all parts of England and Wales, with a fee in each case of at least three hundred guineas.* His first "special retainer" was in the case of Rex. *v.* Shipley, Dean of St Asaph, for a "seditious libel"—which was nothing else than the publication of a "Dialogue between a Gentleman and a Farmer," written by the Dean's brother-in-law, Sir William Jones, in illustration of the general principles of political economy, and quietly recommending some very moderate parliamentary reforms. The jury, in spite of a very adverse summing up of the Judge, found Dr Shipley "guilty of publishing only," but declined to find "whether a libel or not." In the next Michaelmas Term, the case was re-opened, and practically re-heard; and Erskine moved in arrest of judgment, and with success. "This prosecution," says Lord Campbell, "seemed to establish for ever the fatal doctrine that *libel or no libel* was a pure question of law, for the exclusive determination of judges appointed by the Crown. But in the event it led to the subversion of that doctrine, and the establishment of the liberty of the press, under the guardianship of English juries. . . . I have said, and I still think" (he adds), "that this great constitutional triumph is mainly to be ascribed to Lord Camden, who had been fighting in the cause for half a century

* Townsend's Lives of Eminent Judges, i. 423.

and who uttered his last words in the House of Lords in its support ;
but had he not received the invaluable assistance of Erskine, as
counsel for the Dean of St Asaph, the Star-Chamber might have
been re-established in this country." *

While out of Parliament, Erskine appeared occasionally at the
bar of the House of Commons, but his success there was not such
as to make him ambitious of continuing that part of his practice.
He also gave up his circuit business, and confined himself to special
retainers.   He kept up also his intimacy with the leaders of the
Whig party, especially Fox and Sheridan, through whom he became
personally acquainted with the Prince Regent—then a zealous
Whig—who made him his Attorney-General, and gave him reason
to expect hereafter still further promotion.

In the autumn of 1788 occurred the King's illness, which it was
fully expected would at once have placed the heir-apparent on the
throne.   But the near prospect of Erskine's hopes or expectations
of political power were set aside by the King's speedy recovery, and
the prolonged tenure of office by Mr Pitt and his Tory friends.
In the following year, 1789, as counsel for Stockdale the publisher,
he made what Lord Campbell does not hesitate to call " the finest
speech ever delivered at the English bar, and which for ever established the freedom of the press in England," and of which the
Edinburgh Review * says, " It is justly regarded by all English
lawyers as a consummate specimen of the art of addressing a jury—
as a standard and sort of precedent for treating cases of libel." The
offence of Mr Stockdale was the publishing of a pamphlet by the
Rev. Mr Logan, a Scottish minister, in which Warren Hastings was
exculpated from the charges brought against him, and the House
of Commons compared to the tribunal of the Inquisition.   It is
almost needless to add that the speech, which will be found in these
volumes, was followed by a verdict of " Not guilty."

Erskine's reputation as an advocate was now at its height.   In
this year he paid a visit to Paris, from which he returned with his
Liberal opinions strongly confirmed in the democratical direction.
In the autumn he was again returned to Parliament for Ports-
mouth, which he continued to represent until he was raised to the
Peerage.   In May 1791, he seconded Fox's motion for declaring

* Campbell's Lives of the Chancellors, viii. 279.
† Vol. xvi. 109.

the law of libel; in April 1792, on Mr Grey's motion for parliamentary reform, he defended with much spirit the proceedings of the "Society of Friends of the People;" and, true to his opinions, he declined to join the ranks of the "Alarmists,"—as those Whigs were called who, frightened at the progress of democracy in France, were inclined to abandon their Liberal principles, and, with the Prince of Wales, to go over to the Tory camp. By this adherence to his own views and those of Fox, he knew that he was sacrificing all chance of further employment as a law-officer of the Crown; but was contented to waive all his prospects rather than abandon the fixed and deliberate principles with which he had started in public life. Hence he vehemently opposed the idea of striving to suppress Jacobitism by new penal laws; hence he attacked Pitt's "Traitorous Correspondence Bill;" and hence, when he knew that the majority on the other side was overwhelming, he made an elaborate speech in favour of parliamentary reform.

In the following year, contrary to the advice of Lord Loughborough and some of his best friends, he held a brief for "Tom Paine," the author of "The Rights of Man." Here, however, he failed, as he could scarcely have escaped failing, to convince the jury that the book came within the category of useful publications. Nor was the loss of his client's cause his only disappointment. For taking this brief, he was suspended from his office as Attorney-General to the Prince of Wales. He was equally unsuccessful in defending John Frost against a Government prosecution for seditious words spoken in a public-house; but he won a verdict, as counsel for the defence, in a far more important cause, the Government prosecution of Messrs Perry and Grey, the proprietors of the *Morning Chronicle*, for inserting in their paper an address from a society at Derby, complaining of the unsatisfactory state of the representation of the people in Parliament.

The year 1793, and the following years, have been called, in a legal sense, "The Reign of Terror," on account of the constant efforts of the Tory Administration to put down all outward expressions of political dissatisfaction by the strong hand of the law, and by arbitrary and summary prosecutions. It was in consequence of the prevalence of this spirit that Thomas Hardy, a shoemaker, and eleven other obscure individuals, were put upon their trial for high treason, simply as belonging to a society, or societies, whose end was parliamentary reform. Erskine, of course, was engaged for the defence of Hardy, against Sir John Scott, the Attorney-General, and Chief-Justice Eyre, who showed every wish to forward the case for the Crown. But in spite of all the forces that the Crown could bring to bear against the prisoner, Hardy was acquitted, and the speech delivered on that occasion by his advocate will live for ever. The Government, however, with extraordinary infatuation, resolved to try the experiment of repeating the same drama, by putting another of the twelve, John Horne Tooke, on his trial, but with the same result; and, when this too failed, they prosecuted a third person, named Thelwall. Erskine was counsel for the defence in both these cases; and the acquittal of Tooke and Thelwall so thoroughly discomfited the Government, that they resolved not to go on with the prosecution in the case of the rest of their victims. Such was the joy of the people that bonfires were lit in various parts of London, and the mob took the horses from Erskine's carriage, and drew him in triumph back from the court to his house in Serjeant's Inn.

In 1795 he spoke in Parliament with considerable effect against a motion for the repeal of the Habeas Corpus Act, against the Seditious Meetings Bill, and against the bill for making a conspiracy to levy war, without any overt act of warfare, equivalent to high treason. But somewhat, it must be owned, inconsistently with his own principles and antecedents, he was a party, in common with Fox and Sheridan, to the prosecution of Mr John Reeves in the following year, for the publication of a book which dealt in some very abstract criticism on our mixed constitution of King, Lords, and Commons, the strongest passage of which asserted simply that " the kingly government may go on, in all its functions, without Lords or Commons; . . . but without the King, his Parliament is no more." It seems, indeed, absurd that the party which nailed to its mast the flag of " free inquiry into all political subjects " should have crouched down to the King on bended knees, and have asked leave to turn the engine of a political prosecution against a philosophical-minded gentleman for propounding such hypothetical statements in the retirement of his library, and asserting in print his belief that they were abstractly true. They might be quite true, and yet the House of Brunswick might still sit safely on the throne. At all events, such would be our natural comment, looking back upon them after an interval of nearly four-score years. It is only fair to add, however, that Erskine was not actually engaged in the prosecution.

After this misadventure, which sadly dimmed his popularity, Erskine rarely spoke in Parliament, save on one occasion. In attacking Pitt on his motion for an address to the King urging the active prosecution of the war, the accomplished advocate and orator fairly "broke down." He now joined Fox and the other Whig leaders in their secession from active opposition in Parliament, and reserved himself for more auspicious times, amusing his leisure by publishing a pamphlet on "The Causes and Consequences of the War with France," which went through no less than thirty-seven editions.

In 1797, we find him again seconding Mr Grey's annual motion for parliamentary reform. In 1799, he spoke in reprobation of the rejection of the overtures of peace made by Napoleon when First Consul; and about the same time in favour of a bill to make adultery an indictable offence, against the revival of monastic institutions in England, and against the bill which excluded "clerks in holy orders" from seats in the House of Commons.

His next successes were gained as counsel for William Stone, who was prosecuted for treason, and for the Bishop of Bangor, who was indicted for riot and assault. He was employed for the prosecution against Tom Paine for the publication of his "Age of Reason;" and here, too, he was again successful, Paine being found guilty, and sentenced to a year's imprisonment. But his more appropriate sphere, and that in which he shone far better, was as counsel for the defence; and never did his ability come out more strongly than in his defence of Lord Thanet and Mr R. C. Fergusson, who were indicted for a conspiracy to rescue Arthur O'Connor at Maidstone, though he failed to procure their acquittal.

It would be tedious to attempt to enumerate all the cases in which Mr Erskine was engaged at this time; defending now the Whig *Courier* against a prosecution for "libel" against the Emperor of Russia; now Mr Cuthell, the bookseller, for publishing a pamphlet by Gilbert Wakefield; now Hadfield, the madman, for shooting at George III. in Drury Lane Theatre. His speech on the latter occasion is, perhaps, one of the best efforts of his genius, and is of great service to lawyers as a summary and storehouse of the legal distinctions in cases of mental disease. In the case of Day *v*. Day, a long and protracted litigation, in which were repeated the main features of the well-known "Douglas Case," he suffered a discomfiture; but to the last he maintained that he was right, and that Lord Kenyon, before whom it was tried, was wrong, in his law. In cases of criminal conversation he was thought especially to excel, and his speeches in the well-known causes of Markham *v*. Fawcett, Dunning *v*. Turton, and Howard *v*. Bingham, will be found in these volumes.

During the closing years of Mr Pitt's first Administration, and also during that of his successor, Mr Addington, despairing not of his cause, but of his party, Erskine kept very much aloof from politics, and declined the overtures of the latter, who wished to offer him the post of Attorney-General. He was, however, disposed to give Mr Addington a qualified and independent support, and he severely censured Mr Pitt in one of his speeches, first for his refusal to make peace with Napoleon, and then for deserting the helm of the State at a critical juncture.

In 1802 he paid another visit to Paris, where, however, he found himself very inconveniently eclipsed by the greater Whig luminary, Mr Fox, who happened to be there at the same time. In the following year, he was appointed to the command of the Temple Corps of Volunteers, generally called "The Devil's Own,"* in the ranks of which his biographer, then "plain John Campbell," served as a private; but his command was neither very effective nor of very long duration, and only served to prove how little real taste he ever could have felt for the second of the three professions of which he successively became a member. His last speech in the House of Commons was in opposition to the clause which was proposed to be introduced into the Volunteer Consolidation Bill, preventing the resignation of volunteers till the conclusion of a general peace.

On the resignation of Addington, there were again fresh rumours of a Coalition Government, including Grenville and Fox; but the obstinate King would not hear of Fox holding a seat in the Cabinet; so the negotiation fell through, and Pitt returned once more to power. Just at this time, Erskine had the misfortune to lose

---

* The Lincoln's Inn Volunteers went by the name of "The Devil's Invincibles."

his wife. She died in December 1805, and lies buried in Hampstead parish church, where a mural monument records her name and her virtues.

On the death of Pitt, early in the following year—after an ineffectual attempt to form a Cabinet under Lord Hawkesbury, afterwards Earl of Liverpool—Lord Grenville was sent for to form an Administration. Fox now was included in it, and so was Erskine, who attained what may be presumed to have been the height of his ambition as a lawyer—the custody of the Great Seal. He took his seat on the Woolsack of the House of Lords in February 1806, as Baron Erskine,* of Restormel Castle, in the county of Cornwall—one of the ancient inheritances of the Prince of Wales. The appointment, observes Lord Campbell, was "politically natural, and even laudable, but, judicially viewed, indefensible." He observes, with reference to his want of acquaintance with equity, "Better would it have been for him to have accepted the office of Attorney-General, in the expectation that a common-law chief-justiceship might become vacant, the duties of which he might adequately have performed; or to have been content with being *by far the first advocate* that ever practised at the English bar—a position more enviable than that of an indifferent Chancellor, notwithstanding the precedence and power which the Great Seal confers." Of the principles of equity, it must be owned that he knew but little;† and although he did his best, by the aid of other men, and by great attention to the arguments of counsel, to satisfy himself as to the merits of each case, and was eminently fair, honest, and impartial, still we fear that most members of the legal profession would agree that Lord Campbell is scarcely overstating the case against him, when he says that, after the experiment of his Chancellorship, which

---

* When his arms, as a peer, was made out by the Heralds' College, he dropped the motto of his family, and took instead the appropriate words, "*Trial by Jury.*"

† "The decisions *temp.* Erskine are to be found in the 12th and 13th vols. of the Reports of Vesey, jun. I believe that but little *bad* doctrine is to be found in them; yet . . . . it must be admitted that there is, generally speaking, a striking tenuity about them; that, if they do not do injustice to the parties, they lay down few useful rules; and that if they do not disturb, they do little to advance, our code of equity. In the whole series of them, I do not think that there is once an allusion to the civil or foreign jurists; and the illustrations are drawn from *nisi prius* more frequently than from the general principles established by the successive occupiers of the great chair. Luckily for the public, the office of Master of the Rolls was at this time held by Sir William Grant, who comes up to the highest standard that can be formed of judicial excellence."—*Campbell's Lives of the Chancellors*, viii. 379.

was only of a year's duration, "from being the beheld of all behold-ers, Erskine sunk into comparative insignificance." In spite of his obvious unfitness for the post, so great was his personal popularity, that a very warm address of congratulation was drawn up by the Bar, and presented to him; and among those who signed it were many very staunch and inveterate Tories. He presided as Chan-cellor at the impeachment of Lord Melville. This was a fortunate circumstance for his credit in that capacity, as his *nisi prius* know-ledge, and his ability to decide on questions of evidence, stood him here in good stead, and helped to bring out prominently the best of his judicial qualities.

Nor does it appear that either in Parliament or in the Cabinet was his influence great; but he supported the bill for the abolition of the slave-trade, although at the cost of abandoning the opinions which, in early life, he had formed as to the comparative comfort of the position of the slave. He was one of the pall-bearers at the funeral of Fox, in Westminster Abbey; and did his best to bring the stupid old King to his senses in respect of the Roman Catholic claims. In March 1807, however, a change came over the state of political affairs, and, with his party, he was obliged to resign office.

The rest of his story is soon told. He now came forward only on rare occasions, and to oppose measures which he considered thoroughly objectionable. Thus he opposed the expedition to Copenhagen, and even supported a motion for restoring the Danish fleet. He also took an active part in censuring the famous Orders in Council respecting neutral navigation, foretelling that they would lead to complications, if not to a war, with America, and would ultimately have to be abandoned. We now find him busying him-self with such details as opposing a bill allowing arrest for libel, and bringing forward another for prevention of cruelty to dumb animals. Although, on the question of the commitment of Sir Francis Burdett to the Tower, he took the unpopular side, yet he gradually adopted more enlightened views as to the claims of the Roman Catholics; but, as yet, he was not prepared to place them on a perfect equality with their Protestant fellow-countrymen.

In 1810, he supported the views of those who were inclined to place the Regency in the hands of the Prince of Wales, without any restrictions; and for a short time the Great Seal seemed to be once more within his grasp; but from and after the avowed resolution of the Prince Regent to adhere to Mr Spencer Percival and the Tories (1811), he appears, in common with his party, to have renounced all thoughts of public employment, and to have made up his mind to abstain from all further interference in the course of political affairs. He even paid very little attention to the judicial business of the House of Lords, and seems henceforth to have resolved to give himself up to a life of wit and pleasure in West-End society. He still lived at Hampstead, not far from Lord Mansfield's villa of Caen Wood, and would even occupy his leisure hours by taking in hand a spade or a rake. Shortly after this time he sold his house at Hampstead, and bought an estate near Crawley, in Sussex, where he thought, by an attention to the laws of agriculture, and by the practice of the strictest economy, that he should be able to turn a barren district into a smiling park. The latter, however, turned out a barren speculation, and the best crop it could produce was a supply of stunted birch-trees; and as he found himself approaching nearer to old age, without any great provision made against its arrival, he gave it up in despair. He would often enliven the dinner-table at Lincoln's Inn (of which he was a bencher) by anecdotes of his cotemporaries. The best of his *mots*, however (and they were many), was that which he made with respect to the Chancellorship and the Polar expedition. Captain Parry, the Arctic navigator, dining in the hall one day, complained that he and his crew, when frozen up in the Polar regions, had nothing to eat but *seals*. "And very good living too," replied Erskine, "*if you can only keep them long enough!*"

He was frequently present, and often the president, at the ceremony of laying the first stone of buildings of societies and institutions. Nothing pleased him better than to be present at fashionable balls and breakfasts of peculiar *éclat*. He also strove to divert *ennui*, and to recover his lost ground, by publishing his "Armata," an imitation of the "Utopia" of Sir Thomas More and of "Gulliver's Travels," and which was fairly successful in its day, though it is now forgotten.

In 1812 there was some idea that the Whigs would return to office; but Lord Erskine's views, especially with respect to Catholic Emancipation, were in advance of his age; and accordingly he gave up all thoughts of further employment, and continued to devote himself to the pleasures of West-End society.

For the next years of his life he rarely attended the House of Lords, and in spite of the fact that law reform was among the questions of the day, he turned a deaf ear to the subject. About this time he was made a Knight of the Thistle, an honour which he coveted the more, and appreciated the more highly, because it reflected honour on the land of his birth. He took an active and interested part in the Banbury Peerage case, protesting very strongly and vehemently against the decision arrived at by the Lords. In 1819 he supported Lord Grey's amendment to the address, condemning the Manchester massacre, and brought in a bill for the prevention of arrest of the suspected libeller before indictment found against the libeller. He took a strong and active part in mitigation of all the strong measures taken against the multitude by the Regent's Administration, and also in the trial of Queen Caroline, by whom he thoroughly stood against her Royal Consort. His last speech in the House was delivered in her cause.

In 1820 he paid a visit to Scotland (the first since he had left Leith as a middy), wearing the order of the Thistle—an honour of which his fellow-countrymen were extremely proud. He now revisited his old haunts, the place of his birth, and the old familiar stairs up and down which he had trudged, some sixty years ago, a curly-haired stripling. He was well and kindly received by his countrymen, except by Sir Walter Scott, who, as a genuine Tory, stood aloof.

Having parted with his fine house in Lincoln's Inn Fields, and his villa at Hampstead, he spent the remainder of his days in a lodging in Arabella Row, Pimlico, moving occasionally to a cottage on his estate of Holmbush, near Crawley, in Sussex, which he called Buchan Hill. He also contracted a second marriage at Gretna Green, the lady of his choice being a Miss Sarah Buck. In the early part of 1823, by way of proof that to the last he was interested in all questions of the day, he published a pamphlet on the "Agricultural Distress." But it was obvious to his friends that his career was drawing to its close. In the summer of that year he resolved to pay a visit to his brother, the Earl of Buchan, at Dryburgh Abbey, and (as there were no steamers or express trains in those days) he took ship at Blackwall for Edinburgh. On the voyage he was attacked by a serious illness; was landed at Leith, and reaching the residence of his sister-in-law, the Hon.

Mrs Henry Erskine, at Almondell, he died on the 17th of the November following, at the age of seventy-three. He was buried in a family vault at Uphall, in the county of Linlithgow. Had he died in London, it is more than probable that he would have been honoured by a funeral in Westminster Abbey: as it is, his remains repose in a quiet and peaceful country churchyard, far away from the din of law-courts and the busy haunts of men.

By his first wife he had a family of eight children—four sons and four daughters. Of the latter, Frances married the Rev. Dr Holland, precentor and prebendary of Chichester, and died in 1859 ; Elizabeth married the late Sir David Erskine, and died in 1800; Margaret died unmarried in 1857; and the youngest, Mary, married David Morris, Esq., and was left a widow in 1815. Of the sons, the first was David Montagu, second lord; the second, Henry David, some time Dean of Ripon, who married Lady Mary Harriet, third daughter of John, first Earl of Portarlington, and died in 1859; the third, the Right Hon. Thomas Erskine, one of the Judges of the Court of Common Pleas, married Henrietta Eliza, only daughter of Henry Traill, Esq., and died in 1864; and the youngest, Esme Stewart, a lieutenant-colonel in the army, and deputy-adjutant-general, who served as aide-de-camp to the Duke of Wellington at the battle of Waterloo, where he lost an arm, died in 1817.

In his title he was succeeded by his eldest son, David Montagu, some time British Minister at the court of Munich. He married Fanny, the daughter of General Cadwallader of Philadelphia, by whom he had a numerous family; and dying in 1855, was succeeded by his eldest son, Thomas Americus, the present and third Lord Erskine, who was born in 1802, and married in 1830, Louisa, daughter of George Newnham, Esq., of Newtimber Place, Sussex, and widow of Thomas Legh, Esq., of Adlington, Cheshire, which lady died in 1867.

There is no marble monument erected by the nation to Erskine's memory, nor any mural inscription to celebrate his genius and his public services; "but," to use the words of his biographer, Lord Chancellor Campbell, "the collection of his speeches will preserve his name as long as the English language endures;" and a simple narrative of his life will best show his claim to the gratitude of posterity as one who laboured, and not wholly in vain, in the cause of human progress and freedom, and the advancement of enlightened legislation. "Let us imagine to ourselves," adds his biographer, "an advocate inspired by a generous love of fame, and desirous of honourably assisting in the administration of justice by obtaining redress for the injured and defending the innocent,—one who has liberally studied the science of jurisprudence, and has stored his mind and refined his taste by a general acquaintance with elegant literature,—one who has an intuitive insight into human character, and into the workings of human passion,—one who is able not only by his powers of persuasion to give the best chances of success to every client whom he represents in every variety of public causes, but also to defeat conspiracies against the public liberty founded on a perversion of the criminal law,—and one who, by the victories which he gains and the principles which he establishes, helps to place the free constitution of his countrymen on an imperishable basis. Such an advocate was Erskine. . . . Such an advocate, in my opinion, stands quite as high in the scale of true greatness as the parliamentary leader who ably opens a budget, or who lucidly explains a new system of commercial policy, or who dexterously attacks the measures of the existing Government. . . . I will not here enter into a comparison of the respective merits of the different sorts of oratory handed down to us from antiquity ; but I may be allowed to observe, that among ourselves, in the hundred and fifty volumes of "Hansard's Debates," there are no specimens of parliamentary harangues which, as literary compositions, are comparable to the speeches of Erskine at the bar, with the exception of Burke's, and these were delivered to empty benches. . . . There will probably again be a debater equal to the elder or the younger Pitt, to Fox or Sheridan, Burke or Grey, before there arises another advocate equal to Thomas Erskine." *

* Campbell's Lives of the Chancellors, vol. ix.

SPEECHES OF LORD ERSKINE.

SPEECH for Captain BAILLIE, *delivered in the Court of King's Bench, on the 24th of November* 1778. *Taken in shorthand, and published, with the rest of the proceedings, by* Captain BAILLIE *himself, in* 1779.

THE SUBJECT.

CAPTAIN THOMAS BAILLIE, one of the oldest captains in the British Navy, having, in consideration of his age and services, been appointed Lieutenant-Governor of the Royal Hospital for Superannuated Seamen at Greenwich, saw (or thought he saw) great abuses in the administration of the charity ; and prompted, as he said, by compassion for the seamen, as well as by a sense of public duty, had endeavoured by various means to effectuate a reform.

In pursuance of this object, he had at various times presented petitions and remonstrances to the Council of the Hospital, the Directors, and the Lords Commissioners of the Admiralty, and he had at last recourse to a printed appeal addressed to the General Governors of the Hospital. These Governors consisted of all the great officers of state, privy councillors, judges, flag-officers, &c. &c.

Some of the alleged grievances in this publication were, that the health and comfort of the seamen in the Hospital were sacrificed to lucrative and corrupt contracts, under which the clothing, provisions, and all sorts of necessaries and stores were deficient ; that the contractors themselves presided in the very offices appointed by the charter for the control of contracts, where, in the character of counsellors, they were enabled to dismiss all complaints, and carry on with impunity their own system of fraud and peculation.

But the chief subject of complaint (the public notice of which, as Captain Baillie alleged, drew down upon him the resentment of the Board of Admiralty) was, that *landmen* were admitted into the offices and places in the Hospital designed exclusively for *seamen* by the spirit, if not by the letter, of the institution. To these landmen Captain Baillie imputed all the abuses he complained of, and he more than in-

A

sinuated, by his different petitions, and by the publication in question, that they were introduced to these offices for their election services to the Earl of ——, as freeholders of Huntingdonshire.

He alleged further, that he had appealed from time to time to the Council of the Hospital and to the Directors without effect, and that he had been equally unsuccessful with the Lords Commissioners of the Admiralty during the presidency of the Earl of Sandwich; that, in consequence of these failures, he resolved to attract the notice of the General Governors, and, as he thought them too numerous as a body for a convenient examination in the first instance, and besides had no means of assembling them, a statement of the facts through the medium of this appeal, drawn up exclusively for their use, and distributed solely among the members of their body, appeared to him the most eligible mode of obtaining redress on the subject.

In this composition, which was written with great zeal and with some asperity,* the names of the landmen, intruded into the offices for seamen, were enumerated; the contractors also were held forth and reprobated, and the First Lord of the Admiralty himself was not spared.

On the circulation of the book becoming general, the Board of Admiralty suspended Captain Baillie from his office; and the different officers, contractors, &c., in the Hospital, who were animadverted upon, applied to the Court of King's Bench, in Trinity Term, 1778, and obtained a rule upon Captain Baillie to show cause in the Michaelmas Term following why an information should not be exhibited against him for a libel.

All Captain Baillie's leading counsel having spoken on the 23d of November, and, owing to the lateness of the hour, the Court having adjourned the argument till the morning of the 24th, Mr Erskine spoke as follows, from the back row of the Court, we believe for the first time, as he had only been called to the bar on the last day of the term preceding.

THE SPEECH.

My Lord,—I am likewise of the counsel for the author of this supposed libel; and if the matter for consideration had been merely a question of private wrong, in which the interests of society were no farther concerned than in the protection of the innocent, I should have thought myself well justified, after the very able defence made by the learned gentlemen who have spoken before me, in sparing your Lordship, already fatigued with the subject, and in leaving my client to the prosecutor's counsel and the judgment of the Court.

But upon an occasion of this serious and dangerous complexion, when a British subject is brought before a court of justice only for having ventured to attack abuses which owe their continuance to

---

* The foundation for it we do not mean to enter into, the editor being a stranger to all the circumstances, and the preface being only introduced as explanatory of the speech.

the danger of attacking them; when, without any motives but benevolence, justice, and public spirit, he has ventured to attack them, though supported by power, and in that department, too, where it was the duty of his office to detect and expose them, I cannot relinquish the high privilege of defending such a character; I will not give up even my small share of the honour of repelling and of exposing so odious a prosecution.

No man, my Lord, respects more than I do the authority of the laws, and I trust I shall not let fall a single word to weaken the ground I mean to tread, by advancing propositions which shall oppose or even evade the strictest rules laid down by the Court in questions of this nature.

Indeed, it would be as unnecessary as it would be indecent; it will be sufficient for me to call your Lordship's attention to the marked and striking difference between the writing before you, and I may venture to say almost every other, that has been the subject of argument on a rule for a criminal information.

The writings or publications which have been brought before this Court, or before grand juries, as libels on individuals, have been attacks on the characters of private men, by writers stimulated sometimes by resentment, sometimes, perhaps, by a mistaken zeal; or they have been severe and unfounded strictures on the *characters* of public men, proceeding from officious persons taking upon themselves the censorial office, without temperance or due information, and without any call of duty to examine into the particular department of which they choose to become the voluntary guardians—a guardianship which they generally content themselves with holding in a newspaper for two or three posts, and then, with a generosity which shines on all mankind alike, correct every department of the state, and find at the end of their lucubrations that they themselves are the only honest men in the community. When men of this description suffer, however we may be occasionally sorry for their misdirected zeal, it is impossible to argue against the law that censures them.

But I beseech your Lordship to compare these men and their works with my client and the publication before the Court.

Who is he?—What is his duty?—What has he written?—To whom has he written?—And what motive induced him to write?

He is Lieutenant-Governor of the Royal Hospital of Greenwich, a palace built for the reception of aged and disabled men who have maintained the empire of England on the seas, and into the offices and emoluments of which, by the express words of the charter, as well as by the evident spirit of the institution, no landmen are to be admitted.

His Duty—in the treble capacity of Lieutenant-Governor, Director, and a General Governor—is, in conjunction with others, to watch over the internal economy of this sacred charity, to see that the setting days of these brave and godlike men are spent in comfort and peace, and that the ample revenues appropriated by this generous nation to their support are not perverted and misapplied.

HE HAS WRITTEN, that this benevolent and politic institution has degenerated from the system established by its wise and munificent founders; that its Governors consist, indeed, of a great number of illustrious names and reverend characters, but whose different labours and destinations in the most important offices of civil life rendered a deputation indispensably necessary for the ordinary government of the Hospital; that the difficulty of convening this splendid corporation had gradually brought the management of its affairs more particularly under the direction of the Admiralty; that a new charter has been surreptitiously obtained, in repugnance to the original institution, which enlarges and confirms that dependence; that the present First Lord of the Admiralty (who, for reasons sufficiently obvious, does not appear publicly in this prosecution) has, to serve the base and worthless purposes of corruption, introduced his prostituted freeholders of Huntingdon into places destined for the honest freeholders of the seas; that these men (among whom are the prosecutors) are not only landmen, in defiance of the charter, and wholly dependent on the Admiralty in their views and situations, but, to the reproach of all order and government, are suffered to act as Directors and officers of Greenwich, while *they themselves* hold the very subordinate offices, the *control* of which is the object of that direction; and inferring from thence (as a general proposition) that men in such situations cannot, as human nature is constituted, act with that freedom and singleness which their duty requires, he justly attributes to these causes the grievances which his gallant brethren actually suffer, and which are the generous subject of his complaint.

He has written this, my Lord, not *to the public at large*, which has no jurisdiction to reform the abuses he complains of, but to *those only* whose express duty it is to hear and to correct them, and I trust they will be solemnly heard and corrected. He has not PUBLISHED, but only distributed his book among the Governors, to produce inquiry, and not to calumniate.

THE MOTIVE WHICH INDUCED HIM TO WRITE, and to which I shall by and by claim the more particular attention of the Court, was to produce reformation—a reformation which it was his most pointed duty to attempt, which he has laboured with the most indefatigable zeal to accomplish, and against which every other channel was blocked up.

My Lord, I will point to the proof of all this; I will show your Lordship that it was his duty to investigate; that the abuses he has investigated do really exist and arise from the ascribed causes; that he has presented them to a competent jurisdiction, and not to the public; and that he was under the indispensable necessity of taking the step he has done to save Greenwich Hospital from ruin.

Your Lordship will observe, by this subdivision, that I do not wish to form a specious desultory defence, because, feeling that every link of such subdivision will, in the investigation, produce both law and fact in my favour, I have spread the subject open before the eye of the Court, and invite the strictest scrutiny. Your Lordship will likewise observe by this arrangement that I mean to confine myself to the *general* lines of his defence; the various affidavits have already been so ably and judiciously commented on by my learned leaders—to whom, I am sure, Captain Baillie must ever feel himself under the highest obligations—that my duty has become narrowed to the province of throwing his defence within the closest compass, that it may leave a distinct and decided impression.

And first, my Lord, as to its being his *particular duty* to inquire into the different matters which are the subject of his publication, and of the prosecutors' complaint, I believe, my Lords, I need say little on this head to convince your Lordships, who are yourselves Governors of Greenwich Hospital, that the defendant, in the double capacity of Lieutenant-Governor and Director, is most indispensably bound to superintend everything that can affect the prosperity of the institution, either in internal economy or appropriation of revenue; but I cannot help reading two copies of letters from the Admiralty in the year 1742. I read them from the publication, because their authenticity is sworn to by the defendant in his affidavit; and I read them to show the sense of that Board with regard to the right of inquiry and complaint in all officers of the Hospital, even in the departments not allotted to them by their commissions.

" *To Sir John Jennings,*
" *Governor of Greenwich Hospital.*　•

" ADMIRALTY OFFICE, *April* 10, 1742.

" SIR,—The Directors of Greenwich Hospital having acquainted my Lords Commissioners of the Admiralty, upon complaint made to them, that the men have been defrauded of part of their just allowance of broth and pease-soup, by the smallness of the pewter dishes, which in their opinion have been artificially beaten flat, and that there are other frauds and abuses attending this affair, to the prejudice of the poor men, I am commanded by their Lordships to desire you to call the officers together in Council, and to let them know that their Lordships think them very blamable for suffering such abuses to be practised, which could not have been done without their extreme indolence in not looking into the affairs of the Hospital; that their own establishment in the Hospital is for the care and protection of the poor men, and that it is their duty to look daily into everything, and to remedy every disorder, and not to discharge themselves by throwing it upon the under-officers and servants; and that their Lordships, being determined to go to the bottom of this complaint, do charge them to find out and inform them at whose door the fraud ought to be laid, that their Lordships may give such directions herein as they shall judge proper.—I am, Sir, your most obedient servant, THOS. CORBET."

"ADMIRALTY OFFICE, *May* 7, 1742.

"SIR,—My Lords Commissioners of the Admiralty having referred to the Directors of Greenwich Hospital the report made by yourself and officers of the said Hospital in Council, dated the 23d past, relating to the flatness of the pewter dishes made use of to hold the broth and pease-pottage served out to the pensioners, the said Directors have returned hither a reply, a copy of which I am ordered to send you enclosed: they have herein set forth a fact which has a very fraudulent appearance, and it imports little by what means the dishes became shallow; but if it be true, what they assert, that the dishes hold but little more than half the quantity they ought to do, the poor men must have been greatly injured; and the allegations in the officers' report, that the pensioners have made no complaint, does rather aggravate their conduct in suffering the men's patience to be so long imposed upon.

"My Lords Commissioners of the Admiralty do command me to express myself in such a manner as may show their wrath and displeasure at such a proceeding. You will please to communicate this to the officers of the house in Council.

"Their Lordships do very well know that the Directors have no power but in the management of the revenue and estates of the Hospital, and in carrying on the works of the building, nor did they assume any on this occasion; but their Lordships shall always take well of them any informations that tend to rectify any mistakes or omissions whatsoever concerning the state of the Hospital.—I am, Sir, your obedient servant, THOS. CORBET.

"*To Sir John Jennings,*
"*Governor of Greenwich Hospital.*"

From these passages it is plain that the Admiralty *then* was sensible of the danger of abuses in so extensive an institution, that it encouraged complaints from all quarters, and instantly redressed them; for although corruption was not then *an infant*, yet the idea of making a job of Greenwich Hospital never entered her head; and indeed if it had, she could, hardly have found at that time of day, a man with a heart callous enough to consent to such a scheme, or with forehead enough to carry it into public execution.

Secondly, my Lord, that the abuses he has investigated do in truth exist, and arise from the ascribed causes.

And at the word TRUTH I must pause a little to consider how far it is a defence on a rule of this kind, and what evidence of the falsehood of the supposed libel the Court expects from prosecutors, before it will allow the information to be filed, even where no affidavits are produced by the defendant in his exculpation.

That a libel *upon an individual* is not the less so for being true, I do not, *under certain restrictions*, deny to be law; nor is it necessary for me to deny it, because this is not a complaint in THE ORDINARY COURSE OF LAW, but an application to the Court to exert an ECCENTRIC, EXTRAORDINARY, VOLUNTARY JURISDICTION, BEYOND THE ORDINARY COURSE OF JUSTICE; a jurisdiction, which I am authorised from the best authority to say, this Court will not exercise, unless the prosecutors come PURE AND UNPOLLUTED; denying upon oath the truth of every word and sentence which they complain of as injurious: for although, in common cases, the matter may be not the less libellous because true, yet the Court will not interfere by information for guilty or even equivocal characters, but will leave them to its ordinary process. If the Court does not see palpable MALICE and FALSEHOOD on the part of the defendant, and clear innocence on the part of the prosecutor, it will not stir;—it will say, This may be a libel; this may deserve punishment; but go to a grand jury, or bring your actions:—all men are equally entitled to the protection of the laws, but all men are not equally entitled to an extraordinary interposition and protection beyond the common distributive forms of justice.

This is the true constitutional doctrine of informations, and made a strong impression upon me, when delivered by your Lordship in this Court; the occasion which produced it was of little consequence, but the principle was important. It was an information moved for by General Plasto against the printer of the *Westminster Gazette*, for a libel published in his paper charging that gentleman, among other things, with having been tried at the Old Bailey for a felony. The prosecutor's affidavit denied the charges *generally* as foul, scandalous, and false; but did not traverse the aspersion I have just mentioned *as a substantive fact;* upon which your Lordship told the counsel, Mr Dunning, who was too learned to argue against the objection, that the affidavit was defective in that particular, and should be amended before the Court would even grant a rule to show cause: for although such GENERAL denial would be sufficient where the libellous matter consisted of scurrility, insinuation, GENERAL abuse, which is no otherwise traversable than by innuendoes of the import of the scandal, and a denial of the truth of it, yet that when a libel consisted of DIRECT AND POSITIVE FACTS AS CHARGES, the Court required SUBSTANTIVE *traverses of such facts* in the affidavit before it would interpose to take the matter from the cognisance of a grand jury.

This is the law of informations, and by this touchstone I will try the prosecutors' affidavits, to show that they will fall of themselves, even without that body of evidence with which I can in a moment overwhelm them.

If the defendant be guilty of any crime at all, it is for writing THIS BOOK : and the conclusion of his guilt or innocence must consequently depend on the scope and design of it, the general truth of it, and the necessity for writing it ; and this conclusion can no otherwise be drawn than by taking the WHOLE of it together. Your Lordships will not shut your eyes, as these prosecutors expect, to the *design* and *general truth* of the book, and go entirely upon the *insulated* passages, culled out, and set heads and points in their wretched affidavits, without context, or even an attempt to unriddle or explain their sense or bearing on the subject ; for, my Lord, they have altogether omitted to traverse the scandalous facts themselves, and have only laid hold of those warm animadversions which the recital of them naturally produced in the mind of an honest, zealous man, and which, besides, are in many places only conclusions drawn from facts as general propositions, and not aspersions on them as individuals. And where the facts do come home to them AS CHARGES, *not one of them is denied by the prosecutors. I assert, my Lord, that in the Directors' whole affidavit* (which I have read repeatedly, and with the greatest attention) *there is not any one fact mentioned by the defendant which is substantially denied ;* and even when five or six strong and pointed charges are tacked to each other, to avoid meeting naked truth in the teeth, they are not even contradicted by the lump, but a general innuendo is pinned to them all ; a mere illusory averment, that the facts mean to criminate them, and that they are not criminal ; BUT THE FACTS THEMSELVES REMAIN UNATTEMPTED AND UNTOUCHED.

Thus, my Lord, after reciting in their affidavit the charge of their shameful misconduct, in renewing the contract with the Huntingdon butchers, who had just compounded the penalties incurred by the breach of a former contract, and in that breach of contract, the breach of every principle of humanity, as well as of honesty ; and the charge of putting improper objects of charity into the Hospital, while the families of poor pensioners were excluded and starving ; and of screening delinquents from inquiry and punishment *in a pointed and particular instance,* and therefore traversable as a *substantive fact ;* yet not only there is no such traverse, but, though all these matters are huddled together in a mass, there is not even a general denial ; but one loose innuendo, that the facts in the publication are stated with an intention of criminating the prosecutors, and that, *as far as they tend to criminate them,* they are false.

Will this meet the doctrine laid down by your Lordship in the case of General Plasto ? Who can tell what they mean by criminality ? Perhaps they think neglect of duty not criminal,—

perhaps they think corrupt servility to a patron not criminal; and that if they do not ACTIVELY promote abuses, the winking at them is not criminal. But I appeal to the Court, whether the Directors' whole affidavit is not a cautious composition to avoid downright perjury, and yet a glaring absurdity on the face of it; for since the facts are not traversed, the Court must intend them to exist; and if they do exist, they cannot but be criminal. The very existence of such abuses in itself criminates those whose offices are to prevent them from existing. Under the shelter of such qualifications of guilt, no man in trust could ever be criminated. But at all events, my Lord, since they seem to think that the facts may exist without their criminality,—be it so: the defendant then does not wish to criminate them; he wishes only for effectual inquiry and information, that there may be no longer any crimes, and consequently no criminality. But HE trusts, in the meantime, and *I* likewise trust, that, while these facts do exist, the Court will at least desire the prosecutors to clear themselves before the General Council of Governors, to whom the writing is addressed, and not before any *packed* Committee of Directors appointed by a noble Lord, and then come back to the Court acquitted of all criminality, or, according to the technical phrase, with *clean hands*, for protection.

Such are the merits of the affidavits exhibited by the Directors; and the affidavits of the other persons are, without distinction, subject to the same observations. They are made up either of general propositions, converted into charges by ridiculous innuendoes, or else of strings of distinct disjointed facts tied together, and explained by one general averment; and after all, the scandal, such as their arbitrary interpretation makes it, is still only denied with the old jesuitical qualification of criminality—*the facts themselves remaining untraversed, and even untouched.*

They are, indeed, every way worthy of their authors,—of Mr ——, the *good* steward, who, notwithstanding the remonstrances of the captain of the week, received for the pensioners such food as would be rejected by the idle vagrant poor, and endeavoured to tamper with the cook to conceal it; and of Mr ——, who converted their wards into apartments for himself, and the clerks of clerks, in the endless subordination of idleness; a wretch who has dared, with brutal inhumanity, to strike those aged men, who in their youth would have blasted him with a look. As to Mr —— and Mr ——, though I think them reprehensible for joining in this prosecution, yet they are certainly respectable men, and not at all on a level with the rest, nor has the defendant so reduced them. These two, therefore, have in fact no cause of complaint, and, Heaven knows, the others have no title to complain.

In this enumeration of delinquents, the Rev. Mr —— looks round, as if he thought I had forgotten him. He is mistaken; I well remember him: but *his* infamy is worn threadbare: Mr

Murphy has already treated him with that ridicule which his folly, and Mr Peckham with that invective which his wickedness deserves. I shall, therefore, forbear to taint the ear of the Court further with his name,—a name which would bring dishonour upon his country and its religion, if human nature were not happily compelled to bear the greater part of the disgrace, and to share it amongst mankind.

But these observations, my Lord, are solely confined to the prosecutors' affidavits, and would, I think, be fatal to them, even if they stood uncontroverted. But what will the Court say when *ours* are opposed to them, where the truth of every part is sworn to by the defendant? What will the Court say to the collateral circumstances in support of them, where every material charge against the prosecutors is confirmed? What will it say to the affidavit that has been made that no man can come safely to support this injured officer?—that men have been deprived of their places, and exposed to beggary and ruin, merely for giving evidence of abuses which have already by his exertions been proved before your Lordship at Guildhall, whilst he himself has been suspended as a beacon for prudence to stand aloof from, so that in this unconstitutional mode of trial, where the law will not lend its process to bring in truth by *force*, he might stand unprotected by the *voluntary* oaths of the only persons who could witness for him?* His character has, indeed, in some measure, broken through all this malice: the love and veneration which his honest zeal has justly created have enabled him to produce the proofs which are filed in Court; but many have hung back, and one withdrew his affidavit, *avowedly* from the dread of persecution, even after it was sworn in Court. Surely, my Lord, this evidence of malice in the leading powers of the Hospital would alone be sufficient to destroy their testimony, even when swearing collaterally to facts in which they were not themselves interested; how much more when they come as *prosecutors*, stimulated by resentment, and with the hope of covering their patrons' misdemeanours and their own by turning the tables on the defendant, and prosecuting *him* criminally, to stifle all necessary inquiry into the subject of his complaints?

Lieutenant Gordon, the first Lieutenant of the Hospital, and the oldest officer in the navy; Lieutenant William Lefevre; Lieutenant Charles Lefevre, his son; Alexander Moore; Lieutenant William Ansell; and Captain Allright, have all positively sworn that a faction of landmen subsists in the Hospital, and that they do on their consciences believe that the defendant drew upon

* On the trial of a cause, every person acquainted with any fact is bound, under pain of fine and imprisonment, to attend on a subpœna to give evidence before the Court and jury; but there is no process to compel any man to make an affidavit before the Court.

himself the resentment of the prosecutors from his activity in correcting this enormous abuse, and from his having restored the wards that had been cruelly taken away from the poor old men; that on that just occasion the whole body of the pensioners surrounded the apartments of their Governor to testify their gratitude with acclamations, which sailors never bestow but on men who deserve them. This simple and honest tribute was the signal for all that has followed; the leader of these unfortunate people was turned out of office; and the affidavit of Charles Smith is filed in Court, which, I thank my God, I have not been able to read without tears; how, indeed, could any man, when he swears that for this cause alone his place was taken from him; that he received his dismission when languishing with sickness in the infirmary, the consequence of which was, that his unfortunate wife and several of his helpless innocent children died in want and misery; THE WOMAN ACTUALLY EXPIRING AT THE GATES OF THE HOSPITAL. That such wretches should escape chains and a dungeon is a reproach to humanity, and to all order and government; but that they should become PROSECUTORS is a degree of effrontery that would not be believed by any man who did not accustom himself to observe the shameless scenes which the monstrous age we live in is every day producing.

I come now, my Lord, to consider TO WHOM HE HAS WRITTEN. This book is not PUBLISHED. It was not printed for SALE, but for the more commodious distribution among the many persons who are called upon *in duty* to examine into its contents. If the defendant had written it to calumniate, he would have thrown it abroad among the multitude: but he swears he wrote it for the attainment of reformation, and therefore confined its circulation to the proper channel till he saw it was received as a libel, and then he even discontinued that distribution, and only showed it to his counsel to consider of a defence; and no better defence can be made than that the publication was so *limited.*

My Lord, a man cannot be guilty of a libel who presents grievances before a *competent* jurisdiction, although the facts he presents should be false; he may, indeed, be indicted for a malicious prosecution, and even there a probable cause would protect him, but he can by no construction be considered as a libeller.

The case of Lake and King, in 1st Levinz, 240, but which is better reported in 1st Saunders, is directly in point. It was an action for printing a petition to the members of a Committee of Parliament, charging the plaintiff with gross fraud in the execution of his office. I am aware that it was an action on the case, and not a criminal prosecution; but I am prepared to show your Lordship that the precedent on that account makes the stronger for us. The truth of the matter, though part of the plea, was not the point in contest; the justification was the presenting it to a proper jurisdiction, and printing it, as in this case, for more commodious distribution; and it was first of all resolved by the Court that the delivery of the petition to all the members of the Committee was justifiable; and that it was no libel, *whether the matter contained were true or false*, it being an appeal in a course of justice, and because the parties to whom it was addressed had jurisdiction to determine the matter; that the intention of the law in prohibiting libels was to restrain men from making themselves their own judges, instead of referring the matter to those whom the constitution had appointed to determine it; and that to adjudge such reference to be a libel would discourage men from making their inquiries with that freedom and readiness which the law allows, and which the good of society requires. But it was objected he could not justify the PRINTING; for by that means it was published to printers and composers; but it was answered, and resolved by the whole Court, that the printing, *with intent to distribute them among the members of the Committee*, was legal; and that the making many copies by clerks would have made the matter more public. I said, my Lord, that this being an action on the case, and not an indictment or information, made the stronger for us; and I said so because the action on the case is to redress the party in damages for the injury he has sustained as an individual, and which he has a right to recover unless the defendant can show that the matter is true, or, as in this case, whether true or false, that it is an appeal to justice. Now, my Lord, if a defendant's right to appeal to justice could in the case of Lake and King repel a plaintiff's right to damages, although he was actually damnified by the appeal, how much more must it repel a criminal prosecution which can be undertaken only for the sake of public justice, when the law says it is for the benefit of public justice to make such appeal? And that case went to protect even falsehood, and where the defendant was not particularly called upon in duty as an individual to animadvert: how much more shall it protect us, who were bound to inquire, who have written nothing but truth, and who have addressed what we have written to a competent jurisdiction?

I come, lastly, my Lord, to the motives which induced him to write.

The government of Greenwich Hospital is divided into three departments—the Council, the Directors, and the General Governors. The defendant is a member of every one of these, and therefore his duty is universal. The COUNCIL consists of the officers whose duty it is to regulate the internal economy and discipline of the house, the Hospital being, as it were, a large man-of-war, and the Council its commanders; and, therefore, these men, even by the present mutilated charter, ought all to be seamen. Secondly, The

Directors, whose duty is merely to concern themselves with the appropriation of the revenue, in contracting for and superintending supplies, and in keeping up the structure of the Hospital; and, lastly, the General Court of Governors, consisting of almost every man in the kingdom with a sounding name of office—a mere nullity, on the members of which no blame of neglect can possibly be laid; for the Hospital might as well have been placed under the tuition of the fixed stars as under so many illustrious persons, in different and distant departments. From the Council, therefore, appeals and complaints formerly lay at the Admiralty, the Directors having quite a separate duty; and, as I have shown the Court, the Admiralty encouraged complaints of abuses, and redressed them. But since the administration of the present First Lord, the face of things has changed. I trust it will be observed that I do not go out of the affidavit to seek to calumniate: my respect for the COURT would prevent me, though my respect for the said First Lord might not. But the very foundation of my client's defence depending on this matter, I must take the liberty to point it out to the Court.

The Admiralty having placed several landmen in the offices that form the Council, a majority is often artificially secured there; and when abuses are too flagrant to be passed over in the face of day, they carry their appeal to the Directors instead of the Admiralty, where, from the very nature of man, in a much more perfect state than the prosecutors, they are sure to be rejected or slurred over; because these acting Directors themselves are not only under the same influence with the complainants, but the subjects of the appeals are most frequently the fruits of their own active delinquencies, or at least the consequence of their own neglects. By this manœuvre the Admiralty is secured from hearing complaints; and the First Lord, when any comes as formerly from an individual, answers, with a perfect composure of muscle, that it is *coram non judice*—it does not come through the Directors. The defendant positively swears this to be true; he declares that, in the course of these meetings of the Council, and of appeals to the Directors, he has been not only uniformly overruled, but insulted as Governor in the execution of his duty; and the truth of the abuses which have been the subject of these appeals, as well as the insults I have mentioned, are proved by whole volumes of affidavits filed in Court, notwithstanding the numbers who have been deterred by persecution from standing forth as witnesses.

The defendant also himself solemnly swears this to be true. He swears that his heart was big with the distresses of his brave brethren, and that his conscience called on him to give them vent; that he often complained; that he repeatedly wrote to, and waited on, Lord ——, without any effect, or prospect of effect; and that at last, wearied with fruitless exertions, and disgusted with the insolence of corruption in the Hospital, which hates him for his honesty, he applied to be sent, with all his wounds and infirmities, upon actual service again. The answer he received is worthy of observation. The First Lord told him, in derision, that it would be the same thing everywhere else; that he would see the same abuses in a ship; and I do in my conscience believe he spoke the truth, as far as depended on himself.

What, then, was the defendant to do under the treble capacity of Lieutenant-Governor, of Director, and of General Governor of the Hospital? My Lord, there was no alternative but to prepare, as he did, the statement of the abuses for the other Governors, or to sit silent, and let them continue. Had he chosen *the last*, he might have been caressed by the prosecutors, and still have continued the first inhabitant of a palace, with an easy independent fortune. But he preferred the dictates of honour, and he fulfilled them at the expense of being discarded, after forty years' gallant service, covered with wounds, and verging to old age. But he respected the laws while he fulfilled his duty; his object was reformation, not reproach; he preferred a complaint, and stimulated a regular inquiry, but suspended the punishment of public shame till the guilt should be made manifest by a trial. He did not therefore *publish*, as their affidavits falsely assert, but only preferred a complaint *by distribution of copies to the Governors*, which I have shown the Court, by the authority of a solemn legal decision, is NOT A LIBEL.

Such, my Lords, is the case. The defendant,—not a disappointed malicious informer, prying into official abuses, because without office himself, but himself a man in office;—not troublesomely inquisitive into other men's departments, but conscientiously correcting his own;—doing it pursuant to the rules of law, and, what heightens the character, doing it at the risk of his office from which the effrontery of power has already suspended him without proof of his guilt;—a conduct not only unjust and illiberal, but highly disrespectful to this Court, whose judges sit in the double capacity of ministers of the law and governors of this sacred and abused institution. Indeed, Lord —— has, in my mind, acted such a part——

> [*Here Lord Mansfield, observing the counsel heated with his sub-ject, and growing personal on the First Lord of the Admiralty, told him that Lord —— was not before the Court.*]

I know that he is not formally before the Court, but for that very reason *I will bring him before the Court:* he has placed these men in the front of the battle, in hopes to escape under their shelter, but I will not join in battle with them: *their* vices, though screwed up to the highest pitch of human depravity, are not of dignity enough to vindicate the combat with *me*. I will drag *him* to light who is the dark mover behind the scene of iniquity. I assert that the Earl of —— has but one road to escape out of this business without pollution and disgrace: and *that is*, by publicly disavowing the acts of the prosecutors, and restoring Captain Baillie to his command. If he does this, then his offence will be no more than the too common one of having suffered his own *personal* interest to prevail over his *public* duty, in placing his voters in the Hospital. But if, on the contrary, he continues to protect the prosecutors, in spite of the evidence of their guilt, which has excited the abhorrence of the numerous audience that crowd this Court; IF HE KEEPS THIS INJURED MAN SUSPENDED, OR DARES TO TURN THAT SUSPENSION INTO A REMOVAL, I SHALL THEN NOT SCRUPLE TO DECLARE HIM AN ACCOMPLICE IN THEIR GUILT, A SHAMELESS OPPRESSOR, A DISGRACE TO HIS RANK, AND A TRAITOR TO HIS TRUST. But, as I should be very sorry that the fortune of my brave and honourable friend should depend either upon the exercise of Lord ——'s virtues or the influence of his fears, I do most earnestly entreat the Court to mark the malignant object of this prosecution, and to defeat it. I beseech you, my Lords, to consider, that even by discharging the rule, and with costs, the defendant is neither protected nor restored. I trust, therefore, your Lordships will not rest satisfied with fulfilling your JUDICIAL duty, but, as the strongest evidence of foul abuses has, by accident, come collaterally before you, that you will protect a brave and public-spirited officer from the persecution this writing has brought upon him, and not suffer so dreadful an example to go abroad into the world as the ruin of an upright man for having faithfully discharged his duty.

My Lords, this matter is of the last importance. I speak not as an ADVOCATE alone—I speak to you AS A MAN—as a member of a state whose very existence depends upon her NAVAL STRENGTH. If a misgovernment were to fall upon Chelsea Hospital, to the ruin and discouragement of our army, it would be no doubt to be lamented, yet I should not think it fatal; but if our fleets are to be crippled by the baneful influence of elections, WE ARE LOST INDEED! If the seaman who, while he exposes his body to fatigues and dangers, looking forward to Greenwich as an asylum for infirmity and old age, sees the gates of it blocked up by corruption, and hears the riot and mirth of luxurious landmen drowning the groans and complaints of the wounded, helpless companions of his glory,—he will tempt the seas no more. The Admiralty may press HIS BODY, indeed, at the expense of humanity and the constitution, but they cannot press *his mind*—they cannot press the heroic ardour of a British sailor; and instead of a fleet to carry terror all round the globe, the Admiralty may not much longer be able to amuse us with even the peaceable, unsubstantial pageant of a review.*

FINE AND IMPRISONMENT!—The man deserves a PALACE instead

* There had just before been a naval review at Portsmouth.

of a PRISON who prevents the palace, built by the public bounty of his country, from being converted into a dungeon, and who sacrifices his own security to the interests of humanity and virtue.

And now, my Lord, I have done ;—but not without thanking your Lordship for the very indulgent attention I have received, though in so late a stage of this business, and notwithstanding my great incapacity and inexperience. I resign my client into your hands, and I resign him with a well-founded confidence and hope ; because that torrent of corruption which has unhappily overwhelmed every other part of the constitution is, by the blessing of Providence, stopped HERE by the sacred independence of the judges. I know that your Lordships will determine ACCORDING TO LAW ; and, therefore, if an information should be suffered to be filed, I shall bow to the sentence, and shall consider this meritorious publication to be indeed an offence against the laws of this country ; but then I shall not scruple to say, that it is high time for every honest man to remove himself from a country in which he can no longer do his duty to the public with safety ;—where cruelty and inhumanity are suffered to impeach virtue, and where vice passes through a court of justice unpunished and unreproved.

SPEECH for THOMAS CARNAN, *Bookseller, at the Bar of the House of Commons, on the 10th of May* 1779. *As taken in shorthand.*

THE SUBJECT.

By letters-patent of King James I., the Stationers' Company and the Universities of Oxford and Cambridge had obtained the exclusive right of printing almanacs, by virtue of a supposed copyright in the Crown. This monopoly had been submitted to from the date of the grant in the last century, until Mr Carnan, formerly a bookseller in St Paul's Churchyard, printed them, and sold them in the ordinary course of his trade. This spirited and active tradesman made many improvements upon the Stationers' and University almanacs, and, at a very considerable expense, compiled many of the various classes of useful information, by which pocket almanacs have been rendered so very convenient in the ordinary occurrences of life, but which, without the addition of the calendar, few would have been disposed to purchase.

Upon the sale of Carnan's almanacs becoming extensive and profitable, the two Universities and the Stationers' Company filed a bill in the Court of Exchequer, for an injunction to restrain it, praying that the copies sold might be accounted for, and the remainder delivered up to be cancelled.

It appears from the proceedings printed at the time by the late Mr Carnan, that the Court, doubting the validity of the King's charter, on which the right of the Universities and of the Stationers' Company was founded, directed a question upon its legality to be argued before the Court of Common Pleas, whose judges, after two arguments before them, certified that the patent was void in law; the Court of Exchequer thereupon dismissed the bill, and the injunction was dissolved.

Mr Carnan, having obtained this judgment, prosecuted his trade for a short time with increased activity, when a bill was introduced into the House of Commons by the late Earl of Guilford, then Lord North, Prime Minister, and Chancellor of the University of Oxford, *to revest, by Act of Parliament, the monopoly in almanacs, which had fallen to the ground by the above-mentioned judgments in the King's courts.*

The preamble of the bill recited the exclusive right given to the Stationers and Universities by the charter of Charles II., as a fund for the printing of curious and learned books, the uniform enjoyment under it, the judgments of the courts of law upon the invalidity of the charter, and the expediency of regranting the monopoly for the same useful purposes by the authority of Parliament.

The bill being supported by all the influence of the two Universities in the House of Commons, and being introduced by Lord North in the plenitude of his authority, Mr Carnan's opposition to it by counsel was considered at the time as a forlorn hope ; but to the high honour of the House of Commons, it appears from the journals, vol. xxxvii., p. 388, that immediately on Mr Erskine's retiring from the bar, the House divided, and that the bill was rejected by a majority of forty-five votes.

THE SPEECH.

Mr Speaker,—In preparing myself to appear before you, as counsel for a private individual, to oppose the enactment of a *general* and *public* statute, which was to affect the *whole* community, I felt myself under some sort of difficulty.   Conscious that no man, or body of men, had a right to dictate to, or even to argue with Parliament on the exercise of the high and important trust of legislation, and that the policy and expediency of a law was rather the subject of debate in the *House*, than of argument at the *bar*, I was afraid that I should be obliged to confine myself to the special injury which the petitioner, as an individual, would suffer, and that you might be offended with any *general* observations, which, if not applying to him personally, might be thought unbecoming in me to offer to the superior wisdom of the House.

But I am relieved from that apprehension by the great indulgence with which you have listened to the general scope of the question from the learned gentleman (Mr Davenport) who has spoken before me, and likewise by the reflection, that I remember no instance where Parliament has taken away any right conferred by the law as a common benefit, without very satisfactory evidence that the universal good of the community required the sacrifice ; because every unnecessary restraint on the natural liberty of mankind is a degree of tyranny which no wise legislature will inflict.

The general policy of the bill is then fully open to my investigation ; because, if I can succeed in exposing the erroneous principles on which it is founded,—if I can show it to be repugnant to every wise and liberal system of government, I shall be listened to with the greater attention, and shall have the less to combat with, when I come to state the special grounds of objection which I am instructed to represent to you on behalf of the petitioner against it. Sir, I shall not recapitulate what you have already heard from the bar ; you are in full possession of the facts which gave rise to the question, and I shall therefore proceed directly to the investigation of the principles which I mean to apply to them, in opposition to the bill before you—pledging myself to you to do it with as much truth and fidelity, as if I had the honour to speak to you as a member of the House.   I am confident, sir, that, if you will indulge me with your attention, I shall make it appear that the very same principles which emancipated almanacs from the fetters of the prerogative in the courts of law, ought equally to free them from all parliamentary restriction.

On the first introduction of printing, it was considered, as well in England as in other countries, to be a matter of state. The quick and extensive circulation of sentiments and opinions, which that invaluable art introduced, could not but fall under the gripe of governments, whose principal strength was built upon the ignorance of the people who were to submit to them. The PRESS was, therefore, wholly under the coercion of the Crown, and *all printing*, not only of *public* books containing ordinances religious or civil, but *every species of publication whatsoever*, was regulated by the King's proclamations, prohibitions, charters of privilege, and finally by the decrees of the Star-Chamber.

After the demolition of that odious jurisdiction, the Long Parliament, on its rupture with Charles I., assumed the same power which had before been in the Crown; and after the Restoration the same restrictions were re-enacted and re-annexed to the prerogative by the statute of the 13th and 14th of Charles II., and continued down by subsequent acts, till after the Revolution. In what manner they expired at last, in the time of King William, I need not state in this House; their happy abolition, and the vain attempts to revive them in the end of that reign, stand recorded on your own journals, I trust, as perpetual monuments of your wisdom and virtue. It is sufficient to say, that the expiration of these disgraceful statutes, by the refusal of Parliament to continue them any longer, formed THE GREAT ERA OF THE LIBERTY OF THE PRESS IN THIS COUNTRY, and stripped the Crown of every prerogative over it, except that which, upon just and rational principles of government, must ever belong to the executive magistrate in all countries, namely, the exclusive right to publish religious or civil constitutions,—in a word, to promulgate every ordinance which contains the rules of action by which the subject is to live and to be governed. These always did, and, from the very nature of civil government, always ought to, belong to the sovereign, and hence have gained the title of prerogative copies.

When, therefore, the Stationers' Company, claiming the exclusive right of printing almanacs under a charter of King James I., applied to the Court of Exchequer for an injunction against the petitioner at your bar, the question submitted by the barons to the learned judges of the Common Pleas, namely, "WHETHER THE CROWN COULD GRANT SUCH EXCLUSIVE RIGHT?" was neither more nor less than this question—*Whether almanacs were such public ordinances, such matters of state, as belonged to the King by his prerogative, so as to enable him to communicate an exclusive right of printing them to a grantee of the Crown?* For the press being thrown open by the expiration of the licensing Acts, nothing could

remain exclusively to such grantees but the printing of such books
as, upon solid constitutional grounds, belonged to the superintendence of the Crown as matters of authority and state.

The question so submitted was twice solemnly argued in the
Court of Common Pleas; when the judges unanimously certified
that the Crown had no such power; and their determination, as
evidently appears from the arguments of the counsel, which the
Chief-Justice recognised with the strongest marks of approbation,
was plainly founded on this,—that almanacs had no resemblance to
those public acts, religious or civil, which, on principle, fall under
the superintendence of the Crown.

The counsel (Mr Serjeant Glynn and Mr Serjeant Hill), two of
the most learned men in the profession, who argued the case for the
plaintiffs, were aware that the King's prerogative in this particular
had no absolute and fixed foundation, either by prescription or
statute, but that it depended on public policy, and the reasonable
limitation of executive power for the common good ; they felt that
the judges had no other standard by which to determine whether
it *was* a prerogative copy, than by settling upon principles of good
sense *whether it ought to be one;* they laboured, therefore, to show the
propriety of the revision of almanacs by public authority ; they said
they contained the regulation of time, which was matter of public
institution, having a reference to all laws and ordinances,—that they
were part of the Prayer-Book, which belonged to the King as head
of the Church,—that they contained matters which were received as
conclusive evidence in courts of justice, and therefore ought to be
published by authority,—that the trial by almanac was a mode of
decision not unknown,—that many inconveniences might arise to
the public from mistakes in the matters they contained : many
other arguments of the like nature were relied on, which it is unnecessary for me to enumerate in this place, as they were rejected by
the Court ; and likewise, because the only reason of my mentioning
them at all is to show, that the *public expediency or propriety* of
subjecting almanacs to revision by authority, appeared to those
eminent lawyers, and to the Court, which approved of their arguments, as only the standard by which the King's prerogative over
them was to be measured.   For if the judges had been bound to
decide on that prerogative by *strict precedent,* or by any other rule
than a judicial construction of the *just and reasonable* extent of prerogative, these arguments, founded on *convenience, expediency,* and
propriety, would have been downright impertinence and nonsense ;
but taking them, as I do, and as the judges did, they were (though
unsuccessful, as they ought to be) every way worthy of the very able
men who maintained them for their clients.

Thus, sir, the exclusive right of printing almanacs, which, from
the bigotry and slavery of former times, had so long been monopolised as a prerogative copy, was at last thrown open to the subject,

as not falling within the reason of those books, which still remain, and ever must remain, the undisputed property of the Crown.

The only two questions, therefore, that arise on the bill before you are—First, Whether it be wise or expedient for Parliament to revive a monopoly so recently condemned by the courts of law as unjust, from not being a fit subject of a monopoly, and to give it to the very same parties who have so long enjoyed it by usurpation, and who have, besides, grossly abused it? Secondly, Whether Parliament can, consistently with the first principles of justice, overlook the injury which will be sustained by the petitioner *as an individual*, from his being deprived of the exercise of the lawful trade by which he lives,—a trade which he began with the free spirit of an Englishman in contempt of an illegal usurpation,—a trade supported and sanctioned by a decree of one of the highest judicatures known to the constitution?

Surely, sir, the bill ought to be rejected with indignation by this House, under such circumstances of private injustice, independently of public inexpediency. If you were to adopt it, the law would be henceforth a snare to the subject—no man would venture to engage hereafter in any commercial enterprise, since he never could be sure that, although the tide of his fortunes was running in a free and legal channel, its course might not be turned by Parliament into the bosom of a monopolist.

Let us now consider more minutely the two questions for your consideration : the general policy, and the private injury.

As to the first, no doubt the Legislature is supreme, and may create monopolies which the Crown cannot. But let it be recollected, that the very same reasons which emancipated almanacs from the prerogative in the courts below, equally apply against any interference of Parliament. If almanacs be not publications of a nature to fall within the legal construction of prerogative copyrights, why should Parliament grant a monopoly of them, since it is impossible to deny that, if they contain such matters as in *policy* required the stamp or revision of public authority, the exclusive right of printing them would have been inherent in the Crown by prerogative, upon legal principles of executive power, in which case an Act would not have been necessary to protect the charter. And it is equally impossible to deny, on the other hand, that if they be not such publications as require to be issued or reviewed by authority, they then stand on the general footing of all other printing, by which men in a free country are permitted to circulate knowledge. The bill, therefore, is either nugatory, or the patent is void; and, if the patent be void, Parliament cannot set it up again without a dangerous infringement of the general liberty of the press.

Sir, when I reflect that this proposed monopoly is a monopoly in PRINTING, and that it gives, or rather continues it, to the Company of Stationers—the very same body of men who were the literary constables to the Star-Chamber to suppress all the science and information, to which we owe our freedom—I confess I am at a loss to account for the reason or motive of the indulgence: but get the right who may, the principle is so dangerous, that I cannot yet consent to part with this view of the subject.   The bill proposes that Parliament should subject almanacs to the revision of the King's authority, when the judges of the common law, the constitutional guardians of his prerogative, have declared that they do not on principle require that sanction : so that your bill is neither more nor less than the reversal of a decision, admitted to be wise and just ; since, as the Court was clearly at liberty to have determined the patent to have been good, if the principle by which prerogative copies have been regulated in other cases had fairly applied to almanacs, *you*, in saying that such principle *does apply*, in fact arraign that legal judgment.   God forbid, sir, that I should have the indecency to hint that this reasoning concerning public convenience and expediency will ever be extended to reach other publications more important than almanacs ; but certainly the principle might, with much less violence than is necessary to bring them within the pale of authority, upon the principle of the bill before you, subject the most valuable productions of the press to parliamentary regulations, and totally annihilate its freedom.

Is it not, for instance, much more dangerous that the rise and fall of the funds, in this commercial nation, should be subject to misrepresentation than the rise or fall of the tides ?   Are not misconstructions of the arguments and characters of the members of this high assembly more important in their consequences than mistakes in the calendar of those wretched saints which still, to the wonder of all wise men, infest the liturgy of a reformed Protestant Church ?   Prophecies of famine, pestilence, national ruin, and bankruptcy, are surely more dangerous to reign unchecked than prognostications of rain or dust ; yet they are the daily uncontrolled offspring of every private author, and I trust will ever continue to be so ; because the liberty of the press consists in its being subject to no previous restrictions, and liable only to animadversion when that liberty is abused.   But if almanacs, sir, are held to be such matter of public consequence as to be revised by authority, and confined by a monopoly, surely the various departments of science may, on much stronger principles, be parcelled out among the different officers of state, as they were at the first introduction of printing.   There is no telling to what such precedents may lead ; the public welfare was the burden of the preambles to the licensing Acts ; the most tyrannical laws in the most absolute governments speak a kind, parental language to the abject wretches who groan under their crushing and humiliating weight : resisting, therefore, a regulation and supervision of the press *beyond the rules of the common law,* I lose sight of my client, and feel that I am speaking for myself, for every man in England. With such a Legislature as I have now the honour to address, I confess the evil is imaginary. But who can look into the future? This precedent, trifling as it may seem, may hereafter afford a plausible inlet to much mischief: the protection of the LAW may be a pretence for a monopoly in all books on LEGAL subjects; the safety of the *state* may require the suppression of *histories* and *political writings;* even philosophy herself may become once more the slave of the schoolmen, and religion fall again under the iron fetters of the Church.

If a monopoly in almanacs had never existed before, and inconveniences had actually arisen from a general trade in them, the offensive principle of the bill might have been covered by a suitable preamble reciting that mischief; but having existed above a century by convicted usurpation, so as to render that recital impossible, you are presented with this new sort of preamble, in the teeth of facts which are notorious.

[*States the preamble of the bill.*]

First, it recites an exercise and enjoyment under the King's letters-patent, and then, without explaining why the patent was insufficient for its own protection, it proposes to confer what had been just stated to be conferred already, with this most extraordinary addition, "*Any law or usage to the contrary notwithstanding.*" Sir, if the letters-patent were void, they should not have been stated at all, nor should the right be said to have been exercised and enjoyed under them. On the other hand, if they were valid, there could be no law or usage to the contrary, for contradictory laws cannot both subsist. This has not arisen from the ignorance or inattention of the framer of the bill, for the bill is ably and artfully framed; but it has arisen from the awkwardness of attempting to hide the real merits of the case. To have preserved the truth, the bill must have run thus:

Whereas the Stationers' Company and the two Universities have, for above a century last past, CONTRARY TO LAW, *usurped the right of printing almanacs, in exclusion of the rest of His Majesty's faithful people, and have from time to time harassed and vexed divers good subjects of our Lord the King for printing the same, till checked by a late decision of the courts of law:*

Be it therefore enacted, that this usurpation be made legal, and be confirmed to them in future.

This, sir, would have been a curiosity indeed, and would have made some noise in the House, *yet it is nothing but the plain and simple truth.* The bill could not pass without making a sort of bolus of the preamble to swallow it in.

So much for the introduction of the bill, which, ridiculous as it is, has nevertheless a merit not very common to the preambles of modern statutes, which are generally at cross purposes with the enacting part. Here, I confess, the enacting part closes in to a nicety with the preamble, and makes the whole a most CONSISTENT and respectable piece of tyranny, absurdity, and falsehood.

But the correctness and decency of these publications are, it seems, the great objects in reviving and confirming this monopoly, which the preamble asserts to have been hitherto attained by it, since it states "that such monopoly has been found to be convenient and expedient." But, sir, is it seriously proposed by this bill to attain these moral objects by vesting, or rather legalising, the usurped monopoly in the Universities, under episcopal revision, as formerly? Is it imagined that our almanacs are to come to us in future in the classical arrangement of Oxford, fraught with the mathematics and astronomy of Cambridge, printed with the correct type of the Stationers' Company, AND SANCTIFIED BY THE BLESSINGS OF THE BISHOPS?* I beg pardon, sir, but the idea is perfectly ludicrous; it is notorious that the Universities sell their right to the Stationers' Company for a fixed annual sum, and that this act is to enable them to continue to do so. And it is equally notorious that the Stationers' Company make a scandalous job of the bargain, and, to increase the sale of almanacs among the vulgar, publish under the auspices of religion and learning, the most senseless absurdities. I should really have been glad to have cited some sentences from the one hundred and thirteenth edition of Poor Robin's Almanac, published under the revision of the Archbishop of Canterbury and the Bishop of London, but I am prevented from doing it by a just respect for the House. Indeed, I know *no house* but a brothel that could suffer the quotation. The worst part of Rochester is ladies' reading when compared with them.

They are equally indebted to the calculations of their astronomers, which seem, however, to be made for a more *western* meridian than LONDON. PLOW MONDAY falls out on a SATURDAY, and Hilary Term ends on Septuagesima Sunday. In short, sir, their almanacs have been, as everything else that is monopolised must be, uniform and obstinate in mistake and error, for want of the necessary rivalry. It is not worth their while to unset the press to correct mistakes, however gross and palpable, because they cannot affect the sale. If the moon is made to rise in the west, she may continue to rise there for ever. When ignorance, nonsense, and obscenity were thus hatched under the protection of a royal patent, how must they thrive under the wide-spreading fostering wings of an Act of Parliament. Whereas in Scotland and in Ireland, where the trade in almanacs has been free and unrestrained, they have been eminent for exactness and useful information. The act recognises the truth of this remark, and prohibits the importation of them.

But, sir, this bill would extend not only to monopolise almanacs,

* The imprimatur of the Archbishop of Canterbury and Bishop of London was necessary by the letters-patent.

but every other useful information published with almanacs which render the common businesses of life familiar. It is notorious that the various lists and tables, which are portable in the pocket, are not saleable without almanacs. Yet all these, sir, are to be given up to the Stationers' Company, and taken from the public by the large words in the bill of *books, pamphlets, or papers ;* since the booksellers cannot afford to compile these useful works, which, from their extensive circulation, are highly beneficial to trade, and to the revenue of stamps, if they must purchase from the Stationers' Company the almanac annexed to them, because the Company must have a profit, which will enhance their price. In short, sir, Parliament is going to tear a few innocent leaves out of books of most astonishing circulation, and of very general use, by which they will be rendered unsaleable, merely to support a monopoly estab-lished in the days of ignorance, bigotry, and superstition, which has deviated from the ends of its institution, senseless and worthless as they were, and which could not stand a moment, when dragged by a public-spirited citizen into the full sunshine of a MODERN English court of justice.

It would be a strange thing, sir, to see an odious monopoly, which could not even stand upon its legs in Westminster Hall, upon the broad pedestal of prerogative, though propped up with the pre-cedents which the decisions of judges in darker ages had accumu-lated into law,—it would be a strange thing to see such an abuse supported and revived by the Parliament of Great Britain in the eighteenth century, in the meridian of the arts, the sciences, and liberty,—to see it starting up among your numberless acts of liberal toleration, and boundless freedom of opinion. God forbid, sir, that at this time of day we should witness such a disgrace as the mono-poly of a twopenny almanac, rising up like a tare among the rich fields of trade which the wisdom of your laws has blown into a smiling harvest all around the globe.

But, sir, I forget myself; I have trespassed too long upon your indulgence; I have assumed a language fitter, perhaps, for the House than for its bar ; I will now therefore confine myself in greater strictness to my duty as an advocate, and submit to your *private justice,* that, let the *public policy* of this bill be what it may, the individual whom I represent before you is entitled to your protection against it.

Mr Carnan, the petitioner, had turned the current of his fortunes into a channel perfectly open to him in law, and which, when blocked up by usurpation, he had cleared away at a great expense, by the decision of one of the highest courts in the kingdom. Pos-sessed of a decree, founded too on a certificate from the judges of the common law,—was it either weak or presumptuous in an Englishman to extend his views, that had thus obtained the broadest seal of justice ? Sir, he *did* extend them with the same liberal spirit in which he began; he published twenty different kinds of almanacs, calculated for different meridians and latitudes, corrected the blunders of the lazy monopolists, and, supported by the encouragement which laudable industry is sure to meet with in a free country, he made that branch of trade his first and leading object,—and I challenge the framer of this bill (even though he should happen to be at the head of His Majesty's Government) to produce to the House a single instance of immorality, or of any mistake or uncertainty, or any one inconvenience arising to the public from this general trade, which he had the merit of redeeming from a disgraceful and illegal monopoly. On the contrary, much useful learning has been communicated, a variety of convenient additions introduced, and many egregious errors and superstitions have been corrected. Under such circumstances I will not believe it possible that Parliament can deliver up the honest labours of a citizen of London to be damasked and made waste paper of (as this scandalous bill expresses it) by any man or body of men in the kingdom. On the contrary, I am sure the attempt to introduce, through the Commons of England, a law so shockingly repugnant to every principle which characterises the English Government, will meet with your just indignation as an insult to the House, whose peculiar station in the government is the support of *popular freedom.* For, sir, if this Act were to pass, I see nothing to hinder any man, who is turned out of possession of his neighbour's estate by legal ejectment, from applying to you to give it him back again by Act of Parliament. The fallacy lies in supposing that the Universities and Stationers' Company *ever had* a right to the monopoly which they have exercised so long. The preamble of the bill supposes it,—but, as it is a supposition in the very teeth of a judgment of law, it is only an aggravation of the impudence of the application.

And now, Mr Speaker, I retire from your bar, I wish I could say with confidence of having prevailed. If the wretched Company of Stationers had been my only opponents, my confidence had been perfect; indeed so perfect, that I should not have wasted ten minutes of your time on the subject, but should have left the bill to dissolve in its own weakness: but, when I reflect that OXFORD AND CAMBRIDGE are suitors here, I own to you I am alarmed, and I feel myself called upon to say something, which I know your indulgence will forgive. The House is filled with their most illustrious sons, who no doubt feel an involuntary zeal for the interest of their parent Universities. Sir, it is an influence so natural, and so honourable, that I trust there is no indecency in my hinting the *possibility of its operation.* Yet I persuade myself that these learned bodies have effectually defeated their own interests by the sentiments which their liberal sciences have disseminated amongst you; their wise and learned institutions have erected in your minds the august image of an enlightened statesman, which, trampling down all personal interests and affections, looks steadily forward to the great ends of public and private justice, unawed by authority, and unbiassed by favour.

It is from thence my hopes for my client revive. If the Universities have lost an advantage, enjoyed contrary to law, and at the expense of sound policy and liberty, you will rejoice that the courts below have pronounced that wise and liberal judgment against them, and will not set the evil example of reversing it *here*. But you need not therefore forget that the Universities *have* lost an advantage,—and if it be a loss that can be felt by bodies so liberally endowed, it may be repaired to them by the bounty of the Crown, or by your own. It were much better that the people of England should pay ten thousand pounds a year to each of them, than suffer them to enjoy one farthing at the expense of the ruin of a free citizen, or the monopoly of a free trade.*

* According to the seasonable hint at the conclusion of the speech, *which perhaps had some weight* in the decision of the House to reject the bill, a parliamentary compensation was afterwards made to the Universities, and remains as a monument erected by a British Parliament to a free press.

SPEECH for GEORGE STRATTON, HENRY BROOKE, CHARLES FLOYER, *and* GEORGE MACKAY, Esqs. (*the Council of Madras*), *as delivered in the Court of King's Bench, on the 5th February* 1780.

THE SUBJECT.

Time now casts into the shade a proceeding which occupied at the moment a great deal of public interest and attention, viz., the arrest and imprisonment of Lord Pigot, Governor of Madras, by the majority of the Council of that settlement, in the year 1776.

On their recall to Europe by the Directors of the East India Company, a motion was made in the House of Commons for their prosecution, by the Attorney-General, for a high misdemeanour.

Admiral Pigot, the brother of Lord Pigot, being at that time a member of the House, and a most amiable man, connected in political life with the Opposition party in Parliament, an extraordinary degree of acrimony arose upon the subject, and the House of Commons came to a resolution to prosecute Messrs Stratton, and others, in the Court of King's Bench; and an information was accordingly filed against them by the Attorney-General. They were defended by Mr Dunning, and the other leading advocates of that time, but were found guilty; and, on their being brought up to receive the judgment of the Court, Mr Erskine, who was then only junior counsel, made the following speech in mitigation of their punishment.

The principle of the mitigation, as maintained by Mr Erskine, may be thus shortly described : Lord Pigot, considering himself, as President of the Government of Madras, to be an integral part of it, independent of the Council, refused to put a question for decision by the Board, which the members of the Council contended it was his duty ministerially to have done; and he also unduly suspended two of them, to make up a majority in favour of his proceedings. This act of Lord Pigot was held by the majority of the Council to be a subversion and usurpation of the government, which they contended was vested in the President and Council, and not in the President only; and to vindicate the powers of the government, thus claimed to reside in them, they caused Lord Pigot to be arrested and suspended, and directed the act of the majority of Council, which Lord Pigot refused to execute, to be carried into execution. It was, of course, admitted that this act was not legally justifiable; that the defendants were properly convicted, and must, therefore, receive some punishment from the Court; but it was contended in the following speech that the Court was bound to remember and respect the principles which governed our ancestors at the Revolution, and which had dictated so many acts of indemnity by Parliament, when persons, impelled by imminent necessity, had disobeyed the laws.

The defendants were only fined one thousand pounds, without any sentence of imprisonment.

THE SPEECH.

MY LORD,—I really do not know how to ask, or even to expect, the attention of the Court; I am sure it is no gratification to me to try your Lordships' patience on a subject so completely exhausted; I feel, besides, that the array of counsel assembled on this occasion gives an importance and solemnity to the conviction which it little deserves, and carries the air of a painful resistance of an expected punishment, which it would be a libel on the wisdom and justice of the Court to expect.

But in causes that, from their public nature, have attracted the public notice, and in which public prejudices have been industriously propagated and inflamed, it is very natural for the objects of them to feel a pleasure in seeing their actions (if they will bear a naked inspection) repeatedly stripped of the disguise with which the arts of their enemies had covered them, and to expect their counsel to be, as it were, the heralds of their innocence, even after the minds of the judges are convinced. They are apt, likewise, and with some reason, to think that, in *this* stage of a prosecution, surplusage is less offensive, the degree of punishment not being reducible to a point like a legal justification, but subject to be softened and shaded away by the variety of views in which the same facts may be favourably and justly presented, both to the understanding and the heart. Such feelings, my Lord, which I more than guess are the feelings of my injured clients, must be my apology for adding anything to what my learned leaders have already, I think, unanswerably urged in their favour. It will be, however, unnecessary for me to fatigue your Lordship with a minute recapitulation of the facts; I shall confine myself to the prominent features of the cause.

The defendants are convicted of having assumed to themselves the power of the government of Madras, and with having assaulted and imprisoned Lord Pigot. I say, they are convicted of *that*, because, although I am aware that the general verdict of guilty includes, likewise, the truth of the first count of the information, which charges the obstruction of Lord Pigot in carrying into execution the specific orders of the Company, yet it is impossible that the general verdict can at all embarrass the Court in pronouncing judgment, it being notorious on the face of the evidence, first, that there were no direct or specific orders of the Company

touching the points which occasioned either the original or final
differences, the Rajah of Tanjore being, before the disputes arose,
even beyond the letter of the instructions, restored and secured.
Secondly, that the instructions, whatever they were, or however to
be construed, were not given to the single construction of Lord
Pigot, but to him *and his Council, like all the other general instruc-*
tions of that government.

The Company inclined that the Rajah of Tanjore should be
restored without infringing the rights of the Nabob of the Car-
natic; but *how* such restoration and security of the Rajah could,
or was to be effected without the infringement of those rights of
the Nabob which were not to be violated, the Company did not
leave to the single discretion of Lord Pigot, but to the determination of the ordinary powers of the government of Fort St George,
acting to the best of their understandings, responsible only, like
all other magistrates and rulers, for the purity of their intentions.

It is not pretended that the Company's instructions directed the
Rajah's security to be effected by the residence of a civil chief and
council in Tanjore, or by any other civil establishment whatsoever:
on the contrary, they disavow such appropriation of any part of
the revenues of that country; *yet the resisting a civil establishment*
in the person of Lord Pigot's son-in-law, Mr Russel, destined, too,
by the Company for a different and incompatible service, is the
specific obstruction which is the burden of the first count of the
information, and which is there attempted to be brought forward
as an aggravation of the assumption of the general powers of the
government; the obstruction of what was not only *not* ordered by
the Company, but of which their orders implied, and in public
council were admitted by one of Lord Pigot's adherents to imply,
a *disapprobation and prohibition.*

The claims of Mr Benfield, the subject of so much slanderous
declamation without proof, or attempt of proof, and, what is more
extraordinary, without even charge or accusation, are subject to
the same observations: the orders to restore the Rajah to the
possession of his country certainly did not express, and, if my
judgment does not mislead me, could not imply, a restitution of
the crops sown with the Prince's money, advanced to the inhabitants on the credit of the harvest, without which universal famine
would have ensued.

Had the Nabob, indeed, seized upon Tanjore in defiance of the
Company, or even without its countenance and protection, he would,
no doubt, have been a *malâ fide* possessor, *quoad* all transactions
concerning it with the Company's servants, whatever the justice of
his title to it might in reality have been; and the Company's
governors, in restoring the Rajah, paying no respect to such
usurped possession, would have been justifiable in telling any
European who had lent his money on the security of Tanjore—

Sir, you have lent your money with your eyes open, to a person, whose title you knew not to be ratified by our approbation, and we cannot, therefore, consider either his claim or yours derived from it. But when the Nabob was put into possession by the Company's troops; when that possession, so obtained, was ratified in Europe, at least, by the silence of the Company, no matter whether wisely or unwisely, justly or unjustly; and, after the Nabob had been publicly congratulated upon such possession, by the King's pleni-potentiary in the presence of all the neighbouring princes in India; I confess I am at a loss to discover the *absurdity* (as it has been called) of the Nabob's pretensions; and it must be remembered, that Mr Benfield's derivative title was not the subject of dispute, but the title of the Nabob, his principal, from whence it was derived; I am, therefore, supported by the report of the evidence, in saying, that it does not appear that the differences in Council arose, were continued, or brought to a crisis, on points where Lord Pigot had the Company's orders, either express or implied, to give any weight to his single opinion beyond the ordinary weight allotted to it by the constitution of the settlement, so as to justify the Court to consider the dissent of the majority from *his measures*, to be either a criminal resistance of the President, or a disobe-dience of the Company's specific or general instructions.

Thus perishes the first count of the information, even if it had been matter of charge! But much remains behind. I know it is not enough that the Company's orders were not specific touching any of the points on which the differences arose, or that they were silent touching the property of the crop of Tanjore, or that the Nabob's claim to it had the semblance, or even the reality of justice; I admit that it is not sufficient that the defendants had the largest and most liberal discretion to exercise, if that discretion should appear to have been warped by bad, corrupt, or selfish motives; I am aware, that it would be no argument to say, that the acts charged upon them were done in resistance of Lord Pigot's illegal subversion, if it could be replied upon me, and that reply be supported by evidence, that such subversive acts of Lord Pigot, though neither justifiable nor legal, were in laudable opposition to their corrupt combinations. I freely admit that, if such a case were established against me, I should be obliged to abandon their defence; because I could apply none of the great principles of government to their protection; but, if they are clear of such imputations, then I *can* and *will* apply them *all*.

My Lord, of this bad intention there is no proof; no proof did I say? there is no charge! I cannot reply to *slander* here. I will not debase the purity of the Court by fighting with the phantoms of prejudice and party, that are invisible to the sedate and sober eye of justice! If it had been a private cause, I would not have suffered my clients, as far as my advice could have influenced, to have filed a single affidavit in support of that integrity which no complaint attached upon, and which no evidence had impeached; but, since they were bound like public victims, and cast into this furnace, we wished them to come forth pure and white; their innocence is, therefore, witnessed before your Lordships, and before the world, by their most solemn oaths; and it is surely no great boon. to ask credit for facts averred under the most sacred obligations of religion, and subject to criminal retribution *even here*, which you are bound, in the absence of proof, not only in duty as judges, but in charity as men, to believe without any oaths at all.

They have denied every corrupt motive and purpose, and every interest, directly or indirectly, with Mr Benfield, or his claims.— " But," says Mr Rous, " Benfield was a man of straw set up by the *Nabob;*" be it so;—they have positively sworn that they had no interest, directly or indirectly, in the claims of the *Nabob himself;* no interest, directly or indirectly, in the property of the crop of Tanjore; no interest, directly or indirectly, beyond their duty, in the preference of Colonel Stuart's appointment to Mr Russel's; nor any interest, direct or indirect, in any one act which is the subject of the prosecution, or which can, by the most collateral direction, be brought to bear upon it. Such are the affidavits; and if they be defective, the defect is in us. They protested their innocence to us, their counsel, and, telling us that there was no form in which language could convey asseverations of the purity of their motives, which they could not with a safe conscience subscribe to, they left it to *us* to frame them in terms to exclude all evasion.

But *circumstances* come in aid of their credit stronger than all oaths: men may swear falsely; men may be perjured, though a court of justice cannot presume it; but human nature cannot be perjured. They did not do the very thing, when they got the government, for which they are supposed to have usurped it. The history of the world does not afford an instance of men wading through guilt for a purpose which, when within their grasp, they never seized or looked that way it lay.

When Mr Benfield first laid his claims before the Board, Lord Pigot was absent in Tanjore, and Mr Stratton was the legal governor during his absence, who might therefore have, in strict regularity, proceeded to the discussion of them; *but he referred them back to Lord Pigot, and postponed that discussion till his return;* when, on that discussion, they were declared valid by a legal majority, they neither forced them, nor threatened to force them on the Rajah, but only recommended it to him to do justice, leaving the time and the manner to himself; and, when at last they assumed the government, they did not change their tone with their power; the Rajah was left unrestrained as before, and, *at this hour*, the claims remain in the same situation in which they stood at the commencement of the disputes; neither the Nabob nor Mr

Benfield have derived the smallest advantage or support from the revolution in the government.

This puts an end to all discussion of Indian politics, which have been artfully introduced to puzzle and perplex the simple merits of this cause ; I have no more to do with the first or second *Tanjore* war, than with the first or second *Carthaginian* war ; I am sorry, however, my absence yesterday in the House of Commons prevented me from hearing the history of them, because, I am told, Mr Rous spoke with great ability, and, I am convinced from what I know of his upright temper, with a zeal, that, for the moment, justified what he said to his own bosom ; but, if I am not misinformed, his zeal was his only brief; his imagination and resentment spurned the fetters both of fact and accusation, and his acquaintance with Indian affairs enabled him to give a variety to the cause by plausible circumstances beyond the reach of vulgar and ignorant malice to invent. It was calculated to do much mischief, for it was too long to be remembered, and too unintelligible to be refuted ; yet I am contented to demand judgment on my clients on Mr Rous' terms : he tells your Lordship, that their intentions cannot be known till that time when the secrets of all human hearts shall be revealed, and then, in the very same breath, he calls for a punishment as if they were revealed already. It is a new, ingenious, and summary mode of proceeding—*festinum remedium*, an assize of conscience. If it should become the practice, which, from the weight of my learned friend, I have no manner of doubt it will, we shall hear such addresses to juries in criminal courts as this :—Gentlemen, I am counsel for the prosecution, and I must be candid enough to admit that the charge is not proved against the defendants ; there is certainly no legal evidence before you to entitle the Crown to your verdict; but, as there is little reason to doubt that they are guilty, and as this deficiency in the evidence will probably be supplied at the day of judgment, you are well warranted in convicting them ; and if, when the day of judgment comes, both you and I should turn out to be mistaken, they may move for a new trial.

This was the *general* argument of guilt ; and, in the *particulars,* the reasoning was equally close and logical. How, says Mr Rous, can it be believed that the Tanjore crop was not the corrupt foundation of the defendants' conduct, when it appears from day to day, on the face of all the consultations, as the single object of dispute ? That it was the object of dispute, I shall, for argument's sake, admit ; but does Mr Rous's conclusion follow from the admission of his premises ? I will tell him why it does not; it is so very plain a reason, that, when he hears it, he will be astonished he did not discover it himself. Let me remind him, then, that all the inferences which connexions with the *Nabob* so amply supplied on the *one hand,* connexions with the *Rajah* would as amply have supplied on the *other.* If the Tanjore crop was the bone of contention, the Rajah, by *keeping it*, had surely the same opportunity of gratitude to his adherents that the Nabob had to his by *snatching it from him.* The appointment of Mr Russel to the residency of Tanjore—Mr Russel, the friend, the confidant, the son-in-law of Lord Pigot—was surely as good a butt for insinuation as *Colonel Stuart,* for the *whole Council.* The ball might, therefore, have been thrown back with redoubled violence; and I need not remind the Court, that the cause was conducted on our part by a gentleman whose powers of throwing it back it would be folly in me to speak of; but he nobly disdained it; he said he would not hire out his talents to scatter insinuation and abuse, when the administration of right and justice did not require it; and his clients, while they received the full, faithful, and energetic exercise of his great abilities, admired and applauded the delicate manly rectitude of his conduct; they felt that their cause derived a dignity and a security from the MAN greater than the *advocate*, and even than *such* an advocate, could bestow.

I shall follow the example of Mr Dunning... God forbid, my Lord, that I should insult the ashes of a brave man, who, in other respects, deserved well of his country; but let me remind the gentlemen on the other side, that the honour of the LIVING is as sacred a call on humanity and justice as the memory of the DEAD.

My Lord, the case, thus stripped of the false colours thrown upon it by party defamation, stands upon plain and simple principles, and I shall, therefore, discuss it in the same arrangement which your Lordship pursued in summing up the evidence to the jury at the trial, only substituting alleviation for justification.

First, In whom did the ordinary powers of the government of Madras reside?

Secondly, What acts were done by Lord Pigot subversive of that government?

Thirdly, What degree of criminality belongs to the confessedly illegal act of the defendants, in assuming to themselves the whole powers of the government, *so subverted?* I say, *so subverted;* for I must keep it constantly in the eye of the Court that the government was subverted, and was admitted by your Lordship, at the trial, to have been subverted *by Lord Pigot*, before it was assumed by *the majority of the Council.*

First, then, in whom did the government of Fort St George reside? And, in deciding this question, it will not be necessary to go, as some have done, into the general principles of government, or to compare the deputation of a company of merchants with great political governments, either ancient or modern. The East India Company, being incorporated by Act of Parliament, derived an authority from their charter of incorporation, to constitute inferior governments, dependent on them for the purposes of managing their concerns in those distant parts:—had the Company, at the time the charter was granted, been such an immense and powerful body as it has since become from the trade and prosperity of the empire, it might have happened that the forms of these governments would have been accurately chalked out by Parliament, and been made part of the charter; in which case, the charter itself would have been the only place to have resorted to for the solution of any question respecting the powers of such governments, because the Company, by the general law of all corporations, could have made no by-laws, or standing orders, repugnant to it; but, on the other hand, the charter having left them at liberty in this instance, and not having prescribed constitutions for their territorial governments in India, there can be no possible place to resort to for the solution of such questions but to the commissions of government granted by the Company; their standing orders, which may be considered as fundamental constitutions; and such explanatory instructions as they may, from time to time, have transmitted to their servants for the regulation of their conduct;—by these, and these alone, must every dispute arising in the governments of India be determined, except such as fall within the cognizance of the Act 13 George III., for the regulation of the Company's affairs, as well in India as in Europe.

Again, then, as to the commission of government, where the clause on which they build the most is made to run thus:—"And to the end that he might be the better enabled to manage all the affairs of them, the said Company, they appointed certain persons, therein named, to be of their Council at Fort St George." These words would certainly imply the President to be an integral and substantive part distinct from the Council; but, unfortunately, no such words are contained in the commission of government, which speaks a very different language, almost in itself conclusive against the proposition they wish to establish. The words are—"And to the end that the said George Lord Pigot might be the better enabled to manage all the affairs of us, the said Company, we do constitute and ordain George Stratton, Esq., to be SECOND in our Council of Fort St George, to wit, TO BE NEXT IN THE COUNCIL after our said President George Lord Pigot." It is impossible for the English language more plainly to mark out the President to be merely *the first in Council*, and not an integral substantive part, *assisted by a Council;* for, in such case, Mr Stratton, the senior councillor, would, it is apprehended, be called the *first in Council*, instead of the *second* in Council, to wit, next after the President; and this clause in the commission, so explained, not only goes far by itself to resist the claim of independence in the President, but takes off from the ambiguity and uncertainty which would otherwise cloud the construction of the clause that follows, viz.:—"And we do hereby give and grant unto our said

President and Governor, George Lord Pigot, *and to our Council aforenamed*, or the major part of *them*, full power and authority," &c.   The President and Council being here named distinctly, the word *them*, without the foregoing clause, might seem to constitute the President an integral part, and separate from the Council ; but the President, having been before *constructively* named as the *first in Council ;* Mr Stratton, though the senior councillor, being expressly named the *second ;* it is plain the word *them* signifies *the majority of such Council, of which the President is the first*, and, who is named distinctly, not only by way of pre-eminence, but because all public bodies are called and described by their corporate names, and all their acts witnessed by their common seals, whatever their internal constitutions may be.   No heads of corporations have, by the common law of England, any negative on the proceedings of the other constituent parts, unless by express provision in their charters ; yet all their powers are given to them, and exercised by them, in their corporate names, which ever makes the head a party, although he may be dissentient from the act that receives authority from his name.

The standing orders of the Company, published in 1687 and 1702, which may be considered as fundamental constitutions, are plain and unequivocal ; they enjoin, " That all their affairs shall be transacted IN COUNCIL, and ordered and managed as the MAJORITY OF THE COUNCIL shall determine, and not otherwise, on any pretence whatsoever."   And again, " That whatever is agreed on by the MAJORITY shall be the order by which each one is to act ; and every individual person, *even the dissenters themselves*, are to perform their parts in the prosecution thereof."

The agreement of the majority being denominated an ORDER, shows as clearly as language can do that obedience is expected to their determination ; and it is equally plain, that no constituent member of that government can frustrate or counteract such order, since each individual, *even the dissenters themselves*, are commanded to act in conformity to it, and to perform their parts in the prosecution thereof.   In speaking to dispassionate men, it is almost needless to add any arguments to show that the President's claim to refuse to put a question, adopted by a majority of Council, stands upon the very same grounds as his claim to a negative on their proceedings, and that, if the first be overturned, the second must fall along with it ; for if he be not an integral part of the government, and his concurrence be consequently not necessary to constitute an act of it, then his office as President, *with respect to putting questions*, must necessarily be only ministerial, and he cannot obstruct the proceedings by refusing to put them ; for, if he could, his power would be equal in effect to that of an integral part ; and it would be a strange solecism indeed, if, at the same time that all the affairs of the government were to be managed and ordered by the opinions of a majority, the President could prevent such opinions from ever being collected; and, at the same time that their acts would bind him, could prevent such acts from ever taking place. But it is altogether unnecessary to explain, by argument and inference, that which the Company, who are certainly the best judges of their own meaning, have explained in absolute and unequivocal terms by their instructions sent by Mr Whitehill to Madras, explanatory of the new commission, by which they expressly declare the government to be in the *major part of the Council*, giving the President, or the senior councillor in his absence, a casting vote, and directing *that every question proposed in writing by any member of Council shall be put by the Governor, or, in his absence, by the senior member acting as President for the time being; and that every question carried by a majority shall be deemed the act of the President and Council*. Indeed, the uniform determinations of the Directors on every occasion where this question has been referred to them, have been in favour of the majority of Council; even so late as the 21st of April 1777, *subsequent to the disturbances at Madras*, it will be found upon their records to have been resolved by ballot, " *That the powers contended for and assumed by Lord Pigot, are neither known in the constitution of the Company, nor authorised by charter, nor warranted by any orders or instructions of the Court of Directors.*" It is clear, therefore, beyond all controversy, that the President and Council were, at all times, bound and concluded by the decision of the majority, and that it was his duty to put every question proposed by any member of the Board.

Had these regulations been made part of the *new* commission, they might have been considered as a *new* establishment, and not as a recognition of the *former* government; and consequently such regulations subsequent to the disturbances could be no protection for the majority acting under the *former* commission; but the caution of the East India Company, to exclude the possibility of such a construction, is most striking and remarkable: sitting down to frame a new commission under the immediate pressure of the difficulties that had arisen from the equivocal expressions of the former; they, nevertheless, adopt and preserve the very same words in all the parts on which the dispute arose, the two commissions differing in nothing except in the special preamble restoring Lord Pigot; and the object of this caution is self-evident, because, if, instead of thus preserving the same form, and sending out collateral instructions to explain it, they had rendered the new commission more precise and unequivocal by *new modes of expression*, it would have carried the appearance of a *new* establishment of what the government should *in future be*, and not as a recognition and definition of what it *always had been;* but by thus using the same form of commission, and accompanying it with explanatory regulations, they, beyond all dispute, pronounced the former commission always to have implied what they expressly declare the latter to be, as it is impossible to suppose that the Company would make use of the same form of words to express delegations of authority diametrically opposite to each other. But, taking it for argument's sake to be a new establishment rather than a recognition, still it is a strong protection to the defendants. If the question, indeed, was concerning the regularity of an act done by the majority, without the President, coming before the Court by a person claiming a franchise under it, or in any other *civil* shape where the constitution of the government was in issue, my argument, I admit, would not hold; the Court would certainly, *in such case*, be obliged to confine itself strictly to the commission of government, and such explanatory constitutions as were precedent to the act, the regularity of which was the subject of discussion; but it is very different when men are prosecuted *criminally* for subverting a constitution, and abusing delegated authority: they are not to be punished, I trust, for the obscurity of their employers' commissions, if they have been fortunate enough, notwithstanding such obscurity, to construe them as they were intended by their authors: if their employers declare, even after an act done, *This is what we meant should be our government*, that ought to be sufficient to sanction previous acts that correspond with such declarations, more especially declarations made on the spur of the occasion which such previous acts had produced; for otherwise this monstrous supposition must be admitted, viz., That the Company had enlarged the power of their servants, because they had, in defiance of their orders, assumed them when they had them not; whereas, the reasonable construction of the Company's subsequent proceeding is this: *It is necessary that our Council on the President's refusing to perform his duty, should have such powers of acting* WITHOUT HIM, *as they have assumed in the late emergency; the obscurity of our commissions and instructions has afforded a pretence of resistance, which has obliged our servants either to surrender the spirit of their trusts, or to violate the form ; to prevent such disputes in future we do that*, HITHERTO UNKNOWN *; we make a regular form of government, and, at the same time, prescribe a rule of action in case it should not act up to the end of its present institution, to prevent an exercise of discretion always, if possible, to be avoided in every government, but more especially in such as are subordinate.* Therefore, my Lord, whether the late instructions be considered as explanatory or enacting, they ought to be a protection to the defendants *in a criminal court*, unless when their employers are the prosecutors. Neither Parliament nor the Crown ought to interfere; but, as they have done it, no evidence ought to have convicted them of assuming the powers of government, and obstructing the Company's service, but the evidence of the Directors of that Company under whom they acted. They ought not to be judged by blind records and parchments, *whilst the authors of them are at hand to explain them.* It is a shocking absurdity to see men convicted of abusing trusts when the persons who gave them are neither prosecutors nor witnesses against them.

The ordinary powers of the government of Madras being thus proved to have resided in the majority of the Council, it now only remains to show, by a short state of the evidence, the necessity which impelled the extraordinary and otherwise unwarrantable exercise of such powers in suspending and imprisoning Lord Pigot; for they once more enter a protest against being thought to have assumed and exercised such power as incident to their commission while the government subsisted. It is their business to show that, as long as the government continued to subsist, they faithfully acted their parts in it; and that it was not till after a total subversion of it by an arbitrary suspension of the governing powers, that they asserted their own rights, and restored the government by resuming them.

On the 8th of July, Lord Pigot refused, as President, *to put a question* to the Board (upon the regular motion of a member), for rescinding a resolution before entered into. This refusal left the majority no choice between an absolute surrender of their trusts and an exercise of them without his ministerial assistance; there was no other alternative *in the absence of a superior coercive authority, to compel him to a specific performance of his duty;* but they proceeded no further than the necessity justified; they did not extend the irregularity (if any there was) beyond the political urgency of the occasion.—Although their constitutional rights were infringed by the President's claim, they formed no plan for their general vindication; but contented themselves with declaring on that particular occasion, that, as the government resided *in them*, the President ought not to refuse putting the question, and that the resolution ought to be rescinded.

When the President again refused to put the question in the month following, for taking into consideration the draughts of instructions to Colonel Stuart (which was the immediate cause of all the disturbances that followed), they again preserved the same moderation, and never dreamt of any further vindication of their authority, thus usurped, than should become absolutely necessary for the performance of the trusts delegated to them by the Company, which they considered it to be treachery to desert. They lamented the necessity of departing even from form; and, therefore, although the President's resolution to emancipate himself from their constitutional control was avowed upon the public minutes of the consultations, they first adjourned without coming to any resolution at all, in hopes of obtaining formality and regularity to their proceedings by the President's concurrence:—disappointed in that hope by his persevering to refuse, and driven to the necessity of either surrendering their legal authority or of devising some other means of exercising it without his personal concurrence, *having (as before observed) no process to compel him to give it*, they passed a vote approving of the instructions, and wrote a letter to Colonel Harper, containing orders to deliver the command to Colonel Stuart ; but they did not proceed to sign it at that consultation, still hoping, by an adjournment, to gain Lord Pigot's sanction to acts legal in all points by the constitution of the government, except, perhaps, in wanting that *form* which it was his duty to give them.

The use which Lord Pigot made of this slowness of the majority to vindicate the divided rights and spirit of the government, by a departure from even its undecided forms, notwithstanding the political necessity which arose singly from his own illegal refusal, is very luckily recorded by one of his lordship's particular friends in Council, and a party to the transaction, as it would have been, otherwise, too much to have expected full credit to it from the most impartial mind.

" It had been discussed," says Mr Dalrymple, " before the Council met, what measures could be taken to support the government established by the Company, in case the majority should still persist in their resolution to come to no compromise or reference of the matter in question, to the decision of the Court of Directors, but to carry things to extremity. One mode occurred to Lord Pigot, viz., by putting Colonel Stuart in arrest if he obeyed an order without the Governor's concurrence. To this many objections arose. Colonel Stuart might contrive to receive the orders *without* the garrison, and, consequently, by the new military regulations, not be liable to the Governor's arrest: if he *was* arrested, the majority would, of course, refuse to issue a warrant for a court-martial, and confusion and disgrace must be the consequence.

" The only expedient that occurred to any of us, was, to ground a charge in case of making their declaration in the name of the Council, instead of the President and Council ; but here an apprehension arose, that they would see this impropriety, and express their order, not in the name of the Council, as they had hinted, but in the name of the President and Council, maintaining that the majority constituted the efficient Board of President and Council. In this case, we could devise no measure to be pursued consistent with the rules of the service ; but Lord Pigot said there was no fear of this, as he insisted the Secretary would not dare to issue any order in his name when he forbade it. It was impossible to know whether Sir Robert Fletcher would attend or not ; it was necessary to have everything prepared, that nothing might be to be done in Council ; the Company's orders required the charge to be in writing ; *the Governor, therefore, had in his pocket charges prepared for every probable contingency*, whether they began at the eldest or the youngest, and whether the form was an order from themselves or an order to the Secretary; and whether Sir Robert Fletcher was present or not. It was agreed that the first of us to whom the paper was presented for signing should immediately hand it to the President, who was then to produce the charge; the standing orders directing that members against whom a charge is made should have no seat, the members charged were, of course, deprived of their votes. As our ideas went no further than relieving the Governor from the compulsion the majority wanted to lay him under, it was determined to suspend no more than the necessity of the circumstance required."

With this snare laid for them during the interval of that adjournment, *which their moderation had led them to*, the Council met on the 22d of August, and, after having recorded their dissent from the President's illegal claim, to a negative on their proceedings, by refusing to perform his part in the prosecution of them (though strictly enjoined thereto by the standing orders of the Company), and in which refusal he still obstinately persisted, they entered a minute, declaring it as their opinion that the resolution of the Council should be carried into execution without further delay, and that the instructions to Colonel Stuart, and the letter to Colonel Harper, should be signed by the Secretary by order of Council.

This minute was regularly signed by a majority, and the President having again positively refused his concurrence, they prepared a letter to Mr Secretary Sullivan, approving of the instructions to Colonel Stuart, and the letter to Lieutenant-Colonel Harper.

The letter thus written, *in the name of the majority*, and under their most public and avowed auspices, it was the immediate purpose of *all of them* to have signed in pursuance of the minute they had just before delivered in, expressive of their authority to that purpose; but the President, according to the *ingenious* plan preconcerted during the adjournment, snatched the paper from Mr Brooke after he and Mr Stratton had signed it, before the rest of the majority could put their names to it, and pulling a written accusation out of his pocket, charged them as being guilty of an act subversive of the government; put the question of suspension on both at once, and ordered the Secretary to take neither of their votes, which, according to Mr Dalrymple's *economical* scheme of illegality, exactly got rid of the majority, by his own (*the accuser's*) casting vote.

The weakness and absurdity of the *principle* (if it deserves the name) on which this suspension was founded, creates a difficulty in seriously exposing it by argument; yet, as it produced all the consequences that followed, I cannot dismiss it without the following remarks:—

That was a gross violation of the constitution of the government, even admitting Lord Pigot to have been that integral part of it which he assumed to be, as the establishment of that claim

could only have given him a negative on the proceedings of a
majority, but never could have enabled him to fabricate one so as
to do positive acts without one ; the sudden charge and suspension
of Messrs Stratton and Brooke, and breaking the majority by
putting the question on both at once, would therefore have been
irregular, even supposing the concurrence of the majority to the
act which constituted the charge against them to have been
unknown to Lord Pigot and the minority who voted with him : but
when their concurrence was perfectly known ; when the majority of
the Board had just before publicly delivered in a minute expressive
of their right to authorise the Secretary to sign the order, if the
President refused to do it ; when the order was avowedly drawn
out in pursuance of that minute, which made the whole *one act*,
and was in the regular course of signing by the majority, who
had just before declared their authority to sign it ; the snatching
the paper, under such circumstances, while unfinished, and arraigning those who had already signed it under the auspices of the
majority, as being guilty of an act subversive of the government
lodged in that majority, and turning it into a minority by exclud-
ing the votes of the parties charged, was a trick upon the governing
powers which they could neither have submitted to with honour to
themselves or duty to their employers.

Such a power, however, Lord Pigot assumed over the government
of Fort St George, by converting an act of the majority, rendered
necessary by his refusal to do his duty, into a criminal charge
against two members acting under their authority, and by a device
too shallow to impose on the meanest understanding, cut them off
from acting as part of that majority, by which the powers of the
government were subverted, and passed away from them while they
were in the very act of saving them from subversion.

It is unnecessary to say that they were neither called upon in
duty, nor even authorised, had they been willing, to attend the
summons of a Board so constituted by the foulest usurpation ; a
Board at which they must either have sacrificed their consciences
and judgments, or become the vain opposers of measures destructive
to the interests of their employers ; they therefore assembled, and
answered the illegal summons by a public protest against the
usurped authority by which it issued.   To this Council, assembled
for the single purpose of sending such protest, they did not, indeed,
summon the subverters of the government against whom it was
levelled ; affairs were arrived at too dangerous a crisis to sacrifice
substance to forms, which it was impossible should have been regarded.   Lord Pigot and his associates, on receiving the protest
against the proceedings of the 22d of August, completed the subversion of the constitution, by the suspension of the rest of the
majority of the Council, and ordered Sir Robert Fletcher, the com-
mander-in-chief, to be put under arrest, to be tried by a court-

martial, for asserting the rights of the *civil* government as a member of the Council. This is positively sworn to have been done by Lord Pigot before their assumption of the government. Here then was a crisis in which it was necessary to act with decision, and, in asserting their rights by civil authority, to save the impending consequences of tumult and blood.—The period of temporising was past, and there was no doubt of what it was their duty to do. Charged with the powers of the government, they could not surrender them with honour, and it was impossible to maintain them with safety or effect while their legal authority was treated as usurpation and rebellion. They, therefore, held a Council, and agreed that the fortress and garrison should be in their hands, and under their command, as the legal representatives of the Company, and, as there was everything to dread from the intemperance of Lord Pigot's disposition, they, at the same time, authorised Colonel Stuart to arrest his person, if he thought it necessary, to preserve the peace of the settlement. Colonel Stuart *did* think it necessary, and his person was accordingly arrested: but, during his necessary confinement, he was treated with every mark of tenderness and respect.

Such, my Lord, is the case—and it is much to the honour of the defendants that not a single fact appeared, or was attempted to be made appear, at the trial, that did not stand avowed upon the face of their public proceedings; I say, literally none; for I will not wheel into Court that miserable post-chaise, nor its flogged postillion, the only living birth of this mountain which has been two years in its labour; everything, and the reason and motive of everything, appeared, and still appear, to speak and plead for themselves. No cabals—no private meetings—no coming prepared for all possible events—no secret manufacture of charges—no tricks to overcome majorities—but everything fair, open, and manly, to be judged of by the justice of their employers, the equity of their country, and the candour and humanity of the civilised world. As long as the government subsisted, their parts appear to have been acted in it with regularity and fidelity, nor was it till after a total subversion of it, by the arbitrary suspension of the governing powers, *and in the absence of all superior visitation*, that they asserted their own rights, and restored the government by reassuming them. The powers, so assumed, appear to have been exercised with dignity and moderation; the necessary restraint of Lord Pigot's person was not tainted with any unnecessary rigour, but alleviated (notwithstanding the dangerous folly of his friends) with every enlargement of intercourse, and every token of respect; the most jealous disinterestedness was observed by Mr Stratton in not receiving even the lawful profits of magistracy; and the temporary authority, thus exerted for the benefit of their employers, was resigned back into their hands with cheerfulness and submission,—resigned, not like rapacious usurpers, with exhausted revenues, disordered dependencies, and distracted councils, but with such large investments, and such harmonious dispositions, as have been hitherto unknown in the Company's affairs in any settlement in the East.

Your Lordships are, therefore, to decide this day on a question never before decided, or even agitated, in any English court of justice; you are to decide upon the merits of A REVOLUTION— which, as all revolutions must be, was contrary to established law, and not legally to be justified. The only revolutions which have happened in this land have been when Heaven was the only court of appeal, because their authors had no human superiors; and so rapidly has this little island branched itself out into a great empire, that I believe it has never occurred that any disorder in any of its foreign *civil* dependencies has been the subject of judicial inquiry; but, I apprehend that, since the empire has thus expanded itself, and established governments *at distances in-accessible to its own ordinary visitation and superintendence*, all such subordinate governments, all political emanations from them, must be regulated by the same spirit and principles which animate and direct the parent state. Human laws neither do nor can make provision for cases which suppose the governments they establish to fall off from the ends of their institutions; and, therefore, on such extraordinary emergencies, when *forms* can no longer operate, from the absence of a superior power to compel their operation, it strikes me to be the duty of the component parts of such governments to take such steps as will best enable them to preserve the *spirit* of their trusts; in no event whatsoever to surrender them, or submit to their subversion; and, by considering themselves as an epitome of the constitution of their country, to keep in mind the principles by which that constitution has been preserved, and on which it is established.

These are surely fair premises to argue from, when the question is not *technical justification*, but *palliation* and *excuse*. The members of the Council, in the majority of which the efficient government of Madras resided, were certainly as deeply responsible to the India Company in conscience, and on every principle of society, for the preservation of *its* constitution from an undue extension of Lord Pigot's power, as the other component parts of *this* government are answerable to the people of this country for keeping the King's prerogative within its legal limits; there can be no difference but that which I have stated, namely, that the one is subordinate, and the other supreme. But as, in the total absence of the superior power, subordination to it can only operate by an appeal to it for the ratification or annulment of acts already done, and not for directions what to do (otherwise, on every emergency, government must entirely cease), I trust it is not a strained proposition to assert, that there can be no better rule of action, when subordinate rulers must act somehow, owing to their distance from the fountain of authority, than the history of similar emergencies in the government of their country, of which they are a type and an emanation.

Now, my Lord, I believe there is no doctrine more exploded, or more repugnant to the spirit of the British government, because the Revolution is built upon its ruin, than that there must be an imminent political necessity, analogous to natural necessity, to justify the resistance of the other component parts of the government, if one steps out of its delegation, and subverts the constitution. I am not speaking of technical justification. It would be nonsense to speak of law and a revolution in the same sentence. But I say, the British constitution, which is a government of law, knows no greater state necessity than the inviolate preservation of the spirit of a public trust from subversion or encroachment, no matter whether the country would fall into anarchy or blood, if such subversion or encroachment were suffered to pass unresisted. A good Whig would swoon to hear such a qualification of resistance, even of the resistance of an integral part of legislation, much less of a part merely ministerial, which, in all governments, must be subordinate to the legislature, wherever it resides. Such a state necessity, analogous to natural necessity, may be necessary to call out a private man, but is not at all applicable to the powers of a government. The defendants did not act as *private* men, but as *governing powers ;* for, although they were not, technically speaking, the government, when not assembled by the President; yet they were in the spirit of law, and on every principle of human society, the rulers of the settlement. The information charges the act as done by them in the public capacity of members of the Council, in the majority of which the government did reside ; and their act must, therefore, be taken to be a public act, for the preservation of their delegated trusts from subversion by Lord Pigot, which, on the true principle of British government, is sufficient to render resistance meritorious, though not legal.

Where was the imminent state necessity at the Revolution in this country? King James suspended and dispensed with the laws. What laws? Penal laws against both Papists and Protestant Dissenters. Would England have fallen into confusion and blood if the persecuted Papist had been suffered publicly to humbug himself with the mystery of transubstantiation, and the Independent to say his prayers without the mediation of a visible church? Parliament, on the contrary, immediately after the Revolution, repealed many of those intolerant laws, with a preamble to the Act that abolished them, almost copied *verbatim* from the preamble of the proclamation by which the King suspended them ; yet that suspension (although King James was, I trust, something more of an integral part of this government than Lord Pigot was of that of Madras) most justly cost him the crown of these kingdoms. What was the principle of the Revolution? I hope it is well known, understood, and revered by all good men. The principle was, that the trustees of the people were not to suffer an infringement of the constitution, *whether for good or for evil*. All tyrants are plausible and cunning enough to give their encroachments the show of public good. Our ancestors were not to surrender the *spirit* of their trusts, though at the expense of the *form*, and though urged by no imminent state necessity to defend them; no other, at least, than that which I call, and which the constitution has ever since called, the first and most imminent of all state necessities, *the inviolate preservation of delegated trusts from usurpation and subversion*. This is the soul of the British government. It is the very being of every human institution which deserves the name of government; without it, the most perfect model of society is a painful and laborious work, which a madman, or a fool, may, in a moment, kick down and destroy.

Now, why does not the principle apply HERE? Why may not inferiors, in the absence of the superior, *justly*, though not legally, at all events without sanguinary punishment, do, by a *temporary act to be annulled, or ratified, by such superior*, that which the superior would do finally where there is no appeal at all? Will you punish men who were obliged, from their distance from the fountain of authority, to act for themselves, only for having, at all events, refused to surrender their trusts?—only for having saved the government committed to their charge from subversion?—only for having acted as it was the chief glory of our ancestors to have acted? The similitude does not, to be sure, hold throughout; but all the difference is in *our* favour; *our* act was not peremptory and final, but temporary and submissive to annulment; nor is the president of a council equal only to each other individual in it, with an office merely ministerial, to be compared with the condensed executive majesty of this great kingly government with a negative in legislation.

The majority of the Council was the efficient government of Madras, or, in other words, the legislature of the settlement, whose decisions the Company directed should be the order by which each one was to act, without giving any negative in legislation to the President, whose office was consequently (as I have before said) ministerial. This ministerial office he not only refused to perform, but assumed to himself in effect the whole government by dissolving a majority against him. Let me put this plain question to the Court, Ought such arbitrary, illegal dissolution to have been submitted to? Ought the majority, which was, in fact, the whole government in substance, spirit, and effect, though not in regular form, to have suffered itself to be thus crumbled to pieces and destroyed? Was there, in such a case, any safe medium between suffering both spirit and form to go out together, and thus sacrificing the form to preserve the spirit? And could the powers of the government have been assumed or exercised without bloodshed if Lord Pigot had been left at large? I appeal to your Lordships whether human ingenuity could have devised a *middle road* in the absence of all superior control? Ought they to have acquiesced, and waited for the sentence of the Directors, and, on his motion, played at shuttlecock with their trusts across the globe, by referring back questions to Europe which they were sent out to Asia to decide? Where representatives *doubt* what are the wishes of their constituents, it may be proper to make such appeals; but if they were subject to punishment for not consenting to them, whenever one of their body proposed them, government would be a mere mockery. It would be in the power of the President, whenever he pleased, to cripple all the proceedings of the Council. It puts me in mind of the embargo once laid upon corn by the Crown during the recess of Parliament, which was said, in a great assembly, to be but forty days' tyranny at the outside; and it equally reminds me of the celebrated constitutional reply which was made on that occasion, which it would be indelicate for me to cite here, but which, I trust, your Lordship has not forgotten.*

This would have been not only forty days' tyranny at the outside, but four hundred days' tyranny at the inside. It would have been a base surrender of their trusts, and a cowardly compromising conduct unworthy of magistracy.

But the defendants are, notwithstanding all this, CONVICTED; surely, then, either the jury or I mistake. If what I have advanced be sound or reasonable in principle, the verdict must be unjust. By no means. All I have said is compatible with the verdict. Had I been on the jury, I should have found them guilty; but had I been in the House of Commons, I would have given my voice against the prosecution. CONVICTION! Good God! how could I doubt of conviction when I know that our patriot ancestors, who assisted in bringing about the glorious Revolution, could not have stood justified in this Court, though King William sat on the throne, but must have stood self-convicted criminals without a plea to offer in their defence, had not Parliament protected them by Acts of indemnity!

Nothing that I have said could have been uttered without folly to *a jury*. It could not have been uttered with less folly to your Lordships, sitting in judgment on this case, on a *special verdict*. They are not arguments of *law;* they are arguments of *State*, and the State ought to have heard them before it awarded the prosecution; but, having awarded it, *your Lordships now sit in their place to do justice.* If the law, indeed, had prescribed a *specific*

* Lord Mansfield's speech in the House of Lords against the dispensing power.

punishment to the fact charged, the judgment of the law must have followed the conviction of the *fact*, and your Lordship could not have mitigated the sentence. They could only have sued to the state for indemnity. It would, in that case, have been the sentence of the law, not of the judge. But it is not so here. A judge, deciding on a misdemeanour, is bound in conscience, in the silence of law, not to allot a punishment beyond his opinion of what the law, in its distributive justice, would have specifically allotted.

My Lord, if these arguments, drawn from a reflection on the principles of society in general, and of our own government in particular, should, from their uncommonness in a court of justice, fail to make that immediate and decided impression which their justice would otherwise ensure to them, I beseech your Lordship to call to mind that the defendants, who stand here for judgment, stand before you for acts done as the rulers of a valuable, immensely extended, and important country, so placed at the very extremity of the world that the earth itself travels round her orbit in a shorter time than the Eastern deputy can hear the voice of the European superior ; a country surrounded, not only with nations which policy, but which nature—violated nature !—has made our enemies, and where government must, therefore, be always on the watch and in full vigour to maintain dominion over superior numbers by superior policy. The conduct of men in such situations ought not surely to be measured on the narrow scale of municipal law. *Their* acts must not be judged of like the acts of a little corporation within the reach of a mandamus, or of the executive strength of the state. I cannot, indeed, help borrowing an expression from a most excellent and eloquent person, when the conduct of one of our colony governments was, like this, rather hastily arraigned in Parliament. " I am not ripe," said a member of the House of Commons, " to pass sentence on the gravest public bodies, intrusted with magistracies of great weight and authority, and charged with the safety of their fellow-citizens on the very same title that I am ; I really think, that for wise minds, this is not judicious ; for sober minds, not decent ; for minds tinctured with humanity, not mild and merciful." Who can refuse his assent to such admirable, manly sentiments ? What, indeed, can be so repugnant to humanity, sound policy, decency, or justice, as to punish public men, acting in extremities not provided for by positive institution, without a corrupt motive proved, or even charged upon them ? I repeat the words again, that every man's conscience may *force* him to follow me—*without a corrupt motive proved, or even charged upon them.*

Yet it has been said, that PUBLIC EXAMPLE ought to weigh heavily with the Court in pronouncing judgment. I think so too. It ought to weigh heavily indeed ; but all its weight ought to be placed in the saving, not in the vindictive, scale. PUBLIC EXAMPLE requires that men should be secure in the exercise of the great *public*

duties they owe to magistracy, which are paramount to the obligations of obedience they owe to the laws as *private* men.   PUBLIC
EXAMPLE requires that no magistrate should be punished for an
error in judgment, even in the common course of his duty, which
he ought to know, and for which there is a certain rule ; much less
for an act like this, in which he must either do wrong by seizing
the trust of another, or do wrong by surrendering his own.   PUBLIC
EXAMPLE requires that a magistrate should stand or fall by his
HEART ;—that is the only part of a magistrate vulnerable in law in
every civilised country in the world. WHO HAS WOUNDED THE
DEFENDANTS THERE? Even in this fertile age of perjury, where
oaths may be had cheap, and where false oaths might be safe from
the distance of refutation, no one champion of falsehood has stood
forth, but the whole evidence was read out of a book *printed by the
defendants themselves, for the inspection of all mankind.*
   What, then, has produced this virulence of prosecution in a
country so famed for the humanity of its inhabitants, and the mildness of its laws?   *The death of Lord Pigot during the revolution
in the government?*   Strange, that malice should conjure up so
improbable an insinuation as that the defendants were interested
in that unfortunate event ; no event, indeed, could be to them more
truly unfortunate.   If Lord Pigot had lived to return to England,
this prosecution had never been. HIS guilt and his popularity,
gained by other acts than these, would have been the best protection for THEIR friendless innocence. Lord Pigot, besides many
connexions in this country, had a brother, who has, and who
deserves to have, many friends in it. I can judge of the zeal of
his friends from the respect and friendship I feel for him myself—
a zeal which might have misled *me*, as it has many better and
wiser than *me*, if my professional duty had not led me to an early
opportunity of correcting prejudice by truth.   Indeed, some of the
darkest and most dangerous prejudices of men arise from the most
honourable principles of the mind.   When prejudices are caught
up from bad passions, the worst of men feel intervals of remorse to
soften and disperse them ; but when they arise from a generous
though mistaken source, they are hugged closer to the bosom, and
the kindest and most compassionate natures feel a pleasure in fostering a blind and unjust resentment.   This is the reason that the
defendants have not met with that protection from many which
their meritorious public conduct entitled them to, and which has
given rise to a cabal against them so unworthy the legislature of an
enlightened people—a cabal which would stand forth as a striking
blot upon its justice—if it were not kept in countenance by a happy
uniformity of proceeding, as this falling country can well witness.
I believe, indeed, this is the first instance of a criminal trial in
England, canvassed for like an election, supported by defamation,
and publicly persisted in, in the face of a court of justice, without

the smallest shadow of evidence. This deficiency has compelled the
counsel for the Crown to supply the baldness of the cause with the
most foreign invective—foreign, not only in proof, but in accusation.
In justice to them, I use the word *compelled*, as, I believe, none of
them would have been inclined, from what I know of their own
manners and dispositions, to adopt such a conduct without a most
imminent *Westminster Hall necessity*, viz., that of saying something
in support of a cause which nothing but slander and falsehood could
support. *Their* duty as *public* and *private* men was, perhaps, as
incompatible as the duty of my clients ; and they have chosen, like
them, to fulfil the *public* one ; and, indeed, nothing less than the
great ability and eloquence (*I will not say the propriety*) with
which that public duty was fulfilled at the trial, could have saved
the prosecution from ridicule and contempt. As for us, I am sure
we have lost nothing with the world, or with the Court, by our
moderation: nor could the prejudices against us, even if the trial
had not dispelled them, reach us within these venerable walls.
Nothing, unsupported by evidence, that has been said here, or anywhere, will have any other effect upon the Court than to inspire it
with more abundant caution in pronouncing judgment. Judges in
this country are not expected to shut themselves up from society ;
and, therefore, when a subject that is to pass in judgment before
them is of a public and popular nature, and base arts have been
used to excite prejudices, it will only make wise and just magistrates
(such as I know, and rejoice that I am addressing myself to) the
more upon their guard rigidly to confine all their views to the
record of the charge which lies before them, and to the evidence by
which it has been proved, and to be doubly jealous of every avenue
by which human prejudices can force their way to mislead the
soundest understandings, and to harden the most upright hearts.

[The Court, by its judgment, only imposed a fine of one thousand
pounds upon each of the defendants ; a sentence which, we believe, was
considered at the time by the whole profession of the law, and by all others
qualified to consider such a subject, as highly just and proper, under all
the circumstances of the case. The accusation was weighty, but the
judges were bound, by their oaths, to weigh all the circumstances of
mitigation, as they appeared from the facts in evidence, and from the
pleadings of the counsel at the bar. They were not to pronounce a
severe judgment because the House of Commons was the prosecutor.
Mr Burke, however, who had taken a very warm, and, we have no
doubt, an honest part, in the prosecution, took great offence at the
lenient conclusion ; and repeatedly animadverted upon it in the House
of Commons. There can be no doubt of the high value of the privilege
possessed by the representatives of the people to be public accusers ;
but for that very reason they can have no right to determine, or to

interfere with, the judgments of other tribunals, when they themselves are the prosecutors. If judges, indeed, conduct themselves corruptly, or partially, upon a prosecution by the House of Commons, or upon any other judicial proceeding whatsoever, it is a high and valuable privilege of the people's representatives in Parliament to proceed against the offenders by impeachment; but it is not the duty of any member of that high assembly to disparage the decisions of the judges, by invidious observations, without any public proceeding which may bring their merits or demerits into public examination. Such a course is injurious to those who have been the subjects of them; disrespectful to the magistrates who have pronounced them; and contrary to the spirit and character of the British constitution.]

SPEECH for Lord GEORGE GORDON *against Constructive Treason,
delivered in Westminster Hall, Feb.* 1781.

THE SUBJECT.

THE occasion of the prosecution of Lord George Gordon for high treason is but too well remembered; but the general outlines of the extraordinary event which led to it, and of the evidence given upon the trial,
may nevertheless lead to the better understanding of the following
speech.

A bill had been brought into Parliament—the session of 1778—by
Sir George Saville, one of the most upright men which perhaps any age
or country ever produced, to relieve the Roman Catholic subjects of
England from some of the penalties they were subject to by an Act
passed in the eleventh and twelfth year of King William III.—an Act
supposed by many to have originated in faction, and which at all events,
from many important changes since the time of its enactment, had
become unnecessary, and therefore unjust.

On the passing of this bill, which required a test of fidelity from the
Roman Catholics who claimed its protection, many persons of that
religion, and of the first families and fortunes in the kingdom, came
forward with the most zealous professions of attachment to the Government, so that the good effects of the indulgence were immediately felt,
and hardly any murmur from any quarter was heard. This Act of Sir
George Saville did not extend to Scotland; but in the next winter, it
was proposed by persons of distinction in that country to revise the
penal laws in force against the Catholics of that kingdom: at least a
report prevailed of such intention. This produced tumults in Edinburgh, in which some Popish chapels and mass-houses were destroyed,
and the attempt to extend the statute to North Britain was given up.

Upon this occasion a great number of Protestant societies were formed
in Scotland; and the memorable one in London was soon afterwards
erected under the name of the Protestant Association. Large subscrip-
tions were raised in different parts of the kingdom, a secretary was
publicly chosen, and correspondences set on foot between the different
societies in England and Scotland, for the purpose of petitioning Parliament to repeal Sir George Saville's Act, which was represented at
these meetings, and branded in their various publications, as big with
danger to the constitution both of Church and State.

In the month of November 1779, Lord George Gordon, youngest
brother of His Grace the Duke of Gordon, and at that time a member
of the House of Commons, was unanimously invited to become president of the London Association, where he afterwards regularly attended
till the catastrophe of 1780, when he was committed to the Tower.

The object of the Protestant Association was to procure a repeal of the Act of Parliament by petition, as appears from all their resolutions, which were publicly printed and distributed, without any interruption from the magistracy for many months together; and although it was undoubtedly meant, by the numbers and zeal of the petitioners, that Parliament should feel the propriety of repealing the Act, and even an alarm of prudence in refusing to yield to the solicitation of multitudes, not numbered, nor capable of numeration, yet, in all probability, Mr Erskine was justified by the real fact, when he asserted that the idea of *absolute force and compulsion by armed violence*, never was in the contemplation of the prisoner, or of any who afterwards attended him on the memorable 2d of June. So certain is it that the destinations of mobs may not be dictated by their leaders, or even known to themselves—a truth which highly enhances the guilt of assembling them.

After the opening of the Attorney-General, the case for the Crown was introduced by the evidence of William Hay, who had attended the meetings of the Protestant Association, and who swore that the prisoner announced that the associated Protestants amounted to above forty thousand persons, and directed them to assemble on Friday the 2d of June, in four separate columns or divisions, dressed in their best clothes, with blue cockades as a badge of distinction. The witness further swore, that the prisoner declared that the King had broken his coronation oath; and he also spoke to his attendance at the House of Commons on the 2d of June, and his exhortation to the multitude in the lobby to adhere to so good and glorious a cause; for though there was little hope from the House of Commons, they would meet with redress from their mild and gracious Sovereign. Mr Hay also spoke to the burning of the different mass-houses; and, upon his cross-examination, appeared to have been in every quarter where mischief was committing. This gentleman was very ably cross-examined by Mr Kenyon (afterwards Lord Kenyon), and the result of it appears at large in the following speech, where much reliance was placed on it by Mr Erskine, in discredit of the witness, and in protection of the prisoner. It was afterwards proved by Mr Anstruther, M.P., that the prisoner, at Coachmakers' Hall, where the Association assembled, desired the whole body to meet him on the 2d of June, to go up with the petition, declaring that, if there was one less than twenty thousand men, he would not present it, but that they must find another president, as he would have nothing to do with them; that he recommended temperance and firmness, by which he said the Scotch had carried their point, and added that he did not mean them to go into any danger which he would not share, as he would go to death for the Protestant cause. Mr Anstruther further proved the prisoner's directions with regard to the order of the assembling, and his conduct in the lobby of the House of Commons, viz., "that he told them they were called a mob in the House, but that they were peaceable petitioners; that he had no doubt His Majesty would send to his Ministers to repeal the Act when he saw the confusion it created." He further proved that several people called to Lord George, and asked him whether he desired them to disperse, to which he replied, "You are the best judges of what you ought to do; but I will tell you how the matter stands. The House are going to divide

upon the question whether your petition shall be taken into consideration now or on Tuesday. There are for taking it into consideration
now, only myself and six or seven others. If it is not taken into consideration now, your petition may be lost; to-morrow, the House does
not meet; Monday is the King's birthday; and upon Tuesday, the
Parliament may be dissolved or prorogued." The multitude in the
avenues of the Houses of Parliament, and the consequent clamour and
obstruction, it seems, continued after this. Mr Anstruther gave this
evidence with great coolness and precision; and it appears from the
printed trial that the prisoner's counsel thought it prudent to avoid
any cross-examination of him.

Mr Bowen, the chaplain of the House of Commons, proved, that the
prisoner told the multitude that Mr Rous had just moved that the
civil power should be sent for, but that they need not mind it; they
had only to keep themselves cool and steady. The chaplain further
stated that he had advised Lord George to disperse them, and told him
that he had heard in the lobby that they would go if he desired it. That
the prisoner then addressed them from the gallery, advising them to be
quiet and steady; that His Majesty was a gracious sovereign, and when
he heard that the people miles round were collecting, he would send his
ministers private orders to repeal the bill; that an attempt had been
made to introduce a bill into Scotland; that the Scotch had no redress
till they pulled down the mass-houses; that then Lord Weymouth sent
them official assurances that the act should not extend to them. That
he then advised them to be quiet and peaceable, and told them to beware of evil-minded persons, who would mix among them and entice
them to mischief, the blame of which would be imputed to them. That
somebody in the lobby then asked the prisoner if it was not necessary
for them to retire; and that he answered, " I will tell you how it is :
The question was put; I moved that your petition should be taken into
consideration to-night. It was clearly against you, but I insisted upon
dividing the House. *No division can take place when you are there ; * but
to go or not, I leave to yourselves.*" The chaplain then said, that the
prisoner laid hold of his gown, and presented him to the people as the
clergyman of the House of Commons, saying, " Ask him his opinion of
the Popish bill," to which he answered, that the only answer he would
give was, that all the consequences which might arise from that night
would be entirely owing to him ; to which the prisoner made no reply,
but went into the House; and when the Speaker went in, there were
cries of " Repeal, repeal."

Mr Joseph Pearson, the door-keeper of the House of Commons, was
also examined for the Crown. He proved the presence of the mob, and
their cries of " No Popery," and " Repeal, repeal." And with respect
to Lord George Gordon himself, he said that his Lordship came to the
door two or three times, saying, he would come out and let them know
what was going on; that they had a good cause, and had nothing to fear;
that Sir Michael le Fleming had spoken for them like an angel. The
witness added, that as they crowded upon him he called out, " For
God's sake, gentlemen, keep from the door." That the prisoner put his

---

* On a division one part of the House go forth into the lobby.

hand out, waving it, and said, " Pray, gentlemen, make what room you can ; your cause is good, and you have nothing to fear." Other witnesses were examined to what passed in the lobby, the material substance of whose testimony the editor has extracted from the printed trial. The rest of the evidence went to prove those scenes of disorder and violence which are but too well remembered, without narration.

In the course of the evidence for the Crown respecting the riots and burnings in London, a paper was produced by Richard Pond, a witness, who swore that, hearing his house was to be pulled down, he applied to the prisoner for a protection, which he presented to him in the following words, and which was signed by the prisoner :—

"All true friends to Protestants, I hope, will be particular, and do no injury to the property of any true Protestant, as I am well assured the *proprietor* * of this house is a stanch and worthy friend to the cause.
"G. GORDON."

The Attorney-General was also in possession of some letters and papers which Mr Dingwall, a jeweller, was called to establish ; but he said he was not sufficiently acquained with Lord George's hand to prove them.

On the whole of the evidence, the counsel for the Crown contended that the prisoner, by assembling the multitude round the Houses of Parliament, to enforce their purposes by violence and numbers, or even to overawe and intimidate the Legislature in their deliberations, was a levying of war against the King in his realm, within the statute of treasons of the twenty-fifth of Edward III. ; a doctrine which was fully confirmed by the Court ; and they concluded with contending that the overt acts established by the evidence were the only means by which the prisoner's traitorous purposes could possibly be proved. On the close of the evidence for the Crown, the late Lord Kenyon, then Mr Kenyon, senior counsel for the prisoner, addressed the jury in a speech of much ability and judgment, and, according to usual practice, should then have been followed by Mr Erskine, before the examination of the prisoner's witnesses; but it appears from the printed trial that Mr Erskine claimed the right of reserving his address to the jury till after the final close of the whole evidence on both sides, which he said was matter of great privilege to the prisoner, and for which he stated that there was a precedent, the protection of which he should insist upon for his client. This being assented to by the Court, eleven or twelve witnesses were called on the part of the prisoner, the great object of whose examinations was to negative the conclusions drawn by the Crown from the evidence laid before the jury. For this purpose the different expressions culled out from the proceedings at Coachmakers' Hall, and the lobby of the House of Commons, were contrasted with the general tenor of the prisoner's behaviour from his first becoming President of the Protestant Association.

The Rev. Mr Middleton, a member of the Association, was the first witness : he said he had watched all his conduct, and declared that he

* The tenant was a Catholic.

appeared animated with the greatest loyalty to the King, and attach-ment to the constitution ;—that nothing in any of his speeches at the Association contained any expressions disloyal or improper, nor tended directly or indirectly to a repeal of the bill *by force ;*—that he expressed the cockade to be only a badge to prevent disorderly people from mixing in the procession of the Association ;—that he desired them not to carry even sticks, and begged that riotous persons might be delivered up to the constables. Several other witnesses were examined to the same effect as Mr Middleton, particularly Mr Evans, an eminent surgeon, who swore that he saw Lord George in the centre of one of the divisions in Saint George's Fields, and that it appeared at that time, from his conduct and expressions, that, to prevent all disorder, his wish was not to be attended across the bridge by the multitude. This evidence was con-firmed by several other respectable witnesses ; and it appeared also that the bulk of the people in the lobby, and in Palace Yard, were not mem-bers of the Association, but idlers, vagabonds, and pickpockets, who had put cockades in their hats and joined the Association in their progress. This fact was particularly established by the evidence of Sir Philip Jennings Clerke, who said that the people assembled round the House of Commons were totally different, both in appearance and behaviour, from the members of the Association who were assembled by the prisoner, and who formed the original procession to carry up the petition.

The Earl of Lonsdale (then Sir James Lowther) was also examined for the prisoner, and swore that he carried Lord George and Sir Philip Jennings Clerke from the House of Commons ; that the carriage was surrounded with great multitudes, who inquired of Lord George the fate of the petition, who answered that it was uncertain, and earnestly entreated them to retire to their homes and be quiet.

On the close of the evidence, which was about midnight, Mr Erskine rose and addressed the jury in the following speech. The Solicitor-General replied, and the jury, after being charged by the venerable Earl of Mansfield, then Chief-Justice, retired to deliberate. They returned into court about three in the morning, and brought in a verdict *Not Guilty*, which was repeated from mouth to mouth to the uttermost extremities of London by the multitudes which filled the streets.

The editor, though he forbears from observing upon the arguments he has collected, cannot forbear remarking, that the great feature of the following speech is, that it combated successfully the doctrine of con-structive treasons, a doctrine highly dangerous to the public freedom. It is recorded of Dr Johnson that he expressed his satisfaction at the acquittal of this nobleman on that principle. " I am glad," said he, " that Lord George Gordon has escaped, rather than a precedent should be established of hanging a man for constructive treason." *

---

* Boswell's Life of Johnson.

THE SPEECH.

GENTLEMEN OF THE JURY,—Mr Kenyon * having informed the Court that we propose to call no other witnesses, it is now my duty to address myself to you, as counsel for the noble prisoner at the bar, the whole evidence being closed. I use the word closed, because it is certainly not finished, since I have been obliged to leave the place in which I sat, to disentangle myself from the volumes of men's names which lay there under my feet, whose testimony, had it been necessary for the defence, would have confirmed all the facts that are already in evidence before you.

Gentlemen, I feel myself entitled to expect, both from you and from the Court, the greatest indulgence and attention; I am, indeed, a greater object of your compassion than even my noble friend whom I am defending. HE rests secure in conscious innocence, and in the well-placed assurance that it can suffer no stain in your hands: not so with ME; I stand up before you a troubled, I am afraid a *guilty* man, in having presumed to accept of the awful task which I am now called upon to perform,—a task which my learned friend who spoke before me, though he has justly risen by extraordinary capacity and experience to the highest rank in his profession, has spoken of with that distrust and diffidence which becomes every Christian in a cause of blood. If Mr Kenyon has such feelings, think what mine must be. Alas! gentlemen, who am I?—a young man of little experience, unused to the bar of criminal courts, and sinking under the dreadful consciousness of my defects. I have, however, this consolation, that no ignorance nor inattention on my part can possibly prevent you from seeing, under the direction of the Judges, that the Crown has established no case of treason.

Gentlemen, I did expect that the Attorney-General, in opening a great and solemn state prosecution, would have at least indulged the advocates for the prisoner with his notions on the law, as applied to the case before you, in less general terms. It is very common indeed, in little civil actions, to make such obscure introductions by way of trap; but in criminal cases, it is unusual and unbecoming; because the right of the Crown to reply, even where no witnesses are called by the prisoner, gives it thereby the advantage of replying, without having given scope for observations on the principles of the opening, with which the reply must be consistent.

One observation he has, however, made on the subject, in the truth of which I heartily concur—viz., that the crime of which the noble person at your bar stands accused is the very *highest* and

---

* Afterwards Lord Kenyon, and Chief-Justice of the Court of King's Bench.
Mr Erskine sat originally in the front row, under which there were immense piles of papers, and he retired back before he began to address the jury.

most *atrocious* that a member of civil life can possibly commit ; because it is not, like all *other* crimes, merely an *injury* to society from the breach of some of its reciprocal relations, but is an attempt *to utterly dissolve and destroy society altogether.*

In nothing, therefore, is the wisdom and justice of our laws so strongly and eminently manifested, as in the *rigid, accurate, cautious, explicit, unequivocal* definition of what shall constitute this high offence ; for, high treason consisting in the breach and dissolution of that allegiance which binds society together, if it were left ambiguous, uncertain, or undefined, all the other laws established for the personal security of the subject would be utterly useless ; since this offence, which, from its nature, is so capable of being created and judged of by rules of political expediency on the spur of the occasion, would be a rod at will to bruise the most virtuous members of the community, whenever virtue might become troublesome or obnoxious to a bad Government.

Injuries to the persons and properties of our neighbours, considered as individuals, which are the subjects of all other criminal prosecutions, are not only capable of greater precision, but the powers of the state can be but rarely interested in straining them beyond their legal interpretation; but if *treason, where the Government itself is directly offended*, were left to the judgment of its ministers, without any boundaries,—nay, without the most *broad, distinct*, and *inviolable* boundaries marked out by law,—there could be no public freedom, and the condition of an Englishman would be no better than a slave's at the foot of a sultan ; since there is little difference whether a man dies by the stroke of a sabre, without the forms of a trial, or by the most pompous ceremonies of justice, if the crime could be made at pleasure by the state to fit the fact that was to be tried.

Would to God, gentlemen of the jury, that this were an observation of theory alone, and that the page of our history was not blotted with so many melancholy, disgraceful proofs of its truth ; but these proofs, melancholy and disgraceful as they are, have become glorious monuments of the wisdom of our fathers, and ought to be a theme of rejoicing and emulation to us. For from the mischief constantly arising to the state from every extension of the ancient law of treason, the ancient law of treason has been always restored, and the constitution at different periods washed clean, though, unhappily, with the blood of oppressed and innocent men.

When I speak of the ancient law of treason, I mean the venerable statute of King Edward III., on which the indictment you are now trying is framed,—a statute made, as its preamble sets forth, for the more precise definition of this crime, which had not, by the common law, been sufficiently explained ; and consisting of different and distinct members, the plain *unextended letter* of which was thought to be a sufficient protection to the person and honour of the Sovereign, and an adequate security to the laws committed to his execution. I shall mention only two of the number, the others not being in the remotest degree applicable to the present accusation.

To compass or imagine the death of the King; such imagination, or purpose of the mind (visible only to its great Author), being manifested by some open act; an institution obviously directed, not only to the security of his natural person, but to the stability of the Government, the life of the prince being so interwoven with the constitution of the state that an attempt to destroy the one is justly held to be a rebellious conspiracy against the other.

Secondly, which is the crime charged in the indictment, *To levy war against him in his realm;*—a term that one would think could require no explanation, nor admit of any ambiguous construction amongst men who are willing to read laws according to the plain signification of the language in which they are written, but which has nevertheless been an abundant source of that *constructive* cavil which this sacred and valuable Act was made expressly to prevent. The real meaning of this branch of it—as it is bottomed in policy, reason, and justice, as it is ordained in plain, unambiguous words, as it is confirmed by the precedents of justice, and illustrated by the writings of the great lights of the law, in different ages of our history—I shall, before I sit down, impress upon your minds as a safe, unerring standard by which to measure the evidence you have heard. At present, I shall only say that, far and wide as judicial decisions have strained the construction of levying war beyond the warrant of the statute, to the discontent of some of the greatest ornaments of the profession, they hurt not me. As a citizen, I may disapprove of them; but as advocate for the noble person at your bar, I need not impeach their authority, because none of them have said more than this: that war may be levied against the King in his realm, not only by an insurrection to change or to destroy the fundamental constitution of the Government itself by rebellious war, but, by the same war, to endeavour to suppress the execution of the laws it has enacted, or to violate and overbear the protection they afford, not to individuals (which is a private wrong), but to any general class or description of the community, BY PREMEDITATED OPEN ACTS OF VIOLENCE, HOSTILITY, AND FORCE.

Gentlemen, I repeat these words, and call solemnly on the Judges to attend to what I say, and to contradict me if I mistake the law: BY PREMEDITATED, OPEN ACTS OF VIOLENCE, HOSTILITY, AND FORCE;— nothing equivocal; nothing ambiguous; no intimidations, or over-awings, which signify nothing precise or certain, because what frightens one man, or set of men, may have no effect upon another; but that which COMPELS and COERCES; OPEN VIOLENCE AND FORCE.

Gentlemen, this is not only the whole text; but I submit it to the learned Judges, under whose correction I am happy to speak, an accurate explanation of the statute of treason, as far as it relates to the present subject, taken in its utmost extent of judicial construction, and which you cannot but see, not only in its letter, but in its most strained signification, is confined to acts which *immediately*, *openly*, and *unambiguously* strike at the very root and being of government, and not to any other offences, however injurious to its peace.

Such were the boundaries of high treason marked out in the reign of Edward III.; and as often as the vices of bad princes, assisted by weak submissive parliaments, extended state offences beyond the strict letter of that Act, so often the virtue of better princes and wiser parliaments brought them back again.

A long list of new treasons, accumulated in the wretched reign of Richard II., from which (to use the language of the Act that repealed them) " no man knew what to do or say for doubt of the pains of death," were swept away in the first year of Henry IV., his successor; and many more, which had again sprung up in the following distracted arbitrary reigns, putting tumults and riots on a footing with armed rebellion were again levelled in the first year of Queen Mary, and the statute of Edward made once more the standard of treasons. The Acts, indeed, for securing his present Majesty's illustrious house from the machinations of those very Papists *who are now so highly in favour*, have since that time added to the list; but these not being applicable to the present case, the ancient statute is still our only guide, which is so plain and simple in its object, so explicit and correct in its terms, as to leave no room for intrinsic error; and the wisdom of its authors has shut the door against all extension of its plain letter; declaring in the very body of the Act itself, that nothing out of that plain letter should be brought within the pale of treason by inference or construction; but that, if any such cases happened, they should be referred to the Parliament.

This wise restriction has been the subject of much just eulogium by all the most celebrated writers on the criminal law of England. Lord Coke says, " The Parliament that made it was on that account called Benedictum or Blessed;" and the learned and virtuous Judge Hale, a bitter enemy and opposer of constructive treasons, speaks of this sacred institution with that enthusiasm which it cannot but inspire in the breast of every lover of the just privileges of mankind.

Gentlemen, in these mild days, when juries are so free and judges so independent, perhaps all these observations might have been spared as unnecessary; but they can do no harm; and this history of treason, so honourable to England, cannot (even imperfectly as I have given it) be unpleasant to Englishmen. At all events, it cannot be thought an inapplicable introduction to saying that Lord George Gordon, who stands before you indicted for that crime, is not, *cannot* be guilty of it, unless he has levied war against the King in his realm, contrary to the plain letter, spirit, and intention of the Act of 25th Edward III.; to be extended by no *new or occasional constructions; to be strained by no fancied analogies; to be measured by no rules of political expediency; to be judged of by no theory; to be determined by the wisdom of no individual, however wise—but to be expounded by the simple genuine* LETTER *of the law.*

Gentlemen, the only overt act charged in the indictment is—the assembling the multitude, which we all of us remember went up with the petition of the Associated Protestants on the second day of last June; and in addressing myself to a humane and sensible jury of Englishmen, sitting in judgment on the life of a fellow-citizen, more especially under the direction of a Court so filled as this is, I trust I need not remind you that the *purposes* of that multitude, as originally assembled on that day, *and the purposes and acts of him who assembled them*, are the sole objects of investigation; and that all the dismal consequences which followed, and which naturally link themselves with this subject in the firmest minds, must be altogether cut off and abstracted from your attention,—*further than the evidence warrants their admission.* Indeed, if the evidence had been coextensive with these consequences,—if it had been proved that the same multitude, *under the direction of Lord George Gordon*, had afterwards attacked the bank, broke open the prisons, and set London in a conflagration,—I should not now be addressing you. Do me the justice to believe that I am neither so foolish as to imagine I could have defended him, nor so profligate as to wish it, if I could. But when it has appeared, not only by the evidence in the cause, but by the evidence of the thing itself,— BY THE ISSUES OF LIFE, WHICH MAY BE CALLED THE EVIDENCE OF HEAVEN, that these dreadful events were either entirely unconnected with the assembling of that multitude to attend the petition of the Protestants, or, at the very worst, the unforeseen, undesigned, unabetted, and deeply regretted consequences of it, I confess the seriousness and solemnity of this trial sink and dwindle away. Only abstract from your minds all that misfortune, accident, and the wickedness of others have brought upon the scene,—and the cause requires no advocate. When I say that it requires no advocate, I mean that it requires no argument to screen it from the guilt of *treason.* For though I am perfectly convinced of the purity of my noble friend's intentions, yet I am not bound to defend his prudence, nor to set it up as a pattern for imitation; since you are not trying him for imprudence, for indiscreet zeal, or for want of foresight and precaution,—but for a deliberate and malicious predetermination to overpower the laws and government of his country, by HOSTILE, REBELLIOUS FORCE.

The indictment, therefore, first charges that the multitude, assembled on the 2d of June, " WERE ARMED AND ARRAYED IN A WARLIKE MANNER: " which indeed, if it had omitted to charge, we should not have troubled you with any defence at all, because no judgment could have been given on so defective an indictment; for the statute never meant to put an unarmed assembly of citizens on a footing with armed rebellion; and the crime, whatever it is, must always appear on the record to warrant the judgment of the Court.

It is certainly true, that it has been held to be matter of evidence, and dependent on circumstances, what numbers, or species of equipment and order, though not the regular equipment and order of soldiers, shall constitute an army so as to maintain the averment in the indictment of a warlike array; and likewise, what kinds of violence, though not pointed at the King's person, or the existence of the Government, shall be construed to be war against the King. But as it has never yet been maintained in argument in any court of the kingdom, or even speculated upon in theory, that a multitude, without either weapons offensive or defensive of any sort or kind, and yet not supplying the want of them by such acts of violence as multitudes sufficiently great can achieve without them, was a hostile array within the statute;—as it has never been asserted by the wildest adventurer in constructive treason, that a multitude,—armed with nothing,—threatening nothing,—and doing nothing, was an army levying war; I am entitled to say, that the evidence does not support the first charge in the indictment; but that, on the contrary, it is manifestly false;—false in the knowledge of the Crown, which prosecutes it,—false in the knowledge of every man in London who was not bedridden on Friday the 2d of June, and who saw the peaceable demeanour of the Associated Protestants.

But you will hear, no doubt, from the Solicitor-General (*for they have saved all their intelligence for the reply*) that fury supplies arms—*furor arma ministrat;*—and the case of Damaree will, I suppose, be referred ·to, where the people assembled had no banners or arms, but only clubs and bludgeons: yet the ringleader, who led them on to mischief, was adjudged to be guilty of high treason for levying war. This judgment it is not my purpose to impeach, for I have no time for digression to points that do not press upon me. In the case of Damaree, the mob, though not regularly armed, were provided with such weapons as best suited their mischievous .designs:—their designs were, besides, open and avowed, and all the mischief was done that could have been accomplished, if they had been in the completest armour. They burnt dissenting meeting-houses protected by law, and Damaree was taken at their head, *in flagrante delicto*, with a torch in his hand, not only in the very act of destroying one of them, but leading on his followers *in person*, to the *avowed* destruction of all the rest. There could therefore be no doubt of *his* purpose and intention, nor any great doubt that the perpetration of such purpose was, from *its generality*, high treason, if perpetrated by such a force as distinguishes a felonious riot from a treasonable levying of war. The principal doubt, therefore, in that case was, whether such an un-armed riotous force was war, within the meaning of the statute; and on that point very learned men have differed; nor shall I attempt to decide between them, because in this one point they all agree. *Gentlemen, I beseech you to attend to me here.* I say on this point they all agree; *that it is the* INTENTION *of assembling them, which forms the guilt of treason.* I will give it you in the words of high authority, the learned Foster; whose private opinions will, no doubt, be pressed upon you as doctrine and law, and which, if taken together, as all opinions ought to be, and not extracted in smuggled sentences to serve a shallow trick, I am contented to consider as authority.

That great judge, immediately after supporting the case of Damaree as a levying war within the statute, against the opinion of Hale in a similar case, viz., the destruction of bawdy-houses, which happened in his time, says, " *The true criterion, therefore, seems to be*—quo animo *did the parties assemble?—with what intention did they meet?* "

On that issue, then, by which I am supported by the whole body of the criminal law of England,—concerning which there are no practical precedents of the courts that clash, nor even abstract opinions of the closet that differ,—I come forth with boldness to meet the Crown; for even supposing that peaceable multitude,—though not hostilely arrayed,—though without one species of weapon among them,—though assembled without plot or disguise by a public advertisement, exhorting, nay, commanding peace, and inviting the magistrates to be present to restore it, if broken,—though composed of thousands who are now standing around you, unimpeached and unreproved, yet who are all principals in treason, if such assembly was treason; supposing, I say, this multitude to be nevertheless an army within the statute, still the great question would remain behind, on which the guilt or innocence of the accused must singly depend, and which it is your exclusive province to determine—namely, whether they were assembled by my noble client *for the traitorous purpose charged in the indictment?* For war must not only be levied, but it must be levied against the King in his realm—*i.e.*, either directly against his person to alter the constitution of the Government of which he is the head, or to suppress the laws committed to his execution, BY REBELLIOUS FORCE. You must find that Lord George Gordon assembled these men *with that traitorous intention.* You must find not merely a riotous illegal *petitioning,*—not a tumultuous, indecent importunity to influence Parliament,—not the compulsion of motive, from seeing so great a body of people united in sentiment and clamorous sup-plication,—BUT THE ABSOLUTE, UNEQUIVOCAL COMPULSION OF FORCE FROM THE HOSTILE ACTS OF NUMBERS UNITED IN REBELLIOUS CON-SPIRACY AND ARMS.

This is the issue you are to try; for crimes of all denominations consist wholly in the purpose of the human will producing the act: *Actus non facit reum nisi mens sit rea.* The act does not constitute guilt, unless *the mind* be guilty. This is the great text from which the whole moral of penal justice is deduced: it stands at the top of the criminal page throughout all the volumes of our humane and sensible laws; and Lord Chief-Justice Coke, whose chapter on this crime is the most authoritative and masterly of all his valuable works, ends almost every sentence with an emphatical repetition of it.

The indictment *must* charge an open *act*, because the purpose of the mind, which is the object of trial, can only be known by actions; or, again to use the words of Foster, who has ably and accurately expressed it, "The traitorous purpose is the treason, the overt act, the means made use of to effectuate the intentions of the heart." But why should I borrow the language of Foster, or of any other man, when the language of the indictment itself is lying before our eyes? What does it say? Does it directly charge the overt act as in itself constituting the crime? No. It charges that the prisoner "maliciously and traitorously did *compass, imagine, and intend to raise and levy war and rebellion against the King;*" this is the malice-prepense of treason ; and that to fulfil and bring to effect *such traitorous compassings and intentions,* he did, on the day mentioned in the indictment, actually assemble them, and levy war and rebellion against the King. Thus the law, which is made to correct and punish the wickedness of the heart, and not the unconscious deeds of the body, goes up to the fountain of human agency, and arraigns the lurking mischief of the soul, dragging it to light by the evidence of open acts. The hostile *mind* is the crime ; and, therefore, unless the matters which are in evidence before you do, beyond all doubt or possibility of error, convince you that the prisoner is a determined traitor *in his heart,* he is not guilty.

It is the same principle which creates all the various degrees of homicide, from that which is excusable to the malignant guilt of murder. The fact is the same in all ; the death of the man is the imputed crime ; but the *intention* makes all the difference ; and he who killed him is pronounced a murderer, a single felon, or only an unfortunate man, as the circumstances by which his mind is deciphered to the jury show it to have been cankered by deliberate wickedness or stirred up by sudden passions.

Here an immense multitude was, beyond all doubt, assembled on the 2d of June; but whether HE that assembled them be guilty of high treason, of a high misdemeanour, or only of a breach of the Act of King Charles II. against tumultuous petitioning (if such an Act still exists), depends wholly upon the evidence of his purpose in assembling them, to be gathered by you, and *by you alone,* from the whole tenor of his conduct ; and to be gathered, not by *inference* or *probability*, or reasonable *presumption*, but in the words of the Act, *provably;* that is, in the full unerring force of demonstration. You are called upon your oaths to say, *not* whether Lord George Gordon assembled the multitudes in the place charged in the indictment, for that is not denied; but whether it appears by the facts produced in evidence for the Crown, when confronted with the proofs which we have laid before you, that he assembled them *in hostile array, and with a hostile mind, to take the laws into his own hands by main force, and to dissolve the constitution of the Government unless his petition should be listened to by Parliament.*

That it is *your* exclusive province to determine. The Court can only tell you what acts the law, in its general theory, holds to be high treason, on the general assumption that such acts proceed from traitorous purposes: but they must leave it to *your* decision, and to *yours* alone, whether the acts proved appear, in the present instance, under all the circumstances, to have arisen from the causes which form the essence of this high crime.

Gentlemen, you have now heard the law of treason: first in the abstract, and secondly as it applies to the general features of the case: and you have heard it with as much sincerity as if I had addressed you upon my oath from the bench where the Judges sit. I declare to you solemnly, in the presence of that great Being at whose bar we must all hereafter appear, that I have used no one art of an advocate, but have acted the plain unaffected part of a Christian man instructing the consciences of his fellow-citizens to do justice. If I have deceived you on the subject, I am myself deceived; and if I am misled through ignorance, my ignorance is incurable, for I have spared no pains to understand it.

I am not stiff in opinions; but before I change any one of those that I have given you to-day, I must see some direct monument of justice that contradicts them: for the law of England pays no respect to theories, however ingenious, or to authors, however wise; and therefore, unless you hear me refuted by a series of *direct precedents*, and not by vague doctrine, if you wish to sleep in peace, *follow me.*

And now the most important part of our task begins—namely, the application of the evidence to the doctrines I have laid down; for trial is nothing more than the reference of facts to a certain rule of action, and a long recapitulation of them only serves to distract and perplex the memory, without enlightening the judgment, unless the great standard principle by which they are to be measured is fixed and rooted in the mind. When that is done (which I am confident has been done by you), everything worthy of observation falls naturally into its place, and the result is safe and certain.

Gentlemen, it is already in proof before you (indeed, it is now a

matter of history), that an Act of Parliament passed in the session
of 1778, for the repeal of certain restrictions which the policy of
our ancestors had imposed upon the Roman Catholic religion, to
prevent its extension, and to render its limited toleration harmless ;
restrictions imposed, *not* because our ancestors took upon them to
pronounce that faith to be offensive to God, but because it was
incompatible with good faith to man; being utterly inconsistent
with allegiance to a Protestant Government, from their oaths and
obligations, to which it gave them not only a release, but a crown
of glory as the reward of treachery and treason.

It was indeed with astonishment that I heard the Attorney-
General stigmatise those wise regulations of our patriot ancestors
with the title of factious and cruel impositions on the consciences
and liberties of their fellow-citizens.   Gentlemen, they were *at the
time* wise and salutary regulations ; regulations to which this
country owes its freedom, and His Majesty his crown,—a crown
which he wears under the strict entail of professing and protecting
that religion which they were made to repress ; and which I know
my noble friend at the bar joins with me, and with all good men,
in wishing that he and his posterity may wear for ever.

It is not my purpose to recall to your minds the fatal effects
which bigotry has in former days produced in this island.   I will
not follow the example the Crown has set, me by making an attack
on your passions on subjects foreign to the object before you ;   I
will not call your attention from those flames, kindled by a villainous banditti (which they have thought fit, in defiance of evidence,
to introduce), by bringing before your eyes the more cruel flames
in which the bodies of our expiring, meek, patient, Christian
fathers were, little more than a century ago, consuming in Smith-
field.   I will not call up from the graves of martyrs all the precious
holy blood that has been spilt in this land to save its established
Government and its reformed religion from the secret villainy and
the open force of Papists.   The cause does not stand in need even of
such honest arts ; and I feel my heart too big voluntarily to recite
such scenes when I reflect that some of my own, and my best and
dearest progenitors, from whom I glory to be descended, ended
their innocent lives in prisons and in exile, *only because they were
Protestants.*

Gentlemen, whether the great lights of science and of commerce,
which, since those disgraceful times, have illuminated Europe, may,
by dispelling these shocking prejudices, have rendered the Papists
of this day as safe and trusty subjects as those who conform to the
national religion established by law, I shall not take upon me to
determine.   It is wholly unconnected with the present inquiry.   We
are not trying a question either of divinity or civil policy ; and I
shall therefore not enter at all into the motives or merits of the Act
that produced the Protestant petition to Parliament.   It was cer-

tainly introduced by persons who cannot be named by any good
citizen without affection and respect. But this I will say, without
fear of contradiction, that it was sudden and unexpected ; that it
passed with uncommon precipitation, considering the magnitude of
the object ; that it underwent no discussion ; and that the heads of
the Church, the constitutional guardians of the national religion,
were never consulted upon it. Under such circumstances, it is no
wonder that many sincere Protestants were alarmed ; and they had
a right to spread their apprehensions. It is the privilege and *the
duty* of all the subjects of England to watch over their religious
and civil liberties, and to approach either their representatives or
the throne with their fears and their complaints—a privilege
which has been bought with the dearest blood of our ancestors,
and which is confirmed to us by law as our ancient birthright and
inheritance.

Soon after the repeal of the Act, the Protestant Association
began, and from small beginnings extended over England and
Scotland. A deed of association was signed, *by all legal means* to
oppose the growth of Popery: and which of the advocates for the
Crown will stand up and say that such an union was illegal ?
Their union was perfectly constitutional ; there was no obligation
of secresy ; their transactions were all public ; a committee was
appointed for regularity and correspondence ; and circular letters
were sent to all the dignitaries of the Church, inviting them to join
with them in the protection of the national religion.

All this happened before Lord George Gordon was a member of,
or the most distantly connected with it ; for it was not till November 1779 that the London Association made him an offer of
their chair, by a unanimous resolution communicated to him,
unsought and unexpected, in a public letter signed by the secretary in the name of the whole body ; and from that day to the day
he was committed to the Tower, I will lead him by the hand in
your view, that you may see there is no blame in him. Though
all his behaviour was unreserved and public, and though watched
by wicked men for purposes of vengeance, the Crown has totally
failed in giving it such a context as can justify, in the mind of any
reasonable man, the conclusion it seeks to establish.

This will fully appear hereafter ; but let us first attend to the
evidence on the part of the Crown.

The first witness to support this prosecution is—

William Hay—a bankrupt in *fortune* he acknowledges himself
to be, and I am afraid he is a bankrupt in *conscience.* Such a
scene of impudent, ridiculous inconsistency would have utterly
destroyed his credibility in the most trifling civil suit ; and I am,
therefore, almost ashamed to remind you of his evidence when I
reflect that you will never suffer it to glance across your minds on
this solemn occasion.

This man, whom I may now, without offence or slander, point out to you as a dark Popish spy, who attended the meetings of the London Association to pervert their harmless purposes, conscious that the discovery of his character would invalidate all his testimony, endeavoured at first to conceal the activity of his zeal, by denying that he had seen any of the destructive scenes imputed to the Protestants ; yet almost in the same breath it came out, by his own confession, that there was hardly a place, public or private, where riot had erected her standard, in which he had not been, nor a house, prison, or chapel that was destroyed, to the demolition of which he had not been a witness. He was at Newgate, the Fleet, at Langdale's, and at Colman Street ; at the Sardinian Ambassador's, and in Great Queen Street, Lincoln's Inn Fields. What took him to Coachmakers' Hall ? He went there, as he told us, to watch their proceedings, because he expected no good from them ; and to justify his prophecy of evil, he said, on his examination by the Crown, that as early as December he had heard some alarming republican language. What language did he remember ? "Why, that the Lord Advocate of Scotland was called only HARRY DUNDAS." Finding this too ridiculous for so grave an occasion, he endeavoured to put some words about the breach of the King's coronation oath into the prisoner's mouth, as proceeding from himself, which it is notorious he read out of an old Scotch book, published near a century ago, on the abdication of King James II.

Attend to his cross-examination :—He was *sure* he had seen Lord George Gordon at Greenwood's room in January ; but when Mr Kenyon, who knew Lord George had *never* been there, advised him to recollect himself, he desired to consult his notes. First, he is positively sure from his memory that he had seen him there : then he says he cannot trust his memory without referring to his papers ; on looking at them, they contradict him ; and he then confesses that he *never* saw Lord George Gordon at Greenwood's room in January, when his note was taken, *nor at any other time.* But *why* did he take notes ? He said it was because he foresaw what would happen. How fortunate the Crown is, gentlemen, to have such friends to collect evidence by anticipation ! *When* did he begin to take notes ? He said on the 21st of February, which was the *first* time he had been alarmed at what he had seen and heard, although not a minute before he had been reading a note taken at Greenwood's room in *January*, and had sworn that he attended their meetings from apprehensions of consequences as early as *December*.

Mr Kenyon, who now saw him bewildered in a maze of falsehood, and suspecting his notes to have been a villainous fabrication to give the show of correctness to his evidence, attacked him with a shrewdness for which he was wholly unprepared. You remember the witness had said that he always took notes when he attended any meetings where he expected their deliberations might be attended with dangerous consequences. *" Give me one instance,"* says Mr Kenyon, *" in the whole course of your life, where you ever took notes before."* *Poor Mr Hay was thunderstruck;* the sweat ran down his face, and his countenance bespoke despair, not recollection:—" Sir, I must have an instance; tell me when and where?" Gentlemen, it was now too late; *some* instance he was obliged to give, and, as it was evident to everybody that he had one still to choose, I think he might have chosen a better. *He had taken notes at the General Assembly of the Church of Scotland six-and-twenty years before.* What! did he apprehend dangerous consequences from the deliberations of the grave elders of the Kirk. Were THEY levying war against the King? At last, when he is called upon to say to whom he communicated the intelligence he had collected, the spy stood confessed indeed. At first he refused to tell, saying he was his friend, and that he was not obliged to give him up; and when forced at last to speak, it came out to be *Mr Butler,* a gentleman universally known, and who, from what I know of him, I may be sure never employed him or any other spy, because he is a man every way respectable, but who certainly is not only a. Papist, but the person who was employed, in all their proceedings, to obtain the late indulgences from Parliament. He said Mr Butler was his particular friend, yet professed himself ignorant of his religion. I am sure he could not be desired to conceal it; Mr Butler makes no secret of his religion; it is no reproach to any man who lives the life he does; but Mr Hay thought it of moment to *his own* credit in the cause, that *he himself* might be thought a Protestant, unconnected with Papists, and not a Popish spy.

So ambitious, indeed, was the miscreant of being useful in this odious character, through every stage of the cause, that after staying a little in St George's Fields, he ran home to his own house in St Dunstan's Churchyard, and got upon the leads, where he swore he saw *the very same man* carrying *the very same flag* he had seen in the fields. Gentlemen, whether the petitioners employed the same standard-man through the whole course of their peaceable procession is certainly totally immaterial to the cause, but the circumstance is material to show the wickedness of the man. " How," says Mr Kenyon, " do you know that it was the same person you saw in the fields? Was you acquainted with him?"—" No." " How then?"—" Why, he looked like a brewer's servant."—" *Like a brewer's servant!* What! were they not all in their Sunday clothes?"—" Oh! yes, they were all in their Sunday clothes."— ' Was the man with the flag, then, alone in the dress of his trade?" —" No."—" Then, how do you know he was a brewer's servant?" *Poor Mr Hay—nothing but sweat and confusion again.* At last, after a hesitation which everybody thought would have ended in his running out of court, he said he knew him to be a brewer's servant *because there was something particular in the cut of his coat, the cut of his breeches,* AND THE CUT OF HIS STOCKINGS.

You see, gentlemen, by what strange means villainy is sometimes detected; perhaps he might have escaped from me, but he sunk under that shrewdness and sagacity which ability, without long habits, does not provide. Gentlemen, you will not, I am sure, forget, whenever you see a man about whose apparel there is anything particular, to set him down for a brewer's servant.

Mr Hay afterwards went to the lobby of the House of Commons. What took him there? He thought himself in danger; and therefore, says Mr Kenyon, you thrust yourself voluntarily into the very centre of danger. *That would not do.* Then he had a *particular friend,* whom he knew to be in the lobby, and whom he apprehended to be in danger. " Sir, who was that particular friend? Out with it. Give us his name instantly." *All in confusion again. Not a word to say for himself; and the name of this person, who had the honour of Mr Hay's friendship, will probably remain a secret for ever.*

It may be asked, Are these circumstances material? and the answer is obvious. They are material, because, when you see a witness running into every hole and corner of falsehood, and as fast as he is made to bolt out of one, taking cover in another, you will never give credit to what that man relates as to any possible matter which is to affect the life or reputation of a fellow-citizen accused before you. God forbid that you should. I might therefore get rid of this wretch altogether, without making a single remark on that part of his testimony which bears upon the issue you are trying; but the Crown shall have the full benefit of it all. I will defraud it of nothing he has said. Notwithstanding all his folly and wickedness, let us for the present take it to be true, and see what it amounts to. What is it he states to have passed at Coachmakers' Hall? That Lord George Gordon desired the multitude to behave with unanimity and firmness, as the Scotch had done. Gentlemen, there is no manner of doubt that the Scotch behaved with unanimity and firmness in resisting the relaxation of the penal laws against Papists, and that by that unanimity and firmness they succeeded; but it was by the *constitutional* unanimity and firmness of the great body of the people of Scotland, whose example Lord George Gordon recommended, and not by the *riots and burning*, which they attempted to prove had been committed in Edinburgh in 1778.

I will tell you myself, gentlemen, as one of the people of Scotland, that there then existed, and still exist, eighty-five societies of Protestants, who have been, and still are, uniformly firm in opposing every change in that system of laws established to secure the

Revolution; and Parliament gave way in Scotland to their united voice, and not to the firebrands of the rabble.   It is the duty of Parliament to listen to the voice of the people; for they are the servants of the people; and when the constitution of Church or State is believed, whether truly or falsely, to be in danger, I hope there never will be wanting men (notwithstanding the proceedings of to-day) to desire the people to persevere and be firm.   Gentlemen, has the Crown proved that the Protestant brethren of the London Association fired the mass-houses in Scotland, or acted in rebellious opposition to law, so as to entitle it to wrest the prisoner's expressions into an excitation of rebellion against the State, or of violence against the properties of English Papists, by setting up their firmness as an example?   Certainly not.   They have not even proved the naked fact of such violences, though such proof would have called for no resistance, since to make it bear as rebellious advice to the Protestant Association of London, it must have been first shown that such acts had been perpetrated or encouraged by the Protestant societies in the North.

Who has dared to say this?   No man.   The rabble in Scotland certainly did that which has since been done by the rabble in England, to the disgrace and reproach of both countries; but in neither country was there found one man of character or condition, of any description, who abetted such enormities, nor any man, high or low, of any of the associated Protestants here or there, who were either convicted, tried, or taken on suspicion.

As to what this man heard, on the 29th of May, it was nothing more than the proposition of going up in a body to St George's Fields, to consider how the petition should be presented, with the same exhortations to firmness as before.   The resolution made on the motion has been read, and when I come to state the evidence on the part of my noble friend, I will show you the impossibility of supporting any criminal inference from what Mr Hay afterwards puts in his mouth in the lobby, even taking it to be true.   I wish here to be accurate [*looks on a card on which he had taken down his words*].   He says: "Lord George desired them to continue steadfastly to adhere to so good a cause as theirs was; promised to persevere in it himself, and hoped, though there was little expectation at present from the House of Commons, that they would meet with redress from their *mild and gracious Sovereign*, who, no doubt, would recommend it to his Ministers to repeal it."   This was all he heard; and I will show you how this wicked man himself (if any belief is to be given to him) entirely overturns and brings to the ground the evidence of Mr Bowen, on which the Crown rests singly for the proof of words which are more difficult to explain.   Gentlemen, was this the language of rebellion?   If a multitude were at the gates of the House of Commons, to command and insist on a repeal of this law, why encourage their hopes by reminding them

that they had a mild and gracious Sovereign? If war was levying
against him, there was no occasion for his mildness and graciousness. If he had said, " *Be firm and persevere, we shall meet with
redress from the* PRUDENCE of the Sovereign," it might have borne a
different construction; because, whether he was gracious or severe,
his prudence might lead him to submit to the necessity of the times.
The words sworn to were, therefore, perfectly clear and unambiguous
—*Persevere in your zeal and supplications, and you will meet with
redress from a mild and gracious King, who will recommend it to
his Minister to repeal it.* Good God! if they were to wait till the
King, whether from benevolence or fear, should direct his Minister
to influence the proceedings of Parliament, how does it square with
the charge of instant coercion or intimidation of the House of Commons? If the multitude were assembled with the premeditated
design of producing immediate repeal by terror or arms, is it possible to suppose that their leader would desire them to be quiet, and
refer them to those qualities of the prince which, however eminently
they might belong to him, never could be exerted on subjects in
rebellion to his authority? In what a labyrinth of nonsense and
contradiction do men involve themselves, when, forsaking the rules
of evidence, they would draw conclusions from words in contradiction to language, and in defiance of common sense.

The next witness that is called to you by the Crown is Mr Metcalf. He was not in the lobby, but speaks only to the meeting in
Coachmakers' Hall on the 29th of May, and in St George's Fields.
He says that at the former, Lord George reminded them that the
Scotch had succeeded by their unanimity, and hoped that no one
who had signed the petition would be ashamed or afraid to show
himself in the cause;—that he was ready to go to the gallows for
it;—that he would not present the petition of a lukewarm people;
—that he desired them to come to St George's Fields, distinguished
with blue cockades, and that they should be marshalled in four
divisions. Then he speaks to having seen them in the fields in the
order which has been prescribed; and Lord George Gordon in a
coach, surrounded with a vast concourse of people with blue rib-
bons forming like soldiers, but was not near enough to hear whether
the prisoner spoke to them or not. Such is Mr Metcalf's evidence;
and after the attention you have honoured me with, and which I
shall have occasion so often to ask again on the same subject, I shall
trouble you with but one observation, viz., That it cannot without
absurdity be supposed, that if the assembly at Coachmakers' Hall
had been such conspirators as they are represented, their doors
would have been open to strangers like this witness, to come in to
report their proceedings.

The next witness is Mr ANSTRUTHER, who speaks to the language
and deportment of the noble prisoner, both at Coachmakers' Hall on
the 29th of May, and afterwards on the 2d of June, in the lobby of

the House of Commons. It will be granted to me, I am sure, even by the advocates of the Crown, that this gentleman, not only from the clearness and consistency of his testimony, but from his rank and character in the world, is infinitely more worthy of credit than Mr Hay, who went before him; and if the circumstances of irritation and confusion under which the Rev. Mr Bowen confessed himself to have heard and seen what he told you he heard and saw, I may likewise assert, without any offence to the reverend gentleman, and without drawing any parallel between their credits, that where their accounts of this transaction differ, the preference is due to the former. Mr Anstruther very properly prefaced his evidence with this declaration: " I do not mean to speak accurately to words; it is impossible to recollect them at this distance of time." I believe I have used his very expression, and such expression it well became him to use in a *case of blood*. But WORDS, even if they could be accurately remembered, are to be admitted with *great reserve and caution* when the purpose of the speaker is to be measured by them. They are transient and fleeting; frequently the effect of a sudden transport,—easily misunderstood,—and often unconsciously misrepresented. It may be the fate of the most innocent language to appear ambiguous or even malignant, when related in mutilated detached passages, by people to whom it is not addressed, and who know nothing of the previous design either of the speaker or of those to whom he spoke. Mr Anstruther says that he heard Lord George Gordon desire the petitioners to meet him on the Friday following in St George's Fields, and that if there were fewer than twenty thousand people he would not present the petition, as it would not be of consequence enough;—and that he recommended to them the example of the Scotch, who, by their firmness, had carried their point.

Gentlemen, I have already admitted that they did by firmness carry it. But has Mr Anstruther attempted to state any one expression that fell from the prisoner to justify the positive unerring conclusion, or even the presumption, that the *firmness* of the Scotch Protestants, by which the point was carried in Scotland, *was the resistance and riots of the rabble?* No, gentlemen; he singly states the words as he heard them in the hall on the 29th, and all that he afterwards speaks to in the lobby repels so harsh and dangerous a construction. The words sworn to at Coachmakers' Hall are, "that he recommended temperance and firmness." Gentlemen, if his motives are to be judged by words, for Heaven's sake let these words carry their popular meaning in language. Is it to be presumed without proof, that a man means *one* thing because he says *another?* Does the exhortation of temperance and firmness apply most naturally to the constitutional resistance of the Protestants of Scotland, or to the outrages of ruffians who pulled down the houses of their neighbours? Is it possible, with decency, to say in a court of justice that the recommendation of temperance is the excitation to villainy and frenzy? But the words, it seems, are to be construed, not from their own signification, but from that which follows them, viz., *by that the Scotch carried their point.* Gentlemen, *is* it in evidence before you that *by rebellion* the Scotch carried their point, or that the indulgences to Papists were not extended to Scotland because the *rabble* had opposed their extension? Has the Crown authorised either the Court or its law servants to tell you so? Or can it be decently maintained that Parliament was so weak or infamous as to yield to a wretched mob of vagabonds at Edinburgh what it has since refused to the earnest prayers of a hundred thousand Protestants in London? No, gentlemen of the jury; Parliament was not, I hope, so abandoned. But the Ministers knew that the Protestants in Scotland were to a man abhorrent of that law; and though they never held out resistance, if Government should be disposed to cram it down their throats by force, yet such a violence to the united sentiments of a whole people appeared to be a measure so obnoxious, so dangerous, and withal so unreasonable, that it was wisely and judiciously dropped to satisfy the general wishes of the nation, and not to avert the vengeance of those low incendiaries whose misdeeds have rather been talked of than proved.

Thus, gentlemen, the exculpation of Lord George's conduct on the 29th of May is sufficiently established by the very evidence on which the Crown asks you to convict him :—since in recommending *temperance and firmness, after the example of Scotland,* you cannot be justified in pronouncing that he meant more than the firmness of the grave and respectable people in that country, to whose constitutional firmness the Legislature had before acceded, instead of branding it with the title of rebellion; and who, in my mind, deserve thanks from the King for temperately and firmly resisting every innovation which they conceived to be dangerous to the national religion, independently of which His Majesty (without a new limitation by Parliament) has no more title to the Crown than I have.

Such, gentlemen, is the whole amount of all my noble friend's previous communication with the petitioners, whom he afterwards assembled to consider how their petition should be presented. This is all, not only that men of credit can tell you on the part of the prosecution, but all that even the worst vagabond who ever appeared in a court,—the very scum of the earth,—thought himself safe in saying, upon oath on the present occasion. Indeed, gentlemen, when I consider my noble friend's situation, his open, unreserved temper, and his warm and animated zeal for a cause which rendered him obnoxious to so many wicked men;—speaking daily and publicly to mixed multitudes of friends and foes on a subject which affected his passions, I confess I am astonished that

no other expressions than those in evidence before you have found
their way into this court.   That they have not found their way is
surely a most satisfactory proof that there was nothing in his heart
which even youthful zeal could magnify into guilt, or that want of
caution could betray.

Gentlemen, Mr Anstruther's evidence, when he speaks of the
lobby of the House of Commons, is very much to be attended to.
He says, " I saw Lord George leaning over the gallery," which
position, joined with what he mentioned of his talking with the
chaplain, marks the time, and casts a strong doubt on Bowen's
testimony, which you will find stands, in this only material part
of it, single and unsupported.   " I then heard him," continues Mr
Anstruther, " tell them that they had been called a mob in the
House, and that peace-officers had been sent to disperse them,
peaceable petitioners ; but that by steadiness and firmness they
might carry their point, as he had no doubt His Majesty, who
was a *gracious* prince, would send to his Ministers to repeal the
Act when he heard his subjects were coming up for miles round,
and *wishing* its repeal." How coming up ? In rebellion and
arms to compel it ? No ! All is still put on the *graciousness* of
the Sovereign in listening to the unanimous wishes of his people.
If the multitude then assembled had been brought together to
intimidate the House by their firmness, or to coerce it by their
numbers, it was ridiculous to look forward to the King's influence
over it, when the collection of future multitudes should induce him
to employ it.   The expressions were therefore quite unambiguous,
nor could malice itself have suggested another construction of them,
were it not for the fact that the House was at that time surrounded,
not by the petitioners whom the noble prisoner had assembled, but
by a mob who had mixed with them, and who, therefore, when
addressed by him, were instantly set down as his followers.   He
thought he was addressing the sober members of the Association,
who, by " steadiness and perseverance," could understand nothing
more than perseverance in that conduct he had antecedently prescribed, as steadiness signifies a uniformity, not a change of conduct ; and I defy the Crown to find out a single expression, from
the day he took the chair of the Association to the day I am speaking of, that justifies any other construction of " steadiness and
firmness " than that which I put upon it before.

What would be the feelings of our venerable ancestors, who
framed the statute of treasons to prevent their children being drawn
into the snares of death, unless *provably* convicted by overt acts,
if they could hear us disputing whether it was treason to desire
harmless unarmed men to be firm and of good heart, and to trust
to the graciousness of their King ?

Here Mr Anstruther closes his evidence, which leads me to Mr
Bowen, who is the only man—*I beseech you, gentlemen of the jury,
to attend to this circumstance*—Mr Bowen is the *only* man who has

attempted, directly or indirectly, to say that Lord George Gordon uttered a syllable to the multitude in the lobby concerning the destruction of the mass-houses in Scotland.   Not one of the Crown's witnesses—not even the wretched, abandoned Hay, who was kept, as he said, in the lobby the whole afternoon, from anxiety for his pretended friend—has ever glanced at any expression resembling it. They all finish with the expectation which he held out from a mild and *gracious* Sovereign.   Mr Bowen ALONE goes on further, and speaks of the successful riots of the Scotch ; but speaks of them in such a manner as, so far from conveying the hostile idea, *which he seemed sufficiently desirous to convey*, tends directly to wipe off the dark hints and insinuations which have been made to supply the place of proof upon that subject—a subject which should not have been touched on without the fullest support of evidence, and where nothing but the most unequivocal evidence ought to have been received.   He says his Lordship began by bidding them be QUIET, PEACEABLE, and STEADY—*not steady alone ;* though, if that had been the expression, *singly, by itself,* I should not be afraid to meet it ; but be quiet, *peaceable,* and steady.   Gentlemen, I am indifferent what other expressions of dubious interpretation are mixed with these, for you are trying whether my noble friend came to the House of Commons with a decidedly hostile mind ; and as I shall, on the recapitulation of our own evidence, trace him in your view without spot or stain down to the very moment when the imputed words were spoken, you will hardly forsake the whole innocent context of his behaviour, and torture your inventions to collect the blackest system of guilt, starting up in a moment, without being previously concerted, or afterwards carried into execution.

First, what are the words by which you are to be convinced that the Legislature was to be frightened into compliance, and to be coerced if terror should fail ?   " Be quiet, *peaceable,* and steady ; you are a good people, yours is a good cause.   His Majesty is a *gracious* monarch, and when he hears that all his people, ten miles round, are collecting, he will send to his Ministers to repeal the Act."   By what rules of construction can such an address to unarmed, defenceless men be tortured into treasonable guilt ?   It is impossible to do it without pronouncing, even in the total absence of all proof of fraud or deceit in the speaker, THAT QUIET SIGNIFIES TUMULT AND UPROAR, AND THAT PEACE SIGNIFIES WAR AND REBELLION.

I have before observed, that it was most important for you to remember, that with this exhortation to quiet and confidence in the King, the evidence of all the other witnesses closed ; even Mr Anstruther, who was a long time afterwards in the lobby, heard nothing further ; so that if Mr Bowen had been out of the case altogether ; what would the amount have been ?   Why, simply, that Lord George Gordon, having assembled an unarmed, inoffensive multitude in St George's Fields, to present a petition to Parliament, and finding them becoming tumultuous, to the discontent of Parliament and the discredit of the cause, desired them not to give it up, but to continue to show their zeal for the legal object in which they were engaged; to manifest that zeal *quietly and peaceably*, and not to despair of success; since, though the House was not disposed to listen to it, they had a GRACIOUS Sovereign, who would second the wishes of his people. This is the sum and substance of the whole. They were not, even by any one ambiguous expression, encouraged to trust to their numbers as sufficient to overawe the House, or to their strength to compel it, nor to the prudence of the state in yielding to necessity, but to *the indulgence of the King*, in compliance with the wishes of his people. Mr Bowen, however, thinks proper to proceed; and I beg that you will particularly attend to the sequel of his evidence. He stands *single* in all the rest that he says, which might entitle me to ask you absolutely to reject it; but I have no objection to your believing every word of it, *if you can;* because, if inconsistencies prove anything, they prove that there was nothing of that deliberation in the prisoner's expressions which can justify the inference of guilt. *I mean to be correct as to his words.* [*Looks at his words, which he had taken down on a card.*] He says, "That Lord George told the people that an attempt had been made to introduce the bill into Scotland, and that they had no redress till the mass-houses were pulled down. That Lord Weymouth then sent official assurances that it should not be extended to them." Gentlemen, why is Mr Bowen called by the Crown to tell you this? The reason is plain,—because the Crown, conscious that it could make no case of treason from the rest of the evidence in the sober judgment of law, aware that it had proved no purpose or act of force against the House of Commons to give countenance to the accusation, much less to warrant a conviction, found it necessary to hold up the noble prisoner as the wicked and cruel author of all those calamities, in which every man's passions might be supposed to come in to assist his judgment to decide. They therefore made him speak in enigmas to the multitude; not telling them *to do* mischief in order to succeed, but that *by* mischief in Scotland success had been obtained.

But were the mischiefs themselves that did happen here of a sort to support such conclusion? Can any man living, for instance, believe that Lord George Gordon could possibly have excited the mob to destroy the house of that great and venerable magistrate who has presided so long in this high tribunal, that the oldest of us do not remember him with any other impression than he awful form and figure of justice,—a magistrate who had always been the friend of the Protestant dissenters against the ill-timed jealousies of the Establishment—his countryman too—and, without adverting to the partiality not unjustly imputed to men of that country, a man of whom any country might be proud ? No, gentlemen, it is not credible that a man of noble birth and liberal education (unless agitated by the most implacable personal resentment, which is not imputed to the prisoner) could possibly consent to the burning of the house of Lord Mansfield.*

If Mr Bowen, therefore, had ended here, I can hardly conceive such a construction could be decently hazarded, consistent with the testimony of the witnesses we have called ; how much less when, after the dark insinuations which such expressions might otherwise have been argued to convey, the very same person, on whose veracity or memory they are only to be believed, and who must be credited or discredited *in toto*, takes out the sting himself, by giving them such an immediate context and conclusion as renders the proposition ridiculous which his evidence is brought forward to establish ; for he says, that Lord George Gordon instantly afterwards addressed himself thus:—*Beware of evil-minded persons, who may mix among you and do mischief, the blame of which will be imputed to you.*

Gentlemen, if you reflect on the slander which I told you fell upon the Protestants in Scotland by the acts of the rabble there, I am sure you will see the words are capable of an easy explanation. But as Mr Bowen concluded with telling you that he heard them in the midst of noise and confusion, and as I can only take them from *him*, I shall not make an attempt to collect them into one consistent discourse, so as to give them a decided meaning in favour of my client, because I have repeatedly told you, that words, imperfectly heard and partially related, cannot be so reconciled. But this I will say—that he must be a *ruffian* and not a lawyer, who would dare to tell an English jury, that such ambiguous words, hemmed closely in between others not only innocent, but meritorious, are to be adopted to constitute guilt, by rejecting both introduction and sequel, with which they are absolutely irreconcilable and inconsistent: for if ambiguous words, when coupled with actions, decipher the mind of the actor, so as to establish the presumption of guilt, will not such as are plainly innocent and unambiguous go as far to repel such presumption ? Is innocence more difficult of proof than the most malignant wickedness? Gentlemen, I see your minds revolt at such shocking propositions. I beseech you to forgive me ; I am afraid that my zeal has led me to offer observations which I ought in justice to have believed every honest mind would suggest to itself with pain and abhorrence, without being illustrated and enforced.

I now come more minutely to the evidence on the part of the prisoner.

* The house of this venerable nobleman in Bloomsbury Square was one of the first that was attacked by the mob.

I before told you that it was not till November 1779, when the Protestant Association was already fully established, that Lord George Gordon was elected president by the unanimous voice of the whole body, unlooked-for and unsolicited; and it is surely not an immaterial circumstance, that at the very first meeting where his Lordship presided, a dutiful and respectful petition, the same which was afterwards presented to Parliament, was read and approved of,—a petition which, so far from containing anything threatening or offensive, conveyed *not a very oblique reflection* upon the behaviour of the people in Scotland: taking notice that, as England and that country were now ONE, and as official assurances had been given that the law should not pass THERE, they hoped the *peaceable* and *constitutional deportment of the English* Protestants would entitle them to the approbation of Parliament.

It appears by the evidence of Mr Erasmus Middleton, a very respectable clergyman, and one of the committee of the Association, that a meeting had been held on the 4th of May, at which Lord George was not present,—that at that meeting a motion had been made for going up with the petition in a body, but which not being regularly put from the chair, no resolution was come to upon it,—and that it was likewise agreed on, but in the same irregular manner, that there should be no other public meeting previous to the presenting the petition,—that this last resolution occasioned great discontent, and that Lord George was applied to by a large and respectable number of the Association to call another meeting, to consider of the most prudent and respectful method of presenting their petition: but it appears that, before he complied with their request, he consulted with the committee on the propriety of compliance, who all agreeing to it, except the secretary, his Lordship advertised the meeting, which was afterwards held on the 29th of May. The meeting was therefore the act of the *whole* Association; and as to the original difference between my noble friend and the committee on the expediency of the measure, it is totally immaterial, since Mr Middleton, who was one of the number who differed from him on that subject (and whose evidence is therefore infinitely more to be relied on), told you that his whole deportment was so clear and unequivocal, as to entitle him to assure you, on his most solemn oath, that he in his conscience believed his views were perfectly constitutional and pure. This most respectable clergyman further swears, that he attended all the previous meetings of the society, from the day the prisoner became president to the day in question, and that knowing they were objects of much jealousy and malice, he watched his behaviour with anxiety, lest his zeal should furnish matter for misrepresentation; but that he never heard an expression escape him which marked a disposition to violate the duty and subordination of a subject, or which could lead any man to believe that his objects were different from the avowed and legal objects of the Association. We could have examined thousands to the same fact, for, as I told you when I began to speak, I was obliged to leave my place to disencumber myself from their names.

This evidence of Mr Middleton's, as to the 29th of May, must, I should think, convince every man how dangerous and unjust it is in witnesses, however perfect their memories, or however great their veracity, to come into a criminal court where a man is standing for his life or death, retailing scraps of sentences, which they had heard by thrusting themselves, from curiosity, into places where their business did not lead them ; ignorant of the views and tempers of both speakers and hearers, attending only to a part, and, perhaps innocently, misrepresenting that part, from not having heard the whole.

The witnesses for the Crown all tell you that Lord George said he would not go up with the petition unless he was attended by twenty thousand people who had signed it : and there they think proper to stop, as if he had said nothing further ; leaving you to say to yourselves, What possible purpose could he have in assembling such a multitude on the very day the House was to receive the petition ? Why should he urge it, when the committee had before thought it inexpedient ? And why should he refuse to present it, unless he was so attended ? Hear what Mr Middleton says. He tells you that my noble friend informed the petitioners, that if it was decided they were *not* to attend to consider how their petition should be presented, he would with the greatest pleasure go up with it *alone ;* but that, if it was resolved they should attend it in person, he expected twenty thousand at the least should meet him in St George's Fields, for that otherwise the petition would be considered as a forgery : it having been thrown out in the House and elsewhere that the repeal of the bill was not the serious wish of the people at large, and that the petition was a mere list of names in parchment, and not of men in sentiment. Mr Middleton added, that Lord George adverted to the same objections having been made to many other petitions, and he therefore expressed an anxiety to show Parliament how many were actually interested in its success, which he reasonably thought would be a strong inducement to the House to listen to it. The language imputed to him falls in most naturally with this purpose : "I wish Parliament to see who and what you are ; dress yourselves in your best clothes " —which Mr Hay (who, I suppose, had been reading the indictment) thought it would be better to call, ARRAY YOURSELVES. He desired that not a stick should be seen among them, and that if any man insulted another, or was guilty of any breach of the peace, he was to be given up to the magistrates. Mr Attorney-General, to persuade you that this was all colour and deceit, says, " How was a magistrate to face forty thousand men ? How were offenders in such a multitude to be amenable to the civil power?" What a shameful perversion of a plain peaceable purpose! To be sure, if the multitude had been assembled to *resist* the magistrate, offenders could not be secured. But *they themselves* were ordered to apprehend all offenders amongst them, and to deliver them up to justice. *They themselves* were to surrender their fellows to civil authority if they offended.

But it seems that Lord George ought to have *foreseen* that so great a multitude could not be collected without mischief. Gentlemen, we are not trying whether he might or ought to have *foreseen* mischief, but whether he wickedly and traitorously PRECONCERTED AND DESIGNED IT. But if *he* be an object of censure for not foreseeing it, what shall we say to GOVERNMENT, that took no step to prevent it,—that issued no proclamation warning the people of the danger and illegality of such an assembly? If a peaceable multitude, with a petition in their hands, be an army,—and if the noise and confusion inseparable from numbers, though without violence or the purpose of violence, constitute war,—what shall be said of that GOVERNMENT which remained from Tuesday to Friday, knowing that an army was collecting to levy war by public advertisement, yet had not a single soldier, no, nor even a constable, to protect the state?

Gentlemen, I come forth to do that for Government which its own servant, the Attorney-General, has not done. I come forth to rescue it from the eternal infamy which would fall upon its head, if the language of its own advocate were to be believed. But Government has an unanswerable defence. It neither *did* nor *could possibly* enter into the head of any man in authority to prophesy—human wisdom could not divine, that wicked and desperate men, taking advantage of the occasion which, perhaps, an imprudent zeal for religion had produced, would dishonour the cause of all religions by the disgraceful acts which followed.

Why, then, is it to be said that Lord George Gordon is a traitor, who, without proof of any hostile purpose to the Government of his country, only did not foresee,—what nobody else foresaw,—what those people whose business it is to foresee every danger that threatens the state, and to avert it by the interference of magistracy, though they could not but read the advertisement, neither did nor could possibly apprehend?

How are these observations attempted to be answered? Only by asserting, without evidence, or even reasonable argument, that all this was colour and deceit. Gentlemen, I again say that it is scandalous and reproachful, and not to be justified by any duty which can possibly belong to an advocate at the bar of an English court of justice, to declaim, without any proof, or attempt of proof, that all a man's expressions—however peaceable, however quiet, however constitutional, however loyal—are all fraud and villainy. Look, gentlemen, to the issues of life, which I before called the

evidence of Heaven—I call them so still—truly may I call them so
—when out of a book compiled by the Crown from the petition in
the House of Commons, and containing the names of all who signed
it, and which was printed in order to prevent any of that number
being summoned upon the jury to try this indictment, NOT ONE
CRIMINAL, OR EVEN A SUSPECTED NAME IS TO BE FOUND AMONGST
THIS DEFAMED HOST OF PETITIONERS.

After this, gentlemen, I think the Crown ought in decency to be
silent. I see the effect this circumstance has upon you, and I know
I am warranted in my assertion of the fact. If I am not, why did
not the Attorney-General produce the record of some convictions,
and compare it with the list? I thank them, therefore, for the precious compilation, which, though they did not produce, they cannot
stand up and deny.

Solomon says, " O that my adversary would write a book !"—so
say I. My adversary has written a book, and out of it I am entitled
to pronounce that it cannot again be decently asserted that Lord
George Gordon, in exhorting an innocent and unimpeached multitude to be peaceable and quiet, was exciting them to violence against
the state.

What is the evidence, then, on which this connexion with the mob
is to be proved? *Only that they had blue cockades.* Are you or
am I answerable for every man who wears a blue cockade? If a
man commits murder in my livery, or in yours, without command,
counsel, or consent, is the murder ours? In all *cumulative,* constructive treasons, you are to judge from the tenor of a man's
behaviour, not from crooked and disjointed PARTS of it. *Nemo
repente fuit turpissimus.* No man can possibly be guilty of *this*
crime by a *sudden* impulse of the mind, as he may of some others ;
and certainly Lord George Gordon stands upon the evidence at
Coachmakers' Hall as pure and white as snow. He stands so upon
the evidence of a man who had differed with him as to the expediency of his conduct, yet who swears that, from the time he took the
chair till the period which is the subject of inquiry, there was no
blame in him.

You therefore are bound, as Christian men, to believe that when
he came to St George's Fields that morning, he did not come there
with *the hostile purpose* of repealing a law by rebellion.

But still it seems all his behaviour at Coachmakers' Hall was
colour and deceit. Let us see, therefore, whether this body of men,
when assembled, answered the description of ·that which I have
stated to be the purpose of him who assembled them. Were they
a multitude arrayed for terror or force? On the contrary, you
have heard, upon the evidence of men whose veracity is not to be
impeached, that they were sober, decent, quiet, peaceable tradesmen ; that they were all of the better sort; all well dressed and
well behaved ; and that there was not a man among them who had

any one weapon offensive or defensive. Sir Philip Jennings Clerke tells you he went into the Fields, that he drove through them, talked to many individuals among them, who all told him that it was not their wish to persecute the Papists, but that they were alarmed at the progress of their religion from their schools. Sir Philip further told you that he never saw a more peaceable multitude in his life; and it appears upon the oaths of all who were present, that Lord George Gordon went round among them, desiring peace and quietness.

Mark his conduct when he heard from Mr Evans that a low riotous set of people were assembled in Palace Yard. Mr Evans, being a member of the Protestant Association, and being desirous that nothing bad might happen from the assembly, went in his carriage with Mr Spinage to St George's Fields, to inform Lord George that there were such people assembled (probably Papists) who were determined to do mischief. The moment he told him of what he heard, whatever his original plan might have been, he instantly changed it on seeing the impropriety of it. "Do you intend," said Mr Evans, "to carry up all these men with the petition to the House of Commons?"—"Oh no! no! not by any means—I do not mean to carry them all up." "Will you give me leave," said Mr Evans, "to go round to the different divisions, and tell the people it is not your Lordship's purpose?" He answered—"By all means;" and Mr Evans accordingly went, but it was impossible to guide such a number of people, peaceable as they were. They were all desirous to go forward, and Lord George was at last obliged to leave the Fields, exhausted with heat and fatigue, beseeching them to be peaceable and quiet. Mrs Whitingham set him down at the House of Commons; and at the very time that he thus left them in perfect harmony and good order, it appears by the evidence of Sir Philip Jennings Clerke, that Palace Yard was in an uproar, filled with mischievous boys and the lowest dregs of the people.

Gentlemen, I have all along told you that the Crown was aware that it had no case of treason, without connecting the noble prisoner with consequences, which it was in some luck to find advocates to state, without proof to support it. I can only speak for myself; that small as my chance is (*as times go*) of ever arriving at high office, I would not accept of it on the terms of being obliged to produce against a fellow-citizen that which I have been witness to this day: for Mr Attorney-General perfectly well knew the innocent and laudable motive with which the protection was given that he exhibited as an evidence of guilt: yet it was produced to insinuate that Lord George Gordon, knowing himself to be the ruler of those villains, set himself up as a saviour from their fury. We called Lord Stormont to explain this matter to you, who told you that Lord George Gordon came to Buckingham House, and begged to see the King, saying, he might be of great use in quelling the riots;

and can there be on earth a greater proof of conscious innocence?
For if he had been the wicked mover of them, would he have gone
to the King to have confessed it, by offering to recall his followers
from the mischiefs he had provoked? No! But since, notwithstanding a public protest issued by himself and the Association,
reviling the authors of mischief, the Protestant cause was still made
the pretext, he thought his public exertions might be useful, as they
might tend to remove the prejudices which wicked men had diffused.
The King thought so likewise, and therefore (as appears by Lord
Stormont) refused to see Lord George till he had given the test of
his loyalty by such exertions. But sure I am, our gracious Sovereign meant no trap for innocence, nor ever recommended it as such
to his servants.

Lord George's language was simply this:—"The multitude
pretend to be perpetrating these acts under the authority of the
Protestant petition; I assure your Majesty they are not the
Protestant Association, and I shall be glad to be of any service in
suppressing them." I say, by God, that man is a ruffian who
shall, after this, presume to build upon such honest, artless conduct as an evidence of guilt. Gentlemen, if Lord George Gordon
had been guilty of high treason (as is assumed to-day) *in the face
of the whole Parliament,* how are all its members to defend themselves from the misprision of suffering such a person to go at large
and to approach his Sovereign? The man who conceals the perpetration of treason is himself a traitor; but they are all perfectly
safe, for nobody thought of treason till fears arising from another
quarter bewildered their senses. The King, therefore, and his
servants, very wisely accepted his promise of assistance, and he
flew with honest zeal to fulfil it. Sir Philip Jennings Clerke tells
you that he made use of every expression which it was possible for
a man in such circumstances to employ. He begged them, for
God's sake, to disperse and go home; declared his hope that the
petition would be granted, but that rioting was not the way to
effect it. Sir Philip said he felt himself bound, without being
particularly asked, to say everything he could in protection of an
injured and innocent man, and repeated again that there was not
an art which the prisoner could possibly make use of that he did
not zealously employ; but that it was all in vain. I began, says
he, to tremble for myself when Lord George read the resolution of
the House, which was hostile to them, and said their petition
would not be taken into consideration till they were quiet. But
did he say, "*Therefore go on to burn and destroy?*" On the contrary,
he helped to pen that motion, and read it to the multitude, *as one
which he himself had approved.* After this he went into the
coach with Sheriff Pugh in the city; and there it was, in the presence of the very magistrate whom he was assisting to keep the
peace, that he *publicly* signed the protection which has been read

in evidence against him : although Mr Fisher, who now stands in my presence, confessed in the Privy Council that he himself had granted similar protections to various people, *yet he was dismissed as having done nothing but his duty.*

This is the plain and simple truth—and for this just obedience to His Majesty's request do the King's servants come to-day into his Court, where he is supposed in person to sit, to turn that obedience into the crime of high treason, and to ask you to put him to death for it.

Gentlemen, you have now heard, upon the solemn oaths of honest, disinterested men, a faithful history of the conduct of Lord George Gordon from the day that he became a member of the Protestant Association to the day that he was committed a prisoner to the Tower. And I have no doubt, from the attention with which I have been honoured from the beginning, that you have still kept in your minds the principles to which I entreated you would apply it, and that you have measured it by that standard.

You have, therefore, only to look back to the whole of it together ; to reflect on all you have heard concerning him ; to trace him in your recollection through every part of the trans-action ; and, considering it with one manly, liberal view, to ask your own honest hearts whether you can say that this noble and unfortunate youth is a wicked and deliberate traitor, who deserves by your verdict to suffer a shameful and ignominious death, which will stain the ancient honours of his house for ever.

The crime which the Crown would have fixed upon him is, that he assembled the Protestant Association round the House of Commons, not merely *to influence and persuade Parliament by the earnestness of their supplications,* but actually to coerce it *by hostile rebellious force ;* that finding himself disappointed in the success of that coercion, he afterwards incited his followers to abolish the legal indulgences to Papists, which the object of the petition was to repeal, by the burning of their houses of worship and the destruction of their property, which ended at last in a general attack on the property of all orders of men, religious and civil, on the public treasures of the nation, and on the very being of the Government.

To support a charge of so atrocious and unnatural a complexion, the laws of the most arbitrary nations would require the most incontrovertible proof. Either the villain must have been taken in the overt act of wickedness, or, if he worked in secret upon others, his guilt must have been brought out by the discovery of a con-spiracy, or by the consistent tenor of criminality. The very worst inquisitor that ever dealt in blood would vindicate the torture by plausibility at least, and by the semblance of truth.

What evidence, then, will a jury of Englishmen expect from the servants of the Crown of England before they deliver up a brother

accused before them to ignominy and death? What proof will
their consciences require? What will their plain and manly
understandings accept of? What does the immemorial custom of
their fathers, and the written law of this land, warrant them in
demanding? Nothing less, *in any case of blood*, than the clearest
and most unequivocal conviction of guilt. But in *this case* the
Act has not even trusted to the humanity and justice of our general
law, but has said in plain, rough, expressive terms—*provably*—
that is, says Lord Coke, *not upon conjectural presumptions or
inferences, or strains of wit*, but upon DIRECT AND PLAIN PROOF.
" For the King, Lords, and Commons," continues that great
lawyer, "did not use the word *probably*, for then a common argument might have served; but *provably*, which signifies the
highest force of demonstration." And what evidence, gentlemen
of the jury, does the Crown offer to you in compliance with these
sound and sacred doctrines of justice? A few broken, interrupted,
disjointed words, without context or connexion, uttered by the
speaker in agitation and heat, heard by those who relate them to
you in the midst of tumult and confusion, and even those words,
mutilated as they are, in direct opposition to, and inconsistent with,
repeated and earnest declarations, delivered at the very same time,
and on the very same occasion, related to you by a much greater
number of persons, and absolutely incompatible with the whole
tenor of his conduct. Which of us all, gentlemen, would be
safe, standing at the bar of God or man, if we were not to be
judged by the regular current of our lives and conversations, but
by detached and unguarded expressions, picked out by malice, and
recorded, without context or circumstances, against us? Yet such
is the only evidence on which the Crown asks you to dip your
hands and to stain your consciences in the innocent blood of the
noble and unfortunate youth who now stands before you—on the
single evidence of the words you have heard from their witnesses
(*for of what but words have you heard?*) which, even if they had
stood uncontroverted by the proofs that have swallowed them up,
or unexplained by circumstances which destroy their malignity,
could not, *at the very worst*, amount in law to more than a breach
of the Act against tumultuous petitioning (if such an Act still
exists); since the worst malice of his enemies has not been able to
bring up one single witness to say that he ever *directed, countenanced*, or *approved* rebellious force against the Legislature of his
country. It is therefore a matter of astonishment to me that men
can keep the natural colour in their cheeks when they ask for
human life, even on the Crown's original case, *though the prisoner
had made no defence*. But will they still continue to ask for it
after what they have heard? I will just remind the Solicitor-
General, before he begins his reply, what matter he has to
encounter. He has to encounter this:—That the going up in a

body was not even originated by Lord George, but by others in his absence: That when proposed by him officially as chairman, it was adopted by the *whole* Association, and consequently was *their* act as much as his: That it was adopted, not in a conclave, but with open doors, and the resolution published to all the world: That it was known, of course, to the Ministers and magistrates of the country, who did not even signify to him, or to anybody else, its illegality or danger: That decency and peace were enjoined and commanded: That the regularity of the procession, and those badges of distinction, which are now cruelly turned into the charge of an hostile array against him, were expressly and *publicly* directed *for the preservation of peace and the prevention of tumult:* That while the House was deliberating, he repeatedly entreated them to behave with decency and peace, and to retire to their houses; *though he knew not that he was speaking to the enemies of his cause:* That when they at last dispersed, no man thought or imagined that treason had been committed: That he retired to bed, where he lay, unconscious that ruffians were ruining him by their disorders in the night: That on Monday he published an advertisement reviling the authors of the riots, and, as the Protestant cause had been wickedly made the pretext for them, solemnly enjoined all who wished well to it to be obedient to the laws. (*Nor has the Crown even attempted to prove that he had either given, or that he afterwards gave, secret instructions in opposition to that public admonition.*) That he afterwards begged an audience to receive the King's commands: That he waited on the Ministers: That he attended his duty in Parliament; and when the multitude, *amongst whom there was not a man of the Associated Protestants*, again assembled on the Tuesday, under pretence of the Protestant cause, he offered his services, and read a resolution of the House to them, accompanied with every expostulation which a zeal for peace could possibly inspire: That he afterwards, in pursuance of the King's direction, attended the magistrates in their duty; honestly and honourably exerting all his powers to quell the fury of the multitude; a conduct which, to the dishonour of the Crown, has been scandalously turned against him, by criminating him with protections granted publicly in the coach of the Sheriff of London, whom he was assisting in his office of magistracy,—although protections of a similar nature were, to the knowledge of the whole Privy Council, granted by Mr Fisher himself, who now stands in my presence unaccused and unreproved, but who, if the Crown that summoned him *durst have called him*, would have dispersed to their confusion the slightest imputation of guilt.

What, then, has produced this trial for high treason, or given it, when produced, the seriousness and solemnity it wears? What but the inversion of all justice, by judging from *consequences*, in-

stead of from *causes* and *designs?* What but the artful manner in
which the Crown has endeavoured to blend the petitioning in a
body, and the zeal with which an animated disposition conducted
it, with the melancholy crimes that followed?—crimes which the
shameful indolence of our magistrates, which the total extinction
of all police and government, suffered to be committed in broad
day, and in the delirium of drunkenness, by an unarmed banditti,
without a head, without plan or object, and without a refuge from
the instant gripe of justice,—a banditti with whom the Associated
Protestants and their president had no manner of connexion, and
whose cause they overturned, dishonoured, and ruined.

How unchristian, then, is it to attempt, without evidence, to in-
fect the imaginations of men who are sworn dispassionately and
disinterestedly to try the trivial offence of assembling a multitude
with a petition to repeal a law (which has happened so often in all
our memories) by blending it with the fatal catastrophe on which
every man's mind may be supposed to retain some degree of irritation? *Oh, fie! Oh, fie!* Is the intellectual seat of justice to be thus
impiously shaken? Are your benevolent propensities to be thus
disappointed and abused? Do they wish you, while you are listening to the evidence, to connect it with unforeseen consequences, in
spite of reason and truth? Is it their object to hang the millstone
of prejudice around his innocent neck to sink him? If there be
such men, may Heaven forgive them for the attempt, and inspire
you with fortitude and wisdom to discharge your duty with calm,
steady, and reflecting minds!

Gentlemen, I have no manner of doubt that you will. I am
sure you cannot but see, notwithstanding my great inability, increased by a perturbation of mind (arising, thank God! from no
dishonest cause), that there has been not only no evidence on the
part of the Crown to fix the guilt of the late commotions upon the
prisoner, but that, on the contrary, we have been able to resist the
probability—I might almost say the *possibility*—of the charge, not
only by living witnesses, whom we only ceased to call because the
trial would never have ended, but by the evidence of all the blood
that has paid the forfeit of that guilt already,—an evidence that I
will take upon me to say is the strongest, and most unanswerable,
which the combination of natural events ever brought together
since the beginning of the world for the deliverance of the
oppressed; since in the late numerous trials for acts of violence
and depredation, though conducted by the ablest servants of the
Crown, with a laudable eye to the investigation of the subject
which now engages us, no one fact appeared which showed any
plan, any object, any leader; since out of forty-four thousand persons who signed the petition of the Protestants, *not one* was to be
found among those who were convicted, tried, or even apprehended
on suspicion; and since out of all the felons who were let loose

from prisons, and who assisted in the destruction of our property, not a single wretch was to be found who could even attempt to save his own life by the plausible promise of giving evidence to-day.

What can overturn such a proof as this? Surely a good man might, without superstition, believe that such an union of events was something more than natural, and that the divine Providence was watchful for the protection of innocence and truth.

I may now therefore relieve you from the pain of hearing me any longer, and be myself relieved from speaking on a subject which agitates and distresses me. Since Lord George Gordon stands clear of every hostile act or purpose against the Legislature of his country, or the properties of his fellow-subjects; since the whole tenor of his conduct repels the belief of the *traitorous intention* charged by the indictment, my task is finished. I shall make no address to your passions. I will not remind you of the long and rigorous imprisonment he has suffered. I will not speak to you of his great youth, of his illustrious birth, and of his uniformly animated and generous zeal in Parliament for the constitution of his country. Such topics might be useful in the balance of a doubtful case; yet even then I should have trusted to the honest hearts of Englishmen to have felt them without excitation. At present, the plain and rigid rules of justice and truth are sufficient to entitle me to your verdict.

SPEECH in the Court of King's Bench against a New Trial in the Case of Breach of Promise of Marriage, MORTON *v.* FENN.

THE SUBJECT.

THE following speech may appear, at first glance, to be scarcely worthy of a place in a collection of pleadings upon so many interesting subjects ; but it will be found, on examination, to contain very important principles of law. The occasion of it was shortly this. A woman of the name of Morton, who was the plaintiff, in a cause tried before Lord Mansfield at the sittings at Guildhall, in London, had hired herself to be housekeeper to a Mr Fenn, who was the defendant, an old and infirm man. Mrs Morton, the plaintiff, was not a young woman, and had no great personal recommendations. The old gentleman, however, thought otherwise, and, to induce his housekeeper to cohabit with him, had promised to marry her, the breach of which promise was the foundation of an action to recover damages.

The cause was conducted by Lord Erskine, who had not then been long at the bar. There is no note of what passed at the trial, nor is it material, except that, after the plaintiff's case had been opened, and, after some cross-examination of the witness who proved the promise, with a view to ridicule the person and manners of the plaintiff, Mr Wallace, then Attorney-General, and who was a very able *nisi prius* advocate, endeavoured, as the lawyers call it, without calling witnesses, to laugh the cause out of court, by representing that neither of the parties to the contract had any loss from the breach of it, as the plaintiff was an ugly old woman, and the defendant, who was then in court, and whom he pointed out to the jury to make the scene more ludicrous, was not a person, in the loss of whom, as *a husband,* there could be any claim to more than a *farthing* damages. The jury, however, returned a verdict of *two thousand pounds;* and, in the term which followed, a rule having been obtained by the Attorney-General for setting aside the verdict, and for a new trial, on the ground that the damages were *excessive,* the following very short speech was made by Mr Erskine, maintaining his client's right to the whole money, and denying the jurisdiction of the Court, *in such a case,* to impeach the verdict of the jury.

Perhaps there is no subject more important in the whole volumes of the law than that which regards the distinct jurisdictions of judges and juries in that mixed form of trial which is the peculiar and the best feature in the British constitution. The subject, as it applies to criminal cases, is treated of in every possible point of view in the

Dean of St Asaph's case (p. 96 of the present volume); but it is most important, also (even as it regards *civil* cases) that the distinct offices of judges and juries should be thoroughly understood and rigidly maintained. If, in civil actions, the Court had no jurisdiction to set aside verdicts, and to grant new trials, even in cases where the jury may either have mistaken the law, or where they may have assessed damages by no means commensurate with the loss of property, or with the injury sustained by the party complaining ; if in cases where juries may have assessed damages either manifestly and grossly excessive, or unjustly inadequate, the Court had no jurisdiction to send the case to another hearing for more mature consideration, trial by jury, the boast and glory of our country, would be as great a national evil as it is now a benefit and a blessing ;—but if, on the other hand, revisions of verdicts were suffered to take place, unless in cases of *manifest* injustice ; if new trials were to be awarded, because judges might differ from juries upon occasions where men of sense and justice might reasonably differ from one another, such a proceeding would be the substitution of judicial authority, in fixed magistrates, for the discretion lodged by the constitution in the popular jurisdictions of the country. Every pleading, therefore, which accurately marks out and firmly maintains those salutary boundaries, *though already very well understood and ascertained*, is worthy of a faithful report. On the present occasion, the Court refused to set aside the verdict, upon the principles contained in the short speech which follows.

THE SPEECH.

MY LORD,—The jurisdiction exercised by the Court in cases of excessive damages stands upon so sensible and so clear a principle, that the bare stating of it must, in itself, be an answer to the rule for a new trial which the defendant has obtained.

In cases of pecuniary contracts, the damage is matter of *visible* and *certain* calculation ; the Court can estimate it as well as the jury ; and though it never interferes on account of those variations which may be fairly supposed to have arisen from the different degrees of credit given to the evidence, yet where the jury steps beyond every possible estimate of the injury arising from the contract broken, the Court must say that the verdict is wrong ; because this is a subject upon which there can be no difference of judgment amongst reasonable men ; the advantage of a pecuniary contract, and, consequently, the loss following from the breach of it, being a matter of dry calculation. In such cases, therefore, the Court does not set up a jurisdiction over damages in violation, or control, of the constitutional rights of juries, but only prevents the operation either a visible, certain, palpable mistake, or a wilful act of injustice : this is the whole—and without such power in the Court, since attaints have gone into disuse, the constitution would be wretchedly defective.

The same principles apply likewise to all actions of tort founded on injuries to property; the measure of damages in such actions being equally certain. As much as the plaintiff's property is diminished in value by the act of the defendant, so much shall the defendant pay; for he must place the plaintiff in the same condition as if the wrong had not been committed. In such discussions there must be, likewise, many shades of difference in the judgments of men respecting the loss and inconvenience suffered by acts injurious to property, and, as far as these differences can have any reasonable operation, juries have an uncontrolled jurisdiction; as the Court will never set aside their verdict for a difference which might fairly subsist upon the evidence between intelligent and unprejudiced men: but here, too, when they go beyond the *utmost limits of discreet judgment*, the Court interferes, because there is in all cases of injury to *property* a *pecuniary* calculation to govern the jurisdiction it exercises; all attacks on property resolving themselves into pecuniary loss, pecuniary damages are easily adjusted.

But there is a catalogue of wrongs over which juries, where neither favour nor corruption can be alleged against them, ought to have an uncontrolled dominion; not because the Court has not the same superintending jurisdiction in these as in other cases, but because it can rarely have any standard by which to correct the error of the verdict.

There are other rights which society is instituted to protect as well as the right of property, which are much more valuable than property, and for the deprivation of which no adequate compensation in money can be made. What Court, for instance, shall say, in an action for slandering an honest and virtuous character, that a jury has overrated the wrong which honour and sensibility endure at the very shadow of reproach? If a wife is seduced by the adulterer from her husband, or a daughter from the protection of her father, can the Court say this or that sum of money is too much for villainy to pay, or for misery to receive? In neither of these instances can the jury compel the defendant to make an adequate atonement, for neither honour nor happiness can be estimated in gold; and the law has only recourse to pecuniary compensation from the want of power to make the sufferer any other.

These principles apply, in a strong degree, to the case before the Court. It is, indeed, a suit for breach of a contract, but not of a *pecuniary* contract; injury to *property* is an ingredient—but not the *sole* ingredient of the action: there is much personal wrong; and of a sort that is irreparable. There is, upon the evidence reported by your Lordship, loss of health, loss of happiness, loss of protection from relations and friends, loss of honour which had been before maintained (in itself the full measure of ruin to a woman); and, added to all these, there is loss of property in the disappointment of a permanent settlement for life: and for all this, the jury have given two thousand pounds, not more than a year's interest of the defendant's property.

I am, therefore, at a loss to discover any circumstance on the face of your Lordship's report, from which alone the Court must judge of the evidence, that can warrant a judgment that the jury have done wrong; for independent of their exclusive right to settle the degrees of credit due to the witnesses, what was there at the trial, or what is there *now*, to bring their credit into question? Their characters stood before the jury, and stand before the Court, unimpeached; and Mr Wallace's whole argument, if indeed, jest is to be considered as reason, hangs upon the inadmissible supposition that the witnesses exaggerated the case. But the *jury* have decided on their veracity; and, therefore, before the Court can grant a new trial, it must say, that the verdict is excessive and illegal *upon the facts as reported by your Lordship, taking them to be literally as they proceeded from the mouths of the witnesses.* Upon this state of the case, and it is impossible to remove me from it, I think it is not very difficult to make up the defendant's bill for two thousand pounds.

The plaintiff appears to be the daughter of a clergyman, and to have been bred up with the notions of a gentlewoman; she had been before respectably married, in which condition, and during her widowhood, she had preserved her character, and had been protected and respected by her relations and friends. It is probable that her circumstances were very low, from the character in which she was introduced to the defendant, who, being an old and infirm man, was desirous of some elderly person as a housekeeper: and no imputation can justly be cast upon the plaintiff for consenting to such an introduction; for, by Mr Wallace's favour, the jury had a view of this defendant, and the very sight of him rebutted every suspicion that could possibly fall upon a woman of any age, constitution, or complexion. I am sure everybody who was in court must agree with me, that all the diseases catalogued in the dispensatory seemed to be running a race for his life, though the asthma appeared to have completely distanced his competitors, as the fellow was blowing like a smith's bellows the whole time of the trial. His teeth being all gone, I shall say nothing of his gums; and, as to his shape, to be sure a bass-fiddle is perfect gentility compared with it. I was surprised, therefore, that Mr Wallace should be the first to point out this mummy to the jury, and to comment on his imperfections; because they proved to a demonstration that the plaintiff could have no other possible inducement or temptation to cohabit with him, but that express and solemn promise of marriage which was the foundation of the action and the aggravation of the wrong. But besides such plain presumption, it is directly *proof* that she never DID cohabit with him before, nor until under this express promise and condition; so that the whole argument is, that disease and infirmity are excuses for villainy, and extinction of vigour an apology for debauchery. The age of the plaintiff, who is a woman towards fifty, was another topic; so that a crime is argued to be *less* in proportion as the temptation to commit it is *diminished.*

It would be in the defendant's favour if the promise had been improvident and thoughtless, suddenly given, and as suddenly repented; but the very reverse is in evidence, as she lived with him on these terms for several months, and at the end of them, he repeated his promises, and expressed the fullest approbation of her conduct. It is further in proof, that she fell into bad health on her discovering the imposition practised on her, and his disposition to abandon her. He himself admitted her vexation on that account to be the cause of her illness, and his behaviour under that impression was base: having determined to get rid of her, he smuggled her out of his own house to her sister's, under pretence that change of air would recover her; and continued to amuse the poor creature with fresh promises and protestations, till, without provocation, and without notice or apology, he married another woman, young enough to be his daughter, and who, I hope, will manifest her affection by furnishing him with a pair of *horns,* sufficient to defend himself against the sheriff when he comes to levy the money upon this verdict.

By this marriage, the poor woman is abandoned to poverty and disgrace, cut off from the society of her relations and friends, and shut from every prospect of a future settlement in life suitable to her education and her birth: for having neither beauty nor youth to recommend her, she could have no pretensions but in that good conduct and discretion which, by trusting to the honour of the defendant, she has forfeited and lost.

On all these circumstances, no doubt, the jury calculated the damages, and how can your Lordship unravel or impeach the calculation? They are not like the items in a tradesman's account, or the entries in a banker's book; it is—

For loss of character, so much;

For loss of health, so much;

For loss of the society and protection of relations and friends, so much;

And for the loss of a settlement for life, so much.

How is the Court to audit this account, so as to say, that, in every possible state of it, the jury has done wrong? How, my Lord, are my observations, weak as they are as proceeding from me, but strong as supported by the subject, to be answered?—only by ridicule, which the facts do not furnish, and at which even folly, when coupled with humanity or justice, cannot smile. We are, besides, not in a theatre, but in a court of law; and when judges are to draw grave conclusions from facts, which not being under re-examination, cannot be distorted by observation, they will hardly be turned aside from justice by a jest.

I therefore claim for the plaintiff the damages which the jury gave her under these directions from your Lordship, "That they were sò entirely within *their* province, that you would not lead their judgments by a single observation."

The rule for a new trial was discharged.

SPEECH at Shrewsbury, 6th August 1784, *for the* Rev. WILLIAM DAVIES SHIPLEY, *Dean of St Asaph, on his Trial for Publishing a Seditious Libel.*

THE SUBJECT.

IN the year 1783, soon after the conclusion of the calamitous war in America, the public attention was very warmly and generally turned throughout this country towards the necessity of a reform in the representation of the people in the House of Commons. Several societies were formed in different parts of England and Wales for the promotion of it ; and the Duke of Richmond and Mr Pitt, then the Minister, took the lead in bringing the subject before Parliament.

To render this great national object intelligible to the ordinary ranks of the people, Sir William Jones, then an eminent barrister in London, and afterwards one of the judges of the Supreme Court of Judicature at Bengal, composed a dialogue between a scholar and a farmer as a vehicle for explaining to common capacities the great principles of society and government, and for showing the defects in the representation of the people in the British Parliament. Sir William Jones having married a sister of the Dean of St Asaph, he became acquainted with and interested in this dialogue, and recommended it strongly to a committee of gentlemen of Flintshire who were at that time associated for the object of reform, where it was read, and made the subject of a vote of approbation. The Court party, on the other hand, having made a violent attack upon this committee for the countenance thus given to the dialogue, the Dean of St Asaph, considering (as he himself expressed it) that the best means of justifying the composition, and those who were attacked for their approbation of it, was to render it public, that the world might decide the controversy, sent it to be printed, prefixing to it the following advertisement :—

" A short defence hath been thought necessary against a violent and groundless attack upon the Flintshire Committee, for having testified their approbation of the following dialogue, which hath been publicly branded with the most injurious epithets ; and it is conceived that the sure way to vindicate this little tract from so unjust a character will be as publicly to produce it. The friends of the Revolution will instantly see that it contains no principle which has not the support of the highest authority, as well as the clearest reason.

" If the doctrines which it slightly touches in a manner suited to the nature of the dialogue be 'seditious, treasonable, and diabolical,' Lord Somers was an incendiary, Locke a traitor, and the Convention Parliament a pandæmonium ; but if those names are the glory and boast of England, and if that Convention secured our liberty and happiness, then the doctrines in question are not only just and rational, but constitutional and salutary; and the reproachful epithets belong wholly to the system of those who so grossly misapplied it."

The dialogue being published, the late Mr Fitzmaurice, brother to the late Marquis of Lansdowne, preferred a bill of indictment against the Dean for a libel at the great sessions for Denbighshire, where the cause stood to be tried at Wrexham assizes in the summer of 1783, but was put off by an application to the Court, founded upon the circulation of papers to prejudice the trial. At the spring assizes for Wrexham, in 1784, the cause again stood for trial, and the defendant attended by his counsel a second time, when it was removed by the prosecutor into the Court of King's Bench, and came on at last to be tried at Shrewsbury, as being in the next adjacent English county.

The indictment set forth, "That William Davies Shipley, late of Llannerch Park, in the parish of Henllan, in the county of Denbigh, clerk, being a person of a wicked and turbulent disposition, and maliciously designing and intending to excite and diffuse, amongst the subjects of this realm, discontents, jealousies, and suspicions of our Lord the King and his government, and disaffection and disloyalty to the person and government of our Lord the now King; and to raise very dangerous seditions and tumults within this kingdom; and to draw the government of this kingdom into great scandal, infamy, and disgrace; and to incite the subjects of our Lord the King to attempt, by force and violence, and with arms, to make alterations in the government, state, and constitution of this kingdom, on the 1st day of April, in the twenty-third year of the reign of our Sovereign Lord George the Third, now King of Great Britain, and so forth, at Wrexham, in the county of Denbigh aforesaid, wickedly and seditiously published, and caused and procured to be published, a certain false, wicked, malicious, seditious, and scandalous libel of and concerning our said Lord the King, and the government of this realm, in the form of a dialogue between a supposed gentleman and a supposed farmer, wherein the part of the supposed gentleman, in the supposed dialogue, is denoted by the letter G., and the part of the supposed farmer, in such supposed dialogue, is denoted by the letter F., entitled, 'The Principles of Government, in a Dialogue between a Gentleman and a Farmer.' In which said libel are contained the false, wicked, malicious, seditious, and scandalous matters following" (to wit).

The indictment then set forth verbatim the following dialogue, without any averments or innuendoes, except those above mentioned, viz., that by "G." throughout the dialogue was meant *Gentleman*, and by "F." *Farmer*. By "The King" (when it occurred), *The King of Great Britain*; and by "Parliament" (when it occurred), *The Parliament of his kingdom*. The dialogue, therefore, as it follows, is in fact the whole indictment, only without the constant repetition that F. means Farmer, G. King, and P. Parliament.

" The Principles of Government, in a Dialogue between a Gentleman and a Farmer.

" F. Why should humble men like me sign or set marks to petitions of this nature ? It is better for us farmers to mind our husbandry, and leave what we cannot comprehend to the King and Parliament.

" G. You can comprehend more than you imagine ; and, as a free member of a free state, have higher things to mind than you may conceive.

" F. If by free you mean out of prison, I hope to continue so as long as I can pay my rent to the squire's bailiff; but what is meant by a free state ?

" G. Tell me first what is meant by a club in the village, of which I know you to be a member ?

" F. It is an assembly of men who meet after work every Saturday to be merry and happy for a few hours in the week ?

" G. Have you no other object but mirth ?

" F. Yes ; we have a box into which we contribute equally from our monthly or weekly savings, and out of which any members of the club are to be relieved in sickness or poverty ; for the parish officers are so cruel and insolent, that it were better to starve than apply to them for relief.

" G. Did they, or the squire, or the parson, or all together, compel you to form this society ?

" F. Oh, no ; we could not be compelled ; we formed it by our choice.

" G. You did right. But have you not some head or president of your club ?

" F. The master for each night is chosen by all the company present the week before.

" G. Does he make laws to bind you in case of ill-temper or mis-behaviour ?

" F. He make laws ! He bind us ! No ; we have all agreed to a set of equal rules, which are signed by every new-comer, and were written in a strange hand by young Spelman, the lawyer's clerk, whose uncle is a member.

" G. What should you do if any member were to insist on becoming perpetual master, and on altering your rules at his arbitrary will and pleasure ?

" F. We should expel him.

" G. What if he were to bring a sergeant's guard, when the militia are quartered in your neighbourhood, and insist upon your obeying him ?

" F. We would resist if we could ; if not, the society would be broken up.

" G. Suppose that, with his sergeant's guard, he were to take the money out of the box, or out of your pockets ?

" F. Would not that be a robbery ?

" G. I am seeking information from you. How should you act upon such an occasion ?

" F. We should submit perhaps at that time ; but should afterwards try to apprehend the robbers.

" G. What if you could not apprehend them ?

" F. We might kill them, I should think ; and if the King would not pardon us, God would.

"G. How could you either apprehend them, or, if they resisted, kill them, without a sufficient force in your own hands?

"F. Oh! we are all good players at single-stick, and each of us has a stout cudgel or quarter-staff in the corner of his room.

"G. Suppose that a few of the club were to domineer over the rest, and insist upon making laws for them?

"F. We must take the same course; except it would be easier to restrain one man than a number; but we should be the majority with justice on our side.

"G. A word or two on another head. Some of you, I presume, are no great accountants?

"F. Few of us understand accounts; but we trust old Lilly, the schoolmaster, whom we believe to be an honest man; and he keeps the key of our box.

"G. If your money should, in time, amount to a large sum, it might not, perhaps, be safe to keep it at his house, or in any private house.

"F. Where else should we keep it?

"G. You might choose to put it into the funds, or to lend it the squire, who has lost so much lately at Newmarket, taking his bond on some of his fields, as your security for payment, with interest.

"F. We must, in that case, confide in young Spelman, who will soon set up for himself, and, if a lawyer can be honest, will be an honest lawyer.

"G. What power do you give to Lilly, or should you give to Spelman, in the case supposed?

"F. No power; we should give them both a due allowance for their trouble, and should expect a faithful account of all they had done for us.

"G. Honest men may change their nature. What if both or either of them were to deceive you?

"F. We should remove them, put our trust in better men, and try to repair our loss.

"G. Did it never occur to you that every state or nation was only a great club?

"F. Nothing ever occurred to me on the subject; for I never thought about it.

"G. Though you never thought before on the subject, yet you may be able to tell me why you suppose men to have assembled, and to have formed nations, communities, or states, which all mean the same thing?

"F. In order, I should imagine, to be as happy as they can while they live.

"G. By happy, do you mean merry only?

"F. To be as merry as they can without hurting themselves or their neighbours, but chiefly to secure themselves from danger, and to relieve their wants.

"G. Do you believe that any king or emperor compelled them to associate?

"F. How could one man compel a multitude?—a king or an emperor, I presume, is not born with a hundred hands.

"G. When a prince of the blood shall, in any country, be so distinguished by nature, I shall then, and then only, conceive him to be a greater man than you : but might not an army, with a king or general at their head, have compelled them to assemble ?

" F. Yes ; but the army must have been formed by their own choice ; one man of a few can never govern many without their consent.

" G. Suppose, however, that a multitude of men, assembled in a town or city, were to choose a king or governor ; might they not give him high power and authority ?

" F. To be sure ; but they would never be so mad, I hope, as to give him a power of making their laws.

" G. Who else should make them ?

" F. The whole nation or people.

" G. What if they disagreed ?

" F. The opinion of the greater number, as in our village-clubs, must be taken, and prevail.

" G. What could be done if the society were so large that all could not meet at the same place ?

" F. A greater number must choose a less.

" G. Who should be the choosers ?

" F. All who are not upon the parish in our club. If a man asks relief of the overseer, he ceases to be one of us, because he must depend upon the overseer.

" G. Could not a few men, one in seven, for instance, choose the assembly of law-makers as well as a larger number ?

" F. As conveniently, perhaps ; but I would not suffer any man to choose another who was to make laws, by which my money or my life might be taken from me.

" G. Have you a freehold in any county of forty shillings a year ?

" F. I have nothing in the world but my cattle, implements of hus-bandry, and household goods, together with my farm, for which I pay a fixed rent to the squire.

" G. Have you a vote in any city or borough ?

" F. I have no vote at all ; but am able, by my honest labour, to sup-port my wife and four children ; and, whilst I act honestly, I may defy the laws.

" G. Can you be ignorant that the Parliament to which members are sent by this county, and by the next market-town, have power to make new laws, by which you and your family may be stripped of your goods, thrown into prison, and even deprived of life ?

" F. A dreadful power ! Having business of my own, I never made inquiries concerning the business of Parliament ; but imagined the laws had been fixed for many hundred years.

" G. The common laws to which you refer are equal, just, and humane ; but the King and Parliament may alter them when they please.

" F. The King ought therefore to be a good man, and the Parliament to consist of men equally good.

" G. The King alone can do no harm ; but who must judge the good-ness of Parliament men ?

" F. All those whose property, freedom, and lives may be affected by their laws.

" G. Yet six men in seven who inhabit this kingdom have, like you, no votes ; and the petition which I desired you to sign has nothing for its object but the restoration of you all to the right of choosing those law-makers, by whom your money or your lives may be taken from you : attend while I read it distinctly.

" F. Give me your pen. I never wrote my name, ill as it may be written, with greater eagerness.

" G. I applaud you, and trust that your example will be followed by millions. Another word before we part. Recollect your opinion about your club in the village, and tell me what ought to be the consequence if the King alone were to insist on making laws, or on altering them at his will and pleasure.

" F. He too must be expelled.

" G. Oh ! but think of his standing army, and of the militia, which now are his in substance, though ours in form.

" F. If he were to employ that force against the nation, they would, and ought to resist him, or the state would cease to be a state.

" G. What if the great accountants, and great lawyers, the Lillys and Spelmans of the nation, were to abuse their trust, and cruelly injure, instead of faithfully serving, the public ?

" F. We must request the King to remove them, and make trial of others ; but none should implicitly be trusted.

" G. But what if a few great lords or wealthy men were to keep the King himself in subjection, yet exert his force, lavish his treasure, and misuse his name, so as to domineer over the people, and manage the Parliament ?

" F. We must fight for the King and ourselves.

" G. You talk of fighting, as if you were speaking of some rustic engagement at a wake ; but your quarter-staffs would avail you little against bayonets.

" F. We might easily provide ourselves with better arms.

" G. Not so easily. When the moment of resistance came, you would be deprived of all arms ; and those who should furnish you with them, or exhort you to take them up, would be called traitors, and probably put to death.

" F. We ought always, therefore, to be ready, and keep each of us a strong firelock in the corner of his bedroom.

" G. That would be legal as well as rational. Are you, my honest friend, provided with a musket ?

" F. I will contribute no more to the club, and purchase a firelock with my savings.

" G. It is not necessary. I have two, and will make you a present of one, with complete accoutrements.

" F. I accept it thankfully, and will converse with you at your leisure on other subjects of this kind.

" G. In the meanwhile, spend an hour every morning in the next fortnight in learning to prime and load expeditiously, and to fire and charge with bayonet firmly and regularly. I say every morning, because, if you exercise too late in the evening, you may fall into some of the legal snares, which have been spread for you by those gentlemen who would rather secure game for their table than liberty for their nation.

"F. Some of my neighbours, who have served in the militia, will readily teach me: and perhaps the whole village may be persuaded to procure arms, and learn their exercise.

"G. It cannot be expected that the villagers should purchase arms; but they might easily be supplied, if the gentry of the nation would spare a little from their vices and luxury.

"F. May they turn to some sense of honour and virtue!

"G. Farewell, at present, and remember, that a free state is only a more numerous and more powerful club; and that he only is a free man who is member of such a state.

"F. Good-morning, sir: you have made me wiser and better than I was yesterday; and yet, methinks, I had some knowledge in my own mind of this great subject, and have been a politician all my life without perceiving it."

This dialogue (as above set forth verbatim from the indictment) with the intentions, as alleged in the introductory part, constituted the charge, and the publication of it by the Dean's direction constituted the proof.

On the Dean's part, the above-mentioned advertisement prefixed to it was given in evidence to show with what intention he published it, and his conduct in general relating to it was proved. Witnesses were also called to his general character as a good subject.

Mr Bearcroft, as counsel for the Crown, having addressed the jury in a very able and judicious speech, and the evidence being closed for the Crown, Mr Erskine spoke as follows for the Dean of St Asaph.

THE SPEECH.

GENTLEMEN OF THE JURY,—My learned and respectable friend having informed the Court that he means to call no other witnesses to support the prosecution, you are now in possession of the whole of the evidence on which the prosecutor has ventured to charge my reverend client, the Dean of St Asaph, with a seditious purpose to excite disloyalty and disaffection to the person of his King, and an armed rebellion against the state and constitution of his country; which evidence is nothing more than his direction to another to publish this dialogue, containing in itself nothing seditious, with an advertisement prefixed to it containing a solemn protest against all sedition.

The only difficulty, therefore, which I feel in resisting so false and malevolent an accusation is, to be able to repress the feeling excited by its folly and injustice within those bounds which may leave my faculties their natural and unclouded operations; for I solemnly declare to you, that if he had been indicted as a libeller of our holy religion only for publishing that the world was made by its Almighty Author, my astonishment could not have been greater than it is at this moment, to see the little book which I hold in my hand presented by a grand jury of English subjects as a libel upon the government of England. Every sentiment contained in it (if the interpretations of words are to be settled, not according to fancy, but by the common rules of language) is to be found in the brightest pages of English literature, and in the most sacred volumes of English laws: if any one sentence from the beginning to the end of it be seditious or libellous, the Bill of Rights (to use the language of the advertisement prefixed to it) was a seditious libel,—the Revolution was a wicked rebellion,—the existing government is a traitorous conspiracy against the hereditary monarchy of England, —and our gracious Sovereign, whose title I am persuaded we are all of us prepared to defend with our blood, is a usurper of the crowns of these kingdoms.

That all these absurd, preposterous, and treasonable conclusions follow necessarily and unavoidably from a conclusion *upon this evidence,*—that this dialogue is a libel,—following the example of my learned friend, who has pledged *his* personal veracity in support of his sentiments, I assert upon *my* honour to be my unaltered, and I believe I may say unalterable opinion, formed upon the most mature deliberation; and I choose to place that opinion in the very front of my address to you, that you may not in the course of it mistake the energies of truth and freedom for the zeal of professional duty.

This declaration of my own sentiments, even if my friend had not set me the example by giving you his, I should have considered to be my duty in this cause; for although, in ordinary cases, where the private right of the party accused is alone in discussion, and no general consequences can follow from the decision, the advocate and the private man ought, in sound discretion, to be kept asunder; yet there are occasions when such separation would be treachery and meanness. In a case where the dearest rights of society are involved in the resistance of a prosecution,—where the party accused is (as in this instance) but a mere name,—where the whole community is wounded through his sides,—and where the conviction of the private individual is the subversion or surrender of public privileges, the advocate has a more extensive charge:—the duty of the patriot citizen then mixes itself with his obligation to his client, and he disgraces himself, dishonours his profession, and betrays his country, if he does not step forth in his personal character and vindicate the rights of all his fellow-citizens which are attacked through the medium of the man he is defending. Gentlemen, I do not mean to shrink from that responsibility upon this occasion; I desire to be considered the fellow-criminal of the defendant, if by your verdict he should be found one, by publishing in advised speaking (which is substantially equal in guilt to the publication that he is accused of before you) my hearty approbation of every sentiment contained in this little book ; promising here, in the face of the world, to publish them upon every suitable occasion amongst that part of the community within the reach of my precept, influence, and example. If there be any more prosecutors of this denomination abroad among us, they know how to take advantage of these declarations.*

Gentlemen, when I reflect upon the danger which has often attended the liberty of the press in former times from the arbitrary proceedings of abject, unprincipled, and dependent judges, raised to their situations without abilities or worth in proportion to their servility to power, I cannot help congratulating the public that you are to try this indictment with the assistance of the learned Judge before you ;—much too instructed in the laws of this land to mislead you by mistake, and too conscientious to misinstruct you by design.

The days indeed I hope are now past when judges and jurymen upon state trials were constantly pulling in different directions ; the Court endeavouring to annihilate altogether the province of the jury, and the jury in return listening with disgust, jealousy, and alienation to the directions of the Court. Now they may be expected to be tried with that harmony which is the beauty of our legal constitution ;—the jury preserving their independence in judging of the intention, which is the essence of every crime ; but listening to the opinion of the judge upon the evidence and upon the law with that respect and attention which dignity, learning, and honest intention in a magistrate must and ought always to carry along with them.

Having received my earliest information in my profession from the learned Judge himself,† and having daily occasion to observe his able administration of justice, you may believe that I anticipate nothing from the bench unfavourable to innocence ; and I have experienced his regard in too many instances not to be sure of every indulgence that is personal to myself.

These considerations enable me with more freedom to make my address to you upon the merits of this prosecution, in the issue of which your own general rights, as members of a free state, are not less involved than the private rights of the individual I am defending.

Gentlemen, my reverend friend stands before you under circumstances new and extraordinary, and I might add harsh and cruel ; he is not to be tried in the forum *where he lives*, according to the wise and just provisions of our ancient laws ;—he is not to be tried

---

* It will be seen hereafter, that when the dialogue was brought before the Court by Mr Erskine's motion to arrest the judgment, the Court was obliged to declare that it contained no illegal matter.

† Mr Erskine was for some time one of the Judge's pupils as a special pleader before he was raised to the bench.

by the vicinage, who from their knowledge of general character and conduct, were held by our wise and humane ancestors to be the fittest, or rather the only, judges in criminal cases:—he has been deprived of that privilege by the arts of the prosecutor, and is called before *you*, who live in *another* part of the country, and who, except by vague reputation, are utter strangers to him.

But the prosecution itself, abandoned by the public, and left, as you cannot but know it is, in the hands of an individual, is a circumstance not less extraordinary and unjust,—unless as it palpably refutes the truth of the accusation. For if this little book be a libel at all, it is a libel upon *the state and constitution of the nation*, and *not* upon any person under the protection of its laws: it attacks the character of no man in this or any other country; and therefore no man is *individually or personally* injured or offended by it. If it contain matter dangerous or offensive, *the state alone* can be endangered or offended.

And are we, then, reduced to that miserable condition in this country, that, if discontent and sedition be publicly exciting amongst the people, the charge of suppressing it devolves upon Mr Jones? My learned friend, if he would have you believe that this dialogue is seditious and dangerous, must be driven to acknowledge that Government has grossly neglected its trust; for if, as he says, it has an evident tendency in critical times to stir up alarming commotions, and to procure a reform in the representation of the people by violence and force of arms; and if, as he likewise says, a public prosecution is a proceeding calculated to prevent these probable consequences, what excuse is he prepared to make for the Government, which, when according to the evidence of his own witness, an application was made to it for that express purpose, positively, and on deliberation, refused to prosecute? What will he say for one learned gentleman,* who dead is lamented, and for another,† who living is honoured by the whole profession, both of whom, on the appearance of this dialogue, were charged with the duty of prosecuting all offenders against the state, yet who not only read it day after day in pamphlets and newspapers, without stirring against the publishers, but who, on receiving it from the Lords of the Treasury by official reference, opposed a prosecution at the national expense? What will he say of the successors of those gentlemen who hold their offices at this hour, and who have ratified the opinions of their predecessors by their own conduct? And what, lastly, will he say in vindication of Majesty itself, to my knowledge not unacquainted with the subject, yet from whence no orders issued to the inferior servants of the state?

So that, after Mr Fitzmaurice, representing this dialogue as big with ruin to the public, has been laughed at by the King's Ministers

* Mr Wallace, then Attorney-General.
† Mr Lee, late Attorney, then Solicitor-General.

at the Treasury, by the King himself, of whom he had an audience, and by those appointed by his wisdom to conduct all prosecutions, you are called upon to believe that it is a libel, dangerous and destructive; and that while the state, neglected by those who are charged with its preservation, is tottering to its centre, the falling constitution of this ancient nation is happily supported by Mr Jones, who, like another Atlas, bears it upon his shoulders.*

Mr Jones, then, who sits before you, is the only man in England who accuses the defendant. He alone takes upon himself the important office of dictating to His Majesty, of reprobating the proceedings of his Ministers, and of superseding his Attorney and Solicitor-General; and shall I insult your understandings by supposing that this accusation proceeds from pure patriotism and public spirit in him, *or more properly, in that other gentleman, whose deputy upon this occasion he is well known to be?* Whether such a supposition would not indeed be an insult, his conduct as a public prosecutor will best illustrate.

He originally put the indictment in a regular course of trial in the very neighbourhood where its operations must have been most felt, and where, if criminal in its objects, the criminality must have been the most obvious. A jury of that vicinage was assembled to try it; and the Dean having required my assistance on the occasion, I travelled two hundred miles with great inconvenience to myself, to do him that justice which he was entitled to as my friend, and to pay to my country that tribute which is due from every man when the LIBERTY OF THE PRESS is invaded.

The jury thus assembled was formed from the first characters in their county—men who would have most willingly condemned either disaffection to the person of the King, or rebellion against his government: yet, when such a jury was empannelled, and such names were found upon it as Sir Watkyn Williams Wynne, and others not less respectable, this *public-spirited prosecutor, who had no other object than public justice*, was confounded and appalled. He said to himself, " This will never do. All these gentlemen know not only that this paper is not in itself a libel, but that it neither was, nor could be, published by the Dean with a libellous intention. What is worse than all, they are men of too proud an honour to act upon any persuasion or authority against the conviction of their own consciences. But how shall I get rid of them? They are already struck and empannelled, and unfortunately neither integrity nor sense are challenges to jurors."

Gentlemen, in this dilemma he produced an affidavit, which appeared to me not very sufficient for the purpose of evading the

---

* Mr Jones, the present Marshal of the King's Bench, became entangled in the prosecution as the attorney of Mr Fitzmaurice, brother to the late Marquis of Lansdowne. He is esteemed a very worthy man, and has since lived in habits of intimacy and regard with Lord Erskine.

trial; but as those who upon that occasion had to decide that question upon their oaths were of a different opinion, I shall not support my own by any arguments, meaning to conduct myself with the utmost reverence for the administration of justice. I shall therefore content myself with stating that the affidavit contained no other matter than that there had been published at Wrexham an extract from Dr Towers's Biography, containing accounts of trials for libels published above a century ago, from which the jurors (if it had fallen in their way, which was not even deposed to) might have been informed of their right to judge their fellow-citizens for crimes affecting their liberties or their lives—a doctrine not often disputed, and never without the vindication of it, by the greatest and most illustrious names in the law. But, says this *public-spirited* prosecutor, IF THE JURY are to try this, I must withdraw my prosecution, for they are men of honour and sense; they know the constitution of their country, and they know the Dean of St Asaph; and I have therefore nothing left but to apply to the judges, suggesting that the minds of the special jury are so prejudiced by being told that they are Englishmen, and that they have the power of acquitting a defendant accused of a crime, if they think him innocent, that they are unfit to sit in judgment upon him. Gentlemen, the scheme succeeded, and I was put in my chaise and wheeled back again, with the matter in my pocket which had postponed the trial,—matter which was to be found in every shop in London, and which had been equally within the reach of every man who had sat upon a jury since the times of King Charles II.

In this manner, above a year ago, the prosecutor deprived my reverend friend of an honourable acquittal in his own country. It is a circumstance material in the consideration of this indictment, because, in administering public justice, you will, I am persuaded, watch with jealousy to discover whether public justice be the end and object of the prosecution: and in trying whether my reverend client proceeded *malo animo* in the publication of this dialogue, you will certainly obtain some light from examining *quo animo* the prosecutor has arraigned him before you.

When the indictment was brought down again to trial at the next following assizes, there were no more pamphlets to form a pretext for procrastination. I was surprised, indeed, that they did not employ some of their own party to publish one, and have recourse to the same device which had been so successful before; but this mode either did not strike, or was thought to be but fruitlessly delaying that acquittal, which could not be ultimately prevented.

The prosecutor, therefore, secretly sued out a writ of *certiorari* from the Court of King's Bench, the effect of which was to remove the indictment from the Court of Great Sessions in Wales, and to bring it to trial as an English record in an English county. Armed with this secret weapon to defeat the honest and open arm of justice, he appeared at Wrexham, and gave notice of trial, saying to himself, "I will take no notice that I have the King's writ, till I see the complexion of the jury; if I find them men fit for my purpose, either as the prostitutes of power, or as men of little minds, or from their insignificance equally subject to the frown of authority and the blandishments of corruption, so that I may reasonably look for a sacrifice, instead of a trial, I will then keep the *certiorari* in my pocket, and the proceedings will, of course, go forward; but if, on the contrary, I find such names as I found before—if the gentlemen of the county are to meet me—I will then, with His Majesty's writ in my hand, discharge them from giving that verdict of acquittal which their understandings would dictate and their consciences impose."

Such, without any figure, I may assert to have been the secret language of Mr Jones to himself, unless he means to slander those gentlemen in the face of this Court, by saying that the jurors, from whose jurisdiction he, by his *certiorari*, withdrew the indictment, were not impartial, intelligent, and independent men; a sentiment which he dares not presume even to whisper, because in public or in private he would be silenced by all who heard it.

From such a tribunal this public-spirited prosecutor shrunk a second time; and just as I was getting out of my chaise at Wrexham, after another journey from the other side of the island, without even notice of an intention to postpone the trial, he himself in person (his counsel having, from a sense of honour and decency, refused it) presented the King's writ to the Chief-Justice of Chester, which dismissed the Dean for ever from the judgment of his neighbours and countrymen, and which brings him before you to-day.

What opinion, then, must the prosecutor entertain of your honour and your virtues, since he evidently expects from you a verdict which it is manifest from his conduct he did not venture to hope for from such a jury as I have described to you?

Gentlemen, I observe an honest indignation rising in all your countenances on the subject, which, with the arts of an advocate, I might easily press into the service of my friend; but as his defence does not require the support of your resentments, or even of those honest prejudices to which liberal minds are but too open without excitation, I shall draw a veil over all that may seduce you from the correctest and the severest judgment.

Gentlemen, the Dean of St Asaph is indicted by the prosecutor, not for having published this little book; that is not the charge: he is indicted for publishing a false, scandalous, and malicious libel; and for publishing it (I am now going to read the very words of the charge) "with a malicious design and intention to diffuse among the subjects of this realm jealousies and suspicions of the King and his government; to create disaffection to his person; to raise seditions and tumults within the kingdom; and to excite His Majesty's subjects to attempt, by armed rebellion and violence, to subvert the state and constitution of the nation."

These are not words of *form*, but of the very essence of the charge. The defendant pleads that he is not guilty, and puts himself upon you, his country; and it is fit, therefore, that you should be distinctly informed of the effect of a general verdict of guilty on such an issue, before you venture to pronounce it. By such a verdict you do not merely find that the defendant *published the paper in question;* for if that were the whole scope of such a finding, involving no examination into the *merits* of the thing published, the term *guilty* might be wholly inapplicable and unjust, because the publication of that which is not criminal cannot be a crime, and because a man cannot be *guilty* of publishing that which contains in it nothing which constitutes guilt. This observation is confirmed by the language of the record; for if the verdict of guilty involved no other consideration than the simple fact of publication, the legal term would be, *that the defendant* PUBLISHED, not that he was GUILTY of publishing: yet they who tell you that a general verdict of guilty comprehends nothing more than the fact of publishing, are forced in the same moment to confess, that if you found *that fact alone,* without applying to it the epithet of *guilty,* no judgment or punishment could follow from your verdict: and they therefore call upon you to pronounce that guilt which they forbid you to examine into, acknowledging at the same time that it can be legally pronounced by NONE BUT YOU: a position shocking to conscience, and insulting to common sense.

Indeed, every part of the record exposes the absurdity of a verdict of *guilty,* which is not founded on a previous judgment that the matter indicted is a libel, and that the defendant published it with a criminal intention; for if you pronounce the word *guilty,* without meaning to find sedition in the thing published, or in the mind of the publisher, you expose to shame and punishment the innocence which you mean to protect; since the instant that you say the defendant is *guilty,* the gentleman who sits under the Judge is bound by law to record him *guilty in manner and form as he is accused,*—*i.e.,* guilty of publishing a seditious libel, with a seditious intention,—and the Court above is likewise bound to put the same construction on your finding. Thus, without inquiry into the only circumstance which can constitute *guilt,* and without meaning to find the defendant *guilty,* you may be seduced into a judgment which your consciences may revolt at, and your speech to the world deny; but which the authors of this system have resolved that you shall not explain to the Court, when it is proceeding to punish the defendant on the authority of your intended verdict of acquittal.

As a proof that this is the plain and simple state of the question, I might venture to ask the learned Judge what answer I should

receive from the Court of King's Bench, if you were this day to
find the Dean of St Asaph guilty, but without meaning to find
it a libel, or that he published it with a wicked and seditious
purpose ; and I, on the foundation of your wishes and opinions,
should address myself thus to the Court when he was called up for
judgment :—

"My Lords, I hope that, in mitigation of my client's punishment, you will consider that he published it with perfect innocence
of intention, believing, on the highest authorities, that everything
contained in it was agreeable to the laws and constitution of his
country ; and that your Lordships will further recollect that the
jury, at the trial, gave no contrary opinion, finding only *the fact of*
publication."

Gentlemen, if the patience and forbearance of the Judges permitted me to get to the conclusion of such an absurd speech, I
should hear this sort of language from the Court in answer to it :
" We are surprised, Mr Erskine, at everything we have heard from
you.   You ought to know your profession better, after seven years'
practice of it, than to hold such a language to the Court : *you are*
estopped by the verdict of guilty from saying he did not publish
with a seditious intention ; and we cannot listen to the declarations
of jurors in contradiction to their recorded judgment."

Such would be the reception of that defence ; and thus you are
asked to deliver over the Dean of St Asaph into the hands of the
Judges, humane and liberal indeed, but who could not betray *their*
oaths, because you had set them the example by betraying *yours,*
and who would therefore be bound to believe him criminal, because
you had said so on the record, though in violation of your opinions
—opinions which, as ministers of the law, they could not act upon
—to the existence of which they could not even advert.

The conduct of my friend Mr Bearcroft, upon this occasion,
which was marked with wisdom and discretion, is a farther confirmation of the truth of all these observations : for, if your duty
had been confined to the simple question of publication, his address
to you would have been nothing more than that he would call his
witness to prove *the fact that the Dean published this paper,* instead of enlarging to you, as he has done with great ability, on the
libellous nature of the publication.   There is, therefore, a gross
inconsistency in his address to you, not from want of his usual
precision, but because he is hampered by his good sense in stating
an absurd argument, which happens to be necessary for his
purpose ; for he sets out with saying, that if you shall be of
opinion it has no tendency to excite sedition, you must find him
not guilty; and ends with telling you, that whether it *has* or *has not*
such tendency, is a question of *law for the Court,* and foreign to the
present consideration.   It requires, therefore, no other faculty than
that of keeping awake, to see through the fallacy of such doctrines;

and I shall therefore proceed to lay before you the observations I have made upon this dialogue, which you are desired to censure as a libel.

I have already observed, and it is indeed on all hands admitted, that if it be libellous at all, it is a libel on the public government, and not the slander of any private man.

Now, to constitute a libel upon the government, one of two things appears to me to be absolutely necessary. The publication must either arraign and misrepresent the general principles on which the constitution is founded, with a design to render the people turbulent and discontented under it: or, admitting the good principles of the government in the abstract, must accuse the existing administration with a departure from them, in such a manner, too, as to convince a jury of an evil design in the writer.

Let us try this little pamphlet by these touchstones, and let the defendant stand or fall by the test.

The beginning of this pamphlet, and indeed the evident and universal scope of it, is to render our happy constitution, and the principles on which it is founded, well understood by all that part of the community which are out of the pale of that knowledge by liberal studies and scientific reflections; a purpose truly public-spirited, and which could not be better effected than by having recourse to familiar comparisons drawn from common life, more suited to the frame of unlettered minds than abstract observations.

It was this consideration that led Sir William Jones,* a gentleman of great learning and excellent principles, to compose this dialogue, and who immediately after avowing himself to be the author, was appointed by the King to be one of the supreme judges of our Asiatic empire: where he would hardly have been selected to preside if his work had been thought seditious. Of this I am sure, that his intentions were directly the contrary. He thought and felt, as all men of sense must feel and think, that there was no mode so likely to inculcate obedience to government in an Englishman, as to make him acquainted with its principles; since the English constitution must always be cherished and revered exactly in the proportion that it is understood.

He therefore divested his mind of all those classical refinements which so remarkably characterise it, and composed this simple and natural dialogue between a gentleman and a farmer: in which the gentleman, meaning to illustrate the great principles of public government by comparing them with the lesser combinations of society, asks the farmer what is the object of the little club in the village of which he is a member; and if he is a member of it on compulsion, or by his free consent?—if the president is self-

* Sir William Jones is now dead, but his name will live for ever in the grateful memory of his country.

appointed, or rules by election?—if he would submit to his taking the money from the box without the vote of the members? with many other questions of a similar tendency; and being answered in the negative, he very luminously brings forward the analogy by making the gentleman say to him, "Did it never occur to you that every state is but a great club?" or in other words, that the greater as well as the lesser societies of mankind are held together by social compacts, and that the government of which you are a subject is not the rod of oppression in the hands of the strongest, but is of your own creation, a voluntary emanation from yourself, and directed to your own advantage.

Mr Bearcroft, sensible that this is the just and natural construction of that part of the dialogue, was very desirous to make you believe that the other part of it, touching the reform in the representation of the people in Parliament, had no reference to that context; but that it was to be connected with all that follows about bearing arms. I must therefore beg your attention to that part of the publication, which will speak plainly for itself.

The gentleman says to the farmer, on his telling him he had no vote, "Do you know that six men in seven have, like you, no voice in the election of those who make the laws which bind your property and life?" And then asks him to sign a petition which has for its object to render elections co-extensive with the trusts which they repose. And is there a man upon the jury who does not feel that all the other advantages of our constitution are lost to us until this salutary object is attained; or who is not ready to applaud every man who seeks to attain it by means that are constitutional?

But, according to my friend, the means proposed were not constitutional, but rebellious. I will give you his own words, as I took them down: "The gentleman was saying, very intelligibly, Sir, I desire you to rebel—to clothe yourself in armour, for you are cheated of your inheritance. How are you to rectify this? How are you to right yourselves? Learn the Prussian exercise."

But, how does my friend collect these expressions from the words of the passages, which are shortly these: "And the petition which I desired you to sign has only for its object the restoration of your right to choose your law-makers." I confess I am at a loss to conceive how the Prussian exercise finds its way into this sentence. It is a most martial way of describing pen and ink. Cannot a man sign a petition without tossing a firelock? I, who have been a soldier, can do either; but I do not sign my name with a gun. There is, besides, another difficulty in my friend's construction of the sentence. The object of the petition is the choosing of law-makers; but according to him, there is to be an end of all law-makers, and of all laws: for neither can exist under the Prussian exercise. He must be a whimsical scholar who tells a farmer to sign a petition for the improvement of government, his real purpose being to set it upon the die of a rebellion whether there should be any government at all.

But, let me ask you, gentlemen, whether such strained constructions are to be tolerated in a criminal prosecution, when the simple and natural construction of language falls.in directly with the fact? You cannot but know, that at the time when this dialogue was written, the table of the House of Commons groaned with petitions presented to the House from the most illustrious names and characters, representing the most important communities in the nation; not with the threat of the Prussian exercise, but with the prayer of humility and respect to the legislature, that some immediate step should be taken to avert that ruin which the defect in the representation of the people must sooner or later bring upon this falling empire. I do not choose to enter into political discussions here. But we all know that the calamities which have fallen upon this country have proceeded from that fatal source; and every wise man must be therefore sensible that a reform, if it can be attained without confusion, is a most desirable object. But whether it be or be not desirable is an idle speculation; because, at all events, the subject has a right to petition for what he *thinks* beneficial. However visionary, therefore, you may think his petition, you cannot deny it to be constitutional and legal; and I may venture to assert, that this dialogue is the *first abstract speculative writing which has been attacked as a libel since the Revolution;* and from Mr Bearcroft's admission, that the proceeding is not prudent, I may venture to foretell that it will be the last.

If you pursue this part of the dialogue to the conclusion, the false and unjust construction put upon it becomes more palpable. " Give me your pen," said the farmer; "I never wrote my name, ill as it may be written, with greater eagerness." Upon which the gentleman says, " I applaud you, and trust that your example will be followed by millions." What example?—Arms?—Rebellion?—Disaffection? No! but that others might add their names to the petition which he had advised him to sign, until the voice of the whole nation reached Parliament on the subject. This is the plain and obvious construction; and it is not long since that those persons in Parliament with whom my friend associates, and with whom he acts, affected at least to hold the voice of the people of England to be the rule and guide of Parliament; and the gentleman in the dialogue, knowing that the universal voice of the community could not be wisely neglected by the legislature, only expressed his wish that the petitions should not be partial, but universal.

With the expression of this wish everything in the dialogue upon the subject of representation finally closes; and if you will only honour me with your attentions for a few moments longer, I will

show you that the rest of the pamphlet is the most abstract speculation on government to be found in print; and that I was well
warranted when I told you, some time ago, that all its doctrines
were to be found in the brightest pages of English learning, and
in the most sacred volumes of English laws.

The subject of the petition being finished, the gentleman says,
" Another word before we part. What ought to be the consequence if THE KING ALONE were to insist on making laws, or on
altering them at his will and pleasure?"   To which the farmer
answers, " He too must be expelled."   " Oh, but think of his
standing army," says the gentleman, "and of the militia, which
now are his in substance though ours in form."   Farmer, "If he
were to employ that force against the nation, they would and
ought to resist him, or the state would cease to be a state."   And
now you will see that I am not countenancing rebellion; for if
this were pointed to excite resistance to the King's authority, and
to lead the people to believe that His Majesty was, in the present
course of his government, breaking through the laws, and therefore, on the principles of the constitution, was subject to expulsion,
I admit that my client ought to be expelled from this and every
other community.   But is this proved?   No!   It is not even
asserted.   I say this in the hearing of a Judge deeply learned in
the laws, and who is bound to tell you that there is nothing in the
indictment which even charges such an application of the general
doctrine.   The gentleman who drew it is also very learned in his
profession; and if he had intended such a charge, he would have
followed the rules delivered by the twelve judges in the House of
Lords, in the case of the King against Horne,[*] and would have
set out with saying that, at the time of publishing the libel in
question, there were petitions from all parts of England, desiring
a reform in the representation of the people in Parliament; and
that the defendant, knowing this, and intending to stir up rebellion,
and to make the people believe that His Majesty was ruling contrary to law, and ought to be expelled, caused to be published the
dialogue.   This would have been the introduction to such a charge;
and then when he came to the words, " He too must be expelled,"
he would have said, by way of innuendo, *meaning thereby to insinuate that the King was governing contrary to law, and ought to
be expelled;* which innuendo, though void in itself, without antecedent matter by way of introduction, would, when coupled with
the introductory averment on the record, have made the charge
complete.   I should have then known what I had to defend my
client against, and should have been prepared with witnesses to
show you the absurdity of supposing that the Dean ever imagined,
or meant to insinuate, that the present King was governing contrary to law.   But the penner of the indictment, well knowing

* See Mr H. Cowper's Reports.

that you never could have found such an application, and that, if it had been averred as the true meaning of the dialogue, the indictment must have fallen to the ground for want of such finding, prudently omitted the innuendo: yet you are desired by Mr Bearcroft to take that to be the true construction which the prosecutor durst not venture to submit to you by an averment in the indictment, and which, not being averred, is not at all before you.

But if you attend to what follows, you will observe that the writing is *purely speculative*, comprehending *all* the modes by which a government may be dissolved; for it is followed with the speculative case of injury to a government from bad ministers, and its constitutional remedy. Says the gentleman, "What if the great accountants and great lawyers of the nation were to abuse their trust, and cruelly injure, instead of faithfully serving, the public, what in such case are you to do?" Farmer, "We must request the King to remove them, and make trial of others, but none should implicitly be trusted." Request *the King* to remove them! Why, according to Mr Bearcroft, you had expelled *him* the moment before.

Then follows a third speculation of a government dissolved by an aristocracy, the King remaining faithful to his trust; for the gentleman proceeds thus: "But what if a few great lords or wealthy men were to keep the King himself in subjection, yet exert his force, lavish his treasure, and misuse his name, so as to domineer over the people and manage the Parliament?" Says the farmer, "We must fight for the King and for ourselves." What! for the fugitive King whom the Dean of St Asaph had before expelled from the crown of these kingdoms? Here, again, the ridicule of Mr Bearcroft's construction stares you in the face; but taking it as an abstract speculation of the ruin of a state by aristocracy, it is perfectly plain. When he first puts the possible case of regal tyranny, he states the remedy of expulsion; when of bad ministers to a good king, the remedy of petition to the throne; and when he supposes the throne to be overpowered by aristocratic dominion, he then says, "We must fight for the King and for ourselves." If there had been but one speculation, viz., of regal tyranny, there might have been plausibility at least in Mr Bearcroft's argument; but when so many different propositions are put, altogether repugnant to and inconsistent with each other, common sense tells every man that the writer is speculative, since no state of facts can suit them all.

Gentlemen, these observations, striking as they are, must lose much of their force, unless you carry along with you the writing from which they arise; and therefore I am persuaded that you will be permitted to-day to do what juries have been directed by courts to do on the most solemn occasions, that is, to take the supposed libel with you out of Court, and to judge for yourselves whether

it be possible for any conscientious or reasonable man to fasten
upon it any other interpretation than that which I have laid
before you.

If the dialogue is pursued a little further, it will be seen that
all the exhortations to arms are pointed to the protection of the
King's government, and the liberty of the people derived from it.
Says the gentleman, " You talk of fighting as if you were speaking of some rustic engagement ; but your quarter-staff would avail
you little against bayonets." Farmer, " We might easily provide
ourselves with better arms." " Not so easily," says the gentleman ;
"you ought to have a strong firelock." What to do ? Look at
the context,—for God's sake do not violate all the rules of grammar by refusing to look at the next antecedent !—take care to have
a firelock. For what purpose ? " To fight for the King and
yourself," in case the King, who is the fountain of legal government, should be kept in subjection by those great and wealthy
lords, who might abuse his authority and insult his title. This, I
assert, is not only the genuine and natural construction, but the
only legal one it can receive from the Court on this record ; since,
in order to charge all this to be not merely speculative and abstract,
but pointing to the King and his government, to the expulsion of
our gracious Sovereign, whom my reverend friend respects and
loves, and whose government he reverences as much as any man
who hears me, there should have been such an introduction as I
have already adverted to, viz., that there were such views and intentions in *others*, and that *he, knowing it, and intending to improve
and foment them, wrote so and so ;* and then on coming to the
words, *that the King must be expelled*, the sense and application
should have been pointed by an averment, *that he thereby meant
to insinuate to the people of England that the present King ought
in fact to be expelled ;* and not speculatively, that under such circumstances it would be lawful to expel a King.

Gentlemen, if I am well founded in thus asserting that neither
in law nor in fact is there any seditious application of those general
principles, there is nothing further left for consideration than to
see whether they be warranted in the abstract ; a discussion hardly
necessary under the government of his present Majesty, who holds
his crown under the Act of Settlement, made in consequence of the
compact between the King and people at the Revolution. What
part you or I, gentlemen, might have taken if we had lived in the
days of the Stuarts, and in the unhappiest of their days which
brought on the Revolution, is foreign to the present question ;
whether we should have been found among those glorious names
who from well-directed principle supported that memorable era,
or amongst those who from mistaken principle opposed it, cannot
affect our judgments to-day : whatever part we may conceive we
should or ought to have acted, we are bound by the acts of our

ancestors, who determined that there existed an original compact between King and people, who declared that King James had broken it, and who bestowed the crown upon another. The principle of that memorable Revolution is fully explained in the Bill of Rights, and forms the most unanswerable vindication of this little book. The misdeeds of King James are drawn up in the preamble to that famous statute ; and it is worth your attention that one of the principal charges in the catalogue of his offences is, that he caused several of those subjects (whose right to carry arms is to-day denied by this indictment) to be disarmed in defiance of the laws. Our ancestors having stated all the crimes for which they took the crown from the head of their fugitive sovereign, and having placed it on the brows of their deliverer, mark out the conditions on which he is to wear it. They were not to be betrayed by his great qualities, nor even by the gratitude they owed him, to give him an unconditional inheritance in the throne ; but enumerating all their ancient privileges, they tell their new sovereign in the body of the law that while he maintains these privileges, and no longer than he maintains them, *he is King*.

The same wise caution which marked the acts of the Revolution is visible in the Act of Settlement on the accession of the House of Hanover, by which the crown was again bestowed upon the strict condition of governing according to law, maintaining the Protestant religion, and not being married to a Papist.

Under this wholesome entail, *which again vindicates every sentence in this book*, may His Majesty and his posterity hold the crown of these kingdoms for ever !—a wish in which I know I am fervently seconded by my reverend friend, and with which I might call the whole country to vouch for the conformity of his conduct.

But my learned friend, knowing that I was invulnerable here, and afraid to encounter those principles on which his own personal liberty is founded, and on the assertion of which his well-earned character is at stake in the world, says to you with his usual artifice :—" Let us admit that there is no sedition in this dialogue, let us suppose it to *be* all constitutional and legal, *yet it may do mischief ; why tell the people so ?*"

Gentlemen, I am furnished with an answer to this objection, which I hope will satisfy my friend, and put an end to all disputes among us ; for upon this head I will give you the opinion of Mr Locke, the greatest Whig that ever lived in this country, and likewise of Lord Bolingbroke, the greatest Tory in it ; by which you see that Whigs and Tories, who could never accord in anything else, were perfectly agreed upon the propriety and virtue of enlightening the people on the subject of government.

Mr Locke on this subject speaks out much stronger than the

dialogue.   He says in his "Treatise on Government":—"Wherever law ends tyranny begins; and whoever in authority exceeds the power given him by the law, and makes use of the force he has under his command to compass that upon the subject which the law allows not, ceases in that to be a magistrate, and, acting without authority, may be opposed as any other man who by force invades the rights of another.   This is acknowledged in subordinate magistrates.   He that hath authority by a legal warrant to seize my person *in the street,* may be opposed as a thief and a robber if he endeavours to break *into my house* to execute it on me there, although I know he has such a warrant as would have empowered him to arrest me abroad.   And why this should not hold in the highest as well as in the most inferior magistrate I would gladly be informed.   For the exceeding the bounds of authority is no more a right in a great than in a petty officer, *in a king* than *in a constable;* but is so much the worse in him that he has more trust put in him, and more extended evil follows from the abuse of it."

But Mr Locke, knowing that the most excellent doctrines are often perverted by wicked men, who have their own private objects to lead them to that perversion, or by ignorant men who do not understand them, takes the very objection of my learned friend, Mr Bearcroft, and puts it as follows into the mouth of his adversary, in order that he may himself answer and expose it:—"But there are who say that it lays a foundation for rebellion."   Gentlemen, you will do me the honour to attend to this, for one would imagine Mr Bearcroft had Mr Locke in his hand when he was speaking.

"But there are who say that it lays a foundation for rebellion to tell the people that they are absolved from obedience when illegal attempts are made upon their liberties, and that they may oppose their magistrates when they invade their properties contrary to the trust put in them ; and that, therefore, the doctrine is not to be allowed as libellous, dangerous, and destructive of the peace of the world."   But that great man instantly answers the objection, which he had himself raised in order to destroy it, and truly says, " Such men might as well say that the people should not be told that honest men may oppose robbers or pirates, lest it should excite to disorder and bloodshed."

What reasoning can be more just?—for if we were to argue from the possibility that human depravity and folly may turn to evil what is meant for good, all the comforts and blessings which God, the author of indulgent nature, has bestowed upon us, and without which we should neither enjoy, nor indeed deserve, our existence, would be abolished as pernicious, till we were reduced to the fellowship of beasts.

The Holy Gospels could not be promulgated ; for though they

are the foundation of all the moral obligations which unite men together in society, yet the study of them often conducts weak minds to false opinions, enthusiasm, and madness.

The use of pistols should be forbidden; for though they are necessary instruments of self-defence, yet men often turn them revengefully upon one another in private quarrels. Fire ought to be prohibited; for though, under due regulations, it is not only a luxury but a necessary of life, yet the dwellings of mankind and whole cities are often laid waste and destroyed by it. Medicines and drugs should not be sold promiscuously; for though, in the hands of skilful physicians, they are the kind restoratives of nature, yet they may come to be administered by quacks, and operate as poisons. There is nothing, in short, however excellent, which wickedness or folly may not pervert from its intended purpose. But if I tell a man that if he takes my medicine in the agony of disease it will expel it by the violence of its operation, will it induce him to destroy his constitution by taking it while he is in health? Just so when a writer speculates on all the ways by which human governments may be dissolved, and points out the remedies which the history of the world furnishes from the experience of former ages; is he, therefore, to be supposed to prognosticate instant dissolution in the existing government, and to stir up sedition and rebellion against it?

Having given you the sentiments of Mr Locke, published three years after the accession of King William, who caressed the author, and raised him to the highest trust in the state, let us look at the sentiments of a Tory on that subject, not less celebrated in the republic of letters, and on the theatre of the world: I speak of the great Lord Bolingbroke, who was in arms to restore King James to his forfeited throne, and who was anxious to rescue the Jacobites from what he thought a scandal on them, namely the imputation that, because from the union of so many human rights centred in the person of King James, they preferred and supported his hereditary title on the footing of our own ancient civil constitutions, they therefore believed in his claim to govern *jure divino*, independent of the law.

This doctrine of passive obedience, which the prosecutor of this libel must successfully maintain to be the law, and which certainly is the law, if this dialogue be a libel, was resented above half a century ago by this great writer even in a tract written while an exile in France on account of his treason against the House of Hanover. "The duty of the people," says his Lordship, "is now settled upon so clear a foundation, that no man can hesitate how far he is to obey, or doubt upon what occasions he is to resist. Conscience can no longer battle with the understanding; we know that we are to defend the Crown with our lives and fortunes, as long as the Crown protects us, and keeps strictly to the bounds within which the laws have confined it.   We know, likewise, that we are to do it no longer.'

Having finished three volumes of masterly and eloquent discussions on our government, he concludes with stating the duty imposed on every enlightened mind to instruct the people on the principles of our government, in the following animated passage :—
" The whole tendency of these discourses is to inculcate a rational idea of the nature of our free government into the minds of all my countrymen, and to prevent the fatal consequence of those slavish principles which are industriously propagated through the kingdom by wicked and designing men.   He who labours to blind the people, and to keep them from instruction on those momentous subjects, may be justly suspected of sedition and disaffection ; but he who makes it his business to open the understandings of mankind, by laying before them the true principles of their government, cuts up all faction by the roots ; for it cannot but interest the people in the preservation of their constitution when they know its excellence and its wisdom."

But, says Mr Bearcroft, again and again, " Are the multitude to be told all this ? "   I say as often on my part, YES.   I say, that nothing can preserve the government of this free and happy country, in which, under the blessing of God, we live,—that nothing can make it endure to all future ages but its excellence and its wisdom being known, not only to you and the higher ranks of men, who may be overborne by a contentious multitude, but also to the great body of the people, by disseminating among them the true principles on which it is established ; which show them that they are not the hewers of wood and the drawers of water to men who avail themselves of their labour and industry ; but that government is a *trust* proceeding from *themselves;* an emanation from their own strength; a benefit and a blessing, which has stood the test of ages,—that they are governed because they desire to be governed, and yield a voluntary obedience to the laws, because the laws protect them in the liberties they enjoy.

Upon these principles I assert, with men of all denominations and parties who have written on the subject of free governments, that this dialogue, so far from misrepresenting or endangering the constitution of England, disseminates obedience and affection to it as far as it reaches ; and that the comparison of the great political institutions with the little club in the village, is a decisive mark of the honest intention of its author.

Does a man rebel against the president of his club while he fulfils his trust ?   No! because he is of his own appointment, and acting for his comfort and benefit.   This safe and simple analogy, lying within the reach of every understanding, is therefore adopted by the scholar as the vehicle of instruction ; who, wishing the peasant to be sensible of the happy government of this country, and to be acquainted with the deep stake he has in its preservation, truly tells him that a nation is but a great club, governed by the same consent, and supported by the same voluntary compact; impressing upon his mind the great theory of public freedom by the most familiar allusions to the little but delightful intercourses of social life, by which men derive those benefits that come home the nearest to their bosoms.

Such is the wise and innocent scope of this dialogue, which, after it had been repeatedly published without censure, and without mischief, under the public eye of Government in the capital, is gravely supposed to have been circulated by my reverend friend many months afterwards, with a malignant purpose to overturn the monarchy by an armed rebellion.

Gentlemen, if the absurdity of such a conclusion, from the scope of the dialogue itself, were not self-evident, I might render it more glaring by adverting to the condition of the publisher. The affectionate son of a reverend prelate,* not more celebrated for his genius and learning than for his warm attachment to the constitution, and in the direct road to the highest honours and emoluments of that very church which, when the monarchy falls, must be buried in its ruins: nay, the publisher a dignitary of the same church himself at an early period of his life, and connected in friendship with those who have the dearest stakes in the preservation of the government, and who, if it continues, may raise him to all the ambitions of his profession. I cannot therefore forbear from wishing that somebody, in the happy moments of fancy, would be so obliging as to invent a reason, in compassion to our dulness, why my reverend friend should aim at the destruction of the present establishment; since you cannot but see, that the moment he succeeded, down comes his father's mitre, which leans upon the crown; away goes his own deanery, with all the rest of his livings; and neither you nor I have heard any evidence to enable us to guess what he is looking for in their room. In the face, nevertheless, of all these absurdities, and without a colour of evidence from his character or conduct in any part of his life, he is accused of sedition, and under the false pretence of public justice, dragged out of his own country, deprived of that trial by his neighbours, which is the right of the meanest man who hears me, and arraigned before you, who are strangers to those public virtues which would in themselves be an answer to this malevolent accusation. But when I mark your sensibility and justice in the anxious attention you are bestowing, when I reflect upon your characters, and observe from the pannel (though I am personally unknown to you) that you are men of rank in this county, I know how these circumstances of injustice will operate: I freely forgive the prosecutor for having fled from his original tribunal.

* Dr Shipley, then Bishop of St Asaph.

Gentlemen, I come now to a point very material for your consideration; on which even my learned friend and I, who are brought here for the express purpose of disagreeing in everything, can avow no difference of opinion; on which judges of old and of modern times, and lawyers of all interests and parties, have ever agreed; namely, that even if this innocent paper were admitted to be a libel, the publication would not be criminal, if you, the jury, saw reason to believe that it was not published by the Dean with a criminal intention. It is true, that if a paper containing seditious and libellous matter be published, the publisher is *primâ facie* guilty of sedition, the bad intention being a legal inference from the act of publishing: but it is equally true that he may rebut that inference, by showing that he published it innocently.

This was declared by Lord Mansfield, in the case of the King and Woodfall: where his Lordship said, that the fact of publication would in that instance have constituted guilt, if the paper was a libel; because the defendant had given no evidence to the jury to repel the legal inference of guilt, as arising from the publication; but he said at the same time, in the words that I shall read to you, that such legal inference was to be repelled by proof.

"There may be cases where the fact of the publication even of a libel may be justified or excused as lawful or innocent; for no fact which is not criminal, even though the paper be a libel, can amount to a publication of which a defendant ought to be found guilty."

I read these words from Burrow's Reports, published under the eye of the Court, and they open to me a decisive defence of the Dean of St Asaph upon the present occasion, and give you an evident jurisdiction to acquit him, even if the law upon libels were as it is laid down to you by Mr Bearcroft: for if I show you that the publication arose from motives that were innocent, and not seditious, he is not a criminal publisher, even if the dialogue were a libel, and, according even to Lord Mansfield, ought not to be found guilty.

The Dean of St Asaph was one of a great many respectable gentlemen, who, impressed with the dangers impending over the public credit of the nation, exhausted by a long war, and oppressed with grievous taxes, formed themselves into a committee, according to the example of other counties, to petition the Legislature to observe great caution in the expenditure of the public money. This dialogue, written by Sir William Jones, a near relation of the Dean by marriage, was either sent or found its way to him in the course of public circulation. He knew the character of the author; he had no reason to suspect him of sedition or disaffection; and believed it to be, what I at this hour believe, and have represented it to you, a plain, easy manner of showing the people the great interest they had in petitioning Parliament for reforms beneficial to the public. It was accordingly the opinion of the Flintshire committee, and not particularly of the Dean as an individual, that the dialogue should be translated into Welsh and published. It was accordingly delivered, at the desire of the committee, to a Mr -Jones, for the purpose of translation. This gentleman, who will be called as a witness, told the Dean a few days afterwards that there were persons, not indeed from their real sentiments, but from spleen and opposition, who represented it as likely to do mischief, from ignorance and misconception, if translated and circulated in Wales.

Now, what would have been the language of the defendant upon this communication if his purpose had been that which is charged upon him by the indictment? He would have said, " If what you tell me is well founded, *hasten the publication;* I am sure I shall never raise discontent here by the dissemination of such a pamphlet in English : therefore let it be instantly translated, if the ignorant inhabitants of the mountains are likely to collect from it that it is time to take up arms."

But Mr Jones will tell you that, on the contrary, the instant he suggested that such an idea, absurd and unfounded as he felt it, had presented itself, from any motives, to the mind of any man, the Dean, impressed as he was with its innocence and its safety, instantly acquiesced ; he recalled, even on his own authority, the intended publication by the committee ; and it never was translated into the Welsh tongue at all.

Here the Dean's connexion with this dialogue would have ended, if Mr Fitzmaurice, who never lost any occasion of defaming and misrepresenting him, had not thought fit, near three months after the idea of translation was abandoned, to reprobate and condemn the Dean's conduct at the public meetings of the county in the severest terms for his former intention of circulating the dialogue in Welsh, declaring that its doctrines were *seditious, treasonable, and repugnant to the principles of our government.*

It was upon this occasion that the Dean, naturally anxious to redeem his character from the unjust aspersions of having intended to undermine the constitution of his country, conscious that the epithets applied to the dialogue were false and unfounded, and thinking that the production of it would be the most decisive refutation of the groundless calumny cast upon him, directed a few English copies of it to be published in vindication of his former opinions and intentions, prefixing an advertisement to it, which plainly marks the spirit in which he published it. For he there complains of the injurious misrepresentations I have adverted to, and impressed with the sincerest conviction of the innocence, or rather the merit of the dialogue, makes his appeal to the friends of the Revolution in his justification.

[*Mr Erskine here read the advertisement to the jury, as prefixed* *to the dialogue.*]

Now, gentlemen, if you shall believe upon the evidence of the witness to these facts, and of the advertisement prefixed to the publication itself (which is artfully kept back, and forms no part of the indictment), that the Dean, upon the authority of Sir William Jones, who wrote it, of the other great writers on the principles of our government, and of the history of the country itself, really thought the dialogue innocent and meritorious, and that his single purpose in publishing the English copies, after the Welsh edition had been abandoned, was the vindication of his character from the imputation of sedition,—then he is not guilty upon this indictment, which charges the publication with a wicked intent to excite disaffection to the King, and rebellion against his government.

Actus non facit reum nisi mens sit rea is the great maxim of penal justice, and stands at the top of the criminal page in every volume of our humane and sensible laws. The hostile *mind* is the crime which it is your duty to decipher ; a duty which I am sure you will discharge with the charity of Christians ; refusing to adopt a harsh and cruel construction, when one that is fair and honourable is more reconcilable, not only with all probabilities, but with the evidence which you are sworn to make the foundation of your verdict. The prosecutor rests on the single fact of publication, without the advertisement, and without being able to cast an imputation upon the defendant's conduct, or even an observation to assign a motive to give verisimilitude to the charge.

Gentlemen, after the length of time which, very contrary to my inclination, I have detained you, I am sure you will be happy to hear that there is but one other point to which my duty obliges me to direct your attention. I should, perhaps, have said nothing more concerning the particular province of a jury upon this occasion than the little I touched upon it at the beginning, if my friend Mr Bearcroft had not compelled me to it by drawing a line around you, saying (I hope with the same effect that King Canute said to the sea), " Thus far shalt thou go." But since he has thought proper to coop you in, it is my business to let you out ; and to give the greater weight to what I am about to say to you, I have no objection that everything which I may utter shall be considered as proceeding from my own private opinions ; and that not only my professional character, but my more valuable reputa-·tion as a man, may stand or fall by the principles which I shall lay down for the regulation of your judgments.

This is certainly a bold thing to say, since what I am about to deliver may clash in some degree (*though certainly it will not throughout*) with the decision of a great and reverend Judge, who has administered the justice of this country for above half a century with singular advantage to the public, and distinguished reputation to himself; but whose extraordinary faculties and general integrity, which I should be lost to all sensibility and justice if I did not acknowledge with reverence and affection, could not protect him from severe animadversion when he appeared as the supporter of those doctrines which I am about to controvert. I shall certainly never join in the calumny that followed them, because I believe he acted upon that, as upon all other occasions, with the strictest integrity; an admission which it is my duty to make, which I render with great satisfaction, and which proves nothing more than that the greatest of men are fallible in their judgments, and warns us to judge from the essences of things, and not from the authority of names, however imposing.

Gentlemen, the opinion I allude to is, that *libel or not libel* is a question of *law* for the Judge, *your* jurisdiction being confined to the *fact of publication*. And if this were all that was meant by the position (though I could never admit it to be consonant with reason or law), it would not affect me in the present instance, since all that it would amount to would be that the Judge, and not you, would deliver the only opinion which can be delivered from that quarter upon this subject. But what I am afraid of upon this occasion is, that *neither of you are to give it;* for so my friend has expressly put it. "My Lord," says he, "will probably not give you his opinion whether it be a libel or not, because, as he will tell you, it is a question open upon the record, and that if Mr Erskine thinks the publication innocent, he may move to arrest the judgment." Now this is the most artful and the most mortal stab that can be given to justice, and to my innocent client. All I wish for is, that the judgment of the Court should be a guide to yours in determining whether this pamphlet be or be not a libel; because, knowing the scope of the learned Judge's understanding and professional ability, I have a moral certainty that his opinion would be favourable. If therefore libel or no libel be a question of law, as is asserted by Mr Bearcroft, I call for his Lordship's judgment upon that question, according to the regular course of all trials where the law and the fact are blended; in all which cases the notorious office of the Judge is to instruct the consciences of the jury to draw a correct legal conclusion from the facts in evidence before them. A jury are no more bound to return a special verdict in cases of libel than upon other trials, criminal and civil, where law is mixed with fact: they are to find generally upon both, receiving, as they constantly do in every court at Westminster, the opinion of the Judge both on the evidence and the law.

Say the contrary who will, I assert this to be the genuine unrepealed constitution of England; and therefore, if the learned Judge shall tell you that this pamphlet is in the abstract a libel, though I shall not agree that you are therefore *bound* to find the defendant guilty unless you think so likewise, yet I admit his opinion ought to have very great weight with you, and that you should not rashly, nor without great consideration, go against it. But, if *you* are only to find the *fact of publishing*, which is not even disputed, and the Judge is to tell you that the matter of libel being on the record, *he shall shut himself up in silence, and give no opinion at all as to the libellous and seditious tendency of the paper, and yet shall nevertheless expect you to affix the epithet of* GUILTY *to the publication of a thing the* GUILT *of which* YOU *are forbid, and* HE *refuses to examine*, miserable indeed is the condition into which we are fallen! Since if you, following such directions, bring in a verdict of guilty, without finding the publication to be a libel, or the publisher seditious, and I afterwards, in mitigation of punishment, shall apply to that humanity and mercy which is never deaf when it can be addressed consistently with the law, I shall be told in the language I before put in the mouths of the judges, " You are estopped, sir, by the verdict ; we cannot hear you say your client was mistaken but NOT GUILTY, for had *that* been the opinion of the jury, they had a jurisdiction to *acquit* him."

Such is the way in which the liberties of Englishmen are by this new doctrine to be shuffled about from jury to court, without having any solid foundation to rest on. I call this the effect of *new* doctrines, because I do not find them supported by that current of ancient precedents which constitutes English law. The history of seditious libels is perhaps one of the most interesting subjects which can agitate a court of justice; and my friend thought it prudent to touch but very slightly upon it.

We all know that by the immemorial usage of this country, no man in a criminal case could ever be compelled to plead a special plea; for although our ancestors settled an accurate boundary between law and fact, obliging the party defendant who could not deny the latter to show his justification to the Court; yet a man accused of a crime had always a right to throw himself by a general plea upon the justice of his peers; and on such general issue, his evidence to the jury might ever be as broad and general as if he had pleaded a special justification. The reason of this distinction is obvious. The rights of property depend upon various intricate rules, which require much learning to adjust, and much precision to give them stability; but CRIMES consist wholly in intention; and of that which passes in the breast of an Englishman as the motives of his actions, none but an English jury shall judge. It is therefore impossible, in most criminal cases, to separate law from fact; and, consequently, whether a writing be or be not a libel, *never can be an abstract legal question for judges*. And this position is proved by the immemorial practice of courts, the forms of which are founded upon legal reasoning; for that very libel, over which it seems you are not to entertain any jurisdiction, is always read, and often delivered to you out of court for your consideration.

The administration of criminal justice in the hands of the people is the basis of all freedom. While that remains, there can be no tyranny, because the people will not execute tyrannical laws on themselves. Whenever it is lost, liberty must fall along with it, because the sword of justice falls into the hands of men who, however independent, have no common interest with the mass of the people. Our whole history is therefore chequered with the struggles of our ancestors to maintain this important privilege, which in cases of libel has been too often a shameful and disgraceful subject of controversy.

The ancient government of this country not being founded, like the modern, upon public consent and opinion, but supported by ancient superstitions, and the lash of power, saw the seeds of its destruction in a free press. Printing, therefore, upon the revival of letters, when the lights of philosophy led to the detection of prescriptive usurpations, was considered as a matter of state, and subjected to the control of licensers appointed by the Crown; and although our ancestors had stipulated by Magna Charta that no freeman should be judged but by his peers, the courts of Star-Chamber and High Commission, consisting of privy counsellors erected during pleasure, opposed themselves to that freedom of conscience and civil opinion which *even then* were laying the foundations of the Revolution. Whoever wrote on the principles of government was pilloried in the Star-Chamber; and whoever exposed the errors of a false religion was persecuted in the Commission Court. But no power can supersede the privileges of men in society, when once the lights of learning and science have arisen amongst them. The prerogatives which former princes exercised with safety, and even with popularity, were not to be tolerated in the days of the First Charles; and our ancestors insisted that these arbitrary tribunals should be abolished. Why did they insist upon their abolition? Was it that the question of libel, which was their principal jurisdiction, should be determined only by the judges at Westminster? In the present times, even such a reform, though very defective, might be consistent with reason, because the judges are now honourable, independent, and sagacious men; but in those days, they were often wretches—libels upon all judicature; and instead of admiring the wisdom of our ancestors, if that had been their policy, I should have held them up as lunatics, to the scoff of posterity; since, in the times when these unconstitutional tribunals were supplanted, the courts of Westminster Hall were filled with men who were equally the tools of power with those in the Star-Chamber; and the whole policy of the change consisted in that principle which was then never disputed, viz., that the judges.

at Westminster, in criminal cases, were but a part of the Court, and could only administer justice through the medium of a jury.

When the people, by the aid of an upright Parliament, had thus succeeded in reviving the constitutional trial by the country, the next course taken by the Ministers of the Crown was to pollute what they could not destroy. Sheriffs devoted to power were appointed, and corrupt juries packed to sacrifice the rights of their fellow-citizens under the mask of a popular trial. This was practised by Charles II., and was made one of the charges against King James, for which he was expelled the kingdom.

When juries could not be found to their minds, judges were daring enough to browbeat the jurors, and to dictate to them what they called the law; and in Charles II.'s time, an attempt was made which, if it had proved successful, would have been decisive. In the year 1670, Penn and Mead, two Quakers, being indicted for *seditiously* preaching to a multitude *tumultuously* assembled in Gracechurch Street, were tried before the Recorder of London, who told the jury that they had nothing to do but to find whether the defendants had preached or not; for that, whether the matter or the intention of their preaching were seditious, were questions of law, and not of fact, which they were to keep to at their peril. The jury, after some debate, found Penn guilty of speaking to people in Gracechurch Street; and on the Recorder's telling them that they meant, no doubt, that he was speaking to a *tumult* of people there, he was informed by the foreman that they allowed of no such words in their finding, but adhered to their former verdict. The Recorder refused to receive it, and desired them to withdraw, on which they again retired, and brought in a general verdict of acquittal, which the Court, considering as a contempt, set a fine of forty marks upon each of them, and condemned them to lie in prison till it was paid. Edward Bushel, one of the jurors (to whom we are almost as much indebted as to Mr Hampden, who brought the case of ship-money before the Court of Exchequer), refused to pay his fine, and being imprisoned in consequence of the refusal, sued out his writ of Habeas Corpus, which, with the cause of his commitment, viz., *his refusing to find according to the direction of the Court in matter of law*, was returned by the Sheriffs of London to the Court of Common Pleas, when Lord Chief-Justice Vaughan, to his immortal honour, delivered his opinion as follows:—" We must take off this veil and colour of words which make a show of being something, but are in fact nothing. If the meaning of these words, *finding against the direction of the Court in matter of law*, be that if the Judge, having heard the evidence given in court (for he knows no other), shall tell the jury upon this evidence that the law is for the Crown, and they, under the pain of fine and imprisonment, are to find accordingly, every man sees that the jury is but a troublesome delay, great charge, and of no use in determining right and wrong; and therefore the trials by them may be better abolished than continued, which were a strange and new-found conclusion, after a trial so celebrated for many hundreds of years in this country."

He then applied this sound doctrine with double force to criminal cases, and discharged the upright juror from his illegal commitment.

This determination of the right of juries to find a general verdict was never afterwards questioned by succeeding judges; not even in the great case of the seven bishops, on which the dispensing power and the personal fate of King James himself in a great measure depended.

These conscientious prelates were, you know, imprisoned in the Tower, and prosecuted by information for having petitioned King James II. to be excused from reading in their churches the declaration of indulgence which he had published contrary to law. The trial was had at the bar of the Court of King's Bench, when the Attorney-General of that day, rather more peremptorily than my learned friend (who is much better qualified for that office, and whom I should be glad to see in it), told the jury *that they had nothing to do but with the bare fact of publication*, and said he should therefore make no answer to the arguments of the bishops' counsel, as to whether the petition was or was not a libel. But Chief-Justice Wright (no friend to the liberty of the subject, and with whom I should be as much ashamed to compare my Lord, as Mr Bearcroft to that Attorney-General) interrupted him, and said, " Yes, Mr Attorney, I will tell you what they offer, *which it will lie upon you to answer :* they would have you show the jury how this petition has disturbed the Government, or diminished the King's authority." So say I. I would have Mr Bearcroft show you, gentlemen, how this dialogue has disturbed the King's Government, excited disloyalty and disaffection to his person, and stirred up disorders within these kingdoms.

In the case of the bishops, Mr Justice Powell followed the Chief-Justice, saying to the jury, " I have given my opinion; *but the whole matter is before you, gentlemen, and you will judge of it.*" Nor was it withdrawn from their judgment; for although the majority of the Court were of opinion that it was a libel, and had so publicly declared themselves from the bench, yet, by the unanimous decision of all the judges, after the Court's own opinion had been pronounced by way of charge to the jury, the petition itself, which contained no innuendoes to be filled up as facts, was delivered nto their hands, to be carried out of court, for their deliberation. The jury accordingly withdrew from the bar, carrying the libel vith them, and (puzzled, I suppose, by the infamous opinion cf he judges) were most of the night in deliberation; all London urrounding the Court with anxious expectation for that verdict which was to decide whether Englishmen were to be freemen or slaves. Gentlemen, the decision was in favour of freedom, for the reverend fathers were acquitted; and though acquitted in direct opposition to the judgment of the Court, yet it never occurred even to those arbitrary judges, who presided in it, to cast upon them a censure or a frown. This memorable and never to be forgotten trial is a striking monument of the importance of these rights, which no juror should ever surrender; for if the legality of the petition had been referred as a question of law to the Court of King's Bench, the bishops would have been sent back to the Tower, the dispensing power would have acquired new strength, and perhaps the glorious era of the Revolution, and our present happy constitution, might have been lost.

Gentlemen, I ought not to leave the subject of these doctrines which, in the libels of a few years past, were imputed to the noble Earl of whom I formerly spoke, without acknowledging that Lord Mansfield was neither the original composer of them, nor the copier of them from these impure sources. It is my duty to say that Lord Chief-Justice Lee, in the case of the King against Owen, had recently laid down the same opinions before him. But then both of these great judges always conducted themselves on trials of this sort, as the learned Judge will no doubt conduct himself to-day; they considered the jury as open to all the arguments of the defendant's counsel. And in the very case of Owen, who was acquitted against the direction of the Court, the present Lord Camden addressed the jury, not as I am addressing you, but with all the eloquence for which he is so justly celebrated. The *practice*, therefore, of these great judges is a sufficient answer to their *opinions ;* for if it be the law of England that the jury may not decide on the question of libel, the same law ought to extend its authority to prevent their being told by counsel that they may.

There is indeed no end of the absurdities which such a doctrine involves; for suppose that this prosecutor, instead of indicting my reverend friend for publishing this dialogue, had indicted him for publishing the Bible, beginning at the first book of Genesis, and ending at the end of the Revelations, without the addition or subtraction of a letter, and without an *innuendo* to point out a libellous application, only putting in at the beginning of the indictment that he published it with a blasphemous intention. On the trial for such a publication, Mr Bearcroft would gravely say, " Gentlemen of the Jury, you must certainly find by your verdict that the defendant is guilty of this indictment, *i.e.*, guilty of publishing the Bible with the intentions charged by it. To be sure, everybody will laugh when he hears it, and the conviction can do the defendant no possible harm; for the Court of King's Bench will determine that it is not a libel, and he will be discharged from the consequences of the verdict." Gentlemen, I defy the most ingenious man living to make a distinction between that case and the present; and in this way you are desired to sport with your oaths by pronouncing my reverend friend to be a criminal, without either determining yourselves, or having a determination, or even an insinuation from the Judge that any crime has been committed; following strictly that famous and respectable precedent of Rhadamanthus, judge of hell, who punishes first, and afterwards institutes an inquiry into the guilt.

But it seems your verdict would be no punishment, if judgment on it was afterwards arrested. I am sure, if I had thought the Dean so lost to sensibility as to feel it no punishment, he must have found another counsel to defend him. But I know his nature better. Conscious as he is of his own purity, he would leave the court hanging down his head in sorrow, if he were held out by your verdict a seditious subject, and a disturber of the peace of his country. The arrest of judgment which would follow in the term upon his appearance in court as a convicted criminal, would be a cruel insult upon his innocence, rather than a triumph over the unjust prosecutors of his pretended guilt.

Let me, therefore, conclude with reminding you, gentlemen, that if you find the defendant guilty, not believing the thing published to be a libel, or the intention of the publisher seditious, your verdict and your opininions will be at variance; and it will then be between God and your own consciences to reconcile the contradiction.

SUBJECT of the Trial of the Dean of St Asaph.

To enable the reader to understand thoroughly the further proceedings in this memorable cause, and more particularly to assist him in appreciating the vast value and importance of the Libel Bill, which it gave rise to, it becomes necessary to insert at full length Mr Justice Buller's Charge to the Jury, and what passed in court before the verdict was recorded; by which it will appear that the rights of juries, as often established by Act of Parliament, had been completely abandoned by all the profession, except by Mr Erskine. The doctrine insisted and acted upon was, that the jury were confined to the mere act of publishing, and were bound by their oaths to convict of a libel, whatever might be the matter written or published;—a course of proceeding which placed the British press entirely in the hands of fixed magistrates, appointed by the Crown. This doctrine, we say, was so completely fastened upon the public, that the reader will find in the fifth volume of Sir James Burrow's Reports upon the trial of Woodfall for publishing the Letters of Junius, alluded to by Mr Justice Buller in his Charge to the Jury at Shrewsbury, that an objection to that rule of law, as delivered by Lord Mansfield, was considered to be perfectly frivolous. The next time after that decision when it appears to have been again insisted upon, in the trial of the Rev. Mr Bate Dudley, for a libel in the *Morning Herald* on the Duke of Richmond, Lord Mansfield told Mr Erskine the moment he touched upon it in his speech to the jury, that " it was strange he should be contesting points now, which the greatest lawyers in the court had submitted to for years before he was born." The jury, however, acquitted Mr Dudley notwithstanding, and Mr Erskine continued to oppose the false doctrine, which was at last so completely exposed and disgraced by the following speeches in this cause, that Mr Fox thought the time at last ripe for the introduction of the Libel Bill, which he moved soon after in the House of Commons, and was seconded by Mr Erskine. The merits of this most excellent statute, which redeemed, and we trust established for ever, the liberty of the press, and the rights of British juries, will be more easily explained and better understood by perusing the following speeches, which produced at the time a perfect unanimity upon the subject. We have, as a supplement to this volume, printed the Libel Bill itself, and annexed a few observations upon it.

MR JUSTICE BULLER'S CHARGE.

Gentlemen of the Jury,—This is an indictment against William Shipley, for publishing the pamphlet which you have heard, and which the indictment states to be a libel.

The defendant has pleaded that he is not guilty ; and whether he is guilty *of the fact* or not, is the matter for you to decide. On the part of the prosecution to prove the publication, they have called Mr Edwards, who says that the words *gentleman* and *farmer* in the pamphlet, which he now produces, are the Dean of St Asaph's handwriting. He received the pamphlet, which he now produces, from the Dean, with the directions which he has also produced, and which have been read to you. *Those directions are for him to get it printed with an advertisement affixed to it, which is contained in that letter which has been read,* which appears to be dated the 24th of January 1783 ; and in consequence of that letter, which desires him to get the enclosed dialogue printed, he sent it to Marsh, a printer, according to the directions contained in the letter. John Marsh says this pamphlet was printed at their office, from what was sent by Mr Edwards. After some copies were struck off, he saw the Dean ; he told him Mr Jones had had several copies. The Dean seemed then quite surprised that any stir should be made about it. William Jones is then called, who says he bought the second pamphlet produced from Marsh in the month of February 1783. He says he is the prosecutor of the indictment; then he told you that he applied to the Treasury about the prosecution, and they did not take it up. This is the whole of the evidence for the prosecution. For the defendant, Edward Jones has been called, who says he was a member of the Flintshire committee,—that it was intended by them to print this dialogue in Welsh,—that the Dean said he had received the pamphlet so late from Sir William Jones, that he had not had time to read it. He says he told the Dean that he had collected the opinions of gentlemen, which were, that it might do harm. After that the Dean told him that he was obliged to him for his information, that he should be sorry to publish anything that tended to sedition ; and it was for this reason that it was not published in Welsh. This passed on the 7th of January 1783. Some time after, Mr Shipley said he would read it, to show it was not so seditious, but that he read it with a rope about his neck ; and when he had read it, he gave his opinion he did not think it quite so bad.

Mr ERSKINE. I ask your Lordship's pardon. I believe the witness said it was at the county meeting where the Dean said this.

Mr JONES. It was the same day, the 7th of January.

Mr JUSTICE BULLER. Yes, afterwards, at the county meeting, he said he would read it to show it was not so seditious, but that he read it with a rope about his neck ; when he had read it, he said he did not think it so bad. Then he called five gentlemen who spoke to his character. Sir Watkyn Williams Wynne says he has known the defendant eight or nine years. He does not think him a man likely to be guilty of that which is now imputed to him. Sir Roger Mostyn, who is Lord-Lieutenant of Flintshire, says he has known the defendant several years ; that he put him into the commission of the peace, and appointed him a deputy-lieutenant ; that in his opinion he don't think the defendant capable of stirring up sedition or rebellion. Major Williams says he has no reason to believe the defendant capable of being guilty of the crime imputed to him ; on the contrary, he thinks he would be the first that would quell sedition. Colonel Myddelton says he has known the Dean of St Asaph near twelve years ; that he has attended with the Dean at private meetings of the justices, and at quarter sessions, and in his judgment the King has not a better subject. Bennet Williams likewise says he has known the Dean many years ; that the defendant is a peaceable man, not capable of stirring up sedition, and he thinks he is as peaceable a subject as any the King has. Now, gentlemen, this is the whole of the evidence that has been given on the one side and the other. *As to the several witnesses who have been called to give Mr Shipley the character of a quiet and peaceable man, not disposed to stir up sedition, that cannot govern the present case, for the question for you to decide is,* WHETHER HE IS OR IS NOT GUILTY OF PUBLISHING THIS PAMPHLET ?

You have heard a great deal said which really does not belong to the case, and a part of it has embarrassed me a good deal in what manner to treat it. I cannot subscribe to a great deal I have heard from the defendant's counsel, but I do readily admit the truth and wisdom of that proposition which he stated from Mr Locke, that, "wherever the law ends, tyranny begins." The question then is, What is the law as applicable to this business? and, to narrow it still more, What is the law in this stage of the business? *You have been pressed very much by the counsel, and so have I also, to give an opinion upon the question, whether this pamphlet is or is not a libel. Gentlemen, it is my happiness that I find the law so well and so fully settled, that it is impossible for any man who means well to doubt about it;* and the counsel for the defendant was so conscious that the law was so settled, that he himself stated what he knew must be the answer which he would receive from me,— that is, that the matter appears upon the record; and as such, it is not for me, a single judge sitting here at *nisi prius,* to say whether it is or is not a libel. Those who adopt the contrary doctrine, forget a little to what lengths it would go; for if that were to be allowed, the obvious consequence would be what was stated by the counsel in reply; namely, that you deprive the subject of that which is one of his dearest birthrights:—you deprive him of his appeal; you deprive him of his writ of error: for if I was to give an opinion here, that it was not a libel, and you adopted that, the matter is closed for ever. The law acts equally and justly, as the pamphlet itself states,—it is equal between the prosecutor and the defendant; and whatever appears upon the record is not for our decision here, but may be the subject of future consideration in the court out of which the record comes; and afterwards, if either party thinks fit, they have a right to carry it to the dernier resort, and have the opinion of the House of Lords upon it; and therefore that has been the uniform and established answer, not only in criminal but civil cases: the law is the same in both, and there is not a gentleman round this table who does not know that is the constant and uniform answer which is given in such cases. *You have been addressed by the quotation of a great many cases upon libels. It seems to me that that question is so well settled, that gentlemen should not agitate it again; or at least, when they do agitate it, it should be done by stating fairly and fully what has passed on all sides, not by stating a passage or two from a particular case that may be twisted to the purpose that they want it to answer;* AND HOW THIS DOCTRINE EVER COMES TO BE NOW SERIOUSLY CONTENDED FOR, IS A MATTER OF SOME ASTONISHMENT TO ME; FOR I DO NOT KNOW ANY ONE QUESTION IN THE LAW WHICH IS MORE THOROUGHLY ESTABLISHED THAN THAT IS. I know it is not the language of a particular set or party of men, because the very last case that has ever arisen upon a libel was conducted by a very respectable and a very honourable man, who is as warm a partisan (and upon the same side of the question) as the counsel for the defendant, and I believe of what is called the same party. But he stated the case in a few words, which I certainly adopted afterwards, and which I believe no man ever doubted about the propriety of. That case arose not three weeks ago at Guildhall, upon a question on a libel; and in stating the plaintiff's case, he told the jury that there could be but three questions.

The first is, Whether the defendant is guilty of publishing the libel?

The second, Whether the innuendoes or the averments made on the record are true?

The third, which is a question of law, Whether it is a libel or not? Therefore, said he,* the two first are the only questions you have to consider: and this, added he very rightly, is clear and undoubted law; it was adopted by me as clear and undoubted law, and it has been so held for considerably more than a century past. It is indeed admitted by the counsel, that upon great consideration it has been so held, in one of the cases he mentioned, by a noble lord who has presided a great many years, with very distinguished honour, in the first court of criminal justice in this country; and it is worthy of observation how that case came on. For twenty-eight years past, during which time we have had a vast number of prosecutions in different shapes for libels, the uniform and invariable conduct of that noble judge has been to state the questions as I have just stated them to you; and though the cases have been defended by counsel not likely to yield much, yet that point was never found fault with by them; and often as it has been enforced by the Court, they never have attempted yet by any application to set it aside. At last it came on in this way—the noble judge himself brought it on by stating to the Court what his directions had always been, with a desire to know whether, in their opinions, the direction was right or wrong? The Court was unanimously of opinion that it was right, and that the law bore no question or dispute. It is admitted by the counsel, likewise, that in the time that Lord Chief-Justice Lee presided in the Court of King's Bench, the same doctrine was laid down as clear and established; a sounder lawyer, or a more honest man, never sat on the bench than he was. But if we trace the question farther back, it will be found that about the year 1731 (which I suppose has not escaped the diligence of the counsel) another Chief-Justice held the same doctrine, and in terms which are more observable than those in most of the other cases, because they show pretty clearly when and how it was that this idea was first broached. That was an information against one Franklin, I think, for publishing a libel called the *Craftsman.* The then Chief-Justice stated the three questions to the jury in the same way I mentioned. He said, " The first is as to the fact of publication. Secondly, Whether the averments in the information are true or not? And thirdly, Whether it is a libel?" He says, " There are but two questions for your considera-

* Mr John Lee, then Attorney-General.

tion; the third is merely a question of law, with which you the jury having nothing to do, as has now of late been thought by some people who ought to know better; but," says he, " we must always take care to distinguish between matters of law and matters of fact, and they are not to be confounded." With such a train of authorities, it is rather extraordinary to hear that matter *now* broached as a question which admits of doubt. And if they go farther back, they will find it still clearer; for about the time of the Revolution authorities will be found which go directly to the point. In one of them, which arose within a year or two from the time of the case of the seven bishops, which the counsel alluded to, a defendant in an information for a libel, which was tried at bar, said to the Court, " As the information states this to be a scandalous and seditious libel, I desire it may be left to the jury to say whether it is a scandalous and seditious libel or not." The answer then given by the Court was, " That is matter of law; the jury are to decide upon the fact; and if they find you guilty of the fact, the Court will afterwards consider whether it is or not a libel." If one goes still farther back, we find it settled as a principle which admits of no dispute, and laid down so early as the reign of Queen Elizabeth, as a maxim, that " *ad quæstionem facti respondent juratores, ad quæstionem juris respondent judices.*" And in the case that the counsel has thought fit to allude to under the name of Bushell's case, the same maxim is recognised by the Court negatively,—viz., " *ad quæstionem facti non respondent judices, ad quæstionem legis non respondent juratores;*" for, said the Court unanimously, if it be asked of the jury what the law is, they cannot say; if it be asked of the Court what the fact is, they cannot say. Now, so it stands as to legal history upon the business. Suppose there were no authority at all, can anything be a stronger proof of the impropriety of what is contended for by the counsel for the defendant than what they have had recourse to? You have been addressed not as is very usual to address a jury, which you must know yourselves, if you have often served upon them;—you have been addressed upon a question of law, on which they have quoted cases for a century back. Now, are you possessed of those cases in your own minds? Are you apprised of the distinctions on which those determinations are founded? Is it not a little extraordinary to require of a jury that they should carry all the legal determinations in their minds? If one looks a little farther into the constitution, it seems to me that, without recourse to authorities, it cannot admit of a doubt what is the mode of administering justice in this country. The judges are appointed to decide the law, the juries to decide the fact. How? Both under the solemn obligation of an oath : the judges are sworn to administer the law faithfully and truly; the jury are not so sworn, but to give a true verdict according to the evidence. Did ever any man hear of it, or was it ever yet attempted to give evidence of what the law was? If it were done in one instance, it must hold in all. Suppose a jury should say that which is stated upon a record is high treason or murder; if the facts charged upon the record are not so, it is the duty of the Court to look into the record, and they are bound by their oaths to discharge the defendant: the consequence, if it were not so, would be, that a man would be liable to be hanged who had offended against no law at all. It is for the Court to say whether it is any offence or not, after the fact is found by the jury. It would undoubtedly hold in civil cases as well as criminal, and as the counsel for the prosecution has said in reply, by the same reason in the case of an ejectment, you might give a verdict against law. But was it ever supposed that a jury was competent to say what is the operation of a fine, or a recovery, or a warranty, which are mere questions of law? Then the counsel says it is a very extraordinary thing if you have nothing else to decide but the fact of the publication; because then the jury are to do nothing but to decide that which was never disputed. Now, there is a great deal of art in that argument, and it was very ingeniously put by the counsel; but all that arises from the want of distinguishing how the matter comes here, and how it stands now: it is not true that the defendant by the issue admits that he ever published it. No, upon the record he denies it; but when he comes here, he thinks fit to admit it: but that does not alter the mode of trial. Then it is asserted, that if you go upon the publication only, the defendant would be found guilty, though he is innocent. But that is by no means the case; and it is only necessary to see how many guards the law has made, to show how fallacious the argument is. If the fact were, that the defendant never denied the publication, but meant to admit it, and insist that it was not a libel, he had another way in which he should have done it, a way universally known to the profession; he ought to have demurred to the indictment, by which in substance he would have said—I admit the fact of publishing it, but deny that it is any offence. But he is not precluded even now from saying it is not a libel; for if the fact be found by you, that he did publish the pamphlet, and upon future consideration the Court of King's Bench shall be of opinion that it is not a libel, he must then be acquitted.* As to his coming here, it is his own choice.

But, say the counsel further, it is clear in point of law, that in a criminal case the defendant cannot plead specially, therefore he might give anything in evidence that would be a justification if he could plead specially. I admit it; but what does that amount to? You must plead matter of fact; you cannot plead matter of law—the plea is bad if you do. Then admitting that he could give that in evidence upon not guilty, which would in point of law, if pleaded,

* It must be obvious to everybody, that upon this doctrine the press was in the hands of judges appointed by the Crown.

amount to an excuse or a defence, the question still is, What are the facts on which the defence is founded? That brings the case to the question of publication, for the innuendoes are no more than this: the indictment says, that by the letter G. is meant gentleman, and by the letter F. is meant farmer. Now, the title of this pamphlet is, "The Principles of Government, in a Dialogue between a *Gentleman* and a *Farmer.*" The first question is, Whether the *G.* means *Gentleman*, and the *F. Farmer?* The next question is not upon initials or letters that may be doubtful, but whether *the King*, written at length, means *the King of Great Britain*, and whether *the Parliament* means *the Parliament of Great Britain?* These are points I don't know how to state a question upon; and if you are satisfied as to the innuendoes, the only remaining question of fact is as to the publication. Whether Mr Edward Jones's evidence will or will not operate in mitigation of punishment, is not a question for me to give an opinion upon, because it is not for me to inflict the punishment, *if the defendant is found guilty.* But upon his evidence, it stands thus:—The Dean had thoughts of printing the pamphlet in Welsh; but upon what was said to him by Mr Jones, and other gentlemen, his friends, he declined it, but he afterwards published it in English; for this conversation is sworn by Jones to be on the 7th of January; and not till the 24th of January does he send this letter to Edwards with the pamphlet, desiring that it might be published; therefore there is no contradiction as to the publication; and if you are satisfied of this in point of fact, it is my duty to tell you, in point of law, you are bound to find the defendant guilty. I wish to be as explicit as I can in the directions I give, because, if I err in any respect, it is open to the defendant to have it corrected. As far as it is necessary to give any opinion in point of law upon the subject of the trial, I readily do it; beyond that, I don't mean to say a word, because it is not necessary nor proper here. In a future stage of the business, if the defendant is found guilty, he will have a right to demand my opinion; and if ever that happens, it is my duty to give it, and then I will; but till that happens, I do not think it proper, or by any means incumbent upon one who sits where I do, to go out of the case to give an opinion upon a subject which the present stage of the case does not require; therefore I can only say that, if you are satisfied that the defendant did publish this pamphlet, and are satisfied as to the truth of the innuendoes, in point of law you ought to find him guilty; if you think they are not true, you will of course acquit him.

The jury withdrew to consider of their verdict, and in about half an hour returned again into court.

ASSOCIATE. Gentlemen, do you find the defendant guilty or not guilty?

FOREMAN. Guilty of publishing only.

Mr ERSKINE. You find him guilty of publishing only?

A JUROR. Guilty only of publishing.

Mr JUSTICE BULLER. I believe that is a verdict not quite correct. You must explain that one way or the other as to the meaning of the innuendoes. The indictment has stated that G. means Gentleman, F. Farmer; the King the King of Great Britain, and the Parliament the Parliament of Great Britain.

ONE OF THE JURY. We have no doubt of that.

Mr JUSTICE BULLER. If you find him guilty of publishing, you must not say the word *only*.

Mr ERSKINE. By that, they mean to find there was no sedition.

A JUROR. We only find him guilty of publishing. We do not find anything else.

Mr ERSKINE. I beg your Lordship's pardon with great submission. I am sure I mean nothing that is irregular. I understand they say, We only find him guilty of publishing.

A JUROR. Certainly; that is all we do find.

Mr BRODERICK. They have not found that it is a libel of and concerning the King and his Government.

Mr JUSTICE BULLER. If you only attend to what is said, there is no question or doubt. If you are satisfied whether the letter G. means Gentleman, whether F. means Farmer, the King means King of Great Britain, the Parliament the Parliament of Great Britain—if they are all satisfied it is so, is there any other innuendo in the indictment?

Mr LEYCESTER. Yes; there is one more upon the word *votes*.

Mr ERSKINE. When the jury came into court, they gave, in the hearing of every man present, the very verdict that was given in the case of the King against Woodfall; they said, Guilty of publishing only. Gentlemen, I desire to know whether you mean the word *only* to stand in your verdict?

ONE OF THE JURY. Certainly.

ANOTHER JUROR. Certainly.

Mr JUSTICE BULLER. Gentlemen, if you add the word *only*, it will be negativing the innuendoes; it will be negativing that by the word King, it means King of Great Britain; by the word Parliament, Parliament of Great Britain; by the letter F., it means Farmer, and G. Gentleman; that, I understand, you do not mean.

A JUROR. No.

Mr ERSKINE. My Lord, I say that will have the effect of a general verdict of guilty. I desire the verdict may be recorded. I desire your Lordship sitting here as Judge to record the verdict as given by the jury. If the jury depart from the word *only*, they alter their verdict.

Mr JUSTICE BULLER. I will take the verdict as they mean to

give it; it shall not be altered. Gentlemen, if I understand you right, your verdict is this: You mean to say guilty of publishing this libel?

A JUROR. No; the pamphlet. We do not decide upon its being a libel.

Mr JUSTICE BULLER. You say he is guilty of publishing the pamphlet, and that the meaning of the innuendoes is as stated in the indictment.

A JUROR. Certainly.

Mr ERSKINE. Is the word *only* to stand part of your verdict?

A JUROR. Certainly.

Mr ERSKINE. Then I insist it shall be recorded.

Mr JUSTICE BULLER. Then the verdict must be misunderstood. Let me understand the jury.

Mr ERSKINE. The jury do understand their verdict.

Mr JUSTICE BULLER. Sir, I will not be interrupted.

Mr ERSKINE. I stand here as an advocate for a brother citizen, and I desire that the word *only* may be recorded.

Mr JUSTICE BULLER. Sit down, sir. Remember your duty, or I shall be obliged to proceed in another manner.

Mr ERSKINE. Your Lordship may proceed in what manner you think fit. I know my duty as well as your Lordship knows yours. I shall not alter my conduct.

Mr JUSTICE BULLER. Gentlemen, if you say guilty of publishing only, you negative the meaning of the particular words I have mentioned.

A JUROR. Then we beg to go out.

Mr JUSTICE BULLER. If you say guilty of publishing only, the consequence is this, that you negative the meaning of the different words I mentioned to you. That is the operation of the word *only*. They are endeavouring to make you give a verdict in words different from what you mean.

A JUROR. We should be very glad to be informed how it will operate.

Mr JUSTICE BULLER. If you say nothing more but find him guilty of publishing, and leave out the word *only*, the question of law is open upon the record, and they may apply to the Court of King's Bench, and move in arrest of judgment there. If they are not satisfied with the opinion of that Court, either party has a right to go to the House of Lords, if you find nothing more than the simple fact; but if you add the word *only*, you do not find all the facts; you do not find in fact that the letter G. means Gentleman, that F. means Farmer, the King the King of Great Britain, and Parliament the Parliament of Great Britain.

A JUROR. We admit that.

Mr JUSTICE BULLER. Then you must leave out the word *only*.

Mr ERSKINE. I beg pardon. I beg to ask your Lordship this

question : Whether, if the jury find him guilty of publishing, leaving out the word *only*, and if the judgment is not arrested by the Court of King's Bench, whether the sedition does not stand recorded ?

Mr JUSTICE BULLER. No, it does not, unless the pamphlet be a libel in point of law.

Mr ERSKINE. True ; but can I say that the defendant did not publish it seditiously, if judgment is not arrested, but entered in the record ?

Mr JUSTICE BULLER. I say it will not stand as proving the sedition. Gentlemen, I tell it you as law, and this is my particular satisfaction, as I told you when summing up the case, if in what I now say to you I am wrong in any instance, they have a right to move for a new trial. The law is this : if you find him guilty of publishing, without saying more, the question whether libel or not is open for the consideration of the Court.

A JUROR. That is what we mean.

Mr JUSTICE BULLER. If you say guilty of publishing only, it is an incomplete verdict, because of the word *only*.

A JUROR. We certainly mean to leave the matter of libel to the Court.

Mr ERSKINE. Do you find sedition ?

A JUROR. No ; not so. We do not give any verdict upon it.

Mr JUSTICE BULLER. I speak from adjudged cases (I will take the verdict when you understand it yourselves in the words you give it) : if you say, Guilty of publishing only, there must be another trial.

A JUROR. We did not say so ; only guilty of publishing.

Mr ERSKINE. Will your Lordship allow it to be recorded thus, Only guilty of publishing ?

Mr JUSTICE BULLER. It is misunderstood.

Mr ERSKINE. The jury say, Only guilty of publishing. Once more, I desire that that verdict may be recorded.

Mr JUSTICE BULLER. If you say, Only guilty of publishing, then t is contrary to the innuendoes ; if you think the word King means he King of Great Britain, the word Parliament the Parliament f Great Britain, the G. means Gentleman, and the F. Farmer, *ou may say this*, Guilty of publishing ; but whether a libel or not, he jury do not find.

A JUROR. Yes.

Mr ERSKINE. I asked this question of your Lordship in the earing of the jury, whether, upon the verdict you desire them to nd, the sedition which they have not found will not be inferred ↗ the Court if judgment is not arrested ?

Mr JUSTICE BULLER. Will you attend ? Do you give it in this ιy, Guilty of the publication ; but whether a libel or not, you do t find ?

A JUROR. We do not find it a libel, my Lord: we do not decide upon it.

Mr ERSKINE. They find it no libel.

Mr JUSTICE BULLER. You see what is attempted to be done ?

Mr ERSKINE. There is nothing wrong attempted upon my part. I ask this once again, in the hearing of the jury, and I desire an answer from your Lordship as Judge, whether or no, when I come to move in arrest of judgment, and the Court enter up judgment, and say it is a libel, whether I can afterwards say, in mitigation of punishment, the defendant was not guilty of publishing it with a seditious intent, when he is found guilty of publishing it in manner and form as stated; and whether the jury are not thus made to find him guilty of sedition, when in the same moment they say they did not mean to do so. Gentlemen, do you find him guilty of sedition?

A JUROR. We do not, neither one nor the other.

Mr JUSTICE BULLER. Take the verdict.

ASSOCIATE. You say, Guilty of publishing; but whether a libel or not, you do not find ?

A JUROR. That is not the verdict.

Mr JUSTICE BULLER. You say, Guilty of publishing; but whether a libel or not, you do not find,—is that your meaning ?

A JUROR. That is our meaning.

ONE OF THE COUNSEL. Do you leave the intention to the Court ?

A JUROR. Certainly.

Mr COWPER. The intention arises out of the record.

Mr JUSTICE] BULLER. And unless it is clear upon record, there can be no judgment upon it.

Mr BEARCROFT. You mean to leave the law where it is ?

A JUROR. Certainly.

Mr JUSTICE BULLER. The first verdict was as clear as could be; they only wanted it to be confounded.

On the 8th of November, the second day of the ensuing term, Mr Erskine moved the Court of King's Bench to set aside the verdict, for the misdirection of the Judge in the foregoing charge to the jury, and obtained a rule to show cause why there should not be a new trial. There was no shorthand writer in court except a gentleman employed by the editors of the *Morning Herald*, from which paper of the succeeding day the following speech of Mr Erskine was taken.

[Delivered in the Court of King's Bench, on Monday the 8th of November 1784, on his Motion for a new trial in Defence of the DEAN *of* ST ASAPH.]

MR ERSKINE began by stating to the Court the substance of the indictment against the Dean of St Asaph, which charged the publication with an intention to incite the people to subvert the Government by armed rebellion,—the mere evidence of the publication of the dialogue which the prosecutor had relied on to establish that malicious intention,—and the manner in which the defendant had, by evidence of his real motives for publishing it, as contained in the advertisement, rebutted the truth of the epithets charged by the indictment.

He then stated the substance of his speech to the jury at Shrewsbury, maintaining the legality of the dialogue, the right of the jury to consider that legality, the injustice of a verdict affixing the epithet of *guilty* to a publication without first considering whether the thing published contained any *guilt;* and, above all, the right which the jury unquestionably had (even upon the authority of those very cases urged against his client) to take the evidence into consideration, by which the defendant sought to exculpate himself from the seditious intention charged by the indictment.

He said that the substance of Mr Jones's evidence was, *that it had been the intention of the Flintshire committee to translate the dialogue into Welsh ;* that it was delivered to him to give to a Mr Lloyd for that purpose ; that *the Dean had just then received it from Sir William Jones,* and had not had time to read it before he delivered it to the witness. Some days after, Mr Jones wrote to the Dean, telling him that he had collected the opinions of some gentlemen that the translation of it into Welsh might do harm. The Dean's answer (WHO HAD NEVER THEN READ THE THING HIMSELF) was this, " I am very much obliged to you for what you have communicated respecting the pamphlet ; I should be exceeding sorry to publish anything that should tend to sedition." Mr Erskine contended that this was no admission on the Dean's part that he thought it seditious, for he had never read it ; but that his conduct showed that he was not seditiously inclined, since he stopped the publication even in compliance with the affected scruples of men whom he found out, on reading it, to be both

wicked and ignorant; and the translation of it into Welsh was
accordingly dropped.

Mr Jones had further said that many persons afterwards, and
particularly Mr Fitzmaurice, made very free with the Dean's
character for having entertained an idea of translating it into
Welsh. It was publicly mentioned at the general meeting of the
county, and many opprobrious epithets being fastened on the
dialogue itself, the Dean said, "*I am now called upon to show that
it is not seditious, and I read it with a rope about my neck.*"

MR ERSKINE THEN SPOKE AS FOLLOWS VERBATIM.

My Lord,—Although this is not the place for any commentary on
the evidence, I cannot help remarking that this expression was
strong proof that the Dean did not think it seditious; for it is
absurd to suppose that a man, feeling hurt at the accusation of
sedition, should say, I am now called upon to show I am not
seditious, and then proceed to read that aloud which he *felt and
believed* to contain sedition. The words which follow, " I read it
with a rope about my neck," confirm this construction. The
obvious sense of which is—I am now called upon to show that this
dialogue is not seditious. It has never been read by those who call
it so. I will read it in its own vindication, and in mine—" *I read
it with a rope about my neck,*"—that is, if it be treasonable, as is
asserted, it is a misdemeanour to read it; but I am so convinced
of its innocence, that I read it notwithstanding—*meo periculo.*

The only part of Mr Jones's evidence which remains is as
follows :—I asked him, "Did you collect from what the Dean
said that his opinion was that the dialogue was constitutional and
legal ?" His answer was, "Undoubtedly. The Dean said,
Now I have read this, I do not think it so bad a thing; and I
think we ought to publish it, in *vindication of the committee.*" The
question and answer must be taken in fairness together. The
witness was asked if he collected from the Dean that he thought it
innocent and constitutional, and the first term in the answer is
decisive; that the witness did not merely think it LESS criminal
than it had been supposed, but *perfectly constitutional;* for he
says, " *Undoubtedly I collected that he thought so.*" The Dean
said he thought he ought to publish it in vindication of the committee, and it is repugnant to common sense to believe that if the
Dean had supposed the dialogue *in any degree* criminal, he would
have proposed to publish it himself, in vindication of a former
intention of publication by the committee. It would have been a
confirmation, not a refutation, of the charge.

The learned Judge, after reciting the evidence which I have just
been stating (merely as a matter of form, since afterwards it was
laid wholly out of the question), began by telling the jury that he

was astonished at a great deal he had heard from the defendant's counsel; for that he did not know any one question of law more thoroughly settled than the doctrine of libels, as he proposed to state it to them: it then became *my turn* to be astonished.   Mr Justice Buller then proceeded to state, that what had fallen from me, namely, that the jury had a right to consider the libel, *was only the language of a party in this country; but that the contrary of their notions was so well established, that no man who meant well could doubt concerning it.*

It appeared afterwards that Mr Lee and myself were members of this party, though my friend was charged with having deserted his colours, as he was the first authority that was cited against me; and what rendered the authority more curious, the learned Judge mentioned that he had delivered his dictum at Guildhall as counsel for a plaintiff, when these doctrines might have been convenient for the interests of his client, and therefore no evidence of his opinion.   This quotation, however, had perhaps more weight with the jury than all that followed, and certainly the novelty of it entitled it to attention.

I hope, however, the sentiments imputed to my friend were not necessary upon that occasion; if they were, his client was betrayed, for I was myself in the cause alluded to; and I take upon me to affirm that Mr Lee *did not, directly or indirectly,* utter any sentiment in the most remote degree resembling that which the learned Judge was pleased to impute to him for the support of his charge. This I shall continue to affirm, notwithstanding the Judge's declaration to the contrary, until I am contradicted by Mr Lee himself, who is here to answer me if I misrepresent him.   [Mr Lee confirmed Mr Erskine by remaining silent.]

The learned Judge then said that, as to whether the dialogue, which was the subject of the prosecution, was criminal or innocent, he should not even hint an opinion; *for that if he should declare it to be no libel, and the jury, adopting that opinion, should acquit the defendant, he should thereby deprive the prosecutor of his right of appeal upon the record, which was one of the dearest birthrights of the subject.*   That the law was equal as between the prosecutor and defendant, and that there was no difference between criminal and civil cases.   I am desirous not to interrupt the state of the trial by observations, but cannot help remarking that justice to the prosecutor as standing exactly in equal scales with a prisoner, and in the light of an adverse party in a civil suit, was the first reason given by the learned Judge why the jury should at all events find the defendant guilty, without investigating his guilt.   This was telling the jury, in the plainest terms, *that they could not find a general verdict in favour of the defendant without an act of injustice to the prosecutor,* who would be shut out by it from his writ of error, which he was entitled to by law, and which was the best birthright of the subject. It was, therefore, an absolute denial of the right of the jury, and of the Judge also, as no right can exist which necessarily works a wrong in the exercise of it. If the prosecutor had by law a right to have the question on the record, the Judge and jury were both tied up at the trial: the one from directing, and the other from finding a verdict which disappointed that right.

If the prosecutor had a right to have the question upon the record, for the purpose of appeal, by the jury's confining themselves to the fact of publication, which would leave that question open, it is impossible to say that the jury had a right likewise to judge of the question of libel, and to acquit the defendant, which would deprive the prosecutor of that right. There cannot be contradictory rights, the exercise of one destroying and annihilating the other. I shall discuss this new claim of the prosecutor upon a future occasion; for the present, I will venture to say that no man has a right, a property, or a beneficial interest in the punishment of another. A prosecution at the instance of the Crown has public justice alone, and not private vengeance, for its object; in prosecutions for murder, and felonies, and most other misdemeanors, the prosecutor can have no such pretence, since the record does not comprehend the offence. Why he should have it in the case of a libel, I would gladly be informed.

The learned Judge then stated your Lordship's uniform practice in trying libels, for eight and twenty years,—the acquiescence of parties and their counsel, and the ratification of the principle, by a judgment of the Court in the case of the King against Woodfall. He likewise cited a case which, he said, happened within a year or two of the time of the seven bishops, in which a defendant, indicted for a seditious libel, desired it might be left to the jury whether the paper was seditious; but that the Court said the jury were to decide upon *the fact;* and that if they found him guilty of the *fact,* the Court would afterwards decide the question of libel. The learned Judge then cited the maxim, *ad quæstionem facti respondent juratores, ad quæstionem juris respondent judices,* and said that maxim had been confirmed in the sense he put on it in the very case of Bushel, on which I had relied so much for the contrary position.

The learned Judge, after honouring some of my arguments with answers, and saying again, in stronger terms than before, that there was no difference between the province of the jury in civil and criminal cases, notwithstanding the universality of the general issue instead of special pleadings, told the jury *that if they believed that G. meant Gentleman, and F. meant Farmer, the matter for their consideration was reduced to the simple fact of publication.*

The Court will please to recollect that the advertisements explaining the Dean's sentiments concerning the pamphlet, and his motives for the publication of it in English, after it had been given up in Welsh, had been read in evidence to the jury; that Mr Jones had been likewise examined to the same effect, to induce the jury to believe the advertisement to have been prefixed to it *bonâ fide*, and to have spoken the genuine sentiments and motives of the publisher; and that several gentlemen of the first character in the Dean's neighbourhood, in Wales, had been called to speak to his general peaceable deportment, in order to strengthen that proof, and to resist the assent of the jury to the principal averment in the information, viz., *that the defendant published, intending to excite a revolution in the Government, by armed rebellion.* Whether all this evidence, given for the defendant, was adequate to its purpose, is foreign to the present inquiry. I think it was. *But my objection is, that no part of it was left to the consideration of the jury, who were the judges of it.* As to the advertisement, which was part of the pamphlet itself, the learned Judge never even named it, but as part of the prosecutor's proof of the publication, though I had read it to the jury, and insisted upon it as sufficient proof of the defendant's intention, and had called Mr Jones to confirm the construction I put upon it.

As to Mr Jones's testimony, Mr Justice Buller said, "Whether his evidence will or will not operate in mitigation of punishment, is not a question for me to give an opinion upon." And he further declared that if the jury were satisfied as to the fact of the publication, they were BOUND to find the defendant guilty. As to the evidence of character, it was disposed of in the same manner. Mr Justice Buller said, "As to the several witnesses who have been called to give Mr Shipley the character of a quiet and peaceable man, not disposed to stir up sedition, *that cannot govern the present question; for the question you are to decide on is, Whether he be, or be not, guilty of publishing this pamphlet?*"

This charge, therefore, contained an express exclusion of the right of the jury to consider the evidence offered by the defendant, to rebut the inference of sedition arising from the act of publication.

The learned Judge repeated the same doctrine at the end of his charge, entirely removing from the jury the consideration of the whole of the defendant's evidence, and concluded by telling them, ' *That if they were satisfied as to the truth of the innuendoes and the act of publication, they were* BOUND *to find the defendant guilty.*" The jury retired to consider of this charge, and brought in a verdict, "Guilty of publishing ONLY." The learned Judge refused to record it, and I am ready to admit that it was an imperfect verdict. He was not bound to receive it; but when he saw the jury had no doubt of the truth of the innuendoes, and that therefore the word ONLY could not apply to a negation of them, he should have asked them whether they believed the defendant's witnesses, and meant negative the seditious purpose. It was the more his duty to

have asked that question, as several of the jury themselves said
that they gave no opinion concerning seditious intention—a declaration decisive in the defendant's favour, who had gone into
evidence to rebut the charge of intention, and of which the Judge,
who, in the humane theory of the English law, ought to be counsel
for the prisoner, should at the least have taken care to obtain an
explanation from the jury, by asking them what *their* opinion was,
instead of arguing upon the principle of *his own* charge, what it
necessarily must be, if the innuendoes were believed—a position
which gave the go-by to the difficulties of the jury. Their intention
to exclude the seditious purpose was palpable ; and under such circumstances, the excellent remark of the great Mr Justice Foster
never should be forgotten : " When the rigour of the law bordereth
upon injustice, mercy ought to interpose in the administration. It
is not the part of judges to be perpetually hunting after forfeitures,
while the heart is free from guilt. They are the ministers of the
Crown appointed for the ends of public justice, and ought to have
written upon their hearts the obligation which His Majesty is under,
to cause law and justice in mercy to be executed in all his judgments." This solemn obligation is no doubt written upon the
hearts of all the judges ; but it is unfortunate when it happens
to be written in so illegible a hand that a jury cannot possibly
read it.

To every part of the learned Judge's directions I have objections
which appear to me to be weighty. I will state them distinctly
and in their order as shortly or as much at large as the Court shall
require of me.

The first proposition which I mean to maintain as a foundation
for a new trial is this :

That when a bill of indictment is found or an information filed,
charging any crime or misdemeanour known to the law of England,
and the party accused puts himself upon the country by pleading
the general issue, Not guilty, the jury are GENERALLY charged with
his deliverance from that CRIME, and not SPECIALLY from the fact
or facts in the commission of which the indictment or information
charges the crime to consist, much less from any single fact to the
exclusion of others charged upon the same record.

Secondly, I mean to maintain that no act, which the law in its
general theory holds to be criminal, constitutes in itself a crime
abstracted from the mischievous intention of the actor ; and that
the intention, even where it becomes a simple inference of reason
from a fact or facts established, may, and ought to be, collected by
the jury with the Judge's assistance ; because the act charged,
though established as a fact in a trial on the general issue, does
not necessarily and unavoidably establish the criminal intention
by any ABSTRACT conclusion of law ; the establishment of the fact
being still no more than *evidence* of the crime, but not the CRIME

ITSELF, unless the jury render it so themselves by referring it voluntarily to the Court by special verdict.

I wish to explain this proposition.

When a jury can discover no other reasonable foundation for judging of the intention than the inference from the act charged, and doubting what that inference ought to be in law, refer it to the Court by special verdict, the intention becomes by that inference a question of law; but it only becomes so by this voluntary declaration of the jury, that they mean the party accused shall stand or fall by the abstract legal conclusion from the act charged, not being able to decipher his purpose by any other medium.

But this discretionary reference to the Court upon particular occasions, which may render it wise and expedient, does not abridge or contract the power or the duty of a jury, under other circumstances, to withhold their consent from the intention being taken as a legal consequence of the act; even when they have had no evidence capable of being stated on the face of a special verdict, they may still find a general verdict, founded on their judgment of the crime, and the intention of the party accused of it.

When I say that the jury MAY consider the crime and the intention, I desire to be understood to mean, not merely that they have the POWER to do it without control or punishment, and without the possibility of their acquittal being disannulled by any other authority (for that no man can deny); but I mean that they have a constitutional legal RIGHT to do so,—a right, in many cases, proper to be exercised, and intended by the wise founders of the English government to be a protection to the lives and liberties of Englishmen against the encroachments and perversions of authority in the hands of fixed magistrates.

The establishment of both or either of these two propositions must entitle me to a new trial; for if the jury, on the general issue, had a strictly legal jurisdiction to judge of the libellous nature or seditious tendency of the paper (taking that nature or tendency to be law or fact), then the Judge's direction is evidently unwarrantable. If he had said, As libel or no libel requires a legal apprehension of the subject, it is my duty to give you my opinion; and had then said, I think it is a libel, and had left the jury to find it one under his directions, or otherwise, at their discretion, and had at the same time told them that the criminal intention was an inference from the publication of the libel which it was their duty to make,—or if, admitting their right in *general*, he had advised a special verdict in the *particular instance*, I should have stood in a very different situation; but he told the jury (I take the general result of his whole charge) that they had no jurisdiction to consider of the libel or of the intention, both being beyond the compass of their oath.

Mr Bearcroft's position was very different. He addressed the jury with the honest candour of a judge without departing from the proper zeal of an advocate. He said to the jury—I cannot honour him more than by repeating his words; they will long be remembered by those who respect *him* and love the constitution :—

" There is no law in this country," said Mr Bearcroft (thank God, there is not; for it would not be a free constitution if there were), " that prevents a jury, if they choose it, from finding a general verdict; I admit it; I rejoice in it; I admire and reverence the principle as the palladium of the constitution. But does it follow, because a jury *may* do this, that they *must* do it—that they OUGHT to do it?" He then took notice of the case of the seven bishops, and honoured the jury for exercising this right on that occasion.

Mr Bearcroft's position is therefore manly and intelligible. It is simply this: It is the excellence of the English constitution that you may exert this power when you think the season warrants the exercise of it. The case of the seven bishops was such a season; this is not.

But Mr Justice Buller did by no means ratify this doctrine. It is surely not too much to expect that the Judge, who is supposed to be counsel for the prisoner, should keep within the bounds of the counsel for the Crown, when a Crown prosecution is in such hands as Mr Bearcroft's. The learned Judge, however, told the jury from his own authority, and supported it with much history and observation, and many quotations, that they had nothing to do at all with those questions, their jurisdiction over which Mr Bear-croft had rejoiced in as the palladium of the constitution. He did not tell them this by way of advice, as applied to the particular case before them; he did not (admitting their right) advise them to forbear the exercise of it in the *particular instance*. No! the learned Judge fastened a UNIVERSAL ABSTRACT limitation on the province of the jury to judge of the crime, or the criminal purpose of the defendant. His whole speech laid down this limit-ation UNIVERSALLY, and was so understood by the jury; he told them these questions were beyond the compass of their oaths, which was confined to the decision of the fact; and he drove them from the law by the terrors of conscience. The conclusion is short.

If the jury have no jurisdiction, by the law of England, to examine the question of libel, and the criminality or innocence of the intention of the publisher, then the Judge's charge was right ; but if they have jurisdiction, and if their having it be the palla-dium of the Government, it must be wrong. For how, in common sense, can that power in a jury be called the palladium of the con-stitution which can never be exerted but by a breach of those rules of law which the same constitution has established for their government ?

If in no case a jury can entertain such a question without step-ping beyond their duty, it is an affront to human reason to say that the safety of the Government depends on men's violating their oaths in the administration of justice. If the jury have that right, there is no difference between restricting the exercise of it by the terrors of imprisonment, or the terrors of conscience. If there be any difference, the second is the most dangerous; an upright juryman, like Bushel, would despise the first, but his very honesty would render him the dupe of the last.

The two former propositions on which my motion is founded applying to all criminal cases, and a distinction having always been taken between libels and other crimes by those who support the doctrines I am combating, I mean therefore to maintain that an indictment for a libel, even where the slander of an individual is the object of it (which is capable of being measured by precedents of justice), forms no exception to the jurisdiction or duties of juries, or the practice of judges in other criminal cases,—that the argument for the difference, viz., because the whole crime always appears upon the record, is false in fact, and, even if true, would form no solid or substantial difference in law.

I said that the record does not always contain sufficient for the Court to judge of a libel. The Crown may indict part of a publication, and omit the rest, which would have explained the author's meaning, and rendered it harmless. It has done so here; the advertisement is part of the publication, but no part of the record.

The famous case put by Algernon Sydney is the best illustration that can possibly be put.

Suppose a bookseller, having published the Bible, was indicted in these words, "That intending to promote atheism and irreligion, he had blasphemously printed and published the following false and profane libel—There is no God." The learned Judge said that a person unjustly accused of publishing a libel might always demur to the indictment. This is an instance to the contrary; on the face of such a record, by which the demurrer can alone be determined, it contains a complete criminal charge. The defendant, therefore, would plead not guilty, and go down to trial, when the prosecutor of course could only produce the Bible to support the charge, by which it would appear to be only a verse in the Proverbs of Solomon, viz., "The fool has said in his heart, There is no God," and that the context had been omitted to constitute the libel. The jury, shocked at the imposition, would only wait the Judge's direction to acquit; but, consistently with the principles which have governed in the Dean of St Asaph's trial, how could he be acquitted? The Judge must say, You have nothing to do but with the fact that the defendant published *the words laid in the information.*

But, says the adversary, the distinction is obvious; reading the sacred context to the jury would enable them to negative the innuendoes which are within their province to reject, and which,

being rejected, would destroy the charge.   The answer is obvious.
Such an indictment would contain no innuendo on which a negative could be put; for if the record charged that the defendant
blasphemously published that there was no God, it would require
no innuendo to explain it.

Driven from that argument, the adversary must say that the
jury by the context would be enabled to negative the epithets
contained in the introduction, and could never pronounce it to be
blasphemous.   But the answer to that is equally conclusive; for
it was said, in the case of the King against Woodfall, that these
epithets were mere formal inferences of law, from the fact of publishing that which on the record was a libel.

When the defendant was convicted, it could not appear to the
Court that the defendant only published the Bible.   The Court
could not look off the record, which says that the defendant
blasphemously published that there was no God.   The Judge,
maintaining these doctrines, would not, however, forget the respect
due to the *religion* of his country, though the law of it had escaped
him.   He would tell the jury that it should be remembered in
mitigation of punishment, and the honest bookseller of Pater-
noster Row, when he came up in custody to receive judgment,
would be let off for a small fine, upon the Judge's report that he
had only published a new copy of the Bible; but not till he had
been a month in the King's Bench prison, while this knotty point
of divinity was in discussion.   This case has stood invulnerable
for above one hundred years, and it remains still for Mr Bearcroft
to answer.

I said, in opening this proposition, that even if it were true that
the record did contain the whole charge, it would form no substantial difference in law; and I said so, because, if the position be
that the Court is always to judge of the law, when it can be made
to see it upon the record, no case can occur in which there could
be a general verdict, since the law might be always separated
from the facts by finding the latter specially, and referring them
to the judgment of the Court.   By this mode of proceeding, the
crime would be equally patent upon the record as by indictment; and if it be patent there, it matters not whether it appears
on the front or the back of the parchment; on the first by the
indictment, or on the last by the postea.

People who seek to maintain this doctrine do not surely see to
what length it would go; for if it can be maintained that where-
ever, as in the case of a libel, the crime appears upon the record,
the Court alone, and not the jury ought to judge, it must follow,
that where a writing is laid as an overt act of high treason (which
it may be when coupled with publication), the jury might be tied
down to find the fact, and the judges of the Crown might make
state criminals at their discretion, by finding the law.

The answer in these mild and independent days of judicature is this (Mr Bearcroft, indeed, gave it at the trial): Why may not judges be trusted with our liberties and lives, who determine upon our property and everything that is dear to us?

The observation was plausible for the moment, and suited to his situation, but he is too wise a man to subscribe to it. Where is the analogy between ordinary civil trials between man and man, where judges can rarely have an interest, and great state prosecutions, where power and freedom are weighing against each other, the balance being suspended by the servants of the executive magistrate? If any man can be so lost to reason as to be a sceptic on such a subject, I can furnish him with a cure from an instance directly in point. Let him turn to the 199th page of the celebrated Foster, to the melancholy account of Peachum's indictment for treason for a manuscript sermon found in his closet, never published, reflecting on King James I.'s government. The case was too weak to trust without management even by the sovereign to the judges of those days; it was necessary first to sound them; and the great (but on that occasion the contemptible) Lord Bacon was fixed on for the instrument; and his letter to the King remains recorded in history, where, after telling him his successful practice on the puisne judges, he says that when in some dark manner he has hinted this success to Lord Coke, he will not choose to remain singular.

When it is remembered what comprehensive talents and splendid qualifications Lord Bacon was gifted with, it is no indecency to say that all judges ought to dread a trust which the constitution never gave them, and which human nature has not always enabled the greatest men to fulfil.

If the Court shall grant me a rule, I mean to contend, Fourthly, that a seditious libel contains no question of law; but supposing the Court should deny the legality of all these propositions, or admitting their legality, resist the conclusion I have drawn from them, then the last proposition in which I am supported, even by all those authorities on which the learned Judge relies for the doctrines contained in this charge is this:—

PROPOSITION V.

That in all cases where the mischievous intention (which is agreed to be the essence of the crime) cannot be collected by simple inference from the fact charged, because the defendant goes into evidence to rebut such inference, the intention becomes then a pure unmixed question of fact, for the consideration of the jury.

I said the authorities of the King against Woodfall and Almon were with me. In the case of Rex against Woodfall, 5th Burrow, Lord Mansfield expressed himself thus: "Where an act in itself indifferent becomes criminal, when done with a particular intent, there

the intent must be proved and found.   But where the act is itself
unlawful, as in the case of a libel, the PROOF of justification or
excuse lies on the defendant; *and in failure thereof, the law implies
a criminal intent.*"   Most luminously expressed to convey this sentiment, viz., That when a man publishes a libel, and has nothing
to say for himself,—no explanation or exculpation,—a criminal
intention need not be proved: it is an inference of common sense,
not of law.   But the publication of a libel does not exclusively show
criminal intent, but is only an implication of law, in failure of the
defendant's proof.   Lord Mansfield immediately afterwards in the
same case explains this further: "There may be cases where the
publication may be justified or excused as lawful OR INNOCENT;
FOR NO ACT WHICH IS NOT CRIMINAL, *though the paper* BE A LIBEL,
can amount to SUCH a publication of which a defendant ought
to be found guilty."   But no question of that kind arose at the trial
(*i.e.*, trial of Woodfall).   Why?—Lord Mansfield immediately.
says why.   "*Because* the defendant called no witnesses;" expressly
saying that the publication of a libel is not in itself a crime, unless
the intent be criminal ; and that it is not merely in mitigation of
punishment, but that *such* a publication does not warrant a verdict
of guilty, if the seditious intention be rebutted by evidence.

In the case of the King against Almon, a magazine containing
one of Junius's letters was sold at Almon's shop ; there was proof of
that sale at the trial.   Mr Almon called no witnesses, and was found
guilty.   To found a motion for a new trial, an affidavit was offered
from Mr Almon, that he was not privy to the sale, nor knew that
his name was inserted as a publisher, and that this practice of
booksellers being inserted as publishers by their correspondents
without notice was common in the trade.

Lord Mansfield said, "Sale of a book in a bookseller's shop
is *primâ facie* evidence of publication by the master, and the
publication of a libel is *primâ facie* evidence of criminal intent :
it stands good till answered by the defendant : it must stand till
contradicted or explained ; *and if not contradicted, explained, or
exculpated,* BECOMES *tantamount to conclusive when the defendant
calls no witnesses.*"

Mr Justice Aston said, "*Primâ facie* evidence not answered is
sufficient to ground a verdict upon ; if the defendant had a sufficient
excuse, he might have proved it at the trial : his having neglected
it where there was no surprise is no ground for a new one."   Mr
Justice Willes and Mr Justice Ashhurst agreed upon those express
principles.

These cases declare the law beyond all controversy to be, that
publication, even of a libel, is no *conclusive* proof of guilt, but only
primâ facie evidence of it till answered ; and that if the defendant
can show that his intention was not criminal, he completely rebuts
the inference arising from the publication, because, though it remains

true that he published, yet it is, according to Lord Mansfield's express words, not such a publication of which a defendant ought to be *found guilty*. Apply Mr Justice Buller's summing up to this law, and it does not require even a legal apprehension to distinguish the repugnancy.

The advertisement was proved to convince the jury of the Dean's motive for publishing ; Mr Jones's testimony went strongly to aid it ; and the evidence to character, though not sufficient in itself, was admissible to be thrown into the scale. But not only no part of this was left to the jury, *but the whole of it was expressly removed from their consideration;* although, in the cases of Woodfall and Almon, it was as expressly laid down to be within their cognisance, and a complete answer to the charge, if satisfactory to the minds of the jurors.

In support of the learned Judge's charge, there can be therefore but two arguments:—either that the defendant's evidence, namely, the advertisement,—Mr Jones's evidence in confirmation of its having been published *bonâ fide;*—and the evidence to character to strengthen that construction, were not sufficient proof that the Dean believed the publication meritorious, and published it in vindication of his honest intentions;—or else that, even admitting it to establish that fact, it did not amount to such an exculpation as to be evidence on not guilty, so as to warrant a verdict. I give the learned Judge his choice of the alternative.

As to the first, viz., Whether it showed *honest intention* in point of *fact;* that surely was a question for the jury. If the learned Judge had thought it was not sufficient evidence to warrant the jury's believing that the Dean's motives were such as he had declared them, he should have given his opinion of it as a point of evidence, and left it there. I cannot condescend to go farther ; it would be ridiculous to argue a self-evident proposition.

As to the second, That even if the jury had believed from the evidence that the Dean's intention was wholly innocent, it did not amount to an excuse, and therefore should not have been left to them. Does the learned Judge mean to say, that if the jury had declared, " We find that the Dean published this pamphlet, whether a libel or not we do not find ; and we find further, that believing it in his conscience to be meritorious and innocent, he, *bonâ fide,* published it with the prefixed advertisement, as a vindication of his character from the seditious intentions, and not to excite sedition,"—does the Judge mean to say, that on such a special verdict he could have pronounced a criminal judgment ? If, on making the report, he says yes, I shall have leave to argue it.

If he says no, then why was the consideration of that evidence, by which those facts might have been found, withdrawn from the jury, even after they had brought in a verdict, Guilty of publishing only, which, in the case of the King against Woodfall, was only said

not to negative the criminal intention, because that defendant had
called no witnesses? Why did he confine his inquiries to the innuendoes? and finding the jury agreed upon them, why did he declare
them to be bound to affix the epithet of guilty without asking them if
they believed the defendant's evidence to rebut the criminal inference? Some of the jury meant to negative the criminal inference,
by adding the word *only*, and all would have done it, if they had
thought themselves at liberty to enter upon the evidence of the
advertisement. *But they were told expressly that they had nothing
to do with the consideration of that evidence, which, if believed,
would have warranted that verdict.* The conclusion is evident;—
if they had a right to consider it, and their consideration might
have produced such a verdict, and if such a verdict would have
been an acquittal, it must be a misdirection.

It seems to me, therefore, that to support the learned Judge's
directions, the very cases relied on in support of them must be
abandoned; since, even upon their authority, the criminal intention, though a legal inference from the fact of publishing, in the
absence of proof from the defendant, becomes a question of fact,
when he offers proof in exculpation to the jury;—the foundation
of my motion, therefore, is clear.

I first deny the authority of these modern cases, and rely upon
the rights of juries, as established by the ancient law and custom
of England, and hold that the Judge's charge confines that right
and its exercise, though not the power in the jury to find a general
verdict of acquittal.

I assert further, that, whatever were the Judge's intentions, the
jury could not but collect that restriction from his charge;—that
all free agency was therefore destroyed in them, from respect to
authority, in opposition to reason,—and that, therefore, the defendant has had no trial which this Court can possibly sanction by
supporting the verdict. But if the Court should be resolved to
support its own late determinations, I must content myself even
with *their* protection; they are certainly not the shield with which,
in a contest for freedom, I should wish to combat, but they are
sufficient for my protection: it is impossible to reconcile the learned
Judge's directions with any of them.

My Lord, I shall detain the Court no longer at present. The
people of England are deeply interested in this great question; and
though they are not insensible to that interest, yet they do not feel
it in its real extent. The dangerous consequences of the doctrines
established on the subject of libel are obscured from the eyes of
many, from their not feeling the immediate effects of them in daily
oppression and injustice. But that security is temporary and
fallacious; it depends upon the convenience of Government for the
time being, which may not be interested in the sacrifice of individuals, and in the temper of the magistrate who administers the

criminal law, as the head of this court. I am one of those who could almost lull myself by these reflections from the apprehension of *immediate* mischief, even from the law of libel laid down by your Lordship, if you were always to continue to administer it yourself. I should feel a protection in the gentleness of your character ; in the love of justice which its own intrinsic excellence forces upon a mind enlightened by science, and enlarged by liberal education, and in that dignity of disposition which grows with the growth of an illustrious reputation, and becomes a sort of pledge to the public for security : but such a security is as a shadow which passeth away ;—you cannot, my Lord, be immortal, and how can you answer for your successor ? If you maintain the doctrines which I seek to overturn, you render yourself responsible for all the abuses that may follow from them to our latest posterity.

My Lord, whatever may become of the liberties of England, it shall never be said that they perished without resistance when under my protection.

On this motion the Court granted a rule to show cause why there should not be a new trial—and cause was accordingly shown by the counsel for the Crown on the 15th of November following ; their arguments were taken in shorthand by Mr Blanchard, but were never published. They relied, however, altogether upon the authorities cited by Mr Justice Buller, in his charge to the jury, and upon the uniform practice of the Court of King's Bench, for more than fifty years. The following speech, in support of the new trial, which was taken at the same time by Mr Blanchard, was soon after published by Mr Erskine's authority, in order to attract the attention of the public to the Libel Bill, which Mr Fox was then preparing for the consideration of Parliament.

ARGUMENT, in the King's Bench, in support of the Rights of Juries.

I AM now to have the honour to address myself to your Lordship in support of the rule granted to me by the Court upon Monday last, which, as Mr Bearcroft has truly said, and seemed to mark the observation with peculiar emphasis, is a rule for a new trial. Much of my argument, according to his notion, points another way; whether its direction be true, or its force adequate to the object, it is now my business to show.

In rising to speak at this time, I feel all the advantage conferred by the reply over those whose arguments are to be answered; but I feel a disadvantage likewise which must suggest itself to every intelligent mind. In following the objections of so many learned persons, offered under different arrangements upon a subject so complicated and comprehensive, there is much danger of being drawn from that method and order, which can alone fasten conviction upon unwilling minds, or drive them from the shelter which ingenuity never fails to find in the labyrinth of a desultory discourse.

The sense of that danger, and my own inability to struggle against it, led me originally to deliver to the Court certain written and maturely considered propositions, from the establishment of which I resolved not to depart, nor to be removed, either in substance or in order, in any stage of the proceedings, and by which I must, therefore, this day unquestionably stand or fall.

Pursuing this system, I am vulnerable two ways, and in two ways only. Either it must be shown that my propositions are not valid in law; or, admitting their validity, that the learned Judge's charge to the jury at Shrewsbury was not repugnant to them: there can be no other possible objections to my application for a new trial. My duty to-day is, therefore, obvious and simple; it is, first, to re-maintain those propositions; and then to show that the charge delivered to the jury at Shrewsbury was founded upon the absolute denial and reprobation of them.

I begin, therefore, by saying again, in my own original words, that when a bill of indictment is found, or an information filed, charging any crime or misdemeanour known to the law of England, and the party accused puts himself upon the country by pleading the general issue, Not guilty, the jury are GENERALLY charged with his deliverance from that CRIME, and not SPECIALLY from the *fact or facts*, in the commission of which the indictment or information charges the crime to consist; much less from any single fact, to the exclusion of others charged upon the same record.

Secondly, that no act, which the law in its general theory holds to be criminal, constitutes in itself a crime, abstracted from the mischievous intention of the actor. And that the intention, even where it becomes a simple inference of legal reason from a fact or facts established, may and ought to be collected by the jury, with the Judge's assistance. Because the act charged, though established as a fact in a trial *on the general issue*, does not necessarily and unavoidably establish the criminal intention by any ABSTRACT conclusion of law; the establishment of the fact being still no more than full evidence of the crime, but not the crime itself; unless the jury render it so themselves, by referring it voluntarily to the Court by special verdict.

These two propositions, though worded with cautious precision, and in technical language, to prevent the subtlety of legal disputation in opposition to the plain understanding of the world, neither do nor were intended to convey any other sentiment than this, viz., that in all cases where the law either directs or permits a person accused of a crime to throw himself upon a jury for deliverance by pleading *generally* that he is not guilty, the jury, thus legally appealed to, may deliver him from the accusation by a general verdict of acquittal, founded (as in common sense it evidently must be) upon an investigation as general and comprehensive as the charge itself from which it is a general deliverance.

Having said this, I freely confess to the Court that I am much at a loss for any further illustration of my subject; because I cannot find any matter by which it might be further illustrated so clear, or so indisputable, either in fact or in law, as the very proposition itself which upon this trial has been brought into question. Looking back upon the ancient constitution, and examining with painful research the original jurisdictions of the country, I am utterly at a loss to imagine from what sources these novel limitations of the rights of juries are derived. Even the Bar is not yet trained to the discipline of maintaining them. My learned friend Mr. Bearcroft solemnly abjures them; he repeats to-day what he vowed at the trial, and is even jealous of the imputation of having meant less than he expressed; for when speaking this morning of he *right* of the jury to judge of the whole charge, your Lordship orrected his expression by telling him he meant the *power*, and ot the *right;* he caught instantly at your words, disavowed your xplanation, and, with a consistency which does him honour, eclared his adherence to his original admission in its full and bvious extent. "I did not mean," said he, "merely to acknowdge that the jury have the *power*, for their power nobody ever doubted; and, if a Judge was to tell them they had it not, they would only have to laugh at him, and convince him of his error by finding a general verdict which must be recorded.   I meant, therefore, to consider it as a *right*, as an important privilege, and of great value to the constitution."

Thus Mr Bearcroft and I are perfectly agreed: I never contended for more than he has voluntarily conceded.   I have now his express authority for repeating, in my own former words, that the jury have not merely the *power* to acquit, upon a view of the whole charge, without control or punishment, and without the possibility of their acquittal being annulled by any other authority; but that they have a *constitutional, legal right to do it,—a right fit to be exercised*, and intended by the wise founders of the government to be a protection to the lives and liberties of Englishmen against the encroachments and perversions of authority in the hands of fixed magistrates.

But this candid admission on the part of Mr Bearcroft, though very honourable to himself, is of no importance to me ; since, from what has already fallen from your Lordship, I am not to expect a ratification of it from the Court ; it is therefore my duty to establish it.   I feel all the importance of my subject, and nothing shall lead me to-day to go out of it.   I claim all the attention of the Court, and the right to state every authority which applies in my judgment to the argument, without being supposed to introduce them for other purposes than my duty to my client and the constitution of my country warrants and approves.

It is not very usual, in an English Court of Justice, to be driven back to the earliest history and original elements of the constitution in order to establish the first principles which mark and distinguish English law ; they are always assumed, and, like axioms in science, are made the foundations of reasoning without being proved.   Of this sort our ancestors, for many centuries, must have conceived the right of an English jury to decide upon every question which the forms of the law submitted to their final decision ; since, though they have immemorially exercised that supreme jurisdiction, we find no trace in any of the ancient books of its ever being brought into question.   It is but as yesterday, when compared with the age of the law itself, that judges, unwarranted by any former judgments of their predecessors, without any new commission from the Crown, or enlargement of judicial authority from the Legislature, have sought to fasten a limitation upon the rights and privileges of jurors, totally unknown in ancient times, and palpably destructive of the very end and object of their institution.

No fact, my Lord, is of more easy demonstration, for the history and laws of a free country lie open even to vulgar inspection.

During the whole Saxon era, and even long after the establishment of the Norman government, the whole administration of justice, criminal and civil, was in the hands of the people, without the control or intervention of any judicial authority delegated to fixed magistrates by the Crown.   The tenants of every manor administered civil justice to one another in the court-baron of their lord; and their crimes were judged of in the leet, every suitor of the manor giving his voice as a juror, and the steward being only the register, and not the judge.   On appeals from these domestic jurisdictions to the county court, and to the torn of the sheriff, or in suits and prosecutions originally commenced in either of them, the sheriff's authority extended no further than to summon the jurors, to compel their attendance, ministerially to regulate their proceedings, and to enforce their decisions; and even where he was specially empowered by the King's writ of *justices* to proceed in causes of superior value, no *judicial* authority was thereby conferred upon himself, but only a more enlarged juris-diction ON THE JURORS who were to try the cause mentioned in the writ.

It is true that the sheriff cannot now intermeddle in pleas of the Crown; but with this exception, which brings no restrictions on juries, these jurisdictions remain untouched at this day; intri-cacies of property have introduced other forms of proceeding, but the constitution is the same.

This popular judicature was not confined to particular districts, or to inferior suits and misdemeanours, but pervaded the whole legal constitution; for when the Conqueror, to increase the influ-ence of his crown, erected that great superintending Court of Justice in his own palace, to receive appeals criminal and civil from every court in the kingdom, and placed at the head of it the *capitalis justiciarius totius Angliæ*, of whose original authority the Chief Justice of this Court is but a partial and feeble emanation; even that great magistrate was in the *aulá regis* merely ministerial; every one of the King's tenants who owed him service in right of a barony had a seat and a voice in that high tribunal, and the office of justiciar was but to record and to enforce their judgments.

In the reign of King Edward I., when this great office was abolished, and the present Courts at Westminster established by a distribution of its powers, the barons preserved that supreme superintending jurisdiction which never belonged to the justiciar, but to themselves only as the jurors in the King's court: a juris-diction which, when nobility, from being territorial and feodal, became personal and honorary, was assumed and exercised by the peers of England, who, without any delegation of judicial authority from the Crown, form to this day the supreme and final court of English law, judging in the last resort for the whole kingdom, and sitting upon the lives of the peerage, in their ancient and genuine character, as the *pares* of one another.

When the courts at Westminster were established in their present forms, and when the civilisation and commerce of the nation had introduced more intricate questions of justice, the judicial authority in civil cases could not but enlarge its bounds; the rules of property in a cultivated state of society became by degrees beyond the compass of the unlettered multitude; and in certain well-known restrictions undoubtedly fell to the Judges; yet more perhaps from necessity than by consent, as all judicial proceedings were artfully held in the Norman language, to which the people were strangers.

Of these changes in judicature, immemorial custom, and the acquiescence of the legislature, are the evidence, which establish the jurisdiction of the Courts on the true principle of English law, and measure the extent of it by their ancient practice.

But no such evidence is to be found of the least relinquishment or abridgment of popular judicature *in cases of crimes;* on the contrary, every page of our history is filled with the struggles of our ancestors for its preservation. The law of property changes with new objects, and becomes intricate as it extends its dominion; but crimes must ever be of the same easy investigation: they consist wholly in intention; and the more they are multiplied by the policy of those who govern, the more absolutely the public freedom depends upon the people's preserving the entire administration of criminal justice to themselves. In a question of property between two private individuals, the Crown can have no possible interest in preferring the one to the other: but it may have an interest in crushing both of them together, in defiance of every principle of humanity and justice, if they should put themselves forward in a contention for public liberty, against a government seeking to emancipate itself from the dominion of the laws. No man in the least acquainted with the history of nations, or of his own country, can refuse to acknowledge, that if the administration of criminal justice were left in the hands of the Crown or its deputies, no greater freedom could possibly exist than government might choose to tolerate from the convenience or policy of the day.

My Lord, this important truth is no discovery or assertion of mine, but is to be found in every book of the law: whether we go up to the most ancient authorities, or appeal to the writings of men of our own times, we meet with it alike in the most emphatic language. Mr Justice Blackstone, by no means biassed towards democratical government, having in the third volume of his Commentaries explained the excellence of the trial by jury in civil cases, expresses himself thus, vol. iv., p. 349:—" But it holds much stronger in criminal cases; since in times of difficulty and danger, more is to be apprehended from the violence and partiality of Judges appointed by the Crown, in suits between the King and the subject, than in disputes between one individual and another to settle the boundaries of private property. Our law has, therefore, wisely placed this strong and twofold barrier of a presentment and trial by jury between the liberties of the people and the prerogative of the Crown : without this barrier, justices of *oyer* and *terminer* named by the Crown might, as in France or in Turkey, imprison, dispatch, or exile any man that was obnoxious to government, by an instant declaration that such was their will and pleasure. So that the liberties of England cannot but subsist so long as this palladium remains sacred and inviolate, not only from all open attacks, which none will be so hardy as to make, but also from all secret machinations which may sap and undermine it."

But this remark, though it derives new force in being adopted by so great an authority, was no more original in Mr Justice Blackstone than in me : the institution and authority of juries is to be found in Bracton, who wrote above five hundred years before him. " The *curia* and the *pares*," says he, " were necessarily the judges in all cases of life, limb, crime, and disherison of the heir in capite. The King could not decide, for then he would have been both prosecutor and judge ; neither could his justices, for they represent him." *

Notwithstanding all this, the learned Judge was pleased to say at the trial that there was no difference between civil and criminal cases. I say, on the contrary, independent of these authorities, that there is not, even to vulgar observation, the remotest similitude between them.

There are four capital distinctions between prosecutions for crimes and civil actions, every one of which deserves consideration.

First, In the jurisdiction necessary to found the charge.

Secondly, In the manner of the defendant's pleading to it.

Thirdly, In the authority of the verdict which discharges him.

Fourthly, In the independence and security of the jury from all consequences in giving it.

As to the first, it is unnecessary to remind your Lordships that, in a civil case, the party who conceives himself aggrieved states his complaint to the Court, avails himself at his own pleasure of its process, compels an answer from the defendant by its authority, or taking the charge *pro confesso* against him on his default, is entitled to final judgment and execution for his debt without any interposition of a jury. But in criminal cases it is otherwise ; the Court has no cognisance of them, without leave from the people forming a grand inquest. If a man were to commit a capital offence in the face of all the judges of England, their united authority could not put him upon his trial ; they could file no complaint against him, even upon the records of the supreme criminal Court, but could only commit him for safe custody, which is equally competent to every common justice of the peace : the

* *Vide* Mr Reeves' very ingenious History of the English Law.

grand jury alone could arraign him, and in their discretion might likewise finally discharge him, by throwing out the bill, with the names of all your Lordships as witnesses on the back of it. If it shall be said that this exclusive power of the grand jury does not extend to lesser misdemeanours, which may be prosecuted by information, I answer, that for that very reason it becomes doubly necessary to preserve the power of the other jury which is left. In the rules of pleading there is no distinction between capital and lesser offences; and the defendant's plea of not guilty (which universally prevails as the legal answer to every information or indictment, as opposed to special pleas to the Court in civil actions), and the necessity imposed upon the Crown to join the general issue, are absolutely decisive of the present question.

Every lawyer must admit that the rules of pleading were originally established to mark and to preserve the distinct jurisdictions of the Court and the jury, by a separation of the law from the fact, wherever they were intended to be separated. A person charged with owing a debt, or having committed a trespass, &c. &c., if he could not deny the facts on which the actions were founded, was obliged to submit his justification for matter of law by a special plea to the Court upon the record; to which plea the plaintiff might demur, and submit the legal merits to the judges. By this arrangement no power was ever given to the jury by an issue joined before them, but when a right of decision, as comprehensive as the issue, went along with it: if a defendant in such civil actions pleaded the general issue instead of a special plea, aiming at a general deliverance from the charge, by showing his justification to the jury at the trial, the Court protected its own jurisdiction by refusing all evidence of the facts on which such justification was founded. The extension of the general issue beyond its ancient limits, and in deviation from its true principle, has introduced some confusion into this simple and harmonious system; but the law is substantially the same. No man at this day, in any of those actions where the ancient forms of our jurisprudence are still wisely preserved, can possibly get at the opinion of a jury upon any question not intended by the constitution for their decision. In actions of debt, detinue, breach of covenant, trespass, or replevin, the defendant can only submit the mere fact to the jury; the law must be pleaded to the Court: if, dreading the opinion of judges, he conceals his justification under the cover of a general plea in hopes of a more favourable construction of his defence at the trial, its very existence can never even come within the knowledge of the jurors; every legal defence must arise out of facts, and the authority of the Judge is interposed to prevent their appearing before a tribunal which, in such cases, has no competent jurisdiction over them.

By imposing this necessity of pleading every legal justification to the Court, and by this exclusion of all evidence on the trial beyond the negation of the fact, the Courts indisputably intended to establish, and did in fact effectually secure, the judicial authority over legal questions from all encroachment or violation ; and it is impossible to find a reason in law, or in common sense, why the same boundaries between the fact and the law should not have been at the same time extended to criminal cases by the same rules of pleading, if the jurisdiction of the jury had been designed to be limited to the fact, as in civil actions.

But no such boundary was ever made or attempted ; on the contrary, every person, charged with any crime by an indictment or information, has been in all times, from the Norman conquest to this hour, not only permitted, but even bound to throw himself upon his country for deliverance by the general plea of not guilty ; and may submit his whole defence to the jury, whether it be a negation of the fact, or a justification of it in law ; and the Judge has no authority, as in a civil case, to refuse such evidence at the trial, as out of the issue, and as *coram non judice ;* an authority which in common sense he certainly would have, if the jury had no higher jurisdiction in the one case than in the other. The general plea thus sanctioned by immemorial custom so blends the law and the fact together as to be inseparable but by the voluntary act of the jury in finding a special verdict : the general investigation of the whole charge is therefore before them ; and although the defendant admits the fact laid in the information or indictment, he nevertheless, under his general plea, gives evidence of others which are collateral, referring them to the judgment of the jury as a legal excuse or justification, and receives from their verdict a complete, general, and conclusive deliverance.

Mr Justice Blackstone, in the fourth volume of his Commentaries, page 339, says, " The traitorous or felonious intent are the points and very gist of the indictment, and must be answered directly by the general negative, not guilty ; and the jury will take notice of any defensive matter, and give their verdict accordingly, as effectually as if it were specially pleaded."

This, therefore, says Sir Matthew Hale, in his " Pleas of the Crown," page 258, is, upon all accounts, the most advantageous plea for the defendant : " It would be a most unhappy case for the Judge himself, if the prisoner's fate depended upon his directions : —unhappy also for the prisoner ; for if the Judge's opinion must rule the verdict, the trial by jury would be useless."

My Lord, the conclusive operation of the verdict when given, and the security of the jury from all consequences in giving it, render the contrast between criminal and civil cases striking and complete. No new trial can be granted, as in a civil action :—your Lordships, however you may disapprove of the acquittal, have no authority to award one ; for there is no precedent of any such upon record ; and the discretion of the Court is circumscribed by the law.

Neither can the jurors be attained by the Crown.   In Bushel's case, "Vaughan's Reports," page 146, that learned and excellent Judge expressed himself thus: "There is no case in all the law of an attaint for the King, nor any opinion but that of Thyrning's, 10th of Henry IV., title Attaint, 60 and 64, for which there is no warrant in law, though there be other spacious authority against it, touched by none that have argued this case."

Lord MANSFIELD. To be sure it is so.

Mr ERSKINE. Since that is clear, my Lord, I shall not trouble the Court further upon it: indeed I have not been able to find any one authority for such an attaint but a dictum in "Fitzherbert's Natura Brevium," page 107; and on the other hand, the doctrine of Bushel's case is expressly agreed to in very modern times: *vide* "Lord Raymond's Reports," 1st volume, page 469.

If, then, your Lordships reflect but for a moment upon this comparative view of criminal and civil cases which I have laid before you; how can it be seriously contended, not merely that there is no difference, but that there is any the remotest similarity between them? In the one case, the power of accusation begins from the Court;—in the other, from the people only; forming a grand jury. In the one, the defendant must plead a special justification, the merits of which can only be decided by the Judges;—in the other, he may throw himself for general deliverance upon his country. In the first the Court may award a new trial, if the verdict for the defendant be contrary to the evidence or the law;—in the last it is conclusive and unalterable;—and to crown the whole, the King never had that process of attaint which belonged to the meanest of his subjects.

When these things are attentively considered, I might ask those who are still disposed to deny the right of the jury to investigate the whole charge, whether such a solecism can be conceived to exist in any human government, much less in the most refined and exalted in the world, as that a power of supreme judicature should be conferred at random by the blind forms of the law, where no right was intended to pass with it; and which was upon no occasion and under no circumstance to be exercised; which, though exerted notwithstanding in every age and in a thousand instances, to the confusion and discomfiture of fixed magistracy, should never be checked by authority, but should continue on from century to century; the revered guardian of liberty and of life, arresting the arm of the most headstrong governments in the worst of times, without any power in the Crown or its Judges, to touch, without its consent, the meanest wretch in the kingdom, or even to ask the reason and principle of the verdict which acquits him. That such a system should prevail in a country like England, without either the original institution or the acquiescing sanction of the legislature, is impossible. Believe, my Lord, no talents can reconcile, no authority can sanction such an absurdity;—the common sense of the world revolts at it.

Having established this important right in the jury beyond all possibility of cavil or controversy, I will now show your Lordship, that its existence is not merely consistent with the theory of the law, but is illustrated and confirmed by the universal practice of all Judges, not even excepting Mr Justice Forster himself, whose writings have been cited in support of the contrary opinion. How a man expresses his abstract ideas is but of little importance when an appeal can be made to his plain directions to others, and to his own particular conduct: but even none of his expressions, when properly considered and understood, militate against my position.

In his justly celebrated book on the criminal law, page 256, he expresses himself thus: " The construction which the law putteth upon fact STATED AND AGREED OR FOUND by a jury, *is in all cases undoubtedly the proper province of the Court.*" Now if the adversary is disposed to stop here, though the author never intended he should, as is evident from the rest of the sentence, yet I am willing to stop with him, and to take it as a substantive proposition ; for the slightest attention must discover that it is not repugnant to anything which I have said. Facts *stated and agreed*, or facts *found*, by a jury, which amount to the same thing, constitute a special verdict ; and who ever supposed that the law upon a special verdict was not the province of the Court? Where in a trial upon a general issue the parties choose to agree upon facts and to state them, or the jury choose voluntarily to find them without drawing the legal conclusion themselves; who ever denied that in such instances the Court is to draw it? That Forster meant nothing more than that the Court was to judge of the law when the jury thus voluntarily prays its assistance by special verdict, is evident from his words which follow, for he immediately goes on to say, in cases of doubt and REAL difficulty, it is therefore commonly recommended to the jury to state facts and circumstances in a special verdict: but neither here, nor in any other part of his works, is it said or insinuated that they are *bound* to do so, but at their own free discretion ; indeed, the very term *recommended* admits the contrary, and requires no commentary. I am sure I shall never dispute the wisdom or expediency of such a recommendation in those cases of doubt, because the more I am contending for the existence of such an important right, the less it would become me to be the advocate of rashness and precipitation in the exercise of it. It is no denial of jurisdiction to tell the greatest magistrate upon earth to take good counsel in cases of real doubt and difficulty. Judges upon trials, whose authority to state the law is indisputable, often refer it to be more solemnly argued before the Court; and this Court itself often holds a meeting of the twelve Judges before it decides on a point upon its own records, of which the others have confessedly no cognisance till it comes before them by the writ of error of one of the parties. These instances are monuments of wisdom, integrity, and discretion, but they do not bear in the remotest degree upon jurisdiction : the sphere of jurisdiction is measured by what may or may not be decided by any given tribunal with legal effect, not by the rectitude or error of the decision. If the jury, according to these authorities, may determine the whole matter by their verdict, and if the verdict when given is not only final and unalterable, but must be enforced by the authority of the Judges, and executed, if resisted, by the whole power of the state,—upon what principle of government or reason can it be argued not to be law ? That the jury are in this exact predicament is confessed by Forster ; for he concludes with saying, that when the law is clear, the jury, under the direction of the Court, in point of law *may*, and if they are well advised will, *always find a general verdict conformably to such directions.*

This is likewise consistent with my position : if the law be clear, we may presume that the Judge states it clearly to the jury ; and if he does, undoubtedly the jury, if they are well advised, will find according to such directions ; for they have not a capricious discretion to make law at their pleasure, but are bound in conscience as well as Judges are to find it truly ; and, generally speaking, the learning of the Judge who presides at the trial affords them a safe support and direction.

The same practice of Judges in stating the law to the jury, as applied to the particular case before them, appears likewise in the case of the King against Oneby, 2d Lord Raymond, page 1494 :—" On the trial the Judge directs the jury thus : If you believe such and such witnesses who have sworn to such and such facts, *the killing of the deceased appears to be with malice prepense :* but if you do not believe them, then you ought to find him guilty of manslaughter ; and the jury may, if they think proper, give a general verdict of murder or manslaughter : *but if they decline* giving a general verdict, and *will* find the facts specially, the Court is then to form their judgment from the facts found, whether the defendant be guilty or not guilty, *i.e.*, whether the act was done with malice and deliberation, or not." Surely language can express nothing more plainly or unequivocally, than that where the general issue is pleaded to an indictment, the law and the fact are both before the jury ; and that the former can never be separated from the latter, for the judgment of the Court, unless by their own spontaneous act : for their words are, " If they *decline* giving a general verdict, and *will* find the facts specially, the Court is THEN to form their judgment from the facts found." So that, after a general issue joined, the authority of the Court only commences when the jury chooses to decline the decision of the law by a general verdict ; the right of declining which legal determination is a privilege conferred on them by the statute of Westminster 2d, and by no means a restriction of their powers.

But another very important view of the subject remains behind: for supposing I had failed in establishing that contrast between criminal and civil cases, which is now too clear not only to require, but even to justify another observation, the argument would lose nothing by the failure; the similarity between criminal and civil cases derives all its application to the argument from the learned Judge's supposition, that the jurisdiction of the jury over the law was never contended for in the latter, and consequently on a principle of equality could not be supported in the former; whereas I do contend for it, and can incontestably establish it in both.   This application of the argument is plain from the words of the charge: " If the jury could find the law, it would undoubtedly hold in civil cases as well as criminal; but was it ever supposed that a jury was competent to say the operation of a fine, or a recovery, or a warranty, which are mere questions of law ? "

To this question I answer, that the competency of the jury in such cases is contended for to the full extent of my principle, both by Lyttleton and by Coke: they cannot indeed decide upon them *de plano*, which, as Vaughan truly says, is unintelligible, because an unmixed question of law can by no possibility come before them for decision; but whenever (which very often happens) the operation of a fine, a recovery, a warranty, or any other record or conveyance known to the law of England comes forward, mixed with the fact on the general issue, the jury have then most unquestionably a right to determine it; and what is more, no other authority possibly can; because, when the general issue is permitted by law, these questions cannot appear on the record for the judgment of the Court, and although it can grant a new trial, yet the same question must ultimately be determined by another jury.   This is not only self-evident to every lawyer, but, as I said, is expressly laid down by Lyttleton in the 368th section. " Also in such case where the inquest may give their verdict at large, if they will take upon them the knowledge of the law upon the matter, they may give their verdict generally as it is put in their charge : as in the case aforesaid they may well say, that the lessor did not disseise the lessee if they will."   Coke, in his commentary on this section, confirms Lyttleton; saying, that in doubtful cases they should find specially for fear of an attaint; and it is plain that the statute of Westminster the 2d, was made either to give or to confirm the right of the jury to find the matter specially, leaving their jurisdiction over the law as it stood by the common law.   The words of the statute of Westminster 2d, chapter 30th, are, " Ordinatum est quod justitiarii ad assisas capiendas assignati, *non compellant* juratores dicere precise si sit disscisina vel non ; dummodo voluerint dicere veritatem facti et petere

auxilium justitiariorum." From these words it should appear,
that the jurisdiction of the jury over the law when it came before
them on the general issue, was so vested in them by the constitution, that the exercise of it in all cases had been considered to be
compulsory upon them, and that this act was a legislative relief
from that compulsion in the case of an assize of disseisin: it is
equally plain from the remaining words of the act, that their
jurisdiction remained as before; "sed si sponte velint dicere quod
disseisina est vel non, admittatur eorum veredictum sub suo
periculo."

But the most material observation upon this statute, as applicable to the present subject, is, that the terror of the attaint from
which it was passed to relieve them, having (as has been shown)
no existence in cases of crime, the act only extended to relieve the
jury at their discretion from finding the law in civil actions; and
consequently it is only from custom, and not from positive law,
that they are not *even compellable* to give a general verdict
involving a judgment of law on every criminal trial.

These principles and authorities certainly establish that it is the
duty of the judge, on every trial where the general issue is
pleaded, to give to the jury his opinion on the law as applied to
the case before them; and that they must find a general verdict
comprehending a judgment of law, unless they *choose* to refer it
specially to the Court.

But we are here, in a case where it is contended, that the duty
of the judge is the direct contrary of this:—that he is to give no
opinion at all to the jury upon the law as applied to the case
before them; that they likewise are to refrain from all consideration of it, and yet that the very same general verdict comprehending both fact and law, is to be given by them as if the whole legal
matter had been summed up by the one and found by the
other.

I confess I have no organs to comprehend the principle on
which such a practice proceeds. I contended for nothing more at
the trial than the very practice recommended by Forster and Lord
Raymond: I addressed myself to the jury upon the law with all
possible respect and deference, and indeed with very marked
personal attention to the learned Judge: so far from urging the
jury, dogmatically to think for themselves without his constitutional assistance, I called for his opinion on the question of libel;
saying, that if he should tell them distinctly the paper indicted
was libellous, though I should not admit that they were bound at
all events to give effect to it if they felt it to be innocent; yet I
was ready to agree that they ought not to go against the charge
without great consideration: but that if he should shut himself
up in silence, giving no opinion at all upon the criminality of the
paper from which alone any guilt could be fastened on the

publisher, and should narrow their consideration to the publication,
I entered my protest against their finding a verdict affixing the
epithet of *guilty* to the mere fact of publishing a paper, the *guilt*
of which had not been investigated. If, after this address to the
jury, the learned Judge had told them, that in his opinion the
paper was a libel, but still leaving it to their judgments, and likewise the defendant's evidence to their consideration, had further
told them, that he thought it did not exculpate the publication;
and if in consequence of such directions the jury had found a verdict for the Crown, I should never have made my present motion
for a new trial; because I should have considered such a verdict
of Guilty as founded upon the opinion of the jury on the whole
matter as left to their consideration, and must have sought my
remedy by arrest of judgment on the record.

But the learned Judge took a direct contrary course: he gave no
opinion at all on the guilt or innocence of the paper ; he took no
notice of the defendant's evidence of intention : he told the jury, in
the most explicit terms, that neither the one nor the other were
within their jurisdiction ; and upon the mere fact of publication
directed a general verdict comprehending the epithet of *Guilty*,
after having expressly withdrawn from the jury every consideration
of the merits of the paper published, or the intention of the publisher, from which it is admitted on all hands the *guilt* of publication could alone have any existence.

My motion is therefore founded upon this obvious and simple
principle ; that the defendant has had in fact NO TRIAL ; having
been found *guilty* without any investigation of his *guilt*, and without any power left to the jury to take cognisance of his innocence.
I undertake to show, that the jury could not possibly conceive or
believe from the Judge's charge, that they had any jurisdiction to
acquit him ; however they might have been impressed even with
the merit of the publication, or convinced of his meritorious intention in publishing it : nay, what is worse, while the learned Judge
totally deprived them of their whole jurisdiction over the question
of libel and the defendant's seditious intention, he at the same time
directed a general verdict of Guilty, which comprehended a judgment upon both.

When I put this construction on the learned Judge's direction,
I found myself wholly on the language in which it was communicated ; and it will be no answer to such construction, that no such
restraint was meant to be conveyed by it. If the learned Judge's
intentions were even the direct contrary of his expressions, yet if,
in consequence of that which was expressed though not intended,
the jury were abridged of a jurisdiction which belonged to them by
law, and in the exercise of which the defendant had an interest, he
is equally a sufferer, and the verdict given under such misconception of authority is equally void : my application ought therefore

to stand or fall by the charge itself, upon which I disclaim all disingenuous cavilling.   I am certainly bound to show, that from the
general result of it, fairly and liberally interpreted, the jury could
not conceive that they had any right to extend their consideration
beyond the bare fact of publication, so as to acquit the defendant
by a judgment founded on the legality of the dialogue, or the
honesty of the intention in publishing it.

In order to understand the learned Judge's direction, it must be
recollected that it was addressed to them in answer to me, who had
contended for nothing more than that these two considerations
ought to rule the verdict ; and it will be seen that the charge, on
the contrary, not only excluded both of them by general inference,
but by expressions, arguments, and illustrations the most studiously
selected to convey that exclusion, and to render it binding on the
consciences of the jury.   After telling them in the very beginning
of his charge, that the single question for their decision was,
whether the defendant had published the pamphlet? he declared
to them, that it was not even *allowed to him, as the Judge trying
the cause*, to say whether it was or was not a libel : for that if he
should say it was no libel, and they, following his direction, should
acquit the defendant, they would thereby deprive the prosecutor of
his writ of error upon the record, which was one of his dearest
birthrights.   The law, he said, was equal between the prosecutor
and the defendant ; that a verdict of acquittal would close the
matter for ever, depriving him of his appeal ; and that whatever
therefore was upon the record *was not for their decision*, but might
be carried at the pleasure of either party to the House of Lords.

Surely language could not convey a limitation upon the right of
the jury over the question of libel, or the intention of the publisher,
more positive or more universal.   It was positive, inasmuch as it
held out to them that such a jurisdiction could not be entertained
without injustice ; and it was universal, because the principle had
no special application to the particular circumstances of that trial,
but subjected every defendant upon every prosecution for a libel,
to an inevitable conviction on the mere proof of publishing *anything*, though both judge and jury might be convinced that the
thing published was innocent, and even meritorious.

My Lord, I make this commentary without the hazard of contradiction from any man whose reason is not disordered.   For if
the prosecutor in every case has a birthright by law to have the
question of libel left open upon the record, which it can only be
by a verdict of conviction on the single fact of publishing ; no legal
right can at the same time exist in the jury to shut out that question by a verdict of acquittal, founded upon the merits of the publication, or the innocent mind of the publisher.   Rights that are
repugnant and contradictory, cannot be co-existent.   The jury can
never have a constitutional right to do an act beneficial to the

defendant, which, when done, deprives the prosecutor of a right which the same constitution has vested in him. No right can belong to one person, the exercise of which, in *every instance*, must necessarily work a wrong to another. If the prosecutor of a libel has, in *every* instance, the privilege to try the merits of his prosecution before the judges, the jury can have no right in *any* instance to preclude his appeal to them by a general verdict for the defendant.

The jury, therefore, from this part of the charge, must necessarily have felt themselves absolutely limited (I might say even in their powers) to the fact of publication, because the highest restraint upon good men is to convince them that they cannot break loose from it without injustice ; and the power of a good subject is never more effectually destroyed than when he is made to believe that the exercise of it will be a breach of his duty to the public, and a violation of the laws of his country.

But since equal justice between the prosecutor and the defendant is the pretence for this abridgment of jurisdiction, let us examine a little how it is affected by it. Do the prosecutor and the defendant really stand upon an equal footing by this mode of proceeding ? With what decency this can be alleged, I leave those to answer who know that it is only by the indulgence of Mr Bearcroft, of counsel for the prosecution, that my reverend client is not at this moment in prison * while we are discussing this notable equality. Besides, my Lord, the judgment of this Court, though not final in the constitution, and therefore not binding on the prosecutor, is absolutely conclusive on the defendant. If your Lordships pronounce the record to contain no libel, and arrest the judgment on the verdict, the prosecutor may carry it to the House of Lords, and, pending his writ of error, remains untouched by your Lordship's decision. But if judgment be against the defendant, it is only at the discretion of the Crown (as it is said), and not of right, that he can prosecute any writ of error at all ; and even f he finds no obstruction in that quarter, it is but at the best an appeal for the benefit of public liberty, from which he himself can have no personal benefit ; for the writ of error being no supersedeas, he punishment is inflicted on him in the meantime. In the case f Mr Horne,† this Court imprisoned him for publishing a libel pon its own judgment, pending his appeal from its justice ; and e had suffered the utmost rigour which the law imposed upon im as a criminal, at the time that the House of Lords, with the ssistance of the twelve judges of England, were gravely assembled

* Lord Mansfield ordered the Dean to be committed on the motion for the new ial, and said he had no discretion to suffer him to be at large, without consent, ter his appearance in Court on conviction. Upon which Mr Bearcroft gave his nsent that the Dean should remain at large upon bail.

† Afterwards Mr Horne Tooke, whose writings do honour to our language and untry.

to determine whether he had been guilty of any crime. I do not mention this case as hard or rigorous on Mr Horne, as an individual; it is the general course of practice, but surely that practice ought to put an end to this argument of equality between prosecutor and prisoner. It is adding insult to injury to tell an innocent man who is in a dungeon, pending his writ of error, and of whose innocence both judge and jury were convinced at the trial, that he is in equal scales with his prosecutor, who is at large, because he has an opportunity of deciding, after the expiration of his punishment, that the prosecution had been unfounded, and his sufferings unjust. By parity of reasoning, a prisoner in a capital case might be hanged in the meantime for the benefit of equal justice, leaving his executors to fight the battle out with his prosecutor upon the record, through every court in the kingdom, by which, at last, his attainder might be reversed, and the blood of his posterity remain uncorrupted. What justice can be more impartial or equal?

So much for this right of the prosecutor of a libel to *compel* a jury in every case generally to convict a defendant on the fact of publication, or to find a special verdict—a right unheard of before since the birth of the constitution—not even founded upon any equality in fact, even if such a shocking parity could exist in law, and not even contended to exist in any other case where private men become the prosecutors of crimes for the ends of public justice. It can have, generally speaking, no existence in any prosecution for felony, because the general description of the crime in such indictments, for the most part, shuts out the legal question in the particular instance from appearing on the record; and for the same reason, it can have no place even in appeals of death, &c., the only cases where prosecutors appear as the revengers of their own private wrongs, and not as the representatives of the Crown.

The learned Judge proceeded next to establish the same universal limitation upon the power of the jury, from the history of different trials, and the practice of former judges who presided at them; and while I am complaining of what I conceive to be injustice, I must take care not to be unjust myself. I certainly do not, nor ever did, consider the learned Judge's misdirection in his charge to be peculiar to himself; it was only the resistance of the defendant's evidence, and what passed after the jury returned into Court with the verdict, that I ever considered to be a departure from all precedents; the rest had undoubtedly the sanction of several modern cases; and I wish, therefore, to be distinctly understood, that I partly found my motion for a new trial in opposition to these decisions. It is my duty to speak with deference of all the judgments of this Court; and I feel an additional respect for some of those I am about to combat, because they are your Lordship's; but comparing them with the judgments of your predecessors for ages, which is the highest evidence of English law, I must be forgiven if I presume to question their authority.

My Lord, it is necessary that I should take notice of some of them, as they occur in the learned Judge's charge; for although he is not responsible for the rectitude of those precedents which he only cited in support of it, yet the defendant is unquestionably entitled to a new trial, if their principles are not ratified by the Court; for whenever the learned Judge cited precedents to warrant the limitation on the province of the jury imposed by his own authority, it was such an adoption of the doctrines they contained as made them a rule to the jury in their decision.

First then, the learned Judge, to overturn my argument with the jury for their jurisdiction over the whole charge, opposed your Lordship's established practice for eight and twenty years; and the weight of this great authority was increased by the general manner in which it was stated, for I find no expressions of your Lordship's in any of the reported cases which go the length contended for. I find the practice, indeed, fully warranted by them; but I do not meet with the principle which can alone vindicate that practice fairly and distinctly avowed. The learned Judge, therefore, referred to the charge of Chief-Justice Raymond, in the case of the King and Franklin, in which the universal limitation contended for is indeed laid down, not only in the most unequivocal expressions, but the ancient jurisdiction of juries, resting upon all the authorities I have cited, treated as a ridiculous notion which had been just taken up a little before the year 1731, and which no man living had ever dreamed of before. The learned Judge observed that Lord Raymond stated to the jury, on Franklin's trial, that there were three questions: the first was, the fact of publishing the *Craftsman*; secondly, whether the averments in the information were true; but that the third, viz., whether it was a libel, was merely a question of *law*, with which the jury *had nothing to do*, as had been then of late thought by some people who ought to have known better.

This direction of Lord Raymond's was fully ratified and adopted in all its extent, and given to the jury, on the present trial, with several others of the same import, as an unerring guide for their conduct; and surely human ingenuity could not frame a more abstract and universal limitation upon their right to acquit the defendant by a general verdict; for Lord Raymond's expressions amount to an absolute denial of the right of the jury to find the defendant not guilty, if the publication and innuendoes are proved. ' Libel or no libel, is a question of law, with which you, the jury, have *nothing to do*." How then can they have any right to give a general verdict consistently with this declaration? Can any man in his senses collect that he has a right to decide on that with which he has nothing to do?

But it is needless to comment on these expressions, for the jury were likewise told by the learned Judge himself, that, if they believed the fact of publication, they were *bound* to find the defendant guilty ; and it will hardly be contended, that a man has a right to refrain from doing that which he is bound to do.

Mr Cowper, as counsel for the prosecution, took upon him to explain what was meant by this expression ; and I seek for no other construction : " The learned Judge (said he) did not mean to deny the right of the jury, but only to convey, that there was a religious and moral obligation upon them to refrain from the exercise of it." Now, if the principle which imposed that obligation had been alleged to be *special*, applying only to the *particular case of the Dean of St Asaph*, and consequently consistent with the right of the jury to a more enlarged jurisdiction in *other* instances ; telling the jury that they were bound to convict on proof of publication, might be plausibly construed into a recommendation to refrain from the exercise of their right in *that case*, and not to a *general* denial of its existence : but the moment it is recollected that the principle which bound them was not *particular* to the instance, but abstract and universal, binding alike in *every* prosecution for a libel, it requires no logic to pronounce the expression to be an absolute, unequivocal, and universal denial of the right : common sense tells every man, that to speak of a person's right to do a thing, which yet, in every possible instance where it might be exerted, he is religiously and morally bound not to exert, is not even sophistry, but downright vulgar nonsense. But the jury were not only limited by these modern precedents, which certainly have an existence ; but were in my mind limited with still greater effect by the learned Judge's declaration, that some of those ancient authorities on which I had principally relied for the establishment of their jurisdiction, had not merely been overruled, but were altogether inapplicable. I particularly observed how much ground I lost with the jury when they were told from the Bench, that even in Bushel's case, on which I had so greatly depended, the very reverse of my doctrine had been expressly established : the Court having said unanimously in that case, according to the learned Judge's statement, that if the jury be asked what the law is, they cannot say, and having likewise ratified in express terms the maxim, *ad quæstionem legis non respondent juratores.*

My Lord, this declaration from the Bench, which I confess not a little staggered and surprised me, rendered it my duty to look again into Vaughan, where Bushel's case is reported : I have performed that duty, and now take upon me positively to say, that the words of Lord Chief-Justice Vaughan, which the learned Judge considered as a judgment of the Court, denying the jurisdiction of the jury over the law, *where a general issue is joined before them*, were, on the contrary, made use of by that learned and excellent person, to expose the fallacy of such a misapplication of the maxim alluded to, by the counsel against Bushel ; declaring that it had no reference to any case where the law and the fact were incorporated by the plea of not guilty, and confirming the right of the jury to find the law upon every such issue, in terms the most emphatical and expressive. This is manifest from the whole report.

Bushel, one of the jurors on the trial of Penn and Mead, had been committed by the Court for finding the defendant not guilty, against the direction of the Court in matter of law; and being brought before the Court of Common Pleas by *habeas corpus*, this cause of commitment appeared upon the face of the return to the writ. It was contended by the counsel against Bushel, upon the authority of this maxim, that the commitment was legal, since it appeared by the return that Bushel had taken upon him to find the law against the direction of the Judge, and had been, therefore, legally imprisoned for that contempt. It was upon that occasion that Chief-Justice Vaughan, with the concurrence of the whole Court, repeated the maxim, *ad quæstionem legis non respondent juratores*, as cited by the counsel for the Crown, but denied the application of it to impose any restraint upon jurors trying any crime upon the general issue. His language is too remarkable to be forgotten, and too plain to be misunderstood. Taking the words of the return to the *habeas corpus*,—viz., " That the jury did acquit against the direction of the Court in matter of law,"—" These words," said this great lawyer, " taken literally and *de plano*, are insignificant and unintelligible, for no issue can be joined of matter of law;—no jury can be charged with the trial of matter of law barely;—no evidence ever was, or can be given to a jury of what is law or not; nor any oath given to a jury to try matter of law *alone ;* nor can any attaint lie for such a false oath. Therefore we must take off this veil and colour of words, which make a show of being something, but are in fact nothing : for if the meaning of these words, *Finding against the direction of the Court in matter of law*, be, that if the Judge, having heard the evidence given in court (for he knows no other), shall tell the jury upon this evidence that the law is for the plaintiff or the defendant, and they, under the pain of fine and imprisonment, are to find accordingly, every one sees that the jury is but a troublesome delay, great charge, and of no use in determining right and wrong ; which were a strange and new-found conclusion, after a trial so celebrated for many hundreds of years in this country."

Lord Chief-Justice Vaughan's argument is therefore plainly this. Adverting to the arguments of the counsel, he says, You talk of the maxim *ad quæstionem legis non respondent juratores*, but it has no sort of application to your subject. The words of your return,— viz., that Bushel did acquit against the direction of the Court in matter of law, are unintelligible, and, as applied to the case, impossible. The jury could not be asked in the abstract, what was the law: they could not have an issue of the law joined before them: they could not be sworn to try it. *Ad quæstionem legis non respondent juratores*: therefore to say literally and *de plano* that the jury found the law against the Judge's direction is absurd: they could not be in a situation to find it;—an unmixed question of law could not be before them:—the Judge could not give any positive directions of law upon the trial, for the law can only arise out of facts, and the Judge cannot know what the facts are till the jury have given their verdict. Therefore, continued the Chief-Justice, let us take off this veil and colour of words, which make a show of being something, but are in fact nothing: let us get rid of the fallacy of applying a maxim, which truly describes the jurisdiction of the Courts over issues of law, to destroy the jurisdiction of jurors, in cases where law and fact are blended together upon a trial:— since, if the jury at the trial are bound to receive the law from the Judge, every one sees that it is a mere mockery, and of no use in determining right and wrong. This is the plain common sense of the argument; and it is impossible to suggest a distinction between its application to Bushel's case and to the present, except that the right of imprisoning the jurors was there contended for, in order to enforce obedience to the directions of the Judge. But this distinction, if it deserves the name, though held up by Mr Bearcroft as very important, is a distinction without a difference. For if, according to Vaughan, the free agency of the jury over the whole charge, uncontrolled by the Judge's direction, constitutes the whole of that ancient mode of trial, it signifies nothing by what means that free agency is destroyed: whether by the imprisonment of conscience or of body: by the operation of their virtues or of their fears. Whether they decline exerting their jurisdiction from being told that the exertion of it is a contempt of religious and moral order, or a contempt of the Court punishable by imprisonment; their jurisdiction is equally taken away.

My Lord, I should be very sorry improperly to waste the time of the Court, but I cannot help repeating once again, that if, in consequence of the learned Judge's directions, the jury, from a just deference to learning and authority, from a nice and modest sense of duty, felt themselves not at liberty to deliver the defendant from the whole indictment, HE HAS NOT BEEN TRIED: because, though he was entitled by law to plead generally that he was not guilty; though he did in fact plead it accordingly, and went down to trial upon it, yet the jury have not been permitted to try that issue, but have been directed to find at all events a general verdict of guilty, with a positive injunction not to investigate the guilt, or even to listen to any evidence of innocence.

My Lord, I cannot help contrasting this trial with that of Colonel Gordon's but a few sessions past in London. I had in my hand·

but this moment an accurate note of Mr Baron Eyre's* charge to the jury on that occasion ; I will not detain the Court by looking for it amongst my papers, because I believe I can correctly repeat the substance of it.

EARL OF MANSFIELD. The case of the King *v.* Cosmo Gordon ?

Mr ERSKINE. Yes, my Lord: Colonel Gordon was indicted for the murder of General Thomas, whom he had killed in a duel : and the question was, whether, if the jury were satisfied of that fact, the prisoner was to be convicted of murder ? That was, according to Forster, as much a question of law as libel or no libel : but Mr Baron Eyre did not therefore feel himself at liberty to withdraw it from the jury. After stating (greatly to his honour) the hard condition of the prisoner, who was brought to a trial for life, in a case where the positive law and the prevailing manners of the times were so strongly in opposition to one another, that he was afraid the punishment of individuals would never be able to beat down an offence so sanctioned, he addressed the jury nearly in these words : " Nevertheless, gentlemen, I am bound to declare to you what the law is as applied to this case, in all the different views in which it can be considered by you upon the evidence. *Of this law, and of the facts as you shall find them, your verdict must be compounded ;* and I persuade myself, that it will be such a one as to give satisfaction to your own consciences."

Now, if Mr Baron Eyre, instead of telling the jury that a duel, however fairly and honourably fought, was a murder by the law of England, and leaving them to find a general verdict under that direction, had said to them, that whether such a duel was murder or manslaughter, was a question with which neither he nor they had anything to do, and on which he should therefore deliver no opinion ; and had directed them to find that the prisoner was guilty of killing the deceased in a deliberate duel, telling them that the Court would settle the rest, that would have been directly consonant to the case of the Dean of St Asaph. By this direction the prisoner would have been in the hands of the Court, and the judges, not the jury, would have decided upon the life of Colonel Gordon.

But the two learned judges differ most essentially indeed. Mr Baron Eyre conceives himself bound in duty to state the law as applied to the particular facts, and to leave it to the jury. Mr Justice Buller says he is not bound, nor even allowed, so to state or apply it, and withdraws it entirely from their consideration. Mr Baron Eyre tells the jury that their verdict is to be compounded of the fact and the law. Mr Justice Buller, on the contrary, that it is to be confined to the fact only, the law being the exclusive province of the Court. My Lord, it is not for me to settle differences of opinion between the judges of England, nor to pronounce which

* Late Lord Chief-Baron.

of them is wrong; but since they are contradictory and inconsistent, I may hazard the assertion that they cannot both be right:
the authorities which I have cited, and the general sense of mankind, which settles everything else, must determine the rest.

My Lord, I come now to a very important part of the case, untouched I believe before in any of the arguments on this occasion.

I mean to contend that the learned Judge's charge to the jury
cannot be supported even upon its own principles; for, supposing
the Court to be of opinion that all I have said in opposition to
these principles is inconclusive, and that the question of libel, and
the intention of the publisher, were properly withdrawn from the
consideration of the jury, still I think I can make it appear that
such a judgment would only render the misdirection more palpable
and striking.

I may safely assume that the learned Judge must have meant
to direct the jury either to find a general or a special verdict; or,
to speak more generally, that one of these two verdicts must be the
object of every charge; because I venture to affirm, that neither
the records of the courts, the reports of their proceedings, nor the
writings of lawyers, furnish any account of a third. There can be
no middle verdict between both; the jury must either try the
whole issue generally, or find the facts specially, referring the legal
conclusion to the Court.

I may affirm with equal certainty, that the general verdict, *ex
vi termini*, is universally as comprehensive as the issue, and that
consequently such a verdict on an indictment, upon the general
issue, not guilty, universally and unavoidably involves a judgment
of law as well as fact; because the charge comprehends both, and
the verdict, as has been said, is coextensive with it. Both Coke
and Littleton give this precise definition of a general verdict, for
they both say that if the jury will find the law, they may do it by
a general verdict, which is ever as large as the issue. If this be
so, it follows by necessary consequence that if the Judge means to
direct the jury to find generally against a defendant, he must leave
to their consideration everything which goes to the constitution of
such a general verdict, and is therefore bound to permit them to
come to, and to direct them how to form that general conclusion
from the law and the fact, which is involved in the term guilty.
For it is ridiculous to say that guilty is a fact; it is a conclusion
in law from a fact, and therefore can have no place in a special
verdict where the legal conclusion is left to the Court.

In this case the defendant is charged, not with having published
this pamphlet, but with having published a certain false, scandalous,
and seditious libel, with a seditious and rebellious intention. He
pleads that he is not guilty in manner and form as he is accused;
which plea is admitted on all hands to be a denial of the whole
charge, and consequently does not merely put in issue the fact of

publishing the pamphlet, but the truth of the whole indictment, i.e., the publication of the libel set forth in it, with the intention charged by it.

When this issue comes down for trial, the jury must either find the whole charge or a part of it; and admitting, for argument sake, that the Judge has a right to dictate either of these two courses, he is undoubtedly bound in law to make his direction to the jury conformable to the one or the other. If he means to confine the jury to the fact of publishing, considering the guilt of the defendant to be a legal conclusion for the Court to draw from that fact, specially found on the record, he ought to direct the jury to find that fact without affixing the epithet of guilty to the finding. But if he will have a general verdict of guilty, which involves a judgment of law as well as fact, he must leave the law to the consideration of the jury; since when the word guilty is pronounced by them, it is so well understood to comprehend everything charged by the indictment, that the associate or his clerk instantly records that the defendant is guilty in manner and form as he is accused, i.e., not simply that he has *published* the pamphlet contained in the indictment, but that he is *guilty of publishing the libel* with the wicked intentions charged on him by the record.

Now, if this effect of a general verdict of guilty is reflected on for a moment, the illegality of directing one upon the bare fact of publishing will appear in the most glaring colours. The learned Judge says to the jury, whether this be a libel is not for your consideration; I can give no opinion on that subject without injustice to the prosecutor; and as to what Mr Jones swore concerning the defendant's motives for the publication, that is likewise not before you: for if you are satisfied in point of fact that the defendant *published* this pamphlet, you are bound to find him *guilty*. Why guilty, my Lord, when the consideration of guilt is withdrawn? He confines the jury to the finding of a fact, and enjoins them to leave the legal conclusion from it to the Court; yet, instead of directing them to make that fact the subject of a special verdict, he desires them in the same breath to find a general one; to draw the conclusion without any attention to the premises; to pronounce a verdict which, upon the face of the record, includes a judgment upon their oaths that the paper is a libel, and that the publisher's intentions in publishing it were wicked and seditious, although neither the one nor the other made any part of their consideration. My Lord, such a verdict is a monster in law, without precedent in former times, or root in the constitution. If it be true, on the principle of the charge itself, that the fact of publication was all that the jury were to find, and all that was necessary to establish the defendant's guilt, if the thing published be a libel, why was not that fact found like all other facts upon special verdicts? Why was an epithet, which is a legal conclusion from the fact,

extorted from a jury who were restrained from forming it themselves? The verdict must be taken to be general or special : if
general, it has found the whole issue without a coextensive examination ; if special, the word Guilty, which is a conclusion from
facts, can have no place in it. Either this word Guilty is operative
or unessential ; an epithet of substance or of form. It is impossible
to controvert that proposition, and I give the gentlemen their choice
of the alternative. If they admit it to be operative and of real
substance, or, to speak more plainly, that the fact of publication
found specially, without the epithet of guilty, would have been an
imperfect verdict inconclusive of the defendant's guilt, and on
which no judgment could have followed : then it is impossible to
deny that the defendant has suffered injustice, because such an
admission confesses that a criminal conclusion from a fact has
been obtained from the jury, without permitting them to exercise
that judgment which might have led them to a conclusion of innocence ; and that the word Guilty has been obtained from them at
the trial as a mere matter of form, although the verdict without it,
stating only the fact of publication, which they were directed to
find, to which they thought the finding alone enlarged, and beyond
which they had never enlarged their inquiry, would have been an
absolute verdict of acquittal. If, on the other hand, to avoid this
insuperable objection to the charge, the word guilty is to be reduced
to a mere word of form, and it is to be contended that the fact of
publication found specially would have been tantamount : be it so ;
let the verdict be so recorded ; let the word Guilty be expunged
from it, and I instantly sit down ; I trouble your Lordships no
further. I withdraw my motion for a new trial, and will maintain
in arrest of judgment that the Dean is not convicted. But if this
is not conceded to me, and the word Guilty, though argued to be
but form, and though as such obtained from the jury, is still preserved upon the record, and made use of against the defendant as
substance, it will then become us (independently of all consideration as lawyers) to consider a little how that argument is to be
made consistent with the honour of gentlemen, or that fairness
of dealing which cannot but have place wherever justice is administered.

But in order to establish that the word Guilty is a word of
essential substance, that the verdict would have been imperfect
without it, and that therefore the defendant suffers by its insertion,
I undertake to show your Lordship, upon every principle and
authority of law, that if the fact of publication, which was all that
was left to the jury, had been found by special verdict, no judgment
could have been given on it.

My Lord, I will try this by taking the fullest finding which the
facts in evidence could possibly have warranted. Supposing then,
for instance, that the jury had found that the defendant published

the paper according to the tenor of the indictment, that it was written of and concerning the King and his Government, and that the innuendoes were likewise as averred, K. meaning the present King, and P. the present Parliament of Great Britain; on such a finding, no judgment could have been given by the Court, even if the record had contained a complete charge of a libel.   No principle is more unquestionable than that, to warrant any judgment upon a special verdict, the Court, which can presume nothing that is not visible on the record, must see sufficient matter upon the face of it, which, if taken to be true, is conclusive of the defendant's guilt.   They must be able to say, If this record be true, the defendant cannot be innocent of the crime which it charges on him. But from the facts of such a verdict the Court could arrive at no such legitimate conclusion; for it is admitted on all hands, and indeed expressly laid down by your Lordship in the case of the King against Woodfall, that publication even of a libel is not *conclusive* evidence of guilt, for that the defendant may give evidence of an innocent publication.

Looking, therefore, upon a record containing a good indictment of a libel, and a verdict finding that the defendant published it, but without the epithet of guilty, the Court could not pronounce that he published it with the malicious intention which is the essence of the crime; they could not say what might have passed at the trial; for anything that appeared to them, he might have given such evidence of innocent motive, necessity, or mistake, as might have amounted to excuse or justification.   They would say, that the facts stated upon the verdict would have been fully sufficient, in the absence of a legal defence, to have warranted the Judge to have directed, and the jury to have given, a general verdict of guilty, comprehending the intention which constitutes the crime; but that to warrant the Bench, which is ignorant of everything at the trial, to presume that intention, and thereupon to pronounce judgment on the record, the jury must not merely find full evidence of the crime, but such facts as compose its legal definition. This wise principle is supported by authorities which are perfectly familiar.

If, in an action of trover, the plaintiff proves property in himself, possession in the defendant, and a demand and refusal of the thing charged to be converted, this evidence, unanswered, is full proof of a conversion; and if the defendant could not show to the jury why he had refused to deliver the plaintiff's property on a legal demand of it, the Judge would direct them to find him guilty of the conversion.   But on the same facts found by special verdict, no judgment could be given by the Court; the judges would say, the special verdict contains the whole of the evidence given at the trial, the jury should have found the defendant guilty, for the conversion was fully proved; but we cannot declare these facts to amount to a conversion, for the defendant's intention was a fact which the jury should have found from the evidence, over which we have no jurisdiction. So in the case put by Lord Coke, I believe, in his first Institute, 115. If a modus is found to have existed beyond memory till within thirty years before the trial, the Court cannot, upon such facts found by special verdict, pronounce against the modus; but any one of your Lordships would certainly tell the jury that, upon such evidence, they were warranted in finding against it. In all cases of prescription, the universal practice of judges is to direct juries, by analogy to the statute of limitations, to decide against incorporeal rights, which for many years have been relinquished; but such modern relinquishments, if stated upon the record by special verdict, would in no instance warrant a judgment against any prescription. The principle of the difference is obvious and universal; the Court, looking at a record, can presume nothing; it has nothing to do with reasonable probabilities, but is to establish legal certainties by its judgments. Every crime is, like every other complex idea, capable of a legal definition; if all the component parts which go to its formation are put as facts upon the record, the Court can pronounce the perpetrator of them a criminal; but if any of them are wanting, it is a chasm in fact, and cannot be supplied. Wherever intention goes to the essence of the charge, it must be found by the jury; it must be either comprehended under the word guilty in the general verdict, or specifically found as a fact by the special verdict. This was solemnly decided by the Court in Huggins's case, in second Lord Raymond, 1581, which was a special verdict of murder from the Old Bailey.

It was an indictment against John Huggins and James Barnes, for the murder of Edward Arne. The indictment charged that Barnes made an assault upon Edward Arne, being in the custody of the other prisoner, Huggins, and detained him for six weeks in a room newly built over the common sewer of the prison, where he languished and died. The indictment further charged that Barnes and Huggins well knew that the room was unwholesome and dangerous; the indictment then charged that the prisoner Huggins, of his malice aforethought, was present, aiding and abetting Barnes to commit the murder aforesaid. This was the substance of the indictment.

The special verdict found that Huggins was warden of the Fleet by letters-patent; that the other prisoner, Barnes, was servant to Gibbons Huggins, deputy in the care of all the prisoners, and of the deceased, a prisoner there. That the prisoner Barnes, on the 7th of September, put the deceased Arne in a room over the common sewer, which had been newly built, knowing it to be newly built, and damp, and situated as laid in the indictment; *and that fifteen days before the prisoner's death, HUGGINS likewise well knew that the room was new built, damp, and situated as laid.   They found that, fifteen days before the death* of the prisoner, Huggins was present in the room, and saw him there under duress of imprisonment, *but then and there turned away, and Barnes locked the door; and that, from that time till his death, the deceased remained locked up.*

It was argued before the twelve judges in Serjeants' Inn, whether Huggins wás guilty of murder.   It was agreed that he was not answerable, *criminally*, for the act of his deputy, and could not be guilty unless the criminal intention was brought personally home to himself.   And it is remarkable how strongly the judges required the fact of knowledge and malice to be stated on the face of the verdict, as opposed to *evidence* of intention and inference from a fact.

The Court said, It is chiefly relied on that Huggins was present in the room, and saw Arne *sub duritie imprisonamenti, et se avertit;* but he might be present and not know all the circumstances.   The words are VIDIT *sub duritie;* but he might *see* him under duress, and not *know* he was under duress.   It was answered, that seeing him under duress evidently means he knew he was under duress; but, says the Court, "We cannot take things by inference in this manner; his seeing is but evidence of his knowledge of these things, and therefore the jury, if the fact would have borne it, should have found that Huggins knew he was there without his consent; which not being done, we cannot intend these things nor infer them ; we must judge of facts, and not from the evidence of facts ;" and cited Kelynge, 78, that whether a man be aiding and abetting a murder is matter of fact, and ought to be expressly found by a jury.

The application of these last principles and authorities to the case before the Court is obvious and simple.   The criminal intention is a fact, and must be found by the jury, and that finding can only be expressed upon the record by the general verdict of guilty, which comprehends it; or by the special enumeration of such facts as do not merely amount to evidence of, but which completely and conclusively constitute the crime.   But it has been shown, and is indeed admitted, that the publication of a libel is only *prima facie* evidence of the complex charge in the indictment, and not such a fact as amounts in itself, when specially stated, to conclusive guilt ; since, as the judges cannot tell how the criminal inference from the fact of publishing a libel might have been rebutted at the trial, no judgment can follow from a special finding that the defendant published the paper indicted according to the tenor laid in the indictment.   It follows from this, that if the jury had only found the fact of publication, which was all that was left to them, *without affixing the epithet of guilty*, which could only be legally affixed by an investigation not permitted to them,

a *venire facias de novo* must have been awarded because of the
uncertainty of the verdict as to the criminal intention ; whereas
it will now be argued that if the Court shall hold the dialogue to
be a libel, the defendant is fully convicted ; because the verdict
does not merely find that he PUBLISHED, which is a finding consistent with innocence, but finds him GUILTY of publishing, which
is a finding of the criminal publication charged by the indictment.

My Lord, how I shall be able to defend my innocent client
against such an argument I am not prepared to say. I feel all
the weight of it ; but that feeling surely entitles me to greater
attention when I complain of that which subjects him to it without
the warrant of the law. It is the weight of such an argument
that entitles me to a new trial ; for the Dean of St Asaph is not
only found guilty without any investigation of his guilt by the
jury, but without that question being even open to your Lordships
on the record. Upon the record the Court can only say the
dialogue is or is not a libel ; but if it should pronounce it to be
one, the criminal intention of the defendant in publishing it is
taken for granted by the word Guilty ; although it has not only
not been tried, but evidently appears from the verdict itself not to
have been found by the jury. Their verdict is, " Guilty of publishing ; but whether a libel or not, they do not find." And it is,
therefore, impossible to say that they can have found a criminal
motive in publishing a paper on the criminality of which they
have formed no judgment. Printing and publishing that which is
legal contains in it no crime ; the guilt must arise from the publication of a libel ; and there is therefore a palpable repugnancy on
the face of the verdict itself, which first finds the Dean guilty of
publishing, and then renders the finding a nullity, by pronouncing
ignorance in the jury whether the thing published comprehends
any guilt.

To conclude this part of the subject, the epithet of guilty (as I
set out with at first) must either be taken to be substance or form.
If it be substance, and, as such, conclusive of the *criminal* intention of the publisher, should the thing published be hereafter
adjudged to be a libel, I ask a new trial, because the defendant's
guilt in that respect has been found without having been tried ;
if, on the other hand, the word GUILTY is admitted to be but a word
of form, then let it be expunged, and I am not hurt by the verdict.

Having now established, according to my two first propositions,
that the jury, upon every general issue joined in a criminal case,
have a constitutional jurisdiction over the whole charge, I am next,
in support of my third, to contend that the case of a libel forms no
legal exception to the general principles which govern the trial of
all other crimes ; that the argument for the difference, viz., because
the whole charge always appears on the record, is false in fact, and
that, even if true, it would form no substantial difference in law.

As to the first, I still maintain that the whole case does by no means necessarily appear on the record. The Crown may indict part of the publication, which may bear a criminal construction when separated from the context, and the context omitted having no place in the indictment, the defendant can neither demur to it; nor arrest the judgment after a verdict of guilty, because the Court is absolutely circumscribed by what appears on the record, and the record contains a legal charge of a libel.

I maintain likewise, that according to the principles adopted upon this trial, he is equally shut out from such defence before the jury; for though he may read the explanatory context in evidence, yet he can derive no advantage from reading it, if they are tied down to find him guilty of publishing the matter which is contained in the indictment, however its innocence may be established by a view of the whole work. The only operation which, looking at the context, it can have upon a jury, is to convince them that the matter upon the record, however libellous when taken by itself, was not intended to convey the meaning which the words indicted import in language, when separated from the general scope of the writing; but upon the principle contended for, they could not acquit the defendant upon any such opinion, for that would be to take upon them the prohibited question of libel, which is said to be matter of law for the Court.

My learned friend, Mr Bearcroft, appealed to his audience with an air of triumph, whether any sober man could believe that an English jury, in the case I put from Algernon Sidney, would convict a defendant of publishing the Bible, should the Crown indict a member of a verse which was blasphemous in itself, if separated from the context? My Lord, if my friend had attended to me, he would have found that, in considering such supposition as an absurdity, he was only repeating my own words. I never supposed that a jury would act so wickedly, or so absurdly, in a case where the principle contended for by my friend Mr Bearcroft carried so palpable a face of injustice as in the instance which I selected to expose it, and which I therefore selected to show that there were cases in which the supporters of the doctrine were ashamed of it, and obliged to deny its operation; for it is impossible to deny that, if the jury can look at the context in the case put by Sidney, and acquit the defendant on the merits of the thing published, they may do it in cases which will directly operate against the principle seems to support. This will appear from other instances where the injustice is equal, but not equally striking.

Suppose the Crown were to select some passage from Locke upon Government, as for instance, " that there was no difference *between King and the constable when either of them exceeded their authority*." That assertion, under certain circumstances, if taken itself without the context, might be highly seditious, and the question therefore would be *quo animo* it was written ; perhaps the real meaning of the sentence might not be discoverable by the immediate context without a view of the whole chapter,—perhaps of the whole book ; therefore, to do justice to the defendant, upon the very principle by which Mr Bearcroft, in answering Sidney's case, can alone acquit the publisher of his Bible, the jury must look into the whole " Essay on Government," and form a judgment of the design of the author, and the meaning of his work.

Lord MANSFIELD. To be sure, they may judge from the whole work.

Mr ERSKINE. And what is this, my Lord, but determining the question of libel which is denied to-day ? for if a jury may acquit the publisher of any part of Mr Locke on Government, from a judgment arising out of a view of the whole book, though there be no innuendoes to be filled up as facts in the indictment,—what is it that bound the jury to convict the Dean of St Asaph as the publisher of Sir William Jones's Dialogue, on the bare fact of publication, without the right of saying that his observations, as well as Mr Locke's, were speculative, abstract, and legal ?

Lord MANSFIELD. They certainly may, in all cases, go into the whole context.

Mr ERSKINE. And why may they go into the context ? Clearly, my Lord, to enable them to form a correct judgment of the meaning of the part indicted, even though no particular meaning be submitted to them by averments in the indictment ; and therefore, the very permission to look at the context for such a purpose (where there are no innuendoes to be filled up by them as facts), is a palpable admission of all I am contending for, viz., the right of the jury to judge of the merits of the paper, and the intention of its author.*

But it is said, that though a jury have a right to decide that a paper, criminal as far as it appears on the record, is nevertheless legal when explained by the whole work of which it is a part ; yet that they shall have no right to say that the whole work itself, if it happens to be all indicted, is innocent and legal. This proposition, my Lord, upon the bare stating of it, seems too preposterous to be seriously entertained ; yet there is no alternative between maintaining it in its full extent, and abandoning the whole argument.

If the defendant is indicted for publishing part of the verse in the Psalms, " There is no God," it is asserted that the jury may look at the context, and, seeing that the whole verse did not maintain that blasphemous proposition, but only that the fool had said so in his heart, may acquit the defendant upon a judgment that it is no libel to impute such imagination to a fool ; but if the whole verse had been indicted, viz., " The fool has said in his heart, There is no God," the jury, on the principle contended for, would

* The right was fully exercised by the jury who tried and acquitted Mr Stockdale.

be restrained from the same judgment of its legality, and must convict of blasphemy on the fact of publishing, leaving the question of libel untouched on the record.

If, in the same manner, only part of this very dialogue had been indicted, instead of the whole, it is said even by your Lordship that the jury might have read the context, and then, notwithstanding the fact of publishing, might have collected from the whole its abstract and speculative nature, and have acquitted the defendant upon that judgment of it; and yet it is contended that they have no right to form the same judgment of it upon the present occasion, although the whole be before them upon the face of the indictment, but are bound to convict the defendant upon the fact of publishing, notwithstanding they should have come to the same judgment of its legality, which, it is admitted, they might have come to on trying an indictment for the publication of a part. Really, my Lord, the absurdities and gross departures from reason which must be hazarded to support this doctrine, are endless.

The criminality of the paper is said to be a question of law, yet the meaning of it, from which alone the legal interpretation can arise, is admitted to be a question of fact. If the text be so perplexed and dubious as to require innuendoes to explain, to point, and to apply obscure expression or construction, the jury alone, as judges of fact, are to interpret and to say what sentiments the author must have meant to convey by his writing: yet if the writing be so plain and intelligible as to require no averments of its meaning, it then becomes so obscure and mysterious as to be a question of law, and beyond the reach of the very same men who but a moment before were interpreters for the judges; and though its object be most obviously peaceable, and its author innocent, they are bound to say upon their oaths, that it is wicked and seditious, and the publisher of it guilty.

As a question of fact, the jury are to try the real sense and construction of the words indicted, by comparing them with the context; and yet, if that context itself, which affords the comparison, makes part of the indictment, the whole becomes a question of law, and they are then bound down to convict the defendant on the fact of publishing it, without any jurisdiction over the meaning. To complete the juggle, the intention of the publisher may likewise be shown as a fact, by the evidence of any extrinsic circumstances, such as the context to explain the writing, or the circumstances of mistake or ignorance under which it was published; and yet in the same breath, the intention is pronounced to be an inference of law from the act of publication, which the jury cannot exclude, but which must depend upon the future judgment of the Court.

But the danger of this system is no less obvious than its absurdity. I do not believe that its authors ever thought of inflicting death on Englishmen without the interposition of a jury; yet its establishment would unquestionably extend to annihilate the substance of that trial in every prosecution for high treason, where the publication of any writing was laid as the overt act. I illustrated this by a case when I moved for a rule, and called upon my friends for an answer to it, but no notice has been taken of it by any of them. This was just what I expected : when a convincing answer cannot be found to an objection, those who understand controversy never give strength to it by a weak one.

I said, and I again repeat, that if an indictment charges that a defendant did traitorously intend, compass, and imagine the death of the King, and in order to carry such treason into execution, published a paper, which it sets out *literatim* on the face of the record, the principle which is laid down to-day would subject that person to the pains of death by the single authority of the judges, without leaving anything to the jury, but the bare fact of publishing the paper ; for if that fact were proved, and the defendant called no witnesses, the Judge who tried him would be warranted, nay, bound in duty, by the principle in question, to say to the jury— Gentlemen, the overt act of treason charged upon the defendant is the publication of this paper intending to compass the death of the King. The fact is proved, and you are therefore bound to convict him,—the treasonable intention is an inference of law from the act of publishing,—and if the thing published does not upon a future examination intrinsically support that inference, the Court will arrest the judgment, and your verdict will not affect the prisoner.

My Lord, I will rest my whole argument upon the analogy between these two cases, and give up every objection to the doctrine when applied to the one, if upon the strictest examination, it shall not be found to apply equally to the other.

If the seditious intention be an inference of law, from the fact of publishing the paper which this indictment charges to be a libel, is not the treasonable intention equally an inference from the fact of publishing that paper, which the other indictment charges to be an overt act of treason ? In the one case, as in the other, the writing or publication of a paper is the whole charge ; and the substance of the paper so written or published makes all the difference between the two offences. If that substance be matter of law where it is a seditious libel, it must be matter of law where it is an act of treason ; and if, because it is law, the jury are excluded from judging it in the one instance, their judgment must suffer an equal abridgment in the other.

The consequence is obvious. If the jury, by an appeal to their consciences, are to be thus limited in the free exercise of that right which was given them by the constitution, to be a protection against judicial authority, where the weight and majesty of the Crown is put into the scale against an obscure individual, the freedom of the press is at an end. For how can it be said that the press is free because everything may be published without a previous licence, if the publisher of the most meritorious work which the united powers of genius and patriotism ever gave to the world may be prosecuted by information of the King's Attorney-General, without the consent of the Grand Jury,—may be convicted by the petty jury, on the mere fact of publishing (who indeed, without perjuring themselves, must on this system inevitably convict him), and must then depend upon judges who may be the supporters of the very Administration whose measures are questioned by the defendant, and who must therefore either give judgment against him or against themselves.

To all this Mr Bearcroft shortly answers, Are you not in the hands of the same judges, with respect to your property and even to your life, when special verdicts are found in murder, felony, and treason ? In these cases do prisoners run any hazard from the application of the law by the judges to the facts found by the juries ? Where can you possibly be safer ?

My Lord, this is an argument which I can answer without indelicacy or offence, because your Lordship's mind is much too liberal to suppose that I insult the Court by general observations on the principles of our legal government. However safe we might be, or might think ourselves, the constitution never intended to invest judges with a discretion which cannot be tried and measured by the plain and palpable standard of law ; and in all the cases put by Mr Bearcroft, no such loose discretion is exercised as must be entertained by a judgment on a seditious libel, and therefore the cases are not parallel.

On a special verdict for murder, the life of the prisoner does not depend upon the religious, moral, or philosophical ideas of the judges concerning the nature of homicide.   No ; precedents are searched for, and if he is condemned at all, he is judged exactly by the same rule as others have been judged by before him ; his conduct is brought to a precise, clear, intelligible standard, and cautiously measured by it.   It is the law, therefore, and not the Judge, which condemns him.   It is the same in all indictments or civil actions for slander upon individuals.

Reputation is a personal right of the subject, indeed the most valuable of any, and it is, therefore, secured by law, and all injuries to it clearly ascertained.   Whatever slander hurts a man in his trade, subjects him to danger of life, liberty, or loss of property, or tends to render him infamous, is the subject of an action, and in some instances of an indictment.   But in all these cases where the *alus animus* is found by the jury, the judges are in like manner safe repository of the legal consequence, because such libels may be brought to a well-known standard of strict and positive law,—they leave no discretion in the judges,—the determination of what words, when written or spoken of another, are actionable, or the subject of an indictment, leaves no more latitude to a Court sitting in judgment on the record than a question of title does in a special verdict in ejectment.

But I beseech your Lordship to consider by what rule the legality or illegality of this dialogue is to be decided by the Court, as a question of law, upon the record. Mr Bearcroft has admitted in the most unequivocal terms (what indeed it was impossible for him to deny), that every part of it, when viewed in the abstract, was legal ; but he says there is a great distinction to be taken between speculation and exhortation, and that it is this latter which makes it a libel. I readily accede to the truth of the observation ; but how your Lordship is to determine that difference as a question of law is past my comprehension ; for if the dialogue in its phrase and composition be general, and its libellous tendency arises from the purpose of the writer to raise discontent by a seditious application of legal doctrines,—that purpose is surely a question of fact, if ever there was one, and must therefore be distinctly averred in the indictment, to give the cognisance of it as a fact to the jury, without which no libel can possibly appear upon the record. This is well known to be the only office of the innuendo, because the judges can presume nothing which the strictest rules of grammar do not warrant them to collect intrinsically from the writing itself.

Circumscribed by the record, your Lordship can form no judgment of the tendency of this dialogue to excite sedition by anything but the mere words : you must look at it as if it was an old manuscript dug out of the ruins of Herculaneum ; you can collect nothing from the time when, or the circumstances under which, it was published, the person by whom, and those amongst whom it was circulated ; yet these may render a paper at one time, and under some circumstances, dangerously wicked and seditious, which at another time, and under different circumstances, might be innocent and highly meritorious. If puzzled by a task so inconsistent with the real sense and spirit of judicature, your Lordships should spurn the fetters of the record, and, judging with the reason rather than the infirmities of men, should take into your consideration the state of men's minds on the subject of equal representation at this moment, and the great disposition of the present times to revolution in government : if reading the record with these impressions, your Lordships should be led to a judgment not warranted by an abstract consideration of the record, then, besides that such a judgment would be founded on facts not in evidence before the Court, and not within its jurisdiction if they were,—let me further remind your Lordships, that even if those objections to the premises were removed, the conclusion would be no conclusion of law: your decision on the subject might be very sagacious as politicians, as moralists, as philosophers, or as licensers of the press, but they would have no resemblance to the judgments of an English court of justice, because it could have no warrant from the act of your predecessors, nor afford any precedent to your successors.

But all these objections are perfectly removed, when the seditious tendency of a paper is considered as a question of fact: we are then relieved from the absurdity of legal discussion separated from all the facts from which alone the law can arise; for the jury can do what (as I observed before) your Lordships cannot do in judging by the record; they can examine by evidence all those circumstances that tend to establish the seditious tendency of the paper, from which the Court is shut out: they may know themselves, or it may be proved before them, that it has excited sedition already: they may collect from witnesses that it has been widely circulated, and seditiously understood; or, if the prosecution (as is wisest) precedes these consequences, and the reasoning must be *à priori*, surely gentlemen living in the country are much better judges than your Lordship, what has or has not a tendency to disturb the neighbourhood in which they live, and that very neighbourhood is the forum of criminal trial.

If they know that the subject of the paper is the topic that agitates the country around them; if they see danger in that agitation, and have reason to think that the publisher must have intended it; they say he is guilty. If, on the other hand, they consider the paper to be legal, and enlightened in principle; likely to promote a spirit of activity and liberty in times when the activity of such a spirit is essential to the public safety, and have reason to believe it to be written and published in that spirit, they say, as they ought to do, that the writer or the publisher is not guilty. Whereas your Lordships' judgment upon the language of the record must ever be in the pure abstract; operating blindly and indiscriminately upon all times, circumstances, and intentions; making no distinction between the glorious attempts of a Sidney or a Russel, struggling against the terrors of despotism under the Stuarts, and those desperate adventurers of the year forty-five, who libelled the person, and excited rebellion against the mild and gracious government of our late excellent sovereign King George II.

My Lord, if the independent gentlemen of England are thus better qualified to decide from cause of knowledge, it is no offence to the Court to say, that they are full as likely to decide with impartial justice as judges appointed by the Crown. Your Lordships have but a life-interest in the public property, but they have an inheritance in it for their children. Their landed property depends upon the security of the Government, and no man who wantonly attacks it can hope or expect to escape from the selfish lenity of a jury. On the first principles of human action they must lean heavily against him. It is only when the pride of

Englishmen is insulted by such doctrines as I am opposing to-day, that they may be betrayed into a verdict delivering the guilty, rather than surrender the rights by which alone innocence in the day of danger can be protected.

I venture therefore to say, in support of one of my original propositions, that where a writing indicted as a libel, neither contains, nor is averred by the indictment to contain any slander of an individual so as to fall within those rules of law which protect personal reputation, but whose criminality is charged to consist (as in the present instance) in its tendency to stir up general discontent, that the trial of such an indictment neither involves, nor can in its obvious nature involve, any abstract question of law for the judgment of a Court, but must wholly depend upon the judgment of the jury on the tendency of the writing itself, to produce such consequences, when connected with all the circumstances which attended its publication.

It is unnecessary to push this part of the argument further, because I have heard nothing from the Bar against the position which it maintains ; none of the gentlemen have, to my recollection, given the Court any one single reason, good or bad, why the *tendency* of a paper to stir up discontent against Government, separated from all the circumstances which are ever shut out from the record, ought to be considered as an abstract question of law : they have not told us where we are to find any matter in the books to enable us to argue such questions before the Court ; or where your Lordships yourselves are to find a rule for your judgments on such subjects. I confess that to me it looks more like legislation, or arbitrary power, than English judicature. If the Court can say, this is a criminal writing, *not* because we know that mischief was intended by its author, or is even contained in itself, but because fools, believing the one and the other, may do mischief in their folly, the suppression of such writings under particular circumstances may be wise policy in a state ; but upon what principle it can be criminal law in England, to be settled in the abstract by judges, I confess with humility that I have no organs to understand.

Mr Leycester felt the difficulty of maintaining such a proposition by any argument of law, and therefore had recourse to an argument of fact. " If," says my learned friend, " what is or is not a seditious libel, be not a question of law for the Court, but of fact for the jury, upon what principle do defendants found guilty of such libels by a general verdict, defeat the judgment for error on the record ? and what is still more in point, upon what principle does Mr Erskine himself, if he fails in his present motion, mean to ask your Lordships to arrest this very judgment by saying that the Dialogue is not a libel ? "

My Lord, the observation is very ingenious, and God knows the argument requires that it should; but it is nothing more. The arrest of judgment which follows after a verdict of guilty for publishing a writing, which on inspection of the record exhibits to the Court no specific offence against the law is no impeachment of my doctrine. I never denied such a jurisdiction to the Court. My position is, that no man shall be punished for the criminal breach of any law, until a jury of his equals have pronounced him guilty in mind as well as in act. *Actus non facit reum nisi mens sit rea.*

But I never asserted that a jury had the power to make criminal law as well as to administer it; and therefore it is clear that they cannot deliver over a man to punishment if it appears by the record of his accusation, which it is the office of judicature to examine, that he has not offended against any positive law; because, however criminal he may have been in his disposition, which is a fact established by the verdict, yet statute and precedents can alone decide what is by law an *indictable* offence.

If, for instance, a man were charged by an indictment with having held a discourse in words highly seditious, and were found guilty by the jury, it is evident that it is the province of the Court to arrest that judgment; because though the jury have found that he spoke the words as laid in the indictment, with the seditious intention charged upon him, which they, and they only, could find; yet as the words are not punishable by indictment, as when committed to writing, the Court could not pronounce judgment: the declaration of the jury, that the defendant was guilty in manner and form as accused, could evidently never warrant a judgment, if the accusation itself contained no charge of an offence against the law.

In the same manner, if a butcher were indicted for privately putting a sheep to causeless and unnecessary torture in the exercise of his trade, but not in public view, so as to be productive of evil example, and the jury should find him guilty, I am afraid that no judgment could follow; because, though done *malo animo*, yet neither statute nor precedent have perhaps determined it to be an indictable offence; it would be difficult to draw the line. An indictment would not lie for every inhuman neglect of the sufferings of the smallest innocent animals which Providence has subjected to us.

> "Yet the poor beetle which we tread upon,
> In corporal suffering feels a pang as great
> As when a giant dies."

A thousand other instances might be brought of acts base and immoral, and prejudicial in their consequences, which are not yet indictable by law.

In the case of the King against Brewer, in Cowper's Reports, it was held that *knowingly* exposing to sale and selling gold under sterling for standard gold, is not indictable ; because the act refers to goldsmiths only, and private cheating is not a common-law offence. Here too the declaration of the jury that the defendant is guilty in manner and form as accused, does not change the nature of the accusation: the verdict does not go beyond the charge ; and if the charge be invalid in law, the verdict must be invalid also. All these cases, therefore, and many similar ones which might be put, are clearly consistent with my principles. I do not seek to erect jurors into legislators or judges: there must be a rule of action in every society which it is the duty of the legislature to create, and of judicature to expound when created. I only support their right to determine guilt or innocence where the crime charged is blended by the general issue with the intention of the criminal; more especially when the quality of the act itself, even independent of that intention, is not measurable by any precise principle or precedent of law, but is inseparably connected with the time when, the place where, and the circumstances under which, the defendant acted.

My Lord, in considering libels of this nature, as opposed to slander on individuals, to be mere questions of fact, or at all events to contain matter fit for the determination of the jury, I am supported not only by the general practice of Courts, but even of those very practisers themselves who, in prosecuting for the Crown, have maintained the contrary doctrine.

Your Lordships will, I am persuaded, admit that the general practice of the profession, more especially of the very heads of it, prosecuting too for the public, is strong evidence of the law. Attorney-Generals have seldom entertained such a jealousy of the King's judges in state prosecutions, as to lead them to make presents of jurisdiction to juries, which did not belong to them of right by the constitution of the country. Neither can it be supposed that men in high office and of great experience, should in every instance, though differing from each other in temper, character, and talents, uniformly fall into the same absurdity of declaiming to juries upon topics totally irrelevant, when no such inconsistency is found to disfigure the professional conduct of the same men in other cases. Yet I may appeal to your Lordships' recollection, without having recourse to the State Trials, whether upon every prosecution for a seditious libel within living memory, the Attorney-General has not uniformly stated such writings at length to the jury, pointed out their seditious tendency, which rendered them criminal, and exerted all his powers to convince them of their illegality, as the very point on which their verdict for the Crown was to be founded.

On the trial of Mr Horne, for publishing an advertisement in favour of the widows of those American subjects who had been *murdered* by the King's troops at Lexington, did the present Chancellor, then Attorney-General, content himself with saying that he had proved the publication, and that the criminal quality of the paper, which raised the legal inference of guilt against the defendant, was matter for the Court? No, my Lord; he went at great length into its dangerous and pernicious tendency, and applied himself with skill and ability to the understandings and the consciences of the jurors. This instance is in itself decisive of his opinion: that great magistrate could not have acted thus upon the principle contended for to-day:—he never was an idle declaimer;—close and masculine argument is the characteristic of his understanding.

The character and talents of the late Lord Chief-Justice De Grey, no less entitle me to infer his opinion from his uniform conduct. In all such prosecutions while he was in office, he held the same language to juries; and particularly in the case of the King against Woodfall, *to use the expression of a celebrated writer on the occasion,* " he tortured his faculties for more than two hours, to convince them that Junius's letter was a libel."

The opinions of another Crown lawyer, who has since passed through the first offices of the law, and filled them with the highest reputation, I am not driven to collect alone from his language as an Attorney-General; because he carried them with him to the seat of justice. Yet one case is too remarkable to be omitted.

Lord Camden prosecuting Doctor Shebbeare, told the jury that he did not desire their verdict upon any other principle than their solemn conviction of the truth of the information, which charged the defendant with a wicked design to alienate the hearts of the subjects of this country from their King upon the throne.

To complete the account: my learned friend, Mr Bearcroft, though last, not least in favour, upon this very occasion, spoke above an hour to the jury at Shrewsbury, to convince them of the libellous tendency of the Dialogue, which soon afterwards the learned Judge desired them wholly to dismiss from their consideration, as matter with which they had no concern. The real fact is, that the doctrine is too absurd to be acted upon;—too distorted in principle to admit of consistency in practice:—it is contraband in law, and can only be smuggled by those who introduce it:—it requires great talents and great address to hide its deformity:—in vulgar hands it becomes contemptible.

Having supported the rights of juries, by the uniform practice of Crown lawyers, let us now examine the question of authority, and see how this Court itself, and its judges, have acted upon trials for libels in former times; for, according to Lord Raymond, in Franklin's case (as cited by Mr Justice Buller, at Shrewsbury), the principle I am supporting, had, it seems, been only broached about the year 1731, by some men of party spirit, and then, too, for the very first time.

My Lord, such an observation in the mouth of Lord Raymond,

proves how dangerous it is to take up, as doctrine, everything flung out at *nisi prius ;* above all, upon subjects which engage the passions and interests of Government. The most solemn and important trials with which history makes us acquainted, discussed too at the bar of this Court when filled with judges the most devoted to the Crown, afford the most decisive contradiction to such an unfounded and unguarded assertion.

In the famous case of the Seven Bishops, the question of libel or no libel was held unanimously by the Court of King's Bench, trying the cause at the bar, to be matter for the consideration and determination of the jury ; and the Bishops' petition to the King, which was the subject of the information, was accordingly delivered to them when they withdrew to consider of their verdict.

Thinking this case decisive, I cited it at the trial, and the answer it received from Mr Bearcroft was, that it had no relation to the point in dispute between us, for that the Bishops were acquitted, not upon the question of libel, but because the delivery of the petition to the King was held to be no publication.

I was not a little surprised at this statement, but my turn of speaking was then past ; fortunately to-day it is my privilege to speak last, and I have now lying before me the fifth volume of the " State Trials," where the case of the Bishops is printed, and where it appears that the publication was expressly proved,—that nothing turned upon it in the judgment of the Court,—and that the charge turned wholly upon the question of libel, which was expressly left to the jury by every one of the judges. Lord Chief-Justice Wright, in summing up the evidence, told them that a question had at first arisen about the publication, it being insisted on that the delivery of the petition to the King had not been proved ; that the Court was of the same opinion, and that he was just going to have directed them to find the Bishops not guilty, when in came my Lord President (such sort of witnesses were no doubt always at hand when wanted), who proved the delivery to His Majesty. " Therefore," continued the Chief-Justice, " if you believe it was the same petition, it is a publication sufficient, and we must, therefore, come to inquire whether it be a libel."

He then gave his reasons for thinking it within the case *de libellis famosis*, and concluded by saying to the jury, " In short, I must give you my opinion : I do take it to be a libel ; if my brothers have anything to say to it, I suppose they will deliver their opinion." What opinion ? Not that the jury had no jurisdiction to judge of the matter, but an opinion for the express purpose of enabling them to give that judgment which the law required at their hands.

Mr Justice Holloway then followed the Chief-Justice ; and so pointedly was the question of libel or no libel, and not the publication, the only matter which remained in doubt, and which the jury, with the assistance of the Court, were to decide upon, that when the learned Judge went into the facts which had been in evidence, the Chief-Justice said to him, "Look you ; by the way, brother, I did not ask you to sum up the evidence, but only to deliver your opinion to the jury, whether it be a libel or no." The Chief-Justice's remark, though it proves my position, was, however, very unnecessary ; for but a moment before, Mr Justice Holloway had declared he did not think it was a libel, but addressing himself to the jury had said, " *It is left to you, gentlemen.*"

Mr Justice Powell, who likewise gave his opinion that it was no libel, said *to the jury. " But the matter of it is before you, and I leave the issue of it to God and your own consciences ; "* and so little was it an idea of any one of the Court that the jury ought to found their verdict solely upon the evidence of the publication, without attending to the criminality or innocence of the petition ;— that the Chief-Justice himself consented, on their withdrawing from the bar, that they should carry with them all the materials for coming to a judgment as comprehensive as the charge ; and, indeed, expressly directed that the information, the libel, the declarations under the great seal, and even the statute-book, should be delivered to them.

The happy issue of this memorable trial, in the acquittal of the Bishops by the jury, exercising jurisdiction over the whole charge, freely admitted to them as legal even by King James' judges, is admitted by two of the gentlemen to have prepared and forwarded the glorious era of the Revolution.   Mr Bower, in particular, spoke with singular enthusiasm concerning this verdict, choosing (for reasons sufficiently obvious) to ascribe it to a special miracle wrought for the safety of the nation, rather than to the right lodged in the jury to save it by its laws and constitution.

My learned friend, finding his argument like nothing upon the earth, was obliged to ascend into heaven to support it :—having admitted that the jury not only acted like just men towards the Bishops, but as patriot citizens towards their country, and not being able, without the surrender of his whole argument, to allow either their public spirit or their private justice to have been consonant to the laws, he is driven to make them the instruments of Divine Providence to bring good out of evil, and holds them up as men inspired by God to perjure themselves in the administration of justice, in order, by the by, to defeat the effects of that wretched system of judicature, which he is defending to-day as the constitution of England.   For if the King's judges could have decided the petition to be a libel, the Stuarts might yet have been on the throne.

My Lord, this is an argument of a priest, not of a lawyer : and even if faith and not law were to govern the question, I should be as far from subscribing to it as a religious opinion.

No man believes more firmly than I do that God governs the

whole universe by the gracious dispensations of His providence, and that all the nations of the earth rise and fall at His command ; but then this wonderful system is carried on by the natural, though to us the often hidden, relation between effects and causes, which wisdom adjusted from the beginning, and which foreknowledge at the same time rendered sufficient, without disturbing either the laws of nature or of civil society.

The prosperity and greatness of empires ever depended, and ever must depend, upon the use their inhabitants make of their reason in devising wise laws, and the spirit and virtue with which they watch over their just execution : and it is impious to suppose that men, who have made no provision for their own happiness or security in their attention to their government, are to be saved by the interposition of Heaven in turning the hearts of their tyrants to protect them.

But if every case in which judges have left the question of libel to juries in opposition to law is to be considered as a miracle, England may vie with Palestine, and Lord Chief-Justice Holt steps next into view as an apostle, for that great Judge, in Tutchin's case, left the question of libel to the jury in the most unambiguous terms.   After summing up the evidence of writing and publishing, he said to them as follows :—

" You have now heard the evidence, and you are to consider whether Mr Tutchin be guilty.   They say they are innocent papers and no libels, and they say nothing is a libel but what reflects upon some particular person.   But this is a very strange doctrine, to say it is not a libel reflecting on the Government, endeavouring to possess the people that the Government is mal-administered by corrupt persons that are employed in such or such stations either in the navy or army.

" To say that corrupt officers are appointed to administer affairs is certainly a reflection on the Government.   If people should not be called to account for possessing the people with an ill opinion of the Government, no Government can subsist.   For it is very necessary for all Governments that the people should have a good opinion of it, and nothing can be worse to any Government than to endeavour to procure animosities as to the management of it ; this has been always looked upon as a crime, and no Government can be safe without it be punished."

Having made these observations, did the Chief-Justice tell the jury that whether the publication in question fell within that principle, so as to be a libel on Government, was a matter of law for the Court, with which they had no concern ?   Quite the contrary : he considered the seditious tendency of the paper as a question for their sole determination, saying to them—

" Now, you are to consider whether these words I have read to you do not tend to beget an ill opinion of the administration of the

Government; to tell us that those that are employed know nothing of the matter, and those that do know are not employed; men are not adapted to offices, but offices to men, out of a particular regard to their interest, and not to their fitness for the places.   This is the purport of these papers."

In citing the words of judges in judicature I have a right to suppose their discourse to be pertinent and relevant, and that when they state the defendant's answer to the charge and make remarks on it, they mean that the jury should exercise a judgment under their direction This is the practice we must certainly impute to Lord Holt, if we do him the justice to suppose that he meant to convey the sentiments which he expressed.   So that, when we come to sum up this case, I do not find myself so far behind the learned gentleman, even in point of express authority, putting all reason and the analogies of law which unite to support me wholly out of the question.

There is Court of King's Bench against Court of King's Bench; Chief-Justice Wright against Chief-Justice Lee; and Lord Holt against Lord Raymond. As to living authorities, it would be invidious to class them; but it is a point on which I am satisfied myself, and on which the world will be satisfied likewise, if ever it comes to be a question.

But even if I should be mistaken in that particular, I cannot consent implicitly to receive any doctrine as the law of England, though pronounced to be such by magistrates the most respectable, if I find it to be in direct violation of the very first principles of English judicature.   The great jurisdictions of the country are unalterable except by Parliament, and until they are changed by that authority, they ought to remain sacred.   The judges have no power over them.   What parliamentary abridgment has been made upon the rights of juries since the trial of the Bishops, or since Tutchin's case, when they were fully recognised by this Court?—None.   Lord Raymond and Lord Chief-Justice Lee ought therefore to have looked there—to their predecessors—for the law, instead of setting up a new one for their successors.

But supposing the Court should deny the legality of all these propositions, or admitting their legality, should resist the conclusions I have drawn from them, then I have recourse to my last proposition, in which I am supported even by all those authorities on which the learned Judge relies for the doctrines contained in his charge, to wit :—

" That in all cases where the mischievous intention, which is agreed to be the essence of the crime, cannot be collected by simple inference from the fact charged, because the defendant goes into evidence to rebut such inference, the intention becomes then a pure unmixed question of fact for the consideration of the jury."

I said the authorities of the King against Woodfall and Almon were with me.   In the first, which is reported in 5th Burrow, your Lordship expressed yourself thus :—" Where an act, in itself indifferent, becomes criminal when done with a particular intent, there the intent must be proved and found.   But where the act is itself unlawful, as in the case of a libel, the PROOF of justification or excuse lies on the defendant, *and in failure thereof, the law implies a criminal intent.*"   Most luminously expressed to convey this sentiment, viz., that when a man publishes a libel, and has nothing to say for himself, no explanation or exculpation, a criminal intention need not be proved.   I freely admit that it need not ; it is an inference of common sense, not of law.   But the publication of a libel does not exclusively show criminal intent, but is only an implication of law in failure of the defendant's proof.   Your Lordship immediately afterwards in the same case explained this further :—" There may be cases where the publication may be justified or excused as lawful *or innocent,* FOR NO FACT WHICH IS NOT CRIMINAL, though the paper *be a libel,* can amount to *such* a publication of which a defendant ought to be found guilty."   But no question of that kind arose at the trial (*i.e.,* on the trial of Woodfall).   Why ?   Your Lordship immediately explained why— " Because the defendant called no witnesses;" expressly saying that the publication of a libel is not in itself a crime unless the intent be criminal ; and that it is not merely in mitigation of punishment, but that such a publication does not warrant a verdict of guilty.

In the case of the King against Almon, a magazine containing one of Junius's letters was sold at Almon's shop.   There was proof of that sale at the trial.   Mr Almon called no witnesses, and was found guilty.   To found a motion for a new trial, an affidavit was offered from Mr Almon, that he was not privy to the sale, nor knew his name was inserted as a publisher, and that this practice of booksellers being inserted as publishers by their correspondents without notice was common in the trade.

Your Lordship said, " Sale of a book in a bookseller's shop is *primâ facie* evidence of publication by the master, and the publication of a libel is *primâ facie* evidence of criminal intent.   It stands good till answered by the defendant.   It must stand till contradicted or explained, *and if not contradicted, explained, or exculpated,* BECOMES *tantamount to conclusive when the defendant calls no witnesses.*

Mr Justice Aston said, " *Primâ facie* evidence *not answered* is sufficient to ground a verdict upon.   If the defendant had a sufficient excuse, he might have proved it at the trial.   His having neglected it where there was no surprise, is no ground for a new one."   Mr Justice Willes and Mr Justice Ashurst agreed upon those express principles.

These cases declare the law, beyond all controversy, to be, that publication, even of a libel, is no conclusive proof of guilt, but only *primâ facie* evidence of it till answered, and that, if the defendant can show that his intention was not criminal, he completely rebuts the inference arising from the publication, because, though it remains true that he published, yet, according to your Lordship's express words, it is not such a publication of which a defendant ought to be found guilty. Apply Mr Justice Buller's summing up to this law, and it does not require even a legal apprehension to distinguish the repugnancy.

The advertisement was proved to convince the jury of the Dean's motive for publishing. Mr Jones's testimony went strongly to aid it, and the evidence to character, though not sufficient in itself, was admissible to be thrown into the scale. But not only no part of this was left to the jury, but the whole of it was expressly removed from their consideration, although, in the cases of Woodfall and Almon, it was as expressly laid down to be within their cognisance, and a complete answer to the charge if satisfactory to the minds of the jurors.

In support of the learned Judge's charge there can be therefore but the two arguments which I stated on moving for the rule :— Either that the defendant's evidence, namely, the advertisement, Mr Jones's evidence in confirmation of its being *bonâ fide*, and the evidence to character to strengthen that construction, were not sufficient proof that the Dean believed the publication meritorious, and published it in vindication of his honest intentions ; or else, that, even admitting it to establish that fact, it did not amount to such an exculpation as to be evidence on Not Guilty, so as to warrant a verdict. I still give the learned Judge the choice of the alternative.

As to the first, viz., whether it showed honest intention in point of fact, that was a question for the jury. If the learned Judge had thought it was not sufficient evidence to warrant the jury's believing that the Dean's motives were such as he had declared them, I conceive he should have given his opinion of it as a point of evidence, and left it there. I cannot condescend to go further ; it would be ridiculous to argue a self-evident proposition.

As to the second, viz., that even if the jury had believed from the evidence that the Dean's intention was wholly innocent, it would not have warranted them in acquitting, and therefore should not have been left to them upon Not Guilty ; that argument can never be supported. For, if the jury had declared, " We find that the Dean published this pamphlet, whether a libel or not we do not find ; and we find further, that, believing it in his conscience to be meritorious and innocent, he, *bonâ fide*, published it with the prefixed advertisement as a vindication of his character from the reproach of seditious intentions, and not to excite sedition," it is impossible to say, without ridicule, that on such a special verdict the Court could have pronounced a criminal judgment.

Then why was the consideration of that evidence, by which those facts might have been found, withdrawn from the jury, after they brought in a verdict—Guilty of publishing ONLY, which, in the King against Woodfall, was only said not to negative the criminal intention, because the defendant called no witnesses ? Why did the learned Judge confine his inquiries to the innuendoes, and finding them agreed to, direct the epithet of Guilty, without asking the jury if they believed the defendant's evidence to rebut the criminal inference ? Some of them positively meant to negative the criminal inference by adding the word *only*, and all would have done it if they had thought themselves at liberty to enter upon that evidence. But they were told expressly that they had nothing to do with the consideration of that evidence, which, if believed, would have warranted that verdict. The conclusion is evident :—If they had a right to consider it, and their consideration might have produced such a verdict, and if such a verdict would have been an acquittal, it must be a misdirection.

" But," says Mr Bower, " if this advertisement, prefixed to the publication, by which the Dean professed his innocent intention in publishing it, should have been left to the jury as evidence of that intention, to found an acquittal on, even taking the Dialogue to be a libel, no man could ever be convicted of publishing anything, however dangerous ; for he would only have to tack an advertisement to it by way of preface, professing the excellence of its principles and the sincerity of his motives, and his defence would be complete."

My Lord, I never contended for any such position. If a man of education, like the Dean, were to publish a writing so palpably libellous that no ignorance or misapprehension imputable to such a person could prevent his discovering the mischievous design of the author, no jury would believe such an advertisement to be *bona fide*, and would therefore be bound in conscience to reject it, as if it had no existence : the effect of such evidence must be to convince the jury of the defendant's purity of mind, and must therefore depend upon the nature of the writing itself, and all the circumstances attending its publication.

If, upon reading the paper and considering the whole of the evidence, they have reason to think that the defendant did not believe it to be illegal, and did not publish it with the seditious purpose charged by the indictment, he is not guilty upon any principle or authority of law, and would have been acquitted even in the Star-Chamber ; for it was held by that Court in Lambe's case, in the eighth year of King James I., as reported by Lord Coke, who then presided in it, that every one who should be convicted of a libel must be the writer or contriver, or a *malicious* publisher, *knowing* it to be a libel.

This case of Lambe being of too high authority to be opposed, and too much in point to be passed over, Mr Bower endeavours to avoid its force by giving it a new construction of his own : he says, that not knowing a writing to be a libel in the sense of that case, means not knowing the contents of the thing published, as by conveying papers sealed up, or having a sermon and a libel, and delivering one by mistake for the other. In such cases he says, *ignorantia facti excusat*, because the mind does not go with the act. *sed ignorantia legis non excusat ;* and therefore if the party knows the contents of the paper which he publishes, his mind goes with the act of publication, though he does not find out anything criminal, and he is bound to abide by the legal consequences.

This is to make criminality depend upon the consequences of an act, and not upon the knowledge of its quality, which would involve lunatics and children in all the penalties of criminal law ; for whatever they do is attended with consciousness, though their understanding does not reach to the consciousness of offence.

The publication of a libel, not believing it to be one after having read it, is a much more favourable case than publishing it unread by mistake ; the one, nine times in ten, is a culpable negligence which is no excuse at all ; for a man cannot throw papers about the world without reading them, and afterwards say he did not know their contents were criminal : but if a man reads a paper, and not believing it to contain anything seditious, having collected nothing of that tendency himself, publishes it among his neighbours as an innocent and useful work, he cannot be convicted as a criminal publisher. How he is to convince the jury that his purpose was innocent, though the thing published be a libel, must depend upon circumstances ; and these circumstances he may, on the authority of all the cases, ancient and modern, lay before the jury in evidence ; because, if he can establish the innocence of his mind, he negatives the very gist of the indictment.

" In all crimes," says Lord Hale, in his " Pleas of the Crown," " the intention is the principal consideration : it is the mind that makes the taking of another's goods to be felony, or a bare trespass only : it is impossible to prescribe all the circumstances evidencing a felonious intent, or the contrary ; but the same must be left to the attentive consideration of Judge *and jury ;* wherein the best rule is, *in dubiis*, rather to incline to acquittal than conviction."

In the same work he says : " By the statute of Philip and Mary, touching importation of coin counterfeit of foreign money, it must, to make it treason, be with the intent to utter and make payment of the same ; and the intent in this case may be tried and found by circumstances of FACT, by words, letters, and a thousand evidences besides the bare doing of the fact."

This principle is illustrated by frequent practice, where the intention is found by the jury as a fact in a special verdict. It occurred not above a year ago at East Grinstead, on an indictment for burglary, before Mr Justice Ashurst, where I was myself counsel for the prisoner. It was clear upon the evidence that he had broken into the house by force in the night; but I contended that it appeared from proof that he had broken and entered with an intent to rescue his goods, which had been seized that day by the officers of excise; which rescue, though a capital felony by modern statute, was but a trespass, *temp. Henry VIII.*, and consequently not a burglary.

Mr Justice Ashurst saved this point of law, which the twelve judges afterwards determined for the prisoner; but, in order to create the point of law, it was necessary that the prisoner's intention should be ascertained as a fact; and for this purpose the learned Judge directed the jury to tell him with what intention they found that the prisoner broke and entered the house, which they did by answering, "To rescue his goods;" which verdict was recorded.

In the same manner, in the case of the King against Pierce, at the Old Bailey, the intention was found by the jury as a fact in the special verdict. The prisoner having hired a horse, and afterwards sold him, was indicted for felony; but the judges, doubting whether it was more than a fraud, unless he originally hired him intending to sell him, recommended it to the jury to find a special verdict, comprehending their judgment of his intention from the evidence. Here the quality of the act depended on the intention, which intention it was held to be the exclusive province of the jury to determine, before the judges could give the act any legal denomination.

My Lord, I am ashamed to have cited so many authorities to establish the first elements of the law, but it has been my fate to find them disputed. The whole mistake arises from confounding criminal with civil cases. If a printer's servant, without his master's consent or privity, inserts a slanderous article against me in his newspaper, I ought not in justice to indict him; and if I do, the jury *on such proof* should acquit him; but it is no defence to an action, for he is responsible to me *civiliter* for the damage which I have sustained from the newspaper, which is his property. Is there anything new in this principle? So far from it, that every student knows it as applicable to all other cases; but people are resolved, from some fatality or other, to distort every principle of law into nonsense, when they come to apply it to printing, as if none of the rules and maxims which regulate all the transactions of society had any reference to it.

If a man rising in his sleep walks into a china-shop, and breaks everything about him; his being asleep is a complete answer to an *indictment* for a trespass, but he must answer in an *action* for everything he has broken.

If the proprietor of the York coach, though asleep in his bed at that city, has a drunken servant on the box at London, who drives over my leg and breaks it, he is responsible to me in damages for the accident; but I cannot indict him as the criminal author of my misfortune.   What distinction can be more obvious and simple?

Let us only then extend these principles, which were never disputed in other criminal cases, to the crime of publishing a libel; and let us at the same time allow to the jury, as our forefathers did before us, the same jurisdiction in that instance which we agree in rejoicing to allow them in all others, and the system of English law will be wise, harmonious, and complete.

My Lord, I have now finished my argument, having answered the several objections to my five original propositions, and established them by all the principles and authorities which appear to me to apply, or to be necessary for their support.   In this process I have been unavoidably led into a length not more inconvenient to the Court than to myself, and have been obliged to question several judgments which had been before questioned and confirmed.

They, however, who may be disposed to censure me for the zeal which has animated me in this cause, will at least, I hope, have the candour to give me credit for the sincerity of my intentions. It is surely not my interest to stir opposition to the decided authorities of the Court in which I practise: with a seat here within the bar, at my time of life, and looking no farther than myself, I should have been contented with the law as I found it, and have considered *how little* might be said with decency, rather than *how much;* but feeling as I have ever done upon the subject, it was impossible I should act otherwise.   It was the first command and counsel to my youth always to do what my conscience told me to be my duty, and to leave the consequences to God.   I shall carry with me the memory, and, I hope, the practice, of this parental lesson to the grave: I have hitherto followed it, and have no reason to complain that the adherence to it has been even a temporal sacrifice; I have found it, on the contrary, the road to prosperity and wealth, and shall point it out as such to my children.   It is impossible in this country to hurt an honest man; but even if it were possible, I should little deserve that title if I could, upon any principle, have consented to tamper or temporise with a question which involves in its determination and its consequences the liberty of the press; and in that liberty, the very existence of every part of the public freedom.

BEFORE we go on to the final proceeding in this memorable cause, viz., the application to arrest the judgment, on the ground that the Dialogue, as set forth in the indictment, did not contain the legal charge of a libel, it may be necessary to insert the judgment delivered by Lord Mansfield on discharging the rule for a new trial—a judgment which was supported by the rest of the Court, and which confirmed throughout the whole doctrine of Mr Justice Buller, as delivered upon the trial at Shrewsbury.

It was too late in the day, when the counsel finished, for the judges to deliver their opinions, and the Court immediately adjourned; the Lord Chief-Justice declaring that " they were agreed in the judgment they were to give, and would deliver it the next morning."

Accordingly, next day, the 16th of November, at the opening of the Court, the Earl of Mansfield, Lord Chief-Justice, delivered himself as follows :—

In this case of the King against Dr Shipley, Dean of St Asaph, the motion to set aside the verdict, and to grant a new trial upon account of the misdirection of the Judge, supposes that upon this verdict (either as a general, or as minutes of a special verdict to be reduced into form), judgment may be given ; for if the verdict was defective, and omitted finding anything within the province of the jury to find, there ought to be a *venire de novo*, and, consequently, this motion is totally improper; therefore, as I said, the motion supposes that judgment may be given upon the verdict, and it rests upon the objections to the direction of the Judge.

I think they may be reduced to four in number, one of which is peculiar to this case; and therefore I begin with it, viz., *That the Judge did not leave the evidence of a lawful excuse or justification to the jury, as a ground for them to acquit the defendant upon, or as a matter for their consideration.* This is an objection peculiar to this case, and therefore I begin with it, to dispose of it first. Circumstances, merely of alleviation or aggravation, are irrelevant upon the trial ; they are totally immaterial to the verdict, because they do not prevent or conclude the jury's finding for or against the defendant ; they may be made use of when judgment is given to increase or lessen the punishment, but they are totally irrelevant and immaterial upon the trial. Circumstances which amount to a lawful excuse, or a justification, are proper· upon the trial, and can only be used there. Upon every such defence set up of a lawful excuse or justification, there necessarily arise two questions, one of law, the other of fact; the first to be decided by the Court, the second by the jury.

Whether the fact alleged, supposing it true, be a legal excuse, is a question of law; whether the allegation be true, is a question of fact; and according to this distinction, the Judge ought to direct, and the jury ought to follow the direction, though by means of a general verdict they are intrusted with a power of blending law and fact, and following the prejudices of their affections or passions.

The first circumstance in evidence in this cause is a letter of the 24th of January to Edwards, and the advertisement that accompanied it; and what was said by Edward Jones in the conversation that he held with the defendant on the 7th of January. Upon this part of the case, we must suppose the paper seditious or criminal; for, if it is neither seditious nor criminal, the defendant must be acquitted upon the face of the record. Therefore, whether it is an excuse or not, we must suppose the paper to be a libel, or criminal in the eyes of the law. Then how does it stand upon this excuse? Why, the defendant, knowing the paper had been strongly objected to as tending to sedition, or that it might be so understood, publishes it with an advertisement,* avowing and justifying the doctrine; so that he publishes it under the circumstances of avowing and justifying this criminal doctrine.

The next circumstance is from the evidence of Edward Jones: that the defendant was told and knew that the paper was objected to as having a seditious tendency; that it might do mischief if it was translated into Welsh, and therefore that design was laid aside; that he read it at the county meeting, and said he read it *with a rope about his neck;* and, after he had read it, he said *it was not so bad.* And this he knew upon the 7th January; yet he sets this up as an excuse for ordering it to be printed upon the 24th of January.

We are all of opinion clearly, that if the writing be criminal, these circumstances are aggravations, and by no means ought to have been left to the jury as any excuse.

It is a mockery to say it is any excuse. What! when the man himself knows that he reads it *with a rope about his neck;* when he says, admitting it to be bad, that it is not *so bad;* when he has told a company of gentlemen that, for fear of its doing mischief to their country, he would not have it translated into Welsh;—all these circumstances plainly showed him that he should not have published it. Therefore, we are all of opinion it is the same as if no such evidence had been given, and that, if it had been offered by way of excuse, it ought not to have been received. The advertisement was read to the jury, but the Judge did very right not to leave it to them as a matter of excuse, because it was clearly of a contrary tendency.

* For the advertisement prefixed to the Dialogue, *vide supra,* p. 96.

What was meant by saying the advertisement should have been set out in the indictment, I do not comprehend; much less that blasphemy may be charged on the Scripture by only stating half the sentence.

If any part of the sentence qualifies what is set forth, it may be given in evidence, as was expressly determined by the Court so long ago as the case of the King and Bere, in Salkeld, 417, in the reign of King William. Every circumstance which tends to prove the meaning, is every day given in evidence; and the jury are the only judges of the meaning, and must find the meaning; for if they do not find the meaning, the verdict is not complete. So far for the objection upon that part which is peculiar to this case.

The second objection is, that the Judge did not give his own opinion whether the writing was a libel, or seditious, or criminal.

The third, that the Judge told the jury they ought to leave that question upon record to the Court, if they had no doubt of the meaning and publication.

The fourth and last: that he did not leave the defendant's intent to the jury.

The answer to these three objections is, that by the constitution, the jury ought not to decide the question of law, whether such a writing, of such a meaning, published without a lawful excuse, be criminal; and they cannot decide it *finally* against the defendant, because, after the verdict, it remains open upon the record; therefore, it is the duty of the Judge to advise the jury to separate the question of fact from the question of law; and as they ought not to decide the law, and the question remains entire upon the record, the Judge is not called upon necessarily to tell them his own opinion. It is almost peculiar to the form of the prosecution for a libel, that the question of law remains entirely for the Court *upon record*, and that the jury cannot decide it against the defendant; so that a general verdict " that the defendant is guilty," is equivalent to a special verdict in other cases. It finds all which belongs to the jury to find; it finds nothing as to the question of law. Therefore, when a jury have been satisfied as to every fact within their province to find, they have been advised to find the defendant *guilty*, and in that shape they take the opinion of the Court upon the law. No case has been cited of a special verdict in a prosecution for a libel, leaving the question of law upon the record to the Court, though, to be sure, it might be left in that form; but the other is simpler and better.

As to the last objection upon the *intent:* A criminal intent, from doing a thing criminal in itself without a lawful excuse, is an inference of law, and a conclusive inference of law, not to be contradicted but by an excuse, which I have fully gone through. Where an *innocent act* is made criminal, when done with a particular intent, there the intent is a *material* fact to constitute the crime.

This is the answer that is given to these three last objections to the direction of the Judge. The first, I said, was peculiar to this case.

The subject matter of these three objections has arisen upon every trial for a libel since the Revolution, which is now near one hundred years ago. In every reign there have been many such trials both of a private and a public nature. In every reign there have been several defended with all the acrimony of party animosity, and a spirit ready to contest every point, and to admit nothing. During all this time, as far as it can be traced, one may venture to say, that the direction of every Judge has been consonant to the doctrine of Mr Justice Buller; and no counsel has complained of it by any application to the Court. The counsel for the Crown, to remove the prejudices of a jury, and to satisfy the bystanders, have expatiated upon the enormity of the libels; judges, with the same view, have sometimes done the same thing; both have done it wisely, with another view,—to obviate the captivating harangues of the defendant's counsel to the jury, tending to show that they can or ought to find that in law the paper is no libel.

But the formal direction of every Judge (under which every lawyer for near one hundred years, has so far acquiesced as not to complain of it to the Court) seems to me, ever since the Revolution, to have been agreeable to the direction of Mr Justice Buller. It is difficult to cite cases; the trials are not printed. Unless particular questions arise, notes are not taken: nobody takes a note of a direction of course not disputed. We must, as in all cases of tradition, trace backwards, and presume, from the usage which is remembered, that the precedent usage was the same. We know there were many trials for libels in the reign of King William; there is no trace that I know of of any report that at all bears upon the question during that reign, but the case of the King and Bere, which is in Salkeld; that was in the reign of King William, and the only thing there applicable to the present question is, that the Court were of opinion that the writing complained of must be set out *according to the tenor:* Why? That the Court may judge of the very words themselves; whereas, if it was to be *according to the effect,* that judgment must be left to the jury. But there it was determined, and under that authority ever since, the writing complained of is set out according to the tenor.

During the reign of Queen Anne we know several trials were had for libels, but the only one cited is in the year 1704; and there the direction (though Lord Holt, who is said to have done it in several cases, goes into the enormity of the libel) to the jury was, "If you find *the publication* in London, you must find the defendant guilty." Thus it stands, as to all that can be found precisely and particularly in the reigns of King William and Queen Anne. We know that in the reign of George I. there were several trials for libels, but I have seen no note or traces of them, nor any question concerning them. In the reign of King George II. there were others; but the first of which there is a note (for which I am obliged to Mr Manley *), was in February 1729,—the King and Clarke,—which was tried before Lord C.-J. Raymond; and there he lays it down expressly (there being no question about an excuse, or about the meaning), he lays it down, *the fact of printing and publishing only is in issue.*

The *Craftsman* was a celebrated party-paper, wrote in opposition to the ministry of Sir Robert Walpole, by many men of high rank and great talents: the whole party espoused it. It was thought proper to prosecute the famous *Hague* letter. I was present at the trial; it was in the year 1731. It happens to be printed in the State Trials. There was a great concourse of people; it was a matter of great expectation, and many persons of high rank were present to countenance the defendant. Mr Fazakerly and Mr Bootle (afterwards Sir Thomas Bootle) were the leading counsel for the defendant. They started every objection and laboured every point. When the Judge overruled them, he usually said, "If I am wrong, you know where to apply." The Judge was my Lord Raymond, C.-J., who had been eminent at the bar in the reign of Queen Anne, had been Solicitor and Attorney General in the reign of George I., and was intimately connected with Sir Edward Northey, so that he must have known what the ancient practice had been. The case itself was of great expectation, as I have stated to you, and it was so blended with party passion, that it required his utmost attention; yet, when he came to sum up and direct the jury, he does it as of course, just in the same manner as Mr Justice Buller did,—" that there were three points for consideration: the fact of publication; the meaning (those two for the jury); the question of law or criminality, for the Court upon the record." Mr Fazakerly and Mr Bootle were, as we all know, able lawyers; they were connected in party with the writers of the *Craftsman*. They never thought of complaining to the Court of a misdirection: they would not say it was not law: they never did complain. It never was complained of, nor did any idea enter their heads that it was not agreeable to law. Except that case in 1729 that is mentioned, and this, the trials for libels before my Lord Raymond are not printed, nor to be found in any notes. But, to be sure, his direction in all was to the same effect. I, by accident (from memory only I speak now), recollect one where the *Craftsman* was acquitted; and I recollect it from a famous, witty, and ingenious ballad that was made at the time by Mr Pulteney; and though it is a ballad, I will cite the stanza I remember from it, because it will show you the idea of the able men in opposition, and the leaders of the popular party in those days. They had not an idea of assuming that the jury had a right to determine upon a question of law, but they put it

* One of the counsel for the prosecution in this cause.

upon another and much better ground.   The stanza I allude to is
this :

> " For Sir Philip* well knows
> That his *innuendoes*
> Will serve him no longer
> In verse or in prose ;
> For twelve honest men have decided the cause,
> Who are judges of fact, though not judges of laws."

It was the admission of the whole of that party : they put it right ;
they put it upon the *meaning* of the *innuendoes :* upon *that* the
jury acquitted the defendant ; and they never put up a pretence of
any other power, except when talking to the jury themselves.

There are no notes as I know of (and I think the Bar would
have found them out upon this occasion, if there had been any
that were material),—there are no notes of the trials for libel before
my Lord Hardwicke.   I am sure there are none before Lord
Chief-Justice Lee till the year 1752, when the case of the King
and Owen came on before him.   This happens to be printed in
the State Trials, though it is incorrect, but sufficient for the present purpose.   I attended that trial as Solicitor-General.   Lord
Chief-Justice Lee was the most scrupulous observer and follower
of precedents, and he directed the jury, *as of course*, in the same
way Mr Justice Buller has done.

When I was Attorney-General, I prosecuted some libels ; one I
remember from the condition and circumstances of the defendant :
he was found guilty.   He was a common councilman of the city of
London : and I remember another circumstance, it was the first conviction in the city of London that had been for twenty-seven years.
It was the case of the King and Nutt ; and there he was convicted,
under the very same direction, before Lord Chief-Justice Ryder.

In the year 1756 I came into the office I now hold.   Upon the
first prosecution for a libel which stood in my paper,—I think (but I
am not sure), but I think it was the case of the King and Shebbeare,—I made up my mind as to the direction I ought to give.   I
have uniformly given the same in all, almost in the same form of
words.   No counsel ever complained of it to the Court.   Upon
every defendant being brought up for judgment, I have always
stated the direction I gave, and the Court has always assented to
it.   The defence of a *lawful excuse* never existed in any case before
me ; therefore I have told the jury if they were satisfied with the
evidence of the publication, and that the meanings of the *innuendoes*

---

* Sir Philip Yorke, afterwards Lord Chancellor Hardwicke, then Attorney-General.

It appears by a pamphlet printed in 1754, that Lord Mansfield is mistaken.   The
verse runs thus :

> " Sir Philip well knows,
> That his innuendo's
> Will serve him no longer in verse or in prose ;
> For twelve honest men have determin'd the cause,
> Who are judges alike of the facts and the laws."

were as stated, they ought to find the defendant guilty: that the question of law was upon record for the judgment of the Court. This direction being *as of course*, and no question ever raised concerning it in court (though I have had the misfortune to try many libels in very warm times, against defendants most obstinately and factitiously defended), yet the direction being *as of course*, and no objection made, it passed as of course, and there are no notes of what passed. In one case of the King and Woodfall, on account of a very different kind of question (but upon account of another question), there happens to be a report; and there the direction I have stated is adopted by the whole Court as right, and the doctrine of Mr Justice Buller is laid down in express terms. Such a judicial practice in the precise point from the Revolution, as I think, down to the present day, is not to be shaken by arguments of general theory, or popular declamation. Every species of criminal prosecution has something peculiar in the mode of procedure; therefore general propositions, applied to all, tend only to complicate and embarrass the question. No deduction or conclusion can be drawn from what a jury *may* do, from the *form* of procedure, to what they *ought* to do upon the fundamental principles of the constitution and the reason of the thing, if they will act with integrity and good conscience.

The fundamental definition of trial by jury depends upon a universal maxim that is without an exception. Though a definition or maxim in law without an exception, it is said, is hardly to be found; yet this I take to be a maxim without an exception:—*Ad quæstionem juris non respondent juratores; ad quæstionem facti non respondent judices.*

Where a question can be severed by the form of pleading, the distinction is preserved upon the face of the record, and the jury cannot encroach upon the jurisdiction of the Court; where, by the form of pleading, the two questions are blended together and cannot be separated upon the face of the record, the distinction is preserved by the honesty of the jury. The constitution trusts that, under the direction of a Judge, they will not usurp a jurisdiction which is not in their province. They do not know, and are not presumed to know, the law; they are not sworn to decide the law; they are not required to decide the law. If it appears upon the record, they ought to leave it there, or they may find the facts subject to the opinion of the Court upon the law. But further, upon the reason of the thing and the eternal principles of justice, the jury ought not to assume the jurisdiction of the law. As I said before, they do not know, and are not presumed to know, anything of the matter; they do not understand the language in which it is conceived, or the meaning of the terms. They have no rule to go by but their affections and wishes. It is said, if a man gives a *right* sentence upon hearing one side only, he is a wicked Judge, because he is right by chance only, and has neglected taking the proper method to be informed ; so the jury who usurp the judicature of law, though they happen to be right, are themselves wrong, because they are right by chance only, and have not taken the constitutional way of deciding the question. It is the duty of the Judge, in all cases of general justice, to tell the jury how to do right, though they have it *in their power* to do wrong, which is a matter entirely between God and their own consciences.

To be free, is to live under a government by law. The *liberty of the press* consists in printing without any previous license, subject to the consequences of law. The *licentiousness* of the press is *Pandora's* box, the source of every evil. Miserable is the condition of individuals, dangerous is the condition of the State, if there is no certain law, or which is the same thing, no certain administration of law to protect individuals, or to guard the State.

Jealousy of leaving the law to the Court, as in other cases, so in the case of libels, is now, in the present state of things, puerile rant and declamation. The Judges are totally independent of the ministers that may happen to be, and of the King himself. Their temptation is rather to the popularity of the day. But I agree with the observation, cited by Mr Cowper, * from Mr J. Forster, " that a *popular* Judge is an odious and a pernicious character."

The judgment of the Court is not final ; in the last resort it may be reviewed in the House of Lords, where the opinion of all the judges is taken.

In opposition to this, what is contended for ? That the law shall be in every particular cause what any twelve men, who shall happen to be the jury, shall be inclined to think liable to no review, and subject to no control, under all the prejudices of the popular cry of the day, and under all the bias of interest in this town, where thousands, more or less, are concerned in the publication of newspapers, paragraphs, and pamphlets. Under such an administration of law, no man could tell, no counsel could advise, whether a paper was or was not punishable.

I am glad that I am not bound to subscribe to such an absurdity, such a solecism in politics; but that, agreeable to the *uniform* judicial practice since the Revolution, warranted by the fundamental principles of the constitution, of the trial by jury, and upon the reason and fitness of the thing, we are all of opinion that this motion should be rejected, and the rule discharged.†

---

* One of the counsel for the prosecution.

† Although the Court was unanimous in discharging the rule, Mr Justice Willes, in delivering his opinion, sanctioned by his authority Mr Erskine's argument, that upon a plea of not guilty, or upon the general issue on an indictment or information for a libel, the jury had not only the *power*, but a constitutional *right*, to examine, if they thought fit, the criminality or innocence of the paper charged as a libel ; declaring it to be his settled opinion, that, notwithstanding the production of sufficient proof of the publication, the jury might upon such examination acquit the defendant generally, though in opposition to the directions of the Judge. without rendering themselves liable either to attaint, fine, or imprisonment, and that such verdict of deliverance could in no way be set aside by the Court.

THIS judgment may be considered as most fortunate for the public, since, in consequence of the very general interest taken in this cause, the public mind was at last fully ripe for the Libel Bill, which was soon after moved in the House of Commons by Mr Fox, and seconded by Mr Erskine.

The venerable and learned Chief-Justice undoubtedly established by his agument that the doctrine so soon afterwards condemned by the unanimous sense of the Legislature, when it passed the Libel Act, did not originate with himself, and that he only pronounced the law as he found it established by a train of *modern* decisions. But, supported as we now are by this judgment of Parliament, we must venture humbly to differ from so truly great an authority. The Libel Bill does not confer upon the jury any jurisdiction over the law inconsistent with the general principle of the constitution : but considering that the question of libel or no libel is frequently a question of fact rather than of law, and in many cases of fact and law almost inseparably blended together, it directs the Judge, as in other cases, to deliver his opinion to the jury upon the whole matter, including of course the question of libel or no libel, leaving them at the same time to found their verdicts upon such whole matter so brought before them as in all other criminal cases.* The best answer to the apprehensions of the great and eminent Chief-Justice regarding this course of proceeding, as then contended for by

---

* This Act, viz., 32 Geo. III. c. 60, runs thus :—

" Whereas doubts have arisen, whether, on the trial of an indictment or information for the making or publishing any libel, where an issue or issues are joined between the King and the defendant or defendants, on the plea of not guilty pleaded, it be competent to the jury impannelled to try the same to give their verdict upon the whole matter in issue : Be it therefore declared and enacted, by, &c., that on every such trial the jury sworn to try the issue may give a general verdict of guilty or not guilty, upon the whole matter put to issue on such indictment or information; and shall not be required or directed by the Court or Judge, before whom such indictment or information shall be tried, to find the defendant or defendants guilty, merely on the proof of the publication by such defendant or defendants of the paper charged to be a libel, and of the sense ascribed to the same in such indictment or information.

" II. Provided always, that on every such trial, the Court or Judge before whom such indictment or information shall be tried, shall, according to their or his discretion, give their or his opinion or directions to the jury on the matter in issue between the King and the defendant or defendants, in like manner as in all other criminal cases.

" III. Provided also, that nothing herein shall extend, or be construed to extend, to prevent the jury finding a special verdict at their discretion, as in other criminal cases.

" IV. Provided also, that in case the jury find the defendant or defendants guilty, it shall and may be lawful for the said defendant or defendants to move an arrest of judgment on such ground and in such manner as by law he or they might have done before the passing of this Act ; anything herein contained to the contrary notwithstanding."

Mr Erskine, and now established by the Libel Act, is the experience of seventeen years since that Act passed.

Before the statute, it was not difficult for the most abandoned and profligate libeller, guilty even of the most malignant slander upon private men, to connect his cause with the great privileges of the jury to protect innocence. Upon the Judge directing the jury, according to the old system, to find a verdict of guilty upon the fact of publication, shutting out altogether from their consideration the quality of the matter published, ingenious counsel used to seize that occasion to shelter a guilty individual under the mask of supporting great public right; and juries, to show that they were not implicitly bound to find verdicts of guilty upon such evidence alone, were too successfully incited to find improper verdicts of acquittal. But since the passing of the Libel Act, when the whole matter has been brought under their consideration, when the quality of the matter published has been exposed when criminal, and defended when just or innocent, juries have listened to the Judge with attention and reverence, without being bound in their consciences (except in matters of abstract law) to follow his opinion; and instead of that uncertainty anticipated by Lord Mansfield, the administration of justice has been in general most satisfactory, and the public authority been vindicated against unjust attacks with much greater security, and more supported by public opinion, than when juries were instruments in the hands of the fixed magistrates; whilst at the same time public liberty has been secured by leaving the whole matter in all public libels to the judgment and consideration of the people. This reformed state of the law, as it regards the liberty of the press, is now so universally acknowledged, that the highest magistrates have declared in the House of Lords that no new laws are necessary either to support the State or protect the people.

The following argument in arrest of judgment is copied from a newspaper of the succeeding day.

SPEECH in Arrest of Judgment.

Mr ERSKINE moved the Court to arrest the judgment in the case of the King against the Dean of St Asaph upon two grounds: first, because even if the indictment sufficiently charged a libel, the verdict given by the jury was not sufficient to warrant the judgment of the Court: and secondly, because the indictment did not contain any sufficient charge of a libel.

On the first objection, he again insisted on the right of the jury to find a general verdict on the merit of the writing charged on the record as a libel, notwithstanding the late judgment of the Court;— and declared he should maintain it there, and everywhere else, as long as he lived, till the contrary should be settled by Act of Parliament. He then argued at considerable length, that the verdict, as given by the jury, was neither a general nor a special verdict, and complained of the alteration made upon the record without the authority of the Court.

He said, that the only reason for his insisting on his first objection at such length, was the importance of the principle which it involved, and the danger of the precedent it established; although he was so certain of prevailing upon his second objection, that he considered it to be almost injustice to the Court to argue it. All who knew him in and out of the profession, could witness for him, that he had ever treated the idea of ultimately prevailing against him, upon such an indictment, to be perfectly ridiculous, and that his only object in all the trouble which he had given to the Court and to himself, in discussing the expediency of a new trial, was to resist a precedent, which he originally thought, and still continued to think, was illegal and unjustifiable:—the warfare was safe for his client, because he knew he could put an end to the prosecution any hour he pleased, by the objection he would now at last submit to the Court. It did not require the eye of a lawyer to see that even if the Dialogue, instead of being innocent and meritorious, as he thought it, had been the foulest libel ever composed or published, the indictment was drawn in such a manner as to render judgment absolutely impossible. He said, that if he had been answering in his own person to the charge of publishing the Dialogue complained of, he should have rejected with scorn the protection of a deficient indictment, would have boldly met the general question, and holding out defiance to the prosecutor, would have called upon his counsel to show what sentence, or word, though wrested with all the force ingenuity could apply to confound grammar and distort language, could be tortured into a violation of any one principle of the government:—but that, standing as counsel for another, he should not rest his defence even upon that strong foundation, but, after having maintained, as he had done at the trial, the innocence, or rather the merit of the Dialogue, should entrench himself behind every objection which the forms of law enabled him to cast up.

The second objection was, that the indictment did not contain a sufficient charge of a libel of and concerning the King and his government:—that though the Court, by judging of libels of that nature, invested itself with a very large discretion; yet it, nevertheless, was a discretion capable of being measured by very intelligible rules of law, and within which rules he was persuaded the Court would strictly confine itself.

The first was, that the Court, in judging of the libellous or seditious nature of the paper in question, could only collect it from the indictment itself, and could supply nothing from any extrinsic source; and that, therefore, whatever circumstances were necessary to constitute the crime imputed, could not be supplied from any report of the evidence, nor from any inference from the verdict, but must be set out upon the record.

That rule was founded in great wisdom, and formed the boundary between the provinces of the jury and the Court; because, if any extrinsic circumstances, independent of the plain and ordinary meaning of the writing, were necessary to explain it, and point its criminal application, those facts must be put upon the record, for three reasons:—

First, That the charge might contain such a description of the crime, that the defendant might know what crime he was called upon to answer.

Secondly, That the application of the writing to those circumstances which constituted its criminality might be submitted as facts to the jury, who were the sole judges of any meaning which depended upon extrinsic proof.

Thirdly, That the Court might see such a definite crime that they might apply the punishment which the law inflicted.

He admitted, that wherever a writing was expressed in such clear and unambiguous words as in itself to constitute a libel, without the help of any explanation, all averments and innuendoes were unnecessary;—and, therefore, if it could be established that the pamphlet in question, if taken off the dusty shelves of a library, and looked at in the pure abstract, without attention to times or circumstances, without application to any facts not upon record, and without any light cast upon it from without, contained false, pernicious, illegal, and unconstitutional doctrines, in their tendency destructive of the Government, it would unquestionably be a libel. But if the terms of the writing were general, and the criminality imputed to it consisted in criminal allusions or references to matter dehors the writing; then, although every man who reads such a writing might put the same construction on it; yet when it was the charge of a crime, and the party was liable to be punished for it, there wanted something more.

It ought to receive a juridical sense on the record, and, as the facts were to be decided by the jury, they only could decide whether the application of general expressions, or terms of reference, or allusions, as the case might be, to matters extrinsic, was just; nor could the general expressions themselves be extended, even by the jury, beyond their ordinary meaning, without an averment to give them cognisance of such extended import; nor could the Court, even after a verdict of guilty, without such averment infer anything from the finding, but must pronounce strictly according to the just and grammatical sense of the language on the record. The Court, by declaring libel or not libel to be a question of law, must be supposed by that declaration not to assume any jurisdiction over facts, which was the province of the jury; but only to determine that, if the words of the writing, without averment, or with averments found to be true by the jury, contained criminal matter, it would be pronounced to be a libel according to the rules of law:—

whereas, if the libel could only be inferred from its application to something extrinsic, however reasonable or probable such application might be, no court could possibly make it for want of the averment, without which the jury could have no jurisdiction over the facts extrinsic, by reference to which only the writing became criminal.

The next question was, how the application of the writing to any particular object was to be made upon the record : that was likewise settled in the case of the King and Horne.

" In all cases those facts which are descriptive of the charge must be introduced on the record by averments, in opposition to argument and inference."

He said, that where facts were necessary in order to apply the matter of the libel to them, it was done introductorily. And where no new fact was necessary, but only ambiguous words were to be explained, it was done by the innuendo. But that the innuendo could not in itself enlarge the matter which it was employed to explain, without an antecedent introduction to refer to ; but coupled with such introductory matter it could.

He said nothing remained but to apply those unquestionable principles to the present indictment ; and that application divided itself into two heads :—

First, Whether the words of the Dialogue, considered purely in the abstract, without being taken to be a seditious exhortation addressed to the people, in consequence of the present state of the nation, as connected with the subject matter of it, could possibly be considered to be a libel on the King and his Government.

Secondly, Whether, if such reference or allusion was necessary to render it criminal, there were sufficient averments on the record to enable the Court to make the criminal application of otherwise innocent doctrines consistently with the rules of law.

He said he should therefore take the Dialogue, and show the Court that the whole scope and every particular part of it were meritorious.

Here Lord Mansfield said to Mr Erskine, that having laid down his principles of judgment, the counsel for the prosecution should point out the parts they insisted on as sufficiently charged to be libellous, and that he would be heard in reply. On which Mr Bearcroft, Mr Cowper, Mr Leicester, and Mr Bower, were all heard ; and endeavoured with great ingenuity to show that the Dialogue was on the face of it a libel : but on Mr Erskine's rising to reply, the Court said they would not give him any further trouble, as they were unanimously of opinion that the indictment was defective, and that the judgment should be arrested.

The Court went upon the principles of the case of the King against Horne, cited by Mr Erskine, saying there were no averments to point the application of the paper as a libel on the King and his Government; and the Dean is therefore finally discharged from the prosecution.

Mr Justice Willes threw out, that if the indictment had been properly drawn, it might have been supported. But Lord Mansfield and Mr Justice Buller did not give any such opinion, confining themselves strictly to the question before the Court.

The judgment was accordingly arrested, and no new proceedings were ever had upon the subject against the Dean or the printer employed by him. His adversaries were, it is believed, sufficiently disposed to distress him; but they were probably aware of the consequences of bringing the doctrines maintained by the Court of King's Bench into a second public examination.

CASE of the KING *against* JOHN STOCKDALE, *tried in the Court of King's Bench, before* LORD KENYON *and a Special Jury, at Westminster, on the* 9th *of December* 1789, *upon an Information filed against him by the* ATTORNEY-GENERAL, *for a Libel on the* HOUSE OF COMMONS.

THE SUBJECT.

THE trial of Mr John Stockdale, of Piccadilly, is so immediately connected with the well-known impeachment of Mr Hastings, the Governor-General of India, that very little preface is necessary for the illustration of Mr Erskine's defence of him.

When the Commons of Great Britain ordered that impeachment, the articles were prepared by Mr Edmund Burke, who had the lead in all the inquiries which led to it, and, instead of being drawn up in the usual dry method of legal accusation, were expanded into great length, and were characterised by that fervid and affecting language which distinguishes all the writings of that extraordinary person. The articles so prepared, instead of being confined to the records of the House of Commons, until they were carried up to the Lords for trial, were printed and sold in every shop in the kingdom, without question or obstruction by the managers of the impeachment or the House of Commons, and undoubtedly, from the style and manner of their composition, made a very considerable impression against the accused.

To repel the effects of the articles, thus (according to the reasoning of Mr Erskine) prematurely published, the Rev. Mr Logan, one of the ministers of Leith in Scotland, a person eminent for learning, drew up a review of the articles of impeachment (which, as has been already stated, were then in general circulation), and carried them to Mr Stockdale, an eminent and respectable bookseller in Piccadilly, who published them in the usual course of his business. Mr Logan's review was composed with great accuracy and judgment, but undoubtedly with strong severity of observation against the accusation of Mr Hastings ; and having an immediate and very extensive sale, was complained of by Mr Fox to the House of Commons, and upon the motion of that great and eminent person, then one of the managers of the impeachment, the House unanimously voted an address to the King, praying His Majesty to direct his Attorney-General to file an information against Mr Stockdale, as the publisher of a libel upon the Commons House of Parliament, which was filed accordingly.

It is not necessary to lengthen this preface by the passages from Mr Logan's book which were selected by the Attorney-General in forming the information, and which gave the greatest offence to the House of

Commons; neither is it necessary to print the information itself, because the principal passages complained of and contained in it, were read by Lord Chief-Baron Macdonald, then Attorney-General, in his very fair and able address to the jury, which we have printed, as well as his judicious reply, and the summing up of Lord Chief-Justice Kenyon; because this trial, above any other in print, contains the invaluable principles of a free press, and the important privilege of the jury since the passing of the memorable Libel Act. The application of these principles to an acquittal or conviction in this particular instance, is not within our province: but we may state as a fact, that the verdict gave very general satisfaction, and, what is a proud consideration for the subjects of this country, under our invaluable constitution, neither the highest Court in the kingdom, nor the House of Commons, who were the accusers, had a right to question its authority.

The evidence consisted of nothing but the common proof of publication, and is therefore omitted as unnecessary.

The ATTORNEY-GENERAL opened the case as follows:—

GENTLEMEN OF THE JURY,—This information, which it has been my duty to file against the defendant, John Stockdale, comes before you in consequence of an address from the House of Commons. This, you may well suppose, I do not mention as in any degree to influence the judgment which you are by and by to give upon your oath: I state it as a measure which they have taken, thinking it in their wisdom, as everybody must think it, to be the fittest to bring before a jury of the country, an offender against themselves, avoiding thereby, what sometimes indeed is unavoidable, but which they wish to avoid, whenever it can be done with propriety—the acting both as judges and accusers; which they must necessarily have done, had they resorted to their own powers, which are great and extensive, for the purpose of vindicating themselves against insult and contempt, but which, in the present instance, they have wisely forborne to exercise, thinking it better to leave the defendant to be dealt with by a fair and impartial jury.

The offence which I impute to him is that of calumniating the House of Commons: not in its ordinary legislative character, but when acting in its accusatorial capacity, conceiving it to be their duty, on adequate occasions, to investigate the conduct of persons in high stations, and to leave that conduct to be judged of by the proper constitutional tribunal, the peers in Parliament assembled.

After due investigation, as it is well known to the public, the Commons of Great Britain thought it their duty to submit the conduct of a servant of this country, who had governed one of its most opulent dependencies for many years, to an inquiry before that tribunal. One would have thought that every good subject of this country would have forborne imputing to the House of Commons motives utterly unworthy of them, and of those whom they represent : instead of this, to so great a degree now has the licentiousness of the press arisen, that motives the most unbecoming that can actuate any individual who may be concerned in the prosecution of public justice, are imputed to the representatives of the people. No credit is given to them for meaning to do justice to their country, but, on the contrary, private, personal, and malicious motives have been imputed to the Commons of Great Britain.

When such an imputation is made upon the very first tribunal that this country knows, namely, the great inquest of the nation, the Commons in Parliament assembled, carrying a subject, who, as they thought, had offended, to the bar of the House of Lords, I am sure you will think this an attack so dangerous to every tribunal, so dangerous to the whole administration of justice, that if it be well proved, you cannot fail to give it your stigma, by a verdict against the defendant.

Gentlemen, the particular passages which I shall put my finger upon in this libel it will now be my duty to state. You know very well that it is your duty to consider of the meaning that I have imputed to them by the information. If you agree with me in that meaning, you convict ; if you disagree with me, of course you acquit.

The rule of your judgment, I apprehend (with submission to his Lordship), will be the ordinary acceptation of the words, and the plain and obvious sense of the several passages. If there be doubt, or if there be difficulty, if there be screwing or ingenuity, or unworthy straining, on the part of a public prosecutor, you certainly will pay no attention to that ; but, on the contrary, if he who runs may read, if the meanest capacity must understand the words, in their plain and obvious sense, to be the same as imputed in this information, in such a case as that, ingenuity on the other side must be laid aside by you, and you will not be over-anxious to give a meaning to words other than the ordinary and plain one.

In my situation, it does not become me to raise in you more indignation than the words themselves and the plain and simple reading of the libel will do : far be it from me, if it were in my power to do so, to provoke any undue passions or animosity in you against conduct even such as this. The solemnity of the situation in which I am placed on this occasion, obliges me to address the intellect both of the Court and jury, and neither their passions nor their prejudices. For that reason I shall content myself with the few observations I have made, and betake myself merely to the words of the libel ; and leaving that with you, I am most confident that if you follow the rule of interpretation which you always do upon such occasions, it cannot possibly happen that you should differ from me in the construction which I have put upon them.

Gentlemen, this, I should however mention to you, is a libel of a more dangerous nature than the ribaldry that we daily see crowding every one of the prints which appear every morning upon our tables; because it is contained in a work which discovers the author of it to be by no means ignorant of composition, but certainly to be of good understanding, and eminently acquainted with letters. Therefore, when calumny of this sort comes so recommended, and addressing itself to the understandings of the most enlightened part of mankind—I mean those who have had the best education—it may sink deep into the minds of those who compose the thinking and the judging part of the community; and by misleading them, perhaps may be of more real danger than the momentary misleading, or the momentary inflammation, of common minds, by the ordinary publications of the day.

This book is entitled, "A Review of the Principal Charges against Warren Hastings, Esquire, late Governor-General of Bengal."

One passage in it is this: "The House of Commons has now given its final decision with regard to the merits and demerits of Mr Hastings. The grand inquest of England have delivered their charges, and preferred their impeachment: their allegations are referred to proof; and from the appeal to the collective wisdom and justice of the nation in the supreme tribunal of the kingdom, the question comes to be determined, whether Mr Hastings *be guilty or not guilty ?*"

Another is this: "What credit can we give to multiplied and accumulated charges, when we find that they originate from misrepresentation and falsehood?"

Another is: "An impeachment of *error* in *judgment* with regard to the *quantum* of a fine, and for an intention that never was executed, characterises a tribunal of inquisition, rather than a court of Parliament."

In another part it is said: "The other charges are so insignificant in themselves, or founded on such gross misrepresentations, that they would not affect an obscure individual, much less a public character."

And again: "If success, in any degree, attends the designs of the accusers of Mr Hastings, the voice of Britain henceforth to her sons is, Go and serve your country; but if you transgress the line of official orders, though compelled by necessity, you do so at the risk of your fortune, your honour, and your life; if you act with *proper prudence* against the interests of the empire, and bring calamity and disgrace upon your country, you have only to court opposition and coalesce with your enemies, and you will find a party zealous and devoted to support you; you may obtain a vote of thanks from the House of Commons for your *services*, and you may *read your history in the eyes of the mob* by the light of bonfires and illuminations. But if, after exerting all your efforts in the cause of your country, you return, covered with laurels and crowned with success ; if you preserve a loyal attachment to your Sovereign, you may expect the thunders of parliamentary vengeance ; you will certainly be impeached, and probably be undone."

Another passage is this : " The office of calm deliberate justice is to redress grievances as well as to punish offences. It has been affirmed, that the natives of India have been deeply injured ; but has any motion been made to make them compensation for the injuries they have sustained ? Have the accusers of Mr Hastings ever proposed to bring back the Rohillas to the country from which they were expelled ? To restore Cheit Sing to the Zemindary of Benares, or to return the Nabob of Oude the present which the Governor of Bengal received from him for the benefit of the Company ? Till such measures are adopted, and in the train of negotiation, the world has every reason to conclude that the impeachment of Mr Hastings is carried on"—now, gentlemen, I leave you to judge what sort of motives are imputed to the House of Commons here—" from motives of personal animosity, not from regard to public justice."

The general meaning, without specifying it in technical language, which I have thought it my duty to impute to these words, is shortly this : That the House of Commons, without consideration, without reading, without hearing, have not been ashamed to accuse a man of distinguished situation ; and to pervert their accusatorial character from the purposes of deliberate, thoughtful, considerate justice, to immediate, hasty, passionate, vindictive, personal animosity. The work represents that the better a man conducts himself—that the more deserving he has rendered himself of his country's favour from his past conduct, the more he exposes himself to the vindictive proceedings of Parliament ; and that such a man will be impeached and ruined.

In another passage, PERSONAL ANIMOSITY (*the very words are used*) is imputed to the Commons of Great Britain as the motive of their conduct. These are too plain for you, gentlemen, to differ with me in the interpretation.

I do not choose to waste *your* time, and that of the Court, in so plain a case, with much observation ; but, hackneyed as it may be, it is my duty, upon every one of these occasions, to remind you, that the liberty of the press consists in its good regulation: if it be meant that it should be preserved with benefit to the public, it must be from time to time lopped of its unjust excesses, by reasonable and proper verdicts of juries, in fit and clear cases.

The publication having been proved, Mr Erskine addressed the jury as follows : first saying, " I admit that the witness has proved that he bought this book at the shop of Mr Stockdale—Mr Stockdale himself being in the shop—from a young man who acted as his servant."

GENTLEMEN OF THE JURY,—Mr Stockdale, who is brought as a criminal before you for the publication of this book, has, by employing ME as his advocate, reposed what must appear to many an extraordinary degree of confidence, since—although he well knows that I am personally connected in friendship with most of those whose conduct and opinions are principally arraigned by its author —he nevertheless commits to MY hands his defence and justification.

From a trust apparently so delicate and singular, vanity is but too apt to whisper an application to some fancied merit of one's own ; but it is proper, for the honour of the English bar, that the world should know that such things happen to all of us daily, and of course ; and that the defendant, without any knowledge of me, or any confidence that was personal, was only not afraid to follow up an accidental retainer, from the knowledge he has of the general character of the profession. Happy, indeed, is it for this country, that whatever interested divisions may characterise *other places*, of which I may have occasion to speak to-day, however the councils of the highest departments of the State may be occasionally distracted by personal considerations, they never enter these walls to disturb the administration of justice ; whatever may be *our* public principles, or the private habits of *our* lives, they never cast even a shade across the path of our professional duties. If this be the characteristic even of the bar of an English court of justice, what sacred impartiality may not every man expect from its jurors and its Bench ?

As, from the indulgence which the Court was yesterday pleased to give to my indisposition, this information was not proceeded on when you were attending to try it, it is probable you were not altogether inattentive to what passed at the trial of the other indictment, prosecuted also by the House of Commons ; and therefore, without a restatement of the same principles, and a similar quotation of authorities to support them, I need only remind you of the law applicable to this subject, as it was then admitted by the Attorney-General, in concession to my propositions, and confirmed by the higher authority of the Court, viz. :—

First, that every information or indictment must contain such a description of the crime that the defendant may know what crime it is which he is called upon to answer.

Secondly, that the jury may appear to be warranted in their conclusion of guilty or not guilty.

And, lastly, that the Court may see such a precise and definite transgression upon the record, as to be able to apply the punishment which judicial discretion may dictate, or which positive law may inflict.

It was admitted also to follow, as a mere corollary from these propositions, that where an information charges a writing to be composed or published OF AND CONCERNING THE COMMONS OF GREAT BRITAIN, with an intent to bring that body into scandal and disgrace with the public, the author cannot be brought within the scope of such a charge, unless the jury, on examination and comparison of the *whole matter* written or published, shall be satisfied that the particular passages charged as criminal, when explained by the context, and considered as part of *one entire work*, were meant and intended by the author to vilify the House of Commons *as a body*, and were written *of and concerning them* IN PARLIAMENT ASSEMBLED.

These principles being settled, we are now to see what the present information is.

It charges that the defendant " unlawfully, wickedly, and maliciously devising, contriving, and intending to asperse, scandalise, and vilify the Commons of Great Britain in Parliament assembled ; and most wickedly and audaciously to represent their proceedings as corrupt and unjust, and to make it believed and thought as if the Commons of Great Britain in Parliament assembled were a most wicked, tyrannical, base, and corrupt set of persons, and to bring them into disgrace with the public ; " the defendant published—*What?*—*Not* those latter ends of sentences which the Attorney-General has read from his brief, as if they had followed one another in order in this book ; *not* those scraps and tails of passages which are patched together upon this record, and pronounced in one breath, as if they existed without intermediate matter in the same page, and without context anywhere. *No.* This is not the accusation, even mutilated as it is ; for the information charges *that, with intention to vilify the House of Commons,* the defendant published the whole book, describing it on the record by its title, " A Review of the Principal Charges against Warren Hastings, Esq., late Governor-General of Bengal," *in which, amongst other things, the matter particularly selected is to be found.* Your inquiry, therefore, is not confined to whether the defendant published *those selected parts of it ;* and whether, looking at them as they are distorted by the information, they carry in fair construction the sense and meaning which the innuendoes put upon them ; but whether the author of the *entire work*—I say THE AUTHOR, since, if HE could defend himself, THE PUBLISHER unquestionably can,—whether THE AUTHOR wrote the volume which I hold in my hand, as a free, manly, *bona fide* disquisition of criminal charges against his fellow-citizens ; or whether the long eloquent discussion

of them, which fills so many pages, was a mere cloak and cover for
the introduction of the supposed scandal imputed *to the selected
passages;* the mind of the writer, all along, being intent on tra-
ducing the House of Commons, and not on *fairly* answering their
charges against Mr Hastings?

This, gentlemen, is the principal matter for your consideration;
and therefore, if, after you shall have taken the book itself into the
chamber which will be provided for you, and shall have read the
whole of it with impartial attention; if, after the performance of
this duty, you can return here, and with clear consciences pronounce
upon your oaths that the impression made upon you by these pages
is, that the author wrote them with the wicked, seditious, and corrupt intentions charged by the information;—you have then my
full permission to find the defendant guilty. But if, on the other
hand, the general tenor of the composition shall impress you with
respect for the author, and point him out to you as a man mistaken,
perhaps himself, but not seeking to deceive others; if every line of
the work shall present to you an intelligent, animated mind, glowing with a Christian compassion towards a fellow-man, whom he
believed to be innocent, and with a patriot zeal for the liberty of
his country, which he considered as wounded through the sides of
an oppressed fellow-citizen; if *this* shall be the impression on your
consciences and understandings, when you are called upon to deliver
your verdict, then hear from me, that you not only work private
injustice, but break up the press of England, and surrender her
rights and liberties for ever, if you convict the defendant.

Gentlemen, to enable you to form a true judgment of the meaning of this book, and of the intention of its author, and to expose
the miserable juggle that is played off in the information by the
combination of sentences which, in the work itself, have no bearing
upon one another, I will first give you the publication as it is
charged upon the record and presented by the Attorney-General in
opening the case for the Crown; and I will then, by reading the
interjacent matter, which is studiously kept out of view, convince
you of its true interpretation.

The information, beginning with the first page of the book,
charges as a libel upon the House of Common, the following sentence:—" The House of Commons has now given its final decision
with regard to the merits and demerits of Mr Hastings. The
grand inquest of England have delivered their charges, and preferred their impeachment; their allegations are referred to proof;
and from the appeal to the collective wisdom and justice of the
nation in the supreme tribunal of the kingdom, the question comes
to be determined, whether Mr Hastings *be guilty or not guilty?*"

It is but fair, however, to admit that this first sentence, which
the most ingenious malice cannot torture into a criminal construction, is charged by the information rather as introductory to what

is made to follow it, than as libellous in itself; for the Attorney-
General, from this introductory passage in the first page, goes on
at a leap to page *thirteenth*, and reads—almost without a stop, as
if it immediately followed the other—this sentence: " What credit
can we give to multiplied and accumulated charges, when we find
that they originate from misrepresentation and falsehood?"

From these two passages thus standing together, *without the in-
tervenient matter, which occupies thirteen pages*, one would imagine
that, instead of investigating the probability or improbability of
the guilt imputed to Mr Hastings; instead of carefully examining
the charges of the Commons, and the defence of them which had
been delivered before them, or which was preparing for the Lords,
the author had immediately, and in a moment after stating the
mere fact of the impeachment, decided that the act of the Commons
originated from misrepresentation and falsehood.

Gentlemen, in the same manner a veil is cast over all that is
written *in the next seven pages;* for knowing that the context
would help to the true construction, not only of the passages
charged before, but of those in the sequel of this information, the
Attorney-General, aware that it would convince every man who
read it that there was no intention in the author to calumniate the
House of Commons, passes over, by another leap, *to page twenty;*
and in the same manner, without drawing his breath, and as if it
directly followed the two former sentences *in the first and thirteenth
pages*, reads from page twentieth, " An impeachment of error in
judgment with regard to the quantum of a fine, and for an intention that never was executed, and never known to the offending
party, characterises a tribunal of inquisition rather than a court of
Parliament."

From this passage, by another vault, he leaps over *one-and-
thirty pages more, to page fifty-one;* where he reads the following
sentence, which he mainly relies on, and upon which I shall by and
by trouble you with some observations: " Thirteen of them passed
in the House of Commons not only without investigation, but without being read; and the votes were given without inquiry, argument, or conviction. A majority had determined to impeach;
opposite parties met each other, and '*jostled in the dark*,' to perplex the political drama, and bring the hero to a tragic catastrophe."

From thence, deriving new vigour from every exertion, he makes
his last grand stride *over forty-four pages more*, almost to the end
of the book, charging a sentence *in the ninety-fifth page.*

So that out of a volume of *one hundred and ten pages*, the
defendant is only charged with a few scattered fragments of sentences, picked out of *three or four*. Out of a work, consisting of
about *two thousand five hundred and thirty lines*, of manly, spirited
eloquence, only *forty or fifty lines* are culled from different parts of

it, and artfully put together, so as to rear up a libel, out of a false context, by a supposed connexion of sentences with one another, which are not only entirely independent, but which, when compared with their antecedents, bear a totally different construction. In this manner, the greatest works upon government, the most excellent books of science, the sacred Scriptures themselves, might be distorted into libels ; by forsaking the general context, and hanging a meaning upon selected parts : thus, as in the text put by Algernon Sidney, " The fool has said in his heart, There is no God ; " the Attorney-General, on the principle of the present proceeding against this pamphlet, might indict the publisher of the Bible for blasphemously denying the existence of heaven, in printing, " *There is no God.*" For these words alone, without the context, would be selected by the information, and the Bible, like this book, would be *underscored* to meet it. Nor could the defendant in such a case, have any possible defence, unless the jury were permitted to see, BY THE BOOK ITSELF, that the verse, instead of denying the existence of the divinity, only imputed that imagination to a fool.

Gentlemen, having now gone through the Attorney-General's reading, the book shall presently come forward and speak for itself. But before I can venture to lay it before you, it is proper to call your attention to how matters stood at the time of its publication, without which the author's meaning and intention cannot possibly be understood.

The Commons of Great Britain, in Parliament assembled, had accused Mr Hastings, as Governor-General of Bengal, of high crimes and misdemeanours ; and their jurisdiction for that high purpose of national justice was unquestionably competent. But it is proper you should know the nature of this inquisitorial capacity. The Commons, in voting an impeachment, may be compared to a grand jury, finding a bill of indictment for the Crown: neither the one nor the other can be supposed to proceed but upon the matter which is brought before them ; neither of them can find guilt without accusation, nor the truth of accusation without evidence. When, therefore, we speak of the *accuser*, or *accusers*, of a person indicted for any crime, although the grand jury are the accusers *in form*, by giving effect to the accusation, yet in common parlance we do not consider *them* as the responsible authors of the prosecution. If I were to write of a most wicked indictment, found against an innocent man, which was preparing for trial, nobody who read it would conceive I meant to stigmatise the grand jury that found the bill ; but it would be inquired immediately who was the PROSECUTOR, and who were the WITNESSES on the back of it? In the same manner I mean to contend, that if this book is read with only common attention, the whole scope of it will be discovered to be this : That, in the opinion of the author, Mr Hastings had been accused of maladministration in India, from the heat

and spleen of political divisions in Parliament, and not from any zeal
for national honour or justice ; that the impeachment did not originate from Government, but from a faction banded against it,
which, by misrepresentation and violence, had fastened it on an
unwilling House of Commons : that, prepossessed with this sentiment (which, however unfounded, makes no part of the present
business, since the publisher is not called before you for defaming
individual members of the Commons, but for a contempt of the Commons as a body), the author pursues the charges, article by article ;
enters into a warm and animated vindication of Mr Hastings, by regular answers to each of them ; and that, as far as the mind and soul
of a man can be visible, I might almost say embodied, in his writings,
his intention throughout the whole volume appears to have been
to charge with injustice the *private accusers* of Mr Hastings, and ·
not the House of Commons as a body : which undoubtedly rather
reluctantly gave way to, than heartily adopted, the impeachment.
This will be found to be the palpable scope of the book ; and ·
no man who can read English, and who, at the same time, will
have the candour and common sense to take up his impressions
from what is written in it, instead of bringing his own along
with him to the reading of it, can possibly understand it otherwise.

But it may be said, that admitting this to be the scope and
design of the author, what right had he to canvass the merits of
an accusation upon the records of the Commons, more especially
while it was in the course of legal procedure ?   This, I confess,
might have been a serious question ; but the Commons, *as prosecutors of this information*, seem to have waived, or forfeited, their
right to ask it.   Before they sent the Attorney-General into this
place, to punish the publication of *answers* to their charges, they
should have recollected that their own want of circumspection in
the maintenance of their privileges, and in the protection of persons accused before them, had given to the public *the charges themselves*, which should have been confined to *their own journals.*
The course and practice of Parliament might warrant the printing
of them for the use of their own members ; but there the publication should have stopped, and all further progress been
resisted by authority.   If they were resolved to consider *answers to
their charges* as a contempt of their privileges, and to punish the
publication of them by such severe prosecutions, it would have
well become them to have begun first with those printers who, by
publishing *the charges themselves* throughout the whole kingdom,
or rather throughout the whole civilised world, were anticipating
the passions and judgments of the public against a subject of England upon his trial, so as to make the publication of *answers* to
them not merely a privilege, but a debt and duty to humanity and
justice.   The Commons of Great Britain claimed and exercised the

privileges of questioning the innocence of Mr Hastings by their impeachment; but as, however questioned, it was still to be presumed and protected, until guilt was established by a judgment, he whom they had accused had an equal claim upon their justice, to guard him from prejudice and misrepresentation until the hour of trial.

Had the Commons, therefore, by the exercise of their high, necessary, and legal privileges, kept the public aloof from all canvass of their proceedings, by an early punishment of printers who, without reserve or secrecy, had sent out *the charges* into the world from a thousand presses in every form of publication, they would have then stood upon ground to-day from whence no argument of policy or justice could have removed them ; because nothing can be more incompatible with either than appeals to the many upon subjects of judicature, which by common consent a few are appointed to determine, and which must be determined by facts and principles which the multitude have neither leisure nor knowledge to investigate. But then, let it be remembered, that it is for those who have the authority to accuse and punish to set the example of, and to enforce this reserve, which is so necessary for the ends of justice. Courts of law, therefore, in England, never endure the publication of *their* records ; and a prosecutor of an indictment would be attached for such a publication ; and upon the same principle, a defendant would be punished for anticipating the justice of his country by the publication of his defence, the public being no party to it until the tribunal appointed for its determination be open for its decision.

Gentlemen, you have a right to take judicial notice of these matters, without the proof of them by witnesses ; for jurors may not only, without evidence, found their verdicts on facts that are notorious, but upon what they know privately themselves, after revealing it upon oath to one another ; and, therefore, you are always to remember that this book was written when the *charges* against Mr Hastings, *to which it is an answer*, were *to the knowledge of the Commons* (for we cannot presume our watchmen to have been asleep), publicly hawked about in every pamphlet, magazine, and newspaper in the kingdom. You well know with what a curious appetite these charges were devoured by the whole public, interesting as they were, not only from their importance, but from the merit of their composition ; certainly not so intended by the honourable and excellent composer to oppress the accused, but because the most common subjects swell into eloquence under the touch of his sublime genius. Thus, by the remissness of the Commons, *who are now the prosecutors of this information*, a subject of England, who was not even charged with contumacious resistance to authority, much less a proclaimed outlaw, and therefore fully entitled to every protection which the customs and statutes of the kingdom hold out for the protection of British liberty, saw himself pierced with the arrows of thousands and ten thousands of libels.

Gentlemen, before I venture to lay the book before you, it must be yet further remembered (for the fact is equally notorious), that under these inauspicious circumstances the trial of Mr Hastings at the bar of the Lords had actually commenced long before its publication.

There the most august and striking spectacle was daily exhibited which the world ever witnessed. A vast stage of justice was erected, awful from its high authority, splendid from its illustrious dignity, venerable from the learning and wisdom of its judges, captivating and affecting from the mighty concourse of all ranks and conditions which daily flocked into it, as into a theatre of pleasure ; there, when the whole public mind was at once awed and softened to the impression of every human affection, there appeared, day after day, one after another, men of the most powerful and exalted talents, eclipsing by their accusing eloquence the most boasted harangues of antiquity ; rousing the pride of national resentment by the boldest invectives against broken faith and violated treaties, and shaking the bosom with alternate pity and horror by the most glowing pictures of insulted nature and humanity ; ever animated and energetic, from the love of fame, which is the inherent passion of genius ; firm and indefatigable, from a strong prepossession of the justice of their cause.

Gentlemen, when the author sat down to write the book now before you, all this terrible, unceasing, exhaustless artillery of warm zeal, matchless vigour of understanding, consuming and devouring eloquence, united with the highest dignity, was daily, and without prospect of conclusion, pouring forth upon one private unprotected man, who was bound to hear it, in the face of the whole people of England, with reverential submission and silence. I do not complain of this as I did of the publication of the charges, because it is what the law allowed and sanctioned in the course of a public trial : but when it is remembered that we are not angels, but weak, fallible men, and that even the noble judges of that high tribunal are clothed beneath their ermines with the common infirmities of man's nature, it will bring us all to a proper temper for considering the book itself, which will in a few moments be laid before you. But first, let me once more remind you, that it was under all these circumstances, and amidst the blaze of passion and prejudice, which the scene I have been endeavouring faintly to describe to you might be supposed likely to produce, that the author, whose name I will now give you, sat down to compose the book which is prosecuted to-day as a libel.

The history of it is very short and natural.

The Rev. Mr Logan, minister of the gospel at Leith, in Scotland, a clergyman of the purest morals, and, as you will see by and by, of very superior talents, well acquainted with the human character, and knowing the difficulty of bringing back public opinion after it is settled on any subject, took a warm, unbought, unsolicited interest in the situation of Mr Hastings, and determined, if possible, to arrest and suspend the public judgment concerning him. He felt for the situation of a fellow-citizen, exposed to a trial which, whether right or wrong, is undoubtedly a severe one,—a trial certainly not confined to a few criminal acts like those we are accustomed to, but comprehending the transactions of a whole life, and the complicated policies of numerous and distant nations,—a trial which had neither visible limits to its duration, bounds to its expense, nor circumscribed compass for the grasp of memory or understanding; a trial which had therefore broke loose from the common form of decision, and had become the universal topic of discussion in the world, superseding not only every other grave pursuit, but every fashionable dissipation.

Gentlemen, the question you have therefore to try upon all this matter is extremely simple. It is neither more nor less than this: At a time when the charges against Mr Hastings were, by the implied consent of the Commons, in every hand and on every table; when by their managers the lightning of eloquence was incessantly consuming him, and flashing in the eyes of the public; when every man was with perfect impunity saying, and writing, and publishing just what he pleased of the supposed plunderer and devastator of nations; would it have been criminal *in Mr Hastings himself* to have reminded the public that he was a native of this free land, entitled to the common protection of her justice, and that he had a defence in his turn to offer to them, the outlines of which he implored them in the meantime to receive, as an antidote to the unlimited and unpunished poison in circulation against him? This is, without colour or exaggeration, the true question you are to decide; because I assert, without the hazard of contradiction, that if Mr Hastings himself could have stood justified or excused in your eyes for publishing this volume in his own defence, the author, if he wrote it *bonâ fide* to defend him, must stand equally excused and justified; and if the author be justified, the publisher cannot be criminal, unless you had evidence that it was published by him with a different spirit and intention from those in which it was written. The question therefore is correctly what I just now stated it to be: Could *Mr Hastings* have been condemned to infamy for writing this book?

Gentlemen, I tremble with indignation to be driven to put such a question in England. Shall it be endured that a subject of this country (instead of being arraigned and tried for some single act in her ordinary courts, where the accusation, as soon at least as it is made public, is followed within a few hours by the decision) may be impeached by the Commons for the transactions of twenty

years,—that the accusation shall spread as wide as the region of
letters,—that the accused shall stand, day after day, and year after
year, as a spectacle before the public, which shall be kept in a perpetual state of inflammation against him ; yet that he shall not,
without the severest penalties, be permitted to submit anything to
the judgment of mankind in his defence ?   If this be law (which
it is for you to-day to decide) such a man has NO TRIAL ; that great
hall, built by our fathers for English justice, is no longer a court,
but an altar ; and an Englishman, instead of being judged in it by
GOD AND HIS COUNTRY, IS A VICTIM AND A SACRIFICE.

You will carefully remember that I am not presuming to question either the right or the duty of the Commons of Great Britain
to impeach ; neither am I arraigning the propriety of their selecting, as they have done, the most extraordinary persons for ability
which the age has produced to manage their impeachment ; much
less am I censuring the managers themselves, charged with the
conduct of it before the Lords, who were undoubtedly bound, by
their duty to the House and to the public, to expatiate upon the
crimes of the person whom they had accused.   None of these
points are questioned by me, nor are in this place questionable.   I
only desire to have it decided whether, if the Commons, when
national expediency happens to call in their judgment for an impeachment, shall, *instead of keeping it on their own records, and
carrying it with due solemnity to the Peers for trial,* permit it
without censure and punishment to be sold like a common newspaper in the shop of my client, so crowded with their own members
that no plain man, without privilege of Parliament, can hope even
for a sight of the fire in a winter's day, every man buying it, reading it, and commenting upon it ; the gentleman himself who is the
object of it, or his friend in his absence, may not, without stepping
beyond the bounds of English freedom, put a copy of what is thus
published into his pocket, and send back to the very same shop for
publication a *bonâ fide*, rational, able answer to it, in order that
the bane and antidote may circulate together, and the public be
kept straight till the day of decision.   If you think, gentlemen,
that this common duty of self-preservation in the accused himself,
which nature writes as a law upon the hearts of even savages and
brutes, is nevertheless too high a privilege to be enjoyed by an
impeached and suffering Englishman ; or if you think it beyond
the offices of humanity and justice, when brought home to the
hand of a brother or a friend, you will say so by your verdict of
GUILTY—the decision will then be *yours*, and the consolation *mine*
that I laboured to avert it.   A very small part of the misery which
will follow from it is likely to light upon *me ;* the rest will be
divided amongst *yourselves and your children.*

Gentlemen, I observe plainly, and with infinite satisfaction, that
you are shocked and offended at my even supposing it possible you

should pronounce such a detestable judgment; and that you only require of me to make out to your satisfaction (*as I promised*) that the real scope and object of this book is a *bonâ fide* defence of Mr Hastings, *and not a cloak and cover for scandal on the House of Commons.* I engage to do this, and I engage for nothing more. I shall make an open, manly defence; I mean to torture no expressions from their natural constructions, to dispute no innuendoes on the record, should any of them have a fair application; nor to conceal from your notice any unguarded, intemperate expressions, which may perhaps be found to chequer the vigorous and animated career of the work. Such a conduct might, by accident, shelter the defendant; but it would be the surrender of the very principle on which alone the liberty of the English press can stand; and I shall never defend any man from a temporary imprisonment by the permanent loss of my own liberty and the ruin of my country. I mean therefore to submit to you, that though you should find a few lines in page thirteen or twenty-one, a few more in page fifty-one, and some others in other places, containing expressions bearing on the House of Commons, even as a body, which, if written as independent paragraphs by themselves, would be indefensible libels, yet that you have a right to pass them over in judgment, provided the substance clearly appears to be a *bonâ fide* conclusion, arising from the honest investigation of a subject which it was lawful to investigate, and the questionable expressions the visible effusion of a zealous temper, engaged in an honourable and legal pursuit. After this preparation, I am not afraid to lay the book in its genuine state before you.

The pamphlet begins thus: " The House of Commons has now given its final decision with regard to the merits and demerits of Mr Hastings. The grand inquest of England have delivered their charges and preferred their impeachment; their allegations are referred to proof; and from the appeal to the collective wisdom and justice of the nation in the supreme tribunal of the kingdom, the question comes to be determined whether Mr Hastings *be guilty or not guilty ?* "

Now, if immediately after what I have just read to you (which is the first part charged by the information), the author had said, " Will accusations, built on such a baseless fabric, prepossess the public in favour of the impeachment ? What credit can we give to multiplied and accumulated charges when we find that they originate from misrepresentation and falsehood ? "—every man would have been justified in pronouncing that he was attacking the House of Commons, because the groundless accusations mentioned in the second sentence could have no reference but to the House itself, mentioned by name in the first and only sentence which preceded it.

But, gentlemen, to your astonishment, I will now read *what intervenes between these two passages ;* from which you will see, beyond a possibility of doubt, that the author never meant to calumniate the House of Commons, but to say that the accusation of Mr Hastings before the *whole* House grew out of a *Committee of Secrecy* established some years before, and was afterwards brought forward by the spleen of private enemies and a faction in the Government.   This will appear, not only from the grammatical construction of the words, but, from what is better than words, from the meaning which a person writing as a friend of Mr Hastings must be supposed to have intended to convey.   Why should such a friend attack the House of Commons?   Will any man gravely tell me that the House of Commons, *as a body*, ever wished to impeach Mr Hastings?   Do we not all know that they constantly hung back from it, and hardly knew where they were or what to do when they found themselves entangled with it?   My learned friend the Attorney-General is a member of this assembly; perhaps he may tell you by and by what HE thought of it, and whether he ever marked any disposition in the majority of the Commons hostile to Mr Hastings.   But why should I distress my friend by the question?—the fact is sufficiently notorious; and what I am going to read from the book itself (which is left out in the information) is too plain for controversy.

" Whatever may be the event of the impeachment, the proper exercise of such power is a valuable privilege of the British constitution, a formidable guardian of the public liberty and the dignity of the nation.   *The only danger is, that from the influence of faction, and the awe which is annexed to great names, they may be prompted to determine before they inquire, and to pronounce judgment without examination.*"

Here is the clue to the whole pamphlet.   The author trusts to and respects the House of Commons, but is afraid their mature and just examination may be disturbed by *faction*.   Now, does he mean Government by *faction ?*   Does he mean the majority of the Commons by *faction ?*   Will the House, which is the prosecutor here, sanction that application of the phrase ; or will the Attorney-General admit the majority to be the true innuendo of *faction ?*   I wish he would: I should then have gained something at least by this extraordinary debate.   But I have no expectation of the sort.   Such a concession would be too great a sacrifice to any prosecution at a time when everything is considered as *faction* that disturbs the repose of the Minister in Parliament.   But indeed, gentlemen, some things are too plain for argument.   The author certainly means *my* friends, who, whatever qualifications may belong to them, must be contented with the appellation of *faction* while they oppose the Minister in the House of Commons ; but the House, having given this meaning to the phrase of *faction* for its own purposes, cannot in decency change the interpretation in order to convict my client. I take that to be beyond the privilege of Parliament.

The same bearing upon individual members of the Commons, *and not on the Commons as a body*, is obvious throughout. Thus, after saying, in page 9, that the East India Company had thanked Mr Hastings for his meritorious services (which is unquestionably true), he adds, "that mankind would abide by their deliberate decision, rather than by the intemperate assertion of *a committee*."

This he writes after the impeachment was found by the Commons at large; but he takes no account of their proceedings, imputing the whole to the original committee, *i.e.*, *the Committee of Secrecy*; so called, I suppose, from their being the authors of twenty volumes in folio which will remain a secret to all posterity, as nobody will ever read them. The same construction is equally plain from what immediately follows:—" The report of the *Committee of Secrecy* also states, that the happiness of the native inhabitants of India has been deeply affected, their confidence in English faith and lenity shaken and impaired, and the character of this nation wantonly and wickedly degraded."

Here again you are grossly misled by the omission of near *twenty-one pages*. For the author, though he is here speaking of this Committee *by name*, which brought forward the charges to the notice of the House, and which he continues to do onward to the next select paragraph; yet, by arbitrarily sinking the whole context, he is taken to be speaking of the House as a *body*, when, in the passage next charged by the information, he reproaches the *accusers* of Mr Hastings; although, so far is he from considering them as the House of Commons, that, in the very same page, he speaks of the articles as the charges, not even of the Committee, but of Mr Burke alone, the most active and intelligent member of that body, having been circulated in India by a relation of that gentleman :—" The charges of *Mr Burke* have been carried to Calcutta, and carefully circulated in India."

Now, if we were considering these passages of the work as calumniating a body of gentlemen, many of whom I must be supposed highly to respect, or as reflecting upon my worthy friend whose name I have mentioned, it would give rise to a totally different inquiry, which it is neither my duty nor yours to agitate ; but surely, the more that consideration obtrudes itself upon us, the more clearly it demonstrates that the author's whole direction was against the individual accusers of Mr Hastings, and not against the House of Commons, which merely trusted to the matter they had collected.

Although, from a caution which my situation dictates as representing another, I have thought it my duty thus to point out to you the real intention of the author, as it appears by the fair construction of the work, yet I protest that, in my own apprehension,

it is very immaterial whether he speaks of the *Committee* or of
the HOUSE, provided you shall think the whole volume a *bond fide*
defence of Mr Hastings. This is the great point I am, by all my
observations, endeavouring to establish, and which I think no man
who reads the following short passages can doubt. Very intelligent persons have indeed considered them, if founded in facts, to
render every other amplification unnecessary. The first of them
is as follows:—"It was known at that time that Mr Hastings had
not only descended from a public to a private station, but that he
was persecuted with accusations and impeachments. But none of
these *suffering millions* have sent their complaints to this country;
not a sigh nor a groan has been wafted from India to Britain.
On the contrary, testimonies the most honourable to the character
and merit of Mr Hastings have been transmitted by those very
princes whom he has been supposed to have loaded with the
deepest injuries."

Here, gentlemen, we must be permitted to pause together a
little; for in examining whether these pages were written as an
honest answer to the charges of the Commons, or as a prostituted
defence of a notorious criminal, whom the writer believed to be
guilty, *truth becomes material at every step.* For if *in any instance*
he be detected of a *wilful* misrepresentation, he is no longer an
object of your attention.

Will the Attorney-General proceed, then, to detect the hypocrisy
of our author by giving us some details of the proofs by which
these personal enormities have been established, and which the
writer must be supposed to have been acquainted with? I ask
this as the defender of *Mr Stockdale*, not of Mr Hastings, with
whom I have no concern. I am sorry indeed to be so often obliged
to repeat this protest; but I really feel myself embarrassed with
those repeated coincidences of defence, which thicken on me as I
advance, and which were, no doubt, overlooked by the Commons
when they directed this interlocutory inquiry into his conduct. I
ask then, *as counsel for Mr Stockdale*, whether when a great state
criminal is brought for justice, at an immense expense to the
public, accused of the most oppressive cruelties, and charged with
the robbery of princes and the destruction of nations, it is not open
to any one to ask; Who are his accusers? What are the sources
and the authorities of these shocking complaints? Where are the
ambassadors or memorials of those princes whose revenues he has
plundered? Where are the witnesses for those unhappy men in
whose persons the rights of humanity have been violated? How
deeply buried is the blood of the innocent that it does not rise up
in retributive judgment to confound the guilty! These surely are
questions which, when a fellow-citizen is upon a long, painful, and
expensive trial, humanity has a right to propose; which the plain
sense of the most unlettered man may be expected to dictate; and

which all history must provoke from the more enlightened.   When Cicero impeached Verres before the great tribunal of Rome of similar cruelties and depredations in *her* provinces, the Roman people were not left to such inquiries.   All Sicily surrounded the Forum, demanding justice upon her plunderer and spoiler, with tears and imprecations.   It was not by the eloquence of the *orator*, but by the cries and tears of the miserable, that Cicero prevailed in that illustrious cause.   Verres fled from the oaths of his accusers and their witnesses, and not from the voice of Tully.   To preserve the fame of his eloquence, he composed his five celebrated speeches, but they were never delivered against the criminal, because he had fled from the city, appalled with the sight of the persecuted and the oppressed.   It may be said that the cases of Sicily and India are widely different.   Perhaps they may be.   Whether they are or not is foreign to my purpose.   I am not bound to deny the possibility of answers to such questions; I am only vindicating *the right to ask them*.

Gentlemen, the author, in the other passage which I marked out to your attention, goes on thus:—"Sir John Macpherson and Lord Cornwallis, his successors in office, have given the same voluntary tribute of approbation to his measures as Governor-General of India.   A letter from the former, dated the 10th of August 1786, gives the following account of our dominions in Asia:—' The native inhabitants of this kingdom are the happiest and best protected subjects in India.   Our native allies and tributaries confide in our protection; the country powers are aspiring to the friendship of the English; and from the King of Tidore, towards New Guinea, to Timur Shaw, on the banks of the Indus, there is not a State that has not *lately* given us proofs of confidence and respect.'"

Still pursuing the same test of sincerity, let us examine this defensive allegation.

Will the Attorney-General say that he does not believe such a letter from Lord Cornwallis ever existed?   No; for he knows that it is as authentic as any document from India upon the table of the House of Commons.   What then is the letter?   The native inhabitants of this kingdom, says Lord Cornwallis (writing from the very spot), are the happiest and best protected subjects in India, &c., &c., &c.   The inhabitants of *this kingdom !—Of what kingdom!*   Of the very kingdom which Mr Hastings had just returned from governing for thirteen years, and for the misgovernment and desolation of which he stands every day as a criminal, or rather as a spectacle before us.   This is matter for serious reflection, and fully entitles the author to put the question which immediately follows— "Does this authentic account of the administration of Mr Hastings, and of the state of India, correspond with the gloomy picture of despotism and despair drawn by the *Committee of Secrecy* ?"

Had that picture been even drawn by the House of Commons itself, he would have been fully justified in asking this question. But you observe it has no bearing on it. The last words not only entirely destroy that interpretation, but also the meaning of the very next passage which is selected by the information as criminal, *viz.*, " What credit can we give to multiplied and accumulated charges, when we find that they originate from misrepresentation and falsehood?"

This passage, which is charged as a libel on the Commons, when thus compared with its immediate antecedent, can bear but one construction. It is impossible to contend that it charges misrepresentation on the HOUSE, that found the impeachment, but upon the *Committee of Secrecy* just before adverted to, who were supposed to have selected the matter, and brought it before the whole House for judgment.

I do not mean, as I have often told you, to vindicate any calumny on that honourable committee, or upon any individual of it, any more than upon the Commons at large; BUT THE DEFENDANT IS NOT CHARGED BY THIS INFORMATION WITH ANY SUCH OFFENCES.

Let me here pause once more to ask you, whether the book, in its genuine state, as far as we have advanced in it, makes the same impression on your minds now as when it was first read to you in detached passages? and whether, if I were to tear off the first part of it which I hold in my hand, and give it to you as an entire work, the first and last passages which have been selected as libels on the Commons would now appear to be so when blended with the interjacent parts? I do not ask your answer. I shall have it in your verdict. The question is only put to direct your attention, in pursuing the remainder of the volume, to this main point—Is IT AN HONEST, SERIOUS DEFENCE? For this purpose, and as an example for all others, I will read the author's entire answer to the first article of charge concerning Cheit Sing, the Zemindar of Benares, and leave it to your impartial judgments to determine whether it be a mere cloak and cover for the slander imputed by the information to the concluding sentence of it, which is the only part attacked? or whether, on the contrary, that conclusion itself, when embodied with what goes before it, does not stand explained and justified? .

" The first article of impeachment," continues our author, " is concerning Cheit Sing, the Zemindar of Benares. Bulwant Sing, the father of this rajah, was merely an *aumil*, or farmer and collector of the revenues for Sujah ul Dowlah, Nabob of Oude, and Vizir of the Mogul Empire. When, on the decease of his father, Cheit Sing was confirmed in the office of collector for the Vizir, he paid £200,000 as a gift or nuzzeranah, and an additional rent of £30,000 per annum.

" As the father was no more than an *aumil*, the son succeeded only to his rights and pretensions. But by a sunnud granted to him by the Nabob Sujah Dowlah in September 1773, through the influence of Mr Hastings, he acquired a legal title to property in the land, and was raised from the office of *aumil* to the rank of zemindar. About four years after the death of Bulwant Sing, the Governor-General and Council of Bengal obtained the sovereignty paramount of the province of Benares. On the transfer of this sovereignty the Governor and Council proposed a new grant to Cheit Sing, confirming his former privileges, and conferring upon him the addition of the sovereign rights of the Mint, and the powers of criminal justice with regard to life and death. He was then recognised by the Company as one of their zemindars ; a tributary subject, or feudatory vassal, of the British Empire in Indostan. The feudal system, which was formerly supposed to be peculiar to our Gothic ancestors, has always prevailed in the East. In every description of that form of government, notwithstanding accidental variations, there are two associations expressed or understood ; one for internal security, the other for external defence. The king or nabob confers protection on the feudatory baron as tributary prince, on condition of an annual revenue in the time of peace, and of military service, partly commutable for money, in the time of war. The feudal incidents in the Middle Ages in Europe, the fine paid to the superior on *marriage, wardship, relief,* &c., correspond to the annual tribute in Asia. Military service in war, and extraordinary aids in the event of extraordinary emergencies, were common to both.*

" When the Governor-General of Bengal, in 1778, made an extraordinary demand on the Zemindar of Benares for five lacks of rupees, the British Empire, in that part of the world, was surrounded with enemies which threatened its destruction. In 1779, a general confederacy was formed among the great powers of Indostan for the expulsion of the English from their Asiatic dominions. At this

* " Notwithstanding this analogy, the powers and privileges of a zemindar have never been so well ascertained and defined as those of a baron in the feudal ages. Though the office has usually descended to the posterity of the zemindar, under the ceremony of fine and investiture, a material decrease in the cultivation, or decline in the population of the district, has sometimes been considered as a ground to dispossess him. When zemindars have failed in their engagements to the State, though not to the extent to justify expulsion, supervisors have been often sent into the zemindaries, who have farmed out the lands, and exercised authority under the Duannee laws, independent of the zemindar. These circumstances strongly mark their *dependence* on the nabob. About a year after the departure of Mr Hastings from India, the question concerning the rights of zemindars was agitated at great length in Calcutta ; and after the fullest and most accurate investigation, the Governor-General and Council gave it as their deliberate opinion to the Court of Directors, that the property of the soil is not in the zemindar, but in the government; and that a zemindar is merely an officer of government appointed to collect its revenues. Cheit Sing understood himself to stand in this predicament. ' I am,' said he on various occasions, ' the servant of the circar (government), and ready to obey your orders.' The name and office of zemindar is not of Hindoo, but Mogul institution."

crisis the expectation of a French armament augmented the general calamities of the country. Mr Hastings is charged by the committee with making his first demand under the false pretence that hostilities had commenced with France. Such an insidious attempt to pervert a meritorious action into a crime is new—even in the history of impeachments. On the 7th of July 1778, Mr Hastings received private intelligence from an English merchant at Cairo, that war had been declared by Great Britain on the 23d of March, and by France on the 30th of April. Upon this intelligence, considered as authentic, it was determined to attack all the French settlements in India. The information was afterwards found to be premature; but in the latter end of August a secret dispatch was received from England, authorising and appointing Mr Hastings to take the measures which he had already adopted in the preceding month. The Directors and the Board of Control have expressed their approbation of this transaction, by liberally rewarding Mr Baldwyn, the merchant, for sending the earliest intelligence he could procure to Bengal. It was *two days* after Mr Hastings' information of the French war, that he formed the resolution of exacting the five lacks of rupees from Cheit Sing, and would have made *similar exactions* from all the dependencies of the Company in India, had they been in the same circumstances. The fact is, that the great zemindars of Bengal pay as much to Government as their lands can afford. Cheit Sing's collections were above fifty lacks, and his rent not twenty-four.

"The right of calling for extraordinary aids and military service in times of danger, being universally established in India, as it was formerly in Europe during the feudal times, the subsequent conduct of Mr Hastings is explained and vindicated. The Governor-General and Council of Bengal having made a demand upon a tributary zemindar for three successive years, and that demand having been resisted by their vassal, they are justified in his punishment. The necessities of the Company, in consequence of the critical situation of their affairs in 1781, calling for a high fine; the ability of the zemindar, who possessed near two crores of rupees in money and jewels, to pay the sum required; his backwardness to comply with the demands of his superiors; his disaffection to the English interest, and desire of revolt, which even then began to appear, and were afterwards conspicuous, fully justify Mr Hastings in every subsequent step of his conduct. In the whole of his proceedings it is manifest that he had not early formed a design hostile to the zemindar, but was regulated by events which he could neither foresee nor control. When the necessary measures which he had taken for supporting the authority of the Company, by punishing a refractory vassal, were thwarted and defeated by the barbarous massacre of the British troops, and the rebellion of Cheit Sing, the appeal was made to arms, an unavoidable revolution took place in Benares, and the zemindar became the author of his own destruction."

Here follows the concluding passage, which is arraigned by the information :—

"The decision of the House of Commons on this charge against Mr Hastings is one of the most singular to be met with in the annals of Parliament. The Minister, who was followed by the majority, vindicated him in everything that he had *done*, and found him blameable only for what he *intended* to *do ;* justified every step of his *conduct*, and only criminated his proposed *intention* of converting the crimes of the zemindar to the benefit of the State, by a fine of fifty lacks of rupees. An impeachment of *error* in *judgment* with regard to the *quantum* of a fine, and for an *intention* that never was *executed*, and never known to the offending party, characterises a tribunal of *inquisition* rather than a court of Parliament."

Gentlemen, I am ready to admit that this sentiment might have been expressed in language more reserved and guarded; but you will look to the sentiment itself, rather than to its dress ;—to the *mind* of the writer, and not to the bluntness with which he may happen to express it. It is obviously the language of a warm man, engaged in the honest defence of his friend, and who is brought to what he thinks a just conclusion in argument, which, perhaps, becomes offensive in proportion to its truth. Truth is undoubtedly no warrant for writing what is reproachful of any *private* man. If a member of society lives within the law, then if he offends, it is against God alone, and man has nothing to do with him ; and if he transgress the laws, the libeller should arrain him before them, instead of presuming to try him himself. But as to writings on *general subjects*, which are not charged as an infringement on the rights of individuals, but as of a seditious tendency, it is far otherwise. When, in the progress either of legislation, or of high national justice in Parliament, they, who are amenable to no law, are supposed to have adopted through mistake or error a principle which, if drawn into precedent, might be dangerous to the public,— I shall not admit it to be a libel, *in the course of a legal and bonâ fide publication*, to state that such a principle had *in fact* been adopted. The people of England are not to be kept in the dark touching the proceedings of their own representatives. Let us, therefore, coolly examine this supposed offence, and see what it amounts to.

First, Was not the conduct of the right honourable gentleman, whose name is here mentioned, exactly what it is represented ? Will the Attorney-General, who was present in the House of Commons, say that it was not ? Did not the Minister vindicate Mr Hastings in what he *had done*, and was not his consent to that article of the impeachment founded on the *intention only* of levying a fine on the zemindar for the service of the State, beyond the quantum which he, the Minister, thought reasonable? What else is t iis but an impeachment of error in judgment in the quantum of a fine?

So much for the first part of the sentence, which regarding Mr Pitt only, is foreign to our purpose; and as to the last part of it, which imputes the sentiments of the Minister to the majority that followed him with their votes on the question, that appears to me to be giving handsome credit to the majority for having voted from conviction, and not from courtesy to the Minister. To have supposed otherwise, I dare not say, would have been a more *natural* libel, but it would certainly have been a greater one. The sum and substance, therefore, of the paragraph is only this: that an impeachment for error in judgment is not consistent with the theory or the practice of the English Government. So say I. I say, without reserve, speaking merely in the abstract, and not meaning to decide upon the merits of Mr Hastings' cause, that an impeachment for an error in judgment is contrary to the whole spirit of English criminal justice, which, though not binding on the House of Commons, ought to be a guide to its proceedings. I say that the extraordinary jurisdiction of impeachment ought never to be assumed to expose error, or to scourge misfortune, but to hold up a terrible example to corruption and *wilful* abuse of authority by extra legal pains. If public men are always punished with due severity, when the source of their misconduct appears to have been *selfishly corrupt and criminal*, the public can never suffer when their errors are treated with gentleness. From such protection to the magistrate, no man can think lightly of the charge of magistracy itself, when he sees, by the language of the saving judgment, that the only title to it is an honest and zealous intention. If at this moment, gentlemen, or indeed in any other in the whole course of our history, the people of England were to call upon every man in this impeaching House of Commons, who had given his voice on public questions, or acted in authority, civil or military, to answer for the issues of our councils and our wars, and if honest single intentions for the public service were refused as answers to impeachments, we should have many relations to mourn for, and many friends to deplore. For my own part, gentlemen, I feel, I hope, for my country as much as any man that inhabits it; but I would rather see it fall, and be buried in its ruins, than lend my voice to wound any minister, or other responsible person, however unfortunate, who had fairly followed the lights of his understanding and the dictates of his conscience for their preservation.

Gentlemen, this is no theory of mine; it is the language of English law, and the protection which it affords to every man in office, from the highest to the lowest trust of Government. In no one instance that can be named, foreign or domestic, did the Court of King's Bench ever interpose its extraordinary jurisdiction, by information, against any magistrate for the widest departure from the rule of his duty, without *the plainest and clearest proof of corruption.* To every such application, not so supported, the constant answer has been, Go to a grand jury with your complaint. God forbid that a magistrate should suffer from an error in judgment, if his purpose was honestly to discharge his trust. We cannot stop the ordinary course of justice; but wherever the Court has a discretion, such a magistrate is entitled to its protection. I appeal to the noble Judge, and to every man who hears me, for the truth and universality of this position. And it would be a strange solecism indeed to assert, that in a case where the supreme court of criminal justice in the nation would refuse to interpose an *extraordinary,* though a legal jurisdiction, on the principle that the ordinary execution of the laws should never be exceeded but for the punishment of malignant guilt, the Commons, in their higher capacity, growing out of the same constitution, should reject that principle, and stretch them still further by a jurisdiction still more *eccentric.* Many impeachments have taken place, because the law *could not* adequately punish the objects of them; but who ever heard of one being set on foot because the law, upon principle, *would not* punish them? Many impeachments have been adopted for a *higher* example than a prosecution in the ordinary courts, but surely never for a *different* example. The matter, therefore, in the offensive paragraph, is not only an indisputable truth, but a truth in the propagation of which we are all deeply concerned.

Whether Mr Hastings, in the particular instance, acted from corruption or from zeal for his employers, is what I have nothing to do with; it is to be decided in judgment; my duty stops with wishing him, as I do, an honourable deliverance. Whether the Minister or the Commons meant to found this article of the impeachment on mere error without corruption, is likewise foreign to the purpose. The author could only judge from what was said and done on the occasion. He only sought to guard the principle, which is a common interest, and the rights of Mr Hastings under it. He was therefore justified in publishing that an impeachment, founded in error in judgment, was to all intents and purposes illegal, unconstitutional, and unjust.

Gentlemen, it is now time for us to return again to the work under examination. The author, having discussed the whole of the first article through so many pages, without even the imputation of an incorrect or intemperate expression, except in the concluding passage (the meaning of which I trust I have explained), goes on with the same earnest disposition to the discussion of the second charge respecting the princesses of Oude, which occupies EIGHTEEN pages, not one syllable of which the Attorney-General has read, and on which there is not even a glance at the House of Commons. The whole of this answer is indeed so far from being a mere cloak for the introduction of slander, that I aver it to be one of the most masterly pieces of writing I ever read in my life. From thence he goes on to the charge of contracts and salaries, which occupies FIVE pages more, in which *there is not a glance at the House of Commons, nor a word read by the Attorney-General.* He afterwards defends Mr Hastings against the charges respecting the opium contracts. *Not a glance at the House of Commons; not a word by the Attorney-General.* And in short, in this manner he goes on with the others to the end of the book.

Now is it possible for any human being to believe that a man, having no other intention than to vilify the House of Commons (*as this information charges*), should yet keep his mind thus fixed and settled as the needle to the pole, upon the serious merits of Mr Hastings' defence, without ever straying into matter even questionable, except in the two or three selected parts out of two or three hundred pages? This is a forbearance which could not have existed if calumny and detraction had been the malignant objects which led him to the inquiry and publication. The whole fallacy, therefore, arises from holding up to view a few detached passages, and carefully concealing the general tenor of the book.

Having now finished most, if not all, of these *critical* observations, which it has been my duty to make upon this unfair mode of prosecution, it is but a tribute of common justice to the Attorney-General (and which my personal regard for him makes it more pleasant to pay), that none of my commentaries reflect in the most distant manner upon him; nor upon the Solicitor for the Crown, who sits near me, who is a person of the most correct honour: far from it. The Attorney-General, having orders to prosecute, in consequence of the address of the House to his Majesty, had no choice in the mode,—no means at all of keeping the prosecutors before you in countenance but by the course which has been pursued: but so far has he been from enlisting into the cause those prejudices which it is not difficult to slide into a business originating from such exalted authority, he has honourably guarded you against them,—pressing indeed severely upon my client with the weight of his ability, but not with the glare and trappings of his high office.

Gentlemen, I wish that my strength would enable me to convince you of the author's singleness of intention, and of the merit and ability of his work, by reading the whole that remains of it. But my voice is already nearly exhausted; I am sorry my client should be a sufferer by my infirmity. One passage, however, is too striking and important to be passed over; the rest I must trust to your private examination. The author, having discussed all the charges, article by article, sums them all up with this striking appeal to his readers:—

"The authentic statement of facts which has been given, and

the arguments which have been employed, are, I think, sufficient to vindicate the character and conduct of Mr Hastings, even on the maxims of European policy. When he was appointed Governor-General of Bengal, he was invested with a discretionary power to promote the interests of the India Company, and of the British Empire in that quarter of the globe. The general instructions sent to him from his constituents were, ' *That in all your deliberations and resolutions, you make the safety and prosperity of Bengal your principal object, and fix your attention on the security of the possessions and revenues of the Company.*' His superior genius sometimes acted in the spirit, rather than complied with the letter, of the law; but he discharged the trust, and preserved the empire committed to his care in the same way and with greater splendour and success than any of his predecessors in office. His departure from India was marked with the lamentations of the natives and the gratitude of his countrymen; and on his return to England he received the cordial congratulations of that numerous and respectable society whose interests he had promoted, and whose dominions he had protected and extended."

Gentlemen of the jury, if this be a wilfully false account of the instructions given to Mr Hastings for his government, and of his conduct under them, the author and publisher of this defence deserve the severest punishment for a mercenary imposition on the public. But if it be true that he was directed to make the *safety and prosperity of Bengal the first object of his attention*, and that, under his administration, it has been safe and prosperous,—if it be true that the security and preservation of our possessions and revenues in Asia were marked out to him as the great leading principle of his government, and that those possessions and revenues, amidst unexampled dangers, have been secured and preserved,—then a question may be unaccountably mixed with your consideration much beyond the consequence of the present prosecution, involving perhaps the merit of the impeachment itself which gave it birth,—a question which the Commons, as prosecutors of Mr Hastings, should, in common prudence, have avoided; unless, regretting the unwieldy length of their proceedings against him, they wished to afford him the opportunity of this strange anomalous defence. For although I am neither his counsel, nor desire to have anything to do with his guilt or innocence, yet in the collateral defence of my client, I am driven to state matter which may be considered by many as hostile to the impeachment; for if our dependencies have been secured and their interests promoted, I am driven, in the defence of my client, to remark, that it is mad and preposterous to bring to the standard of justice and humanity the exercise of a dominion founded upon violence and terror. It may and must be true that Mr Hastings has repeatedly offended against the rights and privileges of Asiatic government, if he was

the faithful deputy of a power which could not maintain itself for
an hour without trampling upon both: he may and must have
offended against the laws of God and nature, if he was the faithful
viceroy of an empire wrested in blood from the people to whom
God and nature had given it: he may and must have preserved that
unjust dominion over timorous and abject nations by a terrifying,
overbearing, insulting superiority, if he was the faithful adminis-
trator of your Government, which having no root in consent or
affection, no foundation in similarity of interests, nor support from
any one principle which cements men together in society, could
only be upheld by alternate stratagem and force.   The unhappy
people of India, feeble and effeminate as they are from the softness
of their climate, and subdued and broken as they have been by the
knavery and strength of civilisation, still occasionally start up in
all the vigour and intelligence of insulted nature.   To be governed
at all, they must be governed with a rod of iron; and our empire
in the East would, long since, have been lost to Great Britain, if
civil skill and military prowess had not united their efforts to support an authority—which Heaven never gave—by means which it
never can sanction.

Gentlemen, I think I can observe that you are touched with this
way of considering the subject, and I can account for it.   I have
not been considering it through the cold medium of books, but
have been speaking of man and his nature, and of human dominion,
from what I have seen of them myself amongst reluctant nations
submitting to our authority.   I know what they feel, and how such
feelings can alone be repressed.   I have heard them, in my youth,
from a naked savage, in the indignant character of a prince surrounded by his subjects, addressing the governor of a British colony,
holding a bundle of sticks in his hand as the notes of his unlettered
eloquence.   " Who is it?" said the jealous ruler over the desert
encroached upon by the restless foot of English adventure,—" who is
it that causes this river to rise in the high mountains, and to empty
itself into the ocean?   Who is it that causes to blow the loud
winds of winter, and that calms them again in the summer?
Who is it that rears up the shade of those lofty forests, and blasts
them with the quick lightning at his pleasure?   The same Being
who gave to you a country on the other side of the waters, and
gave ours to us; and by this title we will defend it," said the
warrior, throwing down his tomahawk upon the ground, and raising
the war-sound of his nation.   These are the feelings of subjugated
man all round the globe; and depend upon it, nothing but fear
will control where it is vain to look for affection.

These reflections are the only antidotes to those anathemas of
superhuman eloquence which have lately shaken these walls that
surround us, but which it unaccountably falls to my province,
whether I will or no, a little to stem the torrent of, by reminding

you that you have a mighty sway in Asia, which cannot be maintained by the finer sympathies of life, or the practice of its charities and affections. What will they do for you when surrounded by two hundred thousand men with artillery, cavalry, and elephants, calling upon you for their dominions which you have robbed them of? Justice may, no doubt, in such a case forbid the levying of a fine to pay a revolting soldiery; a treaty may stand in the way of increasing a tribute to keep up the very existence of the government; and delicacy for women may forbid all entrance into a zenana for money, whatever may be the necessity for taking it. All these things must ever be occurring. But under the pressure of such constant difficulties, so dangerous to national honour, it might be better perhaps to think of effectually securing it altogether, by recalling our troops and our merchants, and abandoning our Oriental Empire. Until this be done, neither religion nor philosophy can be pressed very far into the aid of reformation and punishment. If England, from a lust of ambition and dominion, will insist on maintaining despotic rule over distant and hostile nations, beyond all comparison more numerous and extended than herself, and gives commission to her viceroys to govern them with no other instructions than to preserve them, and to secure permanently their revenues; with what colour of consistency or reason can she place herself in the moral chair, and affect to be shocked at the execution of her own orders; adverting to the exact measure of wickedness and injustice necessary to their execution, and complaining only of *the excess* as the immorality, considering her authority as a dispensation for breaking the commands of God, and the breach of them as only punishable when contrary to the ordinances of man.

Such a proceeding, gentlemen, begets serious reflections. It would be better, perhaps, for the masters and the servants of all such governments to join in supplication, that the great Author of violated humanity may not confound them together in one common judgment.

Gentlemen, I find, as I said before, I have not sufficient strength to go on with the remaining parts of the book. I hope, however, that, notwithstanding my omissions, you are now completely satisfied, that whatever errors or misconceptions may have misled the writer of these pages, the justification of a person whom he believed to be innocent, and whose accusers had themselves appealed to the public, was the single object of his contemplation. If I have succeeded in that object, every purpose which I had in addressing you has been answered.

It only now remains to remind you, that another consideration has been strongly pressed upon you, and no doubt will be insisted on in reply. You will be told that the matters which I have been justifying as legal and even meritorious, have therefore been not made the subject of complaint; and that whatever intrinsic merit parts of the book may be supposed or even admitted to possess, such merit can afford no justification to the selected passages, some of which, even with the context, carry the meaning charged by the information, and which are indecent animadversions on authority. To this I would answer (still protesting as I do against the application of any one of the innuendoes), that if you are firmly persuaded of the singleness and purity of the author's intentions, you are not bound to subject him to infamy, because, in the zealous career of a just and animated composition, he happens to have tripped with his pen into an intemperate expression in one or two instances of a long work. If this severe duty were binding on your consciences, the liberty of the press would be an empty sound, and no man could venture to write on any subject, however pure his purpose, without an attorney at one elbow, and a counsel at the other.

From minds thus subdued by the terrors of punishment, there could issue no works of genius to expand the empire of human reason, nor any masterly compositions on the general nature of government, by the help of which the great commonwealths of mankind have founded their establishments; much less any of those useful applications of them to critical conjunctures, by which, from time to time, our own constitution, by the exertion of patriot citizens, has been brought back to its standard. Under such terrors, all the great lights of science and civilisation must be extinguished: for men cannot communicate their free thoughts to one another with a lash held over their heads. It is the nature of everything that is great and useful, both in the animate and inanimate world, to be wild and irregular,—and we must be contented to take them with the alloys which belong to them, or live without them. Genius breaks from the fetters of criticism, but its wanderings are sanctioned by its majesty and wisdom when it advances in its path;—subject it to the critic, and you tame it into dulness. Mighty rivers break down their banks in the winter, sweeping away to death the flocks which are fattened on the soil that they fertilise in the summer; the few may be saved by embankments from drowning, but the flock must perish for hunger. Tempests occasionally shake our dwellings and dissipate our commerce; but they scourge before them the lazy elements, which without them would stagnate into pestilence. In like manner, Liberty herself, the last and best gift of God to his creatures, must be taken just as she is;—you might pare her down into bashful regularity, and shape her into a perfect model of severe scrupulous law, but she would then be Liberty no longer; and you must be content to die under the lash of this inexorable justice which you had exchanged for the banners of Freedom.

If it be asked where the line to this indulgence and impunity is to be drawn, the answer is easy. The liberty of the press *on general* *subjects* comprehends and implies as much strict observance of positive law as is consistent with perfect purity of intention, and equal and useful society; and what that latitude is cannot be promulgated in the abstract, but must be judged of in the particular instance, and, consequently, upon this occasion, must be judged of by you without forming any possible precedent for any other case ; —and where can the judgment be possibly so safe as with the members of that society which alone can suffer, if the writing is calculated to do mischief to the public ? You must therefore try the book by that criterion, and say whether the publication was premature and offensive, or, in other words, whether the publisher was bound to have suppressed it until the public ear was anticipated and abused, and every avenue to the human heart or understanding secured and blocked up ? I see around me those by whom, by and by, Mr Hastings will be most ably and eloquently defended ; * but I am sorry to remind my friends, that, but for the right of suspending the public judgment concerning him till their season of exertion comes round, the tongues of angels would be insufficient for the task.

Gentlemen, I hope I have now performed my duty to my client —I sincerely hope that I have ; for, certainly, if ever there was a man pulled the other way by his interests and affections,—if ever there was a man who should have trembled at the situation in which I have been placed on this occasion, it is myself, who not only love, honour, and respect, but whose future hopes and preferments are linked from free choice with those who, from the mistakes of the author, are treated with great severity and injustice. These are strong retardments; but I have been urged on to activity by considerations which can never be inconsistent with honourable attachments, either in the political or social world,—the love of justice and of liberty, and a zeal for the constitution of my country, which is the inheritance of our posterity, of the public, and of the world. These are the motives which have animated me in defence of this person, who is an entire stranger to me—whose shop I never go to—and the author of whose publication, as well as Mr Hastings, who is the object of it, I never spoke to in my life.

One word more, gentlemen, and I have done. Every human tribunal ought to take care to administer justice, as we look hereafter to have justice administered to ourselves. Upon the principle on which the Attorney-General prays sentence upon my client— God have mercy upon us!—instead of standing before Him in judgment with the hopes and consolations of Christians, we must call upon the mountains to cover us ; for which of us can present, for Omniscient examination, a pure, unspotted, and faultless course ? But I humbly expect that the benevolent Author of our being will

* Mr Law, now Lord Ellenborough, Mr Plumer, and Mr Dallas,

judge us as I have been pointing out for your example. Holding up the great volume of our lives of our lives in His hands, and regarding the general scope of them ;—if He discovers benevolence, charity, and good-will to man beating in the heart, where He alone can look ;— if He finds that our conduct, though often forced out of the path by our infirmities, has been in general well directed;—His all-searching eye will assuredly never pursue us into those little corners of our lives, much less will His justice select them for punishment, without the general context of our existence, by which faults may be sometimes found to have grown out of virtues, and very many of our heaviest offences to have been grafted by human imperfection upon the best and kindest of our affections. No, gentlemen, believe me, this is not the course of divine justice, or there is no truth in the Gospels of Heaven. If the general tenor of a man's conduct be such as I have represented it, he may walk through the shadow of death, with all his faults about him, with as much cheerfulness as in the common paths of life ; because he knows, that instead of a stern accuser to expose before the Author of his nature those frail passages, which, like the scored matter in the book before you, chequers the volume of the brightest and best-spent life, His mercy will obscure them from the eye of His purity, and our repentance blot them out for ever.

All this would, I admit, be perfectly foreign and irrelevant, if you were sitting here in a case of property between man and man, where a strict rule of law must operate, or there would be an end of civil life and society. It would be equally foreign, and still more irrelevant, if applied to those shameful attacks upon private reputation which are the bane and disgrace of the press ; by which whole families have been rendered unhappy during life, by aspersions cruel, scandalous, and unjust. Let such libellers remember, that no one of my principles of defence can at any time or upon any occasion ever apply to shield them from punishment ; because such conduct is not only an infringement of the rights of men, as they are defined by strict law, *but is absolutely incompatible with honour, honesty, or mistaken good intentions.* On such men let the Attorney-General bring forth all the artillery of his office, and the thanks and blessings of the whole public will follow him. But this is a totally different case. *Whatever private calumny may mark this work, it has not been made the subject of complaint, and we have therefore nothing to do with that, nor any right to consider it.* We are trying whether the public could have been considered as offended and endangered, if Mr Hastings himself, in whose place the author and publisher have a right to put themselves, had, under all the circumstances which have been considered, composed and published the volume under examination. That question cannot, in common sense, be anything resembling *a question of* LAW, but is a pure question of FACT, to be decided on the principles which I have humbly recommended. I therefore ask of the Court that the book itself may now be delivered to you. Read it with attention, and as you shall find it, pronounce your verdict.

REPLY OF THE ATTORNEY-GENERAL.

GENTLEMEN OF THE JURY,—My learned friend and I stand very much contrasted with each other in this cause. To him belong infinite eloquence and ingenuity, a gift of persuasion beyond that which I almost ever knew fall to any man's share, and a power of language greater than that which ever met my ear.

In *his* situation, it is not only permitted to him, but it is commendable—it is his duty to his client—to exert all those faculties, to comprehend every possible topic that, by the utmost stretch of ingenuity, can possibly be introduced into the most remote connexion with the cause. I, on the other hand, gentlemen, must disclaim those qualities which I ascribe to my learned friend—namely, that ingenuity, that eloquence, and that power of words; but if they did belong to me, we stand contrasted also in this circumstance, that I durst not in my present situation use them, whatever little effort I might make to that effect, acting the part simply of an advocate in a private cause. All that I must abandon to-day, recollecting the situation in which I stand. Gentlemen, however unworthily, yet so it is, that I stand in the situation of the first officer of this high Court; therefore, the utmost fair dealing, the plainest common sense, the clearest argument, the utmost *bona fides* with the Court and jury, are the duties incumbent upon me. In that spirit, therefore, gentlemen, you will not expect from me the discharge of my duty in any other way than by the most temperate observation, and by the most correct and the fairest reasoning in my power.

One should have thought, from the general turn of my learned friend's arguments, that I had in this information imputed it as a crime to the deceased gentleman whom he has named, and whom I think I hardly recollect ever to have heard named before,—that I had imputed it to him as an offence, merely that he reasoned in defence of Mr Hastings ably and eloquently, as is asserted. My learned friend has said that I have picked out passages here and there, disconnected and disjointed, and have omitted a vast variety of other passages. I hardly think that his second observation would have been made had it not been for the sake of his first. But inasmuch as I studiously avoided, and would insert no one single line that consisted of fair reasoning and defence for Mr Hastings, inasmuch as it was no part of my duty so to do, so he has exculpated me by saying that the loading an information with that which was not immediately to the point, was a thing which I had avoided with propriety.

This book, as my learned friend himself has described it to you, and read the greater part of, consists of many different heads. It consists of an historical narration of facts; with which I do not quarrel. It consists of extracts from original papers; with which I do not quarrel. It consists of arguments, of reasoning, and of very good declamation; with that I do not quarrel. But it consists also of a stain, and a deep stain, upon your representatives in Parliament. My learned friend says that this is written with a friendly zeal for Mr Hastings. I commend that zeal; but at the same time you will permit me to distinguish, if that could avail, between the zeal of an author for Mr Hastings, and the cold lucrative motives of the printer of that author's work. It was the duty of that printer to have the work revised by some one else, if he has not the capacity to do it himself, and to see that poison does not circulate among the public. It was his bounden duty to do that; zeal could not excuse or exculpate even the author, much less the mechanical printer; though, perhaps, if this had been shown in manuscript as the work of a zealous friend, great allowance might have been made for that zeal.

My learned friend, for the purposes of argument, deviated into almost every field that it was possible for knowledge such as his, for reading, experience, for knowledge of nature, and everything that belongs to human affairs; he has deviated into them at great length, and nine-tenths of his argument consisted of nothing else. Instead of that, what is this question? The coldest, the dullest, the driest of all possible questions. It is neither more nor less than this, Whether, when the great tribunal of the nation is carrying on its most solemn proceeding, for the benefit and for the interests of the public,—whether, while it is even depending, and not ripe for judgment, the accusers, the House of Commons, who carry up their impeachment to the House of Lords, are slandered by being called persons acting from private and interested animosity; persons who studiously, when they find a meritorious servant of the country come home crowned with laurels (as it is expressed), are sure—to do what?—TO IMPEACH AND TO RUIN HIM?

I shall also studiously avoid anything respecting politics or party, or anything respecting the conduct or opinions of any men in another place; and my learned friend will excuse me also if I do not state my own. These I avoid for this reason, that when we are within these walls we are to betake ourselves to the true and genuine principles of our law and constitution. The justest picture of oppression of one man cannot justify the calumniating other men: it may justify the defending that man, but it will not justify a stain upon the House of Commons of this country. And, gentlemen, surely this author, considerable as he is as a man acquainted with composition, betrays the cause of Mr Hastings, as I should think; at least, he does Mr Hastings no service by going beyond his defence, by deserting and abandoning the declamation and the reasoning, of which he seems to be a considerable master, and deviating into slander and calumny upon the House of Commons, his accusers.

My learned friend has used an analogy. He tells you the House of Commons is a grand jury. I close with him in that analogy. I ask you, as lovers of good order, as men desirous of repressing licentiousness, as persons who wish that your country should be decently and well governed, whether you would endure for an instant if this were an information against a defendant who had published that a grand jury found a bill, not because they thought it a right thing that the person accused should be put upon his trial, but that they found the indictment against him because he was meritorious, that they did it from principles of private animosity, and not with a regard to public justice? If an indictment were brought before you for a slander of that sort upon a grand jury, could you hesitate an instant in saying that it was reprehensible, and a thing not to be endured? Why, then, if the whole representatives of the nation are acting in that capacity, if, after many years' investigation, they bring charges against an individual, is it any apology (justification it cannot be), for an author, in his zeal for his friend, to tack to it that which must be a disgrace to the country if it were true, and, therefore, must not be circulated with impunity? The commendation which even my learned friend has bestowed upon this work, the impassioned and animated manner in which he has recommended it to your perusal, and that of every man in the country, most manifestly prove what I stated in opening this cause, that when such mischief as this is found in a book written by a person of no mean abilities, it comes recommended to, and in fact misleads, the best understandings in the country. I leave any man to judge of the mischievous tendency of such a composition, compared with the squibs, paragraphs, and idle trash of the day, which frequently die away with it. Upon this principle, those passages which I selected and put into this information, and which immediately regard the House of Commons, naturally gave offence to the House; they felt themselves calumniated and aspersed, and entitled to redress from a jury.

My learned friend says, Why don't the House of Commons themselves punish it? Is that an argument to be used in the mouth of one who recommends clemency? Does he recommend that the iron hand of power should come down upon a man of this sort, instead of temperately, wisely, and judiciously submitting to the common law of this country?—saying, Let him be dealt with by that common law. THERE he will have a scrupulously impartial

trial.   There he will have every advantage that the meanest
subject of the country is entitled to.

But, says my learned friend, passages are selected from distant
pages and tacked together; the context between must explain the
meaning of those passages; and he compares it to taking one half
of a sentence, and tells you, that if any man should say, "There is
no God," taking that part alone, he would be a blasphemer; whereas,
taking the whole verse, that "The fool hath said in his heart, there
is no God," in that sense it becomes directly the reverse of blasphemy.   Now, has he found any one garbled sentence in the whole
course of this information ?   Is not every one a clear, distinct, and
separate proposition?   On the contrary, when he himself accuses
me, not personally but officially, of not having stated the whole of
this volume upon record, and undertaking to supply my defects,
he misses this very sentence:—"Assertions so hardy, and accusations so atrocious, ought not to have been introduced into the
preamble of an impeachment, before an assembly so respectable as
the House of Peers, without the clearest and most incontrovertible
evidence.   In all transactions of a political nature, there are many
concealed movements that escape the detection of the world; but
there are some facts so broad and glaring, so conspicuous and
prominent, as to strike the general eye, and meet the common
level of the human understanding."

Now, gentlemen, I only adduce this to show that it is possible
that two leaves may be turned over at once on the defendant's
side of the question, and likewise to show you that I have not, for
the purpose of accusation, culled and picked out every passage that
I might have picked out, or every one that would bear an offensive
construction; but have taken those prominent parts where this
author has abandoned the purpose my learned friend ascribes
to him, that of extenuating the guilt imputed to Mr Hastings,
and of showing that he had merit rather than demerit with the
public.   The passages were selected to show that I have betaken
myself to the fifth head of the work, as I enumerated them before,
where the author does not content himself with executing that
purpose, but holds out the House of Commons as persons actuated
by private malice, not only to the eyes of the subjects of this
country, but also to surrounding nations, whose eyes are unquestionably upon us throughout the whole course of the proceeding.

I ask you whether any reasonable answer has been given to the
interpretation which I put upon the various passages in this book ?
The first of them, I admit, with my learned friend, is simply an
introduction, and is stated in the information merely to show that
the author himself knew the position and state of things, viz.,
that the impeachment had been carried up to the House of Lords,
and was there depending for their judgment.

Then, after having reasoned somewhat upon the introduction to these several articles of impeachment, and after having stated that these had been circulated in India, he goes on to say—

" Will accusations built upon such a baseless fabric prepossess the public in favour of the impeachment ?   What credit can we give to multiplied and accumulated charges when we find that they originate from misrepresentation and falsehood ? "

My learned friend himself told you, in a subsequent part of his speech, that those accusations originated from an inquiry, which lasted two years and a half, by a Secret Committee of the House of Commons (of which I myself was a pretty laborious member). If that be so, what pretence is there here for impregnating the public with a belief that from false, scandalous, and fabricated materials, those charges did originate ?   Is not that giving a directly false impression to the public ?   Are not those to be protected from slander of this sort who take so much pains to investigate what appears to them, in the result, to be a fit matter, not for them to decide ultimately upon, but to put in a course of trial where, ultimately, justice will be done ?

Has my learned friend attempted any explanation, or other interpretation, to be put upon these words, than that which the information imputes ?

" If, after exerting all your efforts in the cause of your country, you return covered with laurels, and crowned with success ; if you preserve a loyal attachment to your Sovereign, you may expect the thunders of parliamentary vengeance,—you will certainly be impeached, and probably be undone."

Is it to be said and circulated in print all over the world, that the House of Commons is composed of such materials ; that exactly in proportion to a man's merit is their injustice and inhuman tyranny ?   Is that to be said or printed freely under the pretext that the author is zealous in the interest of a gentleman under misfortune ?   But it is said there are forty libels every day published against this gentleman, and no one is permitted to defend him.   Let all mankind defend him.   Let every man that pleases write what he will, provided he does it within the verge of the law ; if he does it as a manly and good subject, confining himself to reasonable and good argument.

My learned friend says, If you stop this, the press is gagged ; that it never can be said with impunity that the king and the constable are in the same predicament.   The king and the constable are in one respect in the same predicament, with great difference indeed in the gradation, and in the comparison.   But, without all question, both are magistrates ; the one the highest, to whom we look with awe and reverence ; and to the other with obedience, when within his sphere.   That may be freely said in this country, and ever will be said.   But is it the way to secure the liberty of the press, that, at the time when the nation is solemnly engaged in the investigation of the conduct of one of its first servants, that servant should not only be defended by fair argument and reason, as far as it goes, but that his accusers are to be charged with malice and personal animosity against him ?

If the audacious voice of slander shall go so high as that with impunity, who is there that will ever undertake to be an accuser in this country ?   I am sure I for one, who sometimes am called upon (I hope as sparingly as public exigency will admit of) to exercise that odious and disagreeable task, would with pleasure sacrifice my gown if I saw it established that even the highest accusers that the country knows are, under the pretence of the defence of an individual, to be vilified and degraded.   If this be permitted, can subordinate accusers expect to escape ?

Gentlemen, again give me leave to remind you, that nothing can ever secure a valuable blessing so effectually as by enforcing the temperate, legal, and discreet use of it ; and it cannot be necessary for the *liberty* of the press that it should be *licentious* to such an extreme.   Believe me, that if this country should be worked up, as I expressed it yesterday, to a paroxysm of disgust against the *licentiousness* of the press, which has attacked all ranks of men, and now at last has mounted up to the legislative body, its liberty perhaps never can be in greater danger.   Something may be done in that paroxysm of disgust which might be the gradual means of sapping the foundation of that best of our liberties—A FREE PRESS.

Is it not obvious to common sense, that if the whole country is rendered indignant by the licentiousness of the press knowing no bounds, this is the instant of greatest hazard to its freedom ?   Besides, is the folly of the subjects of Great Britain such, that, in order to enjoy a thing in all its perfection, and to all its good purposes, it is necessary to encourage its extremest licentiousness ?   If you shall encourage this its extremest licentiousness (I venture to call it such when the great accusatorial body of the nation is slandered in this manner), if you give it such encouragement to-day, no man can tell where it will reach hereafter.

Therefore, so far from cramping the press, so far from sapping its foundation, so far from doing it an injury, you are, on the contrary, taking the surest means to preserve it, by distinguishing the two parts of this book, and by saying—True it is that any man is at liberty to expound and to explain in print the conduct of another, to justify it, if he pleases, by stating, in a manly way, that which belongs to his subject ; but the moment that he steps aside and slanders an individual, much more the awful body of the representatives of the people, there he has done wrong, there he has trespassed upon the liberty of the press, and has imminently hazarded its existence.

Gentlemen, lay your hands upon your hearts,—ask yourselves as

men of honour (because I know that binds you as much as your
oaths), ask yourselves whether the true meaning of this libel is not,
that not from public grounds, not from conviction, not with a view
to render public service, but from private pique, from private
malice, from by-motives, which I call corruption, the House of Commons have been induced to send this gentleman to an inquiry before
the proper tribunal, and that too, as the libel expresses it, without
even reading it, without hearing, without consideration ; judge, I
say, whether that be not the true exposition of this libel, and then,
gentlemen, consider with yourselves what the effect will be if you
ratify and confirm such an offence by suffering this defendant to
escape.

Lord KENYON then summed up as follows :—
GENTLEMEN OF THE JURY,—I do not feel that I am called upon
to discuss the nature of this libel, or to state to you what the merit
of the composition is, or what the merit of the argument is, but
merely to state what the questions are to which you are to apply
your judgment, and the evidence given in support of this information. It is impossible, when one reads the preface to it, which
states that the libel was written to asperse the House of Commons,
not to feel that it is a matter of considerable importance ; for I do
not know how far a fixed general opinion that the House of Commons deserves to have crimes imputed to it may go ; for men that
are governed will be thereby much influenced by the confidence
which should be reposed in Government. Mankind will never forget that governors are not made for the sake of themselves, but are
placed in their respective stations to discharge the functions of their
office for the benefit of the public ; and if they should ever conceive
that their governors are so inattentive to their duty as to exercise
their functions only to keep themselves in power, and for their own
emolument, without attending to the interests of the public, government must be relaxed, and at last crumble into dust ; and, therefore, if the case be made out which is imputed to the defendant, it
is no doubt a most momentous case indeed ; but though it is so, it
does not follow that the defendant is guilty : and juries have been
frequently told, and I am bound, in the situation in which I stand,
to tell YOU, that, in forming your judgment upon this case, there
are two points for you to attend to, namely,—
Whether the defendant, who is charged with having published
this, did publish it ? and whether the sense which the Attorney-
General, by his innuendoes in this information, has affixed to the
different passages, is fairly affixed to them ?
From any consideration, as to the first of these points, you are
delivered, because it is admitted that the book was published by the

defendant; but the other is the material point to which you are to apply your judgment. It has been entered into with wonderful abilities, and much in the detail; but it is not enough for a man to say I am innocent,—it belongs alone to the Great Searcher of hearts to know whether men are innocent or not,—*we* are to judge of the guilt or innocence of men (because we have no other rule to go by) by their overt acts, *i.e.*, from what they have done.

In applying the innuendoes, I accede entirely to what was laid down by the counsel for the defendant, and which was admitted yesterday by the Attorney-General, as counsel for the Crown, that you must, upon this information, make up your minds that this was meant as an aspersion upon THE HOUSE OF COMMONS; and I admit also that, in forming your opinion, you are not bound to confine your inquiry to those detached passages which the Attorney-General has selected as offensive matter, and the subject of prosecution. But let me, on the other side, warn you, that though there may be much good writing, good argument, morality, and humanity in many parts of it, yet, if there are offensive passages, the good part will not sanctify the bad part.

Having stated that, I ought also to tell you, that in order to see what is the sense to be fairly imputed to those parts that are culled out as the offensive passages, you have a right to look at all the context,—you have a right to look at the whole book,—and if you find it has been garbled, and that the passages selected by the Attorney-General do not bear the sense imputed to them, the man has a right to be acquitted; and God forbid he should be convicted. It is for you, upon reading the information, which, if you go out of court, you will undoubtedly take with you, and by comparing it with this pamphlet, to see whether the sense the Attorney-General has affixed is fairly affixed: always being guided by this, that where it is truly ambiguous and doubtful, the inclination of your judgment should be on the side of innocence; but if you find you cannot acquit him without distorting sentences, you are to meet this case, and all other cases, as I stated yesterday, with the fortitude of men feeling that they have a duty upon them superior to all leaning to parties, namely, the administration of justice in the particular cause.

It would be in vain for me to go through this pamphlet which has been just put into my hand, and to say whether the sense affixed is the fair sense or not. As far as disclosed by the information, these passages afford a strong bias that the sense affixed to them is the fair sense; but of that you will judge, not from the passages themselves merely, but by reading the context, or the whole book, so much at least as is necessary to enable you to ascertain the true meaning of the author.

If I were prepared to comment upon the pamphlet, in my situation it would be improper for me to do it; my duty is fulfilled when I point out to you what the questions are that are proposed to your judgment, and what the evidence is upon the questions : the result is yours, and yours only.

The jury withdrew for about two hours, when they returned into court with a verdict finding the defendant NOT GUILTY.

THE SUBJECT.

Thomas Paine's work, entitled "The Rights of Man," is so justly odious in England, from the scurrility and indecency with which it reviles and ridicules the principles which have for so many years supported and illustrated the excellent form of government established in this country, that the editor has been induced to vary from his former plan ; and instead of selecting the passages contained in the information, has prefaced the following speech of Mr Erskine for the defendant with a copy of the information itself, including the charges of their evil tendency, which were confirmed by the verdict of the jury ; and with the speech of the Attorney-General in condemnation of the work, which contain in fact all the proceedings material to the cause : the proof of publication, and the reading of the passages selected in the information, being all the evidence adduced at the trial ; and the jury having convicted the defendant, without calling for any reply on the part of the Crown or any summing up from the Judge.

It ought, however, to be noticed, that the letter from Thomas Paine to the Attorney-General, part of which was read by the Attorney-General in the course of his address to the jury, was read in evidence ; the objections taken to it by Mr Erskine having been overruled by the Court. This letter, in addition to those inserted in the argument for the Crown, contained passages replete with most scurrilous matter against the King and Prince of Wales, which we have purposely avoided printing, as they formed no part of the charge which the jury had to try.

The effect of the following trial upon every enlightened mind must be an increased admiration of that free constitution which permitted such a man and such a work to be so defended.

THE INFORMATION.

Of Easter Term, in the 32d Year of King George III.

London, (*tó wit*).—Be it remembered, that Sir Archibald Macdonald, Knight, Attorney-General of our present Sovereign Lord King George the Third, who, for our present Sovereign Lord the King, prosecutes in this behalf in his own proper person, comes into the court of our said present Sovereign Lord the King, before the King himself, at Westminster, in the county of Middlesex, on

Friday next after one month from the feast-day of Easter in this same term; and for our said Lord the King giveth the Court here to understand and be informed, that THOMAS PAINE, late of London, gentleman, being a wicked, malicious, seditious, and ill-disposed person, and being greatly disaffected to our said Sovereign Lord the now King, and to the happy constitution and government of this kingdom, and most unlawfully, wickedly, seditiously, and maliciously devising, contriving, and intending to scandalise, traduce, and vilify the late happy Revolution, providentially brought about and effected under the wise and prudent conduct of His Highness William, heretofore Prince of Orange, and afterwards King of England, France, and Ireland, and the dominions thereunto belonging; and the acceptance of the crown and royal dignity of King and Queen of England, France, and Ireland, and the dominions thereunto belonging, by his said Highness William, and Her Highness Mary, heretofore Prince and Princess of Orange; and the means by which the same Revolution was accomplished, to the happiness and welfare of this realm; and to scandalise, traduce, and vilify the Convention of the Lords Spiritual and Temporal and Commons, at whose request, and by whose advice, their said Majesties did accept the said crown and royal dignity; and to scandalise, traduce, and vilify the Act of the Parliament holden at Westminster in the first year of the reign of their said Majesties King William and Queen Mary, intituled, " An Act declaring the Rights and Liberties of the Subject, and settling the Succession of the Crown," and the declaration of rights and liberties in the said Act contained; and also the limitations and settlements of the crown and regal government of the said kingdoms and dominions as by law established; and also by most wicked, cunning, and artful insinuations to represent, suggest, and cause it to be believed, that the said Revolution, and the said settlements and limitations of the crown and regal government of the said kingdoms and dominions, and the said declaration of the rights and liberties of the subject, were contrary to the right and interest of the subjects of this kingdom in general; and that the hereditary regal government of this kingdom was a tyranny. And also by most wicked, cunning, and artful insinuations, to represent, suggest, and cause it to be believed, that the Parliament of this kingdom was a wicked, corrupt, useless, and unnecessary establishment; and that the King, and the Lords Spiritual and Temporal, and Commons, in Parliament assembled, wickedly tyrannised over and oppressed the subjects of this kingdom in general; and to infuse into the minds of the subjects of this kindom groundless and unreasonable discontents and prejudices against our present Sovereign Lord the King and the Parliament of this kingdom, and the constitution, laws, and government thereof, and to bring them into hatred and contempt, on the sixteenth day of February, in the thirty-second year of the reign of our said present Sovereign Lord the King, with force and arms, at London aforesaid, to wit, in the parish of Saint Mary le Bow, in the ward of Cheap, he, the said Thomas, wickedly, maliciously, and seditiously did write and publish, and cause to be written and published, a certain false, scandalous, malicious, and seditious libel, of and concerning the said late happy Revolution, and the said settlements and limitations of the crown and regal government of the said kingdoms and dominions ; and the said Act declaring the rights and liberties of the subject ; and the said declaration of the rights and liberties of the subject therein contained, and the hereditary regal government of the said kingdoms and dominions ; and also of and concerning the legislature, constitution, government, and laws of this kingdom ; of and concerning our present Sovereign Lord the King that now is ; and of and concerning the Parliament of this kingdom, intituled, " Rights of Man, Part the Second ; combining Principle and Practice : by Thomas Paine, Secretary for Foreign Affairs to Congress, in the American War, and Author of the Work intituled Common Sense, and the First Part of the Rights of Man ; the Second Edition, London, printed for J. S. Jordan, No. 166 Fleet Street, 1792 ; " in which said libel are contained, amongst other things, divers false, scandalous, malicious, and seditious matters. In one part thereof, according to the tenor and effect following (that is to say), " All hereditary government is in its nature tyranny. An heritable crown " (meaning, amongst others, the crown of this kingdom) " or an heritable throne " (meaning, amongst others, the throne of this kingdom), " or by what other fanciful name such things may be called, have no other significant explanation than that mankind are heritable property. To inherit a government, is to inherit the people, as if they were flocks and herds." And in another part thereof, according to the tenor and effect following ; (that is to say), " This Convention met at Philadelphia in May 1787, of which General Washington was elected president. He was not at that time connected with any of the State Governments, or with Congress. He delivered up his commission when the war ended, and since then had lived a private citizen. The Convention went deeply into all the subjects, and having, after a variety of debate and investigation, agreed among themselves upon the several parts of a federal constitution, the next question was the manner of giving it authority and practice. For this purpose, they did not, like a cabal of courtiers, send for a Dutch Stadtholder or a German Elector, but they referred the whole matter to the sense and interest of the country " (thereby meaning and intending that it should be believed that a cabal of courtiers had sent for the said Prince of Orange and King George the First, heretofore Elector of Hanover, to take upon themselves respectively the regal government of the said kingdom and dominions, without referring to the sense and interest of the subjects of the said kingdoms). And in another part thereof, according to the tenor and effect following (that is to say), "The history of the Edwards and Henries" (meaning Edwards and Henries, heretofore Kings of England), "and up to the commencement of the Stuarts" (meaning Stuarts, heretofore Kings of England), "exhibits as many instances of tyranny as could be acted within the limits to which the nation had restricted it. The Stuarts" (meaning Stuarts, heretofore Kings of England) "endeavoured to pass these limits, and their fate is well known. In all those instances, we see nothing of a constitution, but only of restrictions on assumed power. After this, another William" (meaning the said William Prince of Orange, afterwards King of England), "descended from the same stock, and claiming from the same origin, gained possession" (meaning possession of the crown of England); "and of the two evils, James and William" (meaning James the Second, heretofore King of England, and the said William Prince of Orange, afterwards King of England), "the nation preferred what it thought the least; since from circumstances it must take one. The Act called the Bill of Rights" (meaning the said Act of Parliament intituled "An Act declaring the Rights and Liberties of the Subject, and settling the Succession of the Crown") "comes here into view; what is it" (meaning the said Act of Parliament last mentioned) "but a bargain which the parts of the government made with each other to divide powers, profits, and privileges?" (meaning that the last-mentioned Act of Parliament was a bargain which the parts of the government in England made with each other to divide powers, profits, and privileges). "You shall have so much, and I will have the rest; and with respect to the nation it said, For your share you shall have the right of petitioning. This being the case, the Bill of Rights" (meaning the said last-mentioned Act of Parliament) "is more properly a Bill of Wrongs and of Insult. As to what is called the Convention Parliament, it" (meaning the said Convention of Lords Spiritual and Temporal, and Commons, herein before mentioned) "was a thing that made itself, and then made the authority by which it acted. A few persons got together, and called themselves by that name; several of them had never been elected, and none of them for the purpose. From the time of William" (meaning the said King William the Third), "a species of government arose, issuing out of this coalition Bill of Rights" (meaning the said Act intituled "An Act declaring the Rights and Liberties of the Subject, and settling the Succession of the Crown"), "and more so since the corruption introduced at the Hanover succession" (meaning the succession of the heirs of the Princess Sophia, Electress and Duchess-Dowager of Hanover, to the crown and dignity of this kingdom) "by the agency of Walpole, that" (meaning the said species of government) "can be described by no other name than

a despotic legislation.   Though the parts may embarrass each
other, the whole has no bounds; and the only right it acknowledges
out of itself, is the right of petitioning.   Where, then, is the constitution either that gives or that restrains power ?   It is not because a part of the Government" (meaning the Government of this
kingdom) " is elective, that makes it less a despotism, if the persons so elected possess afterwards, as a Parliament, unlimited
powers ; election, in this case, becomes separated from representation, and the candidates are candidates for despotism."   And in
another part thereof, according to the tenor and effect following
(that is to say), " The attention of the Government of England (for
I rather choose to call it by this name than the English Government) appears, since its political connexion with Germany, to have
been so completely engrossed and absorbed by foreign affairs, and
the means of raising taxes, that it seems to exist for no other purposes.   Domestic concerns are neglected ; and with respect to
regular laws, there is scarcely such a thing."   And in another
part thereof, according to the tenor and effect following (that is to
say), " With respect to the two Houses of which the English Parliament " (meaning the Parliament of this kingdom) " is composed,
they appear to be effectually influenced into one, and, as a legislature, to have no temper of its own.   The Minister " (meaning
the Minister employed by the King of this realm in the administration of the government thereof), " whoever he at any time may
be, touches it " (meaning the two Houses of Parliament of this
kingdom) " as with an opium wand ; and it " (meaning the two
Houses of Parliament of this kingdom) " sleeps obedience.   But
if we look at the distinct abilities of the two Houses " (meaning
the two Houses of Parliament of this kingdom), " the difference
will appear so great as to show the inconsistency of placing power
where there can be no certainty of the judgment to use it.   Wretched
as the state of representation is in England " (meaning the state of
representation of the Commons of this kingdom), " it is manhood
compared with what is called the House of Lords " (meaning the
Lords Spiritual and Temporal in Parliament assembled); " and so
little is this nick-named House " (meaning the House of Lords)
" regarded, that the people scarcely inquire at any time what it is
doing.   It " (meaning the said House of Lords) " appears also to
be most under influence, and the furthest removed from the general
interest of the nation."   And in another part thereof, according to
the tenor and effect following, viz., " Having thus glanced at some
of the defects of the two Houses of Parliament " (meaning the Parliament of this kingdom), " I proceed to what is called the Crown "
(meaning the Crown of this kingdom), " upon which I shall be
very concise.   It " (meaning the Crown of this kingdom) " signifies
a nominal office of a million sterling a year, the business of which
consists in receiving the money.   Whether the person " (meaning

the King of this realm) " be wise or foolish, sane or insane, a native or a foreigner, matters not. Every Ministry" (meaning the Ministry employed by the King of this realm in the administration of the government thereof) "acts upon the same idea that Mr Burke writes, namely, that the people" (meaning the subjects of this kingdom) "must be hoodwinked, and held in superstitious ignorance by some bugbear or other; and what is called the Crown" (meaning the Crown of this kingdom), "answers this purpose; and therefore it answers all the purposes to be expected from it. This is more than can be said of the other two branches. The hazard to which this office" (meaning, amongst others, the office of King of this realm) "is exposed in all countries" (meaning, amongst others, this kingdom), "is not from anything that can happen to the man" (meaning the King), "but from what may happen to the nation" (meaning, amongst others, this kingdom); "the danger of its coming to its senses." And in another part thereof, according to the tenor and effect following (that is to say): "I happened to be in England at the celebration of the centenary of the Revolution of 1688. The characters of William and Mary" (meaning the said late King William and Queen Mary) "have always appeared to me detestable; the one" (meaning the said King William) "seeking to destroy his uncle, and the other" (meaning the said Queen Mary) "her father, to get possession of power themselves; yet as the nation was disposed to think something of that event, I felt hurt at seeing it ascribe the whole reputation of it to a man" (meaning the said late King William the Third) "who had undertaken it as a job, and who, besides what he otherwise got, charged six hundred thousand pounds for the expense of the little fleet that brought him from Holland. George the First" (meaning George the First, late King of Great Britain, &c.) "acted the same close-fisted part as William the Third had done, and bought the Duchy of Bremen with the money he got from England, two hundred and fifty thousand pounds, over and above his pay as King; and having thus purchased it at the expense of England, added it to his Hanoverian dominions for his own private profit. In fact, every nation that does not govern itself, is governed as a job; England has been the prey of jobs ever since the Revolution." And in another part thereof, according to the tenor and effect following (that is to say): "The fraud, hypocrisy, and imposition of governments" (meaning, amongst others, the Government of this kingdom), "are now beginning to be too well understood to promise them any long career. The farce of monarchy and aristocracy in all countries is following that of chivalry, and Mr Burke is dressing for the funeral. Let it then pass quietly to the tomb of all other follies, and the mourners be comforted. The time is not very distant when England will laugh at itself for sending to Holland, Hanover, Zell, or Brunswick, for men" (meaning the Kings of these realms, born out of the same, who have acceded to the crown thereof at and since the Revolution), " at the expense of a million a year, who understood neither her laws, her language, nor her interest; and whose capacities would scarcely have fitted them for the office of a parish constable. If Government could be trusted to such hands, it must be some easy and simple thing indeed; and materials fit for all the purposes may be found in every town and village in England." In contempt of our said Lord the King and his laws, to the evil example of all others in the like case offending, and against the peace of our said Lord the King, his crown and dignity. And the said Attorney-General of our said Lord the King, for our said Lord the King, further gives the Court here to understand and be informed, that the said Thomas Paine, being a wicked, malicious, seditious, and ill-disposed person, and being greatly disaffected to our said Sovereign Lord the now King, and to the happy constitution and government of this kingdom, and most unlawfully, wickedly, seditiously, and maliciously devising, contriving, and intending to scandalise, traduce, and vilify the late happy Revolution, providentially brought about and effected under the wise and prudent conduct of His Highness William, heretofore Prince of Orange, and afterwards King of England, France, and Ireland, and the dominions thereunto belonging, and the acceptance of the crown and royal dignity of King and Queen of England, France, and Ireland, and the dominions thereunto belonging, by His said Highness William, and Her Highness Mary, heretofore Prince and Princess of Orange, and the means by which the same Revolution was accomplished, to the happiness and welfare of this realm; and to scandalise, traduce, and vilify the Convention of the Lords Spiritual and Temporal, and Commons, at whose request, and by whose advice, their said Majesties did accept the said crown and royal dignity; and to scandalise, traduce, and vilify the Act of the Parliament holden at Westminster in the first year of the reign of their said Majesties King William and Queen Mary, intituled, "An Act declaring the Rights and Liberties of the Subject, and settling the Succession of the Crown," and the declaration of rights and liberties in the said Act contained; and also the limitations and settlements of the crown and regal government of the said kingdoms and dominions, as by law established; and also by most wicked, cunning, and artful insinuations, to represent, suggest, and cause it to be believed that the said Revolution, and the said settlements and limitations of the crown and regal government of the said kingdoms and dominions, and the said declaration of the rights and liberties of the subject, were contrary to the rights and interest of the subjects of this kingdom in general; and that the regal government of this kingdom was a tyranny; and also by most wicked, cunning, and artful insinuations, to represent, suggest, and cause it to be believed that the Parliament of this kingdom was a wicked, corrupt, useless, and unnecessary establishment; and that the King and Lords Spiritual and

Temporal, and Commons, in Parliament assembled, wickedly tyrannised over and oppressed the subjects of this kingdom in general ; and to infuse into the minds of the subjects of this kingdom groundless and unreasonable discontents and prejudices against our present Sovereign Lord the King, and the Parliament of this kingdom ; and the constitution, laws, and government thereof, and to bring them into hatred and contempt, on the sixteenth day of February, in the thirty-second year of the reign of our said present Sovereign Lord the King, by force and arms, at London aforesaid, to wit, in the parish of Saint Mary-le-Bow, in the ward of Cheap, he, the said Thomas, wickedly, maliciously, and seditiously did print and publish, and cause to be printed and published, a certain false, scandalous, malicious, and seditious libel, of and concerning the said late happy Revolution, and the said settlements and limitations of the crown and regal government of the said kingdoms and dominions ; and the said Act declaring the rights and liberties of the subject, and the said declaration of the rights and liberties of the subject therein contained, and the hereditary regal government of the said kingdoms and dominions ; and also of and concerning the legislature, constitution, government, and laws of this kingdom, and of and concerning our present Sovereign Lord the King that now is, and of and concerning the Parliament of this kingdom, intituled, " Rights of Man, Part the Second ; combining Principle and Practice : by Thomas Paine, Secretary for Foreign Affairs to Congress in the American War, and Author of the Work intituled ' Common Sense,' and the First Part of the Rights of Man ; the Second Edition, London, printed for J. S. Jordan, No. 166 Fleet Street." In which said libel are contained, amongst other things, divers false, scandalous, malicious, and seditious matters. In one part thereof, according to the tenor and effect following (that is to say), " All hereditary government is in its nature tyranny. An heritable crown " (meaning, amongst others, the crown of this kingdom), " or an heritable throne" (meaning amongst others, the throne of this kingdom), " or by what other fanciful name such things may be called, have no other significant explanation than that mankind are heritable property. To inherit a government, is to inherit the people, as if they were flocks and herds." And in another part thereof, according to the tenor and effect following (that is to say), "This Convention met at Philadelphia, in May 1787, of which General Washington was elected president. He was not at that time connected with any of the State Governments, or with Congress. He delivered up his commission when the war ended, and since then had lived a private citizen. The Convention went deeply into all the subjects, and having, after a variety of debate and investigation, agreed among themselves upon the several parts of a federal constitution, the next question was the manner of giving it authority and practice. For this purpose they did not, like a cabal of courtiers, send for a Dutch Stadtholder or a German Elector, but they referred

the whole matter to the sense and interest of the country" (thereby meaning, and intending that it should be believed, that a
cabal of courtiers had sent for the said Prince of Orange and King
George the First, heretofore Elector of Hanover, to take upon
themselves respectively the regal government of the said kingdoms
and dominions, without referring to the sense and interest of the
subjects of the said kingdoms). And in another part thereof,
according to the tenor and effect following (that is to say), " The
history of the Edwards and Henries" (meaning Edwards and
Henries, heretofore Kings of England), " and up to the commencement of the Stuarts" (meaning Stuarts, heretofore Kings of England) " exhibits as many instances of tyranny as could be acted
within the limits to which the nation had restricted it. The
Stuarts " (meaning Stuarts, heretofore Kings of England) " endeavoured to pass those limits, and their fate is well known. In all
those instances, we see nothing of a constitution, but only of
restrictions on assumed power. After this, another William"
(meaning the said William Prince of Orange, afterwards King of
England) " descended from the same stock, and claiming from the
same origin, gained possession " (meaning possession of the crown
of England) ; "and of the two evils, James and William " (meaning James the Second, heretofore King of England, and the said
William Prince of Orange, afterwards King of England), "the nation
preferred what it thought the least ; since, from circumstances it
must take one. The Act called the Bill of Rights" (meaning the
said Act of Parliament, intituled, " An Act declaring the Rights
and Liberties of the Subject, and settling the Succession of the
Crown ") " comes here into view ; what is it " (meaning the said
Act of Parliament last mentioned) " but a bargain which the parts
of the Government made with each other to divide powers, profits,
and privileges ? " (meaning that the said last-mentioned Act of
Parliament was a bargain which the parts of the Government in
England made with each other to divide powers, profits, and
privileges). " You shall have so much, and I will have the rest ;
and, with respect to the nation, it said, For your share you shall
have the right of petitioning. This being the case, the Bill of
Rights " (meaning the said last-mentioned Act of Parliament) "is
more properly a Bill of Wrongs and of Insult. As to what is
called the Convention Parliament, it" (meaning the said Convention of Lords Spiritual and Temporal, and Commons, herein
before mentioned) " was a thing that made itself, and then made
the authority by which it acted. A few persons got together, and
called themselves by that name ; several of them had never
been elected, and none of them for the purpose. From the
time of William" (meaning the said King William the Third),
" a species of government arose, issuing out of this coalition Bill of
Rights " (meaning the said Act, intituled, " An Act, declaring the
Rights and Liberties of the Subject, and settling the Succession of

the Crown"), "and more so since the corruption introduced at the Hanover succession" (meaning the succession of the heirs of the Princess Sophia, Electress and Duchess-Dowager of Hanover, to the crown and dignity of this kingdom) "by the agency of Walpole, that" (meaning the said species of government) "can be described by no other name than a despotic legislation. Though the parts may embarrass each other, the whole has no bounds; and the only right it acknowledges out of itself is the right of petitioning. Where, then, is the constitution either that gives or that restrains power? It is not because a part of the Government" (meaning the Government of this kingdom) "is elective, that makes it less a despotism, if the persons so elected possess afterwards, as a Parliament, unlimited powers; election in this case becomes separated from representation, and the candidates are candidates for despotism." And in another part thereof, according to the tenor and effect following (that is to say), "The attention of the Government of England (for I rather choose to call it by this name than the English Government) appears, since its political connexion with Germany, to have been so completely engrossed and absorbed by foreign affairs, and the means of raising taxes, that it seems to exist for no other purposes. Domestic concerns are neglected; and with respect to regular law, there is scarcely such a thing." And in another part thereof, according to the tenor and effect following (that is to say), "With respect to the two Houses of which the English Parliament" (meaning the Parliament of this kingdom) "is composed, they appear to be effectually influenced into one, and, as a legislature, to have no temper of its own. The Minister" (meaning the Minister employed by the King of this realm in the administration of the government thereof), "whoever he at any time may be, touches it" (meaning the two Houses of Parliament of this kingdom) "as with an opium wand, and it" (meaning the two Houses of Parliament of this kingdom) "sleeps obedience. But if we look at the distinct abilities of the two Houses" (meaning the two Houses of Parliament of this kingdom), "the difference will appear so great, as to show the inconsistency of placing power where there can be no certainty of the judgment to use it. Wretched as the state of representation is in England" (meaning the state of representation of the Commons of this kingdom), "it is manhood compared with what is called the House of Lords" (meaning the Lords Spiritual and Temporal in Parliament assembled) : "and so little is this nicknamed House" (meaning the House of Lords) "regarded, that the people scarcely inquire at any time what it is doing. It" (meaning the said House of Lords) "appears also to be most under influence, and the furthest removed from the general interest of the nation." And in another part thereof, according to the tenor and effect following, viz., "Having thus glanced at some of the defects of the two Houses of Parliament" (meaning the Parliament of this kingdom), "I proceed to what is called the Crown" (meaning the Crown of this kingdom), "upon which I shall be very concise. It" (meaning the Crown of this kingdom) "signifies a nominal office of a million sterling a year, the business of which consists in receiving the money. Whether the person" (meaning the King of this realm) "be wise or foolish, sane or insane, a native or a foreigner, matters not. Every Ministry" (meaning the Ministry employed by the King of this realm in the administration of the government thereof) "acts upon the same idea that Mr Burke writes; namely, that the people" (meaning the subjects of this kingdom) "must be hoodwinked and held in superstitious ignorance by some bugbear or other; and what is called the Crown" (meaning the Crown of this kingdom), "answers this purpose, and therefore it answers all the purposes to be expected from it. This is more than can be said of the other two branches. The hazard to which this office" (meaning, amongst others, the office of King of this realm) "is exposed in all countries" (meaning, amongst others, this kingdom), "is not from anything that can happen to the man" (meaning the King), "but from what may happen to the nation" (meaning, amongst others, this kingdom); "the danger of its coming to its senses." And in another part thereof, according to the tenor and effect following (that is to say), "I happened to be in England at the celebration of the centenary of the Revolution of 1688. The characters of William and Mary" (meaning the said late King William and Queen Mary) "have always appeared to me detestable; the one" (meaning the said late King William) "seeking to destroy his uncle, and the other" (meaning the said Queen Mary) "her father, to get possession of power themselves; yet as the nation was disposed to think something of that event, I felt hurt at seeing it ascribe the whole reputation of it to a man" (meaning the said late King William the Third) "who had undertaken it as a job, and who, besides what he otherwise got, charged six hundred thousand pounds for the expense of the little fleet that brought him from Holland. George the First" (meaning George the First, late King of Great Britain, &c.) "acted the same close-fisted part as William" (meaning the said King William the Third) "had done, and bought the Duchy of Bremen with the money he got from England, two hundred and fifty thousand pounds, over and above his pay as King; and having thus purchased it at the expense of England, added it to his Hanoverian dominions for his own private profit. In fact, every nation that does not govern itself is governed as a job: England has been the prey of jobs ever since the Revolution." And in another part thereof, according to the tenor and effect following (that is to say), "The fraud, hypocrisy, and imposition of Governments" (meaning, amongst others, the Government of this kingdom) "are now beginning to be too well understood to promise them any long career. The farce of monarchy and aristocracy in all countries is following that of chivalry, and Mr Burke is dressing for the funeral. Let it then pass quietly to the tomb of all other follies, and the mourners be comforted. The time is not very distant when England will laugh at itself for sending to Holland, Hanover, Zell, or Brunswick, for men" (meaning the Kings of these realms, born out of the same, who have acceded to the crown thereof at and since the Revolution), "at the expense of a million a year, who understood neither her laws, her language, nor her interest; and whose capacities would' scarcely have fitted them for the office of a parish constable. If government could be trusted to such hands, it must be some easy and simple thing indeed; and materials fit for all the purposes may be found in every town and village in England." In contempt of our said Lord the King and his laws, to the evil example of all others in the like case offending, and against the peace of our said Lord the King, his crown and dignity. And the said Attorney-General of our said Lord the King, for our said Lord the King, further gives the Court here to understand and be informed, that the said Thomas Paine, being a wicked, seditious, and ill-disposed person, and wickedly seditiously, and maliciously intending to scandalise, traduce, and vilify the character of the said late Sovereign Lord King William the Third, and the said late happy Revolution, and the Parliament of England, by whose means the same was established, commonly called the Convention Parliament; and the laws and statutes of this realm limiting and establishing the succession to the crown of this kingdom, and the statute declaring the rights and liberties of the subject, commonly called the Bill of Rights, and the happy constitution and government of this kingdom, as by law established, and to bring the constitution, legislation, and government of this kingdom into hatred and contempt with His Majesty's subjects; and to stir up and excite discontents and seditions among His Majesty's subjects; and to fulfil, perfect, and bring to effect his said wicked, malicious, and seditious intentions, on the said sixteenth day of February, in the thirty-second year aforesaid, at London aforesaid, in the parish and ward aforesaid, he the said Thomas Paine, wickedly, maliciously, and seditiously did write and publish, and cause and procure to be written and published, a certain other false, scandalous, malicious, and seditious libel, in which, amongst other things, are contained certain false, scandalous, malicious, and seditious matters, of and concerning the character of the said late Sovereign Lord King William the Third and the said Revolution and the said Parliament, and the laws and statutes of this realm, and the happy constitution and government thereof, as by law established, according to the tenor and effect following (that is to say), "The history of the Edwards and Henries" (meaning Edwards and Henries, heretofore kings of England), "and up to the commencement of the Stuarts" (meaning Stuarts, heretofore kings of England), " exhibits as many instances of tyranny as could be acted within the limits to which the nation" (meaning England) " had restricted it. The Stuarts" (meaning Stuarts, heretofore kings of England) " endeavoured to pass those limits, and their fate is well known. In all those instances we see nothing of a constitution, but only of restrictions on assumed power. After this another William" (meaning the said late King William the Third), "descended from the same stock, and claiming from the same origin, gained possession" (meaning possession of the crown of England) ; " and of the two evils, James and William " (meaning James the Second, heretofore King of England, and the said King William the Third), " the nation" (meaning England) " preferred what it thought the least, since from circumstances they must take one. The Act called the Bill of Rights" (meaning the said statute declaring the rights and liberties of the subject, commonly called the Bill of Rights) " comes here into view. What is it" (meaning the said last-mentioned statute) " but a bargain which. the parts of the Government made with each other to divide powers, profits, and privileges?" (meaning that the said last-mentioned statute was a bargain which the parts of Government in England made with each other to divide powers, profits, and privileges). " You shall have so much, and I will have the rest. And with respect to the nation" (meaning England), " it said, for your share you shall have the right of petitioning. This being the case, the Bill of Rights" (meaning the said last-mentioned statute), " is more properly a bill of wrongs and of insult. As to what is called the Convention Parliament" (meaning the aforesaid Parliament of England, commonly called the Convention Parliament), " it" (meaning the aforesaid Parliament of England, commonly called the Convention Parliament) " was a thing that made itself, and then made the authority by which it acted. A few persons got together, and called themselves by that name. Several of them had never been elected, and none of them for the purpose. From the time of William" (meaning the said King William the Third), " a species of government" (meaning the government of England) " arose issuing out of this coalition Bill of Rights" (meaning the said statute declaring the rights and liberties of the subject) ; " and more so since the corruption introduced at the Hanover succession" (meaning the succession of the heirs of the Princess Sophia, Electress and Duchess-Dowager of Hanover, to the crown and dignity of this kingdom), " by the agency of Walpole, that" (meaning the said species of government) " can be described by no other name than a despotic legislation. Though the parts may embarrass each other, the whole has no bounds ; and the only right it acknowledges out of itself is the right of petitioning. Where, then, is the constitution either that gives or that restrains power? It is not because a part of the Government" (meaning the Government of this kingdom) " is elective, that makes it less a despotism. If the persons so elected possess afterwards, as a Parliament, unlimited powers, election, in this case, becomes separated from representation, and the candidates are candidates for despotism." In contempt of our said Lord the King and his laws, to the evil example of all others in the like case offending, and against the peace of our said Lord the King, his crown and dignity. And the said Attorney-General of our said Lord the King, for our said Lord the King, further gives the Court here to understand and be informed, that the said Thomas Paine, being a wicked, seditious, and ill-disposed person, and wickedly, seditiously, and maliciously intending to scandalise, traduce, and vilify the character of the said late Sovereign Lord King William the Third, and the said late happy Revolution, and the Parliament of England by whose means the same was established, commonly called the Convention Parliament; and the laws and statutes of this realm, limiting and establishing the succession to the Crown of this kingdom ; and the statute declaring the rights and liberties of the subject, commonly called the Bill of Rights ; and the happy constitution and government of this kingdom as by law established; and to bring the constitution, legislation, and government of this kingdom into hatred and contempt with His Majesty's subjects; and to stir up and excite discontents and seditions among His Majesty's subjects ; and to fulfil, perfect, and bring to effect his said wicked, malicious, and seditious intentions, on the said sixteenth day of February, in the thirty-second year aforesaid, at London aforesaid, in the parish and ward aforesaid, he, the said Thomas Paine, wickedly, maliciously, and seditiously, did print and publish, and cause and procure to be printed and published, a certain other false, scandalous, malicious, and seditious libel, in which, amongst other things, are contained certain false, scandalous, malicious, and seditious matters, of and concerning the character of the said late Sovereign Lord King William the Third, and the said Revolution, and the said Parliament, and the laws and statutes of this realm, and the happy constitution and government thereof, as by law established, according to the tenor and effect following (that is to say), " The history of the Edwards and the Henries" (meaning Edwards and Henries, heretofore Kings of England), "and up to the commencement of the Stuarts " (meaning Stuarts, heretofore Kings of England), "exhibits as many instances of tyranny as could be acted within the limits to which the nation" (meaning England) "had restricted it. The Stuarts" (meaning Stuarts, heretofore Kings of England) " endeavoured to pass those limits, and their fate is well known. In all those instances we see nothing of a constitution, but only of restrictions on assumed power. After this another William" (meaning the said late King William the Third),

" descended from the same stock, and claiming from the same
origin, gained possession " (meaning possession of the crown of
England) ; " and of the two evils, James and William " (meaning
James the Second, heretofore King of England, and the said King
William the Third), " the nation " (meaning England) " preferred
what it thought least, since from circumstances it must take one.
The Act called the Bill of Rights " (meaning the said statute
declaring the rights and liberties of the subject, commonly called
the Bill of Rights) " comes here into view.   What is it " (meaning
the said late-mentioned statute) " but a bargain which the parts of
the government made with each other to divide powers, profits, and
privileges ? " (meaning, that the said last-mentioned statute was a
bargain which the parts of the government in England made with
each other to divide powers, profits, and privileges).   " You shall
have so much, and I will have the rest.   And with respect to the
nation " (meaning England), " it said, For your share you shall
have the right of petitioning.   This being the case, the Bill of
Rights " (meaning the said last-mentioned statute) " is more properly a Bill of Wrongs and of Insult.   As to what is called the
Convention Parliament " (meaning the aforesaid Parliament of
England), " it " (meaning the aforesaid Parliament of England,
commonly called the Convention Parliament) " was a thing that
made itself, and then made the authority by which it acted ; a few
persons got together, and called themselves by that name ; several
of them had never been elected, and none of them for the purpose.
From the time of William " (meaning the said King William the
Third) " a species of government" (meaning the government of
England) " arose, issuing out of this coalition Bill of Rights "
(meaning the said statute declaring the rights and liberties of the
subject), " and more so since the corruption introduced at the Hanover succession " (meaning the succession of the heirs of the
Princess Sophia, Electress and Duchess-Dowager of Hanover, to
the crown and dignity of this kingdom) " by the agency of
Walpole, that " (meaning the said species of government) " can
be described by no other name than a despotic legislation. Though
the parts may embarrass each other, the whole has no bounds; and
the only right it acknowledges, out of itself, is the right of petitioning.   Where then is the constitution either that gives or that
restrains power ?   It is not because a part of the government "
(meaning the government of this kingdom) " is elective, that makes
it less a despotism, if the persons so elected possess afterwards, as a
Parliament, unlimited powers.   Election in this case becomes
separated from representation, and the candidates are candidates
for despotism."   In contempt of our said Lord the King and his
laws, to the evil example of all others in the like case offending,
and against the peace of our said Lord the King, his crown and
dignity.   And the said Attorney-General of our said Lord the

King, for our said Lord the King, further gives the Court here to understand and be informed, that the said Thomas Paine, being a wicked, malicious, seditious, and ill-disposed person, and being greatly disaffected to our said present Sovereign Lord the King, and wickedly, maliciously, and seditiously intending, devising, and contriving to traduce and vilify our Sovereign Lord the King, and the two Houses of Parliament of this kingdom, and the constitution and government of this kingdom, and the administration of, the government thereof, and to stir up and excite discontents and seditions amongst His Majesty's subjects, and to alienate and withdraw the affection, fidelity, and allegiance of his said Majesty's subjects from his said Majesty; and to fulfil, perfect, and bring to effect his said wicked, malicious, and seditious intentions, on the said sixteenth day of February, in the thirty-second year aforesaid, at London aforesaid, in the parish and ward aforesaid, he, the said Thomas Paine wickedly, seditiously, and maliciously did write and publish, and cause to be written and published, a certain other false, scandalous, malicious, and seditious libel; in which libel, amongst other things, are contained certain false, scandalous, malicious, and seditious matters, of and concerning the Crown of this kingdom, and the King's administration of the government thereof, and of and concerning the King and the two Houses of Parliament of this kingdom, according to the tenor and effect following, viz., "Having thus glanced at some of the defects of the two Houses of Parliament" (meaning the Parliament of this kingdom), "I proceed to what is called the Crown" (meaning the Crown of this kingdom), "upon which I shall be very concise. It" (meaning the Crown of this kingdom) "signifies a nominal office of a million sterling a year, the business of which consists in receiving the money. Whether the person" (meaning the King of this realm) "be wise or foolish, sane or insane, a native or a foreigner, matters not. Every Ministry" (meaning the Ministry employed by the King of this realm in the administration of the government thereof) "acts upon the same idea that Mr Burke writes, namely, that the people" (meaning the subjects of this kingdom) "must be hoodwinked, and held in superstitious ignorance by some bugbear or other; and what is called the Crown" (meaning the Crown of this kingdom) "answers this purpose, and therefore it answers all the purposes to be expected from it : this is more than can be said of the other two branches. The hazard to which this office" (meaning, amongst others, the office of King of this realm) "is exposed in all countries" (meaning, amongst others, this kingdom) "is not from anything that can happen to the man" (meaning the King), "but from what may happen to the nation" (meaning, amongst others, this kingdom), "the danger of its coming to its senses." In contempt of our said Lord the King and his laws, to the evil example of all others in the like case offending, and against the peace of our said Lord the King, his crown and dignity. And the said Attorney-General of our said Lord the King, for our Lord the King, further gives the Court here to understand and be informed, that the said Thomas Paine, being a wicked, malicious, seditious, and ill-disposed person, and being greatly disaffected to our said present Sovereign Lord the King, and wickedly, maliciously, and seditiously intending, devising, and contriving to traduce and vilify our Sovereign Lord the King, and the two Houses of Parliament of this kingdom, and the constitution and government of this kingdom, and the administration of the government thereof, and to stir up and excite discontents and seditions amongst His Majesty's subjects, and to alienate and withdraw the affection, fidelity, and allegiance of His said Majesty's subjects from His said Majesty; and to fulfil, perfect, and bring to effect his said wicked, malicious, and seditious intentions, on the said sixteenth day of February, in the thirty-second year aforesaid, at London aforesaid, in the parish and ward aforesaid, he, the said Thomas Paine, wickedly, seditiously, and maliciously did print and publish, and cause to be printed and published, a certain other false, scandalous, malicious, and seditious libel; in which libel, amongst other things, are contained certain false, scandalous, malicious, and seditious matters, of and concerning the Crown of this kingdom, and the King's administration of the government thereof, and of and concerning the King and the two Houses of Parliament of this kingdom, according to the tenor and effect following, viz., "Having thus glanced at some of the defects of the two Houses of Parliament" (meaning of the Parliament of this kingdom), "I proceed to what is called the Crown" (meaning the Crown of this kingdom), "upon which I shall be very concise. It" (meaning the Crown of this kingdom) "signifies a nominal office of a million sterling a year, the business of which consists in receiving the money: whether the person" (meaning the King of this realm) "be wise or foolish, sane or insane, a native or a foreigner, matters not. Every Ministry" (meaning the Ministry employed by the King of this realm in the administration of the government thereof) "acts upon the same idea that Mr Burke writes, namely, that the people" (meaning the subjects of this kingdom) "must·be hoodwinked, and held in superstitious ignorance by some bugbear or other; and what is called the Crown" (meaning the Crown of this kingdom) "answers this purpose, and therefore it answers all the purposes to be expected from it: this is more than can be said of the other two branches. The hazard to which this office" (meaning, amongst others, the office of King of this realm) "is exposed in all countries" (meaning, amongst others, this kingdom), "is not from anything that can happen to the man" (meaning the King), "but from what may happen to the nation" (meaning, amongst others, this kingdom), "the danger of its coming to its senses." In contempt of our said Lord the King and his laws, to the evil example of all others in the like case offending, and against the peace of our said Lord the King, his crown and dignity. And the said Attorney-General of our said Lord the King, for our said Lord the King, further giveth the Court here to understand and be informed, that the said Thomas Paine, being a wicked, malicious, seditious, and ill-disposed person, and being greatly disaffected to our said Lord the King, and the constitution and government of this kingdom, and wickedly, maliciously, and seditiously intending, devising, and contriving to asperse, defame, and vilify the characters of the late Sovereign Lord and Lady William and Mary, heretofore King and Queen of England, and of George the First, heretofore King of Great Britain, &c.; and to asperse, defame, and vilify the happy Revolution, providentially effected under the wise and prudent conduct of the said King William and Queen Mary, and to bring the said Revolution, and the characters of the said King William and Queen Mary, and King George the First, into hatred and contempt with the subjects of this realm, and to stir up and. excite discontents and seditions among His Majesty's subjects, and to alienate and withdraw the affection, fidelity, and allegiance of His Majesty's subjects from His said present Majesty; and to fulfil, perfect, and bring to effect his said wicked, malicious, and seditious intentions, on the said sixteenth day of February, in the thirty-second year of the reign of our Lord the now King, at London aforesaid, in the parish and ward aforesaid, wickedly, maliciously, and seditiously, did write and publish, and cause to be written and published, a certain other false, wicked, malicious, scandalous, and seditious libel; in which same libel, amongst other things, are contained certain false, wicked, malicious, scandalous, and seditious matters, of and concerning the said King William and Queen Mary, and the said King George the First, and the said Revolution, according to the tenor and effect following (that is to say), "I happened to be in England at the celebration of the centenary of the Revolution of 1688" (meaning the said Revolution). "The characters of William and Mary" (meaning the said late King William and Queen Mary) "have always appeared to me detestable; the one" (meaning the said King William) "seeking to destroy his uncle, and the other" (meaning the said Queen Mary) "her father, to get possession of power themselves; yet, as the nation was disposed to think something of that event, I felt hurt at seeing it ascribe the whole reputation of it to a man" (meaning the said late King William the Third) "who had undertaken it as a job; and who, besides what he otherwise got, charged six hundred thousand pounds for the expense of the little fleet that brought him from Holland. George the First" (meaning George the First, late King of Great Britain, &c.) "acted the same close-fisted part as William" (meaning the said King William the Third) had done, and bought the Duchy of Bremen with the money he got from England, two hundred and fifty thousand pounds, over and above his pay as King; and having thus purchased it at the expense of England, added it to his Hanoverian dominions for his own private profit. In fact, every nation that does not govern itself is governed as a job. England has been the prey of jobs ever since the Revolution" (meaning the aforesaid Revolution). In contempt of our said Lord the King and his laws, to the evil and pernicious example of all others in the like case offending, and against the peace of our said Lord the King, his crown and dignity. And the said Attorney-General of our said Lord the King, for our said Lord the King, further gives the Court here to understand and be informed, that the said Thomas Paine, being a wicked, malicious, seditious, and ill-disposed person, and being greatly disaffected to our said Lord the King, and the constitution and government of this kingdom, and wickedly, maliciously, and seditiously intending, devising, and contriving to asperse, defame, and vilify the characters of the late Sovereign Lord and Lady William and Mary, heretofore King and Queen of England, and of George the First, heretofore King of Great Britain, &c., and to asperse, defame, and vilify the happy Revolution, providentially effected under the wise and prudent conduct of the said King William and Queen Mary, and to bring the said Revolution, and the characters of the said King William and Queen Mary, and King George the First, into hatred and contempt with the subjects of this realm, and to stir up and excite discontents and seditions among his Majesty's subjects, and to alienate and withdraw the affection, fidelity, and allegiance of his Majesty's subjects from his said present Majesty; and to fulfil, perfect, and bring to effect, his wicked, malicious, and seditious intentions, on the said sixteenth day of February, in the thirty-second year of the reign of our Lord the now King, at London aforesaid, in the parish and ward aforesaid, wickedly, maliciously, and seditiously did print and publish, and cause to be printed and published, a certain other false, wicked, malicious, scandalous, and seditious libel; in which same libel, amongst other things, are contained certain false, wicked, malicious, scandalous, and seditious matters, of and concerning the said King William and Queen Mary, and the said King George the First, and the said Revolution, according to the tenor and effect following (that is to say), " I happened to be in England at the celebration of the centenary of the Revolution of 1688 " (meaning the said Revolution). " The characters of William and Mary" (meaning the said late King William and Queen Mary) " have always appeared to me detestable; the one " (meaning the said King William) " seeking to destroy his uncle, and the other " (meaning the said Queen Mary) " her father, to get possession of power themselves; yet, as the nation was disposed to think some-

thing of that event, I felt hurt at seeing it ascribe the whole
reputation of it to a man" (meaning the said late King William
the Third) "who had undertaken it as a job; and who, besides
what he otherwise got, charged six hundred thousand pounds for
the expense of the little fleet that brought him from Holland.
George the First" (meaning George the First, late King of Great
Britain, &c.) "acted the same close-fisted part as William" (meaning the said King William the Third) "had done, and bought the
Duchy of Bremen with the money he got from England, two hundred and fifty thousand pounds, over and above his pay as King;
and having thus purchased it at the expense of England, added it
to his Hanoverian dominions for his own private profit. In fact,
every nation that does not govern itself is governed as a job.
England has been the prey of jobs ever since the Revolution"
(meaning the aforesaid Revolution). In contempt of our said
Lord the King and his laws, to the evil and pernicious example of
all others in the like case offending, and against the peace of our
said Lord the King, his crown and dignity. And the said Attorney-
General of our said Lord the King, for our said Lord the King,
further gives the Court here to understand and be informed, that
the said Thomas Paine, being a wicked, malicious, seditious, and
ill-disposed person, and being greatly disaffected to our said Lord
the King, and the constitution and government of this kingdom,
and wickedly, maliciously, and seditiously intending, devising, and
contriving to asperse, defame, and vilify the character of the late
Sovereign Lord William, heretofore King of England, and of
George the First, heretofore King of Great Britain, &c., and to
asperse, defame, and vilify the happy Revolution providentially
effected under the wise and prudent conduct of the said King
William; and to bring the said Revolution and the characters of
the said King William and King George the First into hatred
and contempt with the subjects of this realm; and to stir up and
excite discontents and seditions among his Majesty's subjects, and
to alienate and withdraw the affection, fidelity, and allegiance of
his Majesty's subjects from his said present Majesty; and to fulfil,
perfect, and bring to effect his said wicked, malicious, and seditious
intentions, on the said sixteenth day of February, in the thirty-
second year of the reign of our Lord the now King, at London
aforesaid, in the parish and ward aforesaid, wickedly and maliciously
did write and publish, and cause to be written and published, a
certain other false, wicked, malicious, scandalous, and seditious
libel; in which same libel, amongst other things, are contained
certain false, wicked, malicious, scandalous, and seditious matters,
of and concerning the said King William the Third, and the said
King George the First, and the said Revolution, according to the
tenor and effect following (that is to say), "The fraud, hypocrisy,
and imposition of Governments" (meaning, amongst others, the

Government of this kingdom) "are now beginning to be too well understood to promise them any long career. The farce of monarchy and aristocracy in all countries is following that of chivalry, and Mr Burke is dressing for the funeral. Let it then pass quietly to the tomb of all other follies, and the mourners be comforted. The time is not very distant when England will laugh at itself for sending to Holland, Hanover, Zell, or Brunswick, for men" (meaning the said King William the Third and King George the First), "at the expense of a million a year, who understood neither her laws, her language, nor her interest; and whose capacities would scarcely have fitted them for the office of a parish constable. If government could be trusted to such hands, it must be some easy and simple thing indeed; and materials fit for all the purposes may be found in every town and village in England." In contempt of our said Lord the now King and his laws, to the evil example of all others in the like case offending, and against the peace of our said Lord the King, his crown and dignity. And the said Attorney-General of our said Lord the King, for our said Lord the King, further gives the Court here to understand and be informed, that the said Thomas Paine, being a wicked, malicious, seditious, and ill-disposed person, and being greatly disaffected to our said Lord the King, and the constitution and government of this kingdom, and wickedly, maliciously, and seditiously intending, devising, and contriving to asperse, defame, and vilify the character of the late Sovereign Lord William, heretofore King of England, and of George the First heretofore King of Great Britain, &c., and to asperse, defame, and vilify the happy Revolution providentially effected under the wise and prudent conduct of the said King William, and to bring the said Revolution and the characters of the said King William and King George the First into hatred and contempt with the subjects of this realm; and to stir up and excite discontents and seditions among his Majesty's subjects, and to alienate and withdraw the affection, fidelity, and allegiance of his Majesty's subjects from his said present Majesty; and to fulfil, perfect, and bring to effect his said wicked, malicious, and seditious intentions, on the said sixteenth day of February, in the thirty-second year of the reign of our Lord the now King, at London aforesaid, in the parish and ward aforesaid, wickedly, maliciously, and seditiously did print and publish, and cause to be printed and published, a certain other false, wicked, malicious, scandalous, and seditious libel, in which same libel, amongst other things, are contained certain false, wicked, malicious, scandalous, and seditious matters of and concerning the said King William the Third, and the said King George the First, and the said Revolution, according to the tenor and effect following (that is to say), "The fraud, hypocrisy, and imposition of Governments" (meaning, among others, the Government of this kingdom), "are now beginning to be too well understood to promise them any long career. The farce of monarchy and aristocracy in all countries is following that of chivalry, and Mr Burke is dressing for the funeral. Let it then pass quietly to the tomb of all other follies, and the mourners be comforted. The time is not very distant when England will laugh at itself for sending to Holland, Hanover, Zell, or Brunswick, for men" (meaning the said King William the Third and King George the First), "at the expense of a million a year, who understood neither her laws, her language, nor her interest, and whose capacities would scarcely have fitted them for the office of a parish constable. If government could be trusted to such hands, it must be some easy and simple thing indeed; and materials fit for all the purposes may be found in every town and village in England." In contempt of our said Lord the now King and his laws, to the evil example of all others in the like case offending, and against the peace of our said Lord the King, his crown and dignity. Whereupon the said Attorney-General of our said Lord the King, who for our said Lord the King in this behalf prosecuteth for our said Lord the King, prayeth the consideration of the Court here in the premises, and that due process of law may be awarded against him the said Thomas Paine in this behalf, to make him answer to our said Lord the King touching and concerning the premises aforesaid.

The Information was opened by Mr PERCEVAL.

Mr ATTORNEY-GENERAL then proceeded as follows:—

GENTLEMEN OF THE JURY,—You will permit me to solicit, and for no long space of time, in the present stage of this business, somewhat of your attention to a cause which, considering it on its own merits only, is, in my humble judgment, a plain, a clear, a short, and indisputable case. Were it not, gentlemen, that certain circumstances have rendered it a case of more expectation than ordinary, I do assure you that I should literally have contented myself this day with conducting myself in the manner that I did upon the last occasion that I was called upon to address a jury upon this sort of subject, namely, by simply reading to you the passages which I have selected, and leaving it entirely to your judgment. But, gentlemen, it so happens that the accumulated mischief which has arisen from the particular book that is now before you, and the consequences, which everybody is acquainted with, which have followed from this publication, have rendered it necessary, perhaps, that I should say a few words more in the opening than it would have been my intention to have done, had it not been for those circumstances.

Gentlemen, in the first place, you will permit me, without the imputation, I think, of speaking of myself (a very trifling subject, and always a disgusting one to others), to obviate a rumour which I have heard, namely, that this prosecution does not correspond with my private judgment: that has been said, and has reached my ears from various quarters. The refutation that I shall give to it is this, that I should think I deserved to be with disgrace expelled from the situation with which His Majesty has honoured me in your service, and that of all my fellow-subjects, had I, as far as my private judgment goes, hesitated for one instant to bring this enormous offender, as I consider him, before a jury of his country.

Gentlemen, the publication in question was not the first of its kind which this defendant sent forth into the world. This particular publication was preceded by one upon the same subjects, and handling, in some measure, the same topics. That publication, although extremely reprehensible, and such as, perhaps, I was not entirely warranted in overlooking, I did overlook, upon this principle, that it may not be fitting and prudent at all times for a public prosecutor to be sharp in his prosecutions, or to have it said that he is instrumental in preventing any manner of discussion coming under the public eye, although, in his own estimation, it may be very far indeed from that which is legitimate and proper discussion. Reprehensible as that book was, extremely so, in my opinion, yet it was ushered into the world under circumstances that led me to conceive that it would be confined to the judicious reader; and when confined to the judicious reader, it appeared to me that such a man would refute as he went along.

But, gentlemen, when I found that another publication was ushered into the world still more reprehensible than the former; that in all shapes, in all sizes, with an industry incredible, it was either totally or partially thrust into the hands of all persons in this country, of subjects of every description; when I found that even children's sweetmeats were wrapped up with parts of this, and delivered into their hands in the hope that they would read it; when all industry was used, such as I describe to you, in order to obtrude and force this upon that part of the public whose minds cannot be supposed to be conversant with subjects of this sort, and who cannot therefore correct as they go along, I thought it behoved me, upon the earliest occasion, which was the first day of the term succeeding this publication, to put a charge upon record against its author.

Now, gentlemen, permit me to state to you what it is that I impute to this book, and what is the intention that I impute to the writer of this book. Try it by every test that the human mind can possibly suggest, and see whether, when tried by all the variety of those tests, you will not be satisfied, in the long run, that it does deserve that description which my duty obliges me to give of it.

Gentlemen, in the first place, I impute to it a wilful, deliberate intention to vilify and degrade, and thereby to bring into abhorrence and contempt, the whole constitution of the government of this country; not as *introduced*, that I will never admit, but as *explained* and *restored* at the Revolution: that system of government under which we this day live; and if it shall be attacked by contemptuous expressions; if by dogmatical dicta; if by ready-made propositions, offered to the understandings of men solicitous about the nature of their constitution, properly so (God forbid they ever should be otherwise!), but who, at the same time, may be easily imposed upon to their own destruction, they may be brought to have diffidence, and even abhorrence (for this book goes all that length) of that which is the salvation of the public, and everything that is dear to them.

I impute, then, to this book a deliberate design to eradicate from the minds of the people of this country that enthusiastic love which they have hitherto had for that constitution, and thereby to do the utmost work of mischief that any human being can do in this society.

Gentlemen, further I impute to it that, *in terms*, the regal part of the government of this country, bounded and limited as it is, is represented as an oppressive and an abominable tyranny.

Thirdly, That the whole legislature of this country is directly an usurpation.

Again, with respect to the laws of this realm, which hitherto have been our boast, indiscriminately, and without one single exception, that they are grounded upon this usurped authority, and are therefore in themselves null, or, to use his own words, that there is little or no law in this country.

Then, gentlemen, is it to be held out to a community of ten or twelve millions of people; is it to be held out, as well to the lower as to the better informed classes of these ten or twelve millions, that there is nothing in this society that is binding upon their conduct, excepting such portion of religion or morality as they may individually and respectively entertain?

Gentlemen, are we then a lawless banditti? Have we neither laws to secure our property, our persons, or our reputations? Is it so that every man's arms are unbound, and that he may do whatever he pleases in the society? Are we reduced back again to that savage state of nature? I ask you the question! You, gentlemen, know well what the answer is. But, gentlemen, are we to say that a man who holds this out to those who are not furnished with the means of giving the answer which I know you, and every gentleman who hears me at this moment, will give, is discussing a question? Can anything add to his slander upon the constitution, and upon the separate parts of the Government, so constituted as ours is, more than that sweeping imputation upon the whole system of law that binds us together, namely, that it is null and void, and that there is in reality no such thing to be found?

Gentlemen, in the several passages which I shall read to you, I impute this to him also: that he uses an artifice, gross to those who can observe it, but dangerous in the extreme to those whose minds, perhaps, are not sufficiently cultivated and habituated to reading to enable them to discover it. The artifice, in order to create disgust, is neither more nor less than this: it is stating all the objections that can possibly be urged to monarchy, separately and solely considered, and to pure and simple aristocracy; he never chooses to say a single syllable with respect to those two as combined with a democracy, forbearing also to state, and industriously keeping out of the way, every circumstance that regards that worst of all governments, an unbalanced democracy, which is necessarily pregnant with a democratical tyranny. This is the gross artifice; and when you come to dissect the book in the careful manner that I have done, I believe you and every other reader will easily detect that artifice.

Gentlemen, to whom are the positions that are contained in this book addressed? They are addressed, gentlemen, to the ignorant, to the credulous, to the desperate. To the desperate all government is irksome; nothing can be so palatable to their ears as the comfortable doctrine that there is neither law nor government amongst us.

The ignorant and the credulous we all know to exist in all countries; and perhaps exactly in proportion as their hearts are good and simple, are they an easy prey to the crafty who have the cruelty to deceive them.

Gentlemen, in judging of the malignant intention which I must impute to this author, you will be pleased to take into your consideration the phrase and the manner, as well as the matter. The phrase I state to be insidious and artful; the manner, in many instances scoffing and contemptuous—a short argument, often a prevalent one with the ignorant or the credulous. With respect to the *matter*, in my conscience I call it treason, though technically, according to the laws of the country, it is not; for, gentlemen, balance the inconvenience to society of that which is technically treason, and in this country we must not, thank God, extend it, but keep it within its most narrow and circumscribed definitions; but consider the comparative difference of the mischief that may happen from spreading doctrines of this sort, and that which may happen from any treason whatever.

In the case of the utmost degree of treason, even perpetrating the death of a prince upon the throne, the law has found the means of supplying that calamity in a manner that may save the country from any permanent injury. In many periods of the history of this country, which you may easily recollect, it is true that the reign of a good prince has been interrupted by violence—a great evil; but not so great as this: the chasm is filled up instantly by the constitution of this country, even if that last of treasons should be committed.

But where is the power upon earth that can fill up the chasm of a constitution that has been growing—not for seven hundred years, as Mr Paine would have you believe, from the Norman Conquest—but from time almost eternal, impossible to trace ; that has been growing, as appears from the symptoms Julius Cæsar observed when he found our ancestors nearly savages in the country, from that period until it was consummated at the Revolution, and shone forth in all its splendour ?

In addition to this, this gentleman thinks fit even to impute to the existence of that constitution, such as I have described it, the very evils inseparable from human society, or even from human nature itself. All these are imputed to that scandalous, that wicked, that usurped constitution under which we, the subjects of this country, have hitherto mistakenly conceived that we lived happy and free.

Gentlemen, I apprehend it to be no very difficult operation of the human mind to distinguish reasoning and well-meant discussion from a deliberate design to calumniate the law and constitution under which we live, and to withdraw men's allegiance from that constitution. It is the operation of good sense. It is therefore no difficult operation for a jury of the city of London. Therefore, you will be pleased to observe whether the whole of this book—I should rather say such part as I am at present at liberty to advert to—is not of this description ; that it is by no means calculated to discuss and to convince, but to perform the shorter process of inflammation ; not to reason upon any subject, but to dictate ; and, gentlemen, as I stated to you before, to dictate in such a manner, and in such phrase, and with all such circumstances, as cannot, in my humble apprehension, leave the most remote doubt upon your minds of what was passing in the heart of that man who composed that book.

Gentlemen, you will permit me now to say a word or two upon those passages which I have selected to you, first describing a little what those passages are. I have thought it much more becoming, much more beneficial to the public, than any other course that I could take, to select six or seven, and no more (not wishing to load the record unnecessarily), of those passages that go to the very root of our constitution. That is the nature of the passages which I have selected, and, gentlemen, the first of them is in page 21, where you will find this doctrine :—

" All hereditary government is in its nature tyranny. An heritable crown, or an heritable throne, or by what other fanciful name such things may be called, have no other significant explanation than that mankind are heritable property. To inherit a government is to inherit the people, as if they were flocks and herds."

Now, gentlemen, what is the tendency of this passage—"All hereditary government is in its nature tyranny?" So that no qualification whatever, not even the subordination to the law of the country, which is the only paramount thing that we know of in this country, can take it out of the description of tyranny; the regal office being neither more nor less than a trust executed for the subjects of this country; the person who fills the regal office being understood, in this country, to be neither more nor less than the chief executive magistrate heading the whole gradation of magistracy.

But, without any qualification, he states it roundly that, under all circumstances whatever, hereditary government must in its nature be tyranny. What is that but to hold out to the people of this country that they are nought but slaves? To be sure, if they are living under a tyranny, it is impossible to draw any other consequence.

This is one of those short propositions that are crammed down the throat of every man that is accessible to their arts in this country; this is one of those propositions which, if he believes, must have the due effect upon his mind of saying, The case is come when I understand I am oppressed; I can bear it no longer.

"An heritable crown." Ours is an heritable crown, and therefore it is comprehended in this dogma. "Or by what other fanciful name such things may be called." Is that discussion?   Contemptuous, vilifying, and degrading expressions of that sort are applied to that which we are accustomed to look to with reverence, namely, the representation of the whole body of magistracy and of the law—"have no other significant explanation than that mankind are heritable property. To inherit a government is to inherit the people, as if they were flocks and herds."

Why, gentlemen, are the people of England to be told without further ceremony that they are inherited by a King of this country, and that they are precisely in the case of sheep and oxen?   I leave you to judge if such gross, contemptible, and abominable falsehood is delivered out in bits and scraps of this sort, whether that does not call aloud for punishment?

. Gentlemen, only look at the truth; the converse is directly the case. The King of this country inherits an office under the law; he does not inherit persons. We are not in a state of villenage. The direct reverse to what is here pointed out is the truth of the matter. The King inherits an office, but as to any inheritance of his people, none, you know, belongs to him, and I am ashamed to say anything more upon it.

The next is in page 47, in which this man is speaking of the Congress at Philadelphia in 1787, which was held because the government of that country was found to be extremely defective as at first established.

" This Convention met at Philadelphia, in May 1787, of which General Washington was elected President. He was not at that time connected with any of the State Governments, or with Congress. He delivered up his commission when the war ended, and since then had lived a private citizen.

" The Convention went deeply into all the subjects, and having, after a variety of debate and investigation, agreed among themselves upon the several parts of a federal constitution, the next question was the manner of giving it authority and practice."

What is the conclusion of that? They certainly agreed upon an appointment of their federal constitution in 1787. I should have thought that a man, meaning nothing more than history, would have been very well contented to have stated what actually did happen upon that occasion; but, in order to discuss (as possibly it may be called) something that formerly did pass in this country, he chose to do it in these inflaming and contemptuous terms :—

" For this purpose they did not, like a cabal of courtiers, send for a Dutch Stadtholder or a German Elector; but they referred the whole matter to the sense and interest of the country."

Here again the Revolution and the Act of Settlement stare us in the face, as if the interest and the sense of the country were in no way consulted; but, on the contrary, it was nothing more than a mere cabal of courtiers. Whether that is or is not to be endured in this country, your verdict will show; but, in order to show you how totally unnecessary this passage was, except for the deliberate purpose of calumny, if this passage had been left out, the narration would have been quite perfect. I will read three or four lines just to show how perfect it would have been :—" The next question was about the manner of giving it authority and practice." The passage beyond that which I call a libel :—" They first directed that the proposed constitution should be published ; secondly, that each State should elect a Convention, for the purpose of taking it into consideration, and of ratifying or rejecting it ;" and so the story goes on; but, in order to explain what I mean by a dogma thrust in, I call your attention to this, as one of those which has no earthly connexion with the subject he was then speaking of.

Does not this passage stand insulated between the two parts of the connected story, officiously and designedly thrust in for the purposes of mischief? Gentlemen, the artifice of that book consists also in this—the different wicked passages that are meant to do mischief in this country are spread throughout it, and stuck in here and there in a manner that, in order to see the whole malignity of it, it is necessary to have a recollection of several preceding passages; but these passages, when brought together, manifestly show the full design of the writer, and therefore extracts of it may be made to contain the whole marrow ; and at the same time that each passage, taken by itself, will do mischief enough, any man reading them together will see that mischief come out much clearer than by a mere transient reading.

The next passage I have to observe upon is in page 52, and in page 52 he is pleased to express himself in this manner. He says :—

" The history of the Edwards and the Henries, and up to the commencement of the Stuarts, exhibits as many instances of tyranny as could be acted within the limits to which the nation had restricted it ; the Stuarts endeavoured to pass those limits, and their fate is well known. In all these instances we see nothing of a constitution, but only of restrictions on assumed power."

Then, gentlemen, from the reign of the Edwards and the Henries down to the Revolution, it was a regular progression of tyranny— not a progression of liberty, but of tyranny—till the Stuarts stepped a little beyond the line in the gradation that was going forward, and that begot a necessity for a revolution. But of the Edwards, I should have thought, at least, he might have spared the great founder of our jurisprudence, King Edward I., beside many other princes, the glory and the boast of this country, and many of them regarders of its freedom and constitution. But instead of that, this author would have the people of this country believe that, up to that time, it was a progressive tyranny, and that there was nothing of a constitution—only restrictions on assumed power ; so that all the power that existed at that time was assumption and usurpation.

He thus proceeds :—" After this another William, descended from the same stock, and claiming from the same origin, gained possession ; and of the two evils, James and William, the nation preferred what it thought the least." So that the deliverance of this country by the Prince of Orange was an evil, but the least of the two, "since from circumstances it must take one. The Act called the Bill of Rights comes here into view. What is it but a bargain which the parts of the Government made with each other to divide powers, profits, and privileges ? You shall have so much, and I will have the rest. And, with respect to the nation, it said, For *your share* **you** *shall have the right of petitioning.* This being the case, the Bill of Rights is more properly a BILL OF WRONGS AND OF INSULT. As to what is called the Convention Parliament, it was a thing that made itself, and then made the authority by which it acted. A few persons got together and called themselves by that name. Several of them had never been elected, and none of them for the purpose."

" From the time of William a species of government arose, issuing out of this coalition Bill of Rights, and more so since the corruption introduced at the Hanover succession by the agency of Walpole, that can be described by no other name than a despotic legislation."

Now, gentlemen, this is the description that this man holds out of that on which rest the property, the lives, and liberties, and the privileges of the people of this country. I wonder to God, gentlemen, that any British man (for such this man certainly was, and still is) could utter such a sentence, and that, to use the language of our own poet, when he spoke these words, " A BILL OF WRONGS, A BILL OF INSULT," they did not " stick in his throat." What is that Bill of Rights? It can never be too often read. I will make no comment upon it, because your own heads and hearts will make that comment. You have a posterity to look to. Are desperate ruffians, who are to be found in every country, thus to attack the inalienable rights and privileges which are to descend undiminished to that posterity?

Are YOU not to take care that this shall be sacred to your posterity? Is it not a trust in YOUR hands? It is a trust in YOUR hands as much as the execution of the law is a trust in the hands of the Crown; each has its guardians in this community, but you are the guardians of the Bill of Rights.

Gentlemen, it is this, " That the pretended power of suspending of laws, or the execution of laws, by regal authority, without consent of Parliament, is illegal.

" That the pretended power of dispensing with laws, or the execution of laws, by the regal authority, as it hath been assumed and exercised of late, is illegal."

That is, the law is above all.

" That levying money for, or to the use of, the Crown, by pretence of prerogative, without grant of Parliament, for longer time, or in other manner than the same is or shall be granted, is illegal."

" That it is the right of the subjects to petition the King, and all commitments and prosecutions for such petitions are illegal."

All that you get by the Bill of Rights, according to this man's doctrine, is, that the Commons of this country have the right of petitioning. We all know this alludes to the case of the Seven Bishops; that was a gross violation of the rights of those subjects of this country; therefore he states falsely and maliciously, according to the language of the information, which is perfectly correct in the present case, that the whole that was obtained by the subjects of this country was the right of petitioning; whereas it is declared to be their unalterable right, and ever to have been so, and adverts, as I before stated, to a gross violation of it in a recent case.

" That the raising or keeping a standing army within the kingdom in time of peace, unless it be with consent of Parliament, is against law."

" That the subjects which are Protestants may have arms for their defence, suitable to their conditions, and as allowed by law."

" That elections of members of Parliament ought to be free."

" That the freedom of speech, and debates or proceedings in Parliament, ought not to be impeached or questioned in any court or place out of Parliament."

" That excessive bail ought not to be required, nor excessive fines imposed, nor cruel and unusual punishments inflicted."

" That jurors ought to be duly impannelled and returned ; and jurors which pass upon men in trials for high treason ought to be freeholders."

" That all grants and promises of fines and forfeitures of particular persons, before conviction, are illegal and void."

" And that for the redress of all grievances, and for the amending, strengthening, and preserving of the laws, Parliaments ought to be held frequently."

Further, gentlemen, this Bill goes on to say, " For the ratifying, confirming, and establishing the said declaration, and the articles, clauses, matters, and things therein contained, by the force of a law made in due form, by authority of Parliament, do pray it may be declared and enacted, that all and singular the rights and liberties asserted and claimed in the said declaration are the true, ancient, and indubitable rights and liberties of the people of this kingdom, and so shall be esteemed, allowed, adjudged, deemed, and taken to be ; and that all and every the particulars aforesaid shall be firmly and strictly holden and observed, as they are expressed in the said declaration ; and all officers and ministers whatsoever shall serve their Majesties and their successors according to the same in all times to come."

Such, gentlemen, is the Bill of Wrongs and of Insult. I shall not profane it by saying one more word upon it.

Now, gentlemen, I would ask you, Whether what is said by this man be reasoning or discussion ? or whether it is nothing else but deception, and that deception consisting of a most abominable and complete suppression ? Is there a word of this Act quoted ? Has the poor mechanic, to whom this passage is addressed, who is told that he has been wronged and insulted at the Revolution, has he this statute by him to read ? Would it not have been fair at least to have stated what it was ? But instead of that, unsight, unseen (to use a very vulgar expression), this proposition is tendered to the very lowest man in this country, namely, that the Bill of Rights is a Bill of Wrongs and of Insult.

Pass we then on to another. If you will please to make a memorandum of page 56, you will find that, in the same spirit, and with the same design, this man tells you that—" The intention of the Government of England "—here comes in another contemptuous expression—" (for I rather choose to call it by this name than the English Government), appears, since its political connexion with Germany, to have been so completely engrossed and absorbed by foreign affairs, and the means of raising taxes, that it seems to exist for no other purposes."

The Government of the country, then, does not exist for the purpose of preserving our lives and properties; but the Government, I mean the constitution of the country, King, Lords, and Commons, exists for no purpose but to be the instruments of raising taxes. To enter into any discussion of that is taking up your time unnecessarily: I only beg to draw your attention to the dogmatical and cavalier manner in which these things are asserted. Further, he says, "Domestic concerns are neglected; and with respect to regular law, there is scarcely such a thing."

I stand in the city of London—I am addressing myself to gentlemen eminent in that city. Whether the Legislature, since the Revolution, has or has not adverted to domestic concerns, I think I may appeal to the growing prosperity of this country, from the moment that the nightmare has been taken off its stomach, which pressed upon it up to that moment.

We then proceed to page 63, where, after the whole constitution of this country has been thus treated in gross, he proceeds a little to dissect and consider the component parts of that constitution; and in page 63, in a dogma, we have this:—

"With respect to the two Houses of which the English Parliament is composed, they appear to be effectually influenced into one, and, as a Legislature, to have no temper of its own. The Minister, whoever he at any time may be, touches it, as with an opium wand and it sleeps obedience."

Now, gentlemen, here is another dogma without a single fact, without a single argument; but it is held out to the subjects of this country that there is no energy or activity in either the aristocratical or democratical parts of this constitution, but that they are asleep, and you might just as well have statues there; it is not merely said that it is so now, but it is in the nature of things, says he, that it should be so.

"But if we look at the distinct abilities of the two Houses, the difference will appear so great as to show the inconsistency of placing power where there can be no certainty of the judgment to use it. Wretched as the state of representation is in England, it is manhood compared with what is called the House of Lords; and so little is this nicknamed House regarded, that the people scarcely inquire at any time what it is doing. It appears also to be most under influence, and the furthest removed from the general interest of the nation."

Now, gentlemen, this is again speaking in this man's contemptuous manner at the expense of the aristocratical part of our constitution of Government, an essentially beneficial part, whose great and permanent interest in the country renders it a firm barrier against any encroachment. I am not to suppose that you are so ignorant of the history of your country, as not to know the great and brilliant characters that have sat in that House. No particular period of time is alluded to in this passage. He surely cannot mean the present time ; but I conceive he speaks of all times, and that from the very nature of our Government it must everlastingly be so. Slander upon that very great and illustrious part of the Legislature (untrue at any period), written in this scurrilous and contemptuous manner, is distinguished greatly indeed from any sober discussion of whether an aristocratical part of Government is a good or bad thing, and is calculated only to mislead and inflame.

If you look next to page 107, there you will find that two of the component parts of the Legislature having been thus disposed of, we come up to the throne itself, and this man says very truly of himself :

" Having thus GLANCED at some of the defects of the two Houses of Parliament, I proceed to *what is called the Crown*, upon which I shall be very concise.

" It signifies a nominal office of a million a year, the business of which consists in receiving the money : whether the person be wise or foolish, sane or insane, a native or a foreigner, matters not. Every Minister acts upon the same idea that Mr Burke writes ; namely, that the people must be hoodwinked, and held in superstitious ignorance by some bugbear or other ; and what is called the Crown answers this purpose, and therefore it answers all the purposes to be expected from it. This is more than can be said of the other two branches.

" The hazard to which this office is exposed in all countries," including this among the rest, " is not from anything that can happen to the man, but from what may happen to the nation—the danger of its coming to its senses."

Then, gentlemen, we have been insane for these seven or eight hundred years : and I shall just dismiss this with this observation, that this insanity having subsisted so long, I trust in God that it is incurable.

" In page 116, you have this note—" I happened to be in England at the celebration of the centenary of the Revolution of 1680. The characters of William and Mary have always appeared to me detestable ; the one seeking to destroy his uncle, and the other her father, to get possession of power themselves ; yet as the nation was disposed to think something of that event, I felt hurt at seeing it ascribe the whole reputation of it to a man who had undertaken it as a job, and who, besides what he otherwise got, charged six hundred thousand pounds for the expense of a little fleet that brought him from Holland. George the First acted the same close-fisted part as William had done, and bought the Duchy of Bremen with the money he got from England, two hundred and fifty thousand pounds, over and above his pay as King ; and having thus purchased it at the expense of England, added it to his Hanoverian dominions for his own private profit. In fact, every nation that does not govern itself, is governed as a job. England has been the prey of jobs ever since the Revolution."

Then, gentlemen, what he calls a nation governing itself is something extremely different from a nation having consented from time immemorial to be governed by a democracy, an aristocracy, and an hereditary executive supreme magistrate ; and, moreover, by a law paramount, which all are bound to obey: he conceives, I say, that sort of government not to be a government of the people themselves, but he denominates that sort of government a job, and not a government.

Gentlemen, such are the passages which I have selected to you, as those that disclose the most offensive doctrines in the book ; that is, such as go fundamentally to the overturning the Government of this country. I beg pardon—I have omitted one which contains more of direct invitation than anything I have yet stated. It is in page 161; it is said, " the fraud, hypocrisy, and imposition of Governments are now beginning to be too well understood to promise them any long career. The farce of monarchy and aristocracy in all countries is following that of chivalry, and Mr Burke is dressing for the funeral—let it then pass quietly to the tomb of all other follies, and the mourner be comforted. The time is not very distant when England will laugh at itself for sending to Holland, Hanover, Zell, or Brunswick, for men, at the expense of a million a year, who understood neither her laws, her language, nor her interest, and whose capacities would scarcely have fitted them for the office of parish constable."

This is said of William the Third—this is said of two very illustrious princes of the House of Brunswick, George the First and Second, and extends to the present Sovereign upon the throne.

" If government could be trusted to such hands, it must be some easy and simple thing indeed ; and materials fit for all the purposes may be found in every town and village in England."

The policy of the constitution of this country has ever avoided, excepting when driven to it by melancholy necessity, to disturb the hereditary succession to the throne; and it has wisely thought it more fitting to pursue that system, even though a foreigner should be seated on the throne of these realms, than to break through it. This would insinuate, that the necessary defects of an hereditary monarchy are such as outweigh the advantages attending that which I have stated. Is that so? I would ask any man who hears me, in point of history, whether it is not the permanent defect of elective monarchies that the sovereigns are seldom men of any consideration, and for an obvious reason : most frequently it has happened that turbulent factions, after having desolated their country, one of them (it has so happened, at least in most instances as far as my recollection goes) sets up a tool whom the successful faction can themselves govern at pleasure. Often has it happened that such factions, when a civil war arises, which must almost necessarily be the case in elective monarchies, not choosing to come to the conclusion of an armed contest, have chosen a very weak person, each in hope of strengthening his party by the time the periodical civil war should come round. I believe, upon examination, this will be found to be generally the case, and to have prevailed in elective monarchies to a greater degree than any inconveniences that may have ever arisen from the natural infirmities of princes who succeeded to their thrones by hereditary right, in the constitution of Great Britain; for to that this man alludes.

Has he stated with any sort of fairness, or has he at all stated or adverted, to the many, many remedies we have for any defect of that sort? Has he stated the numerous councils of a King? His council of Parliament—his council of his Judges in matters of law—his Privy Council? Has he stated the responsibility of all those councils? Some in point of character, some of personal responsibility. Has he stated the responsibility of those immediate servants who conduct his executive government? Has he stated the appointment of regents? Has he stated all this, which is indispensably necessary towards a fair and honest discussion (which this book will possibly be called) of this point of his insuperable objection to hereditary monarchy? Can this be called any other than gross suppression and wilful mis-statement, to raise discontent in half-informed minds?

There does come across my mind at this moment, unquestionably, one illustrious exception to that doctrine I have stated, of men not the most capable of government having in general been chosen in the case of elective monarchies; and that is a man whom no indignities, no misfortunes, no disappointments, no civil commotions, no provocations, ever forced from the full and steady possession of a strong mind, which has always risen with elasticity under all the pressures that I have stated; and he, though not in one sense of that word a great *prince*, yet is certainly a great *man*, who will go down as such to the latest posterity: I mean the King of Poland. Don't imagine, gentlemen, that my adverting to this illustrious character is useless. Every gentleman who hears me knows he had a considerable part of his matured education in this country. Here he familiarised himself with the constitution of this country. Here he became informed of the provisions of what this man calls the Bill of Wrongs and Insults, without disparagement to him, for I believe him to be a just and wise prince, of great natural faculties. Here it was that he saw, and could alone learn, how the regal government of a free people was conducted, and that under a prince of the House of Brunswick.

Gentlemen, having stated thus much to you, I will now, for want of suitable expressions (for mine are very feeble), borrow from another: I certainly have formed an opinion upon this subject

precisely similar : to deliver it in plain words would exhaust the
utmost of my powers, but I will borrow the words of a very able
writer, who has most properly, for fear some ill impression should be
made by this book on the weaker part of mankind in America, given
an answer to this book of Mr Paine. That distinguished gentleman, I have reason to believe, though not the chief magistrate in
that country, is the second in the executive government of it ; that
is, he is second in the exercise of the regal part of the government
of that country. He takes care to confute accurately what Mr
Paine says with respect to America ; but, borrowing his *words*, I
beg to be understood that this is my *opinion* of the work before
you, and which I humbly offer for your consideration and adoption.
He says, " His intention appears evidently to be, to convince the
people of Great Britain that they have neither liberty nor a constitution ; that their only possible means to produce those blessings
to themselves is to topple down headlong their present government,
and follow implicitly the example of the French."

Gentlemen, the next passage, which I beg to be understood as
mine (I wish I could express it as well myself), is this :—" Mr Paine,
in reply, cuts the Gordian knot at once, declares the Parliament of
1688 to have been downright usurpers, censures them for having
unwisely sent to Holland for a king, denies the existence of a British
constitution, and invites the people of England to overturn their
present government, and to erect another upon the broad basis of
national sovereignty and government by representation. As Mr
Paine has departed altogether from the principles of the Revolution,
and has torn up by the roots all reasoning from the British constitution, by the denial of its existence, it becomes necessary to examine
his work upon the grounds which he has chosen to assume. If we
judge of the production from its apparent tendency, we may call it
an address to the English nation, attempting to prove that they
have a right to form a new constitution ; that it is expedient for
them immediately to exercise that right, and that, in the formation
of this constitution, they can do no better than to imitate the model
set before them by the French National Assembly. However
immethodical his production is, I believe the whole of its argumentative part may be referred to these three points : if the subject
were to affect only the British nation, we might leave them to reason
and act for themselves ; but these are concerns equally important
to all mankind ; and the citizens of America are called upon, from
high authority " (he alludes to a gentleman in a high situation in
that country, who has published an opinion of this book), " to rally
round the standard of this champion of revolutions. I shall, therefore, now proceed to examine the reasons ; " and so he goes on.

Gentlemen, I would adopt, with your permission, a few more
words from this publication :—" When Mr Paine invited the people
of England to destroy their present government, and form another

constitution, he should have given them sober reasoning, and not flippant witticisms." Whether that is or is not the case, what I have read to you to-day will enable you to judge. "He should have explained to them the nature of the grievances by which they are oppressed, and demonstrated the impossibility of reforming the government in its present organisation; he should have pointed out some possible method for them to act, in their original character, without a total dissolution of civil society among them; he should have proved what great advantages they would reap as a nation from such a revolution, without disguising the great dangers and formidable difficulties with which it must be attended." So much for the passages themselves, and this interpretation, which I humbly submit to your consideration.

The next matter upon which I shall proceed is the evidence which I propose to adduce; and that evidence will go to show, not only the fact of this man's being the writer of this book, by his own repeated admission, and by letters under his own hand, but will likewise go directly to show what is his intent in such publication, which appears, I think, most clearly; and over and above that, I shall produce to you a letter, which this man was pleased to address to myself, in which letter he avows himself in so many words the author, and I shall prove it to be his handwriting; and further than that, there is matter in that letter, apparently showing the intention with which that book was written, namely, to vilify this constitution, and to injure this country irretrievably.

Two letters I shall be under the necessity of reading to you, in which he has stated himself the author. The one is a letter to a person of the name of Jordan, in which he expresses himself in this manner:—

"February 16, 1792" (that was the day on which the book was published): "For your satisfaction and my own, I send you the enclosed, though I do not apprehend there will be any occasion to use it: if in case there should, you will immediately send a line for me, under cover, to Mr Johnston, St Paul's Churchyard, who will forward it to me, upon which I shall come and answer personally for the work; send also for Mr Horne Tooke.   T. P."

The letter enclosed was this, addressed to the same man, Jordan, the bookseller:—" Sir, should any person, under the sanction of any kind of authority, inquire of you respecting the author and publisher of the 'Rights of Man,' you will please to mention me as the author and publisher of that work, and show to such person this letter. I will, as soon as I am acquainted with it, appear and answer for the work personally."

Gentlemen, with respect to his letter written to me, it is in these terms.

Mr ERSKINE. My Lord, the Attorney-General states a letter in the handwriting of Mr Paine, which establishes that he is the author.   I desire to know whether he means to read a letter which may be the subject of a substantive and distinct prosecution—I do not mean to dispute the publication, or even to give him the trouble of proving the letters which he has just stated—whether the Attorney-General will think it consistent with the situation in which he is placed at this moment to read a letter written at a time long subsequent to the publication, containing, as I understand (if I am mistaken in that, I withdraw my objection), but containing distinct, clear, and unequivocal libellous matter, and which I, in my address to the jury, if I am not deceived in what I have heard, shall admit to be upon every principle of the English law a libel. Therefore, if that should turn out to be the case, will your Lord-ship suffer the mind of the jury to be entirely put aside from that matter which is the subject of the prosecution, and to go into matter which hereafter may be, and I cannot but suppose would be, if the defendant were within the reach of the law of this country, the subject of a distinct and independent prosecution.

Lord KENYON. If that letter goes a jot to prove that he is the author of this publication, I cannot reject that evidence.   In prose-cutions for high treason, where overt acts are laid, you may prove overt acts not laid to prove those that are laid.   If it goes to prove him the author of the book, I am bound to admit it.

Mr ATTORNEY-GENERAL. The letter is thus:—"Paris, 11th of November, first year of the Republic. Sir, as there can be no personal resentment between two strangers I write this letter to you as to a man against whom I have no animosity.

"You have, as Attorney-General, commenced a prosecution against me as the author of the 'Rights of Man.'   Had not my duty, in consequence of my being elected a member of the National Convention of France, called me from England, I should have stayed to have contested the injustice of that prosecution; not upon my own account, for I cared not about the prosecution, but to de-fend the principles I had advanced in the work.

"The duty I am now engaged in is of too much importance to permit me to trouble myself about your prosecution ; when I have leisure I shall have no objection to meet you on that ground ; but, as I now stand, whether you go on with the prosecution, or whether you do not, or whether you obtain a verdict or not, is a matter of the most perfect indifference to me as an individual.   If you obtain one (which you are welcome to if you can get it) it cannot affect me either in person, property, or reputation, otherwise than to in-crease the latter ; and with respect to yourself, it is as consistent that you obtain a verdict against the man in the moon as against me ; neither do I see how you can continue the prosecution against me as you would have done against one of *your own people* who had absented himself because he was prosecuted ; what passed at Dover proves that my departure from England was no secret.

"My necessary absence from your country affords the opportunity of knowing whether the prosecution was intended against Thomas Paine or against the rights of the people of England to investigate systems and principles of government; for as I cannot now be the object of the prosecution, the going on with the prosecution will show that something else was the object, and that something else can be no other than the people of England; for it is against *their rights*, and not against me, that a verdict or sentence can operate, if it can operate at all.   Be then so candid as to tell the jury (if you choose to continue the process) whom it is you are prosecuting, and on whom it is that the verdict is to fall."

Gentleman, I certainly will comply with this request.   I am prosecuting both him and his work; and if I succeed in this prosecution he shall never return to this country otherwise than *in vinculis*, for I will outlaw him.

"But I have other reasons than those I have mentioned for writing you this letter; and however you may choose to interpret them, they proceed from a good heart.   The time, sir, is becoming too serious to play with court prosecutions and sport with national rights.   The terrible examples that have taken place here upon men who, less than a year ago, thought themselves as secure as any prosecuting judge, jury, or attorney-general can now do in England, ought to have some weight with men in your situation."

Now, gentlemen, I do not think that Mr Paine judges very well of mankind.   I do not think that it is a fair conclusion of Mr Paine, that men such as you and myself, who are quietly living in obedience to the laws of the land which they inhabit, exercising their several functions peaceably, and I hope with a moderate share of reputation—I do not conceive that men called upon to think, and in the habit of reflection, are the most likely men to be immediately thrown off the hinges by menaces and threats; and I doubt whether men exercising public functions, as you and I do in the face of our country, could have the courage to run away.   All I can tell Mr Paine is this: if any of his assassins are here in London,—and there is some ground to suppose they may be, or the assassins of those with whom he is connected,—if they are here, I tell them that I do in my conscience think that for a man to die of doing his duty, is just as good a thing as dying of a raging fever or under the tortures of the stone.   Let him not think that not to be an incendiary is to be a coward.

He says—"That the government of England is as great, if not the greatest perfection of fraud and corruption, that ever took place since governments began, is what you cannot be a stranger to; unless the constant habit of seeing it has blinded your sense."   Upon my word, gentlemen I am stone-blind: I am not sorry for it.—"But though you may not choose to see it, the people are seeing it very fast, and the progress is beyond what you may choose to believe, or that reason can make any other man believe, that the capacity of such a man as Mr Guelph, or any of his profligate sons, is necessary to the government of a nation."

Now, gentlemen, with respect to this passage, I have this to say, it is contemptuous, scandalous, false, cruel. Why, gentlemen, is Mr Paine, in addition to the political doctrines that he is teaching us in this country,—is he to teach us the morality and religion of IMPLACABILITY? Is he to teach human creatures, whose moments of existence depend upon the permission of a Being, merciful, long-suffering, and of great goodness, that those youthful errors, from which even royalty is not exempted, are to be treasured up in a vindictive memory, and are to receive sentence of irremissible sin at HIS hands? Are they all to be confounded in these slanderous terms, shocking for British ears to hear, and I am sure distressing to their hearts? He is a barbarian who could use such profligate expressions uncalled for by anything which could be the object of his letter addressed to me. If giving me pain was his object, he has that hellish gratification. Would this man destroy that great auxiliary of all human laws and constitutions—"to judge of others as we would be judged ourselves?" This is the bill of wrongs and insults of the Christian religion. I presume it is considered as that bill of wrongs and insults in the heart of that man who can have the barbarity to use those expressions and address them to me in a way by which I could not but receive them.

Gentlemen, there is not perhaps in the world a more beneficial analogy, nor a finer rule to judge by, in public matters, than by assimilating them to what passes in domestic life. A family is a small kingdom, a kingdom is a large family. Suppose this to have happened in private life, judge of the good heart of this man, who thrusts into my hands, the grateful servant of a kind and beneficent master, and that too through the unavoidable trick of the common post, slander upon that master, and slander upon his whole offspring. Lay your hands upon your hearts, and tell me what is *your* verdict with respect to his heart.—I *see* it !

Gentlemen, he has the audacity to say, "I speak to you as one man ought to speak to another." Does he speak to me of those august personages as one man ought to speak to another? Had he spoken these words to me personally, I will not answer for it whether I should not have forgot the duties my office, and the dignity of my station, by being hurried into a violation of that peace, the breach of which I am compelled to punish in others. He says, "And I know also that I speak what other people are beginning to think. That you cannot obtain a verdict (and if you do it will signify nothing) without *packing a jury*, and we *both* know that such tricks are practised, is what I have very good reason to believe." *Mentiris impudentissime.* Gentlemen, I know of no such practice. I know, indeed, that no such practice exists, nor can exist. I know the very contrary of this to be true; and I know too that this letter, containing this dangerous falsehood, was destined for future publication; that I have no doubt of, and therefore I dwell thus long upon it.

"I have gone into coffee-houses and places where I was unknown on purpose to learn the currency of opinion." Whether the sense of this *nation* is to be had in some pot-houses and coffee-houses in this town of his own choosing is a matter I leave to your judgment. "And I never yet saw any company of twelve men that condemned the book—but I have often found a greater number than twelve approving it—and this I think is *a fair way of collecting the natural currency of opinion.* Do not then, sir, be the instrument of drawing twelve men into a situation that may be *injurious* to them afterwards." Injurious to them afterwards!—those words speak for themselves. He proceeds thus:—

"I do not speak this from policy"—(what then?)—"but from"—(Gentlemen, I will give you a hundred guesses)—"BENEVOLENCE! But if you choose to go on with the process, I make it my request that you would read this letter in court, after which the Judge and the jury may do as they please. As I do not consider myself the object of the prosecution, neither can I be affected by the issue one way or the other. I shall, though a foreigner in your country, subscribe as much money as any other man towards supporting the right of the nation against prosecution; and it is for this purpose only that I shall do it.—THOMAS PAINE."

So it is a subscription-defence you hear.

"*P.S.*—I intended, had I stayed in England, to have published the information, with my remarks upon it"—that would have been a decent thing—"before the trial came on; but as I am otherwise engaged, I reserve myself till the trial is over, when I shall reply fully to everything you shall advance." I hope in God he will not omit any one single word that I have uttered to-day, or shall utter in my future address to you. This *conceited* menace I despise, as I do those of a nature more *cut-throat.*

Gentlemen, I do not think that I need to trouble you any further for the present: according as you shall be of opinion that the necessarily mischievous tendency and intent of this book is that which I have taken the liberty (at more length than I am warranted perhaps) to state to you; according as you shall or shall not be of that opinion, so necessarily will be your verdict. I have done my duty in bringing before a jury an offender of this magnitude. Be the event what it may, I have done MY duty; I am satisfied with having placed this great and flourishing community under the powerful shield of your protection.

MR ERSKINE'S SPEECH.

The publication having been proved, and a letter from Mr Paine acknowledging it; the letter to the Attorney-General mentioned in the preface, and the passages selected in the information, having been read; Mr Erskine, as counsel for the defendant, spoke as follows :—

GENTLEMEN OF THE JURY,—The Attorney-General, in that part of his address which referred to a letter supposed to have been written to him from France, exhibited signs of strong sensibility and emotion. I do not, I am sure, charge him with acting a part to seduce you; on the contrary, I am persuaded, from my own feelings, and from my acquaintance with my friend from our child-hood upwards, that HE expressed himself as he felt. But, gentle-men, if he felt those painful embarrassments, you may imagine what MINE must be: he can only feel for the august character whom he represents in this place as a subject for his Sovereign, too far removed by custom from the intercourses which generate affections, to produce any other sentiments than those that flow from a relation common to us all: but it will be remembered that I stand in the same relation * towards another great person more deeply implicated by this supposed letter; who, not restrained from the cultivation of personal attachments by those qualifications which must always secure them, has exalted my duty to a Prince into a warm and honest affection between man and man. Thus circumstanced, I certainly should have been glad to have had an earlier opportunity of knowing correctly the contents of this letter, and whether (which I positively deny) it proceeded from the defendant. Coming thus suddenly upon us, I see but too plainly the impression it has made upon *you*, who are to try the cause, and I feel its weight upon *myself*, who am to conduct it; but this shall neither detach me from my duty, nor enervate me (if I can help it) in the discharge of it.

If the Attorney-General be well founded in the commentaries he has made to you upon the book which he prosecutes; if he be war-ranted by the law of England in repressing its circulation, from the illegal and dangerous matters contained in it; if that suppres-sion be, as he avows it, and as in common sense it must be, the sole object of the prosecution, the public has great reason to lament that his letter should have been at all brought into the service of the cause. It is no part of the charge upon the record; it had no exist-ence for months after the work was composed and published; it was not written by the defendant, if written by him at all, till after he had been in a manner insultingly expelled from the country by

* Mr Erskine was then Attorney-General to the Prince of Wales.

the influence of Government; it was not even written till he had become the subject of another country. It cannot, therefore, by any fair inference, decipher the mind of the author when he composed his work; still less can it affect the construction of the language in which it is written. The introduction of this letter at all is, therefore, not only a departure from the charge, but a dereliction of the object of the prosecution, which is to condemn *the book*: since, if the condemnation of the author is to be obtained, *not by the work itself*, but by *collateral matter*, not even existing when it was written, nor known to its various publishers throughout the kingdom, how can a verdict upon *such* grounds condemn the work, or criminate *other* publishers, strangers to the collateral matter on which the conviction may be obtained to-day? I maintain, therefore, upon every principle of sound policy, as it affects the interests of the Crown, and upon every rule of justice, as it affects the author of " The Rights of Man," that the letter should be wholly dismissed from your consideration.

Gentlemen, the Attorney-General has thought it necessary to inform you; that a rumour had been spread, and had reached his ears, that he only carried on the prosecution as a *public* prosecutor, but without the concurrence of his own judgment; and, therefore, to add the just weight of his *private* character to his public duty, and to repel what he thinks a calumny, he tells you that he should have deserved to have been driven from society if he had not arraigned the work and the author before you. Here, too, we stand in situations very different. I have no doubt of the existence of such a rumour, and of its having reached his ears, because he says so; but for the narrow circle in which any rumour, personally implicating my learned friend's character, has extended, I might appeal to the multitudes who surround us, and ask, which of them all, except the few connected in office with the Crown, ever heard of its existence? But with regard to myself, every man within hearing at this moment, nay, the whole people of England, have been witnesses to the calumnious clamour that, by every art, has been raised and kept up against me: in every place where business or pleasure collect the public together, day after day my name and character have been the topics of injurious reflection. And for what? only for not having shrunk from the discharge of a duty which no personal advantage recommended, and which a thousand difficulties repelled. But, gentlemen, I have no complaint to make, either against the printers of these libels, or even against their authors: the greater part of them, hurried perhaps away by honest prejudices, may have believed they were serving their *country* by rendering *me* the object of its suspicion and contempt; and if there had been amongst them others who have mixed in it from personal malice and unkindness, I thank God I can forgive *them* also. Little, indeed, did they know me, who thought that such calumnies would influence my conduct. I will for ever, at all hazards, assert the dignity, independence, and integrity of the ENGLISH BAR, without which, impartial justice, the most valuable part of the English constitution, can have no existence. From the moment that any advocate can be permitted to say that he *will* or will *not* stand between the Crown and the subject arraigned in the court where he daily sits to practise, from that moment the liberties of England are at an end. If the advocate refuses to defend, from what *he may think* of the charge or of the defence, he assumes the character of the Judge ; nay he assumes it before the hour of judgment ; and in proportion to his rank and reputation, puts the heavy influence of, perhaps, a mistaken opinion into the scale against the accused, in whose favour the benevolent principle of English law makes all presumptions, and which commands the very Judge to be his counsel.

Gentlemen, it is now my duty to address myself without digression to the defence.

The first thing which presents itself in the discussion of any subject is to state distinctly, and with precision, what the question is, and, where prejudice and misrepresentation have been exerted, to distinguish it accurately from what it is NOT. The question, then, is NOT whether the constitution of our fathers—under which we live, under which I present myself before you, and under which alone you have any jurisdiction to hear me—be or be not preferable to the constitution of America or France, or any other human constitution. For upon what principle can a court, constituted by the authority of any Government, and administering a positive system of law under it, pronounce a decision against the constitution which creates its authority, or the rule of action which its jurisdiction is to enforce ? The common sense of the most uninformed person must revolt at such an absurd supposition.

I have no difficulty, therefore, in admitting, that if by accident some or all of you were alienated in opinion and affection from the forms and principles of the English Government, and were impressed with the value of that unmixed representative constitution which this work recommends and inculcates, you could not *on that account* acquit the defendant. Nay, to speak out plainly, I freely admit that even if you were avowed enemies to monarchy, and devoted to republicanism, you would be nevertheless bound by your oaths, as a jury sworn to administer justice according to the English law, to convict the author of " The Rights of Man," if it were brought home to your consciences that he had exceeded those widely-extended bounds which the ancient wisdom and liberal policy of the English constitution have allotted to the range of a free press. I freely concede this, because you have no jurisdiction to judge either the author or the work by any rule but that of English law, which is the source of your authority. But having made this large concession, it follows, by a consequence so inevitable as to be invulnerable to all argument or artifice, that if, on the other hand, you should be impressed (which I know you to be) not only with a dutiful regard, but with an enthusiasm, for the whole form and substance of your own Government; and though you should think that this work, in its circulation amongst classes of men unequal to political researches, may tend to alienate opinion; still you cannot, *upon such grounds*, without a similar breach of duty, convict the defendant of a libel—unless he has clearly stepped beyond that extended range of communication which the same ancient wisdom and liberal policy of the British constitution has allotted for the liberty of the press.

Gentlemen, I admit, with the Attorney-General, that in every case where a court has to estimate the quality of a writing, the *mind* and *intention* of the writer must be taken into the account;—the *bona* or *mala fides*, as lawyers express it, must be examined: for a writing may undoubtedly proceed from a motive, and be directed to a purpose, not to be deciphered by the mere construction of the thing written. But wherever a writing is arraigned as seditious or slanderous, not upon its ordinary construction in language, nor from the necessary consequences of its publication, under *any* circumstances, and at *all* times, but that the criminality springs from some *extrinsic matter*, not visible upon the page itself, nor universally operative, but capable only of being connected with it by evidence, so as to demonstrate the effect of the publication, and the design of the publisher; such a writing, not libellous PER SE, cannot be arraigned as the author's work is arraigned upon the record before the court. I maintain, without the hazard of contradiction, that the law of England positively requires, for the security of the subject, that every charge of a libel complicated with *extrinsic facts and circumstances, dehors the writing*, must appear literally upon the record by an averment of such extrinsic facts and circumstances, that the defendant may know what crime he is called upon to answer, and how to stand upon his defence. What crime is it that the defendant comes to answer for to-day?—what is the notice that I, who am his counsel, have from this parchment of the crime alleged against him? I come to defend his having written *this book*. The record states nothing else:—the general charge of sedition in the introduction is notoriously paper and packthread; because the innuendoes cannot enlarge the sense or natural construction of the text. The record does not state any one *extrinsic fact or circumstance* to render the work criminal at one time more than *another;* it states no peculiarity of time or season or intention, not provable from the writing itself, which is the naked charge upon record. There is nothing, therefore, which gives you any jurisdiction beyond the construction of the *work itself;* and you cannot be justified in finding it criminal because published at *this* time, unless it would have been a criminal publication under any circumstances, or at *any other* time.

The law of England, then, both in its forms and substance, being the only rule by which the author or the work can be justified or condemned, and the charge upon the record being the naked charge of a libel, the cause resolves itself into a question of the deepest importance to us all—THE NATURE AND EXTENT OF THE LIBERTY OF THE ENGLISH PRESS.

But before I enter upon it, I wish to fulfil a duty to the defendant, which, if I do not deceive myself, is at this moment peculiarly necessary to his impartial trial. If an advocate entertains sentiments injurious to the defence he is engaged in, he is not only justified, but bound in duty, to conceal them ; so, on the other hand, if his own genuine sentiments, or anything connected with his character or situation, can add strength to his professional assistance, he is bound to throw them into the scale. In addressing myself, therefore, to gentlemen not only zealous for the honour of English Government, but *visibly* indignant at any attack upon its principles, and who would, perhaps, be impatient of arguments from a suspected quarter, I give my client the benefit of declaring that I am, and ever have been, attached to the genuine principles of the British Government; and that, however the Court or you may reject the application, I defend him upon principles not only consistent with its permanence and security, but without the establishment of which it never could have had an existence.

The proposition which I mean to maintain as the basis of the liberty of the press, and without which it is an empty sound, is this: that every man, not intending to mislead, but seeking to enlighten others with what his own reason and conscience, however erroneously, have dictated to him as truth, may address himself to the universal reason of a whole nation, either upon the subject of governments in general, or upon that of our own particular country: that he may analyse the principles of its constitution, point out its errors and defects, examine and publish its corruptions, warn his fellow-citizens against their ruinous consequences, and exert his whole faculties in pointing out the most advantageous changes in establishments which he considers to be radically defective, or sliding from their object by abuse. All this every subject of this country has a right to do, if he contemplates only what he thinks would be for its advantage, and but seeks to change the public mind by the conviction which flows from reasonings dictated by conscience.

If, indeed, he writes *what he does not think ;* if, contemplating the misery of others, he wickedly condemns what his own understanding approves ; or, even admitting his real disgust against the Government or its corruptions, if he *calumniates living magistrates,* or holds out to individuals that they have a right to run before the public mind in their *conduct;* that they may oppose, by contumacy or force, what private reason only disapproves; that they may disobey the law, because their judgment condemns it; or resist the public will, because they honestly wish to change it—he is then a criminal upon every principle of rational policy, as well as upon the immemorial precedents of English justice; because such a person seeks to disunite individuals from their duty to the whole, and excites to overt acts of *misconduct* in a part of the community, instead of endeavouring to change, by the impulse of reason, that universal assent which, in this and in every country, constitutes the law for all.

I have, therefore, no difficulty in admitting that, if upon an attentive perusal of this work, it shall be found that the defendant has promulgated any doctrines which excite individuals to withdraw from their subjection to the law by which the whole nation consents to be governed; if his book shall be found to have warranted or excited that unfortunate criminal who appeared here yesterday to endeavour to relieve himself from imprisonment by the destruction of a prison, or dictated to him the language of defiance which ran through the whole of his defence; if throughout the work there shall be found any syllable or letter which strikes at the security of property, or which hints that anything less than *the whole nation* can constitute the law, or that the law, be it what it may, is not the inexorable rule of action for every individual, I willingly yield him up to the justice of the Court.

Gentlemen, I say, in the name of Thomas Paine, and in his words as author of " The Rights of Man," as written in the very volume that is charged with seeking the destruction of property—

" The end of all political associations is the preservation of the rights of man, which rights are liberty, property, and security; that the nation is the source of all sovereignty derived from it: the right of property being secured and inviolable, no one ought to be deprived of it, except in cases of evident public necessity, legally ascertained, and on condition of a previous just indemnity."

These are undoubtedly the rights of man—the rights for which all governments are established—and the only rights Mr Paine contends for; but which he thinks (no matter whether right or wrong) are better to be secured by a republican constitution than by the forms of the English Government. He instructs me to admit that, when government is once constituted, no individuals, without rebellion, can withdraw their obedience from it; that all attempts to excite them to it are highly criminal, for the most obvious reasons of policy and justice; that nothing short of the will of a WHOLE PEOPLE can change or affect the rule by which a nation is to be governed; and that no private opinion, however honestly inimical to the forms or substance of the law, can justify resistance to its authority, while it remains in force. The author of "The Rights of Man" not only admits the truth of all this doctrine, but he consents to be convicted, and I also consent for him, unless his work shall be found studiously and painfully to inculcate those great principles of government which it is charged to have been written to destroy.

Let me not, therefore, be suspected to be contending that it is lawful to write a book pointing out defects in the English Government, and exciting individuals to destroy its sanctions, and to refuse obedience. But, on the other hand, I do contend, that it is lawful to address the English nation on these momentous subjects; for had it not been for this inalienable right (thanks be to God and our fathers for establishing it!), how should we have had this constitution which we so loudly boast of? If, in the march of the human mind, no man could have gone before the establishments of the time he lived in, how could our establishment, by reiterated changes, have become what it is? If no man could have awakened the public mind to errors and abuses in our Government, how could it have passed on from stage to stage, through reformation and revolution, so as to have arrived from barbarism to such a pitch of happiness and perfection, that the Attorney-General considers it as profanation to touch it further, or to look for any future amendment?

In this manner power has reasoned in every age; Government, in *its own estimation*, has been at all times a system of perfection; but a free press has examined and detected its errors, and the people have from time to time reformed them. This freedom has alone made our Government what it is; this freedom alone can preserve it; and therefore, under the banners of that freedom, to-day I stand up to defend Thomas Paine. But how, alas! shall this task be accomplished? How may I expect from you what human nature has not made man for the performance of? How am I to address your reasons, or ask them to pause, amidst the torrent of prejudice which has hurried away the public mind on the subject you are to judge?

Was any Englishman ever so brought as a criminal before an English court of justice? If I were to ask you, gentlemen of the jury, what is the choicest fruit that grows upon the tree of English liberty, you would answer, SECURITY UNDER THE LAW. If I were to ask the whole people of England the return they looked for at the hands of Government for the burdens under which they bend to support it, I should still be answered, SECURITY UNDER THE LAW; or, in other words, an impartial administration of justice. So sacred, therefore, has the freedom of trial been ever held in England; so anxiously does justice guard against every possible bias in her path, that if the public mind has been locally agitated upon any subject in judgment, the forum has either been changed, or the trial postponed. The circulation of any paper that brings, or can be supposed to bring, prejudice, or even well-founded know-ledge, within the reach of a British tribunal, *on the spur of an occa-sion*, is not only highly criminal, but defeats itself, by leading to put off the trial which its object was to pervert. On this principle, the noble and learned Judge will permit me to remind him, that on the trial of the Dean of St Asaph for a libel, or rather when he was brought to trial, the circulation of books by a society favour-able to his defence was held by his Lordship, as Chief-Justice of Chester, to be a reason for not trying the cause; * although they contained no matter relative to the Dean, nor to the object of his trial; being only extracts from ancient authors of high reputation on the general rights of juries to consider the innocence as well as the guilt of the accused; yet still, as the recollection of these rights was pressed forward *with a view to affect the proceedings*, the pro-ceedings were postponed.

Is the defendant, then, to be the only exception to these admir-able provisions? Is the English law to judge *him*, stript of the armour with which its universal justice encircles *all others?* Shall we, in the very act of judging him for detracting from the Eng-lish Government, furnish him with ample matter for just repro-bation, instead of detraction? Has not his cause been prejudged through a thousand channels? Has not the work before you been daily and publicly reviled, and his person held up to derision and reproach? Has not the public mind been excited by crying down the very phrase and idea of "The Rights of Man?" Nay, have not associations of gentlemen,—I speak it with regret, because I am persuaded, from what I know of some of them, that they, amongst them at least, thought they were serving the public,—yet have they not, in utter contempt and ignorance of that constitution of which they declare themselves to be the guardians, published the grossest attacks upon the defendant? Have they not, even while the cause has been standing here for immediate trial, published a direct pro-test against the very work now before you; advertising in the same paper, though under the general description of seditious libels, a reward on the conviction of any person who should dare to sell the book itself, to which their own publication was an answer? The Attorney-General has spoken of a forced circulation of this work; but how have these prejudging papers been circulated? We all know how. They have been thrown into our carriages in every street; they have met us at every turnpike; and they lie in the areas of all our houses. To complete the triumph of prejudice, that high tribunal of which I have the honour to be a member (my learned friends know what I say to be true), has been drawn into this vortex of slander; and some of its members,—I must not speak of the House itself,—have thrown the weight of their stations into

* *Vide ante*, pp. 97, 107..

the same scale. By all these means I maintain that this cause has been prejudged.

It may be said, that I have made no motion to put off the trial for these causes, and that courts of themselves take no cognisance of what passes elsewhere, without facts laid before them. Gentlemen, I know that I should have had equal justice from the Court, if I had brought myself within the rule. But when should I have been better in the present aspect of things? And I only remind you, therefore, of all these hardships, that you may recollect that your judgment is to proceed upon that alone which meets you *here*, upon *the evidence* in the cause, and not upon suggestions destructive of every principle of justice.

Having disposed of these foreign prejudices, I hope you will as little regard some arguments that have been offered to you in court. The letter which has been so repeatedly pressed upon you ought to be dismissed even from your recollection. I have already put it out of the question, as having been written long subsequent to the book, and as being a libel on the King, which no part of the information charges, and which may hereafter be prosecuted as a distinct offence. I consider that letter, besides, and indeed have always heard it treated, as a forgery, contrived to injure the merits of the cause, and to embarrass *me personally* in its defence. I have a right so to consider it, because it is unsupported by anything similar at an earlier period. The defendant's whole deportment, previous to the publication, has been wholly unexceptionable: he properly desired to be given up as the author of the book, if any inquiry should take place concerning it: and he is not affected in evidence, either directly or indirectly, with any illegal or suspicious conduct; not even with having uttered an indiscreet or taunting expression, nor with any one matter or thing inconsistent with the duty of the best subject in England. His *opinions* indeed were adverse to our system; but I maintain that OPINION is free, and that CONDUCT alone is amenable to the law.

You are next desired to judge of the author's mind and intention by the modes and extent of the circulation of his work. The FIRST part of the "Rights of Man," Mr Attorney-General tells you he did not prosecute, although it was in circulation through the country for a year and a half together, because it seems it circulated only amongst what he styles the judicious part of the public, who possessed in their capacities and experience an antidote to the poison; but that, with regard to the SECOND part now before you, its circulation had been forced into every corner of society; had been printed and reprinted for cheapness even upon whited-brown paper, and had crept into the very nurseries of children as a wrapper for their sweetmeats.

In answer to this statement, which after all stands only upon Mr Attorney-General's own assertion, unsupported by any kind of proof (no witness having proved the author's personal interference with the sale), I still maintain, that if he had the most anxiously promoted it, the question would remain exactly THE SAME: the question would still be, whether at the time when Paine composed his work, and promoted the most extensive purchase of it, he believed or disbelieved what he had written?—and whether he contemplated the happiness or the misery of the English nation, to which it is addressed? And whichever of these intentions may be evidenced to your judgments upon reading the book itself, I confess I am utterly at a loss to comprehend how a writer can be supposed to mean something different from what he has written, by proof of an anxiety (common, I believe, to all authors) that his work should be generally read. Remember, I am not asking your opinions of the *doctrines themselves,*—you have given them already pretty visibly since I began to address you,—but I shall appeal not only to you, but to those who, without our leave, will hereafter judge, and without appeal, of all that we are doing to-day,—whether, upon the matter which I hasten to lay before you, you can refuse to pronounce, that from his education,—from the accidents and habits of his life,—from the time and occasion of the publication, —from the circumstances attending it,—and from every line and letter of the work itself, and from all his other writings, his conscience and understanding (*no matter whether erroneously or not*) were deeply and solemnly impressed with the matters contained in his book?—that he addressed it to the reason of the nation at large, and not to the passions of individuals?—and that, in the issue of its influence, he contemplated only what appeared to *him* (*though it may not to us*) to be the interest and happiness of England, and of the whole human race? In drawing the one or the other of these conclusions, the book stands first in order, and it shall now speak for itself.

Gentlemen, *the whole of it* is in evidence before you; the particular parts arraigned having only been read by my consent, upon the presumption that, on retiring from the court, you would carefully compare them with the context, and all the parts with the WHOLE VIEWED TOGETHER. You cannot indeed do justice without it. The most common letter, even in the ordinary course of business, cannot be read in a cause to prove an obligation for twenty shillings without THE WHOLE being read, that the writer's meaning may be seen without deception. But in a criminal charge, comprehending only four pages and a half, out of a work containing nearly two hundred, you cannot, with even the appearance of common decency, pronounce a judgment without the most deliberate and cautious comparison. I observe that the noble and learned Judge confirms me in this observation.

If any given part of a work be legally explanatory of every other part of it, the preface, *à fortiori*, is the most material; because the preface is the author's own key to his writing: it is *there* that he takes the reader by the hand, and introduces him to his subject: it is there that the spirit and intention of the whole is laid before him by way of prologue. A preface is meant by the author as a clue to ignorant or careless readers: the author says by it, to every man who chooses to begin where he ought, Look at my plan,—attend to my distinctions,—mark the purpose and limitations of the matter I lay before you.

Let, then, the calumniators of Thomas Paine now attend to his preface, where, to leave no excuse for ignorance or misrepresentation, he expresses himself thus:—

" I have differed from some professional gentlemen on the subject of prosecutions, and I since find they are falling into my opinion, which I will here state as fully but as concisely as I can.

" I will first put a case with respect to any law, and then compare it with a government, or with what in England is or has been called a constitution.

" It would be an act of despotism, or what in England is called arbitrary power, to make a law to prohibit investigating the principles, good or bad, on which such a law, or any other, is founded.

" If a law be bad, it is one thing to *oppose the practice* of it, but it is quite a different thing to *expose its errors,* to *reason* on its defects, and to *show cause* why it should be repealed, or why another ought to be substituted in its place. I have always held it an opinion (making it also my practice), that it is better to obey a bad law, making use at the same time of every argument to show its errors and procure its repeal, than forcibly to violate it; because the precedent of breaking a bad law might weaken the force, and lead to a discretionary violation, of those which are good.

" The case is the same with principles and forms of governments, or to what are called constitutions, and the parts of which they are composed.

" It is for the good of nations, and not for the emolument or aggrandisement of particular individuals, that government ought to be established, and that mankind are at the expense of supporting it. The defects of every government and constitution, both as to principle and form, must, on a parity of reasoning, be as open to discussion as the defects of a law, and it is a duty which every man owes to society to point them out. When those defects and the means of remedying them are generally seen by a NATION, THAT NATION will reform its government or its constitution in the one case as the government repealed or reformed the law in the other."

Gentlemen, you must undoubtedly wish to deal with every man who comes before you in judgment as you would be dealt by; and surely you will not lay it down to-day as a law to be binding here-

after, even upon yourselves, that if you should publish any opinion
concerning existing abuses in your country's government, and point
out to the whole public the means of amendment, you are to be
acquitted or convicted as any twelve men may happen to agree with
you in your *opinions.* Yet this is precisely what you are asked to
lo to another—it is precisely the case before you. Mr Paine expressly says, I obey a law until it is repealed; obedience is not
only my principle but my practice, since my disobedience of a law,
from thinking it *bad,* might apply to justify another man in the
disobedience of a *good one;* and thus individuals would give the
rule for themselves, and not society for all. You will presently see
that the same principle pervades the whole work; and I am the
more anxious to call your attention to it, however repetition may
tire you, because it unfolds the whole principle of my argument;
for, if you find a sentence in the whole book that invests any individual, or any number of individuals, or any community short of
the WHOLE NATION, with a power of changing any part of the law
or constitution, I abandon the cause,—YES, I freely abandon it,
because I will not affront the majesty of a court of justice by maintaining propositions which, even upon the surface of them, are
false. Mr Paine, page 162–168, goes on thus :—

" When a NATION changes its opinion and habits of thinking, it
is no longer to be governed as before ; but it would not only be
wrong, but bad policy, to attempt by force what ought to be accomplished by reason. Rebellion consists in forcibly opposing the
general will of a nation, whether by a party or by a government. There ought, therefore, to be, in every nation, a method of
occasionally ascertaining the state of public opinion with respect to
government.

"There is, therefore, no power but the voluntary will of the
people that has a right to act in any matter respecting a general
reform ; and, by the same right that two persons can confer on
such a subject, a thousand may. The object in all such prelim-
inary proceedings is, to find out what the GENERAL SENSE OF A
NATION is, and to be governed by it. If it prefer a bad or defective
government to a reform, or choose to pay ten times more taxes
than there is occasion for, it has a right so to do ; and, so long as
the majority do not impose conditions on the minority different to
what they impose on themselves, though there may be much error,
there is no injustice ; neither will the error continue long. Reason
and discussion will soon bring things right, however wrong they
may begin. By such a process no tumult is to be apprehended.
The poor, in all countries, are naturally both peaceable and grateful in all reforms in which their interest and happiness are
included. It is only by neglecting and rejecting them that they
become tumultuous."

Gentlemen, these are the sentiments of the author of the "Rights of Man ; " and, whatever *his* opinions may be of the defects in our Government, it never can change ours concerning it, if our sentiments are just ; and a writing can never be seditious in the sense of the English law, which states that the Government leans on the UNIVERSAL WILL for its support.

This universal will is the best and securest title which His Majesty and his family have to the throne of these kingdoms ; and in proportion to the wisdom of our institutions, the title must in common sense become the stronger. So little idea, indeed, have I of any other, that in my place in Parliament, not a week ago, I considered it as the best way of expressing my reverence to the constitution, as established at the Revolution, to declare (I believe in the presence of the Heir-Apparent to the Crown, to whom I have the greatest personal attachment) that His Majesty reigned in England by choice and consent, as the magistrate of the English people ; not indeed a consent and choice by personal election, like a King of Poland,—the worst of all possible constitutions ; but by the election of a family for great national objects, in defiance of that hereditary right, which only becomes tyranny, in the sense of Mr Paine, when it claims to inherit a nation, instead of governing by their consent, and continuing for its benefit. This sentiment has the advantage of Mr Burke's high authority, who says with great truth, in a " Letter to his Constituents,"—" Too little dependence cannot be had at this time of day on names and prejudices : the eyes of mankind are opened ; and communities must be held together by a visible and solid interest." I believe, gentlemen of the jury, that the Prince of Wales will always render this title dear to the people. The Attorney-General can only tell you what he *believes* of him : I can tell you what I KNOW, and what I am bound to declare, since this Prince may be traduced in every part of the kingdom, without its coming in question, till brought in to load a defence with matter collateral to the charge. I therefore *assert* what the Attorney-General can only *hope*, that whenever that Prince shall come to the throne of this country (which I pray, but by the course of nature, may never happen), he will make the constitution of Great Britain the foundation of all his conduct.

Having now established the author's general intention by his own introduction, which is the best and fairest exposition, let us next look at the occasion which gave it birth.

The Attorney-General, throughout the whole course of his address to you (I knew it would be so), has avoided the most distant notice or hint of any circumstance having led to the appearance of the author in the political world, after a silence of so many years : he has not even pronounced, or even glanced, at the name of Mr Burke, but has left you to take it for granted that the defendant volunteered this delicate and momentous subject, and, without being led to it by the provocation of political controversy, had seized a favour-

able moment to stigmatise, from mere malice, and against his own
confirmed opinions, the constitution of this country.

Gentlemen, my learned friend knows too well my respect and
value for him to suppose that I am charging him with a wilful
suppression ; I know him to be incapable of it ; he knew it would
come from me.   He will permit me, however, to lament that it
should have been left for me to inform you, at this late period of
the cause, that not only the work before you, but the first part, of
which it is a natural continuation, were written, *avowedly and upon
the face of them*, IN ANSWER TO MR BURKE.   They were written,
besides, under circumstances to be explained hereafter, in the course
of which explanation I may have occasion to cite a few passages
from the works of that celebrated person.   And I shall speak of
him with the highest respect: for, with whatever contempt he may
delight to look down upon my humble talents, however he may disparage the principles which direct my public conduct, he shall
never force me to forget the regard which this country owes to him
for the writings which he has left upon record as an inheritance to
our most distant posterity.   After the gratitude which we owe to
God for the divine gifts of reason and understanding, our next
thanks are due to those from the fountains of whose enlightened
minds they are fed and fructified.   But, pleading, as I do, the cause
of freedom of opinions, I shall not give offence by remarking that
this great author has been thought to have changed some of his :
and, if Thomas Paine had not thought so, I should not now be
addressing you, because the book which is my subject would never
have been written.   Who may be right and who in the wrong, in
the contention of doctrines, I have repeatedly disclaimed to be the
question.   I can only say that Mr Paine may be right THROUGHOUT,
but that Mr Burke CANNOT.   Mr Paine has been UNIFORM in *his*
opinions, but Mr Burke HAS NOT.   Mr Burke can only be right in
part ; but, should Mr Paine be even mistaken in the whole, still I
am not removed from the principle of his defence.   My defence has
nothing to do with the rectitude of his doctrines.   I admit Mr
Paine to be a republican: you shall soon see what made him one.
I do not seek to shade or qualify his attack upon our constitution ;
I put my defence on no such matter.   He undoubtedly means to
declare it to be defective in its forms, and contaminated with
abuses which, in his judgment, will, one day or other, bring on the
ruin of us all.   It is in vain to mince the matter ; this is the scope
of his work.   But still, if it contain no attack upon the King's
Majesty, nor upon any other LIVING MAGISTRATE ; if it excite to no
resistance to magistracy, but, on the contrary, if it even studiously
inculcate obedience, then, whatever may be its defects, the question
continues as before, and ever must remain, an unmixed question of
the liberty of the press.   I have therefore considered it as no
breach of professional duty, nor injurious to the cause I am defend-

ing, to express my own admiration of the real principles of our constitution,—a constitution which I hope may never give way to any other,—a constitution which has been productive of many benefits, and which will produce many more hereafter, if we have wisdom enough to pluck up the weeds that grow in the richest soils and amongst the brightest flowers. I agree with the merchants of London, in a late declaration, that the English Government is equal to the reformation of its own abuses; and, as an inhabitant of the city, I would have signed it, if I had known, *of my own knowledge*, the facts recited in its preamble. But abuses the English constitution unquestionably has, which call loudly for reformation, the existence of which has been the theme of our greatest statesmen, which have too plainly formed the principles of the defendant, and may have led to the very conjuncture which produced his book.

Gentlemen, we all but too well remember the calamitous situation in which our country stood but a few years ago,—a situation which no man can look back upon without horror, nor feel himself safe from relapsing into again, while the causes remain which produced it. The event I allude to you must know to be the American War, and the still existing causes of it, the corruptions of this Government. In those days it was not thought virtue by the patriots of England to conceal the existence of them from the people; but then, as now, authority condemned them as disaffected subjects, and defeated the ends they sought by their promulgation.

Hear the opinion of Sir George Saville—not his speculative opinion concerning the structure of our Government in the *abstract*, but his opinion of the settled abuses which prevailed in *his own time*, and which continue at *this moment*. But first let me remind you who Sir George Saville was. I fear we shall hardly look upon his like again. How shall I describe him to you? In my own words I cannot. I was lately commended by Mr Burke in the House of Commons for strengthening my own language by an appeal to Dr Johnson. Were the honourable gentleman present at this moment, he would no doubt doubly applaud my choice in resorting to *his own works* for the description of Sir George Saville.

"His fortune is among the largest; a fortune which, wholly unencumbered as it is, without one single charge from luxury, vanity, or excess, sinks under the benevolence of its dispenser. This private benevolence, expanding itself into patriotism, renders his whole being the estate of the public, in which he has not reserved a *peculium* for himself of profit, diversion, or relaxation. During the session, the first in and the last out of the House of Commons, he passes from the senate to the camp; and, seldom seeing the seat of his ancestors, he is always in Parliament to serve his country, or in the field to defend it."

It is impossible to ascribe to such a character any principle but patriotism, when he expressed himself as follows :—

" I return to you baffled and dispirited, and I am sorry that truth obliges me to add, with hardly a ray of hope of seeing any change in the miserable course of public calamities.

" On this melancholy day of account, in rendering up to you my trust, I deliver to you your share of a country maimed and weakened ; its treasure lavished and misspent ; its honours faded ; and its conduct the laughing-stock of Europe : our nation in a manner without allies or friends, except such as we have hired to destroy our fellow-subjects, and to ravage a country in which we once claimed an invaluable share. I return to you some of your principal privileges impeached and mangled. And, lastly, I leave you, as I conceive, at this hour and moment, fully, effectually, and absolutely under the discretion and power of a military force, which is to act without waiting for the authority of the civil magistrates.

" Some have been accused of exaggerating the public misfortunes, nay, of having endeavoured to help forward the mischief, that they might afterwards raise discontents. I am willing to hope, that neither my temper nor my situation in life will be thought naturally to urge me to promote misery, discord, or confusion, or to exult in the subversion of order, or in the ruin of property. I have no reason to contemplate with pleasure the poverty of our country, the increase of our debts and of our taxes, or the decay of our commerce. Trust not, however, to my report : reflect, compare, and judge for yourselves.

" But, under all these disheartening circumstances, I could yet entertain a cheerful hope, and undertake again the commission with alacrity, as well as zeal, if I could see any effectual steps taken to remove the original cause of the mischief. ' Then would there be a hope.'

" But, till the purity of the constituent body, and thereby that of the representative, be restored, there is NONE.

" I gladly embrace this most public opportunity of delivering my sentiments, not only to all my constituents, but to those likewise not my constituents, whom yet, in the large sense, I represent, and am faithfully to serve.

" I look upon restoring election and representation in some degree (for I expect no miracles) to their original purity, to be that, without which all other efforts will be vain and ridiculous.

" If something be not done, you may, indeed, retain the OUTWARD FORM of your constitution, but not the POWER thereof."

Such were the words of that great good man, lost with those of many others of his time, and his fame, as far as power could hurt it, put in the shade along with them. The consequences we have all seen and felt : America, from an obedient affectionate colony, became an independent nation ; and two millions of people, nursed in the very lap of our monarchy, became the willing subjects of a republican constitution.

Gentlemen, in that great and calamitous conflict Edmund Burke and Thomas Paine fought in the same field of reason together, but with very diffcrent successes. Mr Burke spoke to a Parliament in England, such as Sir George Saville describes it, having no ears but for sounds that flattered its corruptions. Mr Paine, on the other hand, spoke TO A PEOPLE, reasoned with them, told them that they were bound by no subjection to any sovereignty, further than their own benefit connected them; and by these powerful arguments prepared the minds of the American people for that GLORI-OUS, JUST, and HAPPY revolution.

Gentlemen, I have a right to distinguish it by these epithets, because I aver that at this moment there is as sacred a regard to property, as inviolable a security to all the rights of individuals, lower taxes, fewer grievances, less to deplore, and more to admire, in the constitution of America, than that of any other country under heaven. I wish indeed to except our own, but I cannot even do that, till it shall be purged of those abuses which, though they obscure and deform the surface, have not as yet, *thank God,* destroyed the vital parts.

Why then is Mr Paine to be calumniated and reviled, because, out of a people consisting of near three millions, *he alone* did not remain attached *in opinion* to a monarchy? Remember that all the blood which was shed in America, and to which he was for years a melancholy and indignant witness, was shed by the authority of the Crown of Great Britain, under the influence of a Parliament such as Sir George Saville has described it, and such as Mr Burke himself will be called upon by and by in more glowing colours to paint it. How then can it be wondered at, that Mr Paine should return to this country in his heart a republican? Was he not equally a republican when he wrote " Common Sense?" Yet that volume has been sold without restraint or prosecution in every shop in England ever since, and which nevertheless (*I appeal to the book, which I have in Court, and which is in everybody's hands*) contains every one principle of government, and every abuse in the British constitution, which is to be found in the " Rights of Man." Yet Mr Burke himself saw no reason to be alarmed at that publication, nor to cry down its contents, even when America, which was swayed by it, was in arms against the Crown of Great Britain. You shall hear his opinion of it in his Letter to the Sheriffs of Bristol, pages 33 and 34.

" The *Court Gazette* accomplished what the abettors of inde-pendence had attempted in vain. When that disingenuous com-pilation, and strange medley of railing and flattery, was adduced as a proof of the united sentiments of the people of Great Britain, here was a great change throughout all America. The tide of popular affection, which had still set towards the parent country, began immediately to turn, and to flow with great rapidity in a contrary course. Far from concealing these wild declarations of enmity, *the author of the celebrated pamphlet** *which prepared the minds of the people for independence*, insists largely on the multitude and the spirit of these addresses; and draws an argument from them which (if the fact were as he supposes) must be irresistible; for I never knew a writer on the theory of government so partial to authority as not to allow that the hostile mind of the rulers to their people did fully justify a change of government; nor can any reason whatever be given why one people should voluntarily yield any degree of pre-eminence to another, but on a supposition of great affection and benevolence towards them. Unfortunately, your rulers, trusting to other things, took no notice of this great principle of connexion."

Such were the sentiments of Mr Burke; but there is a time, it seems, for all things.

Gentlemen, the consequences of this mighty revolution are too notorious to require illustration. No audience would sit to *hear* (what everybody has *seen* and *felt*), how the independence of America notoriously produced, not by remote and circuitous effect, but directly and palpably, the revolutions which now agitate Europe, and which portend such mighty changes over the face of the earth. Let governments take warning. The revolution in France was the consequence of her incurably corrupt and profligate Government. God forbid that I should be thought to lean, by this declaration, upon her unfortunate monarch, bending perhaps at this moment under afflictions which my heart sinks within me to think of: when I speak with detestation of the former politics of the French court, I fasten as little of them upon that fallen and unhappy prince, as I impute to our gracious Sovereign the corruptions of our own. I desire, indeed, in the distinctest manner, to be understood that I mean to speak of His Majesty, not only with that obedience and duty which I owe to him as a subject, but with that justice which I think is due to him from all men who examine his conduct either in public or private life.

Gentlemen, Mr Paine happened to be in England when the French Revolution took place; and notwithstanding what he must be supposed and allowed from his own history to have felt upon such a subject, he remained wholly silent and inactive. The people of this country, too, appeared to be indifferent spectators of the animating scene. They saw, without visible emotion, despotism destroyed, and the King of France, by his own consent, become the first magistrate of a free people. Certainly, at least, it produced none of those effects which are so deprecated by Government at present; nor, most probably, ever would, if it had not occurred to

* " Common Sense," written by Thomas Paine in America.

the celebrated person whose name I must so often mention voluntarily to provoke the subject,—a subject which, if dangerous to be discussed, HE should not have led to the discussion of; for surely it is not to be endured that any private man shall publish a creed for a whole nation: shall tell us that we are not to think for ourselves, shall impose his own fetters upon the human mind, shall dogmatise at discretion, and yet that no man shall sit down to answer him without being guilty of a libel. I assert that if it be a libel to mistake our constitution, to attempt the support of it by means that tend to destroy it, and to choose the most dangerous season for doing so, Mr Burke is that libeller; but not therefore the object of a criminal prosecution: whilst I am defending the motives of one man, I have neither right nor disposition to criminate the motives of another. All I contend for is a fact that cannot be controverted, viz., that *this officious interference was the origin of Mr Paine's book.* I put my cause upon its being the origin of it —the avowed origin—as will abundantly appear from the introduction and preface to both parts, and from the whole body of the work; nay, from the very work of Mr Burke himself, to which both of them are answers.

For the history of that celebrated work, I appeal to itself.

When the French Revolution had arrived at some of its early stages, a few, and but a few, persons (not to be named when compared with the nation) took a visible interest in these mighty events,—an interest well worthy of Englishmen. They saw a pernicious system of government which had led to desolating wars, and had been for ages the scourge of Great Britain, giving way to a system which seemed to promise harmony and peace amongst nations. They saw this with virtuous and peaceable satisfaction; and a reverend divine,* eminent for his eloquence, recollecting that the issues of life are in the hands of God, saw no profaneness in mixing the subject with public thanksgiving, by reminding the people of this country of their own glorious deliverance in former ages. It happened, also, that a society of gentlemen, France being then a neutral nation, and her own monarch swearing almost daily upon her altars to maintain the new constitution, thought they infringed no law by sending a general congratulation. Their numbers, indeed, were very inconsiderable; so much so, that Mr Burke, with more truth than wisdom, begins his volume with a sarcasm upon their insignificance:

"Until very lately he had never heard of such a club. It certainly never occupied a moment of his thoughts; nor, he believed, those of any person out of their own set."

Why then make their proceedings the subject of alarm throughout England? There had been no prosecution against them, nor any charge founded even upon suspicion of disaffection against any

* Dr Price.

of their body.　But Mr Burke thought it was reserved for his eloquence to whip these curs of faction to their kennels.　How he has succeeded, I appeal to all that has happened since the introduction of his schism in the British Empire, by giving to the King, whose title was questioned by no man, a title which it is His Majesty's most solemn interest to disclaim.

After having, in his first work, lashed Dr Price in a strain of eloquent irony for considering the monarchy to be elective, which he could not but know Dr Price, *in the literal sense of election*, neither did or could possibly consider it, Mr Burke published a second treatise; in which, after reprinting many passages from Mr Paine's former work, he ridicules and denies the supposed right of the people to change their governments, in the following words :—

"The French Revolution, *say they*" (speaking of the English societies), " was the act of the majority of the people ; and if the majority of any other people, *the people of England, for instance*, wish to make the same change, they have the same right ; just the same undoubtedly ; that is, none *at all.*"

And then, after speaking of the subserviency of will to duty (in which I agree with him), he, in a substantive sentence, maintains the same doctrine, thus :—

" The constitution of a country being once settled upon some compact, tacit or expressed, there is no power existing of force to alter it, without the breach of the covenant, or the consent of all the parties.　Such is the nature of a contract."

So that if reason, or even revelation itself, were now to demonstrate to us, that our constitution was mischievous in its effects,—if, to use Mr Attorney-General's expression, we had been insane for the many centuries we have supported it ; yet that still, if the King had not forfeited his title to the Crown, nor the Lords their privileges, *the universal voice of the people of England* could not build up a new government upon a legitimate basis.

Passing by, for the present, the absurdity of such a proposition, and supposing it could, beyond all controversy, be maintained ; for Heaven's sake, let wisdom never utter it !　Let policy and prudence for ever conceal it !　If you seek the stability of the English Government, rather put the book of Mr Paine, which calls it bad, into every hand in the kingdom, than doctrines which bid human nature rebel even against that which is the best.　Say to the people of England, Look at your constitution, there it lies before you—the work of your pious fathers,—handed down as a sacred deposit from generation to generation,—the result of wisdom and virtue,—and its parts cemented together with kindred blood : there are, indeed, a few spots upon its surface ; but the same principle which reared the structure will brush them all away : You may preserve your Government—you may destroy it.　To such an address, what would be the answer ?　A chorus of the nation—YES, WE WILL PRESERVE

IT. But say to the *same* nation, even of the very *same* constitution, it is yours, such as it is, for better or for worse;—it is strapped upon your backs, to carry it as beasts of burden,—you have no jurisdiction to cast it off. Let *this* be your position, and you instantly raise up (I appeal to every man's consciousness of his own nature) a spirit of uneasiness and discontent. It is this spirit alone that has pointed most of the passages arraigned before you.

But let the prudence of Mr Burke's argument be what it may, the argument itself is untenable. His Majesty undoubtedly was not elected to the throne. No man can be supposed, in the teeth of fact, to have contended it;—but did not the people of England elect King William, and break the hereditary succession?—and does not His Majesty's title grow out of that election? It is one of the charges against the defendant, his having denied the Parliament which called the Prince of Orange to the throne to have been a legal convention of the whole people; and is not the very foundation of that charge that it *was* such a legal convention, and that it was intended to be so? And *if it was so*, did not the people then confer the Crown upon King William without any regard to hereditary right? Did they not cut off the Prince of Wales, who stood directly in the line of succession, and who had incurred no personal forfeiture? Did they not give their deliverer an estate in the Crown totally new and unprecedented in the law or history of the country? And, lastly, might they not, by the same authority, have given the royal inheritance to the family of a stranger? Mr Justice Blackstone, in his Commentaries, asserts in terms *that they might;* and ascribes their choice of King William, and the subsequent limitations of the Crown, not to want of jurisdiction, but to their true origin, to prudence and discretion in not disturbing a valuable institution further than public safety and necessity dictated.

The English Government stands then on this public consent, the true root of all governments. And I agree with Mr Burke that, while it is well administered, it is not in the power of factions or libels to disturb it; though, when ministers are in fault, they are sure to set down all disturbances to these causes. This is most justly and eloquently exemplified in his own "Thoughts on the Cause of the Present Discontents," pages 5 and 6 :—

" Ministers contend that no adequate provocation has been given or so spreading a discontent, our affairs having been conducted throughout with remarkable temper and consummate wisdom. The wicked industry of some libellers, joined to the intrigues of a few disappointed politicians, have, in their opinion, been able to produce this unnatural ferment in the nation.

" Nothing, indeed, can be more unnatural than the present convulsions of this country, if the above account be a true one. I confess I shall assent to it with great reluctance, and only on the compulsion of the clearest and firmest proofs; because their account

resolves itself into this short but discouraging proposition : ' That
we have a very good Ministry, but that we are a very bad people ; '
that we set ourselves to bite the hand that feeds us: and, with a
malignant insanity, oppose the measures, and ungratefully vilify
the persons of those whose sole object is our own peace and prosperity.
If a few puny libellers, acting under a knot of factious politicians,
without virtue, parts, or character (for such they are constantly
represented by these gentlemen), are sufficient to excite this'disturbance, very perverse must be the disposition of that people, amongst
whom such a disturbance can be excited by such means."
     He says true : never were serious disturbances excited by such
means !
     But to return to the argument.   Let us now see how the rights
of the people stand upon authorities.   Let us examine whether this
great source of government insisted on by Thomas Paine, be not
maintained by persons on whom my friend will find it difficult to
fasten the character of libellers.
     I shall begin with the most modern author on the subject of
government—whose work lies spread out before me, as it often does
at home for my delight and instruction in my leisure hours. I have
also the honour of his personal acquaintance.   He is a man, perhaps
more than any other, devoted tȯ the real constitution of this country,
as will be found throughout his valuable work ; he is a person,
besides, of great learning, which enabled him to infuse much useful
knowledge into my learned friend now near me, who introduced me
to him.*   I speak of Mr Paley, Archdeacon of Carlisle, and of his
work entitled "The Principles of Political and Moral Philosophy,"
in which he investigates the first principles of all governments—a
discussion not thought dangerous *till lately.*   I hope we shall soon
get rid of this ridiculous panic.
     Mr Paley professes to think of governments what the Christian
religion was thought of by its first teachers :—" *If it be of God, it
will stand ;* " and he puts the duties of obedience to them upon free-
will and moral duty.   After dissenting from Mr Locke as to the
origin of governments in compact, he says :—
     " Wherefore, rejecting the intervention of a compact as unfounded
in its principle, and dangerous in the application, we assign for the
only ground of the subjects' obligation, THE WILL OF GOD, AS COL-
LECTED FROM EXPEDIENCY.
     " The steps by which the argument proceeds are few and direct.
' It is the will of God that the happiness of human life be promoted : '
—this is the first step, and the foundation, not only of this, but of
every moral conclusion.   ' Civil society conduces to that end : '—
this is the second proposition.   ' Civil societies cannot be upheld,
unless, in each, the interest of the whole society be binding upon
every part and member of it : '—this is the third step, and conducts

* Lord Ellenborough, then Mr Law.

us to the conclusion, namely,—' That, so long as the interest of the whole society requires it (that is, so long as the established government cannot be resisted or changed without public inconveniency), it is the will of God (which will universally determines our duty) that the established government be obeyed,'—*and no longer.*

"But who shall judge of this? We answer, ' *Every man for himself.*' In contentions between the sovereign and the subject, the parties acknowledge no common arbitrator ; and it would be absurd to commit the decision to those whose conduct has provoked the question, and whose own interest, authority, and fate, are immediately concerned in it. The danger of error and abuse is no objection to the rule of expediency, because every other rule is liable to the same or greater; and every rule that can be propounded upon the subject (like all rules which appeal to or bind the conscience), must, in the application, depend upon private judgment. It may be observed, however, that it ought equally to be accounted the exercise of a man's private judgment, whether he determines by reasonings and conclusions of his own, or submits to be directed by the advice of others, provided he be free to choose his guide."

He then proceeds in a manner rather inconsistent with the principles entertained by my learned friend in his opening to you :—

" No usage, law, or authority whatever, is so binding, that it need or ought to be continued, when it may be changed with advantage to the community. The family of the prince—the order of succession—the prerogative of the crown—the form and parts of the legislature—together with the respective powers, office, duration, and mutual dependency of the several parts ; are all only so many laws, mutable, like other laws, whenever expediency requires, either by the ordinary act of the legislature, or, if the occasion deserve it, BY THE INTERPOSITION OF THE PEOPLE."

No man can say that Mr Paley intended to diffuse discontent by this declaration. He must, therefore, be taken to think with me, that freedom and affection, and the sense of advantage, are the best and the only supports of government. On the same principle he then goes on to say,—" These points are wont to be approached with a kind of awe ; they are represented to the mind as principles of the constitution, settled by our ancestors ; and, being settled, to be no more committed to innovation or debate; as foundations never to be stirred ; as the terms and conditions of the social compact, to which every citizen of the state has engaged his fidelity by virtue of a promise which he cannot now recall. Such reasons have no place in our system."

These are the sentiments of this excellent author; and there is no part of Mr Paine's work, from the one end of it to the other, that advances any other proposition.

But the Attorney-General will say these are the grave speculative opinions of a friend to the English Government, whereas Mr

Paine is its professed enemy; what then? · The principle is, that every man, while he obeys the laws, is to think for himself, and to communicate what he thinks. The very ends of society exact this licence, and the policy of the law, in its provisions for its security, has tacitly sanctioned it. The real fact is, that writings against a free and well-proportioned government need not be guarded against by laws. They cannot often exist, and never with effect. The just and awful principles of society are rarely brought forward but when they are insulted and denied, or abused in practice. Mr Locke's Essay on Government we owe to Sir Robert Filmer, as we owe Mr Paine's to Mr Burke; indeed, between the arguments of Filmer and Burke I see no essential difference, since it is not worth disputing whether a king exists by *divine* right, or by *indissoluble human* compact, if he exists whether we will or no. If his existence be without our consent, and is to continue without benefit, it matters not whether his title be from God, or from man.

That his title is from man, and from every generation of man, without regard to the determination of former ones, hear from Mr Locke: "*All men,*" say they (*i.e.,* Filmer and his adherents), "*are* BORN *under government, and therefore they cannot be at liberty to begin a new one. Every one is born a subject to his father, or his prince, and is therefore under the perpetual tie of subjection and allegiance.* It is plain, mankind never owned nor considered any such natural *subjection that they were born in,* to one or the other, that tied them, without their own consents, to a subjection to them and their heirs."

" It is true, that whatever engagements or promises any one has made for himself, he is under the obligation of them, but cannot, by any compact whatsoever, bind his children or posterity; for his son, when a man, being altogether as free as the father, any *act of the father can no more give away the liberty of the son* than it can of anybody else."

So much for Mr Locke's opinion of the rights of man. Let us now examine his ideas of the supposed danger of trusting him with them.

" Perhaps it will be said that—the people being ignorant, and always discontented—to lay the foundation of government in the unsteady opinion˙and uncertain humour of the people, is to expose it to certain ruin; and no government will be able long to subsist if the people may set up a new legislature whenever they take offence at the old one. To this, I answer, Quite the contrary; people are not so easily got out of their old forms as some are apt to suggest; they are hardly to be prevailed with to amend the acknowledged faults in the frame they have been accustomed to; and if there be any original defects, or adventitious ones introduced by time, or corruption, it is not an easy thing to be changed, even when all the world sees there is an opportunity for it. This slowness and aversion in the people to quit their old constitutions, has, in the many revolutions which have been seen in this kingdom in this and former ages, still kept us to, or, after some interval of fruitless attempts, still brought us back again to our old legislative of kings, lords and commons; and whatever provocations have made the crown be taken from some of our princes' heads, they never carried the people so far as to place it in another line."

Gentlemen, I wish I had strength to go on with all that follows; but I have read enough, not only to maintain the true principles of government, but to put to shame the narrow system of distrusting the people.

It may be said that Mr Locke went great lengths in his positions to beat down the contrary doctrine of divine right, which was then endangering the new establishment. But that cannot be objected to David Hume, who maintains the same doctrine. Speaking of the Magna Charta in his History, vol. ii., page 88, he says, "It must be confessed that the former articles of the great charter contain such mitigations and explanations of the feudal law as are reasonable and equitable; and that the latter involve all the chief outlines of a legal government, and provide for the equal distribution of justice, and free enjoyment of property; the great object for which political society was founded by men, *which the people have a perpetual and unalienable right to recall; and which no time, nor precedent, nor statute, nor positive institution, ought to deter them from keeping ever uppermost in their thoughts and attention.*"

These authorities are sufficient to rest on; yet I cannot omit Mr Burke himself, who is, if possible, still more distinct on the subject. Speaking not of the ancient people of England, but of colonies planted almost within our memories, he says, "If there be one fact in the world perfectly clear, it is this, that the disposition of the people of America is wholly averse to any other than a free government; and this is indication enough to any honest statesman, how he ought to adapt whatever power he finds in his hands to their case. If any ask me what a free government is, I answer, THAT IT IS WHAT THE PEOPLE THINK SO; AND THAT THEY, AND NOT I, ARE THE NATURAL, LAWFUL, AND COMPETENT JUDGES OF THIS MATTER. If they practically allow me a greater degree of authority over them than is consistent with any correct ideas of perfect freedom, I ought to thank them for so great a trust, and not to endeavour to prove from thence, that they have reasoned amiss; and that, having gone so far, by analogy, they must hereafter have no enjoyment but by my pleasure."

Gentlemen, all that I have been stating hitherto has been only to show that there is not that *novelty* in the opinions of the defendant as to lead you to think he does not *bona fide* entertain them, much less when connected with the history of his life, which I

therefore brought in review before you. But still the great question remains unargued: Had he a right to promulgate these
opinions? If he entertained them, I shall argue that he had; and
although my arguments upon the liberty of the press may not to-
day be honoured with your or the Court's approbation, I shall
retire not at all disheartened, consoling myself with the reflection
that a season may arrive for their reception. The most essential
liberties of mankind have been but slowly and gradually received;
and so very late, indeed, do some of them come to maturity, that,
notwithstanding the Attorney-General tells you that the very question I am now agitating is most peculiarly for *your* consideration,
AS A JURY, under our ANCIENT constitution; yet I must remind
both YOU and HIM that your jurisdiction to consider and deal with
it at all in judgment is but A YEAR OLD. Before that late period
I ventured to maintain this very RIGHT OF A JURY over the question
of libel under the same *ancient* constitution (I do not mean before
the noble Judge now present, for the matter was gone to rest in
the courts long before he came to sit where he does, but) before a
noble and reverend magistrate of the most exalted understanding,
and of the most uncorrupted integrity.* He treated me not with
contempt, indeed, for of that his nature was incapable, but he put
me aside with indulgence, as you do a child while it is lisping its
prattle out of season; and if this cause had been tried *then*, instead
of *now*, the defendant must have been instantly convicted on the
proof of the publication, whatever *you* might have thought of his
case. Yet I have lived to see it resolved, by an almost unanimous
vote of the whole Parliament of England, that I had all along been
in the right. If this be not an awful lesson of caution concerning
opinions, where are such lessons to be read?

Gentlemen, I have insisted, at great length, upon the origin of
governments, and detailed the authorities which you have heard
upon the subject, because I consider it to be not only an essential
support, but the very foundation of the liberty of the press. If Mr
Burke be right in HIS principles of government, I admit that the
press, in my sense of its freedom, ought not to be free, *nor free in
any sense at all;* and that all addresses to the people upon the
subject of government, and all speculations of amendment, of what
kind or nature soever, are illegal and criminal, since, if the people
have, without possible recall, delegated all their authorities, they
have no jurisdiction to act, and therefore none to think or write
upon such subjects; and it would be a libel to arraign government,
or any of its acts, before those that have no jurisdiction to correct
them. But, on the other hand, as it is a settled rule in the law of
England that the subject may always address a competent jurisdiction, no legal argument can shake the freedom of the press, in my
sense of it, if I am supported in my doctrines concerning the great

* Earl of Mansfield.

unalienable right of the people, to reform or to change their governments.

It is because the liberty of the press resolves itself into this great issue that it has been, in every country, the last liberty which subjects have been able to wrest from power. Other liberties are held *under* governments; but the liberty of opinion keeps GOVERNMENTS THEMSELVES in due subjection to their duties. This has produced the martyrdom of truth in every age, and the world has been only purged from ignorance with the innocent blood of those who have enlightened it.

Gentlemen, my strength and time are wasted, and I can only make this melancholy history pass like a shadow before you.

I shall begin with the grand type and example.

The universal God of nature, the Saviour of mankind, the Fountain of all light, who came to pluck the world from eternal darkness, expired upon a cross—the scoff of infidel scorn; and His blessed apostles followed Him in the train of martyrs. When He came in the flesh, He might have come like the Mahometan prophet, as a powerful sovereign, and propagated His religion with an unconquerable sword, which even now, after the lapse of ages, is but slowly advancing under the influence of reason over the face of the earth; but such a process would have been inconsistent with His mission, which was to confound the pride, and to establish the universal rights of men. He came, therefore, in that lowly state which is represented in the gospel, and preached his consolations to the poor.

When the foundation of this religion was discovered to be invulnerable and immortal, we find political power taking the church into partnership; thus began the corruptions, both of religion and civil power; and, hand in hand together, what havoc have they not made in the world?—ruling by ignorance and the persecution of truth; but this very persecution only hastened the revival of letters and liberty. Nay, you will find that in the exact proportion that knowledge and learning have been beat down and fettered, they have destroyed the governments which bound them. The Court of Star Chamber, the first restriction of the press of England, was erected previous to all the great changes in the constitution. From that moment, no man could legally write without an Imprimatur from the State; but truth and freedom found their way with greater force through secret channels; and the unhappy Charles, *unwarned by a free press*, was brought to an ignominious death. When men can freely communicate their thoughts and their sufferings, real or imaginary, their passions spend themselves in air, like gunpowder scattered upon the surface; but, pent up by terrors, they work unseen, burst forth in a moment, and destroy everything in their course. Let reason be opposed to reason, and argument to argument, and every good government will be safe.

The usurper, Cromwell, pursued the same system of restraint in support of his government, and the end of it speedily followed.

At the restoration of Charles II. the Star Chamber Ordinance of 1637 was worked up into an Act of Parliament, and was followed up during that reign, and the short one that followed it, by the most sanguinary prosecutions. But what fact in history is more notorious than that this blind and contemptible policy prepared and hastened the Revolution? At that great era these cobwebs were all brushed away. The freedom of the press was regenerated, and the country, ruled by its affections, has since enjoyed a century of tranquillity and glory. Thus I have maintained, by English history, that, in proportion as the press has been free, English government has been secure.

Gentlemen, the same important truth may be illustrated by great authorities. Upon a subject of this kind resort cannot be had to law cases. The ancient law of England knew nothing of such libels; they began, and should have ended, with the Star Chamber. What writings are slanderous of *individuals* must be looked for where these prosecutions are recorded; but upon *general* subjects we must go to *general* writers. If, indeed, I were to refer to obscure authors, I might be answered that my very authorities were libels, instead of justifications or examples; but this cannot be said with effect of great men, whose works are classics in our language, taught in our schools, and repeatedly printed under the eye of Government.

I shall begin with the poet Milton, a great authority in all learning. It may be said, indeed, he was a republican, but that would only prove that republicanism is not incompatible with virtue. It may be said too that the work which I cite was written against previous licensing, which is not contended for to-day. But if every work were to be adjudged a libel which was adverse to the wishes of Government, or to the opinions of those who may compose it, the revival of a licenser would be a security to the public. If I present my book to a magistrate appointed by law, and he rejects it, I have only to forbear from the publication. In the forbearance I am safe; and he too is answerable to law for the abuse of his authority. But, upon the argument of to-day, a man must print at his peril, without any guide to the principles of judgment upon which his work may be afterwards prosecuted and condemned. Milton's argument therefore applies, and was meant to apply, to every interruption to writing, which, while they oppress the individual, endanger the State.

"We have them not," says Milton, "that can be heard of, from any ancient state, or polity, or church, nor by any statute left us by our ancestors, elder or later, nor from the modern custom of any reformed city, or church abroad; but from the most antichristian council, and the most tyrannous inquisition that ever existed. Till *then*, books were ever as freely admitted into the world as any other birth ; *the issue of the brain was no more stifled than the issue of the womb.*

To the pure all things are pure ; not only meats and drinks, but all kind of knowledge, whether good or evil. The knowledge cannot defile, nor consequently the books, if the will and conscience be not defiled.

"Bad books serve in many respects to discover, to confute, to forewarn, and to illustrate. Whereof, what better witness can we expect I should produce than one of your own, now sitting in Parliament, the chief of learned men reputed in this land, *Mr Selden*, whose volume of natural and national laws proves, not only by great authorities brought together, but by exquisite reasons and theorems almost mathematically demonstrative, that all opinions, YEA ERRORS, known, read, and collated, are of main service and assistance toward the speedy attainment of what is truest.

"Opinions and understanding are not such wares as to be monopolised and traded in by tickets, and statutes, and standards. We must not think to make a staple commodity of all the knowledge in the land, to mark and license it like our broadcloth and our woolpacks.

"Nor is it to the common people less than a reproach ; for if we be so jealous over them that we cannot trust them with an English pamphlet, what do we but censure them for a giddy, vicious, and ungrounded people ; in such a sick and weak estate of faith and discretion as to be able to take nothing down but through the pipe of a licenser ? That this is care or love of them we cannot pretend.

"Those corruptions which it seeks to prevent break in faster at doors which cannot be shut. To prevent men thinking and acting for themselves by restraints on the press is like to the exploits of that gallant man who thought to pound up the crows by shutting his park gate.

"This obstructing violence meets, for the most part, with an event utterly opposite to the end which it drives at. Instead of suppressing books, it raises them and invests them with a reputation. The punishment of wits enhances their authority, saith the Viscount St Albans, and a forbidden writing is thought to be a certain spark of truth that flies up in the face of them who seek to tread it out."

He then adverts to his visit to the famous Galileo, whom he found and visited in the Inquisition, "for not thinking in astronomy with the Franciscan and Dominican monks." And what event ought more deeply to interest and affect us ? THE VERY LAWS OF NATURE were to bend under the rod of a licenser. This illustrious astronomer ended his life within the bars of a prison, because, in seeing the phases of Venus through his newly-invented telescope,

he pronounced that she shone with borrowed light, and from the
sun as the centre of the universe.   This was the *mighty crime*, the
placing the sun in the centre: that sun which now inhabits it
upon the foundation of mathematical truth, which enables us to
traverse the pathless ocean, and to carry our line and rule amongst
other worlds, which, but for Galileo, we had never known, perhaps
even to the recesses of an infinite and eternal God.

Milton then, in his most eloquent address to the Parliament,
puts the liberty of the press on its true and most honourable
foundation :—

" Believe it, Lords and Commons, they who counsel ye to such
a suppressing of books, do as good as bid you suppress yourselves,
and I will soon show how.

" If it be desired to know the immediate cause of all this free
writing and free speaking, there cannot be assigned a truer than
your own mild, and free, and humane government.   It is the
liberty, Lords and Commons, which your own valorous and happy
counsels have purchased us ; liberty, which is the nurse of all great
wits.   This is that which hath rarefied and enlightened our spirits
like the influence of heaven.   This is that which hath enfranchised,
enlarged, and lifted up our apprehensions degrees above themselves.
Ye cannot make us now less capable, less knowing, less eagerly
pursuing the truth, unless ye first make yourselves that made us
so, less the lovers, less the founders of our true liberty.   We can
grow ignorant again, brutish, formal, and slavish, as ye found us ;
but you then must first become that which ye cannot be, oppressive, arbitrary, and tyrannous, as they were from whom ye have freed
us.   That our hearts are now more capacious, our thoughts now
more erected to the search and expectation of greatest and exactest
things, is the issue of your own virtue propagated in us.   Give me
the liberty to know, to utter, and to argue freely according to
conscience, above all liberties."

Gentlemen, I will yet refer you to another author, whose opinion
you may think more in point, as having lived in our own times,
and as holding the highest monarchical principles of government.
I speak of Mr Hume, who, nevertheless, considers that this liberty
of the press extends not only to abstract speculation, but to keep
the public on their guard against all the acts of their Government.

After showing the advantages of a monarchy to public freedom,
provided it is duly controlled and watched by the popular part of
the constitution, he says, " These principles account for the great
liberty of the press in these kingdoms, beyond what is indulged in
any other Government.   It is apprehended that arbitrary power
would steal in upon us were we not careful to prevent its progress,
and were there not an easy method of conveying the alarm from
one end of the kingdom to the other. *The spirit of the people
must frequently be roused in order to curb the ambition of the Court,*

and the dread of rousing this spirit must be employed to prevent that ambition. Nothing is so effectual to this purpose as the liberty of THE PRESS, by which all the learning, wit, and genius of the nation may be employed on the side of freedom, and every one be animated to its defence. *As long, therefore, as the republican part of our Government can maintain itself against the monarchical, it will naturally be careful to keep the press open, as of importance to its own preservation."*

There is another authority contemporary with the last, a splendid speaker in the Upper House of Parliament, and who held during most of his time high offices under the King. I speak of the Earl of Chesterfield, who thus expressed himself in the House of Lords:—" One of the greatest blessings, my Lords, we enjoy is liberty ; but every good in this life has its alloy of evil. Licentiousness is the alloy of liberty, it is"——

Lord KENYON. Doctor Johnson claims to pluck that *feather* from Lord Chesterfield's wing. He speaks, I believe, of the eye of the political body.

Mr ERSKINE. My Lord, I am happy that it is admitted to be a feather. I have heard it said that Lord Chesterfield borrowed that which I was just about to state, and which his Lordship has anticipated.

Lord KENYON. That very speech which did Lord Chesterfield so much honour is supposed to have been written by Doctor Johnson.

Mr ERSKINE. Gentlemen, I believe it was so, and I am much obliged to his Lordship for giving me a far higher authority for my doctrine. For though Lord Chesterfield was a man of great wit, he was undoubtedly far inferior in learning, and, what is more to the purpose, in *monarchical* opinion, to the celebrated writer to whom my Lord has now delivered the work by his authority. Doctor Johnson then says, " One of the greatest blessings we enjoy, one of the greatest blessings a people, my Lords, can enjoy, is liberty ; but every good in this life has its alloy of evil. Licentiousness is the alloy of liberty. It is an ebullition, an excrescence ; it is a speck upon the eye of the political body, but which I can never touch but with a gentle, with a trembling hand, lest I destroy the body, lest I injure the eye upon which it is apt to appear.

" There is such a connexion between licentiousness and liberty, that it is not easy to correct the one without dangerously wounding the other: it is extremely hard to distinguish the true limit between them : like a changeable silk, we can easily see there are two different colours, but we cannot easily discover where the one ends, or where the other begins."

I confess I cannot help agreeing with this learned author. THE DANGER OF TOUCHING THE PRESS IS THE DIFFICULTY OF MARKING ITS LIMITS. My learned friend, who has just gone out of Court, has drawn no line, and unfolded no principle. He has not told us, if *this* book is condemned, *what* book may be written. If I may not write against the existence of a monarchy, and recommend a republic, may I write against any part of the Government? May I say that we should be better without a House of Lords, or a House of Commons, or a Court of Chancery, or any other given part of our establishment? Or if, as has been hinted, a work may be libellous for stating even *legal* matter with *sarcastic* phrase, the difficulty becomes the greater, and the liberty of the press more impossible to define.

The same author, pursuing the subject, and speaking of the fall of Roman liberty, says, " But this sort of liberty came soon after to be called licentiousness ; for we are told that Augustus, after having established his empire, restored order in Rome by restraining licentiousness. God forbid we should in this country have order restored or licentiousness restrained, at so dear a rate as the people of Rome paid for it to Augustus !

" Let us consider, my Lords, that arbitrary power has seldom or never been introduced into any country at once. It must be introduced by slow degrees, and as it were step by step, lest the people should see its approach. The barriers and fences of the people's liberty must be plucked up one by one, and some plausible pretences must be found for removing or hoodwinking, one after another, those sentries who are posted by the constitution of a free country for warning the people of their danger. When these preparatory steps are once made, the people may then, indeed, with regret, see slavery and arbitrary power making long strides over their land ; but it will be too late to think of preventing or avoiding the impending ruin.

" The stage, my Lords, and the press, are two of our out-sentries : if we remove them, if we hoodwink them, if we throw them in fetters, the enemy may surprise us."

Gentlemen, this subject was still more lately put in the justest and most forcible light by a noble person high in the magistracy, whose mind is not at all tuned to the introduction of disorder by improper popular excesses: I mean Lord Loughborongh, Chief Justice of the Court of Common Pleas. I believe I can answer for the correctness of my note, which I shall follow up with the opinion of another member of the Lords' House of Parliament, the present Earl Stanhope ; or rather, I shall take Lord Stanhope first, as his Lordship introduces the subject by adverting to this argument of Lord Loughborough's. " If," says Lord Stanhope, " our boasted liberty of the press were to consist only in the liberty to write *in praise* of the constitution, this is a liberty enjoyed under many *arbitrary* governments. I suppose it would not be deemed quite an unpardonable offence, even by the Empress of Russia, if any man were to take into his head to write a panegyric upon the Russian form of government. Such a liberty as that might therefore properly be termed the *Russian liberty of the press*. But, the *English liberty of the press* is of a very different description : for, by the law of England, it is not prohibited to publish speculative works upon the constitution, whether *they contain praise or censure* " (*Lord Stanhope's Defence of the Libel Bill*).

You see, therefore, as far as the general principle goes, I am supported by the opinion of Lord Stanhope, for otherwise the noble Lord has written a libel himself, by exciting other people to write *whatever they may think*, be it good or evil, of the constitution of the country. As to the other high authority, Lord Loughborough, I will read what applies to this subject—" Every man," said Lord Loughborough, "may publish at his discretion his opinions concerning forms and systems of government. If they be wise and enlightening, the world will gain by them; if they be weak and absurd, they will be laughed at and forgotten; and if they be *bonâ fide*, they cannot be criminal, however ERRONEOUS. On the other hand, the purpose and the direction may give a different turn to writings whose common construction is harmless, or even meritorious. · Suppose men, assembled in disturbance of the peace, to pull down mills or turnpikes, or to do any other mischief, and that a mischievous person should disperse among them an excitation to the planned mischief known to both writer and reader, *To your tents, O Israel;* that publication would be criminal ;—not as a libel, not as an abstract writing, but as an act; and the act being the crime, *it must be stated as a fact extrinsic on the record :* for otherwise, a Court of Error could have no jurisdiction but over the *natural construction of the writing ;* nor would the defendant have any notice of such matter at the trial, without a charge on the record. To give the jury cognisance of any matter beyond the construction of the writing, the averment should be, in the case as I have instanced, that certain persons were, as I have described, assembled; and that the publisher, intending to excite these persons so assembled, wrote *so and so.* Here the crime is complete, and consists in an *overt act of wickedness evidenced by a writing.*"

In answer to all these authorities, the Attorney-General may say that, if Mr Paine had written his observations with the views of those high persons and under other circumstances, he would be protected and acquitted :—to which I can only answer, that no facts or circumstances attending his work are either *charged or proved ;*—that you have *no* jurisdiction whatever, but over the natural construction of the work before you, and that I am therefore brought without a flaw to the support of the passages which are the particular subject of complaint.

Gentlemen, I am not unmindful how long I have already trespassed upon your patience ; and, recollecting the nature of the human mind, and how much, for a thousand reasons, I have to

struggle against at this moment, I shall not be disconcerted if any
of you should appear anxious to retire from the pain of hearing me
further. It has been said, in the newspapers, that my vanity has
forwarded my zeal in this cause ;—but I might appeal even to the
authors of those paragraphs, whether a situation ever existed which
vanity would have been fonder to fly from—the task of speaking
against every known prepossession—with every countenance, as it
were, planted and lifted up against me. But I stand at this bar to
give to a criminal arraigned before it the defence which the law of
the country entitles him to. If any of my arguments be indecent,
or unfit for the Court to hear, the noble Judge presides to interrupt them : if all, or any of them, are capable of an answer,
they will be answered: or if they be so unfounded in your own
minds, who are to judge of them, as not to call for refutation,
your verdict in a moment will overthrow all that has been said.
We shall then have all discharged our duties. It is your unquestionable province to judge, and mine not less unquestionably to
address your judgments.

When the noble Judge and myself were counsel for Lord George
Gordon in 1781, it was not considered by that jury, nor imputed
to us by anybody, that we were contending for the privileges of
overawing the House of Commons, or recommending the conflagration of this city. *I* am doing the same duty now which *my Lord
and I* then did in concert together ; and, whatever may become of
the cause, *I expect to be heard ;* conscious that no just obloquy can
be, or will in the end be, cast upon me for having done my duty in
the manner I have endeavoured to perform it.—Sir, I shall name
you presently.*

Gentlemen, I come now to observe on the passages selected by
the information ; and with regard to the first, I shall dispose of it
in a moment.

" All *hereditary* government is in its nature tyranny. An heritable crown, or an heritable throne, or by what other fanciful
name such things may be called, have no other significant explanation than that mankind are heritable *property.* To *inherit*
a government is to *inherit* the *people* as if they were flocks and
herds."

And is it to be endured, says the Attorney-General, that the
people of this country are to be told that they are driven like oxen
or sheep ? Certainly not. I am of opinion that a more dangerous
doctrine cannot be instilled into the people of England. But who
instils such a doctrine ? I deny that it is instilled by Mr Paine.
When he maintains that hereditary monarchy inherits a people
like flocks and herds, it is clear from the context (*which is kept
out of view*), that he is combating the proposition in Mr Burke's

---

* This expression was provoked by the conduct of one of the jury, which this
rebuke put an end to.—ED.

book, which asserts that the hereditary monarchy of England is
fastened upon the people of England by *indissoluble compact.*
Mr Paine, on the contrary, asserts the King of England to be the
magistrate of the people, existing by their consent, which is utterly
incompatible with their being driven like herds. His argument,
therefore, is this, and it retorts on his adversary: he says, Such
a king as *you*, Mr Burke, represent the King of England to be,
inheriting the people by virtue of conquest, or of some compact,
which, having once existed, cannot be dissolved while the original
terms of it are kept, *is an inheritance like flocks and herds.* But
I deny that to be the King of England's title. He is *the magistrate
of the people*, and that title I respect. It is to your own imaginary
King of England therefore, and not to His Majesty, that your unfounded innuendoes apply. It is the monarchs of Russia and Prussia,
and all governments fastened upon unwilling subjects by hereditary
indefeasible titles, who are stigmatised by Paine as inheriting the
people like flocks. The sentence, therefore, must either be taken
in the pure abstract, and then it is not only merely speculative, but
the application of it to our own Government fails altogether, or it
must be taken connected with the matter which constitutes the
application, and then it is Mr BURKE'S KING OF ENGLAND, and
NOT His Majesty, whose title is denied.

I pass, therefore, to the next passage, which appears to be an
extraordinary selection. It is taken at a leap from page 21 to page
47, and breaks in at the words " This convention." The sentence
selected stands thus: " This convention met at Philadelphia in
May 1787, of which General Washington was elected president.
He was not at that time connected with any of the State governments, or with Congress. He delivered up his commission when
the war ended, and since then had lived a private citizen.

" The convention went deeply into all the subjects; and having,
after a variety of debate and investigation, agreed among themselves upon the several parts of a federal constitution, the next
question was, the manner of giving it authority and practice.

" For this purpose, they did not, like a cabal of courtiers, send
for a Dutch stadtholder, or a German elector; but they referred
the whole matter to the sense and interest of the country."

This sentence, standing thus by itself, may appear to be a mere
sarcasm on King William, upon those who effected the Revolution,
and upon the Revolution itself, without any reasoning or deduction; but when the context and sequel are looked at and compared,
it will appear to be a serious historical comparison between the
Revolution effected in England in 1688, and the late one in
America when she established her independence; and no man
can doubt that his judgment on that comparison was sincere. But
where is the libel on the Constitution? For whether King William was brought over here by the sincerest and justest motives of

the whole people of England, each man acting for himself, or from the motives and through the agencies imputed by the defendant, it signifies not one farthing at this time of day to the establishment itself. Blackstone properly warns us not to fix our obedience or affection to the Government on the motives of our ancestors, or the rectitude of their proceedings, but to be satisfied with what is established. This is safe reasoning, and, for my own part, I should not be differently affected to the constitution of my country, which my own understanding approved, whether angels or demons had given it birth.

Do any of you love the Reformation the less because Henry the Eighth was the author of it? or because lust and poverty, not religion, were his motives? He had squandered the treasures of his father, and he preferred Anne Bullen to his queen: these were the causes which produced it. What then? Does that affect the purity of our reformed religion? Does it undermine its establishment, or shake the King's title, to the exclusion of those who held by the religion it had abolished? Will the Attorney-General affirm that I could be convicted of a libel for a whole volume of asperity against Henry the Eighth, merely because he effected the Reformation; and if not, why against King William, who effected the Revolution? Where is the line to be drawn? Are one, two, or three centuries to constitute the statute of limitation? Nay, do not our own historians detail this very cabal of courtiers from the records of our own country? If you will turn to Hume's History, volume the eighth, page 188, &c., &c., you will find that he states, at great length, the whole detail of intrigues which paved the way for the Revolution, and the interested coalition of parties which gave it effect.

But what of all this, concerning the motives of parties, which is recorded by Hume? The question is, *What is the thing brought about—Not*, HOW *it was brought about.* If it stands, as Blackstone argues it, upon the consent of our ancestors, followed up by our own, no individual can withdraw his obedience. If he dislikes the establishment, let him seek elsewhere for another; I am not contending for uncontrolled *conduct*, but for freedom of *opinion*.

With regard to what has been stated of the *Edwards* and *Henries*, and the other princes under which the author can only discover " *restrictions on power, but nothing of a constitution ;*" surely my friend is not in earnest when he selects that passage as a libel.

Paine insists that there was no constitution under these princes, and that English liberty was obtained from usurped power by the struggles of the people. So SAY I. And I think it for the honour and advantage of the country that it should be known. Was there any freedom after the original establishment of the Normans by conquest? Was not the MAGNA CHARTA wrested from John by *open force of arms* at Runnymede? Was it not again re-enacted whilst menacing arms were in the hands of the people? Were not its stipulations broken through, and two-and-forty times re-enacted by Parliament, upon the firm demand of the people in the following reigns? I protest it fills me with astonishment to hear these truths brought in question.

I was formerly called upon, under the discipline of a college, to maintain them, and was rewarded for being thought to have suc-cessfully maintained that our present Constitution was by no means a remnant of Saxon liberty, nor any other institution of liberty, but the pure consequence of the oppression of the Norman tenures, which, spreading the spirit of freedom from one end of the kingdom to another, enabled our brave fathers, inch by inch, not to reconquer, *but for the first time to obtain* those privileges which are the un-alienable inheritance of all mankind.

But why do we speak of the Edwards and Henries, when Hume himself expressly says, notwithstanding all we have heard to-day of the antiquity of our Constitution, that our monarchy was nearly absolute till the middle of last century. It is his " Essay on the Liberty of the Press," vol. i., page 15—

" All absolute governments, and such in a great measure was England till the middle of the last century, *notwithstanding the numerous panegyrics on* ANCIENT *English liberty*, must very much depend on the administration."

This is Hume's opinion; the conclusion of a grave historian from all that he finds recorded as the materials for history: and shall it be said that Mr Paine is to be punished for writing to-day what was before written by another, who is now a distinguished classic in the language? All the verdicts in the world will not make such injustice palatable to an impartial public or to posterity.

The next passage arraigned is this (page 56) : " The attention of the Government of England (for I rather choose to call it by this name than the English Government) appears, since its politi-cal connexion with Germany, to have been so completely engrossed and absorbed by foreign affairs, and the means of raising taxes, that it seems to exist for no other purposes. Domestic concerns are neglected ; and with respect to regular law, there is scarcely such a thing."

That the Government of this country has, in consequence of its connexion with the continent, and the continental wars which it has occasioned, been continually loaded with grievous taxes, no man can dispute : and I appeal to your justice, whether this sub-ject has not been, for years together, the constant topic of unre-proved declamation and grumbling.

As to what he says with regard to there hardly existing such a thing as regular law, he speaks *in the abstract* of the complexity of our system ; he does not arraign the administration of justice *in its practice.* But with regard to criticisms and strictures on the general system of our Government, it has been echoed over and over again by various authors, and even from the pulpits of our country. I have a sermon in court, written during the American war by a person of great eloquence and piety, in which he looks forward to an exemption from the intolerable grievances of our old legal system in the infant establishment of the New World :—

" It may be in the purposes of Providence, on yon western shores, to raise the bulwark of a purer reformation than ever Britain patronised : to found a less burdensome, more auspicious, stable, and incorruptible government than ever Britain has enjoyed ; and to establish there a system of law more just and simple in its principles, less intricate, dubious, and dilatory in its proceedings, more mild and equitable in its sanctions, more easy and more certain in its execution ; wherein no man can err through ignorance of what concerns him, or want justice through poverty or weakness, or escape it by legal artifice, or civil privileges, or interposing power ; wherein the rule of conduct shall not be hidden or disguised in the language of principles and customs that died with the barbarism which gave them birth ; wherein hasty formulas shall not dissipate the reverence that is due to the tribunals and transactions of justice ; wherein obsolete prescripts shall not pervert, nor entangle, nor impede the administration of it, nor in any instance expose it to derision or to disregard ; wherein misrepresentation shall have no share in deciding upon right and truth ; and under which no man shall grow great by the wages of chicanery, or thrive by the quarrels that are ruinous to his employers."

This is ten times stronger than Mr Paine; but who ever thought of prosecuting Mr Cappe ? *

In various other instances you will find defects in our jurisprudence pointed out and lamented, and not seldom by persons called upon by their situations to deliver the law in the seat of magistracy : therefore, the author's *general* observation does not appear to be that species of attack upon the magistracy of the country as to fall within the description of a libel.

With respect to the two Houses of Parliament, I believe I shall be able to show you that the very person who introduced this controversy, and who certainly is considered by those who now administer the government, as a man usefully devoted to maintain the constitution of the country in the present crisis, has himself made remarks upon these assemblies, that upon comparison you will think more severe than those which are the subject of the Attorney-General's animadversion. The passage in Mr Paine runs thus :

" With respect to *the two Houses* of which the English Parlia-

* A late eminent and pious minister at York.

ment is composed, they appear to be effectually influenced into one, and, as a legislature, to have no temper of its own. The minister, whoever he at any time may be, touches it as with an opium wand, and it sleeps obedience.

" But if we look at the distinct abilities of the two Houses, the difference will appear so great as to show the inconsistency of placing power where there can be no certainty of the judgment to use it. Wretched as the state of representation is in England, it is manhood compared with what is called the House of Lords ; and so little is this nicknamed House regarded, that the people scarcely inquire at any time what it is doing. It appears also to be most under influence, and the furthest removed from the general interest of the nation."

The conclusion of the sentence, and which was meant by Paine as evidence of the previous assertion, the Attorney-General has omitted in the information and in his speech ; it is this : " In the debate on engaging in the Russian and Turkish war, the majority in the House of Peers in favour of it was upwards of ninety, when in the other House, which is more than double its numbers, the majority was sixty-three."

The terms, however, in which Mr Burke speaks of the House of Lords are still more expressive : " It is something more than a century ago since we voted the House of Lords useless. They have now voted themselves so, and the whole hope of reformation (*speaking of the House of Commons*) is cast upon us." This senti-ment Mr Burke not only expressed in his place in Parliament, where no man can call him to an account ; but it has been since repeatedly printed amongst his works. Indeed his opinion of BOTH THE HOUSES OF PARLIAMENT, which I am about to read to you, was originally published as a separate pamphlet, and applied to the settled habitual abuses of these high assemblies. Remember, I do not use them as *argumenta ad hominem*, or *ad invidiam* against the author; for if I did, it could be no defence of Mr Paine. But I use them as high authority, the work * having been the just foundation of substantial and lasting reputation. Would to God that any part of it were capable of being denied or doubted !

" Against the being of Parliament I am satisfied no designs have ever been entertained since the Revolution. Every one must perceive that it is strongly the interest of the Court to have some second cause interposed between the ministers and the people. The gentlemen of the House of Commons have an interest equally strong in sustaining the part of that intermediate cause. However they may hire out the *usufruct* of their voices, they never will part with the *fee and inheritance*. Accordingly, those who have been of

* Mr Burke's " Thoughts on the Cause of the Present Discontents," published in 1775.

the most known devotion to the will and pleasure of a Court, have at the same time been most forward in asserting an high authority in the House of Commons. *When they knew who were to use that authority, and how it was to be employed, they thought it never could be carried too far.* It must be always the wish of an unconstitutional statesman, that an House of Commons *who are entirely dependent upon him, should have every right of the people dependent upon their pleasure.* FOR IT WAS DISCOVERED THAT THE FORMS OF A FREE AND THE ENDS OF AN ARBITRARY GOVERNMENT, WERE THINGS NOT ALTOGETHER INCOMPATIBLE.

" The power of the Crown, almost dead and rotten as prerogative, has grown up anew, with much more strength and far less odium, under the name of influence. An influence which operates without noise and violence,—which converts the very antagonist into the instrument of power,—which contains in itself a perpetual principle of growth and renovation ; and which the distresses and the prosperity of the country equally tend to augment,—was an admirable substitute for a prerogative that, being only the offspring of antiquated prejudices, had moulded in its original stamina irresistible principles of decay and dissolution. The ignorance of the people is a bottom but for a temporary system ; but the interest of active men in the state is a foundation perpetual and infallible."

Mr Burke, therefore, in page 66, speaking of the same Court party, says :—

" Parliament was indeed the great object of all these politics, the end at which they aimed, as well as the INSTRUMENT by which they were to operate."

And pursuing the subject in page 70, proceeds as follows :—

" They who will not conform their conduct to the public good, and cannot support it by the prerogative of the Crown, have adopted a new plan. They have totally abandoned the shattered and old-fashioned fortress of Prerogative, and made a lodgment in the stronghold of Parliament itself. If they have any evil design to which there is no ordinary legal power commensurate, they bring it into Parliament. *There the whole is executed from the beginning to the end ; and the power of obtaining their object absolute ; and the safety in the proceeding perfect ; no rules to confine, nor after-reckonings to terrify.* For Parliament cannot with any great propriety punish others for things in which they themselves have been ACCOMPLICES. Thus its control upon the executory power is lost, because it is made to partake in every considerable act of government ; *and impeachment, that great guardian of the purity of the constitution, is in danger of being lost even to the idea of it.*"

" Until this time, the opinion of the people, through the power of an Assembly, still in some sort popular, led to the greatest honours and emoluments in the gift of the Crown. Now the principle is reversed ; and the favour of the Court is the only sure way of obtaining and holding those honours which ought to be IN THE DISPOSAL OF THE PEOPLE."

Mr Burke, in page 100, observes with great truth, that the mischiefs he complained of did not at all arise from the monarchy, but from the Parliament, and that it was the duty of the people to look to it. He says, " The distempers of monarchy were the great subjects of apprehension and redress, in the *last century* ; *in this*, the distempers of Parliament."

Not the distempers of Parliament in this year or the last, but in *this century*, *i.e.*, its settled habitual distemper. " It is not in Parliament alone that the remedy for parliamentary disorders can be completed ; and hardly indeed can it begin there. Until a confidence in Government is re-established, the people ought to be *excited* to a more strict and detailed attention to the conduct of their representatives. Standards for judging more systematically upon their conduct ought to be settled in the meetings of counties and corporations, and frequent and correct lists of the voters in all important questions ought to be procured.

" By such means something may be done, since it may appear who those are, that, by an indiscriminate support of all administrations, have totally banished all integrity and confidence out of public proceedings; have confounded the best men with the worst; and weakened and dissolved, instead of strengthening and compacting, the general frame of Government."

I wish it was possible to read the whole of this most important volume—but the consequences of these truths contained in it were all eloquently summed up by the author in his speech upon the reform of the household.

" But what I confess was uppermost with me, what I bent the whole course of my mind to, was the reduction of that corrupt influence which is itself the perennial spring of all prodigality and disorder ; which loads us more than millions of debt ; which takes away vigour from our arms, wisdom from our councils, and every shadow of authority and credit from the most venerable parts of our constitution."

The same important truths were held out to the whole public, upon a still later occasion, by the person now at the head of His Majesty's councils ; and so high (as it appears) in the confidence of the nation.* *He*, not in the *abstract*, like the author before you, but upon the *spur of the occasion*, and in the teeth of what had been just declared in the House of Commons, came to, and acted upon, resolutions which are contained in this book †—resolutions pointed to the purification of a Parliament dangerously corrupted into the very state described by Mr Paine. Remember here, too, that I impute no censurable conduct to Mr Pitt. It was the most

---

* Mr Pitt. † Mr Erskine took up a book.

brilliant passage in his life, and I should have thought his life a better one if he had continued uniform in the support of opinions which it is said he has not changed, and which certainly have had nothing to change them. But at all events, I have a right to make use of the authority of his splendid talents and high situation, not merely to protect the defendant, but the public, by resisting the precedent,—that what one man may do in England with approbation and glory, shall conduct another man to a pillory or a prison.

The abuses pointed out by the man before you led that right honourable gentleman to associate with many others of high rank, under the banners of the Duke of Richmond, whese name stands at the head of the list, and to pass various public resolutions concerning the absolute necessity of purifying the House of Commons; and we collect the plan from a preamble entered in the book: " Whereas the life, liberty, and property of every man is or may be affected by the law of the land in which he lives, and every man is bound to pay obedience to the same.

" And whereas, by the constitution of this kingdom, the right of making laws is vested in three estates, of King, Lords, and Commons, in Parliament assembled, and the consent of all the three said estates, comprehending the whole community, is necessary to make laws to bind the whole community. And whereas the House of Commons represents all the Commons of the realm, and the consent of the House of Commons binds the consent of all the Commons of the realm, and in all cases on which the legislature is competent to decide.

" And whereas no man is, or can be actually represented who hath not a vote in the election of his representative.

" And whereas it is the right of every commoner of this realm (infants, persons of insane mind, and criminals incapacitated by law, only excepted) to have a vote in the election of the representative who is to give his consent to the making of laws by which he is to be bound.

" And whereas the number of persons who are suffered to vote for electing the members of the House of Commons, do not at this time amount to one-sixth part of the whole commons of this realm, whereby far the greater part of the said commons are deprived of their right to elect their representatives ; and the consent of the majority of the whole community to the passing of laws, is given by persons whom they have not delegated for such purposes ; and to which the said majority have not in fact consented by themselves or by their representatives.

" And whereas the state of election of members of the House of Commons hath in process of time so grossly deviated from its simple and natural principle of representation and equality, that in several places the members are returned by the property of one man ; that the smallest boroughs send as many members as the largest counties, and that a majority of the representatives of the whole nation are chosen by a number of votes not exceeding twelve thousand."

These, with many others were published, not as *abstract, speculative writings*, but within a few days after the House of Commons had declared that no such rights existed, and that no alteration was necessary in the representation. It was *then* that they met at the Thatched House and published their opinions and resolutions to the country at large. Were any of them prosecuted for these proceedings? Certainly not, for they were legal proceedings. But I desire you, as men of honour and truth, to compare all this with Mr Paine's expression of the minister's touching Parliament with his opiate wand, and let equal justice be done—*that is all I ask*—let all be punished, or none. Do not let Mr Paine be held out to the contempt of the public upon the score of his observations on Parliament, while others are enjoying all the sweets which attend a supposed attachment to their country, who have not only expressed the same sentiments, but have reduced their opinions to practice.

But *now* every man is to be cried down for such opinions. I observed that my learned friend significantly raised his voice in naming Mr Horne Tooke, as if to connect him with Paine, or Paine with him. This is exactly the same course of justice: for, after all, he said nothing of Mr Tooke. What could he have said, but that he was a man of great talents, and a subscriber with the great names I have read in proceedings which they have thought fit to desert?

Gentlemen, let others hold their opinions, and change them at their pleasure; I shall ever maintain it to be the dearest privilege of the people of Great Britain to watch over everything that affects their happiness, either in the system of their government or in the practice, and that for this purpose THE PRESS MUST BE FREE. It has always been so, and much evil has been corrected by it. If Government finds itself annoyed by it, let it examine its own conduct, and it will find the cause; let it amend it, and it will find remedy.

Gentlemen, I am no friend to sarcasms in the discussion of grave subjects, but you must take writers according to the view of the mind at the moment; Mr Burke, as often as anybody, indulges in it. Hear his reason, in his speech on reform, for not taking away the salaries from Lords who attend upon the British Court. " You would," said he, " have the Court deserted by all the nobility of the kingdom.

" Sir, the most serious mischiefs would follow from such a desertion. Kings are naturally lovers of low company; they are so elevated above all the rest of mankind, that they must look upon all their subjects as on a level : they are rather apt to hate than to love their nobility on account of the occasional resistance to their will, which will be made by their virtue, their petulance, or their pride. It must indeed be admitted, that many of the nobility are as perfectly willing to act the part of flatterers, tale-bearers, parasites, pimps, and buffoons, as any of the lowest and vilest of mankind can possibly be. But they are not properly qualified for this object of their ambition. The want of a regular education, and early habits, with some lurking remains of their dignity, will never permit them to become a match for an Italian eunuch, a mountebank, a fiddler, a player, or any regular practitioner of that tribe. The Roman emperors, almost from the beginning, threw themselves into such hands ; and the mischief increased every day till its decline and its final ruin. It is, therefore, of very great importance (provided the thing is not overdone), to contrive such an establishment as must, almost whether a prince will or not, bring into daily and hourly offices about his person a great number of his first nobility ; and it is rather an useful prejudice that gives them a pride in such a servitude : though they are not much the better for a Court, a Court will be much the better for them. I have, therefore, not attempted to reform any of the offices of honour about the King's person."

What is all this but saying that a King is an animal so incurably addicted to low company as generally to bring on by it the ruin of nations ; but nevertheless, he is to be kept as a necessary evil, and his propensities bridled by surrounding him with a parcel of miscreants still worse, if possible, but better than those he would choose for himself. This, therefore, if taken by itself, would be a most abominable and libellous sarcasm on kings and nobility ; but look at the whole speech, and you observe a great system of regulation ; and no man, I believe, ever doubted Mr Burke's attachment to monarchy. To judge, therefore, of any part of a writing, THE WHOLE MUST BE READ.

With the same view, I will read to you the beginning of Harrington's " Oceana ; " but it is impossible to name this well-known author without exposing to just contempt and ridicule the ignorant or profligate misrepresentations which are vomited forth upon the public, to bear down every man as desperately wicked who in any age or country has countenanced a republic, for the mean purpose of prejudging this trial.

[Mr Erskine took up a book, but laid it down again without reading from it, saying something to the gentleman who sat near him, in a low voice, which the reporter did not hear.]

Is this the way to support the English constitution ? Are these the means by which Englishmen are to be taught to cherish it ? I say, if the man upon trial were stained with blood instead of ink, if he were covered over with crimes which human nature would start at the naming of, the means employed against him would not be the less disgraceful.

For this notable purpose, then, Harrington, *not above a week ago*,* was handed out to us as a low, obscure wretch, involved in the murder of the monarch and the destruction of the monarchy, and as addressing his despicable works at the shrine of an usurper. Yet this very Harrington, this low blackguard, was descended (you may see his pedigree at the Heralds' Office for sixpence) from eight dukes, three marquises, seventy earls, twenty-seven viscounts, and thirty-six barons, sixteen of whom were knights of the Garter ; a descent which I think would save a man from disgrace in any of the circles of Germany. But what was he besides ? A BLOOD-STAINED RUFFIAN ? Oh, brutal ignorance of the history of the country ! He was the most affectionate servant of Charles the First, from whom he never concealed his opinions ; for it is observed by Wood, that the King greatly affected his company ; but when they happened to talk of a commonwealth, he would scarcely endure it. " I know not," says Toland, " which most to commend: the King, for trusting an honest man, though a republican ; or Harrington, for owning his principles while he served a King."

But did his opinions affect his conduct ? Let history again answer. He preserved his fidelity to his unhappy prince to the very last, after all his fawning courtiers had left him to his enraged subjects. He stayed with him while a prisoner in the Isle of Wight ; came up by stealth to follow the fortunes of his monarch and master ; even hid himself in the boot of the coach when he was conveyed to Windsor ; and, ending as he began, fell into his arms and fainted on the scaffold.

After Charles's death, the " Oceana" was written, and as if it were written from justice and affection to his memory; for it breathes the same noble and spirited regard, and asserts that it was not CHARLES that brought on the destruction of the *monarchy*, but the feeble and ill-constituted nature of monarchy *itself*.

But the book was a flattery to Cromwell. Once more and finally let history decide. The " Oceana" was seized by the Usurper as a libel, and the way it was recovered is remarkable. I mention it to show that Cromwell was a wise man in himself, and knew on what governments must stand for their support.

Harrington waited on the Protector's daughter to beg for his book, which her father had taken, and on entering her apartment, snatched up her child and ran away. On her following him with surprise and terror, he turned to her and said, " I know what you feel as a mother, feel then for ME : your father has got MY child :" meaning the " Oceana." The " Oceana" was afterwards restored

* A pamphlet had been published just before putting T. Paine and Harrington on the same footing—as obscure blackguards.

on her petition: Cromwell answering with the sagacity of a sound politician, " Let him have his book ; if my government is made to stand, it has nothing to fear from PAPER SHOT." He said true. No GOOD government will ever be battered by paper shot. Montesquieu says that " In a free nation, it matters not whether individuals reason well or ill; it is sufficient that they *do* reason. Truth arises from the collision, and from hence springs liberty, which is a security from the effect of reasoning." The Attorney-General has read extracts from Mr Adams's answer to this book. Let others write answers to it, like Mr Adams; I am not insisting upon the infallibility of Mr Paine's doctrines ; if they are erroneous, let them be answered, and truth will spring from the collision.

Milton wisely says, that a disposition in a nation to this species of controversy is no proof of sedition or degeneracy, but quite the reverse. [I omitted to cite the passage with the others.] In speaking of this subject, he rises into that inexpressibly sublime style of writing wholly peculiar to himself. He was, indeed, no plagiary from anything human ; he looked up for light and expression, as he himself wonderfully describes it, by devout prayer to that great Being who is the source of all utterance and knowledge ; and who sendeth out His seraphim with the hallowed fire of His altar to touch and purify the lips of whom He pleases. " When the cheerfulness of the people," says this mighty poet, " is so sprightly up as that it has not only wherewith to guard well its own freedom and safety, but to spare and to bestow upon the solidest and sublimest points of controversy and new invention, it betokens us not degenerated nor drooping to a fatal decay, but casting off the old and wrinkled skin of corruption, to outlive these pangs, and wax young again, entering the glorious ways of truth and prosperous virtue, destined to become great and honourable in these latter ages. Methinks I see, in my mind, a noble and puissant nation rousing herself, like a strong man after sleep, and shaking her invincible locks : methinks I see her as an eagle muing her mighty youth, and kindling her undazzled eyes at the full mid-day beam ; purging and unscaling her long-abused sight at the fountain itself of heavenly radiance ; while the whole noise of timorous and flocking birds, with those also that love the twilight, flutter about, amazed at what she means, and in their envious gabble would prognosticate a year of sects and schisms."

Gentlemen, what Milton only saw in his mighty imagination, I see in fact; what he expected, but which never came to pass, I see now fulfilling: methinks I see this noble and puissant nation, not degenerated and drooping to a fatal decay, but casting off the wrinkled skin of corruption to put on again the vigour of her youth. And it is because others as well as myself see this that we have all this uproar !—France and its constitution are the mere pretences. It is because Britons begin to recollect the inheritance of their own constitution, left them by their ancestors:—it is because they are awakened to the corruptions which have fallen upon its most valuable parts, that forsooth the nation is in danger of being destroyed by a single pamphlet. I have marked the course of this alarm: it began with the renovation of those exertions for the public which the alarmists themselves had originated and deserted; and they became louder and louder when they saw them avowed and supported by my admirable friend Mr Fox, the most eminently honest and enlightened statesman that history brings us acquainted with: a man whom to name is to honour, but whom in attempting adequately to describe, I must fly to Mr Burke, my constant refuge when eloquence is necessary: a man, who to relieve the sufferings of the most distant nation, "put to the hazard his ease, his security, his interest, his power, even his darling popularity, for the benefit of a people whom he had never seen." How much more then for the inhabitants of his native country!—yet this is the man who has been censured and disavowed in the manner we have lately seen.

Gentlemen, I have but a few more words to trouble you with: I take my leave of you with declaring, that all this freedom which I have been endeavouring to assert is no more than the ancient freedom which belongs to our own inbred constitution. I have not asked you to acquit Thomas Paine upon any new lights, or upon any principle but that of the law, which you are sworn to administer:—my great object has been to inculcate, that wisdom and policy, which are the parents of the government of Great Britain, forbid this jealous eye over her subjects; and that, on the contrary, they cry aloud in the language of the poet, adverted to by Lord Chatham on the memorable subject of America, *unfortunately without effect*—

> " Be to their faults a little blind,
> Be to their virtues very kind ;
> Let all their thoughts be unconfined,
> And clap your padlock on the mind."

Engage the people by their affections,—convince their reason,—and they will be loyal from the only principle that can make loyalty sincere, vigorous, or rational,—a conviction that it is their truest interest, and that their government is for their good. Constraint is the natural parent of resistance, and a pregnant proof that reason is not on the side of those who use it. You must all remember Lucian's pleasant story: Jupiter and a countryman were walking together, conversing with great freedom and familiarity upon the subject of heaven and earth. The countryman listened with attention and acquiescence while Jupiter strove only to convince him; but happening to hint a doubt, Jupiter turned hastily round and threatened him with his thunder. "Ah, ah!" says the countryman, "now, Jupiter, I know that you are wrong; you are always wrong when you appeal to your thunder."

This is the case with me—I can reason with the people of England, but I cannot fight against the thunder of authority.

Gentlemen, this is my defence for free opinions.   With regard to myself, I am, and always have been, obedient and affectionate to *the law* :—to that rule of action, as long as I exist, I shall ever give voice and my conduct; but I shall ever do as I have done to-day, maintain the dignity of my high profession, and perform, as I understand them, all its important duties.

[Mr Attorney-General arose immediately to reply to Mr Erskine, when Mr Campbell (the foreman of the jury) said,—My Lord, I am authorised by the jury to inform the Attorney-General that a reply is not necessary for them, unless the Attorney-General wishes to make it, or your Lordship.   Mr Attorney-General sat down, and the jury gave in their verdict,—GUILTY.]

SPEECH *on the Prosecution of the Publisher of the "Age of Reason."*

THE SUBJECT.

To the trial of Thomas Paine we subjoin Lord Erskine's speech on the prosecution of the printer and publisher of the "Age of Reason," written by the same author. We print it in this place, though much out of the chronological order, as it appears to have been delivered in the year 1797, for two reasons—first, because, in preserving arguments illustrating the principles of British liberty, we are desirous not to be considered as in any manner sanctioning invectives against our admirable constitution ; secondly, because we owe it to Lord Erskine himself, whose speech upon the following prosecution may be considered as containing his own opinions and principles ; it appearing to have been spoken more in his own personal character than as an advocate ; and the result seems rather to be against the full application of the arguments maintained by his Lordship in defending the publication of the "Rights of Man." Because, if it be law that though a man may reason upon controversial points of divinity, however directly his reasonings may contravene the Scriptures as they are received and interpreted by our ecclesiastical establishment, yet that he may not, without being guilty of a misdemeanour, revile in gross and indecent terms the authority and doctrines of the Gospel, it seems to follow, that Thomas Paine, though he might legally have impugned, by argument, the principles of the British Government, yet could not, without being guilty of a libel, defame and ridicule the very foundation of it. in the gross and indecent terms which characterise the second part of the "Rights of Man," for which Mr Paine was indicted. We conceive, therefore, that we have the authority of Lord Erskine himself to deny the application of his own unquestionable principles to the support of his argument in the case of the "Rights of Man," which we can only consider as the argument of an advocate, bound to give the best assistance to a client.

It would be disgusting and indecent to bring before the reader the matter contained in the "Age of Reason," even as it appears in the terms of the indictment ;—and the more so, as it is unnecessary to the understanding the case. It is sufficient to say, that it was by no means an argumentative consideration of the authority of the Old and New Testament, but an attack upon their authenticity in language the most shocking and opprobrious. Lord Erskine laid the case before the jury as follows.

THE SPEECH.

GENTLEMEN OF THE JURY,—The charge of blasphemy, which is put upon the record against the publisher of this publication, is not an accusation of the servants of the Crown, but comes before you sanctioned by the oaths of a grand jury of the country. It stood for trial upon a former day; but it happening, as it frequently does, without any imputation upon the gentlemen named in the pannel, that a sufficient number did not appear to constitute a full special jury, I thought it my duty to withdraw the cause from trial till I could have the opportunity of addressing myself to *you*, who were originally appointed to try it.

I pursued this course from no jealousy of the common juries appointed by the laws for the ordinary service of the Court, since my whole life has been one continued experience of their virtues; but because I thought it of great importance that those who were to decide upon a cause so very momentous to the public. should have the highest possible qualifications for the decision; that they should not only be men capable from their educations of forming an enlightened judgment, but that their situations should be such as to bring them within the full view of their country to which, in character and in estimation, they were in their own turns to be responsible.

Not having the honour, gentlemen, to be sworn for the King as one of his counsels, it has fallen much oftener to my lot to defend indictments for libels than to assist in the prosecution of them; but I feel no embarrassment from that recollection. I shall not be found to-day to express a sentiment, or to utter an expression, inconsistent with those invaluable principles for which I have uniformly contended in the defence of others. Nothing that I have ever said, either professionally or personally, for the liberty of the press, do I mean to-day to contradict or counteract. On the contrary, I desire to preface the very short discourse I have to make to you, with reminding you, that it is your most solemn duty to take care that it suffers no injury in your hands. A free and unlicensed press, *in the just and legal sense of the expression*, has led to all the blessings, both of religion and government, which Great Britain or any part of the world at this moment enjoys, and it is calculated to advance mankind to still higher degrees of civilisation and happiness. But this freedom, like every other, must be limited to be enjoyed, and, like every human advantage, may be defeated by its abuse.

Gentlemen, the defendant stands indicted for having published this book, which I have only read from the obligations of professional duty, and which I rose from the reading of with astonishment and disgust. Standing here with all the privileges belonging to the highest counsel for the Crown, I shall be entitled to reply to any defence that shall be made for the publication. I shall wait with patience till I hear it.

Indeed, if I were to anticipate the defence which I hear and read of, it would be defaming by anticipation the learned counsel who is to make it; since, if I am to collect it from a formal notice given to the prosecutors in the course of the proceedings, I have to expect that, instead of a defence conducted according to the rules and principles of English law, the foundation of all our laws, and the sanctions of all justice, is to be struck at and insulted. What gives the Court its jurisdiction? What but the oath which his Lordship, as well as yourselves, have sworn upon the Gospel to fulfil? Yet, in the King's court, where His Majesty is himself also sworn to administer the justice of England,—in the King's court, who receives his high authority under a solemn oath to maintain the Christian religion as it is promulgated by God in the Holy Scriptures, I am nevertheless called upon as counsel for the prosecution to "*produce a certain book described in the indict-ment to be* THE HOLY BIBLE." No man deserves to be upon the Rolls who has dared, as an attorney, to put his name to such a notice. It is an insult to the authority and dignity of the court of which he is an officer, since it calls in question the very founda-tions of its jurisdiction. If this is to be the spirit and temper of the defence; if, as I collect from that array of books which are spread upon the benches behind me, this publication is to be vindicated by an attack of all the truths which the Christian religion promulgates to mankind, let it be remembered that such an argument was neither suggested nor justified by anything said by me on the part of the prosecution.

In this stage of the proceedings I shall call for reference to the sacred Scriptures, not from their merits, unbounded as they are, but from their authority in a Christian country—not from the obligations of conscience, but from the rules of law. For my own part, gentlemen, I have been ever deeply devoted to the truths of Christianity, and my firm belief in the Holy Gospel is by no means owing to the prejudices of education (though I was re-ligiously educated by the best of parents), but has arisen from the fullest and most continued reflections of my riper years and under-standing. It forms at this moment the great consolation of a life which, as a shadow, passes away, and without it I should consider my long course of health and prosperity (too long, perhaps, and too uninterrupted to be good for any man) only as the dust which the wind scatters, and rather as a snare than as a blessing.

Much, however, as I wish to support the authority of Scripture from a reasoned consideration of it, I shall repress that subject for the present. But if the defence, as I have suspected, shall bring them at all into argument or question, I must then fulfil a duty which I owe, not only to the Court, as counsel for the prosecution, but to the public, and to the world, to state what I feel and know concerning the evidences of that religion which is denied without being examined, and reviled without being understood.

I am well aware that by the communications of a FREE PRESS all the errors of mankind, from age to age, have been dissipated and dispelled, and I recollect that the world, under the banners of reformed Christianity, has struggled through persecution to the noble eminence on which it stands at this moment, shedding the blessings of humanity and science upon the nations of the earth.

It may be asked, then, by what means the Reformation would have been effected if the books of the Reformers had been suppressed, and the errors of now exploded superstitions had been supported by the terrors of an unreformed state? or how, upon such principles, any reformation, civil or religious, can in future be effected? The solution is easy:—Let us examine what are the genuine principles of the liberty of the press, as they regard writings upon general subjects, unconnected with the personal reputations of private men, which are wholly foreign to the present inquiry. They are full of simplicity, and are brought as near perfection by the law of England as, perhaps, is attainable by any of the frail institutions of mankind.

Although every community must establish supreme authorities, founded upon fixed principles, and must give high powers to magistrates to administer laws for the preservation of government, and for the security of those who are to be protected by it; yet, as infallibility and perfection belong neither to human individuals nor to human establishments, it ought to be the policy of all free nations, as it is most peculiarly the principle of our own, to permit the most unbounded freedom of discussion, even to the detection of errors in the constitution of the very Government itself; so as that common decorum is observed, which every State must exact from its subjects, and which imposes no restraint upon any intellectual composition, fairly, honestly, and decently addressed to the consciences and understandings of men. Upon this principle, I have an unquestionable right—a right which the best subjects have exercised—to examine the principles and structure of the constitution, and by fair, manly reasoning, to question the practice of its administrators. I have a right to consider and to point out errors in the one or in the other, and not merely to reason upon their existence, but to consider the means of their reformation.

By such free, well-intentioned, modest, and dignified communication of sentiments and opinions, all nations have been gradually improved, and milder laws and purer religions have been established. The same principles which vindicate civil controversies, honestly directed, extend their protection to the sharpest contentions on the subject of religious faiths. This rational and legal course of improvement was recognised and ratified by Lord Kenyon as the law of England in a late trial at Guildhall, where he looked back with gratitude to the labours of the Reformers, as the fountains of our religious emancipation, and of the civil blessings that followed in their train. The English constitution, indeed, does· not stop short in the toleration of religious *opinions,* but liberally extends it to *practice.* It permits every man, EVEN PUBLICLY, to worship God according to his own conscience, though in marked dissent from the national establishment, so as he professes the general faith, which is the sanction of all our moral duties, and the only pledge of our submission to the system which constitutes the State.

Is not this freedom of controversy, and freedom of worship, sufficient for all the purposes of human happiness and improvement? Can it be necessary for either that the law should hold out indemnity to those who wholly abjure and revile the Government of their country, or the religion on which it rests for its foundation? I expect to hear, in answer to what I am now saying, much that will offend me. My learned friend, from the difficulties of his situation, which I know from experience how to feel for very sincerely, may be driven to advance propositions which it may be my duty, with much freedom, to reply to ; and the law will sanction that freedom. But will not the ends of justice be completely answered by my exercise of that right in terms that are decent and calculated to expose its defects? Or will my argument suffer, or will public justice be impeded, because neither private honour and justice, nor public decorum, would endure my telling my very learned friend, because I differ from him in opinion, that he is a fool, a liar, and a scoundrel, in the face of the Court? This is just the distinction between a book of free legal controversy, and the book which I am arraigning before you. Every man has a right to investigate, with decency, controversial points of the Christian religion ; but no man, consistently with a law which only exists under its sanctions, has a right to deny its very existence, and to pour forth such shocking and insulting invectives as the lowest establishments in the gradations of civil authority ought not to be subjected to, and which soon would be borne down by insolence and disobedience if they were.

The same principle pervades the whole system of the law, not merely in its abstract theory, but in its daily and most applauded practice. The intercourse between the sexes, which, properly regulated, not only continues, but humanises and adorns our natures, is the foundation of all the thousand romances, plays, and novels which are in the hands of everybody. Some of them lead to the confirmation of every virtuous principle ; others, though with the same profession, address the imagination in a manner to lead the passions into dangerous excesses. But though the law does not nicely discriminate the various shades which distinguish these works from one another, so as to suffer many to pass, through its liberal spirit, that upon principle ought to be suppressed, would it, or does it tolerate, or does any decent man contend that it ought to pass by unpunished, libels of the most shameless obscenity, · manifestly pointed to debauch innocence, and to blast and poison the morals of the rising generation? This is only another illustration to demonstrate the obvious distinction between the work of an author who fairly exercises the powers of his mind in investigating the religion or government of any country, and him who attacks the rational existence of every religion or government, and brands with absurdity and folly the State which sanctions, and the obedient tools who cherish, the delusion. But this publication appears to me to be as cruel and mischievous in its effects as it is manifestly illegal in its principles, because it strikes at the best, sometimes, alas! the only, refuge and consolation amidst the distresses and afflictions of the world. The poor and humble, whom it affects to pity, may be stabbed to the heart by it. THEY have more occasion for firm hopes beyond the grave than the rich and prosperous, who have other comforts to render life delightful. I can conceive a distressed but virtuous man, surrounded by his children, looking up to him for bread when he has none to give them, sinking under the last day's labour, and unequal to the next, yet still, supported by confidence in the hour when all tears shall be wiped from the eyes of affliction, bearing the burden laid upon him by a mysterious Providence which he adores, and anticipating with exultation the revealed promises of his Creator, when he shall be greater than the greatest, and happier than the happiest of mankind. What a change in such a mind might be wrought by such a merciless publication! Gentlemen! whether these remarks are the overcharged declamations of an accusing counsel, or the just reflections of a man anxious for the public happiness, which is best secured by the morals of a nation, will be soon settled by an appeal to the passages in the work that are selected by the indictment for your consideration and judgment. You are at liberty to connect them with every context and sequel, and to bestow upon them the mildest interpretation.

[Here Mr Erskine read and commented upon several of the selected passages, and then proceeded as follows]:—

Gentlemen, it would be useless and disgusting to enumerate the other passages within the scope of the indictment. How any man can rationally vindicate the publication of such a book, in a country where the Christian religion is the very foundation of the law of the land, I am totally at a loss to conceive, and have no ideas for the discussion of. How is a tribunal, whose whole jurisdiction is founded upon the solemn belief and practice of what is here denied as falsehood, and reprobated as impiety, to deal with such an anomalous defence? Upon what principle is it even offered to the Court, whose authority is contemned and mocked at? If the religion proposed to be called in question is not previously adopted in belief, and solemnly acted upon, what authority has the Court to pass any judgment at all of acquittal or condemnation? Why am I now, or upon any other occasion, to submit to his Lordship's authority? Why am I now, or at any time, to address twelve of my equals, as I am now addressing you, with reverence and submission? Under what sanction are the witnesses to give their evidence, without which there can be no trial? Under what obligations can I call upon you, the jury representing your country, to administer justice? Surely upon no other than that you are SWORN TO ADMINISTER IT UNDER THE OATHS YOU HAVE TAKEN. The whole judicial fabric, from the King's sovereign authority to the lowest office of magistracy, has no other foundation. The whole is built, both in form and substance, upon the same oath of every one of its ministers to do justice, AS GOD SHALL HELP THEM HEREAFTER. WHAT GOD? AND WHAT HEREAFTER? That God, undoubtedly, who has commanded kings to rule, and judges to decree justice; who hath said to witnesses, not only by the voice of nature, but in revealed commandments—THOU SHALT NOT BEAR FALSE TESTIMONY AGAINST THY NEIGHBOUR; and who has enforced obedience to them by the revelation of the unutterable blessings which shall attend their observance, and the awful punishments which shall await upon their transgressions.

But it seems this is an AGE OF REASON, and the time and the person are at last arrived that are to dissipate the errors which have overspread the past generations of ignorance. The believers in Christianity are many, but it belongs to the few that are wise to correct their credulity. Belief is an act of reason, and superior reason may therefore dictate to the weak. In running the mind along the long list of sincere and devote Christians, I cannot help lamenting that Newton had not lived to this day to have had his shallowness filled up with this new flood of light. But the subject is too awful for irony. I will speak plainly and directly. Newton was a Christian! Newton, whose mind burst forth from the fetters fastened by nature upon our finite conceptions—Newton, whose science was truth, and the foundation of whose knowledge of it was philosophy—not those visionary and arrogant presumptions which too often usurp its name, but philosophy resting upon the basis of mathematics, which, like figures, cannot lie—Newton, who carried the line and rule to the uttermost barriers of creation, and explored the principles by which all created matter exists and is held together. But this extraordinary man, in the mighty reach of his mind, overlooked, perhaps, the errors which a minuter investigation of the created things on this earth might have taught him. What shall then be said of the great Mr Boyle, who looked

into the organic structure of all matter, even to the inanimate sub-
stances which the foot treads upon ?   Such a man may be supposed
to have been equally qualified with Mr Paine to look up through
nature to nature's God.   Yet the result of all *his* contemplations
was the most confirmed and devout belief in all which the other
holds in contempt as despicable and drivelling superstition.   But
this error might, perhaps, arise from a want of due attention to the
foundations of human judgment, and the structure of that understanding which God has given us for the investigation of truth.
Let that question be answered by Mr Locke, who, to the highest
pitch of devotion and adoration, was a Christian—Mr Locke, whose
office was to detect the errors of thinking, by going up to the very
fountains of thought, and to direct into the proper tract of reasoning the devious mind of man, by showing him its whole process,
from the first perceptions of sense to the last conclusions of ratioci-
nation—putting a rein upon false opinion, by practical rules for
the conduct of human judgment.

But these men, it may be said, were only deep thinkers, and lived
in their closets, unaccustomed to the traffic of the world, and to the
laws which practically regulate mankind.   Gentlemen ! in the
place where we now sit to administer the justice of this great country
the never-to-be-forgotten Sir Matthew Hale presided, whose faith
in Christianity is an exalted commentary upon its truth and reason,
and whose life was a glorious example of its fruits ; whose justice,
drawn from the pure fountain of the Christian dispensation, will
be, in all ages, a subject of the highest reverence and admiration.
But it is said by the author that the Christian fable is but the tale
of the more ancient superstitions of the world, and may be easily
detected by a proper understanding of the mythologies of the
heathens.   Did Milton understand those mythologies ?   Was he
less versed than Mr Paine in the superstitions of the world ?   No ;
they were the subject of his immortal song ; and though shut out
from all recurrence to them, he poured them forth from the stores
of a memory rich with all that man ever knew, and laid them in
their order as the illustration of real and exalted faith, the unquestionable source of that fervid genius which has cast a kind of shade
upon all the other works of man—

> " He passed the bounds of flaming space,
> Where angels tremble while they gaze—
> He saw,—till, blasted with excess of light,
> He closed his eyes in endless night."

But it was the light of the BODY only that was extinguished :
" The CELESTIAL LIGHT shone inward, and enabled him to justify
the ways of God to man."   The result of his thinking was nevertheless not quite the same as the author's before us.   The mysterious incarnation of our blessed Saviour (which this work
blasphemes in words so wholly unfit for the mouth of a Christian,

or for the ear of a court of justice, that I dare not, and will not, give them utterance) Milton made the grand conclusion of his " Paradise Lost," the rest from his finished labours, and the ultimate hope, expectation, and glory of the world.

> " A Virgin is His Mother, but His Sire,
> The power of the Most High ;—He shall ascend
> The throne hereditary, and bound His reign
> With earth's wide bounds, His glory with the heavens."

The immortal poet, having thus put into the mouth of the angel the prophecy of man's redemption, follows it with that solemn and beautiful admonition, addressed in the poem to our great first parent, but intended as an address to his posterity through all generations :—

> " This having learned, thou hast attained the sum
> Of wisdom; hope no higher, though all the stars
> Thou knew'st by name, and all th' ethereal pow'rs,
> All secrets of the deep, all Nature's works,
> Or works of God in heaven, air, earth, or sea,
> And all the riches of this world enjoy'st,
> And all the rule, one empire; only add
> Deeds to thy knowledge answerable, add faith,
> Add virtue, patience, temperance, add love,
> By name to come called Charity, the soul
> Of all the rest : then wilt thou not be loth
> To leave this paradise, but shalt possess
> A paradise within thee, happier far."

Thus you find all that is great, or wise, or splendid, or illustrious, amongst created beings—all the minds gifted beyond ordinary nature, if not inspired by its universal Author for the advancement and dignity of the world, though divided by distant ages, and by clashing opinions, yet joining as it were in one sublime chorus to celebrate the truths of Christianity, and laying upon its holy altars the never-fading offerings of their immortal wisdom.

Against all this concurring testimony, we find suddenly, from the author of this book, that the Bible teaches nothing but " LIES, OBSCENITY, CRUELTY, and INJUSTICE." Had he ever read our Saviour's sermon on the mount, in which the great principles of our faith and duty are summed up? Let us all but read and practise it ; and lies, obscenity, cruelty, and injustice, and all human wickedness, will be banished from the world !

Gentlemen, there is but one consideration more, which I cannot possibly omit, because I confess it affects me very deeply. The author of this book has written largely on public liberty and government ; and this last performance, which I am now prosecuting, has, on that account, been more widely circulated, and principally among those who attached themselves from principle to his former works. This circumstance renders a public attack *upon all revealed religion* from *such a writer* infinitely more dangerous. The religious and moral sense of the people of Great Britain is the great anchor which alone can hold the vessel of the State amidst the storms which agitate the world; and if the mass of the people were debauched from the principles of religion—the true basis of that humanity, charity, and benevolence which have been so long the national characteristic, instead of mixing myself, as I sometimes have done, in political reformations, I would retire to the utmost corners of the earth to avoid their agitation, and would bear not only the imperfections and abuses complained of in our own wise establishment, but even the worst government that ever existed in the world, rather than go to the work of reformation with a multitude set free from all the charities of Christianity, who had no other sense of God's existence than was to be collected from Mr Paine's observation of nature, which the mass of mankind have no leisure to contemplate, which promises no future rewards to animate the good in the glorious pursuit of human happiness, nor punishments to deter the wicked from destroying it even in its birth. The people of England are a religious people, and, with the blessing of God, so far as it is in my power, I will lend my aid to keep them so.

I have no objections to the most extended and free discussions upon doctrinal points of the Christian religion; and *though the law of England does not permit it*, I do not dread the reasonings of deists against the existence of Christianity itself, because, as was said by its divine author, if it be of God, it will stand. An intellectual book, however erroneous, addressed to the intellectual world upon so profound and complicated a subject, can never work the mischief which this indictment is calculated to repress. Such works will only incite the minds of men enlightened by study to a deeper investigation of a subject well worthy of their deepest and continued contemplation. The powers of the mind are given for human improvement in the progress of human existence. The changes produced by such reciprocations of lights and intelligences are certain in their progressions, and make their way imperceptibly by the final and irresistible power of truth. If Christianity be founded in falsehood, let us become deists in this manner, and I am contented. But this book has no such object, and no such capacity; it presents no arguments to the wise and enlightened. On the contrary, it treats the faith and opinions of the wisest with the most shocking contempt, and stirs up men without the advantages of learning or sober thinking to a total disbelief of everything hitherto held sacred; and consequently, to a rejection of all the laws and ordinances of the State, which stand only upon the assumption of their truth.

Gentlemen, I cannot conclude without expressing the deepest regret at all attacks upon the Christian religion by authors who profess to promote the civil liberties of the world. For under what other auspices than Christianity have the lost and subverted liberties of mankind in former ages been re-asserted ? By what zeal but the warm zeal of devout Christians have English liberties been redeemed and consecrated ? Under what other sanctions, even in our own days, have liberty and happiness been spreading to the uttermost corners of the earth ? What work of civilisation, what commonwealth of greatness, has this bald religion of nature ever established ? We see, on the contrary, the nations that have no other light than that of nature to direct them sunk in barbarism or slaves to arbitrary governments; whilst, under the Christian dispensation, the great career of the world has been slowly but clearly advancing—lighter at every step—from the encouraging prophecies of the gospel, and leading, I trust in the end, to universal and eternal happiness. Each generation of mankind can see but a few revolving links of this mighty and mysterious chain; but by doing our several duties in our allotted stations, we are, sure that we are fulfilling the purposes of our existence. You, I trust, will fulfil YOURS this day.

THE SUBJECT.

THE following case of Mr John Frost, an attorney of the Court of King's Bench, who was tried before Lord Kenyon and a special jury, in Hilary Term, 1793, for seditious words, requires but little preface, as the whole of the circumstances appear with sufficient clearness in the speech of the Attorney-General, and in the evidence, which we have prefixed to the defence by Mr Erskine, as the best illustration of his arguments.

The indictment having been opened by Mr Wood, the Attorney-General spoke as follows :—

GENTLEMEN OF THE JURY,—Though I have the honour to attend you in my official character, it will not have escaped your attention that this charge is brought against the present defendant by an indictment.

Gentlemen, the transaction with the guilt of which the defendant is charged happened upon the 6th of November last. I hope I shall not be thought guilty of stating anything that can be considered as improper, when I call your attention to a fact that is notorious to the whole country: that about that period public representations had been made that the minds of men were alienated from that constitution which had long been the subject of the warmest encomiums of the best-informed men in this country, which we have been in the habit of considering as the best birthright which our ancestors could have handed down to us, and which we have been long in the habit of considering as the most valuable inheritance that we had to transmit to our posterity. This constitution had been represented as that from which the affections of the country had become altogether alienated ; we were told that this disaffection was moving along the country with the silence of thought ; and something like a public challenge was written to meet men who are fond of other systems, by fair appeals to the public, who are finally to decide upon every question between every individual of this country and the Government.

Gentlemen, the Attorney-General of that day, who found himself, by the duty of his office, called upon to watch over what he considered a property and inheritance of inestimable value, thought it necessary to meet this sort of observation by stripping himself of what belonged to him in his official character, and appealing, as far as he could appeal, to the tribunals of the country, which the wisdom of the constitution had established, for the purpose of protecting men from improper accusations; and he did not, therefore, call upon those whom he thought proper to prosecute by the exercise of any official authority of his own, putting them and himself at issue upon these points, as it were, before a jury of the country; but he directed indictments to be carried to the grand juries of the country, to take their sense upon the subject, and to have their opinion whether it was fit that persons propagating such doctrines as this defendant stands charged with, should, or should not, be suffered in this country to state them with impunity?

Gentlemen, in consequence of this determination, the present defendant stands indicted; and before I state the words to you, I think it my duty to mention to you, that he is now to be tried upon the second indictment which a grand jury of this country has found. When the first indictment was carried before the grand jury, this defendant was abroad; a warrant was issued for his apprehension, and he returned to this country in the month of February last; he appeared to the indictment, and gave bail to it; by some accident he had been indicted by a name which does not belong to him, and pleaded the misnomer in abatement. Another indictment was carried before the second grand jury, who found that second indictment without any hesitation; and it is in consequence of that proceeding that he is called upon to-day to deny the truth of the charges which this information contains, or to state to you upon what grounds he is to contend that his conduct, as stated in this indictment, is to be considered as legal.

Gentlemen, the transaction which the indictment charges him with happened on the 6th of November last; you will find from the conversation, as it will be given in evidence to you, that Mr Frost had, I think, returned from France shortly before; that he had dined with a set of gentlemen, whom I believe to be very respectable, at the Percy Coffee-house upon that day; he came into the public coffee-house between nine and ten in the evening, as nearly as I am able to ascertain the time, and a gentleman, who had long been acquainted with him, to whom, I believe I may venture to say Mr Frost was certainly under no disobligations in life, seeing him, addressed him as an acquaintance, asked whether he was lately come from France, and how matters went on in that country? Mr Frost told him he was lately come from France, and expected soon to go there again; he then added the words that have been read to you from the indictment: "I am for equality: I can see no reason why any man should not be upon a footing with another: it is every man's birthright."

Gentlemen, some persons present in this coffee-room, the general conduct of all of whom, I think, will have some influence upon your judgment, with respect to the mind with which Mr Frost conducted himself upon that day, immediately asked him what he meant by equality, to which he answered, " *Why, I mean* no King." "What! dare you to own, in any public or private company in this country, such sentiments?" " Yes; *I mean no King;* the constitution of this country is a bad one."

Gentlemen, what were the other particulars of the conversation that passed I am unable to state to you; but you will find the zeal and anxiety which a number of respectable persons acted with upon this occasion, made it very difficult for Mr Frost to pursue this sort of conversation any further; and in what manner Mr Frost left the coffee-house, and under what feelings and apprehensions in the minds of those who were there, I shall leave to you to collect from the witnesses, rather than attempt to state it myself.

Now, gentlemen, it is for you to decide whether, in cases of this nature, prosecutions shall be carried on against defendants who think proper to use language so contemptuous to the Sovereign of the country; and surely I need not in this place contend, that anything that is contemptuous to the Sovereign of the country, any thing grossly reflecting upon the administration of the magistracy of this country, or persons holding the offices of magistrates, according to the law of this country, such as it is, and such as I hope it will continue to be, has never been suffered with impunity.

Gentlemen, when you consider, not merely whether the prosecution is to produce a verdict of guilty, but whether the prosecution is expedient and proper, it is not unnecessary to advert to the circumstances of the times, and the temper with which the particular defendant may have proceeded, who is charged with guilt by an indictment brought before a jury of his country.

Gentlemen, this doctrine of equality and no king has been held in this country, which never did, and which, I hope, never will, interfere with the right of free, of temperate, of sober, and of ample discussion, conducted under those restraints, upon every political subject, in which the interests and the happiness of Englishmen can be concerned: but, gentlemen, when a doctrine of this sort, equality and no king,—a doctrine which either means this, or it means nothing—that there shall be no distinction of ranks in society, is brought forward, under circumstances so peculiar as those which attended the statement of this doctrine by the defendant, it becomes the duty of those who are entrusted with watching over the laws of this country, under the control of juries, who are finally to decide between them and individuals who may be charged with a breach of them, at least to do their duty in stating this to the public, that no one *shall dare* to hold language like this, without being prepared to tell a jury of this country upon what grounds he conceives himself justifiable in holding it under the circumstances of the present case.

Gentlemen, advert a little to the time—this was in November 1792. There does not exist upon the face of the earth, I hope, a man more zealously attached to this doctrine than I am. I mean, that every man in this country, and in every country, has an equal right to equal laws, to an equal protection of personal security, to an equal protection of personal liberty, to an equal protection of that without which it requires no reasoning to prove, that neither personal security nor personal liberty ever can exist—I mean to an equal protection of property—that property which the labour of his life, under the blessing of Providence, may have gained to him, or which the superior kindness of Providence may have given him, without bestowing the labour of life in order to acquire it; all this sort of equality *is that which the constitution of Great Britain has secured to every man who lives under it*, but is not the equality which was connected with the doctrine No King, upon the 6th of November 1792.

Gentlemen, that country, from which it appears, from this conversation, Mr Frost came, and to which it appears, from this conversation, that he expected to go, in the year 1789, had framed what was called a constitution; and almost everything that was valuable in it was borrowed from the constitution of this country in which we live, which had provided for the equal rights of man to equal laws; it laid down in doctrine, however ill or well it supported the principle, the equal right of every man to the protection of his personal liberty, of his personal security, and of his property. But in 1792, that first year of equality, as it was called, a different system of equality, connected materially with this system of No King, had been established: a system which, if it meant anything, meant this: it meant equality of property, for all other equality had been before provided for.

Gentlemen of the jury, it is every man's birthright to have a certain species of equality secured to him; but it neither requires reasoning, nor is it consistent with common sense, and cannot be consistent with reason and common sense, because it is not consistent with the nature of things, as established by the Author of nature, that any other system of equality should exist upon the face of the world.

Gentlemen, this equality, recommended by this gentleman, advisedly, as I think you will be satisfied in this transaction of the 6th of November 1792, is a system which has destroyed all ranks — is a system which has destroyed all property—is a system of universal proscription—is a system which is as contrary to the order of moral nature as it is contrary to the order of political nature— it is a system which cuts up by the roots all the enjoyments that result from the domestic relations of life, or the political relations of life—it is a system which cuts up by the roots every incentive to virtuous and active industry, and holds out to the man who chooses to live a life of profligacy and idleness that he may take from him who has exerted through life a laborious and virtuous conduct those fruits which the God of justice, and every law of justice, have endeavoured to secure to him.   This is the only sort of equality that can be connected with this doctrine of No King, upon the 6th of November 1792.

Gentlemen, I am ready to agree, that where the charge is, that words have been spoken, it is fit for those who prosecute for the public to remember, that in that situation they are in a certain degree advocates for the defendant; for no man can do his duty who wishes to press a defendant, charged upon the part of the public with acting more improperly than he shall appear, upon the candid examination of the circumstances, to have acted ; it is fit for me also to observe, that the degree of criminality of these words will depend very much upon the temper, the circumstances, the *quo animo*, with which this gentleman thought proper to utter them.

Gentlemen, I will not depart from this principle, which I have before stated, that if men will dare to utter words, expressions of more serious import than those which produced the mischief to which I have been alluding in other places, it will be the duty of persons in official situations to watch for you and the public over that which they conceive to be a blessing to you and the public ; at least to inform those gentlemen that they must account for their conduct ; it will be for them, if they can, to account for it satisfactorily.

Gentlemen, you will hear from the witnesses with what temper, with what demeanour, and in what manner these words were uttered ; and I allude again to that which will be described to you, I mean the feelings of the persons present, as some degree of evidence, which will have its due, and not more than its due weight, in your minds.

Gentlemen, I will read to you the words of Mr Justice Forster, as containing the principle upon which, though the law holds seditious expressions as an exceeding high misdemeanour, it has not thought proper to consider them as a crime of the magnitude of high treason.   He says, " As to mere words, supposed to be treasonable, they differ widely from writings in point of real malignity and proper evidence.   They are often the effect of mere heat of blood, which, in some natures, otherwise well disposed, carrieth a man beyond the bounds of decency or prudence ; they are always liable to great misconstruction from the ignorance and inattention of the hearers, and too often from a motive truly criminal.   *Loose words, therefore, not relative to any act or design,* are not overt acts of treason, but words of advice or persuasion, and all consultations for the traitorous purposes treated of in this chapter, are certainly so ; they are uttered in contemplation of some traitorous purpose, actually on foot or intended, and in prosecution of it.

Gentlemen of the jury, it is competent to Mr Frost, and he will give me leave to say, I think it is incumbent upon him, having made use of words of this sort, to state to you that, in the sentiment which that language conveys, he does not express those sentiments by which his general conduct in life is regulated. For aught I know, he is otherwise well disposed; and I am sure, if evidence of that sort is given to you, you will feel the propriety of giving to it, not only a candid, but you have my leave to give it the very utmost consideration that can possibly be given to it. Gentlemen, you observe, too, that words are not made treason, because words may be spoken to by witnesses from a motive truly criminal. You will be to judge whether the evidence of the witnesses to be called to you to-day proceeds from motives truly criminal, or whether laudable zeal for the constitution of their country is not their only motive for stating to you the conduct of this defendant.

Gentlemen, there is another circumstance. I will say but a word to you upon it; that is this: that the propriety of prosecuting for words of this sort depends a *great deal upon the time and season* at which those words are uttered.

Gentlemen, we know that in this country the legislature found it necessary to interfere, and by a positive law to enact, that any man who should dare to affirm that the King and Parliament could not regulate the succession to the Crown, should be guilty of high treason. God forbid the time should ever come, and I do not believe it ever can come, when the Legislature, acting upon the same principle, shall be obliged to say, that if it is at this hour high treason for men deliberately to affirm that the King and Parliament of this country cannot regulate the succession to the Crown, it shall be innocent for men to say that the King and Parliament of this country have no right to continue any government in this country. Why, then, gentlemen, if this doctrine of equality and No King has been attended with such consequences as it is notorious to all mankind it has been attended with, the notoriety of the fact renders it incumbent upon those whose duty it is to bring such defendants before a jury of their country, for that jury to say, as between the country and individuals, whether, under such circumstances as will be laid before you, he is to be publicly permitted to hold such doctrines as those which are stated, in a manner that seems to evince that they are not stated for any useful purpose, but that they are stated for the purpose of trying whether there is any law in this country that will secure the government of the country from attacks, which mean nothing but to display the audacity with which men dare to attack that government? And if you shall be convinced, upon the whole of the evidence before you, that the case is such as I have stated it to be, this I am sure of, that you will duly weigh the consequences of the verdict, however you shall be diposed to give it, for the Crown or for the defendant ; and I am sure *the Crown, upon the temperate consideration of what the jury does, will not be dissatisfied with that verdict,* let it be what it may. The constitution of this country, if it be excellent, if it has really handed down to us those great and invaluable blessings which, I believe, ninety-nine persons out of a hundred are convinced it has, and if it be a matter of anxiety to transmit them to our posterity, you will remember that the stability of those blessings finally and ultimately depends upon the conduct of juries. It is with them, by their verdicts, to establish their fellow-subjects in the enjoyment of those rights ; it is with them to say in what cases those rights have been invaded ; and the same constitution that has left it to them to say in what cases those rights have been invaded, has also bound every honest man to say, that when they have given their decision upon it, they have acted properly between the country and the individual who is charged with the offence.

Gentlemen, under these circumstances, I shall proceed to lay the case before you, and I have only again to repeat, if you shall find, upon a due consideration of this case, that this is a hasty, an unguarded, and unadvised expression of a gentleman otherwise well disposed, and who meant no real mischief to the country, you will be pleased, with my consent, to deal with the defendant as a person under those circumstances ought to be dealt with. I never will press a jury for a verdict in a case in which, whatever may be the strictness of the law as between man and man, acting upon moral and candid feelings, it ought not to be asked for ; and having given you my sentiments, I leave the defendant in your hands.

EVIDENCE FOR THE CROWN.

JOHN TAITT, of Oxford Street, upholsterer, sworn.—*Examined by* Mr SOLICITOR-GENERAL.

Q. Do you know Mr John Frost ?

A. I never saw him but *that evening* in my life.

Q. What evening ?

A. The 6th of November last.

Q. Where were you that evening ?

A. In the Percy Coffee-house.

Q. Who was with you ?

A. Mr Paul Savignac.

Q. Were there any other persons in the coffee-house ?

A. Yes, several gentlemen.

Q. Can you name any ?

A. Mr Yatman was there, Mr Bullock ; there were not many that I knew.

Q. Did you see Mr Frost there?

A. Yes.

Q. At what time?

A. About ten in the evening.

Q. Where did Mr Frost come from?

A. He came from a room above-stairs with several gentlemen into the coffee-room.

Q. What did you first perceive with respect to Mr Frost?

A. He addressed himself, I think, first to Mr Yatman, but of that I am not certain; he was asked how long he had been returned from France.

Lord KENYON. Was he asked that by Mr Yatman?

A. By Mr Yatman or some of the other gentlemen; he said he was very lately returned.

Mr SOLICITOR-GENERAL. What did he say more?

A. He asked him what they were doing there, and he said, things were going on very well there, they were doing very well.

Q. Did you hear him say anything more?

A. That he should very shortly return there.

Q. What more?

A. There was nothing more, till, a few minutes after, he went into the body of the coffee-room, two or three boxes from where I was. I heard him exalting his voice, and he was for equality—" I am for equality"—upon which I got off my seat, and I went forward, and inquired, " Who are you, sir?"

Lord KENYON. You asked him.

A. Yes, because I did not know him. Mr Yatman answered, That is Mr Frost; upon which I asked him how he dared to utter such words? He *still continued,* " I am for equality, and no King." Mr Yatman asked him if he meant no King in this country, and he said, Yes, no King or no Kings; I rather think it was in the plural number. That the constitution of this country was a *very* bad one.

Q. Did he say anything more?

A. He said nothing more. I said he ought to be turned out of the coffee-room; upon which he walked up the room and placed his back to the fire, and wished, I believe, rather to retract, if he could have retracted, what he had said; but he still continued, he was for no King, and he was for equality. He quitted the room very shortly after by a general hiss from all the company.

Q. How long did he continue there?

A. I suppose not above five minutes.

Cross-examined by Mr ERSKINE.

Q. You went, I suppose, to the coffee-house just in the ordinary course of your recreation, I take for granted?

A. It is a coffee-house I very seldom go to.

Q. How came you there that night?

A. I went there to sup.

Q. You have been there often?

A. Very often.

Q. Then of course you went to have your supper and read the newspaper?

A. Exactly so.

Q. I take it you remember all the conversation that passed between Mr Savignac and you that night?

A. I believe Mr Savignac wrote down to the same effect.

Q. I dare say you wrote down this?

A. I wrote none down.

Q. But do you recollect the conversation between Mr Savignac and you?

A. No.

Q. Mr Frost had been above-stairs?

A. Yes.

Q. With whom he was dining you do not know?

A. No.

Q. Can you get out of that room without going through the coffee-room?

A. I don't know.

Q. Don't you know the contrary?

A. I do not.

Q. You must have seen people coming from above-stairs, having frequented that house?

A. Yes.

Q. Then you know the way from up-stairs is through the coffee-room?

A. Yes.

Q. You say, you are not certain that Mr Frost addressed himself first to Mr Yatman?

A. No, I am not.

Q. The first of the conversation you will venture to swear to was a question put by Yatman to him?

A. Yes.

Q. Will you venture to swear, that when Mr Frost came down-stairs, he was not going straight through the coffee-house into the street, till Mr Yatman stopped him, and asked him that question?

A. That I cannot say.

Q. What time was it?

A. About ten in the evening, rather before than after.

Q. Mr Frost was perfectly sober, I suppose?

A. I cannot say whether he was or not.

Q. There was a good dinner, where a number of gentlemen had been present?

A. I cannot say.

Q. You saw other gentlemen come down ?

A. Yes.

Q. Were they not all drunk ?

A. They might be ; I don't know.

Q. He asked Mr Frost how long he had been from France, and he told him he was lately returned; *the conversation went about France?*

A. Yes.

Q. Will you venture to swear the conversation did not continue between Mr Yatman and Mr Frost from the time it first began till the time you heard him say he was for equality ?

A. I cannot say ; I did not attend to it till he exalted his voice, and said he was for equality.

Q. Then what question was put to him, and what turn the conversation was taking, you don't know, till you heard him exalt his voice ?

A. No.

Q. Then you did not know whether the conversation respected France or England ; but hearing the word Equality, you was all agog ?

A. No, I was not all agog.

Q. You were in another part of the coffee-house ?

A. I was in the next box.

Q. By your own account you don't appear to have been very attentive ; but hearing his voice louder than before, you immediately went up, and asked him, how he dared to utter such words ?

A. Yes.

Q. You said that in a tone of voice that showed that you felt yourself insulted ?

A. Yes.

Q. Before you knew to what his words alluded ; for he had been talking about France, you know, and how things went on there, and you immediately then interfered. I believe several other persons interfered in the same insulting manner ?

A. Yes, I believe they did.

Q. At this time you make use of an expression which probably may be owing to my dulness, but I cannot understand you. You said, he seemed to wish to retract, but still continued to do the same thing over again ?

A. He did not say much.

Q. You said, he ought to be put upon the fire, you know ?

A. Yes.

Q. Somebody talked of sending for a constable ?

A. Yes ; and *he said every man there was a constable.*

Mr Solicitor-General. Did Mr Frost appear to be disabled by liquor ?

A. If I had known him before, I should have been better able to say, but I think there was hardly a doubt but he might; but as I don't know, I cannot say whether he was or no, but I rather believe he was.

Q. Did he repeat the words more than once?

A. I don't think he did.

Q. You said, he wished to retract, but still continued that he was for no King and equality?

A. He did not repeat that *twice.*

Q. What did you mean by saying he wished to retract?

A. I rather thought he was sorry for what he had said; that is what I mean by it.

PAUL SAVIGNAC, of Carshalton, in Surrey, sworn.—*Examined by* Mr BEARCROFT.

Q. Do you remember being at the Percy coffee-house with Mr Taitt, upon the 6th of November last?

A. Yes.

Q. Do you remember seeing Mr Frost there?

A. I saw a person whom they called Mr Frost, but I never saw him before nor since.

Q. That gentleman that sits there?—(*pointing to Mr Frost.*)

A. I cannot say.

Q. What time in the evening did you see him in the room?

A. Between nine and ten.

Q. Did you hear any particular expressions he made use of?

A. When he passed the box I was sitting in, he was in the company of Mr Yatman, and I heard him say, " I am for equality and no King."

Lord KENYON. What did he say?

A. He was not in the box; he was walking up the middle of the coffee-room; and he said, " I am for equality and no King." I heard Mr Yatman, pressing his brow, say, " What! equality and no King in this country? " Upon which Mr Frost answered, " Yes, no King; there ought to be no King." I heard nothing more in conversation pass. I stepped from the box, and asked him, how he dared to hold a doctrine of that kind in a public coffee-room? He made some reply as before, that he was for equality and no King. I told him, if he was not under the protection of the very King he was then reviling, I would kick him out of the coffee-room. Upon which he asked me if I doubted his courage. I told him, certainly he would not have made use of such expressions without, because I should have supposed it to be an insult to make use of such expressions in a public coffee-house. He· was then handled by other gentlemen, and I sat down; but very soon afterwards he left the room, under the execrations and hisses of all the room.

Q. Did you see him when he first came down into the public coffee-room ?

A. I don't know that I might. I saw him soon after I saw Mr Yatman.

Q. Recollect yourself, and tell me how long you can speak to it, as near as you can—recollect how long he was in the public coffee-room before he went away.

A. Not ten minutes, not more I am sure.

Q. I would ask you whether this conduct and these expressions of his produced any, and what kind of notice in the company ?

A. That every gentleman there was under the same idea with me, that he ought to be kicked out of the coffee-room.

Cross-examined by Mr Serjeant RUNNINGTON.

Q. You don't live in that neighbourhood, do you ?

A. No, in Carshalton, in Surrey.

Q. How long had you been in the coffee-room, before you saw Mr Frost come in ?

A. He was up-stairs.

Q. Was he obliged to come through the coffee-room from up-stairs to go into the street ?

A. I cannot say.

Q. How far were you from Mr Yatman ?

A. They were walking up the coffee-room close to me.

Q. Did anything pass from Mr Yatman to Mr Frost ?

A. Yes.

Q. Before Mr Frost spoke at all ?

A. No.

Q. Do you recollect Mr Yatman saying, as he came down-stairs, " Well, Mr Equality, where are you going to ? "

A. No, I do not.

MATTHEW YATMAN, of Percy Street, sworn.—*Examined by* Mr BALDWIN.

Q. Was you at the Percy Coffee-house, on the 6th of November, in the evening ?

A. I was.

Q. Did you see Mr Frost there ?

A. I did.

Q. You have long known Mr Frost ?

A. Mr Frost was in the commission for watching and lighting the street in which I live, and I am one of the commissioners.

Q. Tell us what passed between Mr Frost and you at the Percy Coffee-house ?

A. *He came from the room where he dined*, into the coffee-

room ; he came up to where I was, and knowing he was lately
come from France, *I said,* " *Well, how do they go on in France ?* "
He seemed to be *stimulated at the question,* and he extended his
arm, and exalted his voice sufficiently to be heard up-stairs, if the
door had been opened, " I am for equality and no King." "What!"
says I, "*no King in this country ?*"   " No *King !* " as loud as he
could hollow.

Q. Did anything more pass between you and your *old friend ?*

A. No, I had enough.   Upon this, the gentlemen in the coffee-
room seemed to be *stimulated* with anger, and Mr Taitt and Mr
Savignac got up, and so enraged at him, I supposed they would have
kicked him out of the coffee-room, and I believe it would have been
done, but one gentleman got him to the door, and *prevailed* on him
to go out.

Q. Did he say anything more that you recollect ?

A. No, it was all confusion after that.

Q. And the manner of it was as you have described it ?

A. Yes.

Q. With vehemence ?

A. Yes, he was very warm.

Cross-examined by Mr ERSKINE.

Q. It was all general confusion after Mr Taitt had interfered ?

A. Yes.

Q. I believe Mr Frost said this extremely loud, that he might
have been heard up-stairs ?

A. I am just of that opinion.

Q. And then it was that Mr Taitt interfered ?

A. Yes.

Q. After that all was confusion ?

A. Yes.

Mr BALDWIN. Though there was confusion afterwards, there was
not when he spoke those words ?

A. No.

Q. Did he speak it coolly or otherwise, excepting the warmth
with which you have spoken ?   How was he in his understanding ?

*A. He spoke it very distinctly, and wished to be heard by every-
body.*

Q. Was he sober or no ?

A. Certainly he was not drunk.

Mr ERSKINE. It was ten o'clock, was it not ?

A. Between nine and ten.   I don't know whether it was quite
ten.

Q. Do you mean to say he was just as sober as he might be at
twelve o'clock in the day ?

A. That *he walked*.

Q. Do you mean to stake your character and your *honour* before the jury, by saying he was as sober as if you had seen him before dinner?

A. I don't say he was sober.

Q. I ask you, whether you mean to stake your *character* and your honour before the jury, by saying that he was as sober as at twelve o'clock at day?

A. I should not have known that he was not by his conversation and *his walk : whether he was in his right senses when he used those words is another thing*.

Q. Do you mean to say he spoke in the manner and the pitch of voice like a sober man?

A. He was *stimulated*.

Q. He extended his arm?

A. Yes.

Q. You think that a mark of sobriety, do you?

A. I do not think it a mark of good sense.

—— BULLOCK, of ——, sworn.—*Examined by* Mr WOOD.

Q. Was you at the Percy Coffee-house on the 6th of November last?

A. I was.

Q. Did you see Mr Frost there?

A. I did.

Q. Be so good as tell us whether you heard him say anything, and what it was?

A. I did not attend to the conversation, till I heard what I thought very treasonable words, upon which I committed them to paper: I wrote it at the time, with an idea of having it signed.

Q. Be so good as to read it slowly.

A. (*Reads*.) Percy Coffee-house, 6th of November 1792. We, the undermentioned, do hereby certify, that at about ten o'clock this evening, Mr John Frost came into this coffee-room, and did then, and in our presence, openly declare *that he wished to see equality prevail in this country*, and no King, in a loud and *factious* way; and upon being asked whether he meant that there should be no King in this country, he answered, *Yes*.—That is all I recollect of *seditious words*.

Lord KENYON. You put this down with a view that they might have been signed?

A. I did.

Mr WOOD. Was Mr Frost drunk or sober at that time?

A. I never saw Mr Frost before that time, but he did not appear to me to be a man in liquor, not in the least so.

Q. Have you ever seen him at any other time?

A. I have frequently since.

Q. Where may that be?

A. In Paris.

Q. How soon after this was it?

A. I arrived at Paris on the 27th of December, I think, to the best of my recollection; and I saw him a few days after my arrival there.

Mr ERSKINE. We have surely nothing to do with what passed in Paris?

Lord KENYON. I think I may hear it; if words in this country, constituting a different offence, that might be prosecuted here; but this is quite a new question. In common slander this is always allowed.

Mr ERSKINE. I confess I cannot help entering my protest against it, and upon this plain principle, that it may be recollected that that question did arise, and that the defendant may have the benefit of it.

Mr ATTORNEY-GENERAL. I believe Mr Erskine has misunderstood what I meant by putting the question. I meant merely whether he had ever seen Mr Frost at any future time anywhere, and whether, from any conversation he had with him, he can take upon him to judge of the state in which Mr Frost was upon the 6th of November 1792; that is, comparing his modes of conversing at future times, near or distant, from that 6th of November 1792. I I don't wish to ask a single question respecting Mr Frost's conversation since that time, whatever the law may be upon the subject. I have a still more important reason for not asking it.

Mr ERSKINE. My objection is by no means cured, but still more important. The question was this, Whether the witness shall be allowed to say from conversations with Mr Frost——

Mr BULLOCK. I believe I can save you a great deal of trouble. I know nothing about it.

Lord KENYON. I am clearly of opinion that it might have been asked in the way in which the Attorney-General put it,—if by his general deportment afterwards he could judge whether he was in liquor or not? I have not the least particle of doubt.

Mr ERSKINE. Neither have I certainly upon that point, my Lord.

Q. Where have you seen him since?

A. At Calais the first time.

Lord KENYON. I will not have all his life and conversation brought forward. I would not have him give evidence from conjecture or knowledge of what he was doing at Paris. All that I mean to allow is, whether, from his general deportment at other times, he thinks he was sober at that time?

Q. How many times might you see him, think you?

A. It is impossible to say; I have frequently seen him at a coffee-house.

Q. Are you able to judge from that whether he was sober or not when you saw him at Percy Street Coffee-house?

A. He was what you may call a sober man.

Mr ERSKINE. Was he like a man that had been drinking?

A. Drinking moderately.

Q. Two bottles of port,—what do you say to that?

A. I cannot say.

Q. It is very difficult to judge by weights and scales?

A. I thought he was sober by his manner.

SPEECH BY MR ERSKINE.

GENTLEMEN OF THE JURY,—I rise to address you under circumstances so peculiar, that I consider myself entitled, not only for the defendant arraigned before you, but personally for myself, to the utmost indulgence of the Court. I came down this morning with no other notice of the duty cast upon me in this cause, nor any other direction for the premeditation necessary to its performance, than that which I have ever considered to be the safest and the best, namely, the records of the Court, as they are entered here for trial, where, for the ends of justice, the charge must always appear with the most accurate precision, that the accused may know what crime he is called upon to answer, and his counsel how he may defend him. Finding, therefore, upon the record which arraigns the defendant a simple, unqualified charge of seditious words, unconnected and uncomplicated with any extrinsic events, I little imagined that the conduct of my client was to receive its colour and construction from the present state of France, or rather of all Europe, as affecting the condition of England. I little dreamed that the 6th day of November (which, reading the indictment, I had a right to consider like any other day in the calendar) was to turn out an epoch in this country (for so it is styled in the argument), and that, instead of having to deal with idle, thoughtless words, uttered over wine, through the passage of a coffee-house, with whatever *at any time* might belong to them, I was to meet a charge of which I had no notice or conception, and to find the *loose dialogue*, which, even upon the face of the record itself, exhibits nothing more than a casual sudden conversation, exalted to an accusation of the most premeditated, serious, and alarming nature, verging upon high treason itself, by its connexion with the most hostile purposes to the State, and assuming a shape still more interesting from its dangerous connexion with certain mysterious conspiracies, which, in confederacy with French republicans, threaten, *it seems*, the constitution of our once happy country.

Gentlemen, I confess myself much unprepared for a discussion
of this nature, and a little disconcerted at being so; for though (as
I have said) I had no notice from the record that the politics of
Europe were to be the subject of discourse, yet experience ought to
have taught me to expect it; for what act of Government has for a
long time past been carried on by any other means?—*when* or
where has been the debate, or *what* has been the object of authority, in which the affairs of France have not taken the lead? The
affairs of France have, indeed, become the common stalking-horse for
all State purposes. I know the honour of my learned friend too well
to impute to him the introduction of them for any improper or dishonourable purpose. I am sure he connects them in his own mind
with the subject, and thinks them legally before you. I am bound
to think so, because the general tenor of his address to you has
been manly and candid. But I assert, that neither the actual condition of France, nor the supposed condition of this country, are, or
can be, in any shape before you; and that upon the trial of this
indictment, supported only by the evidence you have heard, the
words must be judged of as if spoken by any man or woman in the
kingdom, at any time from the Norman Conquest to the moment I
am addressing you.

I admit, indeed, that the particular time in which words are
spoken, or acts committed, *may* most essentially alter their quality
and construction, and give to expressions, or conduct, which in another season might have been innocent, or at least indifferent, the
highest and most enormous guilt; but for that very reason, the
supposed particularity of the present times, as applicable to the
matter before you, is absolutely shut out from your consideration
—shut out upon the plainest and most obvious principle of justice
and law, because, wherever *time* or *occasion* mix with an act, affect
its quality, and constitute or enhance its criminality, they then
become an essential part of the misdemeanour itself, and must consequently be charged as such upon the record. I plainly discover
I have his Lordship's assent to this proposition. If, therefore, the
Crown had considered this cause originally in the serious light
which it considers it to-day, it has wholly mistaken its course. If
it had considered the Government of France as actively engaged in
the encouragement of disaffection to the monarchy of England, and
that her newly-erected republic was set up by her as the great
type for imitation and example here; if it had considered that
numbers, and even classes of our countrymen, were ripe for disaffection, if not for rebellion, and that the defendant, as an emissary
of France, had spoken the words with the premeditated design of
undermining our Government, this situation of things might and
ought to have been put *as facts upon the record*, and as facts established by evidence, instead of resting, as they do to-day, upon assertion. By such a course, the crime indeed would have become of

the magnitude represented ; but on the other hand, as the conviction could only have followed from the proof, *the defendant, upon the evidence of to-day, must have an hour ago been acquitted*, since not a syllable has been proved of any emissaries from France to debauch our monarchical principles; not even an insinuation *in evidence that, if there were any such, the defendant was one of them ;* not a syllable of proof, either directly or indirectly, that the condition of the country, when the words were uttered, differed from its ordinary condition in times of prosperity and peace.   It is therefore a new and most compendious mode of justice that the facts which wholly constitute, or at all events lift up the dignity and danger of the offence, should not be charged upon record, *because they could not be proved*, but are to be taken for granted in the argument, so as to produce the same effect upon the trial, and in the punishment, as if they had been actually charged, and completely established.   If the affairs of France, as they are supposed to affect this country, had been introduced without a warrant from the charge or the evidence, I should have been wholly silent concerning them ; but as they have been already mixed with the subject in a manner so eloquent and affecting as too probably to have made a strong impression, it becomes my duty to endeavour at least to remove it.

The late revolutions in France have been represented to you as not only ruinous to their authors, and to the inhabitants of that country, but as likely to shake and disturb the principles of this and all other Governments; you have been told that though the English people are generally well affected to their government—ninety-nine out of one hundred, upon Mr Attorney-General's own statement—yet that wicked and designing men have long been labouring to overturn it, and that nothing short of the wise and spirited exertions of the present Government (of which this prosecution is, it seems, one of the instances), have hitherto averted, or can continue to avert, the dangerous contagion which misrule and anarchy are spreading over the world ; that bodies of Englishmen, forgetting their duty to their own country and its constitution, have congratulated the Convention of France upon the formation of their monstrous Government; and that the conduct of the defendant must be considered as a part of a deep-laid system of disaffection which threatened the establishments of this kingdom.

Gentlemen, this state of things having no support whatever from any evidence before you, and resting only upon *opinion*, I have an equal right to *mine*, having the same means of observation with other people of what passes in the world; and as I have a very clear one upon this subject, I will give it you in a few words.

I am of opinion, then, that there is not the smallest foundation for the alarm which has been so industriously propagated ; in which

I am so far from being singular, that I verily believe the authors of it are themselves *privately* of the same way of thinking; but it was convenient for *certain persons*, who had changed their principles, to find some plausible pretext for changing them; it was convenient for those who, when *out of* power, had endeavoured to lead the public mind to the necessity of reforming the corruptions of our own Government, to find *any* reasons for their continuance and confirmation, when they operated as engines to support themselves in the exercise of powers which were only odious when in *other hands*. For this honourable purpose, the sober, reflecting, and temperate character of the English nation was to be represented as fermenting into sedition, and into an insane contempt for the revered institutions of their ancestors; for this honourable purpose the wisest men, the most eminent for virtue, the most splendid in talents, the most independent for rank and property in the country, were, for no other crime than their perseverance in those sentiments which *certain persons had originated and abandoned*, to be given up to the licentious pens and tongues of hired defamation, to be stabbed in the dark by anonymous accusation, and to be held out to England, and to the whole world, as conspiring under the auspices of cut-throats to overturn everything sacred in religion, and venerable in the ancient government of our country. Certain it is that the whole system of government, of which the business we are now engaged in is no mean specimen, came upon the public with the suddenness of a clap of thunder, without one act to give it foundation, *from the very moment that notice was given of a motion in Parliament to reform the representation of the people.* Long, long before that time, the "Rights of Man" and other books, though not complained of, had been written; equally long before it, the addresses to the French Government, which have created such a panic, had existed; but as there is a give-and-take in this world, they passed unregarded. Leave but the *practical* corruptions, and they are contented to wink at the *speculations* of theorists, and the compliments of public-spirited civility; but the moment the national attention was awakened *to look to things in practice, and to seek to reform corruptions at home*, from that moment, as at the ringing of a bell, the whole hive began to swarm, and every man in his turn has been stung.

This, gentlemen, is the real state of the case; and I am so far from pushing the observation beyond its bearing for the defence of a client, that I am ready to admit Mr Frost, in his conduct, has not been wholly invulnerable, and that in some measure he has brought this prosecution upon himself.

Gentlemen, Mr Frost must forgive me if I take the liberty to say that, with the best intentions in the world, he formerly pushed his observations and conduct respecting Government further than many would be disposed to follow him. I cannot disguise or conceal from you that I find his name in this green.book * as associated with Mr Pitt and the Duke of Richmond at the Thatched House Tavern, in St James's Street; that I find him also the correspondent of the former, and that I discover in their publications on the structure and conduct of the House of Commons expressions which, however merited, and in my opinion commendable, would now be considered not merely as intemperate and unguarded, but as highly criminal.†

* Mr Erskine read the following minutes from Mr Pitt's handwriting:—

"THATCHED HOUSE TAVERN, *May* 18, 1782.

"At a numerous and respectable meeting of members of Parliament friendly to a constitutional reformation, and of members of several committees of counties and cities, the Duke of Richmond, Lord Surry, Lord Mahon, The Lord Mayor, Hon. William Pitt, Sir Watkin Lewes, Rev. Mr Wyvill, Mr Falconer, Mr Redman, Mr Withers, Mr Bodely, Mr Vardy, Mr Sheridan, Mr Alderman Turner, Mr Trecothick, Mr Vincent, Sir C. Turner, Mr Taylor, Mr Amherst, Mr Duncombe, Mr J. Martin, Mr Alderman Townsend, Mr Alderman Creighton, Mr Alderman Wilkes, Rev. Mr Bromley, Mr B. Hollis, Mr Disney Fitche, Mr Edmunds, General Hale, Sir Cecil Wray, Mr B. Hayes, Sir J. Norcliffe, Dr John Jebb, Major Cartwright, Mr Hill, Mr Baynes, Mr Shove, Mr Churchill, Mr Tooke, Mr Horne, Mr Frost, Mr Trevanion, Dr Brocklesby, Rev. Dr Rycroft, Colonel Byron, Major Parry, Mr Green, &c. &c.:

"Resolved unanimously,—That the motion of the Honourable William Pitt, on the 7th instant, for the appointment of a committee of the House of Commons to inquire into the state of the representation of the people of Great Britain in Parliament, and to report the same to the House ; and also what steps it might be proper in their opinion to take thereupon, having been defeated by a motion made for the order of the day, it is become indispensably necessary that application should be made to Parliament by petitions from the collective body of the people in their respective districts, requesting a substantial reformation of the Commons House of Parliament.

"Resolved unanimously,—That this meeting, considering that a general application by the collective body to the Commons House of Parliament cannot be made before the close of the present session, is of opinion that the sense of the people should be taken at such times as may be convenient this summer, in order to lay their several petitions before Parliament early in the next session, when their proposition for a Parliamentary reformation, *without which neither the liberty of the nation can be preserved, nor the permanence of a wise and virtuous administration can be secured,* may receive that ample and mature discussion which so momentous a question demands.

"Resolved unanimously,—That the thanks of this meeting be given to the Honourable William Pitt for moving, John Sawbridge, Esq., for seconding, and the one hundred and forty-one other members who supported, the motion for a committee to inquire into the state of Parliamentary representation, and to suggest what in their opinion ought to be done thereupon ; as well as to the Duke of Richmond, Lord John Cavendish, Mr Secretary Fox, and every other member of the present Ministry, or of either House of Parliament, who has in any way promoted the necessary reform that was the object of the foregoing motion. WM. PLOMER, *Chairman.*

"And they resolved to have another meeting at the same place, on Saturday, June 1."

† [COPY.]

"LINCOLN'S INN, *Friday, May* 10.

" DEAR SIR,—I am extremely sorry that I was not at home when you and the other gentlemen from the Westminster Committee did me the honour to call.

"May I beg the favour of you to express that I am truly happy to find that the motion of Tuesday last has the approbation of such zealous friends to the public, and to assure the Committee that my exertions shall never be wanting in support of a measure *which I agree with them in thinking essentially necessary to the independence*

Gentlemen, the fashion of this world speedily passeth away. We find these glorious restorers of equal representation determined, *as ministers*, that, so far from every man being an elector, the metropolis of the kingdom should have no election at all, but should submit to the power, or to the softer allurements, of the Crown. Certain it is, that, for a short season, Mr Frost being engaged *professionally as agent for the Government candidate*, did not (indeed he could not) oppose this inconsistency between the doctrine and practice of his friends, and *in this interregnum of public spirit* he was, in the opinion of Government, a perfect patriot, a faithful friend to the British constitution. As a member of the law he was therefore trusted with Government business in matters of revenue, and was, in short, what all the friends of Government of course are, the best and most approved; to save words, he was like all the rest of them,—just what he should be. But the election being over, and, with it, professional agency; and Mr Frost, as he lawfully might, continuing to hold his former opinions, which were still avowed and gloried in, though not acted on by his ancient friends, he unfortunately did not change them the other day, when they were thrown off by others; on the contrary, he rather seems to have taken fire with the prospect of reducing them to practice; and being, as I have shown you, bred in a school which took the lead in boldness of remonstrance of all other reformers before or since, he fell, in the heat and levity of wine, into expressions which have no correspondence with his sober judgment; which would have been passed over or laughed at in you or me, but which, coming from him, were never to be forgiven by Government. This is the genuine history of his offence,—for this he is to be the subject of prosecution,—not the prosecution of my learned friend,—not the prosecution of the Attorney-General, —not the prosecution of His Majesty; but the prosecution of Mr Yatman, who wishes to show you his great loyalty to the State and constitution, which were in danger of falling, had it not been for the drugs of this worthy apothecary.

With regard to the new Government of France, since the subject has been introduced, all I can say of it is this: that the good or evil of it belongs to themselves; that they had a right, like every other people upon earth, to change their government; that the

of Parliament, and the liberty of the people.—I have the honour to be, with great respect and esteem, Sir, your most obedient and most humble servant,

W. PITT.

"*John Frost, Esq., Percy Street.*"

"LINCOLN'S INN, *May* 12, 1782.

"SIR,—I have received the favour of your note, and shall be proud to receive the honour intended me by the gentlemen of the Middlesex Committee, at the time you mention.—I am, with great regard, Sir, your most humble servant,

W. PITT.

"*John Frost, Esq., Percy Street.*"

system destroyed was a system disgraceful to free and rational beings, and if they have neither substituted, nor shall hereafter substitute a better in its stead, they must eat the bitter fruits of their
own errors and crimes. As to the horrors which now disfigure and
desolate that fine country, all good men must undoubtedly agree in
condemning and deploring them, but they may differ nevertheless
in deciphering their causes : men to the full as wise as those who
pretend to be wiser than Providence, and stronger than the order
of things, may perhaps reflect that a great fabric of unwarrantable
power and corruption could not fall to the ground without a
mighty convulsion,—that the agitation must ever be in proportion
to the surface agitated,—that the passions and errors inseparable
from humanity must heighten and swell the confusion, and that
perhaps the crimes and ambition of other nations, under the mask
of self-defence and humanity, may have contributed not a little to
aggravate them,—may have tended to embitter the spirits and to
multiply the evils which they condemn,—to increase the misrule
and anarchy which they seek to disembroil, and in the end to
endanger their own governments, which by carnage and bloodshed,
instead of by peace, improvement, and wise administration, they
profess to protect from the contagion of revolution.

As to the part which bodies of men in England have taken,
though it might in some instances be imprudent and irregular, yet
I see nothing to condemn, or to support the declamation which we
daily hear upon the subject. The congratulations of Englishmen
were directed to the fall of corrupt and despotic power in France,
and were animated by a wish of a milder and freer government,
happier for that country, and safer for this ; they were, besides, addressed to France when she was at peace with England, and when
no law was therefore broken by the expression of opinion or satisfaction. They were not congratulations on the murders which
have since been committed, nor on the desolations which have since
overspread so large a portion of the earth, neither were they traitorous to the Government of this country. This we may safely take
in trust, *since not one of them, even in the rage of prosecution, has
been brought before a criminal court.* For myself, I never joined in
any of these addresses, but what I have delivered concerning them
is all I have been able to discover, and Government itself, as far as
evidence extends, has not been more successful. I would therefore
recommend it to his His Majesty's servants to attend to the
reflections of an eloquent writer, at present high in their confidence
and esteem, who has admirably exposed the danger and injustice
of general accusations. " *This way of proscribing the citizens by
denominations and general descriptions*, dignified by the name of
reason of State, and security for constitutions and commonwealths,
is nothing better at bottom than the miserable invention of an
ingenerous ambition, which would fain hold the sacred trust of

power without any of the virtues or energies that give a title to it;
a receipt of policy, made up of a detestable compound of malice,
cowardice, and sloth.   They would govern men against their will ;
but in that, Government would be discharged from the exercise of
vigilance, providence, and fortitude ; and therefore that they may
sleep on their watch, consent to take some one division of the
society into partnership of the tyranny over the rest.   But let
Government, in whatever form it may be, comprehend the whole in
its justice, and restrain the suspicious by its vigilance, let it keep
watch and ward ; let it discover by its sagacity, and punish by its
firmness, all delinquency against its power, whenever it exists in the
overt acts, and then it will be as safe as God and nature intended
it should be.   Crimes are the acts of individuals, and not of
denominations ;   and therefore arbitrarily to class men under
general descriptions, in order to proscribe and punish them in the
lump for a presumed delinquency, of which perhaps but a part,
perhaps none at all, are guilty, is indeed a compendious method,
and saves a world of trouble about proof ; but such a method, instead of being law, is an act of unnatural rebellion against the
legal dominion of reason and justice, and a vice in any constitution that entertains it, which at one time or other will certainly
bring on its ruin." *

Gentlemen, let us now address ourselves to the cause disembar-
rassed by foreign considerations ; let us examine what the charge
upon the record is, and see how it is supported by the proofs ; for,
unless the whole indictment, or some one count of it, be in form
and substance supported by the evidence, the defendant must be
acquitted, however in other respects you may be dissatisfied with
his imprudence and indiscretion.   The indictment charges, " That
the defendant, being a person of an impious, depraved, seditious
disposition, and maliciously intending to disturb the peace of the
kingdom, to bring our most serene Sovereign into hatred and
contempt with all the subjects of the realm, and to excite them to
discontent against the Government, *he, the said defendant, his
aforesaid wicked contrivances and intentions to complete, perfect,
and render effectual, on the 6th day of November,*" spoke the words
imputed to him by the Crown.   This is the indictment, and it is
drawn with a precision which marks the true principle of English
criminal law.   It does not merely charge the speaking of the
words, leaving the wicked intention to be supplied and collected by
necessary and unavoidable inference, because such inference may
or may not follow from the words themselves, according to circumstances, which the evidence alone can disclose ; it charges therefore
the wicked intention *as a fact*, and as constituting the very essence
of the crime, stating, as it must state, to apprise the defendant
of the crime alleged against him, the overt act by which such

* Edmund Burke.

malicious purpose was displayed, and by which he sought to render it effectual. No man can be criminal without a criminal intention, —*actus non facit reum nisi mens sit rea.* God alone can look into the heart, and man, could he look into it, has no jurisdiction over it, until society is disturbed by its actions ; but the criminal mind being the source of all criminality, the law seeks only to punish actions which it can trace to evil disposition : it pities our errors and mistakes,—makes allowances for our passions, and scourges only our crimes.

Gentlemen, my learned friend the Attorney-General, in the conclusion of his address to you, did more than ratify these propositions; for, with a liberality and candour very honourable to himself, and highly advantageous to the public which he represents, he said to you, that if the expressions charged upon the defendant should turn out, in your opinion, to be unadvised and unguarded, arising on the sudden, and unconnected with previous bad intention, he should not even insist upon the strictness of the law, whatever it might be, nor ask a verdict, but such as between man and man, acting upon moral and candid feelings, ought to be asked and expected. These were the suggestions of his own just and manly disposition, and he confirmed them by the authority of Mr Justice Forster, whose works are so deservedly celebrated ; but judging of my unfortunate client, not from his own charity, but from the false information of others, he puts a construction upon an expression of this great author which destroys much of the intended effect of his doctrine ; a doctrine which I will myself read again to you, and by the right interpretation of which I desire the defendant may stand or fall. In the passage read to you, Forster says, " As to mere words, they differ widely from writings in point of REAL MALIGNITY AND PROPER EVIDENCE; they are often the effect of mere heat of blood, which in some natures, otherwise well disposed, carrieth the man beyond the bounds of prudence : they are always liable to great misconstruction from the ignorance or inattention of the hearers, and too often from a motive truly criminal." Forster afterwards goes on to contrast such loose words " *not relative to any act or design,*" for so he expresses himself, with " words of advice and persuasion *in contemplation of some traitorous purpose actually on foot or intended, and in prosecution of it.*" Comparing this rule of judgment with the evidence given, one would have expected a consent to the most favourable judgment—one would have almost considered the quotation as a tacit consent to an acquittal ; but Mr Attorney-General, still looking through the false medium of other men's prejudices, lays hold of the words " *otherwise well disposed,*" and engrafts upon them this most extraordinary requisition. Show me, he says, that Mr Frost is *otherwise well disposed.* Let him bring himself within the meaning of Forster, and *then* I consent that he shall have the fullest benefit of his indulgent principle of judgment. Good God, gentlemen, are we in an English court of justice? Are we sitting in judgment before the Chief-Justice of England, with the assistance of a jury of Englishmen? and am I, in such a presence, to be called upon to prove the good disposition of my client before I can be entitled to the protection of those rules of evidence which apply equally to the just and to the unjust, and by which an evil disposition must be proved before it shall even be suspected? I came here to resist and to deny the existence of legitimate and credible proof of disloyalty and disaffection; and am I to be called upon to prove that my client has *not* been, nor is disloyal or disaffected? Are we to be deafened with panegyrics upon the English constitution, and yet to be deprived of its first and distinguishing feature, that innocence is to be presumed until guilt be established? Of what avail is that sacred maxim, if upon the bare assertion and imputation of guilt, a man may be deprived of a rule of evidence, the suggestion of wisdom and humanity, as if the rule applied only to those who need no protection, and who were never accused? If Mr Frost, by any *previous overt acts*, by which alone any disposition, good or evil, can be proved, had shown a disposition leading to the offence in question, it was evidence for the Crown. Mr Wood, whose learning is unquestionable, undoubtedly thought so when, with the view of crimination, he asked where Mr Frost had been before the time in question, for he is much too correct to have put an irregular and illegal question in a criminal case; I must therefore suppose his right to ask it appeared to him quite clear and established, and I have no doubt that it was so. Why then did he not go on and follow it up by asking what he had done in France? what declarations he had made *there*, or what part he proposed to act *here*, upon his return? The charge upon the record is, that the words were uttered with malice and premeditation; and Mr Attorney-General properly disclaims a conviction upon any other footing. Surely then it was open to the Crown, upon every principle of common sense, to have proved the previous malice by all previous discourses and previous conduct, *connected with the accusation;* and yet, after having wholly and absolutely failed in this most important part of the proof, we are gravely told that the Crown, having failed in the *affirmative*, we must set about establishing the *negative*, for that otherwise we are not within the pale or protection of the very first and paramount principles of the law and government of the country.

Having disposed of the stumbling-block in the way of sound and indulgent judgment, we may now venture to examine THIS *mighty offence as it is proved by the witnesses for the Crown, supposing the facts neither to have been misstated from misapprehension, nor wilfully exaggerated.*

Mr Frost, the defendant, a gentleman who upon the evidence

stands wholly unimpeached of any design against the public peace, or any indisposition to the constitution of the kingdom, appears to have dined at the tavern over the Percy coffee-house—not even with a company met upon any political occasion, good or evil, but, as has been admitted in the opening, with a society for the *Encouragement of Agriculture*, consisting of most reputable and inoffensive persons, neither talking nor thinking about Government or its concerns: so much for the preface to this dangerous conspiracy. The company did not retire till the bottle had made many merry circles; and it appears upon the evidence for the Crown that Mr Frost, *to say the least*, had drunk very freely; but was it then that, with the evil intention imputed to him, he went into this coffee-house to circulate his opinions, and to give effect to designs he had premeditated. *He could not possibly go home without passing through it ;* for it is proved that there was no other passage into the street from the room where he had dined; but having got there by accident, did he even then stop by design and collect an audience to scatter sedition? So far from it, that Mr Yatman, the very witness against him, admits that he interrupted him as he passed in silence towards the street, and fastened the subject of France upon *him ;* and every word which passed (*for the whole is charged upon the very record as a dialogue with this witness*), in answer to his *entrapping questions*, introduced with the familiarity of a very old acquaintance, and in a sort of banter too, which gave a turn to the conversation which renders it ridiculous as well as wicked to convert it into a serious plan of mischief. "Well," says Mr Yatman, " well, Mr Equality, so you have been in France—when did you arrive? I suppose you are for equality and no kings ? " " Oh, yes," says Mr Frost, " certainly I am for equality ; I am for no kings." Now, beyond all question, when this answer was made, whether in jest or in earnest, whether when drunk or sober, it neither had nor *could* have the remotest relation to ENGLAND OR ITS GOVERNMENT. France had just abolished its new constitution of monarchy, and set up a republic ; she was at that moment divided and in civil confusion on the subject ; the question therefore, and the answer, as they applied to France, were sensible and relevant ; but to England or to English affairs they had not (except in the *ensnaring* sequel) the remotest application. Had Yatman therefore ended here, the conversation would have ended, and Mr Frost would have been the next moment in the street ; but still the question is forced upon him, and he is asked, " What ! no kings in England ?" although his first answer had no connexion with England ; the question, therefore, was self-evidently a snare ; to which he answered, " No kings in England," which seemed to be all that was wanted, for in a moment everything was confusion and uproar ; Mr Frost, who had neither delivered nor meant to deliver any serious opinion concerning government, and finding himself in-

juriously set upon, wished, as was most natural, to explain himself,
by stating to those around him what I have been just stating to
you; but all in vain: they were in pursuit of the immortal fame
of the very business we are engaged in at this moment, and were
resolved to hold their advantage,—his voice was immediately
drowned by the clamours of insult and brutality,—he was baited
on all sides like a bull, and left the coffee-house without the possibility of being heard either in explanation or defence.   An indictment was immediately preferred against him, and from that moment
the public ear has been grossly and wickedly abused upon the
subject, his character shamefully calumniated, and *his cause prejudged before the day of trial.*

Gentlemen, it is impossible for me to form any other judgment
of the impression which such a proceeding altogether is likely to
make upon your minds but from that which it makes upon *my
own.*   In the first place, is society to be protected by the breach of
those confidences, and in the destruction of that security and tranquillity, which constitute its very essence everywhere, but which,
till of late, most emphatically characterised the life of an Englishman?   Is Government to derive dignity and safety by means which
render it impossible for any man who has the least spark of honour
to step forward to serve it?   Is the time come when obedience to the
law and correctness of conduct are not a sufficient protection to the
subject, but that he must measure his steps, select his expressions,
and adjust his very looks in the most common and private intercourses
of life?   Must an English gentleman in future fill his wine by a
measure, lest, in the openness of his soul, and whilst believing his
neighbours are joining with him in that happy relaxation and freedom of thought which is the prime blessing of life, he should find
his character blasted and his person in a prison?   Does any man
put such constraint upon himself in the most private moment of
his life, that he would be contented to have his loosest and lightest
words recorded, and set in array against him in a court of justice?
Thank God, the world lives very differently, or it would not be
worth living in.   There are moments when jarring opinions may
be given without inconsistency, when truth herself may be sported
with without the breach of veracity, and where well-imagined nonsense is not only superior to, but is the very index to wit and wisdom.
I might safely assert, taking too for the standard of my assertion,
the most honourably correct and enlightened societies in the kingdom, that if malignant spies were properly posted, scarcely a dinner
would end without a duel and an indictment.

When I came down this morning and found, contrary to my expectation, that we were to be stuffed into this miserable hole in the
wall,* to consume our constitutions, suppose I had muttered along

* The King's Bench sat in the small court of Common Pleas, the impeachment
having shut up its own court.—ED.

through the gloomy passages, "What! is this cursed trial of Hastings going on again? Are we to have no respite? Are we to die of the asthma in this damned corner? I wish to God that the roof would come down and abate the impeachment, Lords, Commons, and all together." *Such a wish, proceeding from the mind*, would be desperate wickedness, and the serious expression of it a high and criminal contempt of Parliament. Perhaps the bare utterance of such words, even without meaning, would be irreverend and foolish. But still, if such expressions had been gravely imputed to me as the result of a malignant mind, seeking the destruction of the Lords and Commons of England, how would they have been treated in the House of Commons on a motion for my expulsion? How! The witness would have been laughed out of the House before he had half finished his evidence, and would have been voted to be too great a blockhead to deserve a worse character. Many things are indeed wrong and reprehensible, that neither do nor can become the objects of criminal justice, because the happiness and security of social life, which are the very end and object of all law and justice, forbid the communication of them; because the spirit of a gentleman, which is the most refined morality, either shuts men's ears against what should not be heard, or closes their lips with the sacred seal of honour.

This tacit but well understood and delightful compact of social life is perfectly consistent with its safety. The security of free governments, and the unsuspecting confidence of every man who lives under them, are not only compatible but inseparable. It is easy to distinguish where the public duty calls for the violation of the private one; criminal intention, but not indecent levities—not even grave opinions unconnected with conduct—are to be exposed to the magistrate; and when men, which happens but seldom, without the honour or the sense to make the due distinctions, force complaints upon governments which they can neither approve of nor refuse to act upon, it becomes the office of juries, as it is yours to-day, to draw the true line in their judgments, measuring men's conduct by the safe standards of human life and experience.

Gentlemen, the misery and disgrace of society, under the lash of informers, running before the law and hunting men through the privacies of domestic life, is described by a celebrated speaker * with such force and beauty of eloquence, that I will close my observations on this part of the subject by repeating what cannot, I am persuaded, be uttered amongst Englishmen without sinking deep into their hearts:—" A mercenary informer knows no distinction. Under such a system, the obnoxious people are slaves, not only to the Government, but they live at the mercy of every individual; they are at once the slaves of the whole community and of

* Edmund Burke.

every part of it; and the worst and most unmerciful men are those on whose goodness they most depend.

"In this situation men not only shrink from the frowns of a stern magistrate, but are obliged to fly from their very species. The seeds of destruction are sown in civil intercourse and in social habitudes. The blood of wholesome kindred is infected. Their tables and beds are surrounded with snares. All the means given by Providence to make life safe and comfortable are perverted into instruments of terror and torment. This species of universal subserviency, that makes the very servant who waits behind your chair the arbiter of your life and fortune, has such a tendency to degrade and abase mankind, and to deprive them of that assured and liberal state of mind which alone can make us what we ought to be, that I vow to God, I would sooner bring myself to put a man to immediate death for opinions I disliked, and so to get rid of the man and his opinions at once, than to fret him with a feverish being, tainted with the jail distemper of a contagious servitude, to keep him above ground, an animated mass of putrefaction, corrupted himself and corrupting all about him."

If these sentiments apply so justly to the reprobation of persecution for opinions, even for opinions which the laws, however absurdly, inhibit—for opinions though certainly and maturely entertained, though publicly professed, and though followed up by corresponding conduct; how irresistibly do they devote to contempt and execration all evesdropping attacks upon loose conversations, casual or convivial, more especially when proceeding from persons conforming to all the religious and civil institutions of the State, unsupported by general and avowed profession, and not merely unconnected with conduct, but scarcely attended with recollection or consciousness! Such a vexatious system of inquisition, the disturber of household peace, began and ended with the Star-Chamber; the venerable law of England never knew it; her noble, dignified, and humane policy soars above the little irregularities of our lives, and disdains to enter our closets without a warrant founded upon complaint. Constructed by man to regulate human infirmities. and not by God to guard the purity of angels, it leaves to us our thoughts, our opinions, and our conversations, and punishes only overt acts of contempt and disobedience to her authority.

Gentlemen, this is not the specious phrase of an advocate for his client; it is not even my exposition of the spirit of our constitution, but it is the phrase and letter of the law itself. In the most critical conjunctures of our history, when Government was legislating for its own existence and continuance, it never overstepped this wise moderation. To give stability to establishments, it occasionally bridled opinions concerning them, but its punishments, though sanguinary, *laid no snares for thoughtless life*, and took no man by surprise.

Of this the Act of Queen Anne, which made it high treason to deny the right of Parliament to alter the succession, is a striking example. The hereditary descent of the Crown had been recently broken at the Revolution by a minority of the nation, with the aid of a foreign force, and a new inheritance had been created by the authority of the new establishment, which had but just established itself. Queen Anne's title, and the peaceable settlement of the kingdom under it, depended wholly upon the constitutional power of Parliament to make this change; the superstitions of the world, and reverence for antiquity, which deserves a better name, were against this power and the use which had been made of it; the dethroned King of England was living in hostile state at our very doors, supported by a powerful monarch at the head of a rival nation, and our own kingdom itself full of factious plots and conspiracies, which soon after showed themselves in open rebellion.

If ever, therefore, there was a season when a narrow jealousy could have been excusable in a Government,—if ever there was a time when the sacrifice of some private liberty to common security would have been prudent in a people, it was at such a conjuncture; yet, mark the reserve of the Crown, and the prudence of our ancestors, in the wording of the statute. Although the denial of the right of Parliament to alter the succession was tantamount to the denial of all legitimate authority in the kingdom, and might be considered as a sort of abjuration to the laws, yet the statute looked at the nature of man, and to the private security of individuals in society, while it sought to support the public society itself;—it did not, therefore, dog men into taverns and coffee-houses, nor lurk for them at corners, nor watch for them in their domestic enjoyments. The Act provides, "That every person who should maliciously, advisedly, and directly, by *writing or printing*, affirm that the Queen was not the rightful Queen of these realms; or that the Pretender had any right or title to the Crown; or that any other person had any right or title, otherwise than according to the Acts passed since the Revolution for settling the succession; or that the Legislature hath not sufficient authority to make laws for limiting the succession, should be guilty of high treason, and suffer as a traitor;" and then enacts, "That if any person shall *maliciously* and *directly*, by *preaching, teaching*, or *advised speaking*, declare and maintain the same, he shall incur the penalties of a *præmunire*."

"I will make a short observation or two," says Forster, "on the Act:—First, The positions condemned by them had as direct a tendency to involve these nations in the miseries of an intestine war, to incite Her Majesty's subjects to withdraw their allegiance from her, and to deprive her of her crown and royal dignity, as any general doctrine, any declaration *not relative to actions or designs*, could possibly have; and yet in the case of bare words, positions of this dangerous tendency, though maintained *maliciously, advisedly, and directly*, and even in the solemnities of *preaching and teaching*, are not considered as overt acts of treason.

"Secondly, In no case can a man be *argued* into the penalties of the Act by inferences and conclusions drawn from what he hath affirmed; the criminal position must be *directly* maintained to bring him within the compass of the Act.

"Thirdly, Nor will every rash, hasty, or unguarded expression, owing perhaps to natural warmth, or thrown out in the heat of disputation, render any person criminal within the Act; the criminal doctrine must be maintained *maliciously and advisedly.*"

He afterwards adds: "Seditious writings are permanent things; and, if published, they scatter the poison far and wide. They are acts of deliberation, capable of satisfactory proof, and not ordinarily liable to misconstruction; at least they are submitted to the judgment of the Court naked and undisguised, as they came out of the author's hands. Words are transient and fleeting as the wind; the poison they scatter is, at the worst, confined to the narrow circle of a few hearers; they are frequently the effect of a sudden transport, easily misunderstood, and often misreported."

Gentlemen, these distinctions, like all the dictates of sound policy, are as obvious to reason as they are salutary in practice. What a man writes that is criminal and pernicious, and disseminates when written, is conclusive of his purpose;—he manifestly must have deliberated on what he wrote, and the distribution is also an act of deliberation. *Intention in such cases* is not, therefore, matter of legal proof, but of reasonable *inference*, unless the accused, by proof on his side, can rebut what reason must otherwise infer: since he who writes to others undoubtedly seeks to bring over other minds to assimilate with his own. So he who advisedly speaks to others upon momentous subjects, may be presumed to have the same intention; but yet, so frail is memory—so imperfect are our natures—so dangerous would it be to place *words*, which, to use the language of Forster, are transient and fleeting, upon a footing with deliberate *conduct*, that the criminating letter of the law itself interposes the check, and excludes the danger of a rash judgment, by curiously selecting from the whole circle of language an expression which cannot be mistaken: for nothing said upon the sudden, without the evidence of a context, and sequel in thought or conduct, can in common sense deserve the title of advised speaking. Try the matter before you upon the principle of the statute of Queen Anne, and examine it with the caution of Forster.

Suppose, then, that instead of the words imputed by this record, the defendant, coming half-drunk through this coffee-house, had, in his conversation with Yatman, denied the right of Parliament to alter the succession. Could he have been adjudged to suffer death for high treason under the statute of Queen Anne? Reason and humanity equally revolt at the position; and yet the decision asked from you is precisely that decision; for if you could not have found advised speaking to bring it within that statute of treason, so neither can you find it as the necessary evidence of the intention charged upon the present indictment, which intention constitutes the misdemeanour.

If anything were wanting to confirm these principles of the law and the commentaries of its ablest judges, as applicable to words, they are in another way emphatically furnished by the instance before us;—for in the zeal of these coffee-house politicians to preserve the defendant's expressions, they were instantly to be put down in writing, and signed by the persons present; yet the paper read by Colonel Bullock, and written, as he tells you, at the very moment with that intention, contains hardly a single word, from the beginning to the end of it, either in meaning or expression, the same as has been related by the witnesses. It sinks, in the first place, the questions put to the defendant; and the whole dialogue, which is the best clue to the business, and records "*that Mr Frost came into the coffee-house, and declared,*" an expression which he never used, and which wears the colour of deliberation, "*that he wished to see equality prevail in this country.*" Another expression which it is now agreed on all hands he never uttered, and which conveys a very different idea from saying, in answer to an impertinent or a taunting question, "Oh, yes! I am for equality." I impute nothing at all to Colonel Bullock, who did not appear to me to give his evidence unfairly: he read his paper as he wrote. But this is the very strength of my observation: for suppose the case had not come for months to trial, the other witnesses (and honestly too) might have let their memories lean on the written evidence, and thus you would have been trying, and perhaps condemning, the defendant for speaking words, stript too of their explanatory concomitants, which it stands *confessed at this moment were never spoken at all.*

Gentlemen, the disposition which has of late prevailed to depart from the wise moderation of our laws and constitution, under the pretext or from the zeal of preserving them, and which has been the parent of so many prosecutions, is an awful monument of human weakness. These associators to prosecute, who keep watch of late upon our words and upon our looks, are associated, it seems, to preserve our excellent constitution from the contagion of France, where an arbitrary and tyrannous democracy, under the colour of popular freedom, destroys all the securities and blessings of life. But how does it destroy them? How, but by the very means that these new partners of executive power would themselves employ, if we would let them—by inflicting, from a mistaken and barbarous state necessity, the severest punishments for offences never defined by the law;—by inflicting them upon suspicion instead of evidence, and in the blind, furious, and indiscriminate zeal of persecution, instead of by the administration of a sober and impartial jurisprudence. Subtracting the horrors of invading armies, which France cannot help, what other mischief has she inflicted upon herself? From what has she suffered but from this undisciplined and cruel spirit of accusation and rash judgment? A spirit that will look at nothing dispassionately, and which, though proceeding from a zeal and enthusiasm for the most part honest and sincere, is nevertheless as pernicious as the wicked fury of demons, when it is loosened from the sober dominion of slow and deliberate justice. What is it that has lately united all hearts and voices in lamentation? What but these judicial executions, which we have a right to style murders, when we see the axe falling and the prison closing upon the genuine expressions of the inoffensive heart: sometimes for private letters to friends, unconnected with conduct or intention; sometimes for momentary exclamations in favour of royalty, or some other denomination of government different from that which is established.

These are the miseries of France—the unhappy attendants upon revolution; and united as we all are in deploring them, upon what principle of common sense shall we vex and terrify the subjects of our own country in the very bosom of peace, and disgust them with the Government which we wish them to cherish, by unusual, irritating, and degrading prosecutions?

Indeed, I am very sorry to say that we *hear* of late too much of the excellence of the British Government, and *feel* but too little of its benefits. They too who pronounce its panegyrics, are those who alone prevent the entire public from acceding to them; the eulogium comes from a suspected quarter when it is pronounced by persons enjoying every honour from the Crown, and treating the people, upon all occasions, with suspicion and contempt. The three estates of the kingdom are co-ordinate, all alike representing the dignity, and jointly executing the authority, of the nation: yet all our loyalty seems to be wasted upon one of them. How happens it else, that we are so exquisitely sensible, so tremblingly alive to every attack upon the CROWN, OR THE NOBLES that surround it, yet so completely careless of what regards THE ONCE RESPECTED AND AWFUL COMMONS OF GREAT BRITAIN?

If Mr Frost had gone into every coffee-house from Charing Cross to the Exchange, lamenting the dangers of popular government, reprobating the peevishness of opposition in Parliament, and wishing, in the most advised terms, that we could look up to the throne and its excellent ministers alone for quiet and comfortable government, do you think that we should have had an indictment? I ask pardon for the supposition: I can discover that you are laughing at me for its absurdity. Indeed, I might ask you whether it is not the notorious language of the highest men, in and out of Parliament, to justify the alienation of the popular part of the Government from the spirit and principle of its trust and office, and to prognosticate the very ruin and downfall of England, from a free and uncorrupted representation of the great body of the people ?   I solemnly declare to you, that I think the whole of this system leads inevitably to the dangers we seek to avert: it divides the higher and the lower classes of the nation into adverse parties, instead of uniting and compounding them into one harmonious whole : it embitters the people against authority, which, when they are made to feel and know is but their own security, they must, from the very nature of man, unite to support and cherish.   I do not believe that there is any set of men to be named in England— I might say that I do not know an individual—who seriously wishes to touch the Crown, or any branch of our excellent constitution ; and when we hear peevish and disrespectful expressions concerning any of its functions, depend upon it, it proceeds from some practical variance between its theory and its practice.   These variances are the fatal springs of disorder and disgust : they lost America, and in that unfortunate separation laid the foundation of all that we have to fear ; yet instead of treading back our steps, we seek recovery in the system which brought us into peril.   Let Government in England always take care to make its administration correspond with the true spirit of our genuine constitution, and nothing will ever endanger it.   Let it seek to maintain its corruptions by severity and coercion, and neither laws nor arms will support it.   These are my sentiments, and I advise you, however unpopular they may be at this moment, to consider them before you repel them.

If the defendant, amongst others, has judged too lightly of the advantages of our Government, reform his errors by a beneficial experience of them ; above all, let him feel its excellence to-day in its beneficence : let him compare, in his trial, the condition of an English subject with that of a citizen of France, which he is opposed in theory to prefer.   These are the true criterions by which, in the long run, individuals and nations become affectionate to governments, or revolt against them : for men are neither to be talked nor written into the belief of happiness and security, when they do not practically feel them, nor talked or written out of them, when they are in the full enjoyment of their blessings : but if you condemn the defendant upon this sort of evidence, depend upon it, he must have his adherents, and, as far as that goes, I must be one of them.

Gentlemen, I will detain you no longer, being satisfied to leave you, as conscientious men, to judge the defendant as you yourselves would be judged ; and if there be any amongst you who can say the rest that he has no weak or inconsiderate moments—that all *his* words and actions, even in the most thoughtless passages of his life, are fit for the inspection of God and man, he will be the fittest person to take the lead in a judgment of guilty, and the most proper foreman to deliver it with good faith and firmness to the Court.

I know the privilege that belongs to the Attorney-General to reply to all that has been said; but perhaps, as I have called no witnesses, he may think it a privilege to be waived. It is, however, pleasant to recollect, that if it should be exercised, even with his superior talents, his honour and candour will guard it from abuse.

REPLY OF THE ATTORNEY-GENERAL.

GENTLEMEN OF THE JURY,—The experience of some years has taught me, that in the useful administration of justice, as it is administered by the juries in this country, little more is necessary than to lay before them correctly the facts upon which they are to form their judgment, with such observations as naturally arise out of those facts.

Gentlemen, feeling that very strongly at present, I am certainly bound in some measure to account to you why I feel it my duty, in this stage of this proceeding, to avail myself of that liberty which my learned friend has stated to belong to me in addressing you again.

Gentlemen, my learned friend has thought proper to state this prosecution as the prosecution of informers,—of men whom he cannot call mercenary informers, but certainly whom he has been anxious to represent as officious informers,—as a prosecution which it was my duty, independently of any considerations that I might feel myself upon the subject, to bring before you,—that it was what I could not approve of, but what I was bound to persevere in till I received your verdict.

Gentlemen, with respect to bringing the cause before the Court, my learned friend has not confined his observations to that point. He has stated also,—and everything that falls from him, and more especially in a case that concerns the Crown and an individual, deserves and must have an answer from me,—he has given you a comment upon words, upon which I likewise offered you some humble observations: I mean the words, "otherwise well-disposed." I remarked, that where words in their natural meaning did import a seditious mind, it would be competent to a defendant to show, upon a general principle, that whatever might be the words uttered, the circumstances attending the expression of them might be stated to the jury, in order to give a different sense to them from their primary import.

Gentlemen, I hold it to be my duty, standing here responsible to the public for the acts that I do, deeply impressed with a consciousness that I am so responsible, to state to you, that I must be extremely guilty of a breach of my duty if I should now call upon you for a verdict, or if I should now take your opinion; because there is not a tittle of evidence before you which was not before me when the indictment was laid. I protest against that doctrine that the Attorney-General of England is bound to prosecute because some other set of men choose to recommend it to him to prosecute, he disapproving of that prosecution. I know he has it in his power to choose whether he will or not, and he will act according to his sense of duty. Do not understand me to be using a language so impertinent as to say, that the opinions of soberminded persons in any station in life, as to the necessity that calls for a prosecution, ought not deeply to affect his judgment. But I say, it is his duty to regulate his judgment by a conscientious pursuance of that which is recommended to him to do. And if anything is recommended to him which is thought by other persons to be for the good of the country, but which he thinks is not for the good of the country, no man ought to be in the office who would hesitate to say, " My conscience must direct me, your judgment shall not direct me." And I know I can do this: I can retire into a situation in which I shall enjoy what, under the blessings of that constitution thus reviled, is perhaps the best proof of its being a valuable constitution,—I mean the fair fruits of an humble industry, anxiously and conscientiously exercised, in the fair and honourable pursuits of life. I state, therefore, to my learned friend, that I cannot accept that compliment which he paid me when he supposed it was not my act to bring this prosecution before you, because it was not what I myself could approve. Certainly this prosecution was not instituted by me—but it was instituted by a person whose conduct in the humane exercise of his duty is well known; and I speak in the presence of many who have been long and often witnesses to it: and when it devolved upon me to examine the merits of this prosecution, it was my bounden duty to examine, and it was my bounden duty to see if this was a breach of the sweet confidences of private life. If this is a story brought from behind this gentleman's chair by his servants, I can hardly figure to myself the case in which the public necessity and expediency of a prosecution should be so strong as to break in upon the relations of private life. But, good God! is this prosecution to be so represented—when a man goes into a coffee-house, who is from his profession certainly not ignorant of the respect which the laws of his country require from him as much as from any other man; and when he, in that public coffee-house (provided it was an advised speaking), uses a language which I admit it is clear upon the evidence given you to-day provoked the indignation (if you please so to call it) of all who heard it,—when persons, one, two, three, or more, come to ask him what he meant by it,—when he gives them the explanation, and when he makes the offensive words still more offensive by the explanation that he repeatedly gives—will any man tell me, that if he goes into a public coffee-house, whether he comes into it from up-stairs, or whether he goes into it from the street, that he is entitled to the protection that belongs to the confidences of private life, or that it is a breach of the duties that result out of the confidences of private life ?

Gentlemen, I call upon you seriously to consider the case, to act with candour, to act with indulgence to him, if you please, but at the same time to act with firmness as between him and the country. My learned friend has tried me in some measure to-day. Now I avow it again—when *respectable persons* will state to me that such circumstances did pass, I will not take upon myself to say that it is consistent with my duty to the King, or that it is consistent with my duty to the country, for whose benefit it is that he is King, that I should hear that such things have passed unnoticed. , And when it is stated by such men as these are,—unimpeached,—feeling something, though their political theories are not the same as those of this defendant, surely they may be allowed to feel and to express at least with zeal their indignation, if not to assert with industry their right to what they enjoyed through the blessing of Providence, and the constitution under which they lived. It was a case which excited the honest zeal and the fair and reasonable indignation of a great number of gentlemen,—all respectable men, and competent to sit in that jury-box, as between this or any other individual and the justice of the country. But, gentlemen, according to my learned friend, I was to do one of these things : I was to say to Mr Frost, which I certainly should have been glad to have said to him, or any man who stands in the situation of a defendant, if I could do it with propriety, " What is this story, Mr Frost ?" Can I ask a defendant, whom I am to prosecute, upon the *primâ facie* evidence laid before me, what he is to say for himself in that stage of the business ? It was open to Mr Frost in every stage of the business to have explained his conduct. He does not come upon this record to say, as many persons have said, I admit I spoke the words, I will not give you the trouble to prove the words : I spoke them in a degree of heat. I am (what he has never yet said, for he only seemed to retract), I am sorry for the words I have used.

Gentlemen, my learned friend says I should have said nothing to you upon the subject of France, and he particularly alludes to a question put by my learned friend, who will do me the justice to say that I had no communication with him upon any such question. But I will explain myself upon that, as I think I ought to do upon everything which occurs in a cause.

Gentlemen, if words of this sort spoken in France are a crime, I know from his Lordship's authority, as well as the authority of every principle of settled law, that I cannot give them in evidence; and if acts done in France amount to a crime against the law of this country, I know also I ought not to give in evidence upon an indictment such as this is any evidence with respect to the acts so done. They ought to be the subject of a separate prosecution; and if my opinion had risen higher upon that subject than it does, I would not in the prosecution of this case have even risked such a question as that, whether certain acts can be done and declarations made in another country by a subject of this country, without his being amenable to the law of this country. It is a question that ought to be tried, if it is to be tried at all, in a more solemn form than taken as a mere collateral point in evidence. But was not I entitled to speak about France? Did not this gentleman state that things were going on well in France,—that he had come from France,—that it was his intention to go again to France, and that, according to that intention, he did go to France? Is not this evidence that he knew what he was saying,—that he was speaking that which his future acts confirmed? Then how does it appear that he was drunk, or at least so much so, that he could not speak about anything,—that he could not correctly speak his opinion? It is clear that he stated a fact with respect to what he was to do, that the future act of his life corresponded with; and yet my learned friend says he did not speak advisedly at all.

Gentlemen, another observation that fell from my learned friend was with respect to what I have stated as to the words, "otherwise well-disposed." Gentlemen, give me leave, in the first place, to call your attention, as far as my Lord may think your attention ought to be called to it, to what I take to be a clear distinction in the law of England. Gentlemen, if words of their own efficacy and import manifest a seditious intention, the uttering those words is a misdemeanour. I do not desire you to try this question in that manner, because I again repeat what I said towards the conclusion of what I before addressed to you, that if you should be of opinion that Mr Frost did not utter the words advisedly and knowingly, and with an intention to work the mischief this record imputes to him, I do not desire his conviction; but I will say this, that it is a very clear distinction in law with respect to words as they amount to high treason. What did the Legislature say in those just and beautiful passages that were read to you by Mr Erskine from Mr Justice Forster's Reports, that the penalties in high treason are so exceedingly great, that, although treasonable words were spoken, yet if not spoken with such intention, they would not, as in the case of high treason, expose the subject to those pains and penalties: did they mean to say, they should be no offence at all, if the conscience of the jury should be satisfied that they were used in a way to make them criminal? By no means. But if you are of opinion

that these words were advisedly spoken, if the words themselves import that seditious intent which this record ascribes
to them, I say it falls directly within the principle of Mr Justice Forster, namely, that it would be competent to the defendant to give evidence of his general demeanour as a good subject
of the country, to show that he had not that meaning, which
is the *primâ fucie* sense of the words: if that principle be just,
I say that Mr Frost has not found in the company below-stairs,
nor has he found upon the face of the earth, a single person
to state to you, that from his general demeanour, when he uttered
these words, he must not have had the fair use of that judgment
and disposition which conducts him through general life. I say
no more about it. I am sure it would have been competent to
him have produced such witnesses. Gentlemen, it would not only
have been competent to him, but from the turn the cause has taken,
it was made almost necessary. If Mr Frost was drunk, as my
learned friend wishes you to believe, from what Mr Taitt said,—
though I think his evidence will bear no such sense,—was there
no man up-stairs who could have stated it? Was there no man who
saw Mr Frost in the course of that evening that could have stated
it? Then what is it that Mr Taitt says upon the subject? He
does not mean to say that he had not drunk; he says he might be
in liquor, and he did say he did not doubt but he was in liquor,
but he had not seen him before. The question is, whether, when
he made use of those expressions, he made use of them as expressing his judgment upon the subject, and with the intent that this
record ascribes to him? or whether he was so far bereaved of his
judgment by ebriety as to stand before you, entitling himself to the
benefit of this excuse, that he ought not to be answerable for the
consequences of these acts upon that ground?—and it would be extremely strange if a jury, upon this ground, could acquit Mr Frost.
Here are these gentlemen, *respectable in their situation*, and what
have they done? According to what they conceived to be their
duty as subjects of the country, they have been furnishing the
means of this prosecution, and they have not thought that it would
disgrace them to bring before a jury of their country Mr Frost, to
relate this story, that he stood in that situation of mind in which
my learned friend's cross-examination would endeavour to place
him. Whatever is your verdict, it is contrary to my duty to press
for it against your impression of the real nature of the case; but
the true question will be (and here I will not avail myself at any
length of that privilege my learned friend says belongs to me),
whether these words were advisedly spoken? Mr Frost goes into
a public coffee-room, asserts that they were doing very well in
France, and at the same time he asserts, that it was because there
was a doctrine of equality, and a doctrine of no King at that time
established. But was it an equality such as my learned friend has

stated to you? No;—the equality of right to personal security, to personal liberty and property, and a right to equal laws, was asserted indeed in the constitution of the year 1789 ; it was an equality which left every man in possession of that situation which the constitution assigned him, from the King on the throne to the meanest subject; who would be equally entitled to the benefit of the law of the country as any man in it; but that equality did not live till the 6th of November 1792. Why, then, equality might mean one thing, or it might mean another: it might mean the equality of 1789, or it might mean the equality of 1792. Then a stranger comes up to Mr Frost, and feeling a great deal of indignation at hearing this doctrine held, he says, "Sir, what do you mean by equality?" Now, did the Duke of Richmond,—did Mr Pitt, the present Minister of State, who has been alluded to,—did my learned friend, and the other persons, who are very respectable men, as I readily admit them to be, —did they ever give such an answer as Mr Frost gave? I am free to declare this is a country in which every man has a right to his opinion temperately discussed. I am free to say, with respect to my learned friend, I believe he and some of the most respectable persons in the country have their opinions upon that subject. I believe the actual quantum of political happiness that is enjoyed in this country is, upon the present system of government, far beyond that which the providence and favour of God has ever dispensed to any nation that ever lived upon the face of the earth. I have never been able to find in the discordant systems of those respectable persons argument enough to lead my mind to doubt for a moment whether I should not sacrifice my duty to my country if I risked a change upon any principles that they have stated. But, gentlemen, do not understand me to say, that I am wiser than they—far from it ; but I say it is my duty to exercise my best judgment, and act according to it.

Gentlemen, what was the answer that Mr Frost gave? "I will tell you what I mean by equality ; I mean no King." Have any of those gentlemen stated such language? But that is not all; for that which is no act of deliberation is followed up by another question. "Why, surely, you cannot mean that there is to be no King in this country?" Says Mr Frost, "Yes, no King in any country." Why, gentlemen, the single question is, Is it the law of England that these words can be spoken under such circumstances with impunity? I am free to say, that upon the best information I can give myself upon the subject, I cannot feel a doubt that the law of England does not permit it. I say it is the law of England, that where men will hold language of this sort, they shall be deemed guilty of an offence against the law of England. Why, then, what am I to do, if I, standing in this situation, am to govern myself by the wisdom of the law? I say it is my duty to submit to your decision the fact upon the law as it stands. If my learned friend is satisfied that the law is not so, he has one course before him; or if he thinks that the law ought not to be so, he has another before him. But is the Attorney-General of this country to say,—"I will, in the regulation of my official conduct, take upon me to say that I am wiser than the Legislature of this country : I will enforce what I please, let the exigency of the country be what it may ?"

Gentlemen, in the first place, it is to be observed, that the language of that Act of Parliament is exceedingly strong with respect to malicious and advised speaking, and it points out to a jury that they are to have distinct evidence of the intention. This species of the intention may fall under a different consideration. But I do not wish to examine it upon a different consideration; because if in this case the words import the intent that the record attributes to them, you have that case in point of law that justifies you in finding the defendant guilty.

Gentlemen, having stated thus much, rather with a view of explaining my conduct to you than for the purpose of troubling you with particular observations upon the evidence, I will leave the case here. I think, upon the best consideration that I can give the case, that the late Attorney-General did right to bring it before the public. I should not have appeared here to-day, if I had not thought it right so far as to bring it before the public ; and the reason I do it is, that when a considerable number of His Majesty's subjects in a *respectable situation* feel—my learned friend says your verdict is to secure us from being in a situation like France—but when they feel that these words were uttered in a manner that has led them to think that some of the most valuable blessings they enjoy under the constitution of this country, wedded to it as they are, are in danger when this language is publicly held,—I say it is fit, as between the Attorney-General and such persons, that a jury of the country should say whether such words shall be spoke with absolute impunity. It does appear to me that they ought not to escape with absolute impunity ; but if you have any doubt in your minds, you will find a verdict for the defendant.

Lord KENYON, having summed up the evidence, the jury retired for an hour 'and a half, and then returned with a verdict, GUILTY.

TRIAL of Mr PERRY *and* Mr LAMBERT, *Editor and Printer of the " Morning Chronicle," for a Libel.*

THE SUBJECT.

THE following speech for Mr Perry and Mr Lambert, the editor and printer of the *Morning Chronicle*, strongly illustrates our observation in the preface concerning the difficulty of access to genuine trials at distant periods.

These gentlemen were tried for the publication of a libel, on the information of the Attorney-General, on the 9th of December, 1793, and the trial was at the time in very general circulation. Yet it was so wholly out of print that it made no part of the present work as originally prepared for the press ; but on its being referred to by Mr Perry in his able defence of himself on his late trial, we procured from him the copy (the only one to be found) from which we have printed the following pages.

The Attorney-General's information charged the defendants, Mr Perry and Mr Lambert, as editor and printer of the *Morning Chronicle*, with publishing an address of a Society for political information, held at the Talbot Inn, at Derby, which had been sent to the *Morning Chronicle* for insertion, in the ordinary course of business; neither Mr Perry nor Mr Lambert having had any kind of connexion or correspondence with the authors.

This trial being the first after the passing of the Libel Act, we have thought it best to print the whole of it as originally published, with the advertisement prefixed to it by Mr Perry.

ADVERTISEMENT.

In presenting the following trial to the public, at a period the most critical, perhaps, with respect to prosecutions, that ever occurred in the annals of this country, the editor was chiefly influenced by two considerations :—

First, the question, which arose in an early stage of the proceedings, with respect to juries, determined a very important rule of practice, namely, *that the first special jury, struck and reduced according to law, must try the issue joined between parties.* This decision of a controverted point, in the manner most consistent with common sense, and, as appeared from the pleadings, agreeable to the ancient practice of the Courts, and founded upon the statute law of the realm, is certainly to be estimated as an acquisition of no common magnitude to the subject.

Secondly, this is the first trial, since the Libel Bill passed into a law, completely conducted upon the principles of that bill, and may serve as the best illustration of the wise and excellent provisions of the law, as it now stands, with respect to libel ; a law admirably calculated to remove obscurity, to defeat improper influence, to facilitate the ends of justice by simplifying its operations, and to afford additional security for the full enjoyment of the most valuable privilege of Englishmen.

Impressed, then, with the view of this trial, as connected with great principles, and involving consequences the most important, both to the present age and to posterity, I have been anxious to render the following statement of the proceedings as full and correct as possible. Fidelity and accuracy are the only merits of a reporter ; these I have carefully studied. It is not allowed to him who transmits the sentiments of others to boast of his labours, or to claim the reward of public approbation. In this instance, I find myself sufficiently repaid with the pleasing reflection that I have been called, *in an age of prosecutions*, to record *one verdict* gained to the cause of freedom.

We print the parts of the address selected by the Attorney-General from the information itself, with the innuendoes, which run as follow :—

" We" (meaning the Society aforesaid) " feel too much not to believe that deep and alarming abuses exist in the British Government" (meaning his said Majesty's government of this kingdom), " yet we are at the same time fully sensible that our situation is comfortable compared with that of the people of many European kingdoms, and that, as the times are in some degree moderate, they ought to be free from riot and confusion. III. Yet we think there is sufficient cause to inquire into the necessity of the payment of seventeen millions of annual taxes, exclusive of poor-rates, county rates, expenses of collection, &c., &c., by seven millions of people. We think that these expenses may be reduced without lessening the true dignity of the nation" (meaning this kingdom) " or the Government" (meaning the Government of this kingdom), " and therefore wish for satisfaction in this important matter. IV. We view with concern the frequency of wars" (meaning, amongst others, the wars of his said Majesty and his subjects with foreign powers) ; " we are persuaded that the interests of the poor can never be promoted by accession of territory when bought at the expense of their labour and blood ; and we must say, in the language of a celebrated author, we who are only the people, but who pay for wars with our substance and our blood, will not cease to tell kings or governments that to them alone wars are profitable ; that the true and just conquests are those which each makes at home by comforting the peasantry, by promoting agriculture and manufactories, by multiplying men and the other productions of nature; that then it is that kings may call themselves the image of God, whose will is perpetually directed to the creation of new beings. If they continue to make us fight and kill one another in uniform, we will continue to write and speak until nations shall be cured of this folly. We are certain our present heavy burdens" (meaning burdens of the subjects of this kingdom) "are owing, in a great measure, to cruel and impolitic wars" (meaning cruel and impolitic wars entered into by his said Majesty against foreign powers), "and therefore we will do all on our part, as peaceable citizens, who have the good of the community at heart, to enlighten each other, and protest against them. V. The present state of the representation of the people" (meaning the representation of the people of this kingdom in the Parliament thereof) "calls for the particular attention of every man who has humanity sufficient to feel for the honour and happiness of his country, to the defects and corruptions of which we are inclined to attribute unnecessary wars, &c. &c. We think it a deplorable case when the poor" (meaning the poor of this kingdom) "must support a corruption" (meaning corruption of the representation of the people of this kingdom in the Parliament thereof) "which is calculated to oppress them" (meaning the poor of this kingdom), "when the labourer must give his money to afford the means of preventing him having a voice in its disposal, when the lower classes may say, "We give you our money for which we have toiled and sweat, and which would save our families from cold and hunger; but we think it more hard that there is nobody whom we have delegated to see that it is not improperly and wickedly spent." We have none to watch over our interests; the rich only are represented. The form of government" (meaning the government of this kingdom) "since the Revolution is in somo" (meaning some) "respects changed for the worse by the triennial and septennial Acts" (meaning Acts of the Parliament of this kingdom). "We lost annual Parliaments; besides which, the wholesome provisions for obligfno" (meaning obliging) "privy councillors to subscribe thair" (meaning their) "advice with their names, and against placemen and pensioners sitting in Parliament" (meaning the Parliament of this kingdom), "have been repealed. It is said that the voice of the people is the constitutional control of Parliament" (meaning the Parliament of this kingdom); "but what is this but saying that the representatives" (meaning the representatives of the people in the Parliament of this kingdom) "are naturally inclined to support wrong measures, and that the people most" (meaning must) "be constantly assembling to oblige them to do their duty. An equal and uncorrupt representation" (meaning representation in the Parliament of this kingdom) "would, we are persuaded, save us from heavy expenses, and deliver us from many oppressions. We will therefore do our duty to procure this reform, which appears to us of the utmost im-

portance. VI. In short, we see with the most lively concern an
army of placemen, pensioners" (meaning persons holding places
and pensions under the Government of this kingdom), "&c.,
fighting in the cause of corruption and prejudice, and spreading
the contagion far and wide; a large and highly expensive military
establishment" (meaning the military establishment of this kingdom), "though we have a well-regulated militia; the increase of
all kinds of robberies, riots, executions, &c., though the nation"
(meaning this kingdom) "pays taxes equal to the whole land
retail" (meaning rental) "of the kingdom in order to have his
property protected and secured, and is also obliged to enter into
separate associations against felonious depredations—a criminal
code of laws" (meaning the criminal code of laws of this kingdom)
"sanguine and inefficacious—a civil code" (meaning the civil code
of laws of this kingdom) "so voluminous and mysterious as to
puzzle the best understandings, by which means justice is denied
to the poor" (meaning the poor of this kingdom) "on account of
the expense attending the obtaining it. Corporations" (meaning
corporations of this kingdom) "under ministerial or party influence,
swallowing up the importance, and acting against the voice of the
people" (meaning the people of this kingdom); "penaltie" (meaning
penalties) "inflicted on those who accept of offices without conforming to the violation of their consciences and their rights; the
voice of free inquiry drowned in prosecutions, and the clamours of
the pensioned and interested; and we view with the most poignant
sorrow a part of the people" (meaning the people of this kingdom)
"deluded by a cry of the constitution and church in danger,
fighting with the weapons of savages under the banners of
prejudice against those who have their true interest at heart; we
see with equal sensibility the present outcry against reforms, and
a proclamation" (meaning his said Majesty's royal proclamation)
"tending to cramp the liberty of the press, and discredit the true
friends of the people, receiving the support of numbers of our
countrymen; we see the continuation of oppressive game-laws"
(meaning the game-laws of this kingdom) "and destructive
monopolies; we see the education and comfort of the poor" (meaning the poor of this kingdom) "neglected, notwithstanding the
enormous weight of the poor-rates; we see burdens multiplied,
the lower classes" (meaning the lower classes of the subjects of
this kingdom) "sinking into poverty, disgrace, and excesses; and
the means of these shocking abuses increased for the purposes of
revenue for the same, and the excise laws" (meaning the excise
laws of this kingdom), "those badges and sources of oppression,
kept up and multiplied; and when we cast our eyes on a people
just formed in a free community, without having had time to grow
rich under a government by which justice is duly administered,
the poor taught and comforted, property protected, taxes few and

easy, and at an expense as small as that of our pension list—we ask ourselves, Are we in England? Have our forefathers fought, and bled, and conquered, for liberty? And did they not think that the fruits of their patriotism would be more abundant in peace, plenty, and happiness? Are we always to stand still, or go backward? Are our burdens" (meaning the burdens of the subjects of this kingdom) "to be as heavy as the most enslaved people? Is the condition of the poor" (meaning the poor of this kingdom) "never to be improved? Great Britain must have arrived at the highest degree of national happiness and prosperity, and our situation must be too good to be mended, or the present outcry against reforms and improvements is inhuman and criminal. But we hope our condition will be speedily improved, and to obtain so desirable a good is the object of our present association, au" (meaning an) "union founded on principles of benevolence and humanity, disclaiming all connexion with riots and disorders, but firm in our purpose, and warm in our affections for liberty. VII. Lastly, We invite the friends of freedom throughout Great Britain to form similar societies, and to act with unanimity and firmness, till the people" (meaning the people of Great Britain) "be too wise to be imposed upon, and their influence in the government be commensurate with their dignity and importance: then shall we be free and happy. By order of the Society. S. Eyre, chairman" (meaning the chairman to the said Society).

In Trinity Term a rule was made in the usual way, on the motion of the prosecutor, for a special jury. Forty-eight jurors were struck; and in Easter Term they were reduced by the parties to twenty-four. In the sittings after Easter, the cause came on, and seven of the special jurors came into the box. Sir John Scott, the then Attorney-General, did not pray a *tales*, and the trial went off as a *remanet pro defectu juratorum*.

In Michaelmas Term the prosecutor, on a motion of course, took out a rule for a new special jury. This the defendants thought irregular.

On Friday, the 15th day of November, the Hon. Thomas Erskine moved the Court as follows:—

MY LORD,—The motion which I am about to address to the Court will deserve your Lordship's particular attention, as it relates to one of the most essential rights and liberties of the subject, the trial by jury.

Your Lordship may recollect that at the sittings after the last term in this place, an information, filed by the Attorney-General, against the proprietors and printer of the *Morning Chronicle*, for a supposed libel in that newspaper, was called on for trial in the ordinary course of things. Seven of the special jurors, struck under the rule obtained by the Crown itself for the trial of the cause, appeared,

and came into the box to be sworn; but the Attorney-General did
not think proper to pray a *tales* to complete the pannel.   The cause
therefore, of course, went off, *pro defectu juratorum.*

My Lord, if any special reason existed why the jury so appearing
should not be permitted to try the information when it came on
again for trial, and the Crown had moved, upon such special matter,
verified by affidavit, to discharge the original rule under which the
jury was appointed, I should, according to the nature of the objections, have been prepared to give them an answer.   But, my Lord,
no such proceedings have been had or attempted.   The Crown has
made no objection to the jurors, nor any motion in Court to discharge the original rule under which the jury was impannelled:
but assuming it to be the law that the rule was spent and expired,
by the trial going over, for defect of jurors, they have, as a motion,
of course (drawn up, upon the signature of counsel out of court),
obtained a second rule for striking a jury, as if no former rule had
ever existed, and as if no jury had been struck under it.

I confess I was not a little surprised at this attempt to impannel
a jury without the consent of the defendants, between whom and
the Crown the former had been reduced and ascertained under the
first rule.   On their part, I therefore now object to the proceeding,
as totally illegal and hostile to the freedom of trial; and I humbly
move that this new rule may be discharged.

I do not know that I am able to state, at this moment, any
direct precedent for my motion, nor is it necessary that I should,
because I found my application upon the whole statute law of the
kingdom respecting the trial by jury, which is positive and unequivocal on the subject, which no practice can shake, and which
no decisions of the Court, if there were any, could repeal or
overrule.

Lord KENYON. The application crosses all my ideas of the law
upon the subject.   It would be highly dangerous to impartial trial
if the juries were known to the parties so long before the trial.   It
is very strange if the law be so.

Mr ERSKINE. My Lord, the authors of our laws seem to have
thought differently on this subject.   They seem to have entertained
no jealousy that the trial by the country, which was instituted for
the people's protection, could ever be too favourable to them; on
the contrary, the most ancient statutes of the kingdom express no
fears for the Crown, but for the subject only, and provide that
jurors shall be struck so long before the day of trial, that the
defendant may know them, and be prepared to take his challenges.
The Act of the 42d of Edward III., chap. 11, expressly gives this
reason.   After stating that divers of the people had been disheartened and oppressed, from not having had knowledge beforehand of those who were to pass in the inquest, it enacts, that the
names of the jurors should be returned into court in the term

before the assizes, and that, in the meantime, the parties on demand should view the same.

The whole statute law, from that period, speaks the same language, down to the famous statutes of King William and Queen Anne, which give to defendants accused of high treason the names and abodes, not merely of the jurors, but of the very witnesses to be examined against them on the trial. So far, indeed, is it from being true that, by the common law, a jury, once summoned, and not attending, could not be distrained again to appear at a future day, as is supposed by Mr Justice Page, in Masterman's note, that they were bound to give their attendance from assizes to assizes, *in infinitum*, until the reign of William the Third.

The statute of the 13th Edward I., chap. 30, had expressly directed that, upon the default of jurors, the justices should put in the inquest no other than those first summoned ; and this regulation was so much the settled law, that *the Act of William, for the ease of jurors, and the regulation of trial*, recites that, as the law then stood, it often happened that upon causes going off at the assizes for defect of jurors, the same jurors were obliged to attend again and again at the trial of one and the same cause, to their great expense and trouble ; and after this preamble, a new *venire facias*, for the first time in the history of the law, was given to the parties, to bring in a new jury, upon the default of those impannelled under the first writ. It is, therefore, only by the effect of this statute that a jury, once summoned, is discharged before trial ; and the statute not extending, nor indeed relating at all, to special juries, they remain upon the old footing. Special juries do not exist, as many people seem to suppose, by the authority of a statute ; on the contrary, they are as ancient as the law itself, and were always truck, as they are at this day, by direction of the Court, when trials were had at the bar and not at *nisi prius;* the Act of the 3d of George II., chap. 25, having no relation to such juries, except as removes a doubt with regard to the legality of striking them for the trial of misdemeanors. This legality the statute recognises; and putting special juries, struck in the Crown Office, on the same footing with those in civil cases, directs them to be struck by rule, as they anciently were in cases of trials at bar, and enacts that *the iury so struck shall be the jury to try the cause.*

Indeed, so notorious is it that a jury summoned, and not attending, could be distrained to appear again (till the law, as far as it lated to common juries, was altered by the statute of King William), that we know that the whole jury process of the courts this day is founded upon that law ; for the *venire* is always turnable on the last day of the term before trial, at which day it entered on record, as of course, that default was made by the jurors summoned, and then the *distringas* issues to bring them in the day in banc, in the term following. unless the Justices shall come to the assizes in the interval; under which clause of *nisi prius* the trials are all bad. So that the process at this day, building fiction on reality, to give precision and uniformity to practice, ratifies that which is supposed now to have been contrary to all practice whatsoever. In ancient times, every man, in a civil cause, knew, upon the return of the *venire* in term, the jury that was to come at the assizes. The Sheriff now, by the Act of the 3d of George II., returns one pannel for all, which effectually prevents a defect of jurors; but special juries remain untouched by that statute. The reason and justice of the thing, moreover, support my construction. The Attorney-General alone can pray a *tales* in a criminal cause; for the statutes go no farther than to give defendants a right to pray the *tales* in penal actions, prosecuted *qui tam* with the Crown, but not in cases where the Crown is the prosecutor alone. It is true that the Attorney-General now grants his warrant of course to a defendant to pray one, but he may legally refuse it; and the subject's liberties are not to rest upon the courtesies of the officers of the Crown. What, then, is contended for in this right to change the jury? Why, nothing short of this: that if the Attorney-General does not like his jury, he may forbear to pray a *tales* himself; he may also refuse his warrant, without which the defendant cannot pray one; and this he may do *toties quoties*, until he has got a jury to his fancy. I am not arguing that Mr Attorney-General is likely to attempt this practice for such purposes; but the country is not to hold its rights upon the courtesy of the prerogative, or the honesty of those who may occasionally represent it.

Mr ERSKINE then proceeded to state the modern cases, which clearly showed that the practice of the Court bore him out in the law on the subject. He stated the King *v.* Hart, and the King *v.* Joliffe; but he relied implicitly, he said, on the law.

One of the officers of the Crown Office handed up to Mr Justice Buller, an opinion of Judge Page, in the 13th of George II., that a new jury ought to be granted; but Mr Justice Buller said, the defendants should take a rule to show cause, as it was of great importance to be argued and ascertained.

Lord KENYON said, he thought it scarcely necessary; but granted they might take a rule. A rule was therefore granted.

On Monday the 25th of November 1792, the rule came on to be argued.

Mr BEARCROFT, on the part of the Crown, contended that the cases cited by Mr Erskine were not in point. In the case of the King against Hart, the special jury of forty-eight had not been reduced to twenty-four by the parties, and the jurors had not come into court. In the case of the King against Joliffe, the cause had been put off on account of some publications which might have influenced the jury.   In the next term, a new jury was struck, so that the case was in point for the Crown, and it was so much the more so, as the new jury was moved for by a solicitor as well versed in the general practice as any solicitor of that Court.   Their Lordships would agree with him in this description, when they heard that the solicitor for the defendant in that cause was Mr Lowten, and he was solicitor also for the present defendants.   In that cause, then, Mr Lowten had moved for a new trial, and here he opposed a new jury.

[Mr Bearcroft was set right in the case of Joliffe.   In that instance the trial first went off, because, from the publications which had been made, the Court thought that the jury might be influenced.   In the term after this, the cause came on again, and both parties agreed to have a new jury.   A second time it was put off, through the delicacy of Mr Justice Gould; and on the third time it was brought on again, and the prosecutor moved for a new jury, without any pretext of influence, or of any other argument for a new jury.   This, Mr Lowten, as solicitor for the defendant (and who had not been employed in the beginning of the cause) objected to, and the Court *refused*.]

Mr BEARCROFT read from the notes of the late Mr Masterman, one of the secondaries of the Crown Office, a case, where it was his opinion that a new jury was conformable to the practice ; and he quoted also a cause against Lord Charles Fitzroy, where Mr Lowten had also, as solicitor for the defendant, moved for a new jury, and had succeeded ; but he owned that in this case it had been consented to by both parties.

Mr BEARCROFT then said he would argue the question on the *reason* of the rule.   It struck him as a most important point indeed that juries should not be continued from term to term, as they might be tampered with by the parties ; a thing so outrageous to justice, and so opposite to the spirit of our jurisprudence, that it had been ever the study of the Courts, and indeed the very aim of Parliament in making the statute third George II., to prevent juries from becoming permanent, or from being so long known beforehand as to be subject to influence.   That in regard to the prayer for a *tales*, though undoubtedly the defendant must have the warrant of the Attorney-General to enable him to pray a *tales*, yet the Attorney-General never denied such a warrant.   Another argument against the continuance of a jury was, that it must subject gentlemen to great inconvenience,—they never would know when they were to be discharged.   Here seven of them attended to do their duty, and they were again to be called upon ; eleven of them might attend, and still be subject to be called again.   There was no end of this, and he owned he did not know how they could call upon them again, for he did not know an instance of an *alias distringas* to bring up special jurors.

Mr ADAM stated, on the part of the defendants, that there were many instances in the books, especially in Brooke's Abridgment, where an *alias distringas* had gone to compel the attendance of jurors of all descriptions.

Mr Justice BULLER said, that as this case comprehended so important a rule of practice, he had taken pains to inform himself on the point, and he had found a case which, in his mind, determined the rule. He would read it, and then Mr Bearcroft would see what he could make of the argument. Mr Justice Buller then read a manuscript note of the case the King *v.* Franklin, the publisher of the famous paper called the *Craftsman*. It was important to remark the time and the judges—it was the fifth of George II., only three years after the law recognising special juries in misdemeanours had passed, and the judges on the bench were Mr Justice, afterwards Lord Chief-Justice, Lee, Mr Justice Page,* &c. ; and the Crown lawyers were men of the first eminence. Franklin was convicted of printing and publishing a libel in the *Craftsman*. The case was only so far different from the present, that the defendant there moved the Court to reverse the judgment, because the cause, after being put off from one term to another, had not been tried by a new jury. Here the defendants moved to continue the same jury. The doctrine was the same in both cases, only that in this case it is upon the application of the Attorney-General that the new jury is required ; in that case the Attorney-General or the Crown contended that the old jury should continue. Chief-Justice Lee pronounced the opinion of the Court, which Mr Justice Buller read. The opinion of the Court was, that the words of the statute were express, and could not be departed from, unless cause could be shown that there had been some irregularity in the striking of the jury, or in the reducing, or in some part of the proceeding, or in the writ of *venire*, or otherwise. The words of the statute were, " that the jury so struck and so reduced shall be the jury to try the issue joined in such cause." The jury were not dissolved until the cause was determined, and an *alias distringas* might issue. The opinion was at great length, and detailed the practice of striking juries by the ancient statutes downwards, and showed that, by the Act then recently passed, eleventh George II., the alteration with respect to juries related only to the common jury, and left the practice as to special jurors exactly as it stood by the ancient law, except as it declared that special jurors might be demanded by the Crown in cases of misdemeanour. In regard to common juries, it was thought hard and severe to compel their attendance from time to time ; but the special jury was left by that Act precisely as it stood before. This opinion, Mr Justice Buller said, delivered so soon after the Act had passed, so solemnly and argumentatively, in a question discussed by such great legal characters, must, in his

* The same judges who are supposed to have decided the case of the King *v.* Waring.

mind, determine the question. He concluded with saying, that he could not see how the Crown officers could go on without creating error on the record.

Lord Chief-Justice KENYON said, he must bow to such great authority, though the inclination of his disposition was the other way. But a point so solemnly argued (and where such a man as Mr Pulteney, Earl of Bath, being implicated, error *would* have been pleaded, if they could have found error on the record) must decide the present case. He made no inquiry at all, and did not take into his consideration the merits of the question at issue between the present parties; but it was, in his opinion, of the utmost interest to criminal jurisprudence that juries should not be subject to influence. It was that consideration which gave rise to the law for the balloting-box. Every lawyer knew the necessity that there was for that statute; as all the provisions which had been previously made to guard against influence had proved ineffectual, though any person convicted of trying to influence jurors was subject to a penalty of ten times the amount of the object at issue in the cause. What held good as to civil suits was equally applicable to criminal prosecutions. The principle of the balloting-box was equally applicable to both; but it was impossible to resist the precedent, standing as it did upon so high authority.

Mr Justice GROSE and Mr Justice ASHURST were of the same opinion.

The case of the King *v.* Franklin,* therefore, decided this ques-

---

* In consequence of that case, viz., the King *v.* Franklin, it became unnecessary for Mr Erskine and Mr Adam, as counsel for the defendants, to say anything on the part of the defendants; but it may not be unacceptable to know, by a short statement, how far the old practice confirms the good sense and authority of the case, the King *v.* Franklin.

Special juries existed long before the statute of third George II. by the act of the parties; and that as well in misdemeanour as in other cases. One party applied for special jury, and the other party consented; so that the special jury was then the result of compact between the parties. But when the parties had so contracted, the authority of the Court was necessary to give validity to the compact. Accordingly the Court, upon application, made a rule for a special jury; and that rule ran in the same words before the statute that are used now since the statute: an observation very material, especially in considering the last words. The rule ordered then, and orders now, that forty-eight shall be returned; that the prosecutor shall strike twelve, and the defendant twelve; *and that twenty-four, the remainder of the forty-eight, shall be the jury returned for the trial of the issue joined in that cause.*

This being agreed between the parties, and enforced by a rule of Court, the parties, before the statute, chose their forum, and by this forum their own compact and the authority of the rule of Court compelled them to abide; insomuch, that they could not get quit of the jury by the common mode of *challenging the array;* that is, challenging the whole pannel of jurors; such challenge, after the rule of Court, being deemed, like every other breach of the authority of the Court, a contempt by the party who should so challenge.

This had met with a decision in several cases, but particularly in the case of the King *v.* Burridge, for a misdemeanour, which came before the Court of King's Bench, Trinity Term, ten George I., a very short time before the passing of the Act rejecting special juries.

That case is reported in Lord Strange's Reports, vol. i., p. 593; in Lord Raymond,

tion; and the Court determined that the rule for another special jury, obtained upon the motion of the Crown lawyers, must be discharged.

On the 9th of December 1793, the cause having been called on for trial, Mr Attorney-General opened the case for the Crown as follows :—

1364; in Andrew's Reports, 52; in 8 Modern Reports, 245; and in many other books; and the case, as reported in all of them, not only confirms the argument and statement above given, but explains the only remaining difficulty in the case, viz., the meaning to be put upon the words in the rule of Court, *that the twenty-four shall be the jury returned for the trial of the issue in that cause.*

For the judges, in the reports given of their opinions, consider as synonymous, and meaning the same thing, the above phrase; and that they shall be the jury who shall actually try the cause; contrary to the construction contended for by the Crown on the present occasion, where it was pressed that the statute and the rule were both satisfied when the jury had been returned, although they had not actually tried the cause.

Soon after this case—that is, in third George II.—came the statute; and it is very material to observe that the statute transcribes *verbatim* the latter words of the rule used before the statute. Therefore, whatever was the construction of those words in the rule, the same must be their construction in the statute. It has been shown in what sense the judges considered the words in the rule, and it will not be contended that the words in the statute, "which said jury, so struck, shall be the jury returned for the trial of the said issue," can bear a different construction. There is, therefore, judicial authority, added to that of common sense, to settle the meaning of these words. The only other consideration in this case is, what change the statute made in the rights of the parties, if it made none from the words of the rule; and it is evident that it did no more than convert into a statutory obligation, carried into execution by a rule of Court, what had been a matter of compact, executed by a rule of Court; but that in all other respects, except that the one party was, after the statute, bound to agree to a special jury, if the other proposed it, the consequences were the same.

The disobedience to the rule remained a contempt, and the rule remained valid, unless the Court, for particular cause of corruption or undue interference, properly verified, should see ground to have another jury; but that, otherwise, the jury of compact or statute must continue.

This was the more material because of the Attorney-General's power to refuse the defendant a warrant to have a *tales* to make up the special jury, if deficient, and of the common jury; which was so far from being an idle right, as mentioned by Mr Bearcroft, that there was a case in which it was solemnly agitated, and which formed a ground of decision that the Attorney *could* and *ought*, in certain cases, to exercise the right. The King *v.* Jacob Banks, 6 Modern Reports, p. 246, as follows :—

"And as to another objection that was made, 'that such a course, if tolerated, would be of great mischief; for then most profligate offenders would get themselves acquitted by surprise, or over-hastening the trial, without allowing the Queen convenient time to manage her prosecution :'

"It was answered, 'that there could be none, because in Crown causes there cannot be *nisi prius* or *tales* without a warrant from the Attorney-General, *who shall be sure to grant none if he find any such danger.*'" And that such a thing may be at least by consent appears 1 Keb. 195, Rex *v.* Jones. And the granting a *nisi prius* amounts to a consent.

THE ATTORNEY-GENERAL'S SPEECH.

GENTLEMEN OF THE JURY,—The information charges the defendants with having printed and published a seditious libel, the contents of which you have now heard stated. The information originally was not filed by me, but by my predecessor in office, who then was, as you now are, sworn to discharge an important duty to the public according to the best of his judgment. It has since fallen to my lot to execute that duty, in stating to you the grounds upon which this information has been filed. And I have no difficulty in saying that, previous to my coming forward for this purpose, I thought it incumbent upon me to consider whether, in the office which I now hold, I should, of my own accord, have instituted this prosecution; because I thought that it became me not merely to follow up the measures of that highly respectable character, and to bring his opinion before a jury, but to be able, in so doing, to say that I approved of those measures, and concurred in that opinion, and to act exactly as he had done, according to the best of my judgment, for the public. Had I been clearly of opinion that this paper was not fit for the consideration of a jury, I have no hesitation in confessing that I should certainly have discontinued the prosecution. You, gentlemen of the jury, I am sure, will do me the justice to believe that I am not capable of the impertinence of saying, that because I may think this paper fit for prosecution, and may think the defendants guilty, you, therefore, must think so too. The prosecution does nothing more than declare that the paper is a proper subject for the discussion of a jury, and, as such, that I consider myself as bound to bring it forward in the course of my professional duty. With respect to that guilt or innocence of the defendants in publishing this paper, the question, which falls to your consideration, I am perfectly satisfied to leave to your decision. This is a cause of the highest importance, as, indeed, every cause which involves a criminal charge must be important, but this more particularly so from the nature of the charge. It is connected with the press, which has ever been deemed the great palladium of British freedom. In every case in which it is concerned, it is natural, therefore, that the most watchful attention of Englishmen should be excited. It is of great consequence, then, in the first instance, to ascertain what properly constitutes the liberty of the press, what are its bounds, and how far it extends; and on this subject I shall take the liberty of reading to you the sentiments of a character of the highest legal authority, namely, the late Mr Justice Blackstone.

"In this and the other instances which we have lately considered, where blasphemous, immoral, treasonable, schismatical, seditious, or scandalous libels are punished by the English law, some with a greater, others with a less degree of severity, the *liberty of the press*, properly understood, is by no means infringed or violated. The liberty of the press is indeed essential to the nature of a free state; but this consists in laying no *previous* restraints upon publications, and not in freedom from censure for criminal matter, when published. Every freeman has an undoubted right to lay what sentiments he pleases before the public; to forbid this is to destroy the freedom of the press; but if he publishes what is improper, mischievous, or illegal, he must take the consequence of his own temerity. To subject the press to the restrictive power of a licenser, as was formerly done, both before and since the Revolution, is to subject all freedom of sentiment to the prejudices of one man, and make him the arbitrary and infallible judge of all controverted points in learning, religion, and government; but to punish (as the law does at present) any dangerous or offensive writings, which, when published, shall, on a fair and impartial trial, be adjudged of a pernicious tendency, is necessary for the preservation of peace and good order, of government and religion, the only solid foundations of civil liberty. Thus the will of individuals is still left free; the abuse only of that free will is the object of legal punishment. Neither is any restraint hereby laid upon freedom of thought or inquiry; liberty of private sentiment is still left; the disseminating or making public of bad sentiments, destructive of the ends of society, is the crime which society corrects. A man (says a fine writer on this subject) may be allowed to keep poisons in his closet, but not publicly to vend them as cordials. And to this we may add, that the only plausible argument heretofore used for the restraining the just freedom of the press, 'that it was necessary to prevent the daily abuse of it,' will entirely lose its force when it is shown (by a seasonable exertion of the laws) that the press cannot be abused to any bad purpose, without incurring a suitable punishment; whereas it never can be used to any good one when under the control of an inspector. So true will it be found, that to censure the licentiousness is to maintain the liberty of the press." *

These principles of the law of England, thus laid down by this great man, must be admitted to be incontrovertible. The law allowed defendants in this as in every other case, a fair impartial trial, upon the result of which they were to be adjudged guilty or acquitted of the charge exhibited against them : and this principle has been explained by the last Act of Parliament for removing doubts of the functions of juries in cases of libel, the meaning of which Act I take to be, that the jury shall try these charges of libels precisely as they try any other charge of a criminal nature ; that they shall hear the case with attention, and hear it impartially :

* Blackstone's Commentaries, vol. iv., page 151, 8vo edition, 1791.

that they shall hear the advice of the Bench in point of law, and then apply the law, as they understand it, to the facts that appear in evidence, and then they shall acquit or find guilty as to them shall appear right. The question in this case is, "Whether, upon the facts as they shall appear in evidence, under the law as you shall understand it, after the advice of the learned Judge, the defendants be guilty, as the information charges them to be?" With respect to the fact, the paper stated in the information appeared in the *Morning Chronicle* on the 25th of December 1792. And here I must particularly beg the attention of the jury to the date of the libel. This paper, charged to be the libel, is dated at the Talbot Inn, at Derby, on the 16th of July 1792, and it did not appear in the *Morning Chronicle* till the 25th of December 1792. Thus you will observe that the date of the paper preceded its appearance in the *Morning Chronicle* six months. Having said this upon the paper itself, it is now my duty to the defendants to state, that it appeared not to be a publication actually composed by the defendants, but was said to be, with what truth I do not know, composed and agreed to at a society for political information, held at the Talbot Inn, Derby, signed S. Eyre, chairman. Whether there was such a person, or, if there was, whether he was the author, is to me entirely unknown. It was said to be unanimously agreed to by the persons holding the meeting, and ordered to be printed; how it happened that that order was not executed till the 25th of December I am unable to explain to you. But be that circumstance as it may, the defendants are the persons interested in the property and management of the newspaper in which this publication appeared. And I apprehend that the proprietors, printers, and publishers of a newspaper are responsible for whatever it may contain, unless it be admitted as a doctrine that men may carry on a trade which is a source of great profit and emolument, entirely through the medium of servants, without being themselves in the smallest degree accountable. Can it be deemed a sufficient apology for the evil tendency of a publication, of which they reap the advantage, that they are not its authors, or that they had no immediate hand in its insertion, and, therefore, are not bound to answer for what they themselves did not actually commit? On the contrary, I apprehend that, by adopting any publication, they become liable in law for the consequences of that publication, as much as if they were themselves the authors. It is true that there are many circumstances to be considered, either by me in moving judgment, or when it comes to be determined by the Court, what ought to be the nature and extent of the penalty. The consideration of the degree of guilt incurred by the particular act might then be attended to, independent of the law of the case. Negligence, omission, inadvertence, all of which, however, constituted a degree of criminality, might then, perhaps, properly be urged as circum-

stances of extenuation.   Though this paper, therefore, appeared in
the *Morning Chronicle*, not as the projected act of the defendants,
or of either of them, but as an advertisement signed by a Mr
Eyre, still it was a publication for which the defendants, in their
capacity, as connected with this paper, were clearly answerable.
Another circumstance which deserves your attention is the time at
which this advertisement was brought forward.   You will find in
the same paper in which it appeared a vast number of advertisements from various associations in different parts of the kingdom,
stating that there had lately been many seditious writings circulated
with the greatest industry, and from the worst intentions, which
had already done much mischief, and expressing a determination to
take every method in future to discountenance and suppress such
publications.   You are then to consider how far these advertisements might operate as an antidote to the statement contained in
this publication.   You are to take into review the whole of the paper
and advertisements, that you may be able to judge fairly of the
tendency of the contents, and the intention of the writers; you will
then decide whether this paper was published with a peaceable
temper, and from upright intentions.   I have nothing to say in
order to exaggerate the case, or influence your decision.   I have
never had occasion to do so in any instance.   It is neither my duty
nor my wish in the present, and I trust that no man in my situation will ever do so upon any future occasion.   All cases of which
the law takes cognisance, and which are to be determined by ascertaining facts, and applying the law to them, are, thank God, safe in
the hands of a jury, the best guardians of our rights.   Everything
in this country that deserves to be called a blessing is indisputably
deposited in their hands, as well as the power to apply a remedy,
wherever their interference was called for to check the progress of
an evil.   It was from our blessings being vested in their hands
that we derived our security for their enjoyment, and our confidence
in their duration.   It is for you, gentlemen of the jury, exercising
your privilege in its full extent, from the facts which I shall now
lay before you, to judge of the tendency of this paper, which is the
subject of prosecution : from the Bench you will hear laid down,
from the most respectable authority, the law which you are to
apply to those facts.   The right of every man to represent what he
may conceive to be an abuse or grievance existing in the government of the country, if his intentions in so doing be honest, and the
statement made upon fair and open grounds, can never for a
moment be questioned.   I shall never think it my duty to prosecute
any person for writing, printing, and publishing fair and conscientious opinions on the system of the government and constitution of
this country ; nor for pointing out what he may honestly conceive
to be grievances ; nor for proposing legal means of redress.   But
was this the case with respect to the present publication ?   Did the

mode in which the writers exposed what they considered as the abuses of the constitution indicate a peaceable temper, or honest intentions, and a desire only to obtain redress by legal and constitutional means? Did not this paper, on the contrary, describe the whole system as one mass of abuse, grievances, misery, corruption, and despair, not so much as bringing forward one alleviating circumstance, or affording even a ray of hope. [Here Mr Attorney-General read some extracts from the paper]. It attacked the Government in every branch, in its legislature, in its courts of justice, which had ever been deemed sacred; and, in short, represented all as equally corrupt and oppressive. There was no circumstance mentioned fairly, that the public might be left to judge freely upon their situation. What could be the tendency of such a representation but to excite murmurs and inflame discontent, without effecting one good purpose? If a man wishes to state honestly what he conceives to be a grievance, let him do it candidly, and propose what he conceives to be the proper means of redress. Let him not take one side of the picture only, or confine himself entirely to an unfavourable view of the subject, but let him balance the good with the evil, let him enumerate the blessings as well as the inconveniences of the system, and while he points out abuses and errors, not forget, likewise, to enumerate wise and salutary regulations; such a conduct only could answer the purposes of candid and useful discussion. The contrary conduct adopted in this paper could only have a tendency to unsettle men's minds, and stir up sedition and anarchy in the kingdom. I never will dispute the right of any man fully to discuss topics respecting government, and honestly to point out what he may consider as a proper remedy of grievances; every man has a right so to do, if the discussion be fairly and temperately conducted; I never will stand against such a person, even though I should differ with him in my opinion of the grievance, or disapprove of the proposed means of remedy. But when men publish on these points, they must not, as in the present instance, do it unfairly and partially; they must not paint the evil in the most glowing colours, while they draw a veil over the good. The writers of this paper, in describing the government of this country as productive only of one scene of misery, must have acted contrary to their own knowledge of its blessings, and in opposition to the sense which they could not but perceive was entertained by the people at large of the happiness of their condition. To what motives, I will ask, can such a representation be ascribed, or what are the effects to which it is naturally calculated to lead? Are the motives such only as can be set down to fair and honest intention, and the effects only such as can terminate in a legal and peaceable line of conduct? We are to consider, too, that this mode of representation is adopted with respect to a constitution which has been the admiration of the wisest and best men in all ages, who have thought it barely possible that a constitution should exist so nearly approaching to a model of perfection. It is a constitution under which a greater degree of happiness has been enjoyed than by the subjects of any Government whatever; and the sense entertained of its blessings depends not upon the vague result of theory, but the solid conviction of experience. These blessings have, in a great measure, sprung from the properly-regulated freedom of the press; a freedom, therefore, which it is more dangerous to abuse; and on maintaining that freedom on its proper principles chiefly depends our security for the enjoyment of those blessings. That this country has enjoyed a greater sum of happiness under its present constitution than any other, depends not merely upon the testimony of our own experience; let us recur to the evidence of history, we shall be more deeply impressed with a sense of our present felicity; let us take a view of the situation of the subjects of the other European Governments, we shall be more strongly convinced of the superiority of our own. What, then, do the writers of this paper mean when they say "that we feel too much not to believe that deep and alarming abuses exist in the British Government; yet we are at the same time fully sensible that our situation is comfortable compared with that of the people of many European kingdoms; and that as the times are in some degree moderate, they ought to be free from riot and confusion." Let this paragraph be taken by way of illustration. When they talk of our situation being comfortable compared with that of *many* European kingdoms, what need, I will ask, for this qualification? Is there any European Government that in point of real liberty and actual comfort can be compared with the British constitution? In this country we have the fullest security for the possession of our liberty and the enjoyment of our property, the acquisition of which must be the greatest spur to every honest and laudable exertion. But on the 25th December 1792, while this country was actually experiencing the blessings resulting from its admirable constitution, the principles which this paper seemed to recommend were producing very different effects in a neighbouring country. The effects which had there been produced did not surely hold out to British subjects any encouragement to adopt a system of experiment and innovation. The result of this in my mind is, that no man should be at liberty, without a specific object, to state truly or falsely what appears to him to be a grievance merely for the purpose of exciting a spirit of general discontent, which, I will venture to say, never can be called into action without endangering the public prosperity and happiness. We have always been in the habit of regarding the Revolution as the greatest blessing that ever befell this country. But how do the writers of this paper reason with respect to this event? They enumerate all the abuses which they pretend have since crept into the constitution, while they mention none of the many improvements which have taken place since that period. Is this, I will ask, a fair mode of stating the question? Besides, they show themselves ignorant of that Revolution by talking of the annual Parliaments which we then lost. What was the end of all this? The cause of truth and justice can never be hurt by fair and temperate discussion. If you, gentlemen of the jury, consider this paper as coming under that description, you will, of course, acquit the defendants. Look at the beginning and conclusion of their paper. You will find that they set out with declaring *that they are in pursuit of truth in a peaceable, calm, and unbiassed manner, and from an opinion that the cause of truth and of justice can never be hurt by temperate and honest discussion ; that they claim the right to associate together merely for the communication of thoughts, the formation of opinions, and to promote the general happiness.* You will find that they conclude thus : " We hope our condition will be speedily improved, and to obtain so desirable a good is the object of our present association ; an union founded on principles of benevolence and humanity, disclaiming all connexion with riots and disorder, but firm in our purpose, and warm in our affections for liberty." It is with you to decide whether you think the general tenor of this paper consistent with the principles assumed at the beginning and asserted at the end. If you shall judge that it contains matter very inconsistent with these principles, you are then to consider whether, in a case like this, *humble language ought to ransom strong faults.* If you shall be clearly of opinion that the paper has a different tendency from that which is professed in the outset and conclusion, and that the defendants themselves were aware of this tendency, you are then bound by your oath, and by the law of the country, to find the defendants guilty. Once more, as to the contents of this paper ; you will find that the taxes are loudly complained of, but that not a word is said of the general wealth and prosperity of the kingdom. But let a deduction be made of the national taxes from the amount of the national wealth, and I am confident that this country will appear in a higher state of opulence and prosperity than it ever was at any former period. What purpose, then, can such partial and unfair statements answer, except to inflame the discontented and encourage the seditious? Whatever I have said of the tendency of this paper I have stated only as my own opinion : it does not follow that the Society at Derby might not view the subject in a very different light. All that my duty demands is, solemnly to declare that I considered this prosecution, though not originating with myself, as a proper case to be submitted to the consideration of a jury. You have now heard from me almost all that I intended to say at present, or thought necessary to submit to you, except what may fall from my learned friend shall require me to add some farther observations in reply. You will hear from the evidence all the facts which the defendants have to urge in their own justification, and from his Lordship all that shall appear to him to be the law on this subject. I now leave the matter to your decision. If you think the defendants ought to be acquitted, I shall retire from the Court with a full conviction, not inconsistent however with that respect which I owe to your decision, that, in bringing this matter before you, I have acted according to the best of my judgment.

Mr Wood, the junior counsel on the part of the prosecution, was then proceeding to call witnesses; and Mr Berry was called, when the counsel for the defendants said he was instructed to save the Court all this trouble, as the defendants were anxious to try the question on its own merits. As counsel for the defendants, he therefore admitted that John Lambert, charged in the information as printer of the *Morning Chronicle*, was in fact printer of that paper; that the paper was purchased at the printing-house; and that the defendants, James Perry and James Gray, charged in the information as proprietors of the same paper, were in fact so. If these were the facts meant to be ascertained by witnesses, they would spare the Court unnecessary time and trouble by admitting them fully and unequivocally.

The Attorney-General said these were all the facts they meant to establish by proof; he thanked his learned friend for the admission.

———————

The Honourable THOMAS ERSKINE then rose for the defendants.

With the two gentlemen charged in the information as proprietors of the *Morning Chronicle*, I have been long and well acquainted. Of Mr John Lambert, who conducts the mechanical part of the printing business, I have no personal knowledge; but from my intimate acquaintance with the other two, I have no difficulty in saying that if I had in my soul the slightest idea that they were guilty, as charged in the information, of malicious and wicked designs against the State, I should leave the task of defending them to others. Not that I conceive I have a right to refuse my professional assistance to any man who demands it, but I have for a day or two past been so extremely indisposed that I feel myself scarcely equal to the common exertion of addressing the Court; and it is only from the fullest confidence in the innocence of the defendants that I came forward for a very short space to solicit the attention of the jury. You, gentlemen, indeed, are the sole arbitrators in this cause, and to you it belongs to decide on the whole merits of the question. Mr Attorney-General has already given a history of the prosecution, which was originally taken up

by his predecessor, now called to a high situation in his profession.
I do not mean, by anything I shall say, to impute unbecoming conduct to either of those respectable gentlemen for the part which
they have taken in this business; they no doubt brought it forward because they considered it as a proper matter for the discussion of a jury. I take it for granted that they would not have acted
so but from a sense of duty. Be this, however, as it may, the
weight of their characters ought to have no influence upon your
minds against the defendants. It would be dangerous to justice
indeed if, because a charge was brought by a respectable Attorney-
General, it were to be received as an evidence of guilt which ought
at all to bias the judgment or affect the decision of the jury. It is
the privilege of every British subject to have his conduct tried by
his peers, and his guilt or innocence determined by them. In this
case, Mr Attorney-General has given no judgment; he has taken
up the business merely in the course of his professional duty. The
whole of the matter comes before you, gentlemen of the jury, who
of course will reject everything that can have a tendency to influence your decision independently of the merits of the cause; you
will suffer no observation that may fall from my learned friend, or
from myself, to interfere with your own honest and unbiassed judgments. You are to take everything that relates to the case into
your own consideration; you are to consult only *your own* judgments; you are to decide, as you are bound by your duty, according to your own consciences; and your right to decide fully, on
every point, is clearly ascertained by the law of libels. To the Act
lately passed you are to look as the only rule of your conduct in
the exercise of your functions.

With respect to the interpretation of that Act, I must confess
that my learned friend and I materially differ. In one principle,
however, we entirely agree—that a case of libel is to be tried
exactly as any other criminal case; this point, indeed, he has most
correctly stated. When a man accused of a libel is brought before
a jury, they are to consider only the mind and intention with which
the matter was written, and accordingly as they shall find that
they are to form their decision of guilt or innocence. They are to
dismiss every other consideration, and allow themselves to be
biassed by no motive of party or political convenience. There is
this essential difference between criminal and civil cases: in
criminal cases, the jury have the subject entirely in their own
hands; they are to form their judgment upon the whole of it, not
only upon the act alleged to be criminal, but the motive by which
it was influenced, the intention with which it was committed; and,
according to their natural sense of the transaction, they ought to
find a man innocent or guilty, and their verdict is conclusive. Not
so in civil cases. In these the jury are bound to abide in their
decision by the law as explained by the Judge; they are not at

liberty to follow their own opinions.   For instance, if I am deprived
of any part of my property, the loss of my property lays a foundation for an action, and the fact being found, the jury are bound to
find a verdict against the person who has occasioned my loss, whatever might be his intentions.   Here the Judge pronounces the law,
the jury only find the fact.   The law and the fact are as distinct
and separate as light from darkness; nor can any verdict of a jury
pass for a farthing in opposition to the law, as laid down by the
Judge, since the courts have a power to set such a verdict aside.
But in criminal cases, the very reverse has been immemorially
established; the law and the fact have been inseparably joined;
the intention of the party accused is the very gist of the case.   We
are CRIMINAL only in the eyes of God and man, as far as the mind
and intention in committing any act has departed from the great
principles of rectitude by which we are bound as moral agents, and
by the indispensable duties of civil society.   It is not the act itself,
but the motive from which it proceeds, that constitutes guilt; and
the general plea, therefore, in all criminal cases, is not guilty.
Such is the answer which the justice and clemency of our laws
have put into the mouth of the accused, leaving him the right of
acquittal if the circumstances of the transaction shall be found to
exculpate his motives.

The criminality of a person under the Libel Act is not to be
taken as an inference of law from the fact, as Mr Attorney-General
has stated it, but (if as one of the authors of that bill I may be
allowed to interpret its meaning) it connects and involves the law
and the fact together, and obliges the jury to find in this crime, as
in all others, by extrinsic as well as intrinsic means, the mind and
intention with which the fact was committed.   Nothing can be
more simple than the doctrine.   It goes directly to the reason of
the thing.   Two men, for instance, are in company, and one of
them is killed.   It is not an inference in the law from the fact of
the killing that the person was guilty of murder; it might be manslaughter, justifiable homicide, chance-medley, or it might be murder: the fact does not infer the crime; it is the intention with
which the act was committed, and this the jury are bound to discover and decide upon from all the accompanying circumstances.
If I had been wrong in holding this opinion, all my opposition to
that great luminary of the law now departed, but who will always
live in public memory, was wrong and false.   I revered his venerable authority; I admired the splendour of his talents, which illustrated the age he lived in; and perhaps ages will pass without producing his rival.   I still opposed him, in the meridian of his fame,
on the doctrine that the law of libel was an inference from the fact;
and now the Legislature have solemnly confirmed my opinion, that
the law and fact are compounded together, and are both to be found
by the jury.   I could not have held up my head in this court, nor

in the world, if it had been adjudged otherwise; and how my learned friend can hold an opinion that the question of libel is to be tried precisely like all other criminal cases, and yet that criminal intent is an inference of law, I am utterly at a loss to comprehend. I aver that you are solemnly set in judgment on the hearts of the defendants in the publication of this paper; you are to search for their intention by every means which can suggest itself to you; you are bound to believe in your consciences that they are guilty of malicious and wicked designs, before you can pronounce the verdict of GUILTY. It is not because one of them published the paper, or because the others are proprietors of it, but because they were, or were not, actuated by an evil mind, and had seditious intentions, that you must find them guilty or not guilty. Such was the opinion of the venerable Hale. He clearly stated that such should be the charge given to you by the Judge. It is their sacred function to explain to you their opinion, but not to force it upon you as a RULE for yours. A jury will always listen with reverence to the solemn opinion of the Judge; but they are bound to examine that opinion as rigorously as that of an advocate at the Bar; they cannot, and they ought not, to forget that a judge is human, like themselves, and of course not exempt from the infirmities of man. I do not say this to inspire you with any jealousy of the explanations which may be given you by the noble and learned Judge who presides here with so much wisdom, integrity, and candour; and whose ability in explaining the law derives both force and lustre from the impartiality which so eminently distinguishes him in the discharge of the duties of his office.

I now come to the consideration of the question: What is the charge against the defendants? Let us look to the indictment, which sets out with referring to His Majesty's proclamation which had appeared against all seditious writings previous to the publication of the libel. I will not here talk of the propriety of that proclamation; it is not now my business here to enter into political questions; I have a privilege to discuss them in another place. I will suppose the proclamation to have been dictated by a wise and prudent policy; I will give credit to it as a measure of salutary precaution and useful tendency. I will only remind its authors when it was issued. It was issued at a period the most extraordinary and eventful which ever occurred in the annals of mankind; at a period when we beheld ancient and powerful monarchies overturned—crumbled into dust, and republics rising upon their ruins; when we beheld despotic monarchy succeeded by the despotism of anarchy. In this state of alarm, confusion, and devastation in other countries, the defendants are accused by this information of wickedly, maliciously, and seditiously endeavouring to discharge His Majesty from the hearts of his subjects, and to alienate the people of England from what their affections were riveted on—a limited and well-regulated monarchy. The proclamation appeared professedly to check a spirit of innovation which had already displayed itself by such alarming effects in a neighbouring country, and which it was feared, by its authors, might in its progress become fatal to all establishments. How, then, can this paper be deemed seditious in the spirit of that proclamation? It was not surely against a reform in our own constitution, which this paper recommends, that the proclamation was pointed, but against those who, in imitation of that neighbouring country, wished to establish a republican anarchy. Can any man produce a single expression which, in the smallest degree, countenances such a system? How, then, can this paper be urged to be published in defiance of His Majesty's authority, or to have a tendency to alienate the minds of his subjects from his government? A proclamation is always considered as the act of Ministers; it becomes the fair subject of discussion; nor do the contents of this paper at all breathe a spirit either disrespectful to His Majesty's person or injurious to his government.

If you, gentlemen of the jury, can think that the defendants were actuated by the criminal motive, not of wishing to reform and restore the beautiful fabric of our constitution, somewhat impaired by time, but to destroy and subvert it, and to raise on its ruins a democracy or anarchy—an idea at which the mind of every honest man must shudder—you will find them guilty. Nay, if any one man knows or believes them to be capable of entertaining such a wish, or will say he ever heard or had cause to know that one sentence intimating anything of that nature ever fell from the lips of any one of them, I will give them up. How they came to be so charged upon the record I cannot tell: there are not among His Majesty's subjects men better disposed to the Government under which they live than the defendants. There have appeared in the *Morning Chronicle*, day after day, advertisements to a vast number warning the people of this country against seditious persons, and against the effects of seditious publications. How any jury can be brought to think the defendants are what they are stated to be on the record I know not. The information states that the defendants being wicked, malicious, seditious, and ill-disposed persons, did *wilfully, wickedly, maliciously, and seditiously*, publish a certain *malicious, scandalous, and seditious* libel against the Government of this kingdom, against its peace and tranquillity, and to stir up revolt, and to encourage his Majesty's subjects to resistance against his person and government. This is the charge. All records have run in this form from the most remote antiquity in the law of England, for the purpose of charging the defendant expressly and emphatically with an evil intention. So we charge a man accused of treason—so of murder—so of all worst and most dangerous crimes: first, we begin with the intention, and then we state the overt act as evidence of that intention which constitutes the crime. Now the record charges these defendants with this evil intention, and that, in order to give effect to that intention, they did publish the paper now before the jury. Such is the charge. Mr Attorney-General has stated to you in his opening, that if it shall appear to you that the paper in question was not *written with a good intention by its authors,* then the defendants are guilty of the crime imputed to them upon the record. This I deny. Your Lordship will recollect the case of the King and Stockdale ; and I shall leave to the jury in *this,* as your Lordship did in *that* case, the question of the intention of the party from the context of the whole publication, and the circumstances attending it ; and upon this I will maintain that it is not sufficient that it should appear the paper was written with a criminal intention by its author, or that the paper itself was criminal, but that it must also appear that the defendants *published it with a criminal intention.* Here, as in every other case, the great maxim of the law is to be recollected—*actus non facit reum ;* the mere act, taken by itself, and separated from the intention, can never in any instance constitute guilt. There is no evidence who are the authors of this paper ; the Attorney-General has not proved or shown in any way that the person who composed the paper was of the description which the record states the defendants to be. If the design of the writers of this paper was so mischievous, then the Society that gave it birth were seditious and evil-disposed men.. What steps have been taken to discover and hunt out this treason ? Have the Society been prosecuted, or any of its members ? Has the writer been sought after and punished ? No such thing. At Derby all is quiet. No sedition has been found lurking there—no prosecution has been instituted against any person whatever for this paper. But it has been said the paper itself will prove the seditious design. After reading it over and over again, and paying to it all the attention possible, I protest I cannot discover any such tendency ; on the contrary, I can very well conceive that the man who wrote it might honestly be induced to write and circulate it, not only with the most unblemished intentions, but from motives of the purest attachment to the constitution of the country, and the most ardent wishes for the happiness of the people.

I can conceive that he had no other object in pointing out the defects of the constitution than to show the necessity of a reform which might bring it back to its ancient principles, and establish it in its original purity. Animated by these wishes, the author was naturally enough led to advert to what was passing on the continent of Europe, and to consider how far it might affect the interests of his country and the attainment of his favourite object. He was thence led to conclude that nothing could be more fatal to us, or more likely to increase the calamities under which we have already suffered, than an interference in those destructive wars which were ravaging Europe, and against which every good citizen, as well as every friend to humanity, ought to enter his protest. This may be gathered from the conclusion of the fourth section of the paper :— "We are certain our present heavy burdens are owing, in a great measure, to cruel and impolitic wars, and therefore we will do all on our part, as peaceable citizens, who have the good of the community at heart, to enlighten each other, and to protest against them." Here it is evident that the author considers the state of the representation as the cause of our present evils, and to a constitutional reform of Parliament he looks as their remedy. In the conclusion of the fifth section he thus explicitly states his sentiments : —"An equal and uncorrupt representation would, we are persuaded, save us from heavy expenses, and deliver us from many oppressions ; we will therefore do our duty to procure this reform, which appears to us of the utmost importance." How is it proposed to procure this reform ? Why, "by constitutional means—by the circulation of truth in a peaceable, calm, unbiassed manner." Can this then be maliciously intended ? Does it fall within the Attorney-General's description of sedition ? Is it fit that a subject of this country should be convicted of a crime, and subjected to heavy punishment for publishing that abuses subsist in the government of this country, and arguing from thence the necessity for reform ? Mr Attorney-General seems to admit that a man may publish, if he pleases, the evils which appear to him to subsist ; but he qualifies it by saying, that when he points out the defects he should point out also the advantages arising from our representation—that he should state the blessings we enjoy from the mixed nature of our monarchy—that if he draws the gloomy part, he should present us also with the bright side of the picture, in order that we may see the whole together, and be able to compare what is beautiful with what is deformed in the structure of our Government. I must own I was rather surprised to hear such an argument from my learned friend ; I can hardly think the observation fair, or by any means worthy of his enlightened understanding. He must know that when a zealous man pours out his thoughts, intent on urging a particular point, HE confines himself to the question he has in view—he directs his whole attention to illustrate and enforce it, and does not think it necessary to run into every angle and corner to rake together heterogeneous materials, which, though they may be connected with the general subject, are foreign to his particular purpose.

No man, if he felt himself goaded by the excise laws, could be expected, in his petition for redress, to state all the advantages which arose to the State out of the other branches of the revenue. If this were to be adopted as a rule, a man could not complain of a grievance, however intolerable he felt it to himself, without also stating the comforts which were enjoyed by others. Is a man not to be permitted to seek redress from any part of the government under which he lives, and to support which he contributes so much, unless, in enumerating his particular grievance, he enters into a general panegyric on the constitution? Will Mr Attorney-General say to-day that this is the law of libel?

This very point has been most admirably touched upon by a person who ranks in the highest class of genius, and whose splendid and powerful talents, once exerted in the cause of the people, may possibly bear away the palm in the minds of posterity from the most illustrious names of Greece and Rome.

Mr Burke, in his "Reflections on the Affairs of France," at the commencement of the Revolution, most justly observes, that when a man has any particular thing in view, he loses sight for a time even of his own sentiments on former occasions: when that right honourable gentleman was asked by those who had so often listened to his eloquence in favour of the people, why he had excluded his former favourite topic from a share in his work, and made monarchy the sole subject of his vindication and panegyric? Whatever may belong to the work itself, the answer which he gave upon that occasion must be admitted to be sound and forcible. When the rights of the people appeared to him to be in danger, from the increasing and overpowering influence of the Crown, he brought forward, he said, sentiments favourable to such rights. But when monarchy was in danger, monarchy became the object of his protection; the rights of the people were nothing to him then; they did not form the subject of his book; his object was to show where the danger lay; and the beautiful illustration from Homer, relative to the death of Hector, was most applicable :—" When his body was placed before the aged king, his other sons surrounded him, anxious to afford that consolation which so great a calamity required ; the unhappy father, as if offended with their tenderness, flung his affectionate offspring from him like a pestilence. Was it that the inanimate and useless corpse was dearer to the parent than the living children? No. But his mind was so absorbed, so buried in the fate of Hector, that he was for a while incapable of entertaining any other impression." So said the author of that book, and it was well said ; for when a man writes upon a particular subject he centres his mind in, he calls forth all its powers and energy to the discussion, and allows nothing that has not an immediate relation to the object he has in view to divide his feelings or distract his attention. But if the observations of Mr Attorney-General are to be adopted as a rule, it will be impossible to discuss any point of a question without entering into the whole merits ; no man will dare to complain of any abuse of the constitution, without, at the same time, enumerating all its excellences, or venture to touch upon a topic of grievance, without bringing forward a recital of blessings.

A paragraph would be swelled to a pamphlet, and an essay expanded to a dissertation.

But it seems the circumstances of the times render any opinion in favour of a reform of Parliament peculiarly improper, and even dangerous, and that the recommendation of it, as the only remedy for our grievances must, therefore, in the present moment, be ascribed to mischievous intentions. Were I impressed with a sense of that corruption which has, to a certain degree, impaired and defaced the fair fabric of our constitution, and which, if not stopped in its progress, may lead to its decay and ruin : were I to address you, gentlemen of the jury, to petition for a reform of Parliament, I would address you particularly NOW, as the season most fit for the purpose ; I would address you NOW, because we have seen in other countries the effect of suffering evils to prevail so long in a government, and to increase to such a pitch, that it became impossible to correct them, without bringing on greater evils than those which it was the first object of the people to remove ; that it became impossible to remedy abuses without opening a door to revolution and anarchy. There are many diseases which might be removed by gentle medicines in their beginning, and even corrected by timely regimen, which, when neglected, are sure to bring their victims to the grave. A slight wound, which may be certainly cured by the simplest application seasonably administered, if left to itself, will end in gangrene, mortification, and death. If experience can be of any service to warn men of their danger, and to instruct them how to avoid it, this is the season to teach men the best sort of wisdom, that wisdom which comes in time to be useful. I have myself no hesitation in subscribing to all the great points in this declaration of the meeting at Derby. To the abuses of our representative system they ascribe our unnecessary war, our heavy burdens, our many national calamities. And at what period have not the best and wisest men whom this country ever produced adopted the same sentiments and employed the same language ? The illustrious Earl of Chatham has dignified the cause by the noblest specimens of eloquence. And who has not read the beautiful and energetic letter of Sir George Saville to his constituents on the same subject, a letter which is so much in point that I must beg leave to repeat it to you.

" I return to you baffled and dispirited, and I am sorry that truth obliges me to add, with hardly a ray of hope of seeing any change in the miserable course of public calamities.

" On this melancholy day of account, in rendering up to you my trust, I deliver to you your share of a country maimed and weakened ; its treasure lavished and misspent ; its honours faded ; and its conduct the laughing-stock of Europe : our nation in a manner without allies or friends, except such as we have hired to destroy our fellow-subjects, and to ravage a country in which we once claimed an invaluable share. I return to you some of your principal privileges impeached and mangled. And, lastly, I leave you, as I conceive, at this hour and moment, fully, effectually, and absolutely, under the discretion and power of a military force, which is to act without waiting for the authority of the civil magistrates.

"Some have been accused of exaggerating the public misfortunes, nay, of having endeavoured to help forward the mischief, that they might afterwards raise discontents. I am willing to hope, that neither my temper nor my situation in life will be thought naturally to urge me to promote misery, discord, or confusion, or to exult in the subversion of order or in the ruin of property. I have no reason to contemplate with pleasure the poverty of our country, the increase of our debts and of our taxes, or the decay of our commerce. Trust not, however, to my report: reflect, compare, and judge for yourselves.

" But under all these disheartening circumstances, I could yet entertain a cheerful hope, and undertake again the commission with alacrity, as well as zeal, if I could see any effectual steps taken to remove the original cause of the mischief. Then would there be a hope.

" But till the purity of the constituent body, and thereby that of the representative, be restored, there is NONE.

" I gladly embrace this most public opportunity of delivering my sentiments, not only to all my constituents, but to those likewise not my constituents, whom yet, in the large sense, I represent, and am faithfully to serve.

" I look upon restoring election and representation in some degree (for I expect no miracles) to their original purity, to be that without which all other efforts will be vain and ridiculous.

" If something be not done, you may indeed retain the outward form of your constitution, but not the power thereof."

Such were the words of that great and good man, surely equally forcible with any of those employed in the declaration of the meeting at Derby, yet who ever imputed to him mischievous intentions, or suspected him of sedition? Yet this letter he published and circulated, not only among his constituents in the extensive county of York, but addressed it to the nation at large, and recommended it to their attention. Who does not recollect the conduct which had been adopted on the same subject by the persons now nearest His Majesty's person, and highest in his counsels? Had not the same truths published in this declaration been repeatedly asserted and enforced by them? Names it is unnecessary to mention ; the proceedings to which I refer are sufficiently known : but at the same time, I beg leave to be understood to convey no personal reflection or reproach. I am the more anxious, in this instance, to

guard against misrepresentation from what happened to me upon
a late occasion, when, in consequence of my argument being misunderstood, an observation was put into my mouth, which would
have disgraced the lips of an idiot. It was ascribed to me to have
said, that if any man had written a libel, and could prove the publication of the same libel by another person before, he might justify himself under that previous publication. I cannot conceive
how so egregious a blunder could have been committed. What I
said was, that a man may show he was misled by another in adopting his opinion, and may use that circumstance as evidence of the
innocence of his intention in a publication; or where the writing is
not defamatory of an individual which may be brought to a known
standard of positive law, but is only criminal from a supposed
tendency in fact to excite sedition and disorder, he may repel that
tendency by showing the jury, who alone are to judge of it, that
the same writing had before been in extensive circulation, without
either producing, or being supposed to produce, sedition; and he
may also repel the inference of criminal intention by showing that
the wisest and most virtuous men in other times had maintained
the same doctrines, not merely with impunity, but with the approbation and rewards of the public. This I maintained to be the law
in the case of Mr Holt, the printer, and this I shall continue to
maintain upon every suitable occasion.

To bring home the application. The first men in the present
Government have held and published every doctrine contained in
this paper. I studiously avoid all allusion which may seem to
convey reproach to the high persons to whom I have referred, on
account of any change apparent in their conduct and sentiments,
because I conceive it to be unnecessary to my present argument,
and because I have a privilege to discuss their conduct in another
place, where they are themselves present to answer. Besides, a
man has a right to his sentiments, and he has a right to change
them;—on that score I attack no man, I only defend my clients.
But thus far I am entitled to say, that if they published sentiments
without having it imputed to them that they were seditious, evil-
minded, and wicked, it is but fair and reasonable to allege, that
others, in bringing forward the same sentiments, may be equally
exempted from impure motives. I repeat that every man has a
right to publish what he thinks upon matters of public concern, to
point out the impolicy of wars, or the weight of taxes, to complain
of grievances, and to expose abuses. It is a right which has ever
been exercised, and which cannot be annihilated without at the
same time putting an end to all freedom of discussion. If we talk
of the circumstances of the times, do the present afford less ground
for remonstrance and complaints than former periods? I might
read you many extracts from the writings of Mr Burke, who, to
eloquence, the fame of modern times, adds the most extensive and

universal acquaintance with the history both of his own country and of every other. Mr Burke (it is a merit I never can forget), with no less vehemence, and in language not less pointed and forcible than we find in this declaration, exposes the same abuses, and laments the same evils. What HE wrote during the American war are not the writers of this declaration justified in writing at present ? To the defects and abuses of our system of representation, may, in my opinion, be ascribed all the calamities that we then suffered, that we are now suffering, or are still apparently doomed to suffer. The evils which we now lament originated from the same source with those which we formerly suffered. To the defects of our representation we owe the present war, as to them also we owe that disastrous and unprincipled conflict which ended in the separation of Great Britain from her colonies. The events, indeed, were nearly connected : that mighty republic beyond the Atlantic gave birth to the new republic in Europe with which we are at present engaged in hostilities. From all the consequences, which we have already experienced, which we now suffer, and which we have yet to anticipate in reserve, I will venture to say, that a reform in the representation, applied seasonably, would have effectually saved the country. Is it likely, while this fruitful source of misfortune remains, that we shall not continue to suffer ? And if a man really entertains this opinion, is it not his duty to publish his thoughts, and to urge the adoption of a fair and legal remedy ? Is he to be set down as a seditious and evil-minded man because he speaks the truth and loves his country ? Of the war in which this country is engaged I will here say nothing ; it will soon come to be discussed in another place, where I have not failed to exercise that privilege which I there possess, to deliver my opinion of its dreadful consequences. But of all these consequences, there is none which I conceive to be more dreadful and alarming than that I CAN SEE NO END TO IT ; and I believe wiser persons than myself are equally at a loss to predict its termination. This paper, which so justly reprobates wars, is rumoured to come from the pen of a writer whose productions justly entitle him to rank as the first poet of the age ;—who has enlarged the circle of the pleasures of taste, and embellished with new flowers the regions of fancy. It was brought forward in a meeting, in a legal and peaceable manner, and I have never heard that either the author, or any of the members present at the meeting, have been prosecuted, or that the smallest censure has fallen upon their conduct. But even if they had been made the objects of the prosecution, sanctioned as they are in what they have written by every principle of the constitution, and supported their conduct by its best and most virtuous defenders in all times, I should have had little difficulty in defending them. How much less, in the case of the defendants, who are not stated to be the authors of this paper, who only published it in the course of

their business, and who published it under such peculiar circumstances as, even if the contents could have admitted any criminal
interpretation, must have done away on their part all imputation
of any criminal intention.   They have in a manly way instructed
me, however, to meet the question upon its own merits ; not because
they could not have proved a very peculiar alleviation, but because
they have always presented a fair and unequivocal responsibility for
the conduct of their paper.   Let me particularly call your attention
to this circumstance, that for the number of years during which the
defendants have conducted a newspaper, they have never before, in
a single instance, been tried for any offence, either against an individual or against the State ; they have, in the execution of their
task, assiduously endeavoured to enlighten the minds of their fellow-
subjects, while they have avoided everything that might tend to
endanger their morals.   They have displayed, in the conduct of
their paper, a degree of learning, taste, and genius, superior to what
has distinguished any similar undertaking.   They have done their
fellow-citizens a most essential service, by presenting them with
the most full and correct intelligence of what has been passing on
the political theatre of Europe, neither sullied by prejudice, nor
disguised by misrepresentation.   The attention which they have
paid to the important occurrences which have taken place in a
neighbouring country, and the impartiality with which they have
stated them, do them the greatest credit.   I trust that it will be
no objection to them in their character of editors, that they have
sought only for the truth, and, wherever they have found facts, have
not hesitated to bring them before the public.   They have thus
enabled their readers to judge for themselves, and have furnished
them with the means to form a proper judgment.   This is the true
value of a free press.   The more men are enlightened, the better
will they be qualified to be good subjects of a good Government ;
and the British constitution, as it has nothing to fear from comparison, so it can receive no support from those arts which disguise
or suppress the truth respecting other nations.   Wherever they
have been called to deliver their sentiments upon public occurrences,
they have equally avoided being misled by the credulity of alarm
and the frenzy of innovation ; and have reprobated, with the same
spirit and boldness, the abuse of freedom and the perversion of
power,—the outrages of a sanguinary mob, and the oppressions of
an unprincipled despot.   Whatever may have been their political
partialities, they are such as cannot but do them the highest honour,
and their partialities have been the result of honest conviction.
Though uniformly consistent in their friendships, they have never
been accused by those who know them of being partisans for
interest.   Their opinions have been honest, as well as steady ; and
through life they have maintained and asserted the pure principles
of rational freedom, and given the most strenuous support to the

best interests of man.   They have, in their daily task, ever preserved reverence for private character, and in no instance violated
the decorums of life by low ribaldry or wanton defamation. Though
adverse in their sentiments to Ministers and their measures, they
have confined themselves to manly discussion and fair argument,
and never descended to indecent attack or scurrilous abuse.

My learned friend cannot produce a single instance in the course
of seventeen years (the term of my acquaintance with them), in
which they have been charged in any court with public libel or with
private defamation : and I challenge the world to exhibit a single
instance in which they have made their journals the vehicles of
slander, or where from interest, or malice, or any other base motive,
they have published a single paragraph to disturb the happiness of
private life, to wound the sensibility of innocence, or to outrage the
decencies of well-regulated society.   I defy the world to produce
a single instance.   Men who have so conducted themselves are
entitled to protection from any Government, but certainly they are
particularly entitled to it where a free press is part of the system.
In the fair and liberal management of their paper, fifteen shillings
out of every guinea which they receive flows directly into the public
Exchequer ; and besides the incessant toil and the unwearied
watching, all the expenses by which this great gain to Government
is produced are borne exclusively by them.   They essentially
contribute, therefore, by their labours to the support of Government, and they are as honestly and fervently attached to the true
principles of the British constitution, to the Crown, and to the mixed
system of our Government, as any subject of his Majesty ; but at
the same time they are ready to acknowledge that they ever have
been advocates for a temperate and seasonable reform of the
abuses which have crept into our system.   Their minds are to be
taken from the whole view of their conduct.   It is a curious, and I
will venture to say, in times so convulsed, an unexampled thing,
that in all the productions of my friends, that in all the variety of
their daily miscellany, the Crown officers have been able to pick
out but one solitary advertisement from all that they have published,
on which to bring a charge of sedition ; and of this advertisement,
if they thought fit to go into the detail, they could show, even by
internal evidence, that it was inserted at a very busy moment, without revision or correction, and at the very time that this advertisement appeared, seven hundred declarations, in support of the King's
Government, appeared in the same paper, which they revised and
corrected for publication.   You are not therefore to take one advertisement, inserted in their paper, as a criterion of their principles,
but to take likewise the other advertisements which appeared along
with it.   Would the readers, then, of this paper, while they read in
this advertisement a recital of the abuses of the constitution, not be
in possession of a sufficient antidote from the enumeration of its

blessings? While the admirers of the constitution came forward
with an unqualified panegyric of its excellences, were not the
friends of reform justified in coming forward with a fair statement
of grievances? If it is alleged that the pecuniary interest which
the proprietors have in a newspaper ought to subject them to a
severe responsibility for its contents, let it be recollected that they
have only an interest in common with the public. I again call
upon Mr Attorney-General to state whether the fact appears to
him clearly established that the writers of this paper were influenced
by seditious motives. I put it to you, gentlemen of the jury, as
honest men, as candid judges of the conduct, as fair interpreters of
the sentiments of others, whether you do not in your hearts and
consciences believe that these men felt as they wrote—that they
complained of grievances which they actually experienced, and
expressed sentiments with the truth of which they were deeply
impressed? If you grant this—if you give them the credit of honest
feelings and upright intentions, on my part any farther defence is
unnecessary; we are already in possession of your verdict; you
have already pronounced them not guilty; for you will not condemn
the conduct when you have acquitted the heart. You will rather
desire that British justice should resemble that attribute of Heaven
which looks not to the outward act, but the principle from which
it proceeds—to the intention by which it is directed.

In summing up for the Crown, I would never wish to carry the
principles of liberty farther than Mr Attorney-General has done,
when he asserted the right of political discussion, and desired you
only to look to the temper and spirit with which such discussion
was made,—when he asserted that it was right to expose abuses,
to complain of grievances, provided always that it were done with
an honest and fair intention. Upon this principle, I appeal to you
whether this advertisement might not be written with a *bonâ fide*
intention, and inserted among a thousand others, without any seditious purpose or desire to disturb the public peace?

Undoubtedly our first duty is the love of our country; but this
love of our country does not consist in a servile attachment and
blind adulation to authority. It was not so that our ancestors
loved their country; because they loved it, they sought to discover
the defects of its government: because they loved it, they endeavoured to apply the remedy. They regarded the constitution not
as slaves with a constrained and involuntary homage, but they
loved it with the generous and enlightened ardour of free men.
Their attachment was founded upon a conviction of its excellence,
and they secured its permanence by freeing it from blemish. Such
was the love of our ancestors for the constitution, and their posterity surely do not become criminal by emulating their example.
I appeal to you whether the abuses stated in this paper do not exist in
the constitution, and whether their existence has not been admitted

by all parties, both by the friends and enemies of reform? Both, I have no doubt, are honest in their opinions; and God forbid that honest opinion in either party should ever become a crime. In their opinion of the necessity of a reform, as the best and perhaps only remedy of the abuses of the constitution, the writers of this paper coincide with the most eminent and enlightened men. On this ground I leave the question, secure that your verdict will be agreeable to the dictates of your consciences, and be directed by a sound and unbiassed judgment.

Mr ATTORNEY-GENERAL,—There are some propositions which my learned friend (Mr Erskine) has brought forward for the defendants, which not only I do not mean to dispute, as an officer of the Crown carrying on this prosecution, but which I will also admit to their full extent. Every individual is certainly in a considerable degree interested in this prosecution; at the same time I must observe, that I should have, in my own opinion, betrayed my duty to the Crown if I had not brought this subject for the consideration of a jury. Considering, however, every individual as under my protection, I think it a duty which I owe to the defendants to acknowledge, that in no one instance before this time were they brought to the bar of any Court to answer for any offence either against Government or a private individual. This is the only solitary instance in which they have given occasion for such charge to be brought against them. In everything, therefore, that I know of the defendants, you are to take them as men standing perfectly free from any imputation but the present; and I will also say, from all I have ever heard of the defendants, and from all I have ever observed of their morals in the conduct of their paper, I honestly and candidly believe them to be men incapable of wilfully publishing any slander on individuals, or of prostituting their paper to defamation or indecency. But my learned friend, Mr Erskine, has stated some points which my duty calls upon me to take notice of. I bound myself by the contents of the paper only; I did not know the author of it. I did not know any society from which the paper purported to have originated. It is said to be the production of a man of great abilities; I do not know that he is the author,—at any rate, this is the first time I ever heard of that circumstance. There is one fact on which we are all agreed, that the paper itself was dated on the 16th of July 1792, and that it appeared in the *Morning Chronicle* on the 25th of December 1792. It was then presented to the public with a variety of other advertisements, which it will be proper for you to peruse, and for that purpose you will carry out the paper with you, if you find it necessary to withdraw, in order to see what the intent of the defendants was in publishing this paper. A bill, I also admit, passed into a law the last session of Parliament upon the subject of libels; but it would be exceedingly unfortunate for the subjects of this country if my learned friend and myself were to be allowed to give evidence in a court of justice of what was our intention in passing that bill. The bill has now become a solemn act of the Legislature, and must speak for itself by its contents; but, however, it has in my opinion done what it was intended to do. It refers the question of guilt to the jury in cases of libels precisely as in every other criminal case. My learned friend has insisted that criminal intention is matter of fact mixed with matter of law. I agree to this description; but then the law says that such and such facts are evidence of such and such intention. Treason, for instance, depends upon intention; but such and such acts are evidence of a criminal intention; and if the jury entertain any doubts upon any part of the charge, his Lordship will only do his duty by giving them his advice and direction, which will be, that he who does such and such things, if he does them with a criminal intention, is amenable to the law, and that such and such acts are evidence of the criminal intention; and then the jury must decide upon that evidence, and upon that advice, whether the defendant was or was not guilty: so says Mr Erskine, and so I say; for it is a matter of plain common sense, coming home to the understanding of every man. Mr Erskine has contended that the jury must not draw the inference of criminal intention from the mere fact of publishing a paper. Certainly not; but they may draw the inference of guilty intention if they discover in the contents of the paper a wicked and malicious spirit, evidently pursuing a bad object by unwarrantable means. If I should put a paper into the hands of the jury desiring them to put my learned friend to death, would not that prove an evil intention against my friend's life? In all cases of publication containing anything improper, the bad intention of the person publishing was clear, unless on his own part he could prove the contrary. Such has always been the law of England in criminal cases of this description. Mr Erskine has desired you to carry out the paper, and look at the other advertisements: upon this I am bound to remark, that there is not one of them, except that in question, which is not dated in the month of December, while this advertisement is dated on the 16th of July, though it did not find its way into the *Morning Chronicle* until the end of the month of December. How that came to happen I cannot tell; it must be left to you to determine: but it does appear that at a very critical moment to the constitution of this country, it was brought out to counteract the intention and effect of all the other declarations in support of Government. At what time the defendants received the paper in question, they had not attempted to prove. Why, if they received it in July, they did not then insert it, they did not say. They had brought no exculpatory evidence whatever to account for the delay. It was urged that the defendants only published it in the way of business as an advertisement, and therefore they could not be said to be guilty. If I should be brought to admit this as a sufficient answer, and never institute a prosecution where such was the case, I should in so doing deliver the jury, and every man in this country, to the mercy of every newspaper printer in this kingdom, to be traduced and vilified just as the malice of any man who chose to pay for vending his own scandal should dictate. I therefore entreat you to bring the case home to your own bosoms, and to act for the public as in such an instance you would wish to act for yourselves. I must likewise say, that if you are to look at the intention of the defendants in the other matter contained in the same paper, you will find various strong and even intemperate things. Among others, you will find the following, which, if it did not show a seditious, did not breathe a very temperate spirit:—" Well might Mr Fox call this the most momentous crisis that he ever heard of in the history of England; for we will venture to say, there is not any one species of tyranny which might not, in the present day, be tried with impunity; no sort of oppression which would not find, not merely advocates, but supporters; and never, never, in the most agitated moments of our history, were men so universally tame or so despicably feeble."

This paragraph is no advertisement; it came from no society; and will, I take it for granted, not be disavowed by the defendant.

Upon the question of a reform of Parliament, I remain of the same opinion which I have always entertained; and whatever may have been said or thought by Mr Fox, Mr Pitt, the Duke of Richmond, the late Earl of Chatham, or the late Sir George Saville, or by any man, let his authority have been ever so great, never while I live will I consent to vote for a reform in Parliament until I see something specific to be done, and can be very sure that the good to be gained will make it worth while to hazard the experiment.

In this way of thinking I am the more confirmed, from the circumstance, that of all the wise and excellent men who have at different times agitated the question of reform, none of them have ever been able to agree upon any one specific plan. And I declare that I would rather suffer death than consent to open a door for such alterations in the government of this country as chance or bad men might direct; or even good men, misled by bad, might, in the first instance, be inclined to adopt. I shudder, indeed, when I reflect on what have been the consequences of innovation in a neighbouring country. The many excellent men who there began to try experiments on government, confining their views within certain limits of moderation, and having no other object than the public good, little did they foresee in their outset the excesses and

crimes which would follow in the progress of that revolution of
which they were the authors, and of which they were themselves
destined to become the victims.   They are now lying in the
sepulchres of the dead and the tombs of mortality; and most
willingly, I am persuaded, would they have consigned themselves
to their fate, if by their death they could have saved their unhappy
country from the horrors and miseries of that dreadful anarchy
into which it has fallen.   Never, with such examples before my
eyes, will I stake the blessings which we possess under the Government of this country upon the precarious consequences of innovation; nor consent to any alteration of which, whatever may be
stated as its object, the precise effects can never be ascertained.
Indeed, I must think that my friend Mr Erskine, in his propositions with respect to a reform, allows himself to talk like a child,
and does not sufficiently consult that excellent judgment which he
displays upon every other occasion.   But let me entreat him to reflect on the situation in which both of us are now placed, and
which, if twenty years ago any person told me I should have attained, I should have regarded it as madness.   If we, by our industry (my friend, indeed, with the advantage of his superior
talents), have acquired a degree of opulence and distinction which
we could not reasonably have looked for, let us be thankful to that
Government to whose protection and favour we are in a great
measure indebted for our success.   And do not let us, by any rash
attempt upon our constitution, put it out of the power of our children to rise to similar situations, or deprive them of those blessings
which we have ourselves so signally experienced.   Do not let us
pull down a fabric which has been the admiration of ages, and
which it may be impossible to erect anew.   Let me again call
your attention to the paper upon which this prosecution is founded.
[Here Mr Attorney-General read several extracts from the declaration.]   After what you have heard, I think it is impossible to doubt
of the libellous tendency of this publication.   It states, as I have
already said, the whole of our government as one mass of grievances
and abuses, while it does not so much as enumerate a single blessing or advantage with which it is attended.   It represents it as
corrupt and oppressive in every branch, as polluted in its very
source, its legislature, and its courts of justice.   What, I ask, can
be supposed to be the spirit by which such representations are dictated, and the consequences to which they are calculated to lead?
Can you admit such representations to have been brought forward
bonâ fide, and from no other motive than the wish to procure a
peaceable and legal redress of grievances?   If you can admit this,
you will of course find the defendants not guilty.   But if it shall
appear otherwise, let me remind you of that duty which you owe
to the public, with whose safety and protection you are intrusted,
and whose interests you are to consult in the verdict which you

shall give. Let me remind you of the necessity of checking, in proper time, the spirit of sedition, and frustrating the designs of the factious, before it be too late. Let me conclude with observing, that I have brought forward this prosecution as a servant of the public, influenced by my own judgment, and acting from what I conceived to be my duty. I had no other view than the public advantage; and should you be of opinion that the defendants ought to be declared not guilty, I trust you will acquit me of any intention of acting either impertinently with respect to you or oppressively to the defendants.

I shall then retire, conscious of having done my duty in having stated my opinion, though inclined, in deference to your verdict, to suppose myself mistaken.

Lord KENYON then gave a charge in substance as follows:—

GENTLEMEN OF THE JURY,—There are no cases which call forth greater exertions of great abilities than those that relate to political libels. And as this cause, both on the part of the prosecution and also on behalf of the defendants, has been so amply discussed that the subject is exhausted, I should have satisfied myself with what has been already said, if there was not a duty lying on me which by the law of the land it is incumbent on me to discharge.

The liberty of the press has always been, and has justly been, a favourite topic with Englishmen. They have looked at it with jealousy whenever it has been invaded; and though a licenser was put over the press, and was suffered to exist for some years after the coming of William, and after the Revolution, yet the reluctant spirit of English liberty called for a repeal of that law; and from that time to this it has not been shackled and limited more than it ought to be.

Gentlemen, it is placed as the sentinel to alarm us, when any attempt is made on our liberties; and we ought to be watchful, and to take care that the sentinel is not abused and converted into a traitor. It can only be protected by being kept within due limits, and by our doing those things which we ought, and watching over the liberties of the people; but the instant it degenerates into licentiousness, we ought not to suffer it to exist without punishment. It is therefore for the protection of liberty that its licentiousness is brought to punishment.

A great deal has been said respecting a reform of Parliament, that is, an alteration of Parliament. If I were called upon to decide on that point, before I would pull down the fabric, or presume to disturb one stone in the structure, I would consider what those benefits are which it seeks, and whether they, to the extent to which they are asked, ought to be hazarded; whether any imaginary reform ought to be adopted, however virtuous the breast, or however able the head, that might attempt such a reform. I should be a little afraid that, when the water was let out, nobody could tell how to stop it. If the lion was once let into the house, who would be found to shut the door? I should first feel the greater benefits of a reform, and should not hazard our present blessings out of a capricious humour to bring about such a measure.

The merits or demerits of the late law respecting libels I shall not enter into. It is enough for me that it is the law of the land, which by my oath I am bound to give effect to, and it commands me to state to juries what my opinion is respecting this or any other paper brought into judgment before them. In forming my opinion on this paper, or on any other, before I arrive at a positive decision on that point, I would look about and see what the times were when the publication took place. I would look at all the attendant circumstances, and, with that assistance I would set about to expound the paper. The observations which this cause calls for form a part of the notorious history of the country. How long this paper was penned before it appeared in this newspaper I know not: the 25th of December is the day when it was published, and it is dated the 16th of July 1792.

Gentlemen, you will recollect the appearance of public affairs and the feelings of every mind in the country at the time that Parliament met, and for some time after, in December last. I do not know whether I colour the picture right when I say very gloomy sensations had pervaded the whole country. It is for you to say whether at that time there were not emissaries from a neighbouring country making their way, as well as they could, in this country. It is for you to say, looking at the great anarchy and confusion of France, whether they did not wish to agitate the minds of all orders of men, in all countries, and to plant their tree of liberty in every kingdom in Europe. It is for you to say whether their intention was not to eradicate every kind of government that was not sympathetic with their own. I am bound, gentlemen, to declare my opinion on this paper, and to do so I must take within my consideration all the circumstances of the time when it appeared. I have no hesitation in saying, then, that they were most gloomy. The country was torn to its centre by emissaries from France. It was a notorious fact, every man knows it, I could neither open my eyes nor my ears without seeing and hearing them. Weighing thus all the circumstances, that, though dated in July, it was not published till December, when those emissaries were spreading their horrid doctrines; and believing there was a great gloominess in the country (and I must shut my eyes and ears if I did not believe that there was); believing also that there were emissaries from France wishing to spread the maxims prevalent in that country in this; believing that the minds of the people of this country were much agitated by these political topics, of which the mass of the population never can form a true judgment; and reading this paper, which appears to be calculated to put the people in a state of discontent with everything done in this country, I am bound on my oath to answer that I think this paper was published with a wicked malicious intent to vilify the Government, and to make the people discontented with the constitution under which they live. That is the matter charged in the information, that it was done with a view to vilify the constitution, the laws, and the government of this country, and to infuse into the minds of His Majesty's subjects a belief that they were oppressed; and on this ground I consider it as a gross and seditious libel. This is the question put to you to decide.

It is admitted the defendants are the proprietors of the paper in which this address was published.

There is one topic more. It is said they were not the authors of the address, and that it got inadvertently into their paper. It never was doubted, and I suppose it never will be doubted, that the publishers of a newspaper are answerable for the contents of it. Those who think most favourably for the defendants will go no farther than to say that the parties publishing ought to give an account how they published it, and if there is anything baneful in the contents, to show how it came to them, and whether it was inserted inadvertently or otherwise. If anything of that sort had been offered, I certainly should have received it as evidence. But nothing of the kind has been offered, and the defendants stand as the proprietors and publishers of the paper, without the slightest evidence in alleviation being offered in their favour.

It is not for human judgment to dive into the heart of man to know whether his intentions are good or evil. We must draw our conclusions with regard to his intentions from overt acts, and if an evil tendency is apparent on the face of any particular paper, it can only be traced by human judgment *primâ facie* to a bad intention, unless evidence is brought to prove its innocence. This cause is destitute of any proof of that kind.

It is said that this paper contains other advertisements and paragraphs, and therefore, from the moral good tendency of the whole, for aught I know to the contrary, you are to extract an opinion that the meaning was not bad. I cannot say that the travelling into advertisements, which have nothing to do with this business, is exactly the errand you are to go upon. From this paper itself, and all the contents of it, you will extract the meaning, and if upon the whole you should think the tendency of it is good, in my opinion the parties ought to be acquitted. But it is not sufficient that there should be in this paper detached good morals in part of it, unless they gave an explanation of the rest. The charge will be done away if those parts which the Attorney-

General has stated are so explained as to leave nothing excepted.

There may be morality and virtue in this paper, and yet, apparently, *latet anguis in herbâ.* There may be much that is good in it, and yet there may be much to censure. I have told you my opinion. Gentlemen, the constitution has intrusted it to you, and it is your duty to have only one point in view—Without fear, favour, or affection, without regard either to the prosecutor or the defendants, look at the question before you, and on that decide on the guilt or innocence of the defendants.

The jury then withdrew. It was two o'clock in the afternoon. The noble and learned Judge, understanding that they were divided, and likely to be some time in making up their minds, retired from the bench, and directed Mr Lowten to take the verdict. At seven in the evening they gave notice that they had agreed on a special verdict, which Mr Lowten could not receive. They went up in coaches, each attended by an officer, to Lord Kenyon's house. The special verdict was—*Guilty of publishing, but with no malicious intent.*

Lord KENYON. I cannot record this verdict; it is no verdict at all.

The jury then withdrew, and, after sitting in discussion till within a few minutes of five in the morning, they found a general verdict of NOT GUILTY.

TRIAL of Mr Thomas Walker *of Manchester, Merchant, and six other Persons, indicted for a Conspiracy to overthrow the Constitution and Government of this Kingdom, and to aid and assist the French, being the King's enemies, in case they should invade this Kingdom. Tried at Lancaster, before* Mr Justice Heath, *one of the Judges of the Court of Common Pleas, and a Special Jury, on the* 2d *of April* 1794.

THE SUBJECT.

We have not found it necessary, for the full understanding of this interesting and extraordinary case, to print the evidence given upon the trial; because, to the honour of Lord Ellenborough, then Mr Law, who conducted the prosecution for the Crown, after hearing positive contradiction of the only witness in support of it, by several unexceptionable persons, he expressed himself as follows :—

"I know the characters of several of the gentlemen who have been examined, particularly of Mr Jones. I cannot expect one witness alone, unconfirmed, to stand against the testimony of all these witnesses : I ought not to desire it." To which just declaration, which ended the trial, Mr Justice Heath said, "You act very properly, Mr Law."

The jury found Mr Walker Not Guilty; and the witness was immediately committed, indicted for perjury, and convicted at the same assizes.

We have printed Mr Law's able and manly speech to the jury, which contains the whole case, afterwards proved by the witness who was disbelieved. The speech of Mr Erskine in answer to it states the evidence afterwards given to contradict him.

Mr Walker was an eminent merchant at Manchester, and a truly honest and respectable man ; and nothing can show the fever of those times more than the alarming prosecution of such a person upon such evidence. It is not to every Attorney-General that such a case could have been safely trusted. The conduct of Mr Law was highly to his honour, and a prognostic of his future character as a Judge.

MR LAW'S SPEECH.

The indictment having been opened by Mr James, Mr Law addressed the jury as follows :—

Gentlemen of the Jury,—The indictment which has been read to you, imputes to the defendants a species of treasonable misdemeanour second only in degree, and inferior only in malignity, to the crime of high treason itself. It imputes to them a conspiracy for the purpose of adhering with effect to the King's enemies, in case the calamity of foreign invasion, or of internal and domestic tumult, should afford them the desired opportunity of so doing—a conspiracy for the purpose of employing against our country those arms which should be devoted to its defence; and of overthrowing a constitution, the work of long-continued wisdom and virtue in the ages that have gone before us, and which, I trust, the sober-minded virtue and wisdom of the present age will transmit unimpaired to ages that are yet to succeed us. It imputes to them a conspiracy, not indeed levelled at the person and life of our Sovereign, but at that constitution at the head of which he is placed, and at that system of beneficial laws which it is his pride and his duty to administer; at that constitution which makes us what we are—a great, free, and, I trust, with a few exceptions only, a happy and united people. Gentlemen, a conspiracy formed for these purposes, and to be effected eventually by means of arms; a conspiracy which had either for its immediate aim or probable consequence the introduction into this country, upon the model of France, of all the miseries that disgrace and desolate that unhappy land, is the crime for which the defendants stand arraigned before you this day: and it is for you to say, in the first instance, and for my Lord hereafter, what shall be the result and effect in respect to persons against whom a conspiracy of such enormous magnitude and mischief shall be substantiated in evidence.

Gentlemen, whatever subjects of political difference may subsist amongst us, I trust we are in general agreed in venerating the great principles of our constitution, and in wishing to sustain and render them permanent. Whatever toleration and indulgence we may be willing to allow to differences in matters of less importance, upon some subjects we can allow none. To the friends of France, leagued in unity of council, inclination, and interest with France, against the arms and interests of our country, however tolerant in other respects, we can afford no grains of allowance—no sentiments of indulgence or toleration whatsoever. To do so at a time when those arms and councils are directed against our political and civil—against not our national only, but natural existence (and at such a period you will find that the very conspiracy now under consideration was formed), would be equally inconsistent with every rule of law and every principle of self-preservation: it would be at once to authorise every description of mischievous persons to carry their destructive principles into immediate and' fatal effect; in other words, it would be to sign the doom and downfall of that constitution which protects us all.

I am sure, therefore, that for the *crime*, such as I have represented it to be, my learned friend will not, in the exercise of his own good sense, choose to offer any defence or apology; but he

will endeavour to make the evidence I shall lay before you appear
in another point of view : he will endeavour to conceal and soften
much of that malignity which I impute, and I think justly, to the
intentions and actings of these defendants.

It was about the close of the year 1792 that the French nation
thought fit to hold out to all the nations on the globe, or rather,
I should say, to the discontented subjects of all those nations, an
encouragement to confederate and combine together for the purpose of subverting all regular established authority amongst them,
by a decree of the 19th of November 1792, which I consider as
the immediate source and origin of this and other mischievous
societies. That nation, in convention, pledged to the discontented
inhabitants of other countries its protection and assistance, in case
they should be disposed to innovate and change the form of government under which they had heretofore lived. Under the influence
of this fostering encouragement, and meaning, I must suppose, to
avail themselves of the protection and assistance thus held out to
them, this and other dangerous societies sprung up and spread
themselves within the bosom of this realm.

Gentlemen, it was about the period I mentioned, or shortly after,
I mean in the month of December, which followed close upon the
promulgation of this detestable decree, that the society on which I
am about to comment—ten members of which are now presented
on trial before you—was formed.* The vigilance of those to whom
the administration of justice and the immediate care of the police
of the country is primarily intrusted, had already prevented or
dispersed every numerous assembly of persons which resorted to
public-houses for such purposes; it therefore became necessary for
persons thus disposed to assemble themselves, if at all, within the
walls of some private mansion. The president and head of this
society, Mr Thomas Walker, raised to that bad eminence by a
species of merit which will not meet with much favour or encouragement here, opened his doors to receive a society of this sort at
Manchester, miscalled the Reformation Society. The name may,
in some senses, indeed, import and be understood to mean a society
formed for the purpose of beneficial reform ; but what the real
purposes of this society were you will presently learn from their
declared sentiments and criminal actings. He opened his doors,
then, to receive this society : they assembled, night after night,
in numbers, to an amount which you will hear from the witnesses :
sometimes, I believe, the extended number of such assemblies
amounting to more than a hundred persons. There were three
considerable rooms allotted for their reception. In the lower part
of the house, where they were first admitted, they sat upon business
of less moment, and requiring the presence of smaller numbers. In

The Manchester Constitutional Society was instituted in October 1790; the
Reformation Society in March 1792 ; the Patriotic Society in April 1792.

the upper part, they assembled in greater multitudes, and read, as in a school, and, as it were, to fashion and perfect themselves in everything that is seditious and mischievous, those writings which have been already reprobated by other juries sitting in this and other places, by the courts of law, and, in effect, by the united voice of both Houses of Parliament. They read, amongst other works, particularly the works of an author whose name is in the mouth of everybody in this country—I mean the works of Thomas Paine: an author who, in the gloom of a French prison, is now contemplating the full effects, and experiencing all the miseries, of that disorganising system of which he is, in some respects, the parent—certainly the great advocate and promoter.

The works of this author, and many other works of a similar tendency, were read aloud by a person of the name of Jackson, who exercised, upon those occasions, the mischievous function of reader to this society. Others of the defendants had different functions assigned them: some were busy in training them to the use of arms, for the purpose, avowedly, in case there should be either a landing of the French, with whom we were then, I think, actually at war, or about immediately to be at war; or in case there should take place a revolt in the kingdoms of Ireland or Scotland, to minister to their assistance, either to such invasion or to such revolt, That they met for such purposes is not only clear from the writings that were read aloud to them, and the conversations that were held, but by the purposes which were expressly declared and avowed by those who may be considered as the mouthpieces and organs of the society upon these occasions.

The first time, I think, that the witness Dunn, whom I shall presently produce to you, saw the defendant Mr Walker, Mr Walker declared to him, "*that he hoped they should soon overthrow the constitution.*" The witness I have alluded to was introduced to the society by two persons, I think, of the names of M'Callum and Smith, and who, if I am not misinformed, have since taken their flight from this country to America. The first night he was there he did not see their president, Mr Walker; but on the second night that he went there, Mr Walker met him as he entered the door, and observing from his dialect that he was a native of Ireland, Mr Walker inquired of him how the volunteers went on; and said, with a smile, as he passed him in his way up-stairs to the rest of the associated members, " *We shall overthrow the constitution by and by.*" The witness was then ushered into this room, where he saw assembled nearly to the number of a hundred or a hundred and fifty persons. The room was, I understand, a large warehouse at the top of the house; there were about fourteen or fifteen persons then actually under arms, and some of those whose names are to be found in this record were employed in teaching others the military exercise. It would be endless, as well as useless, to relate to you the whole of what passed at these several meetings.

Upon some occasions Mr Walker would talk in the most con-tumelious and abominable language of the sacred person of our Sovereign. In one instance, when talking of monarchy, he said, "Damn kings! what have we to do with them? what are they to us?" and, to show the contempt in which he held the lives of all kings, and particularly that of our own Sovereign, taking a piece of paper in his hand and tearing it, he said, "If I had the King here, I would cut off his head as readily as I tear this paper."

Upon other occasions, others of the members, and particularly a person of the name of Paul, who I believe is now in court, held similar language; damning the King, reviling and defaming him in the execution of his high office, representing the whole system of our public government as a system of plunder and rapacity, representing particularly the administration of a neighbouring kingdom by a Lord-Lieutenant as a scheme and device merely invented to corrupt the people, and to enrich and aggrandise the individual to whose care the government of that kingdom is more immediately delegated; in short, arraigning every part of our public economy as directly productive of misgovernment and oppression. The King himself was sometimes more particularly pointed at by Mr Walker. He related of him a strange, incredible, and foolish fable, which I never heard suggested from any other quarter:—"That his Majesty was possessed of seventeen millions of money in some bank or other at Vienna, which he kept locked up there, and would not bestow a single penny of it to relieve the stresses and indigence of any part of his own subjects." Many other assertions of this sort were made, and conversations of a similar import held between Mr Walker and the persons thus assembled.

About three months after the formation, as far as I can collect of this society, that is, about the month of March 1793, a person of the name of Yorke—Yorke, of Derby, I think he is called—arrived at Manchester, with all the apparatus of a kind of apostolic mission, addressed to the various assemblies of seditious persons in that quarter of the kingdom. He harangued them upon such topics as were most likely to interest and inflame them; he explained to them the object of the journey he was then making through the country; he said he was come to visit all the combined societies, in order to learn the numbers they could respectively muster, in case there should be an invasion by the French, which was then talked of, and is yet, I am afraid, talked of but upon too much foundation; to know, in short, what number they could add to the arms of France, in case these arms should be hostilely directed against Great Britain itself. He stated that the French were about to land in this country, to the number of forty or fifty thousand men, and that he was collecting, in the different societies, the names of such persons as could be best depended upon, in order to ascertain what number in the whole could actually be brought into the field upon such an emergency.

When this person was present, there seems to have been a sort of holiday and festival of sedition. Each member strove with his fellow which should express sentiments the most injurious and hostile to the peace and happiness of their country. Dunn, the witness I have already alluded to, will speak to the actual communication of all the several persons who are defendants upon this record in most of the mischievous councils which were then held, and which are the subject of this prosecution. They met during a considerable length of time he attended (and here you will not be called upon to give credit to a loose and casual recollection of a few random expressions, uttered upon one or two accidental occasions, capable of an innocent or doubtful construction), but he attended, I believe, at nearly forty of these meetings. He attended them from about the month of December or January down to the month of June, when, either through compunction for the share he had himself borne in those mischievous proceedings, or whatever else might be his motive—I trust it was an honourable one, and that it will in its effects prove beneficial to his country—he came forward and detailed this business to the magistrates of this county. It became them, having such circumstances related to them, and having it also confirmed by other evidence that there were numerous nightly meetings of this sort held at stated intervals at the house of Mr Walker,—upon having the objects of these meetings detailed and verified to them, it became them, I say, to use means for suppressing a mischief of such extent and magnitude. It was accordingly thought proper to institute this prosecution for the purpose of bringing these enormous proceedings into public discussion and inquiry before a jury of the country, and for the purpose of eventually bringing to condign punishment the persons immediately concerned in them.

Gentlemen, the evidence of this person, the witness I have mentioned, will unquestionably be assailed and attacked by a great deal of attempted contradiction. His character will, I have no doubt, be arraigned and drawn in question from the earliest period to which the defendants can have any opportunities of access for materials respecting it. Upon nothing but upon the effectual impeachment of the character of this witness can they bottom any probable expectations of acquittal; to that point, therefore, their efforts will be mainly directed. I wish their efforts had been hitherto directed innocently towards the attainment of this object, and that no opportunities had been recently taken, in occasional meetings and conversations, to attempt to tamper with the testimony of this witness. There are other practices which, next to an actual tampering with the testimony of a witness, are extremely mischievous to the regular course and administration of justice. I mean attempts to lure a witness into conversations respecting the subject of his testimony. Of this we have seen many very blameable instances in the course of the present circuit, where conversations have been set on foot for the purpose of catching at some particular expressions inadvertently dropt by a witness, and of afterwards bringing them forward, separately and detached from the rest of the conversation, in order to give a different colour and complexion to the substance of his evidence, and to weaken the effect and credit of the whole.

Gentlemen, these attempts are too commonly made. Happily, however, for public justice, they are commonly unsuccessful, because they do and must, with every honourable mind, recoil upon the party making them. Private applications to a person not only known to be an adverse witness, but to be the very witness upon whose credit the prosecution most materially depends—private conversations with such a witness, for the purpose of getting from him declarations which may be afterwards opposed in seeming contradiction to his solemn testimony upon oath, are of themselves so dishonourable, that, with every well-disposed and well-judging mind, they will naturally produce an effect directly contrary to the expectations of the persons who make them.

I know, gentlemen, what I have most to fear upon this occasion ; I know the vigour and energy of the mind of my learned friend. I have long felt and admired the powerful effect of his various talents. I know the ingenious sophistry by which he can mislead, and the fascination of that eloquence by which he can subdue, the minds of those to whom he addresses himself. I know what he can do to-day by seeing what he has done upon many other occasions before. But, at the same time, gentlemen, knowing what he is, I am somewhat consoled in knowing you. I have practised for several years in this place ; I know the sound discretion and judgment by which your verdicts are generally governed ; and, upon the credit of that experience, I trust that it will not be in the power of my friend, by any arts he is able to employ, to seduce you a single step from the sober paths of truth and justice. You will hear the evidence with the attention which becomes men who are deciding on the fate of others. If these defendants be innocent, and my learned friend is able to substantiate their innocence to your satisfaction, for God's sake let them be acquitted ; but if that innocence cannot be clearly and satisfactorily established, I stand here, interested as I am in common with him in the acquittal of innocence, at the same time, however, demanding the rights of public justice against the guilty. It imports the safety of yourselves, it imports the safety of our country, it imports the existence and security of everything that is dear to us, if these men be not innocent, that no considerations of tenderness and humanity, no considerations of any sort short of what the actual abstract justice of the case may require, should prevent the hand of punishment from falling heavy on them.

Having, therefore, gentlemen, given you this short detail and explanation of the principal facts which are about to be laid before you in evidence, I will now close the first part of the trouble I must give you. I shall by and by, when my learned friend has adduced that evidence by which he will attempt to assail the character and credit of the principal witness for the prosecution, have an opportunity of addressing you again, and I trust, in the meantime, whatever attention you may be disposed to pay to the exertions of those who will labour to establish the innocence of the persons now arraigned before you, that you will, at the same time, steadily bear in mind the duties which you owe to yourselves and to your country, recollecting, as I am sure you will, that we all look up to your firmness and integrity at this moment for the protection of that constitution from which we derive every blessing we individually or collectively enjoy.

MR ERSKINE'S SPEECH.

Gentlemen of the Jury,—I listened with the greatest attention (and in honour of my learned friend I must say with the greatest approbation) to much of his address to you in the opening of this cause ;—it was candid and manly, and contained many truths which I have no interest to deny ; one in particular which involves in it indeed the very principle of the defence,—the value of that happy constitution of Government which has so long existed in this island. I hope that none of us will ever forget the gratitude which we owe to the Divine Providence, and, under its blessing, to the wisdom of our forefathers, for the happy establishment of law and justice under which we live, and under which, thank God, my clients are this day to be judged. Great, indeed, will be the condemnation of any man who does not feel and act as he ought to do upon this subject; for surely if there be one privilege greater than another which the benevolent Author of our being has been pleased to dispense to His creatures since the existence of the earth which we inhabit, it is to have cast our lots in this age and country. For myself, I would in spirit prostrate myself daily and hourly before Heaven to acknowledge it, and instead of coming from the house of Mr Walker, and accompanying him at Preston (the only truths which the witness has uttered since he came into Court), if I believed him capable of committing the crimes he is charged with,

I would rather have gone into my grave than have been found as a friend under his roof.

Gentlemen, the crime imputed to the defendant is a serious one indeed. Mr Law has told you, and told you truly, that this indictment has not at all for its object to condemn or to question the particular opinions which Mr Walker and the other defendants may entertain concerning the principles of this Government, or the reforms which the wisest governments may from time to time require. He is indeed a man of too enlarged a mind to think for a moment that his country can be served by interrupting the current of liberal opinion, or overawing the legal freedom of English sentiment by the terrors of criminal prosecution. He openly disavows such a system, and has, I think, even more than hinted to us that there may be seasons when an attention to reform may be salutary, and that every individual under our happy establishment has a right, upon this important subject, to think for himself.

The defendants, therefore, are not arraigned before you, nor even censured in observation, for having associated at Manchester to promote what they felt to be the cause of religious and civil liberty ;—nor are they arraigned or censured for seeking to collect the sentiments of their neighbours and the public concerning the necessity of a reform in the constitution of Parliament. These sentiments and objects are wholly out of the question: but they are charged with having unlawfully confederated and conspired to destroy and overthrow the Government of the kingdom by OPEN FORCE AND REBELLION, and that to effect this wicked purpose they exercised the King's subjects with arms, perverting that which is our birthright, for the protection of our lives and property, to the malignant purpose of supporting the enemies of this kingdom in case of an invasion : in order, as my friend has truly said (for I admit the consequence if the fact be established), in order to make our country that scene of confusion and desolation which fills every man's heart with dismay and horror when he only reads or thinks of what is transacting at a distance upon the bloody theatre of the war that is now desolating the world. This, and nothing different or less than this, is the charge which is made upon the defendants, at the head of whom stands before you a merchant of honour, property, character, and respect, who has long enjoyed the countenance and friendship of many of the worthiest and most illustrious persons in the kingdom, and whose principles and conduct have more than once been publicly and gratefully acknowledged by the community of which he is a member, as the friend of their commerce and liberties, and the protector of the most essential privileges which Englishmen can enjoy under the laws.

Gentlemen, such a prosecution against such a person ought to have had a strong foundation. Putting private justice and all respect of persons wholly out of the question, it should not, but

upon the most clear conviction and the most urgent necessity, have
been instituted at all. We are at this moment in a most awful and
fearful crisis of affairs. We are told authentically by the Sovereign
from the throne that our enemies in France are meditating an
invasion, and the kingdom from one end to another is in motion to
repel it. In such a state of things, and when the public transactions
of government and justice in the two countries pass and repass from
one another as if upon the wings of the wind, is it politic to prepare
this solemn array of justice upon such a dangerous subject, without
a reasonable foundation, or rather without an urgent call? At a
time when it is our common interest that France should believe us
to be, what we are and ever have been, one heart and soul to protect our country and our constitution,—is it wise or prudent, putting
private justice wholly out of the question, that it should appear to
the councils of France—apt enough to exaggerate advantages—
that the Judge representing the Government in the northern district
of this kingdom should be sitting here in judgment, in the presence
of all the gentlemen whose property lies in this great county, to
trace and to punish the existence of a rebellious conspiracy to
support an invasion from France,—a conspiracy not existing in a
single district alone, but maintaining itself by criminal concert and
correspondence in every district, town, and city in the kingdom,—
projecting nothing less than the utter destruction and subversion of
the Government? Good God! can it be for the interest of Government that such an account of the state of this country should go
forth? Unfortunately, the rumour and effect of this day's business
will spread where the evidence may not travel with it to serve as
an antidote to the mischief; for certainly the scene which we have
this day witnessed can never be imagined in France or in Europe,
where the spirit of our law is known and understood;—it never
will be credited that all this serious process has no foundation either
in fact or probability, and that it stands upon the single evidence
of a common soldier, or rather a common vagabond, discharged as
unfit to be a soldier;—of a wretch, lost to all reverence for God
and religion, who avows that he has none for either, and who is
incapable of observing even common decency as a witness in the
court. This will never be believed; and the country, whose best
strength at home and abroad is the soundness of all its members,
will suffer from the very credit which Government will receive for
the justice of this proceeding.

What, then, can be more beneficial than that *you* should make
haste, as public and private men, to undeceive the world, to do
justice to your fellow-subjects, and to vindicate your country?
What can be more beneficial than that you, as honest men, should
upon your oaths pronounce and record by your verdict that, however Englishmen may differ in religious opinions, which in such a
land of thinking ever must be the case;—that, however they may

separate in political speculations as to the wisest and best formation of a House of Commons;—that though some may think highly of the Church and its establishment, whilst others, but with equal sincerity, prefer the worship of God with other ceremonies, or without any ceremonies;—that though some may think it unsafe to touch the constitution at this particular moment, and some, that at no time it is safe to touch it, while others think that its very existence depends upon immediate reformation;—what, I repeat, can be more beneficial than that your verdict should establish that though the country is thus divided upon these political subjects, as it ever has been in every age and period of our history, yet that we all recollect our duty to the land which our fathers have left us as an inheritance—that we all know and feel we have one common duty and one common interest? This will be the language of your verdict, whatever you yourselves may think upon these topics connected with but still collateral to the cause:—whether you shall approve or disapprove of the opinions or objects of the defendants, I know that you will still with one mind revolt with indignation at the evidence you have heard, when you shall have heard also the observations I have to make upon it, and, what is far more important, the facts I shall bring forward to encounter it. To these last words I beg your particular attention. I say, when you shall hear *the facts with which I mean to encounter the evidence.* My learned friend has supposed that I had nothing wherewith to support the cause but by railing at his witness, and endeavouring to traduce his character by calling others to reproach it. He has told you that I could encounter his testimony by *no one fact*, but that he had only to apprehend the influence which my address might have upon you;—as if I, an utter stranger here, could have any possible weight or influence to oppose to him, who has been so long known and honoured in this place.

But although my learned friend seems to have expected no adverse evidence, he appears to have been apprehensive for the credit and consistency of his own; since he has told you that we have drawn this man into a lure not uncommon for the purpose of entrapping witnesses into a contradiction of testimony;—that we have ensnared him into the company of persons who have drawn him in by insidious questions, and written down what he has been made to declare to them, in destruction of his original evidence, for the wicked purpose of attacking the sworn testimony of truth, and cutting down the consequences which would have followed from it to the defendants. If such a scene of wickedness had been practised, it must have been known to the witness himself; yet my learned friend will recollect, that though he made this charge in his hearing before his examination, he positively denied the whole of it. I put it to him point by point, pursuing the opening as my guide, —and he denied that he had been drawn into any lure;—he denied that any trap had been laid for him ;—he denied that he had been asked any questions by anybody.   If I am mistaken, I desire to be corrected, and particularly so by my learned friend, because I wish to state the evidence as it was given.   He has, then, denied all these things; he has further sworn that he never acknowledged to Mr Walker that he had wronged or injured him, or that the evidence he had given against him was false ;—that he never had gone down upon his knees in his presence to implore his forgiveness ;—that he never held his hands before his face, to hide the tears that were flowing down his cheeks in the moment of contrition or of terror at the consequence of his crimes : all this he has positively and repeatedly sworn in answer to questions deliberately put to him : and instead of answering with doubt, or as trying to recollect whether anything approaching such a representation had happened, he put his hands to his sides, and laughed, as you saw, at me who put the questions, with that sneer of contempt and insolence which accompanied the whole of his evidence, on my part at least of his examination.   If nothing, therefore, was at stake but the destruction of this man's evidence, and with it the prosecution which rests for its whole existence upon it, I should proceed at once to confound him with testimony, the truth of which my learned friend himself will, I am sure, not bring into question.   But as I wish the whole conduct of my clients to stand fairly before you, and not to rest merely upon positive swearing destructive of opposite testimony, and as I wish the evidence I mean to bring before you, and the falsehood of that which it opposes, to be clearly understood, I will state to you how it has happened that this strange prosecution has come before you.

The town of Manchester has been long extremely divided in religious and civil opinions ; and while I wish to vindicate those whom I represent in this place, I desire not to inflame differences which I hope in a short season will be forgotten.   I am desirous, on the contrary, that everything which proceeds from me may be the means of conciliating rather than exasperating dissensions which have already produced much mischief, and which perhaps, but for the lesson of to-day, might have produced much more.

Gentlemen, you all know that there have been for centuries past in this country various sects of Christians worshipping God in different forms, and holding a diversity of religious opinions ; and that the law has for a long season deprived numerous classes, even of his Majesty's Protestant subjects, of privileges which it confers upon the rest of the public, setting as it were a mark upon them, and keeping them below the level of the community by shutting them out from offices of trust and confidence in the country. Whether these laws be wise or unwise, whether they ought to be continued or abolished, are questions for the Legislature, and not for us ; but thus much I am warranted in saying, that it is the undoubted privilege of every man, or class of men, in England, to petition Parliament for the removal of any system or law which either actually does aggrieve, or which is thought to be a grievance. Impressed with the sense of this inherent privilege, this very constitutional society, which is supposed by my learned friend the Attorney-General to have started up on the breaking out of the war with France for the purpose of destroying the constitution,—this very society owed its birth to the assertion of this indisputable birthright of Englishmen, which the authors of this prosecution most rashly thought proper to stigmatise and resist. It is well known that in 1790 the Dissenters in the different parts of the kingdom were solicitous to bring before Parliament their application to put an end for ever to all divisions upon religious subjects, and to make us all, what I look forward yet to see, one harmonious body, living like one family together. It is also well remembered with what zeal and eloquence that great question was managed in the House of Commons by Mr Fox, and the large majority with which the repeal of the Test Acts was rejected. It seems, therefore, strange that the period of this rejection should be considered as an era either of danger to the Church or of religious triumph to Christians. Nevertheless, a large body of gentlemen and others at Manchester, whose motives I am far from wishing to scrutinise or condemn, considered this very wish of the Dissenters as injurious to their rights, and as dangerous to the Church and State. They published advertisements expressive of these sentiments ; and the rejection of the bill in the Commons produced a society styled the Church-and-King Club, which met for the first time to celebrate what they called the glorious decision of the House of Commons in rejecting the prayer of their dissenting brethren.

Gentlemen, it is not for me to say that it was unjust or impolitic in Parliament to reject the application ; but surely I may, without offence, suggest that it was hardly a fit subject of triumph that a great number of fellow-subjects,—amounting, I believe, to more than a million in this country,—had miscarried in an object which they thought beneficial, and which they had a most unquestionable right to submit to the Government under which they lived. Yet for this cause alone—France and every other topic of controversy being yet unborn—the Church and King were held forth to be in danger ; a society was instituted for their protection, and an uniform appointed with the Church of Manchester upon the button.

Gentlemen, without calling for any censure upon this proceeding, but leaving it to every man's own reflection, is it to be wondered at or condemned that those who thought more largely and liberally on subjects of freedom, both civil and religious, but who found themselves persecuted for sentiments and conduct the most avowedly legal and constitutional, should associate for the support of their rights and privileges as Englishmen, and assemble to consider how they might best obtain a more adequate representation of the people of Great Britain in Parliament?

Gentlemen, this society continued with these objects in view until the issuing of the proclamation against republicans and levellers, calling upon the magistrates to exert themselves throughout the kingdom to avert some danger with which, it seems, our rulers thought this kingdom was likely to be visited. Of this danger, or the probability of it, either *generally*, or at Manchester *in particular*, my learned friend has given no evidence from any quarter but that of Mr Dunn;—he has not proved that there has been in any one part of the kingdom anything which could lead Government to apprehend that meetings existed for the purposes pointed at. But that is out of the question. Government had a right to think for itself, and to issue the proclamation. The publicans, however (as it appears upon the cross-examination of the witness), probably directed by the magistrates, thought fit to shut up their houses, opened by immemorial law, to all the King's subjects, and to refuse admission to all the gentlemen and tradesmen of the town who did not associate under the banners of this Church-and-King Club. This illegal proceeding was accompanied with an advertisement containing a vehement libel against all those persons who, under the protection of the laws, thought themselves as much at liberty to consider their various privileges as others were to maintain the establishment of the Church. Upon this occasion Mr Walker honourably stood forth, and opened his house to this constitutional society at a time when they must otherwise have been in the streets by a combination of the publicans to reject them. Now, gentlemen, I put it to you as men of honour, whether it can be justly attributed to Mr Walker as seditious that he opened his house to a society of gentlemen and tradesmen,—whose good principles he was acquainted with,—who had been wantonly opposed by this Church-and-King Club, whose privileges they had never invaded or questioned, and against whom, in this day of trial, there is no man to be found who can come forward to impeach anything they have done or a syllable they have uttered? Vehement as the desire most apparently has been to bring this gentleman and his associates, as they are called, to justice, yet not one magistrate, no man of property or figure in this town or its neighbourhood, no person having the King's authority in the county, has appeared to prove one fact or circumstance from whence even the vaguest suspicion could arise that anything criminal had been intended or transacted: no constable who had ever been sent to guard lest the peace might be broken, or to make inquiries for its preservation; not a paper seized throughout England, nor any other prosecution instituted except upon the unsupported evidence of the same miserable wretch who stands before you ; the town, neighbourhood, and county remaining in the same profound state of tranquillity as it is at the moment I am addressing you.

Gentlemen, when Parliament assembled at the end of 1792, previous to the commencement of the war, these unhappy differences were suddenly (and, as you will see, from no fault of Mr Walker's) brought to the crisis which produced this trial. A meeting was held in Manchester to prepare an address of thanks to the King for having embodied the militia during the recess of Parliament, and for having put the kingdom into a posture of defence. I do not seek to question the measure of Government which gave rise to this approbation, or the approbation itself, which the approvers had a right to bestow ; but others had an equal right to entertain other opinions. On all public measures the decision undoubtedly is with Government ; but the people at the same time have a right to think upon them, and to express what they think. Surely war, of all other subjects, is one which the people have a right to consider ? Surely it can be no offence for those whose properties were to be taxed, and whose inheritances were to be lessened by it, to pause a little upon the eve of a contest the end of which no man can foresee, the expenses of which no man can calculate, or estimate the blood to flow from its calamities ? Surely it is a liberty secured to us by the first principles of our constitution, to address the Sovereign, or instruct our representatives, to avert the greatest evil that can impend over a nation.

Gentlemen, one of those societies, called the Reformation Society, met to exercise this undoubted privilege, and, in my mind, upon the fittest occasion that ever presented itself. Yet mark the moderation of Mr Walker, whose violence is arraigned before you. Though he was no member of that body, and though he agreed in the propriety of the measure in agitation, yet he suggested to them that their opposition might be made a pretence for tumult; that tranquillity in such a crisis was by every means to be promoted; and therefore advised them to abstain from the meeting; so that the other meeting was left to carry its approbation of Government and of the war without a dissenting voice. If ever, therefore, there was a time when the Church and King might be said to be out of danger at Manchester, it was at this moment; yet, *on this very day*, they hoisted the banners of alarm to both ; they paraded with them through every quarter of the town ; mobs, by degrees, were collected, and in the evening of this very 11th of December the houses of Mr Walker and others were attacked. You will observe that, *before this day*, no man has talked about arms at Mr Walker's. If an honourable gentleman upon the jury, who has been carefully taking notes of the evidence, will have the goodness to refer to them, he will find that it was not till near a week after this (so Dunn expresses it) that a single firelock had been seen ; nor, indeed, does any part of the evidence go back beyond this time, when Mr Walker's house was thus surrounded and attacked by a riotous and disorderly mob.   He was aware of the probable consequences of such an attack ; he knew, by the recent example of Birmingham, what he and others professing sentiments of freedom had to expect ; he therefore got together a few firearms which he had long had publicly by him, and an inventory of which, with the rest of his furniture at Barlow Hall, had been taken by a sworn appraiser long before anything connected with this indictment had an existence ; and with these, and the assistance of a few steady friends, he stood upon his defence.   He was advised, indeed, to retire for safety ; but knowing his own innocence, and recollecting the duty he owed to himself, his family, and the public, he declared he would remain there to support the laws, and to defend his property ; and that he would perish rather than surrender those privileges which every member of the community is bound, both from interest and duty, to maintain.   To alarm the multitude, he fired from the windows over their heads, and dispersed them ; but when, the next morning, they assembled in very great numbers before his house, and when a man got upon the churchyard wall, and read a most violent and inflammatory paper, inciting the populace to pull the house down, Mr Walker went out amongst them, and expostulated with them, and asked why they had disgraced themselves so much by attacking him the night before, adding that if he had done any of them, or any person whom they knew, any injury, he was, upon proof of it, ready to make them every satisfaction in his power. He also told them that he had fired upon them the night before because they were mad, as well as drunk ; that if they attacked him again, he would, under the same circumstances, act as he had done before ; but that he was then alone and unarmed in the midst of them, and if he had done anything wrong, they were then sober, and had him completely in their power.

Gentlemen, this was most meritorious conduct.   You all live at a distance from the metropolis, and were probably, therefore, fortunate enough neither to be within or near it in 1780, when, from beginnings smaller than those which exhibited themselves at Birmingham, or even at Manchester, the metropolis of the country, and with it the country itself, had nearly been undone.   The beginning of these things is the season for exertion.   I shall never indeed forget what I have heard the late mild and venerable magistrate, Lord Mansfield, say upon this subject, whose house was one of the first attacked in London.   I have more than once heard him say that perhaps some blame might have attached upon himself and others in authority for their forbearance in not having directed force to have been *at the first moment* repelled by force, it being the highest humanity to check the infancy of tumults.

Gentlemen, Mr Walker's conduct had the desired effect ; he

watched again on the 13th of December, but the mob returned no more, and the next morning the arms were locked up in a bed-chamber in his house, where they have remained ever since, and where, of course, they never could have been seen by the witness, whose whole evidence commences above a week subsequent to the 11th of December, when they were finally put aside.   This is the genuine history of the business; and it must therefore not a little surprise you that when the charge is wholly confined to the use of arms, Mr Law should not even have hinted to you that Mr Walker's house had been attacked, and that he was driven to stand upon his defence, as if such a thing had never had an existence; indeed, the armoury, which must have been exhibited in such a statement, would have but ill suited the indictment or the evidence, and I must therefore undertake the description of it myself.

The arms having been locked up, as I told you, in the bed-chamber, I was shown last week into this house of conspiracy, treason, and death, and saw exposed to view the mighty armoury which was to level the beautiful fabric of our constitution, and to destroy the lives and properties of ten millions of people.   It consisted, first, of six little swivels, purchased two years ago at the sale of Livesey, Hargrave, & Co. (of whom we have all heard so much), by Mr Jackson, a gentleman of Manchester, who is also one of the defendants, and who gave them to Master Walker, a boy about ten years of age.   Swivels, you know, are guns so called because they turn upon a pivot; but these were taken off their props, were painted, and put upon blocks resembling carriages of heavy cannon, and in that shape may be fairly called children's toys; you frequently see them in the neighbourhood of London adorning the houses of sober citizens, who, strangers to Mr Brown and his improvements, and preferring grandeur to taste, place them upon their ramparts at Mile-End or Islington.   Having, like Mr Dunn (I hope I resemble him in nothing else)—having, like him, served his Majesty as a soldier (and I am ready to serve again if my country's safety should require it), I took a closer review of all I saw, and observing that the muzzle of one of them was broke off, I was curious to know how far this famous conspiracy had proceeded, and whether they had come into action, when I found the accident had happened on firing a *feu-de-joie* upon his Majesty's happy recovery, and that they had been afterwards fired upon the Prince of Wales' birthday.   These are the only times that, in the hands of these conspirators, these cannon, big with destruction, had opened their little mouths—once to commemorate the indulgent and benign favour of Providence in the recovery of the Sovereign, and once as a congratulation to the heir-apparent of his crown on the anniversary of his birth.

I went next, under the protection of the master-general of this ordnance (Mr Walker's chambermaid), to visit the rest of this formidable array of death, and found a little musketoon, about so high [*describing it*]; I put my thumb upon it, when out started a little bayonet like the Jack-in-a-box which we buy for children at a fair. In short, not to weary you, gentlemen, there was just such a parcel of arms of different sorts and sizes as a man collecting amongst his friends, for his defence against the sudden violence of a riotous multitude, might be expected to have collected. Here lay three or four rusty guns of different dimensions, and here and there a bayonet or broadsword covered over with dust and rust, so as to be almost undistinguishable; for, notwithstanding what this infamous wretch has sworn, we will prove by witness after witness, till you desire us to finish, that they were principally collected on the 11th of December, the day of the riot; and that from the 12th in the evening, or the 13th in the morning, they have lain untouched as I have described them; that their use began and ended with the necessity; and that, from that time to the present, there never has been a firearm in the warehouse of any sort or description. This is the whole on which has been built a proceeding that might have brought the defendants to the punishment of death, for both the charge and the evidence amount to high treason—high treason, indeed, under almost every branch of the statute, since the facts amount to levying war against the King, by a conspiracy to wrest by force the government out of his hands, to an adherence to the King's enemies, and to a compassing of his death, which is a necessary consequence of an invading army of republicans, or of any other enemies of the State; yet, notwithstanding the notoriety of these facts, the unnamed prosecutors (and, indeed, I am afraid to slander any man, or body of men, by even a guess upon the subject) have been beating up, as for volunteers, to procure another witness to destroy the lives of the gentlemen before you, against many of whom warrants for high treason were issued to apprehend them. Mr Walker, among the rest, was the subject of such a warrant; and as soon as he knew it, he behaved (as he has throughout) like a man and an Englishman. He wrote immediately to the Secretary of State, who was summoned here to-day, and whose absence I do not complain of, because we have, by consent, the benefit of his testimony. He wrote three letters to Mr Dundas, one of which was delivered by Mr Wharton, informing him that he was in London on his business as a merchant; that if any warrant had been issued against him, he was ready to meet it, and for that purpose delivered his address where it might be executed. This Mr Walker did when the prosecutors were in search of another witness, and when this Mr Dunn was walking like a tame sparrow through the New Bailey, fed at the public or some other expense, and suffered to go at large, though arrested upon a criminal charge, and sent into custody under it.

And to what other circumstances need I appeal for the purity of the defendants than that, under the charge of a conspiracy, extensive enough to comprehend in its transactions (if any existed) the whole compass of England, the tour of which was to have been made by Mr Yorke, there has not been one man found to utter a syllable about them,—no, not one man, thanks be to God, who has so framed the characteristics of Englishmen,—except the solitary infamous witness before you, who, from what I heard since I began to address you, may have spoken the truth when he claimed my acquaintance, as I have reason to think he has seen me before in a criminal court of justice.

Having now, for the satisfaction of the defendants, rather than from the necessity of the case, given you an account of their whole proceedings as I shall establish them by proof, let us examine the evidence that has been given against them, and see how the truth of it could stand with reason or probability, supposing it to have been sworn to by a witness the most respectable.

According to Dunn's own account, Mr Walker had not been at the first meeting, so that when he first saw Dunn he did not know either his person or his name; he might have been a spy (God knows there are enow of them), and at that season in particular informers were to be expected. Mr Walker is supposed to have said to him, "What is your business here?" to which he answered, "I am going to the society," which entitled him at once to admission without further ceremony; there was nobody to stop him. Was he asked his name?—was he balloted for?—was he questioned as to his principles? No, he walked in at once; but first, it seems, Mr Walker, who had never before seen him, inquired of him the news from Ireland (observing by his voice that he was an Irishman), and asked what the volunteers were about, as if Mr Walker could possibly suppose that such a person was likely to have been in a correspondence with Ireland which told him more than report must have told everybody else. Mr Dunn tells you indeed he was no such person; he was a friend, as he says, to the King and constitution, which Mr Walker would have found by asking another question; but, without further inquiry, he is supposed to have said to him at once, "We shall overthrow the constitution by and by;" which the moment Dunn had heard, up walked that affectionate subject of our Sovereign Lord the King into Mr Walker's house, where the constitution was to be so overthrown. But then he tells you he thought there was no harm to be done, that it was only for the benefit of the poor and the public good. But how could he think so after what he had that moment heard? But he did not know, it seems, what Mr Walker meant. Gentlemen, do you collect, from Mr Dunn's discourse and deportment to-day that he could not tell but that a man meant good when he had heard even him express *a wish* to overthrow the Government? Would you pull a feather out of a sparrow's wing

upon the oath of a man who swears that he believed a person to
have been a good subject in the very moment he was telling him
of an intended rebellion ?   But why should I fight a phantom with
argument ?   Could any man but a driveller have possibly given
such an answer as is put into Mr Walker's mouth to a man he had
never seen in his life ?   However many may differ from Mr Walker
in opinion, everybody, I believe, will admit that he is an acute, intelligent man, with an extensive knowledge of the world, and not
at all likely to have conducted himself like an idiot.   What follows
next ?   Another night he went into the warehouse, where he saw
Mr Yorke called to the chair, who said he was going the tour of
the kingdom. in order to try the strength of the different societies,
to join fifty thousand men that were expected to land from France
in this country ; and that Mr Walker then said, " Damn all kings—
I know our King has seventeen millions of money in the Bank of
Vienna, although he won't afford any of it to the poor."   Gentlemen, is this the language of a man of sense and education ?   If
Mr Walker had the malignity of a demon, would he think of giving
effect to it by such a senseless lie ?   When we know that, from
the immense expense attending his Majesty's numerous and illustrious family, and the great necessities of the state, he has been
obliged over and over again to have recourse to the generosity and
justice of Parliament to maintain the dignity of the Crown, could
Mr Walker ever have thought of inventing this nonsense about the
Bank of Vienna, when there is a bank too in our own country
where he might legally invest his property for himself and his
heirs ?   But Mr Walker did not stop there ; he went on and said,
" I should think no more of taking off the King's head than I
should of tearing this piece of paper."   All this happened soon
after his admission ; yet this man, who represents himself to you
upon his oath this day as having been uniformly a friend to the
constitution as far as he understood it,—as having left the society
as soon as he saw their mischievous inclinations, and as having
voluntarily informed against them,—I say this same friend of the
constitution tells you, almost in the same breath, that he continued
to attend their meetings from thirty to forty times, *where high
treason was committing with open doors;* and that, instead of
giving information of his own free choice, he was arrested in the
very act of distributing some seditious publication.

Gentlemen, it is really a serious consideration that upon such
testimony a man should even be put upon his defence in the courts
of this country.   Upon such principles what man is safe ?   I was
indeed but ill at ease myself when Mr Dunn told me he knew me
better than I supposed.   What security have I at this moment
that he should not swear that he had met me under some gateway
in Lancaster, and that I had said to him, " Well, Dunn, I hope
you will not swear against Mr Walker, but that you will stick to

the good cause: damn all kings: damn the constitution." If the witness were now to swear this, into gaol I must go; and if my client is in danger from what has been sworn against *him*, what safety would there be for *me* ?—The evidence would be equally positive, and I am equally an object of suspicion as Mr Walker. It is said of *him* that he has been a member of a society for the reform of Parliament; so have *I*, and so am *I* at this moment, and so at all hazards I will continue to be: and I will tell you why, gentlemen, because I hold it to be essential to the preservation of all the ranks and orders of the state,—alike essential to the prince and to the people. I have the honour to be allied to his Majesty in blood, and my family has been for centuries a part of what is now called the aristocracy of the country; I can therefore have no interest in the destruction of the constitution.

In pursuing the probability of this story (since it must be pursued), let us next advert to whether anything appears to have been done in other places which might have been exposed by this man's information. The whole kingdom is under the eye and dominion of magistracy, awakened at that time to an extraordinary vigilance; yet has any one man been arrested even upon the suspicion of any correspondence with the societies of Manchester, good, bad, or indifferent ? or has any person within the four seas come to swear that any such correspondence existed ? So that you are desired to believe, upon Mr Dunn's single declaration, that gentlemen of the description I am representing, without any end or object, or concert with others, were resolved to put their lives into the hands of any miscreant who might be disposed to swear them away, by holding public meetings of conspiracy with open doors, and in the presence of all mankind, liable to be handed over to justice every moment of their lives, since every tap at the door might have introduced a constable as readily as a member; and, to finish the absurdity, these gentlemen are made to discourse in a manner that would disgrace the lowest, and most uninformed classes of the community.

Let us next see what interest Mr Walker has in the proposed invasion of this peaceable country. Has Mr Law proved that Mr Walker had any reason to expect protection from the French, from any secret correspondence or communication, more than you or I have, or that he had prepared any means of resisting the troops of this country ? How was he to have welcomed these strangers into our land ? What! with this dozen of rusty muskets, or with those conspirators whom he exercised ? But who are they ? They are, it seems, " to the jurors unknown," as my learned friend has called them, who drew this indictment, and he might have added, *who will ever remain unknown to them*. But has Mr Walker nothing to lose, like other men who dread an invasion ? He has long had the acquaintance and friendship of some of the best men in this kingdom, who would be destroyed if such an invasion should take place. Has he, like other men, no ties of a nearer description? Alas! gentlemen, I feel at this moment that he has many. Mr Dunn told you that I was with Mr Walker at Manchester; and it enables me to say, of my own knowledge, that it is impossible he could have had the designs imputed to him. · I have been under his roof, where I have seen him the husband of an amiable and affectionate woman, and the happy parent of six engaging children; and it hurts me not a little to think what they must feel at this moment. Before prosecutions are set on foot, those things ought to be considered; we ought not, like the fool in the Proverbs, to scatter firebrands and death, and say, " Am I not in sport?" Could we look at this moment into the dwelling of this unfortunate gentleman, for so I must call him, I am persuaded the scene would distress us; his family cannot but be unhappy; they have seen prosecutions, equally unjust as even this is, attended with a success of equal injustice; and we have seen those proceedings, I am afraid by those who are at the bottom of this indictment, put forward for your imitation. I saw to my astonishment, at Preston, where, as a traveller, I called for a newspaper, that this immaculate society (the Manchester Church-and-King Club) had a meeting lately, and had published to the world the toasts and sentiments which they drank; some of them I like, some of them deserve reprobation : " The Church and King;" very well. " The Queen and Royal Family;" be it so. " The Duke of York and the Army;" be it so. But what do you think came next?

[Here Mr Justice Heath interrupted Mr Erskine by saying, " We are not to go into this, of which you cannot give evidence."]

Mr ERSKINE. I don't know what effect these publications may have upon the administration of justice. Why drink " *The Lord Advocate and the Court of Justiciary in Scotland,*" just when your Lordship is called upon to administer justice according to the laws of *England?* If I had seen the King and his judges upon the Northern Circuit published as a toast——

Mr JUSTICE HEATH. You know you cannot give this in evidence.

Mr ERSKINE. Gentlemen, considering the situation in which my client stands at this moment, I expressed the idea which occurred to me, and which I thought it right not to suppress; but let it pass —this is not the moment for controversy. It is my interest to submit to any course his Lordship may think proper to dictate; the evidence is more than enough for my purpose—so mainly improbable, so contrary to everything in the course of human affairs, that I know you will reject it, even if it stood unanswered. What then will you say, when I shall prove to you, by the oaths of the various persons who attended these societies, that no propositions of the sort insinuated by this witness ever existed—that no hint, directly or indirectly, of any illegal tendency, was ever whispered—that their real objects were just what were *openly professed*, be they right or wrong, be they wise or mistaken, namely, *reformation in the constitution of the House of Commons*, which my learned friend admitted they had a right by constitutional means to promote. This was their object. They neither desired to touch the King's authority, nor the existence or privileges of the House of Lords ; but they wished that those numerous classes of the community who (by the law as it now stands) are excluded from any share in the choice of members to the Parliament, should have an equal right with others in concerns where their interests are equal. Gentlemen, this very county furnishes a familiar instance. There are, I believe, at least thirty thousand freeholders in Lancashire, each of whom has a vote for two members of Parliament ; and there are two boroughs within it (if I mistake not), Clithero and Newton, containing a handful of men who are at the beck of *two individuals*, yet these two little places send for themselves, *or rather for these two persons*, two members each, which makes four against the whole power and interest of this county in Parliament, touching any measure, how deeply soever it may concern their prosperity. Can there be any offence in meeting together to consider of a representation to Parliament suggesting the wisdom of alteration and amendment in such a system ?

Mr JUSTICE HEATH. *There can be no doubt but that a petition to Parliament, for reform or anything else, can be no offence.*

Mr ERSKINE. Gentlemen, I expected this interruption from the learning of the Judge ; certainly it can be no offence, and consequently my clients can be no offenders.

Having now exposed the weakness of Dunn's evidence from its own intrinsic defects, and from the positive contradiction every part of it is to receive from many witnesses, I shall conclude with the still more positive and unequivocal contradiction which the whole of it has received from Dunn himself. You remember that I repeatedly asked him whether he had not confessed that the whole he had sworn to-day was utterly false, whether he had not confessed it to be so with tears of contrition, and whether he had not kneeled down before Mr Walker to implore his forgiveness. My learned friend, knowing that this would be proved upon him, made a shrewd and artful observation to avoid the effects of it. He said that such things had fallen often under the observation of the Court upon the circuit, where witnesses had been drawn into similar snares by artful people to invalidate their testimony. This may be true, but the answer to its application is, that not only the witness himself has positively denied that any such snare was laid for him, but the witnesses I have to call, both in respect of number and credit, will put a total end to such a suggestion. If I had indeed but one witness, my friend the Attorney-General might undoubtedly put it to you in reply whether his or mine was to be believed ; but I will call to you *not one* but *four or five*, or, if necessary, *six witnesses*, ABOVE ALL SUSPICION, in whose presence Dunn voluntarily confessed the falsehood of his testimony, and, with tears of apparent repentance, offered to make any reparation to these injured and unfortunate defendants.   This I pledge myself to prove to your satisfaction.

Gentlemen, the object of all public trial and punishment is the security of mankind in social life.   We are not assembled here for the purposes of vengeance, but for the ends of justice—to give tranquillity to human life, which is the scope of all government and law.   You will take care, therefore, how, in the very administration of justice, you disappoint that which is the very foundation of its institution—you will take care that, in the very moment you are trying a man as a disturber of the public happiness, you do not violate the rules which secure it.

The last evidence I have been stating ought by itself to put an instant end to this cause.   I remember a case very lately which was so brought to its conclusion, where, upon a trial for perjury of a witness who had sworn against a captain of a vessel in the African trade, it appeared that the witnesses who swore to the perjury against the defendants had themselves made deliberate declarations which materially clashed with the testimony they were giving.   Lord Kenyon, who tried the cause, would after this proceed no further, and asked me, who was counsel for the prosecution, whether I would urge it further, saying emphatically, what I hope every judge under similar circumstances will think it his duty to say also, " No man ought or can be convicted in England unless the judge and the jury have *a firm assurance* that innocence cannot by any possibility be the victim of conviction and sentence." And how can the jury or his Lordship have that assurance here, when the only source of it is brought into such serious doubt and question ?   Upon the whole, then, I cannot help hoping that my friend the Attorney-General, when he shall hear my proofs, will feel that a prosecution like this ought not to be offered for the seal and sanction of your verdict.   Unjust prosecutions lead to the ruin of all governments.   Whoever will look back to the history of the world in general, and of our own particular country, will be convinced that exactly as prosecutions have been cruel and oppressive, and maintained by inadequate and unrighteous evidence, in the same proportion, and by the same means, their authors have been destroyed instead of being supported by them ; as often as the principles of our ancient laws have been departed from in weak and wicked times, so often the governments that have violated them have been suddenly crumbled into dust ; and therefore, wishing as I sincerely do the preservation and prosperity of our happy constitution, I desire to enter my protest against its being supported by means that are likely to destroy it. Violent proceedings bring on the bitterness of retaliation, until all justice and moderation are trampled down and subverted. Witness those sanguinary prosecutions previous to the awful period in the last century when Charles the First fell. That unfortunate prince lived to lament those vindictive judgments by which his impolitic, infatuated followers imagined they were supporting his throne—he lived to see how they destroyed it ; his throne, undermined by violence, sunk under him, and those who shook it were guilty in their turn (such is the natural order of injustice) not only of similar but of worse and more violent wrongs; witness the fate of the unhappy Earl of Strafford, who, when he could not be reached by the ordinary laws, was impeached in the House of Commons, and who, when still beyond the consequences of that judicial proceeding, was at last destroyed *by the arbitrary wicked mandate of the Legislature.* James the Second lived to ask assistance in the hour of his distress from those who had been cut off from the means of giving it by unjust prosecutions ; he lived to ask support from the Earl of Bedford, after his son the unfortunate Lord Russell had fallen under the axe of injustice. " I once had a son," said that noble person, " who could have served your Majesty upon this occasion," but there was then none to assist him.

I cannot possibly tell how others feel upon these subjects, but I do know how it is their interest to feel concerning them. We ought to be persuaded that the only way by which Government can be honourably or safely supported, is by cultivating the love and affection of the people,—by showing them the value of the constitution by its protection,—by making them understand its principles by the practical benefits derived from them ; and, above all, by letting them feel their security in the administration of law and justice. What is it, in the present state of that unhappy kingdom, the contagion of which fills us with such alarm, that is the just object of terror ? What, but that accusation and conviction are the same, and that a false witness or power without evidence is a warrant for death ! Not so here ! Long may the countries differ ! And I am asking for nothing more than that you should decide according to our own wholesome rules, by which our Government was established, and by which it has been ever protected. Put yourselves, gentlemen, in the place of the defendants, and let me ask, If you were brought before your country upon a charge supported by no other evidence than that which you have heard to-day, and encountered by that which I have stated to you, what would you say, or your children after you, if you were touched in your persons or your properties by a conviction ? May you never be put to such reflections, nor the country to such disgrace ! The best service we can render to the public is, that we should live like one harmonious family, that we should banish all animosities, jealousies, and sus-

picions of one another; and that, living under the protection of a
mild and impartial justice, we should endeavour, with one heart,
according to our best judgments, to advance the freedom and maintain the security of Great Britain.

Gentlemen, I will trouble you no further; I am afraid, indeed, I
have too long trespassed on your patience; I will therefore proceed
to call my witnesses.

On the examination of the witnesses to the matters mentioned
by Mr Erskine in his speech, the witness for the Crown, Thomas
Dunn, was so entirely contradicted, that Mr Law interposing, in
the manner stated in the preface, the trial ended, and Mr Walker
and the other defendants were acquitted.

END OF VOLUME I.

PRINTED BY BALLANTYNE AND COMPANY
EDINBURGH AND LONDON